5 Historical Romances
Buoyed by the Sea

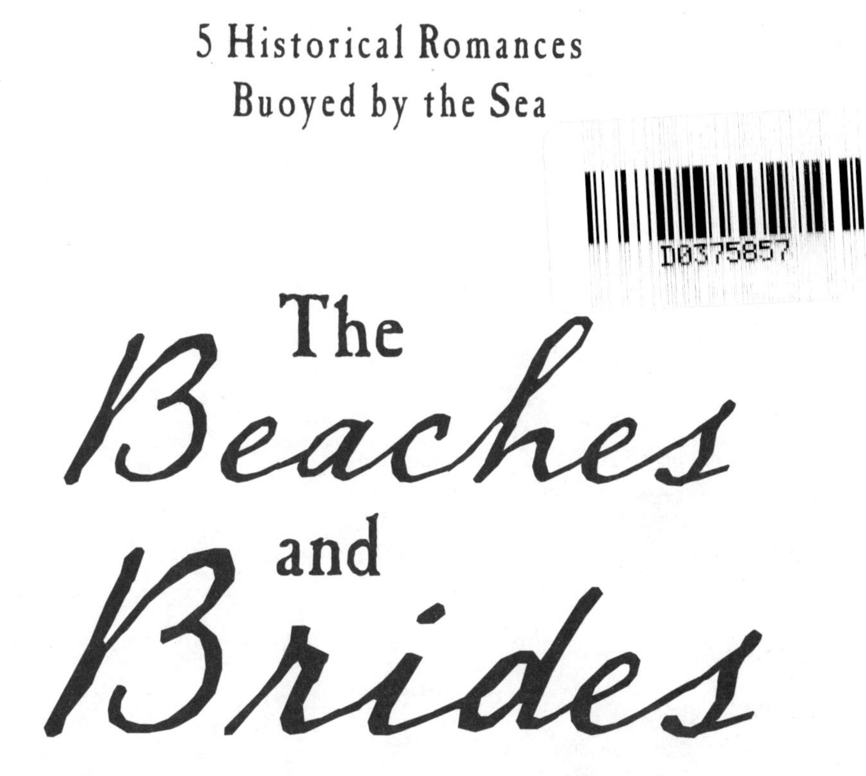

The Beaches and Brides

ROMANCE COLLECTION

Cathy Marie Hake,
Lynn A. Coleman, Mary Davis,
Susan Page Davis & Paige Winship Dooly

BARBOUR
PUBLISHING

Print ISBN 978-1-62836-194-0

eBook Editions:
Adobe Digital Edition (.epub) 978-1-63058-105-3
Kindle and MobiPocket Edition (.prc) 978-1-63058-106-0

All scripture quotations are taken from the King James Version of the Bible.

This book is a work of fiction. Names, characters, places, and incidents are either products of the author's imagination or used fictitiously. Any similarity to actual people, organizations, and/or events is purely coincidental.

Published by Barbour Publishing, Inc., P.O. Box 719, Uhrichsville, Ohio 44683, www.barbourbooks.com

Our mission is to publish and distribute inspirational products offering exceptional value and biblical encouragement to the masses.

ecpa Member of the Evangelical Christian Publishers Association

Printed in Canada.

Contents

A Time to Embrace by Lynn A. Coleman 5
The Captain's Wife by Mary Davis 101
The Castaway's Bride by Susan Page Davis. 197
The Lightkeeper's Daughter by Paige Winship Dooly 295
Restoration by Cathy Marie Hake 387

A TIME TO EMBRACE

by Lynn A. Coleman

Dedication

I'd like to dedicate this book to my loving parents,
Ron and Ellie Putnam.
Without them I wouldn't be here,
nor would I have had full use of their houseboat
in Key West for my research.
May I continue to be a sparkle of joy in your eyes.
All my love, Lynn

Chapter 1

Key West, Florida, 1865

Bea scanned the approaching coastline. "Dear Lord," she exclaimed, her thoughts a jumble of fear and curiosity, "this is like heaven on earth." The crystal-blue sea, the lush green palm trees, flowers bright and full of color in November—could this really be possible? So unlike the waters and shoreline of the New York harbor she had left a week earlier.

Yet she wanted to cling to Richard.

As her arm encircled the four-year-old boy's shoulders, the thought of parting with him tore at her heart. Poor, sweet Richard. Now that both of his parents were dead, it was her entrusted duty to bring him to Key West to live with his uncle. She grasped the ship's rail tighter. Ellis Southard had to be the most self-centered, uncaring man she had ever known. Not that she really knew him at all, but since he had received word of his brother's death, he had done nothing but upset her and Richard's world.

"Nanna, look!" Richard tugged at her skirt. "What are those birds?"

Bea turned to look in the direction that the child pointed. A huge bird, larger than any goose she had ever seen, bobbed up and down on the waves. Its long bill stretched down from its head and nestled in its chest. "I'm not certain, Richie. Perhaps we can ask your uncle Ellis when we see him."

If she could recognize his uncle Ellis. No pictures of Ellis were to be found in the Southard's home. From what she could recall from her conversations with Elizabeth, Ellis had left home to seek his fortune when he was a mere teenaged boy. Still, she hoped he would have some family resemblance, despite the fact that he was several years younger than his brother, Richard Southard II.

Bea donned her fingerless mitts, all the rage of new fashion, then nervously tapped at the ship's railing as she surveyed the crowd now gathering to meet the ship. The long dock reached far into the harbor. Effortlessly, the captain maneuvered the vessel up to the massive wooden structure. The seamen tossed heavy lines, and the pilings creaked under the strain of capturing the great vessel and bringing it to a standstill. As the boat lunged to a halt, Bea lost her footing and mentally chided herself for not remembering to use an onboard stance—feet slightly apart—to maintain her balance.

"Nanna, where's Uncle Ellis?"

"I'm certain he is here, Richard. Calm down, child, and let us wait for the captain's orders."

"Yes, Ma'am."

Bea smiled and tousled the boy's golden blond locks. He looked like the mirror image of his mother—her dear friend. They had been neighbors, Elizabeth older by two years. But as teens, the age difference hadn't mattered. Nearly every day they spent some time together, even after Elizabeth married Richard.

He had been the man next door. Richard was twelve years older than Elizabeth, and thus never the boy next door.

Almost sensing her weakened condition would not improve, Elizabeth pleaded with Bea to come and live with her, to help care for the baby. So many years ago. So many changes.

"I love you, Richie."

"I love you, Nanna." He grabbed her by the hand and pulled her to the gangplank. "Come, let's find Uncle Ellis."

Bea's heart tightened. How could she ever give this child up? He was as much a part of her as life itself. Her father thought it time for her to marry and produce her own children. But Elizabeth had counted on her to nurture this child.

Young Richard, straining on her right hand, led her off the ship and down the dock, casting imploring looks at strangers, yet too afraid to ask.

"Let's wait on the dock, Richie. Perhaps your uncle has been detained." A stunningly handsome man with reddish-brown hair and a trim beard nodded as he passed.

Perhaps father was right, she thought fleetingly. *Perhaps I should consider a husband and marriage.* Oh, she had some offers back home. However, with her responsibilities to young Richard, she never accepted any suitors. How could she possibly fall in love and simply toss the child aside? No, she couldn't do that.

Even the boy's mother, Elizabeth, had known she was asking a lot from Bea to give up her life, her own chance at the happiness of raising her own child. But they both agreed it was best for the baby. When it became clear that Elizabeth would lose her fight to stay alive, she assured Bea that, if Richard Sr. were to ever fall in love with her, she would have her blessing.

Bea smiled, remembering the day. Richard passed as a fairly handsome man, and perhaps she would have married him for the sake of little Richard, but she didn't fancy herself falling in love with him. He seemed too concerned with work, and he had little time for Elizabeth, though he did adore her in his own way. Bea couldn't imagine him having any time for her.

All that didn't matter. He was gone now, joined in heaven with his love, leaving Bea here with their child. Young Richard was now her responsibility. And his uncle obviously cared little for his welfare, or else he would have been here waiting for the ship. They had arrived on time. Perhaps she should just march back on the ship and leave, leave with Richard, and raise him herself. Her mind made up, Bea turned Richard toward the ship, marched briskly back down the weathered dock, and up the gangplank.

Ellis visually scoured the decks of the *Justice,* unable to spot his nephew or the nanny. One thing he disliked most in people was lack of punctuality. He wondered if she had arrived at the New York harbor in time. He'd given her two weeks to pack and make her way to the city. "She certainly should have had enough time," he grumbled. He had noticed only one woman with her child on the docks. The child looked as if he could have been the right age, but his coloring seemed all wrong for a Southard. All Southards had various shades of brown hair, and only he had been blessed with blue-gray eyes. The rest of the family had brown eyes. *Always had, always would,* he reckoned.

Spying Captain Brighton by the cargo hold, he decided to inquire about two things. One, if he would be returning to New York or traveling to Cuba before returning. Two, if his nephew had actually made it on board.

"Good morning, Jed."

Jed returned a hearty handshake. " 'Morning, Ellis. How's the sponge business?"

"Doing well. Are you heading back to New York?"

"After a trip to Cuba. Have some cargo?"

"Yes, but if you're returning from Cuba before going back to New York, I'll have more."

Jed rubbed his beard. "Wasn't planning on it; let me think a spell. I'll be picking up a healthy load of sugarcane."

"I'll take any available space you can give me."

"That's the thing about sponges, they take up room but not too much weight."

"Did my nephew make it on board?"

"Handsome lad. Sure did. I saw him and his nanny on deck a few moments ago. They can't be too far."

"I must have missed them."

"They could have gone back to their cabin to get some of their bags."

"Must be it."

"This will be my last voyage for awhile. The war's over. I'm tired, planning on settling down."

"Ah, a woman?" Ellis inquired.

"Hardly! The war took a toll on me. Privateering carries no honor, now that the war is over. During the war it was necessary. Now, well. . .now, folks just take you for a common thief."

"Sorry to hear it. I know you, Jed, you're an honorable man. Besides, I hate losing one of the fastest vessels to deliver my cargo."

"Aye, but perhaps a woman wouldn't be so bad either.

"Here comes your nephew and the prettiest nanny I've ever seen."

Ellis turned. The woman and fair-haired child. How. . . ?

She was stunning—with lily-white complexion and hazel eyes. Worried eyes. Young eyes. Weren't nannies old and gray? Shouldn't they be?

"Pardon me, Captain Brighton, but we seem to have a problem."

The captain stood with the handsome stranger she had noticed earlier. Perhaps she shouldn't interrupt, but she did want another glimpse at the gentleman with such strong shoulders and distinguished face. *What's wrong with noticing a striking man?* she rationalized.

"Miss Smith, may I introduce you to Mr. Ellis Southard."

Ellis Southard? She examined him closely. He had brown hair, but redder than she expected. Perhaps the tropical sun had painted it. His eyes, oh my, they were so like little Richard's eyes—the same blue-gray, same shape, though older, more mature. More passionate. Bea swallowed.

"Forgive me, Miss Smith, I assumed you were the child's mother." Ellis bent down on one knee before the boy. "You must be Richard?"

"Yes, Sir. Are you my uncle Ellis?"

"That I am, Son, that I am."

Richard stepped out farther from behind Bea's skirt, but still clung to it. For all the child's excitement at meeting his uncle, he remained naturally afraid of a stranger. Why wouldn't he be? The poor child already had so much loss in his short life, and was now about to lose the only mother he'd known. Bea had hoped to stay on for awhile to transition the child into a relationship with his uncle, but now uncertainty loomed. The man was too dangerously appealing.

Ellis extended a hand. Richard took it. "Tell me, Son, what do you think of this tropical isle?"

Richard's other hand trembled with fear on her skirt. Bea placed her hand on his back. "Richard, perhaps your uncle Ellis knows what kind of bird that is." She pointed to the one that had caught his attention earlier.

Ellis Southard followed her lead. "It's a pelican. Did you know those particular birds can swallow fish whole?"

"Pelican?" Richard answered.

"Yes, pelican. Their beaks have a floppy pouch they fill with fish and water. When the bird closes its beak, it spits out the water and swallows the fish."

Richard's eyes bulged as he strained to watch the interesting new bird.

"I've been unable to find a nanny for the child," Ellis said, standing again and meeting Bea's eyes. "Would you be willing to stay on for a week or so, Miss Smith?"

What an answer to prayer! On the other hand, her attraction to this man scared her. "It would be my privilege, Mr. Southard."

"Excellent. If you would excuse me, I need to take care of a bit of business. Then I'll bring you and the child to my home."

The child! He can't even call Richard by his name? Bea fumed. *O Lord, this man can't possibly be meant to care for Richie. He has the compassion of a gnat!*

Rather than speak her mind, she stepped back and led Richie to the railing of the ship where he kept a vigil on the exotic bird. She could see his mind working. She knew he hoped the bird would get hungry so he could watch it eat.

"Nanna, why can't you stay with me?"

"Because I live in New York." Of course, the idea of moving back into her family home after she'd been a nanny for four years bothered her tremendously. She loved her folks, but having tasted independence, she didn't want to go back to the waiting season of balls and having men call on her. Well, perhaps gentlemen callers wouldn't be so bad, but. . .she wanted to do things on her own. Her folks talked about having another coming-out party on her behalf since she had been kept from social events for years.

"But why?" Richard interrupted her reverie.

Bea knelt down beside Richard and pulled him into her arms. "I will visit as often as I can, Richie. I love you as if you were my own. Your uncle Ellis is family; he will take good care of you."

She prayed she wasn't lying to him. She had serious questions about the man's parenting abilities, despite his brief attempts at friendliness toward Richie. Besides, what would a single man do with a child?

Perhaps he had married. She hadn't heard news from him prior to his letter concerning the house, the lands, and the arrangements for her to bring Richard to him. She supposed it amounted, in part, to what bothered her the most about him. He hadn't come to New York to take care of family business himself. Instead he barked out his orders and dictated from Key West.

His brother had been no different, telling his ailing wife he was going off to war. Then he arranged for people to run the farm and left. Well, he had spent several private days with his wife before going. And he had come back as often as possible to oversee the house, look in on his son, and do whatever he could with his few days' leave. But those times had been rare. Of course, he had come as soon as he had received word of Elizabeth's passing. Bea had even seen him weeping at her grave. He truly did love her, Bea believed. He just didn't see marriage as a partnership.

Bea's parents, on the other hand, worked hand-in-hand. True, Mother took care of most of the social activities. Nevertheless, Bea had often heard her parents discussing matters of investments together. She knew her father was a rare man. Not many took stock in a woman's opinion when it came to business. But her mother had a head for numbers. "God's special blessing," her father always said.

She kissed Richard's cheek. "Shh, my love, everything will be all right. God is watching over you and He loves you far more than I."

Richie hugged her hard and returned her kiss. Bea held back the tears burning the edge of her lids.

"Miss Smith, if you are through coddling the child, it is time to be on our way."

Bea stood up straight and eased the child down to the deck. *O Lord, please tell me this isn't a mistake. This man is insufferable.*

Chapter 2

Ellis caught Jed's chastising glance and realized he had been abrupt, possibly even rude, with Miss Smith. Quickly coming to his own defense, he rationalized how women on Key West were rare commodities, and to know he was going to have a beautiful one in his house with a tender loving touch. . .he would definitely need to be on his guard.

She nodded in his direction, her lips tight, her jaw tense. *Yes sir, this woman will definitely need to be kept at a distance.* Even angry she looked appealing. With all the men on Key West, Miss Smith would surely have more invitations to social activities than he'd had for the past year. Ellis felt oddly uncomfortable with the prospect. It might be best to have the temptation of a pretty face gone. On the other hand, the idea of another man. . . Well, he just wouldn't allow himself to follow that particular line of thinking.

"I have a carriage to bring your baggage to the house," he said, trying to ease the tension.

"Uncle Ellis, do you have a boat?"

"Yes, a small one. Did you enjoy the sail from New York, Richard?"

"Yes, Sir. I've never been on a sailboat before."

"May I suggest, on the evenings I'm able, we go for a sail and perhaps do some fishing."

"Can I, Nanna?"

"Of course, Dear. Whatever your uncle Ellis would like. He's your parent now."

Richard knitted his brows. "My daddy died in the war."

"I know, Son." Ellis was still coming to terms with his brother's death. He was amazed at how well the child was handling the tragedy.

"Did you know my daddy?"

"We were brothers. I grew up with him." Ellis looked over to Miss Smith. What had she told the lad about him? She glanced away after acknowledging she had discussed him with the child.

"Nanna told me you were my daddy's brother. I don't have a brother."

"I know, Richard," Ellis replied.

"But Billy has a brother, and his brother lives with him. How come you didn't live with my daddy?"

Ellis reached for Richard's hand, then thought better of it. He was so timid a few minutes ago. He didn't want to spook the child. "That, Son, is a very long story. Let me take you to my home and get Miss Smith out of this hot sun."

Richard nodded.

"Mistress Smith, my carriage is this way." Ellis thought long and hard, trying to remember the woman's first name, but for the life of him he couldn't remember. He was not a man given to forgetfulness. This was indeed something else to ponder. She seemed as beguiling as some of the stories he'd heard of sea sirens in ancient mythology.

Her thick, dark dress would be far too exhausting in this region. He hoped she had brought her summer apparel, as he had requested, along with Richard's belongings. A simple wool coat for the coldest of days in the winter was all that was needed. He reckoned she didn't have a clue what November in the Florida Straits would be like. At least her hat had a wide brim and would protect her fair skin from the hot rays of the sun.

Bea followed Ellis Southard's lead. He seemed to talk with compassion to Richard, and he certainly gave him his full attention. She found this a surprising and welcome relief, compared to the way most adults generally ignored children.

The port was busy. Ships of all shapes and sizes lined the harbor. Few horses and carriages lined the streets, but activity flourished. She had tried to learn about this island, so new to the territory, but little was written. Richard Sr. had informed her of a troop of Union soldiers stationed on the island from the beginning of the Civil War, and she had seen the fort. He had wanted to be stationed here, in the hope of spending some time with his brother, but Richard had spent most of his time in Virginia and other areas of heavy fighting.

Bea wondered if Ellis was a Southern sympathizer. The war was over, but she knew so little of the man. Her mother had told her, on more than one occasion, political matters were for men and she'd best not get involved. For the most part she heeded her mother's admonition, but only due to the fact she was busy caring for a small child. At one point she had followed Elizabeth's instructions and buried the family silver in the yard. It had been passed down for several generations and no war, no matter what the issue, would take that away from the Southards. They, of course, had fed many of the troops as they worked their way south. Never had she felt her life, or little Richard's, was in danger, but it was a weary time. Reports of families being torn apart, brothers fighting against brothers, cousins against cousins—such an ugly mess.

However, Bea was convinced slavery was cruel and heartless. Now, as she looked around the island, she saw black men, white men, and Hispanics working side by side. Could this place truly be a paradise?

She fanned herself. The sun was high in the sky and she was suffocating. Why had she worn such a heavy dress today? The first several days at sea were cold. Very cold. But the last two days, the temperatures had been warming. Now, the intense heat of the bright afternoon sun against the perfect sky of blue made her thirsty and a bit weak.

She needed to get out of these warm clothes. "Pardon me, Mr. Southard. How far must we travel until we reach your home?"

"Not far at all. The island is quite small. You could walk to my home in a few minutes' time."

Walk? The idea worried her. "I thought you said you had a carriage?"

"I did, and I do. As soon as we arrive at my home I'll show you the guest house. You'll be staying in the cottage, and Richard will be staying with me in the main house."

The guest house? She wouldn't be sleeping next to Richard? What if he cried out for her in the middle of the night? Of course he hadn't done that for a long time, not since he was sick the last time, but still. . . .

"Miss Smith, I don't believe it is proper for a man to have a single woman in his home without staff who also live in the home."

"Oh." Bea blushed. He did have a point. But she was the child's nanny. Wasn't that considered staff?

"Since you're no longer the child's nanny, I think it improper."

Could he read her mind? Bea nodded and bit back her counterargument. As far as she was concerned, she was more than a nanny to Richard. But he was right. Her time of releasing and letting the child go had come. "A time to embrace, and a time to refrain from embracing," Ecclesiastes 3:5, came to mind. Wasn't that the scripture the Lord had been working on her heart for months now? Bea let out a deep breath and stepped up into the carriage while Ellis stowed their baggage.

The carriage moved slowly from the docks. The variety of trees, flowers, and unfamiliar sights took Bea's mind off her present discomfort. Farther in from the shore were more trees and a gentle breeze. Mixed with the shade, they eased her discomfort.

The house, a two-story wooden structure with shutters, stood proudly within a tropical garden. Fruit trees of every imaginable kind lined the yard. In the rear of the yard stood a cute cottage, looking to Bea for all the world as if a ship were buried in the earth from the deck down. The cottage gave the appearance of a ship's cabin, perhaps the captain's quarters.

Ellis jumped down and helped Bea to the ground. His firm hands on her waist as he guided her down the long step from the carriage gave her reason to catch his eyes, blue gray and as deep as the northern seas.

He released her the instant her feet were on the ground. Her sides ached for his touch. Bea shook her head slightly, fussing with herself to take a logical approach to all this. She suddenly felt faint from the heat. She'd been to sea for days, perhaps her equilibrium was off. The sight of a handsome face certainly couldn't account for it, especially since the man was so impersonal and seemed to care only for the harsh reality of profit-making.

"The guest cottage was a ship's cabin. The former owner of this property, Captain Curtis, salvaged it and turned it into this cottage."

"It's quite unique." The place really was charming, she had to admit. But she was still agitated over Ellis's comment at the boat about her coddling Richard. *Perhaps feminine words and gestures are not endearing to the gentleman,* she thought, fighting back the sarcasm.

"I trust you will find everything you need. Dinner is served at five—you'll join us for meals."

Was that an order? Bea fought down her defensive posture and thanked him.

He pointed out the outdoor water closet and other necessities for her comfort.

Richard pouted. "I want to stay with Nanna."

"Richie, your uncle Ellis has a room just for you in his big house." Bea stroked his blond hair and smiled.

"Son." Ellis knelt down beside the child. He'd done that before. Maybe he did have a heart of compassion for the lad. "If after seeing your new room you still wish to spend the night out here in the cottage, it will be all right. Miss Smith will be close by. In fact, you can look out your window and see her cottage."

"Really?" Richard's eyes implored his uncle's. Two pairs of similar eyes searched each other. Bea turned. She couldn't allow Richard to see her pain.

"Naturally. Shall I show you your new room so that Miss Smith can have some privacy and gain some comfort from this heat?"

Richard propelled himself from the cottage. *He has only just met his uncle,* Bea lamented silently, *and is already willing to leave me, even forgetting to say good-bye.* Tears edged her eyes. No, she wouldn't cry. Not now. Not yet. Later, perhaps. When no one would know.

The memory of Miss Smith's delicate waist in his hands to aid her descent from his carriage had reinforced his decision to put her in the guesthouse. Face-to-face, day in, day out with a beautiful woman, together with the present shortage of women on the island, would press any sane man to his limits. He couldn't fault little Richie for wanting to stay close to her. Who wouldn't?

He mounted the porch stairs of his newly acquired home two at a time. "Come on, Richard, let me show you to your brand-new room." Curious in Miss Smith's presence, he'd felt the need to be formal, dignified, quite the opposite of his normal boisterous self. He reached down and scooped Richard up, placing him on his shoulders. "So tell me, Son. Does your Nanna have a first name?"

"Nanna!"

Of course. Wasn't his own mother always "Mom"? Ellis chuckled. "I guess I should say, what do other people call Miss Smith?"

"Bea."

Bea. Beatrice. That's it! How could he have forgotten? After all, that was his maternal grandmother's name.

"So, do you like fishing, Richard?"

Ellis could feel the child nod against the back of his head and neck. "Here we are, Son, do you like it?" Together they surveyed the room's single oak-framed bed, an old sea captain's chest he had purchased for the child's toys, and a small chest of drawers he had acquired from a recent wrecking expedition. A small bamboo fishing pole leaned up against the chest of drawers, just the right size for a young boy. One of the things Ellis enjoyed about Key West was the variety of items that came to port. Wrecking, or rather ship salvaging, had been the island's primary income before the war, as ships from around the world ran aground off the various coral reefs.

He settled Richard down to the floor and watched as the lad soaked up his surroundings. His eyes focused on the fishing pole.

"For me?"

"For you. I thought perhaps we could go fishing together. Would you like that?"

Richard nodded his head and tentatively reached for the pole.

"Go ahead, pick it up." Ellis sat on the bed. "How does it feel in your hands?"

Richard worked his tongue between his teeth as he held the pole in his hands, his eyes wide with excitement. Ellis breathed a sigh of relief. He didn't know anything about raising kids but figured he'd focus on things he had enjoyed doing when he was a boy.

His only problem would be caring for the child when he was at work. He had been prone to spend long days away from the house, sunup to sundown. With young Richard now depending on him, he would have to adjust his schedule. But he would need to work, and he would need a nanny to watch over the lad.

His mind raced back to the beautiful woman in his guest house. He hoped she was well. She had looked completely exhausted from the heat. He made a mental note to talk with Cook and have some lemonade taken over to her. She would need to drink a lot to become acclimated to this climate.

"Uncle Ellis? Can Nanna go fishing with us?"

"If she would like." He hadn't known many women from New York who liked to fish. Here in Key West it wasn't unusual, but someone from New York. . .well, he'd never seen it. "Have you been fishing before?"

Richard nodded his head. It seemed he didn't speak often. Ellis wondered if it was just shyness.

"Who took you fishing? Your daddy?"

"Nanna. Daddy was at war." Richard placed the pole back where he had found it.

She took the boy fishing? *Hmm, maybe she doesn't coddle the child after all.* "Did she teach you to bait a hook?"

"Nanna does that. She says it's hard to get the worm to stay on the hook."

Ellis grinned. The image of the fair-skinned, very proper young woman wrapping a worm on a hook intrigued him.

"Well, let me introduce you to Cook."

"Cook?"

"She's someone I hired to prepare meals and do some cleaning for me."

Richard knitted his eyebrows together. “Nanna cooks.”

“Come on, I’ll introduce you.”

Ellis scooped the child into his arms and had him ride on his hip. A pleasing sense of comfort seemed to wrap the inside of his body even as little Richard’s small frame wrapped the outside. He hoped and prayed it brought comfort to Richard as well.

“Good afternoon, Cook. How are you today?”

“Fine, Mr. Ellis. Would this be young Master Southard I’ve been hearin’ about?”

“That’s right. Richard, this is Cook. Cook, this is Richard, my nephew.”

“Fine lookin’ young lad. He has your eyes, Mr. Ellis. But his hair is much fairer than yours.”

“My mommy had blond hair,” Richard stated proudly. “Nanna says I have her hair.”

“Nanna?” Cook inquired.

“Nanna is his term for his nanny. She’s in the guest house. Would you be so kind as to run over and give her some of your fine lemonade?”

“No, Sir, but I’ll give her some limeade.”

Ellis chuckled. “Whatever you think best, Cook.” He turned to Richard, still in his arms. “Richard, do you wish to explore the house or help me with your baggage?”

“Can I explore?”

“Sure can. I haven’t explored it all yet. If you find anything of interest, let me know.” Ellis watched the boy run out of the kitchen and down the hall.

Cook’s broad smile disappeared from her dark, round face. “Now, why is the boy’s nanny out all alone in the guest house?” she demanded, planting her strong hands on ample hips, her full figure going rigid.

“Because you won’t move into my house. How’s a man to keep up with proper etiquette if he has a single woman living with him?”

“Fiddlesticks, ain’t no high society image here to maintain. What’s the real reason? I fixed up the spare room, just like you asked.”

Chapter 3

Ellis shifted nervously. He'd never been able to keep Cook from prying. The woman was incredible. He couldn't imagine her children ever getting away with anything. "Once you meet her, you'll understand."

"Ah, so she struck your fancy."

Ellis blushed. A retreat was his only option, before she learned more than he had a mind to let her know. "Please, take her some limeade." He turned around and quickly made his exit. Two steps out of the room, he heard Cook chuckling under her breath.

Inventory ledgers, exporting records—all needed posting. Ellis tried for the fifteenth time to concentrate on the books before him. He dabbed the pen in the inkwell one more time. He had planned the day off, giving himself and his nephew time to get acquainted. He hadn't planned on his nephew's nanny creating within him a driving force to flee back to work at the docks.

Maybe that isn't a bad idea. Ellis pushed back his chair and walked over to the window facing the small cottage. His hands clasped behind his back, he stood there, staring absentmindedly. A moment later Cook scurried toward the cottage with a tray and a pitcher of limeade. He watched as the door opened, but Miss Smith remained in the shadows as Cook entered the cottage. Disappointed, he turned around and faced the room.

Why was he disappointed?

Breaking his reverie, Richard's scream assaulted his ears. "Uncle Ellis!"

He bolted out of his office down the hall toward the direction of the scream. His heart racing, blood pumping, he found the lad, perfectly well, standing in the parlor.

"Richard, what on earth is the matter?" Ellis barely held back from exploding.

"Nothing."

"Nothing? You scream like that for nothing?"

"I just called you."

Ellis searched the boy's eyes. He truly was puzzled over his uncle's reaction. Was it possible that all boys yelled like that? *Well, not in my house.*

"I thought you were hurt, Son. Sit down, please."

Richard sat on the tall, straight-back sofa. "If you need me, come find me. Don't yell."

Holding back tears, Richard nodded his head.

Ellis calmed himself down and sat beside the boy, wrapping his arm around him. "What was it you called me for?"

Richard pointed to the stereoscope on the table.

Seeing the object, Ellis said, "Would you like to look at some pictures?" Against his arm, he felt Richard trembling with fear. Ellis scooped the boy up and placed him on his lap. "I'm sorry, Richard. I didn't mean to scare you."

Richard wound his soft-skinned arms up around his uncle's neck. His blond curls buried deep into Ellis's chest. Overcome with compassion, Ellis kissed the top of Richard's head and held him tight.

Bea liked Cook. At first she figured the woman for a slave, but soon her forward mannerisms revealed that wasn't the case. Whomever this woman was, she wasn't a pawn to someone else's wishes.

The limeade was refreshing, not as sweet as lemonade, yet the sour of the limes seemed a bit more gentle than that of lemons. Cook told her the limes had grown on a tree on Ellis Southard's property.

The shade of the trees around the cottage helped ease the summer-like temperatures. A gentle breeze blew through the windows. Bea loved the cottage. It was small, but wonderfully decorated, just like a captain's quarters on a ship. The wood paneling, the berth that held the bed, everything was so similar to that of the *Justice* where she had been the guest of Captain Brighton for meals during her trip from New York.

Cook's words brought her back to the present. "Your bed is made. Now remember what ol' Cook says and don't do too much today or tomorrow. Your body needs to adjust to this heat."

"Yes. Thank you."

"Dinner will be served at five. I leave to be with my family by six."

"I understand."

And Bea understood more than Cook realized. In New York the servants were ordered about. Their personal lives had no bearing on the time they were to devote to the family for whom they were employed. Their wealthy employers seldom gave thought to the possibility that their servants' families might have needs, too. Here was another reason to be grateful for her parents' example. They were sensitive to their servants' needs. But in Cook's case, she seemed to be the one giving the orders. Bea grinned.

"What be on your mind, Child?" Cook inquired.

"Oh, nothing."

"The devil be in you! Don't go lying to me. You had a thought, and a funny one at that."

"I like you, Cook. You know your mind."

" 'Tis true, but I've been known to speak when I should have kept my mouth shut. The Good Lord knows He has a problem with me in regards to that." Cook slowly wagged her head. "It's not like I don't try. Well, perhaps I don't. Guess I'm getting set in my ways.

"Now, stay in your chemise in the house and drink lots of fluids. Just for a day or two. You may not think it proper, but child, forget propriety. You need to become acclimated."

"Thank you, Cook. I can get over the immodesty as long as I'm sure no one will come knocking at my door."

"Other than the child, I don't expect you to have visitors. I'll see you for dinner. . ."

"At five," they said in unison and chuckled.

Bea lay down after Cook left. She was exhausted. The heat had worn her out. Without Cook's help, she'd still be laced in a corset. Learning that they were rarely worn down here helped in her decision to leave it off for a couple of days. She took another sip of the cool limeade and rolled over for a nap.

The pounding on her door woke her. "Nanna! Nanna!" Bea fumbled for her housecoat and came to the door.

"Hi, Richie, what's the matter?"

"Cook says it is time for dinner."

"Oh. Thanks. Tell Cook I'll be right over." Richard ran off, and Bea closed the door behind him. She fumbled to put on one of her light cotton dresses. Fortunately, she had packed a couple.

She found the house's decor tasteful, yet it had some of the strangest items she'd ever seen.

The table and chairs in the dining area were of a French style, and the hutch, more of a Spanish design. Oddly enough, the eclectic blend worked. Bea wondered who had decorated the house. She'd never known a man to bother with such things.

"Miss Smith." Ellis held a chair out for her to be seated.

The trestle table was set with fine china and well-polished silver. The stemware was crystal, with flowers delicately etched on each goblet. Ellis Southard apparently had made his fortune.

"Thank you, Mr. Southard."

Ellis nodded and took his place at the head of the table.

"Can I show Nanna my room after dinner?" Richard asked.

Bea watched Ellis from the corner of her eye, sitting up straight, careful not to show too much interest. After all, the man already thought she pampered the child.

"Yes, you may, Son."

Bea was pleased to see admiration in Richard's eyes for his uncle. Perhaps he had taken some interest in the child.

Cook served the dinner and sat with them at the table. It seemed odd to Bea, yet, on the other hand, perhaps it explained the familiarity with which she spoke of Ellis Southard.

"Shall we pray?" Ellis offered a brief prayer of thanksgiving.

At least he prayed over his meal, she thought. Was it possible he was a Bible-believing Christian? That would answer at least one of her prayers for Richard and his future life with his uncle.

"Cook and I often eat together, Miss Smith. She's been invited to move in and live here, but she prefers her own small cottage with relatives cluttering up the place." Ellis forked another morsel of fish.

Can the man read my mind? Bea scrutinized Ellis's blue-gray eyes, catching the hint of a smile within them. Her heart warmed a bit.

"Mr. Southard, you know that isn't the way of it. I'm the elder of the family and they expect me to keep the order."

"Now, Cook, your son is old enough to be the elder. You just like telling folks what they ought to do."

Bea found the playful bantering comforting and informative.

"Nanna," Richard broke in, "Uncle Ellis bought me a fishing pole and he said we could go fishing."

"That's wonderful, Richie."

"Richie?" Ellis whispered the question.

"I'm sorry. Richard," Bea corrected herself. She needed to remember this man was very formal.

"Richie seems a fine name for the boy," Cook muttered, and played with a morsel of fish on her plate.

"Nanna always calls me Richie."

"Enough," Ellis snapped.

Bea fought back a surge of anger. She did not intend to have this child raised by a brute. She saw no cause for him to bellow.

Ellis continued. "If you wish to be called 'Richie' by Miss Smith that is fine."

Cook quickly finished her meal. Bea hustled down the rest of her dinner in silence. No sense lingering and possibly angering Mr. Southard again. Richard excused himself from the table as soon as he swallowed his last bite. He walked around and stood by Bea's side.

"Nanna, can I show you my room now?"

"Yes, I would like that."

Bea couldn't retreat up the stairs fast enough. Richard slipped his tiny hand in hers. She cherished his touch, and her heart tightened again. How could she possibly live without him?

Richie's quarters seemed to shout out "boy's room." Intrigued by the fact that Ellis had managed to acquire a few toys, she found herself suddenly wobbly and confused. Perhaps it was the heat? She sat down on the bed and patted it. "Richie, bring me a book and I'll read to you."

He grabbed one of his favorites. "Nanna, I want to sleep with you tonight."

Bea kissed the top of his head. "Oh, Richie, you'll be fine in your new room. Didn't your uncle Ellis say you can look over to my cottage from your window?"

"Yes."

"I've got an idea. What if I place a candle in my window for you to see? Then you'll know I'm there."

Richard simply nodded.

"I love you, Richie."

"I love you, Nanna." He turned in her arms and embraced her hard. He was scared. This would be the first night he didn't have her close by his side. She held him tight. It would be the first night in four years she wouldn't be close to his side either. *O Lord, thanks for this time of embracing.* She swallowed her tears, not allowing them to flow.

"Nanna?"

"Yes, Richard."

"Can you sing 'In Peace' for me?"

"Sure, honey." And Bea began to sing the familiar Bible verse she had turned into a lullaby so many years before.

> "In peace I will both lie down and sleep.
> For thou alone, O Lord,
> makest me to dwell in safety.
> Psalm four: eight."

Ellis stood just outside Richard's doorway, his heart heavy like a sack of salt. Compassion for this woman and his nephew overwhelmed him. How could he separate them? They truly loved and cared for one another. *She's the only mother the boy has ever known,* he realized. Elizabeth died when Richard was barely one. So much death for such a small child.

He shouldn't have snapped at the dinner table. His words with Cook after they departed were not pleasant. She chastised him for his behavior. How could he explain that he was still having a hard time dealing with the loss of his brother? They had been close as children and had corresponded constantly as adults. He knew Richard's intimate thoughts about war and the massive destruction of humanity he had seen. He knew how such things had grieved his brother.

He also knew that Richard had a problem being home alone with his son—that he saw his beloved wife etched in his features—that each glance brought back the painful memory of her death and rekindled his guilt for having gone to fight the accursed war. Ellis knew all the secret thoughts of a man unable to cope with his wife's death. His brother had even been tempted to just leave the child in his nanny's care and head for the western frontier. And yet there were other times when responsibility and duty were paramount in his brother's life. He had planned to train young Richard to run the farm, teach him business and how to turn a profit.

Ellis eventually concluded that war played havoc with a man's mind. He wished never to partake in such an event. He had been in Key West when Florida seceded from the Union and when the Union soldiers took over Fort Zachary Taylor. The captain ordered all those sympathetic with the South off the island, and the rest were given the option to stay on the island and not fight. Thankfully, few left the island before the orders to leave were rescinded.

Ellis never had to fight. He'd never been forced to take sides. Now that the war was over, the island was beginning to recover financially from its losses.

The beauty of Bea's voice lulled him away from his thoughts as he watched her caress the gentle blond strands of Richard's hair. He longed for a woman to stroke him with such a loving caress.

How long had it been? Ten? No, fifteen years since he walked away from Heather, her father, and his shotgun. They had been foolish young people who thought they were in love, only to discover it was simply infatuation. Had it been love, he would have returned for her when he was older and brought her to live with him. Instead, once out of her sight, her memory, their "love" had grown cold.

No, he was not a man to be trusted with a beautiful woman. He groaned inwardly and left them to their own loving union.

Chapter 4

The warm glow of morning sunlight lapped the palm fronds outside her window as a rooster crowed. Bea ached to be with Richard. This was the first time since his birth she hadn't been at his side, the first morning she wasn't in the kitchen making breakfast for him. She felt useless. She snuggled back under the sheet, having discarded the other bedcovers within minutes of retiring last evening. The small nub of a candle remained on her windowsill. She'd let it burn far longer than needed, just in case Richie would call out for her.

Needed her? She snickered. "He's adjusting just fine with his uncle, Lord. I'm the one who is having a hard time with it. Perhaps I should return home."

She waited for some earth-shattering revelation to bellow from the heavens. At this point she'd even settle for that still small voice spoken of in the Bible. Something, anything. She needed advice, direction. Her world was collapsing and the only verse of Scripture that seemed to placate her was Ecclesiastes 3:5, "A time to embrace. . ."

Disgusted with her self-remorse, Bea flung the sheet off and sprang out of bed. The room spun. She sat back down on the bed, clasping the edge of the mattress for balance. Her body trembled uncontrollably. Her hands felt clammy. What was happening to her? She closed her eyes. Her head began to pound.

She'd lived through hot weather before. Cook said to stay in her chemise and she had. So why was she so unsteady on her feet?

Beatrice's shaky hand grasped the water glass beside her bed and slowly lifted it to her mouth. Snow hadn't fallen yet back home in upstate New York, but she knew the pond was icing over. In a week's time she'd gone from freezing temperatures to sweltering heat. She dipped her handkerchief in the basin and dampened her brow.

Perhaps she should remain in bed. Bea eased her body slowly back upon the mattress. "O Lord, help me, I'm so dizzy and weak," she mumbled in prayer, then closed her eyes and collapsed into the cool darkness of her mind.

Ellis couldn't get over Richard's constant chattering. Questions, he had a million of them. Carefully, he answered them one at a time. Richard was a handsome child, and his eyes were so penetrating. When those eyes looked at him, Ellis felt as if they pierced his soul.

"Uncle Ellis?"

"Yes, Richard?" Ellis scooped another section of passion fruit from its yellow rind.

Richard held up his half-section of the fruit and asked, "What's this called?"

"They call it passion fruit. Some, I've heard, call it grapefruit."

"That's silly."

"Why?"

"Because it doesn't look like a grape, and it's much bigger."

Ellis chuckled. "I suppose you're right, Son."

"Uncle Ellis?"

"Yes, Richard."

"How come Nanna isn't having breakfast with us?"

"I don't know. Perhaps she overslept this morning."

"But Nanna always is up before I am."

It was odd that Beatrice hadn't come over for breakfast. He had told her the precise time for meals, and she was expected to join them. "Possibly she's tired from the heat."

"How come it's so hot here?" Richard asked, working his spoon back and forth until the fruit spit at him.

"Because this part of the earth is closer to the sun."

"How come?"

"I don't know, other than that's the way the Good Lord made it."

"Oh." Richard popped a seed out of his fruit.

"Uncle Ellis?"

Ellis didn't think he'd ever heard his named called out as many times as this lad had called him in the past hour. "What is it, Son?"

He held up the large seed. "If I plant this seed will it grow?"

"I reckon so. Would you like to do that?"

Richard's blue eyes sparkled with excitement. "Can I?"

"Sure, but we need to let the seed dry for a day or two first."

"We had to do that with the corn.

"Uncle Ellis, did you live at my daddy's farm when you were a boy?"

"I sure did. Even helped plant some corn."

"How come I never saw you?"

Out of the mouths of innocent children, Ellis inwardly lamented. "I was busy here with my sponge business."

"How do you grow sponges? Do you plant seeds like corn?"

If he answered that question, he'd be late for certain. Ellis wiped his mouth with a cloth napkin. "Richard, I'd love to tell you all about sponge-fishing, but if I don't get to work, my men will not go to work, and work is what pays to put the food on the table and roof over our heads. So maybe we can revisit this later?"

"All right." Richard grabbed his napkin, wiped his mouth and hands, and promptly stood. "Where do we go to work?"

The boy intended to go to work with him. Ellis took in a deep breath. He needed a break. But he wanted to be accessible for the child.

"Richard," Cook called. "I need you to go and visit your Nanna."

Ellis didn't pass up the opportunity. "Would you look after Nanna today? I'm sure she's having trouble with this heat. You'd be a big help to me if you kept an eye on her."

"All right." Richard scurried out of the dining hall, his feet pattering down the hall.

"Thanks, Cook." Ellis turned to her and smiled.

"The boy is most curious, I'd say. But he's a smart one. Truth be told, I'm worried about Miss Smith. She should have been up here by now. I haven't seen any movement in the house. I'm a bit concerned."

"She'll need your care today. Can you handle the child as well?"

Cook raised her hands to her ample hips. "Now who do you think cared for my young 'uns?"

Ellis held back a grin. He'd known she'd rise to the challenge. But if he had asked her straight out, she would have given him an hour-long lecture about how she wasn't "hired to be no nanny."

"Now, you take that smirk right off your face. I know what you be thinkin'. Besides, I like the gal."

Ellis chuckled and left before anyone could cause him further delay. He was already a half-hour late, though he'd still arrive before his men.

"Nanna! Nanna!"

Bea heard the pounding at her door. She even heard Richie calling her. Yet try as she might, she couldn't roll her body out of bed. Every time she tossed herself over to her side she became dizzy. Her voice was weak.

"Richie," she breathed. Could he hear her? *O God, help me.*

"Uncle Ellis, help!" His nephew's scream reached his ears just as he rounded the gate. "Help!"

Beatrice. . .Miss Smith. . .trouble. Ellis turned back and ran toward the cottage.

Richard stood outside the door, crying. "Help, Uncle Ellis, Nanna won't come."

Ellis lifted the iron latch and flung open the door. He rushed toward the bedroom and found Beatrice wrapped in her bed-sheet. "Richard, go get Cook."

"Is she all right?"

"She will be, Son. Please, go get Cook."

Thankfully, Richard didn't have any more questions. Beatrice was as red as a cooked lobster, and he knew what that meant. She needed to be cooled down and quickly. He reached for a rag in the basin. The water was warm. He dampened it anyway and applied it to her forehead.

The cistern will be the best place for her, he thought, his mind racing. *It should be full this time of year.* Ellis scooped her up and carried her out to the backyard, to the large coral trough protected by a weathered shed. He'd often thought the cistern was far too big, but today it would prove its worth. He set her on the top step, her feet dangling in the pool of water. He held her in his left arm and reached into the pool to dampen the rag again. This time it would be more refreshing.

Gently he applied the cool cloth over her face and neck, her arms and legs, carefully avoiding her torso.

Cook burst into the shed, huffing and gasping for breath. "Mr. Ellis, what's the matter with the poor child?"

"I'm no doctor, but I'd say she has a serious case of heatstroke. Cool her down, Cook. Keep her cool. I'll fetch the doctor."

"I'll take care of the child," she replied, immediately taking Beatrice from Ellis, cradling her like a mother with child.

Richard stood next to Cook trembling, tears streaming down his face. "Is Nanna going to die?" he asked.

"No, Son. She's going to be just fine." Ellis knelt beside him and held his hands. *So much death in this little one's life, Lord. Please make his Nanna all right,* he silently prayed. "Would you help Cook keep Nanna wet?"

Frightened eyes stared inquiringly into his uncle's.

"She'll be fine, Richard, trust me."

Richard nodded.

Cook continued to pour the water over Beatrice's lethargic body.

"Can you help her, Son?"

"Yes."

"Good. Strip down to your shorts and stand in the water next to Cook. Keep pouring water on her. I'll get the doctor."

Richard began stripping off his clothes. Ellis figured the water would help the child as well. While he didn't appear to be having any trouble with the heat, he might later. A good dip in the cool cistern would be helpful for him. Ellis headed for town, thanking God for living in such a small community with the doctor a few blocks away.

"Miss Smith."

Someone was calling her, but who? The gentle lull of a woman's voice continued to penetrate her muddled thoughts.

"Come on, Child, I know you can hear me."

"Nanna!" Richie cried.

Richard, crying. Beatrice opened her eyes wide and tried to bolt upright. Water? She was in a tub? With Richard? And. . .and. . .Cook? What was going on here?

Cook's warm chocolate face broke into a grin, and her eyes sparkled. "Glad to see you're feeling better."

"Where am I? What's going on?"

"A touch of the heat. Didn't drink enough, I reckon."

"Nanna!" Richie exclaimed and jumped on her. The boy was soaking wet, she quickly realized, and in this. . .this huge tub.

Bea embraced Richard. "Where am I? Where are we?"

"This here be a cistern. Folks on the island have them all over. We collect the water during the rainy season and have it for the dry season. When the troops came to the island in the twenties, folks realized they wouldn't have enough fresh water in the wells. So they built these. Come in pretty handy."

Handy—the water was downright wonderful. Beatrice gathered in her surroundings. She was sitting on a white coral step at a rectangular pool of water with walls of coral as well. A small wooden roof with short sides stood over the area with a hatch-like opening at the peak of the roof. She cupped a handful of the refreshing water and sipped. It was cool and very energizing.

"Drink slowly. Your body has had quite a shock."

"How'd I get here?"

"Mr. Southard brought you."

Bea's cheeks flamed. She was in her undergarments. "Oh my," she gasped.

"Don't be fussing about modesty now, child. He had you wrapped in a bedsheet. I took that off."

"Oh."

"Mr. Southard is a perfect gentleman. He's gone to fetch the doctor. I reckon he'll be here shortly."

"Doctor? What happened?"

"Near as I can figure, you passed out from the heat. Your skin was bright red when I first came on you."

Bea looked at her arms. They were pink, but certainly not red.

"Your color's almost back to normal," Cook said.

Richie sat on the step beside Beatrice. "Isn't this great?" Richie wiggled his toes in the water.

Bea reached out to him, found she was still dizzy, and put her hand back down on the steps to steady herself.

"Now don't you go moving too quickly, Miss."

"I can't believe how shaky I am."

"Comes with the heat, if you don't take care of yourself. Now sit back and enjoy the water." Cook rose from her step and sat down on the top stair.

"Nanna, do you think Uncle Ellis will let me go swimming in here?"

"I doubt your uncle will want you swimming in here, Child," Cook answered. "We've got a big ocean out there, plenty of water for a boy to go swimming if'n he has a mind to."

"Can I go swimming in the ocean, Nanna?"

"Give your Nanna some time to rest."

Richard's shoulders sagged. "All right."

Bea couldn't possibly keep Richard's questions straight in her mind. It took all of her energy just to try to stay awake.

"She's in the cistern, Doc." Ellis pointed to the backyard shed covering the cistern.

"Quick reasoning, Ellis," Dr. Hanson replied.

"Cook and my nephew are back there with her. Unless you think you need me, I think for propriety's sake I best stay out front."

"I understand."

"Thanks, Doc. Send the boy to me. I'll take him with me to work."

"Sure." Doc Hanson headed to the backyard.

Ellis paced his front yard, picking up some fallen palm fronds and tossing them in a pile. A house, a yard, a child—all brought more burdens, and more responsibility into his life. Not to mention a guest who had almost died. A pain shot through Ellis's chest. She had such lily-white skin, made even more beautiful by the few freckles dotting her cheeks. The woman weighed next to nothing in his arms. She didn't have the strength to even protest. Never in a million years would he forget her lifeless form draped across his arms. Why hadn't he checked on her sooner, when she hadn't appeared for breakfast?

Ellis kicked a coral rock out of his path. Life sure had changed in a little over a month. Then, he had been a man of no worries. Oh, perhaps a few regarding the success of his business, but then he only had himself to provide for. His bank account grew. He had more than he needed.

He had sunk a tremendous portion of his savings into this old house—a house he had purchased upon learning he was to raise his brother's son. Oh, how the tables had turned.

He had hired Cook to fix his dinner and clean his rented room in town. The owner of the boardinghouse, Ana White, could no longer care for her boarders in that fashion, so he found Cook. In the end, Cook worked for just about everyone in the house, including Ana. She was quite a woman for her age.

He was thankful she had come to work for him here. But he knew she still wandered over to the boardinghouse and took care of a few folks there as well.

"Uncle Ellis."

Ellis spun around to see the child, dripping wet, his rumpled clothes in his arms and fear knotting his forehead.

"How is she, Son?"

"She's awake."

"Good."

"Do I have to go with you?"

How could he take the child away? "Not if you don't want to. But I thought we could walk down to the dock, speak to my workers, and come right back."

"Really?" Richard's eyes widened. A curl of a smile edged on the side of his mouth.

"Sure. Do you want to come with me or stay?"

Richard turned and looked back at the cistern. "Will she be all right?"

"Yes, Son. Cook and the doctor can handle things from here. But I'm sure you helped a great deal."

Richard puffed out his chest. "I did like you said. I got her real wet."

Ellis chuckled. "Good, Son, real good."

Chapter 5

Ellis worked out the tension in his back then walked hand in hand with Richard toward his dock. The sun was bright, the sky a vivid blue, a few clouds lining the horizon. "Richard." Ellis pointed to his right. "See those tall clouds that look like a top?"

"Uh-huh."

"Those are funnel clouds. The air is swirling around real fast."

"Really? How does it work?"

"Hmmm, tell you what. When we get to my office I'll show you how the wind spins and the cloud is formed." The ploy worked; the boy seemed to have taken his mind off his nanny. On the other hand, Ellis found himself wondering how she was doing—if they had her out of the cistern yet and back in her cottage. He'd have moved her into the house to care for her, but the cottage was actually a tad cooler than his home.

"Uncle Ellis?"

"Yes, Son."

"Did you make this dock?"

"No, I bought it from the man who built it."

"How come it's so long? New York had little docks."

The child was amazing, noticing little things like that. "In New York harbor the water becomes deep quickly. In Key West, you have to go out a long way from shore before the water gets deep, so the dock goes out to the deep water to enable the ships to come up to them."

"Oh." Richard pointed toward the mounds of sponges drying on his dock. "What are those?"

"Sponges. They grow in the ocean. My men take small boats out and dive into the water to bring up the sponges."

"Can you teach me how to swim?"

"Sure."

"Nanna plays in the pond with me at the farm. But I don't think she knows how to swim."

"Hmmm, it's possible. Growing up on the farm, I learned to swim in the pond. Is that where Nanna took you to play?"

"Yes, by the big rock."

Ellis smiled. How many leaps had he taken off that rock into the cool, crisp water below? He couldn't possibly count. "The water in Key West is much warmer than back home."

"That's 'cause we are closer to the sun, right?"

Ellis grinned broadly. Richard was a very bright boy indeed. He walked his nephew to the end of his pier where he had a small building which housed his office and tools for the men. Inside he showed him the sharp knives the sponge fishermen used for tools, and the nets they tied to their waists. Some of the men preferred an odd scissors-shaped tool to the knife, depending on which method the man had been taught.

"Uncle Ellis, what's this?" Richard pointed to a long pole with a two-pronged iron hook.

"That's for hooking the sponges from inside the boat."

"Do you go sponge-fishing too?"

"Sometimes, but not too often. Most of the time I have to work in the office here, or with the sponges after they've been harvested.

"Go take a whiff of that pile of sponges over there."

Richard scurried over. He wrinkled his face and looked back at Ellis. "They stink like dead fish."

Ellis chuckled.

Bea raised her head off the soft, down-feather pillow. She inhaled the freshness of the clean white sheets Cook had remade her bed with. "Cook, what were you and the doctor whispering about before he left?"

"Not worth repeatin'. He was just making sure I knew how to care for ya. I'll be spending the night with ya, too."

"I'm fine," Beatrice protested.

"Land sakes, Child, you are exhausted from that heat. I've got to make sure you drink enough fluids."

"But you have a family."

"True, but the doc, he's a-sending a message to my house. My children are all grown with children of their own. They feed themselves now, since I cook dinner for Mr. Ellis, and they insists I eat with him."

"I don't mean to pry, but were you a slave?"

"No, Ma'am. My family was set free when I was no higher than your knee. There's always been good pay for honest work for Bahamians on Key West. So my husband, George, brought us here right after we married. We bought our own home after a few years, and though things been tough at times, we've had a good life here on the island."

"What about the war?"

"Truth be told, the island wasn't much a part of the war. Granted, some of the folks who were wreckers suffered hard times when they weren't allowed to do no salvaging. And, what with the navy being here, there weren't quite so many wrecks."

"Tell me about this island of Key West. Where'd it get its name?"

"Original name was Cayo Hueso. That's Spanish for 'Island of Bones.' Folks say, for a long time the island was just a watering hole for sailors. Belonged to Cuba back then. Eventually, the king of Spain gave it to a man for faithful service. That fella, in turn, sold it to four businessmen from Connecticut. And they was the ones that started building a town here. Soon after, the navy put up a base. But 'twas the wrecking industry what brought a lot of money to the island." Cook leaned back and gave a low laugh, slapping her hands on her broad lap. "Listen to me rattle on."

"No, I'm interested, really."

Cook set her ample figure down on a rocker beside Bea's bed. "I can tell a tale or two about this here island. It's very different from the Bahamas, but I'm most comfortable here."

Beatrice's eyes were getting heavy. "Were there pirates living here?"

"Sure. Still are."

Beatrice pulled the sheet up to her chin.

Cook's robust laughter filled the room. "Most of 'em are retired. They made their money. Now they've settled down, got married, had kids. Got respectable, you might say."

"Really?" The word slipped past Bea's lips before she could catch herself.

"Wreckers salvaged whatever was worth taking from ships. Story goes, years ago, before the law came to the island, some folks would put a light out on the water to confuse the sailors so they'd run their ships aground on the reefs."

"No."

"Don't know if it be true or not. Just know that's what some say, is all. But it woke you up, didn't it?"

Bea chuckled. "Yes."

"Good, you need to stay alert, keep drinking. Rest will come later. But the doctor wants you awake for a mite longer before you sleep again."

"All right. Perhaps you can tell me some more tales of Key West."

"Why don't you tell me something about yourself?"

"Like what?"

"Why are you a nanny at such a young age?"

"Oh, well, that's easy. My best friend was Elizabeth Southard, Richard's mother. She had a terrible time when she was with child. We weren't even sure she was going to pull through. Elizabeth decided she needed some help, and she didn't want just anyone. Richard's family was gone, so they were alone on the farm. And she, being so weak. . .well, she asked me."

"You was a good friend." Cook tapped Bea's hand and proceeded to dip a cloth in the bowl of water. "Go on, I'll keep you cool while you tell me more."

"At first I was supposed to help only until shortly after Richard was born. But Elizabeth never fully recovered. So she asked me to stay. My parents weren't too happy. They'd had my coming-out party just before Elizabeth turned ill. Nevertheless, they understood the closeness between us, and knew that, if it were me who was so desperately ill, Elizabeth would have constantly been at my side.

"Elizabeth worsened after Richard was born. She developed a cough and never shook it." A tear edged her eye. "A year after Richard's birth, she passed on. But not before begging me to stay and continue to watch over Richard. Not that she had to beg me for anything regarding that little one."

"He's a charmer," Cook agreed. "You should have seen him this morning. Had his uncle tied up in knots just trying to figure out where all the boy's questions came from."

Bea laughed, her parched lips feeling brittle. She reached for a glass of Cook's refreshing limeade, noticing her hand still shook, though it was much stronger than earlier this morning. "I can't believe I fainted."

"Praise be to the Almighty! If little Richard hadn't come to check on you right away, you would have been far worse."

"He was so frightened."

"That he was, Child. But the Good Lord was with us, and you're going to be fine. You should have seen him pouring the water on you. He just kept doing what his uncle Ellis told him to do. You've raised a fine lad there, Miss. You should be proud."

"Don't know that I've done all that much, really. Just loved him as if he were my own."

"It shows, Child. It shows." Cook finished applying the damp cloth to Bea's limbs and sat back down on the wooden chair beside the bed. She brushed the gray hair, streaked with black, off her face. "Tell me where the child's father was during all these years."

"The war."

"How could I forget that? Mr. Ellis sure was broken up by his brother's death. I never seen a grown man so close to someone so far away."

"Close? Elizabeth never even spoke of him."

"I've been carin' for Mr. Ellis for a number of years now. He been receivin' a letter from his brother at least once a month."

"Even during the war?"

"Truly a miracle, I say. Yes'm, he managed to get some mail out with a Captain Brighton.

Seems the captain was working for the North, privateering. 'Course, you talk with a Southern sympathizer, they'd call him an outright pirate."

Bea chuckled. "I guess it all depends on which side of the war you're on." So, the *Justice*'s captain was a pirate or a privateer. Interesting.

"You speak a lot of truth there, Child.

"You mentioned your 'coming-out party.' Is that when your family says you're now ready for courtin' and marriage?"

Bea felt her cheeks heat up and she weakly answered, "Yes."

"I'm sure you left a few men lamentin' your status as a nanny."

"I wasn't one to seek the attention of a man. Never cared to, really. I suppose I never found one that was interesting enough." Bea placed her empty glass back on the nightstand.

"Uncle Ellis, who buys the sponges?" Richard asked, squatting on a tall chair beside him at his desk. Mounds of paperwork needed going over. But his mind was yet again on a hazel-eyed sea siren. His thoughts lingered on whether she'd survive this heat. He felt certain he had caught her before she became critical. The cistern was a true blessing from God. But he was still worried for the sake of the child. How would Richard handle losing another person close to him? Ellis shuddered and rubbed the gooseflesh off his arms.

"Uncle Ellis, can we go see Nanna now?"

Ellis plopped down his pencil. "Sure, Son. I was just thinking about her myself."

Richard's bright blue eyes smiled as he jumped off the tall chair he had been perched on. "I'm ready."

"Great, give me a minute to put these books together so I can take them home."

"Why do you write in your books? Nanna said I mustn't write in my books."

"Your Nanna is right. But these are special books for keeping track of a business's money. How much a business spends, how much it makes."

"How much money do you have, Uncle Ellis?"

"Enough." Ellis placed his large masculine hands on top of Richard's head and ruffled his curls, just like he had seen Miss Smith do on more than one occasion.

Richard smiled. "Nanna says I have a lot of money too."

"She did, did she?" What was this woman telling this child? Why would a boy need to worry himself about money at his age? He would need to have a word with Miss Smith when she was feeling better. At least one word.

Richard nodded. "Nanna said when my mommy died she had money put in a special place for me when I became a man."

"I see."

"Nanna said it was to buy my own farm, or go places, or whatever I want."

"That is a special gift, Son."

"Nanna says a wise man thinks before he spends his money."

Maybe he wouldn't need to speak with the woman after all.

"Nanna says some men spend their money on silly things."

"I see."

"Nanna says wise money is like planting corn. If you plant it right it grows and makes more."

"Your Nanna is a pretty smart woman."

"Nanna says Grandpa Smith taught her about wise money."

"I see," he said for the third time. And perhaps he was beginning to see more than he ever expected. As the child's nanny, she was responsible for his schooling, and she knew that

Richard's job would be caring for the farm one day. Maybe she wasn't as overprotective as he'd suspected.

"Uncle Ellis?"

"Yes, Son?" Ellis scooped the child into his arms, figuring they would make it home faster if he carried him. The child was a wonder, his mind so quick with facts and details. He soaked up knowledge like his sponges soaked up water. He was a remarkable lad who had a remarkable teacher. Ellis pondered the possibility of asking a certain Miss Beatrice Smith to stay on as the child's nanny. Of course, he'd probably have to offer her holidays to visit with her family in New York. . . . Still, the idea was plausible.

"Who taught you about money?"

"My dad and your father."

"Was my daddy wise with money?"

"Yes."

Richard nodded. A somber expression creased his delicate face. "I miss my daddy."

Ellis swallowed back a gasp. He hadn't expected Richard to be so honest with his emotions.

Ellis paused in the street. He lowered the child down and knelt before him, face-to-face. "I do, too, Son. I do, too."

Chapter 6

Nanna!" Richard cried from the doorway of her cottage.

"Come in here, Richie, I'm lying down."

"All right."

The old wooden rocking chair creaked as Cook eased herself up. "I'm going to speak with Mr. Ellis, Miss. I'll be back in a minute."

Beatrice nodded. Richard stood by her bed. She tapped the covers. "Come on up."

He climbed up and sat beside her. Bea wrapped her arm lovingly around him.

"Are you okay?" he asked.

"I'll be fine. I feel silly for not drinking as much as I should have for this heat."

"Uncle Ellis said you'd be all right."

"I'll need to stay in bed the rest of the day, but perhaps tomorrow we can get to your lessons."

"Nanna, I can play tomorrow so you can rest more."

Bea chuckled. "I'll see that your lessons are fun. Tell me, did you go to work with your uncle Ellis?"

Enthusiastically he nodded his head. "He fishes for sponges and they stink like dead fish. Uncle Ellis says he washes them so they don't smell."

"Interesting." *Sponges and the other natural wonders this island brings will make exciting lessons for Richard and myself,* Bea thought. Then she remembered she wouldn't be teaching Richard for much longer. Bea fought back her discouragement and tried concentrating on what Richard was telling her. Something about Ellis writing in his books.

". . .Uncle Ellis says he writes his money in a book."

"You mean keeps track of his money in his books. That's good, he uses his money like a good farmer."

"I told him about corn money."

"You did?"

"Uh-huh."

Bea smiled. The man probably thought she was a fool for putting money in the terms of seeds, but it seemed like the best way to explain it to a four year old.

Cook walked in with a broad smile. "Richard, I think you need to let your Nanna rest. You best go with your uncle now."

Richard nodded and slid off the bed. " 'Bye, Nanna. I'll come later."

" 'Bye, Richie. You mind your uncle, and I'll be up tomorrow."

"All right." He ran from the room.

"Now, I say you close those heavy eyes of yours and get some rest. I'll wake you later for some more to drink and maybe a light broth." Cook applied the damp cloth over her body again.

Bea struggled to keep her eyes open. Perhaps she should rest for a moment. Slowly she let them close, the burning at the back of her lids finding relief. So tired, so exhausted, she needed sleep. . . .

Bea awoke to Cook's delicate touch.

"Good morning, Child. You slept well."

"I feel better, but still weak."

"You'll be that way for most of the day. You rest and start getting some good food into your body. Hopefully, you'll be feeling better by evening."

Beatrice grasped Cook's soft, leathered hands. "Thank you." No other words fit. She was deeply indebted to this woman, this stranger who no longer seemed a stranger, but a friend.

"You're welcome. Don't you be carryin' on about how much I did. Just watched over you is all. Any good Christian woman would have."

"I don't know what I would have done without you."

"You would have been stuck with Mr. Ellis pacing all night and young Richard wanting to sleep with you to make sure you were all right."

She grinned at the image of Richie cradled beside her in bed. They had shared many lonely nights that way. However, she couldn't quite figure why Mr. Ellis, as Cook called him, would be pacing the floor on account of her. As far as he was concerned, she was an over-protective nursemaid who would need to return home on the first possible ship. Her grin slipped into a rigid slim line.

"Did you sleep at all, Cook?"

"Some. I'm fine, Child. But if you be fine, I'm going to the house to fix up some breakfast. What would you like?"

"Nothing. I still don't feel like eating."

"Hurumph. You'll be eating something. I'll make it light. Lay back down; I'll return shortly."

"Thank you." Bea watched Cook waddle out of her room. There would be no denying that woman. If she brought you something to eat, you'd better eat it. Cook's ways brought back memories of an old school matron, Miss Arno. The woman was not one to trifle with. She bellowed orders and you followed, or you were left cleaning boards, desks, floors, windows, anything the woman could think of. Bea shook her head and attempted to get up.

Slowly she draped her feet over the side of the bed. She waited for the dizziness to return. Thank the good Lord there was none. Feeling a bit more sure of herself, she eased her feet to the floor and continued holding the edge of the mattress. Carefully she straightened up. Her legs wobbled, her body felt exhausted. Should she dare take a couple steps to sit in the old wooden rocker?

Tentatively she lifted her right foot and slid it forward. Then her left. Yes, she could make it. She would just need to be careful. Easing herself into the rocker, she clasped her hands in her lap and proceeded with her morning prayers. She had a lot to be thankful for this morning, and a lot to petition the Lord about as well.

As always, Richard was in the forefront of all her prayers. "Father God, You know my heart, You know my love for this child. If there is any way I could remain on as his nanny, I'd appreciate it. But I do trust him into Your hands and Your protection for him. You are the Creator, and You do know what's best for him. I'm trying to refrain from embracing, to let go and trust him to You, removing myself. But it is difficult, Father. I love him so."

Ellis groaned as he dragged his body out of bed. He'd been up most of the night. Finally, Cook had told him not to come back to the cottage again; she needed some rest, too. Then, the nagging torment that he was ultimately responsible for the nanny's condition kept his eyes from closing while his feet wore out the floorboards. She was doing well, fortunately. She would recover. But he couldn't forgive himself for having been so insensitive. He had a pretty clear understanding of the amount of undergarments a woman wore up north, and this heat was not fit for a lady of such refinement. Many of the wives of the local residents refused to live here year-round because of the heat. But that number was changing as the women developed a taste for Spanish clothing, a far more agreeable attire for this climate.

A disheveled face in the mirror stared back at him, his eyes bloodshot from the lack of sleep. His beard needed a good trimming and brushing. He worked the stray hairs with his hand into a some semblance of order. Hoping the water would revive him, he rinsed his face one more time.

Ellis worked his way down the stairs to make breakfast for everyone, feeling it was the least he could do. Cook needed some rest, too, having been up most of the night herself. Of course, some of that was due to his wandering over there half a dozen times to check on Miss Smith's condition.

"What are you doing here?" he barked, seeing Cook busy at the stove.

"I'm fixin' breakfast."

"You should be with Miss Smith, Cook. I'll fix breakfast."

"Don't you be bellowing at me, Sir. Beatrice is fine. I appreciate your offer to make the morning meal, but. . ."

"Sorry, Cook," Ellis apologized.

"The lady needs something she can get down, not your idea of a breakfast," Cook teased.

Ellis raised a hand to his chest, feigning injury. *"Moi?"*

"Don't be using no fancy talk. You know you can't cook, that's why you hired me."

"I must have been out of my mind," Ellis mumbled. He truly loved Cook. She kept him in order. But, at times, the woman had an attitude which could make a man's toes curl.

"Probably so, but the good Lord knew you needed me in your life," Cook admonished.

Ellis chuckled. "You're quite a handful, Cook. How did your husband manage?"

"Quite well, thank you," she winked in reply. "Mr. Ellis," Cook lowered her voice, "Bea is going to be fine. She had a good night. She looks well this morning. Another day of rest and she'll be fit as an oyster in its shell."

"Thanks for all your help, Cook. I don't know what I would have done."

"Found some other lady to take care of her, I'm certain. But God doesn't put people in the wrong place at the wrong time. Remember that, Mr. Ellis. She's not here by mistake."

"But. . ."

"But nothin'. God knows, God controls, if you let Him."

Duly admonished, Ellis left the breakfast preparations in the capable hands of Cook. She was right as always. If he genuinely trusted God, he shouldn't have been so worried and shouldn't have been so riddled with guilt. God had placed Beatrice Smith in the position of caring for his nephew, and He knew that they would be coming to live with him in these tropical temperatures. So why was he still blaming himself?

Because if he hadn't commited that act in the past, he would have gone home and picked up his nephew. But fear of entering his hometown, the threat of arrest, the threat of disgracing the family name and losing the farm. . .he simply couldn't risk it. So, was it ultimately still his fault that Beatrice Smith was sick?

Ellis worked the tension out of the back of his neck. "Perhaps not," he spoke to his empty office. But, just maybe, he was still responsible.

"Uncle Ellis, can I go see Nanna now?" Richard yelled down the hall.

When was that child going to learn not to yell? Ellis took a deep breath. Now was not the time to chastise him. He stepped into the hall just as Richard rounded the corner at a run to head into his office.

"Ugh!" Ellis groaned.

"Sorry. Can I?" Richard implored sheepishly.

"Yes, go right in and see how she's doing. Tell her Cook will bring breakfast shortly."

"All right." Richard turned to walk away, then paused, looking over his shoulder, and said, "Good morning, Uncle Ellis."

Ellis broke into a wide grin. " 'Morning, Son. Now shoo." At that, the boy was off, running down the hall, slipping on one small carpet but handling the corner without falling. *Did I run that much when I was a boy?* He had no memory of it. He ran outside, of course, but in the house? Nah, he couldn't have. His mother would have tanned his hide. Come to think of it. . . Ellis rubbed his backside. . .maybe she had.

Bea heard the patter of Richard's feet long before she heard him call, preceded by the slam of the screen door.

"Nanna."

"Come in, Richard. I'm in my room." She straightened the sheet modestly over herself.

"Hi. Uncle Ellis said I could come over."

"I'm glad you came."

"Are you better?"

"Yes, thanks."

"Are you allowed to sit in a chair?"

"I believe so, why do you ask?"

"'Cause yesterday you had to stay in bed. Doctor said so."

"True, but I can sit up for awhile now. Would you like me to read you a story?"

Richard nodded his head.

"Do you want to pick out a book or should I?"

"Can we do the story after breakfast?"

"Sure."

"Cook's making bacon." Richard's eyes sparkled.

"We can read after you have your bacon." As much as Bea enjoyed bacon, she couldn't imagine eating something so greasy at the moment. She silently prayed Cook would not ask her to.

"Nanna?"

"Yes, Richie."

He placed his small hands on his hips and stood with his feet slightly apart. "Are you drinking?"

Bea couldn't help but giggle. "Yes, Son. I'm drinking my juice."

He shook his finger. "Cook said you need to keep drinking or you'll get sick."

"I know. I'll be careful, I promise."

Richard gave one swift nod of the head and relaxed his stance. If Cook was having this effect on the child already, Ellis Southard would have his hands full raising the boy. "Do you think you better go back to the house for your breakfast? I think I can smell the bacon now."

Richard sniffed the air. His smile blossomed. "I'll be back, Nanna," he said, then spun around and ran out the door.

The boy was always running. Beatrice wondered if his father had been a runner as well, or his uncle.

His uncle. The image of the man brought a shiver down her spine. He was so handsome, and she was so infuriatingly attracted to him. Maybe she shouldn't ask to stay on as the child's nanny. She probably should go home and do as the Lord says, "refrain from embracing," to let little Richard go on to be the man he was meant to become. Staying in Key West would mean staying next to temptation, and Bea wasn't all that sure she could handle it.

It would be different, she thought, if she had fancied herself interested in some boys when she was younger. But they were just silly creatures, boys were. They often would start behaving like roosters near a hen house trying to get a woman's attention. Such silliness did not endear her to the male part of the species. Grown men, however, like her father, were acceptable. They either outgrew this boyish behavior or, like her father, had not been given to such childishness. She wondered if she dared ask. Her brother hadn't been one given to such nonsense until Abigail Wilson moved into town. Around her, he degenerated into "one of the roosters."

Bea tossed her head from side to side. Young boys like Richard didn't seem to have this problem. She wondered if it had anything to do with coming of age. Perhaps she would never know. She certainly wouldn't be around when young Richard would be turning sixteen.

A rap sounded at her door. "Miss Smith."

Bea flushed. She was naked. . .well, maybe not naked exactly, but close enough. "Mr. Southard, I'm not presentable. Please do not come in."

"I. . .I. . .mean you no disrespect, Ma'am. I just wanted to let you know that I'm going to work now. Cook will be here and calling on you often. Richard will be in Cook's care, but I've given him permission to visit you as often as you wish today."

"Thank you, Sir. I'm certain I'll be about tomorrow."

"Take the time to recover, Miss Smith. We don't want a repeat of yesterday." His words were almost kind, but there was a slight edge of anger in them too, she suspected.

"I'm drinking regularly and getting my rest, thank you." Regular enough that she thought she could float away if she didn't stop soon.

"Fine," he coughed. "Good day, Miss Smith."

"Good day, Sir."

She wondered again if Ellis Southard truly was as cold as he appeared. What had Cook said earlier? That he would have kept her up all night with his pacing? Was he truly concerned about her? If so, he was a kind man with a cold exterior, Bea noted to herself. That was it. A man with a tender heart, who hid it well, she reasoned.

"Miss Bea," Cook called as she entered the house. "I've got some tea and some white rice for you."

"Rice?"

"Best thing to keep you from dehydrating. Problem some folks have with a new area is the water isn't the same as back home. They, hmm, well, they. . ."

"I understand." And Bea had. The Key West water was already having that "cleansing" effect on her body.

"Black tea, white rice, best medicine there is for diarrhea."

"Thanks, I think." Was there anything her body would get used to about this area? Maybe it didn't matter. Fact was, she wouldn't be staying all that long. But she wanted to be her best for the last days she spent with Richard. "Father, God, please help me get well and stay well," she moaned.

Chapter 7

The next morning Bea woke to the gentle lull of exotic birdsong outside her window. She quietly watched them flit from branch to branch, their vivid colors as beautiful and enchanting as they were different from their cousins in the North. This truly felt as if she were in a whole new world.

Today, perhaps, she could explore this tropical wonder. But would Cook allow her the pleasure? On the other hand, would her body survive it? "What could it hurt, Lord, to walk a few blocks to the center of town?" Without waiting for an answer, her thoughts skipped ahead to the quaint stores filled with merchandise to explore.

Even Ellis Southard's sponge business was so uniquely Caribbean, she reflected, as she climbed out of bed to get ready for the day. She picked up the personal sponge Cook had given her for bathing. After the very first use her skin had felt smoother, cleaner, and softer than she remembered it feeling in years.

Working into the most lightweight outfit she could find, she thought about purchasing some of the Spanish-style skirts and blouses like the ones Cook wore. They looked so comfortable.

Although she wouldn't purchase many. The island clothing would be totally unacceptable back home. There a woman was to always be properly dressed. And while Cook quite naturally wore this new casual apparel, Bea was certain the women of her social class never would, even in these tropical temperatures.

Fortunately, no one here knew of Bea's northern social status, so no heads would turn when and if she wore those outfits. What mattered was to stay covered and cool and to avoid another touch of heatstroke. In her few remaining days with Richard, she wanted to be fit and able to enjoy the merriment and wonder of seeing this place for the first time.

Perhaps she was a bit jealous of the time Ellis played with Richard each evening before he went to bed. She'd heard them laughing and longed to be in the middle of such joyous activity. Each night she had lit the candle in her window for Richard, although Cook had been the keeper of the flame in her weakened state.

She watched from behind her closed screen door as Ellis Southard marched proudly off to work. His broad shoulders straight and firm, he walked with confidence but didn't strut with arrogance. His beard seemed shorter, more groomed this morning; its red highlights seemed to beam his contentment with life and his job.

"Snap out of it, Woman," Bea chastised herself. "Why am I longing so much for this man, a stranger?" She prayed with her head bent low. "We've spoken maybe ten minutes in the three days I've been here. Well, perhaps a few more than ten. But it's been nothing, Lord. I barely know him and yet I'm attracted to him. Why? It must be the heat. Help me keep my mind together, Lord. Don't allow me to turn into some silly, swooning female."

Now what was it she had been thinking before she saw Ellis. . .Mr. Southard. . . she amended. "Ah yes, shopping." Bea opened the screen door and headed toward the main house. It was her first time in the house since falling ill. Cook had brought all her meals to the cottage, with Richard's help, of course. She smiled at the thought. He was so proud, being able to help care for her. Bea's eyes started to water. "How am I going to leave this child, Lord?" she whispered.

"Come on, men, let's get out there before the day is half over," Ellis hollered at his crew lounging on wood blocks and crates scattered around the dock. A few groaned, but all got up and shuffled over to the small boats that would sail out to fetch the sponges. The nets empty, a couple men per boat, he had a good business.

" 'Morning, Ellis, I see your crew has expanded." Ellis turned to see Marc Dabny approach, wearing his usual Union blue army slacks, though he had retired from the military right after the war to live on the island. His premature balding head glistened in the morning sunlight.

" 'Morning, Marc. What can I do for you?"

"Heard your nephew's come to live with you." Marc stopped his approach a couple feet away from Ellis.

"That's right, he's a great kid."

Marc looked down at his feet and cleared his throat. "Heard his nanny came with him, too."

Ellis examined the man more closely. What was he after?

"Yes," he admitted.

"I was wondering if I could. . .well, if I could come and call upon the lady."

What? How dare the man!

On the other hand, Marc had been raised to seek out the gal's father to request permission to court. But he wasn't Beatrice's father, wasn't even close. Still, Beatrice was a guest in his home, and he supposed folks naturally assumed she was now working for him as the child's nanny. But he certainly didn't want to declare open hunting season for Beatrice Smith.

"Marc, the lady's been ill. Stricken with a bad case of heatstroke. By the time she's strong again, I imagine she'll be on a ship heading north."

"She won't be staying?"

"No, Sir." He handled that well, he thought. Didn't lie, but didn't make her available either. "And given the severity of her heatstroke, I imagine she's anxious to leave this place."

"Heard she was a looker. And I've been wanting to settle down now since the war is over. You know, get married and have a handful of kids. Besides, havin' a woman who's pleasant to look at wouldn't be a bad way to spend the rest of your life." Marc winked.

Ellis's stomach flip-flopped. The man wasn't looking for a companion. He was looking for a nursemaid plus a few wifely benefits. That certainly didn't describe Beatrice Smith, who was excellent with children and had a sharp mind. She needed a man with whom she could have a relationship, not be some prize—used whenever the prizewinner suited.

"Afraid that wouldn't be Miss Smith. I believe she has family waiting on her back home." That was also not untrue, but he really hadn't talked with her about it, just assumed. In fact, he knew next to nothing about Beatrice Smith and her family. Everything he knew was through the eyes of his nephew—his love for her, and the things she'd taught him. No, he really didn't know the woman at all.

"Well, I figured I should ask you first. Didn't know if you had other plans for the lady. Didn't want to ask the lady and upset you."

"I appreciate it, Marc, but like I say, she's not staying."

"Mind if I try and persuade her anyway?"

The man deserved some credit for his persistence.

Besides, do I really have the right to say who could or could not court Miss Smith? Ellis felt like he ought to, but knew he didn't. "I don't suppose I could stop you from approaching her, but please give her another day to recover. I was quite concerned at first that she wouldn't even make it."

"Thank you. I come from a long line of Dabnys who've been known to have a way with women. So don't be too surprised if the lady decides to stay right here in Key West."

No matter what Marc Dabny thought about his family heritage, Ellis couldn't see Beatrice

Smith on this man's arm. On the other hand, not being a woman himself, he didn't have a clue as to what a lady would find appealing.

"I won't be keeping you from your work, just felt I ought to speak with you first. I know we don't run on pomp and circumstance down here, but since you and I both hail from the North, I thought I'd better ask."

"I appreciate it. Have a good day, Marc."

"Adios," Marc answered in Spanish. The blend of Spanish and English added to the island's uniqueness.

Ellis worked his shoulders in circles trying to ease the tension that had stiffened his back.

Four days. The woman had been here for only four days and the vultures were already swarming. Ellis shook his head as he walked to his office. Of course, given Miss Beatrice Smith's beauty, it was a wonder no one had approached him days ago. Maybe the fact that she was so ill had made it through the island gossip chain and had kept the pursuers at bay. In any case, she was fair game for the men of Key West, and he had no right to do anything about it.

Frustrated, he absentmindedly worried his lower lip. Why did the thought bother him? Wasn't it possible that some man on Key West might be Beatrice Smith's future husband? She certainly would make a man a good wife and mother, or at least it appeared that way. But the very idea of Marc Dabny pursuing her made him tense. Marc seemed like a decent enough sort on the surface. He was respectable and followed his orders. He wouldn't make a bad husband, Ellis supposed. But then again, Marc wasn't looking for a woman who would challenge him as a man; he was looking for someone to clean his house, cook his food, and bear his children.

Ellis rubbed his temples. This was going nowhere. He wasn't Beatrice Smith's keeper. The woman could court anyone she had a mind to. It wasn't his concern. His concern was providing for his nephew and bringing him up in a manner that would have made the boy's father proud. And to do that he needed to get to work and stop this lollygagging.

"Nanna, are you all right?" Richard questioned.

Bea's legs shook. Her arms felt prickly, as if being stabbed with lots of tiny needles all at once. "I feel a bit weak."

Richard ran to the house they were in front of and banged on the door. An older woman with graying hair came to the door. "May I help you?"

"Nanna doesn't feel well. Can she sit down?"

"Oh, gracious, bring her here, Child."

Bea didn't know whether to be proud or embarrassed by Richard's actions. They hadn't gone a quarter of a mile, but she had apparently gone too far. Richard helped her up the stairs onto the woman's porch.

"Sit in the rocker, dear, I'll fetch you some water."

"Thank you." Beatrice sat down on the wooden rocker facing the street. A small front porch with a wooden floor and white painted handrail stretched across the front of the house. A couple steps and you were to the door.

"Nanna, I'll get Uncle Ellis."

The last thing she needed was to have Ellis Southard come to her rescue. "I'll be fine. No sense worrying your uncle."

"What about Cook? She's closer." Richard's worried eyes pleaded with her to let him help.

"Come here, Richie." She scooped him up and placed him on her lap. She worked his wonderful blond curls from his face with her right hand. "I'm fine, really. I just wasn't up for this yet."

"Nanna, I don't want you to be sick."

"I'm getting better. I just have to be patient and wait for my body to recover a bit more."

"All right." Richard snuggled his head into her chest.

Bea looked up at the sound of the screen door swinging on old hinges to see the elderly woman coming out with a tall glass of lemonade. "Here you go, Miss," she said, steadying herself with her free hand on the back of Bea's chair.

Bea clasped her fingers around the glass. "Thank you." Carefully she brought it to her lips and sipped. How perfectly embarrassing to weaken in such a short amount of time. At mid-morning, the full intensity of the heat wouldn't peak for two to three hours yet.

Bea's hostess sat down in the wicker chair to her left. "My name is Vivian. You're new here, aren't you, dear?"

Bea nodded her head.

"Nanna and I came from New York on a big ship. We're living with my uncle Ellis."

"With those steel-blue eyes, I should have noticed you were Mr. Southard's nephew."

Richard looked at Bea in bewilderment.

"Miss. . .I'm afraid I don't know your last name." Bea flushed.

"Sorry, its Matlin. Mrs. Joseph Matlin."

Bea nodded. "Richard, Mrs. Matlin noticed your eyes have the same coloring as your uncle Ellis's."

"Oh. That's because my daddy and uncle Ellis are brothers."

Vivian chuckled. "That's generally how it works, Son. Can I give you something to drink, and a sweet biscuit perhaps?"

"Can I, Nanna?"

"Sure." Vivian took Richard by the hand and led him into her home. A cool breeze blew across the porch, and Bea laid her head back on the chair and closed her eyes to let the refreshing air sweep across her face. Cook had warned her to be careful, and a race to the corner of the street had clearly exceeded her limits.

She could still feel the pulse in her legs, beat after beat, protesting her stupidity. She hadn't exerted herself that much, having let Richard win. Yet she had done far more than her body could apparently handle. *How long does it take to recover from heatstroke?*

Vivian came back out with a small china plate, with Richard in tow. "Would you like one, dear?"

Bea wasn't really hungry, but the biscuits did smell good. "Thank you. I'm sorry to impose upon you in such a way."

"It's no trouble at all, dear." Vivian sat back down on the chair opposite Beatrice and straightened her apron. "All I know is that you serve as Richard Southard's nanny. I don't know your name, dear."

"Forgive me. . .Beatrice Smith. . .heatstroke seems to be affecting me in more ways than one."

"I know what you mean, Beatrice. May I call you Beatrice?"

"Bea is fine. Have you ever suffered with this ailment?" Bea wiped the crumbs from her lap.

"Years ago, when I first came here. Came about the same time of year as you. The first week was very difficult."

"A whole week? I'll be on a ship back to New York by the end of a week. I do want to take in some of the sights prior to my departure." *Maybe the good Lord just doesn't want me in this climate and I shouldn't get comfortable here.* Another lesson in learning to refrain from embracing, embracing a new way of life, a new culture, a new environment. It wasn't her time, and she just needed to accept the fact that she was to return home to New York.

At the end of the workday Ellis returned home for his evening meal and found the house quiet.

"Hello? Anyone home?" Not a sound. *That's odd,* he thought and proceeded to clean up and change from his work clothes into something casual. From his bedroom window he could see Cook, Richard, and Miss Smith sitting under the shade of the large banyan tree. Even from this distance Beatrice seemed pale, weak, and sorrowful. The woman was so vulnerable, so frail, and yet showed a remarkable ability to hold her own in adversity. Could this change in her demeanor be from the heatstroke?

Ellis slipped his arms into the sleeves of a cool cotton shirt, buttoning it as he made his way down the hall to the stairs and out through the kitchen to the back door. "I wondered where all of you were."

"Uncle Ellis!" Richard declared, jumping up from his spot and scampering over to him. Ellis smiled. *Well, the boy runs outside as well as inside,* he mused.

"Just takin' in the cool night air," Cook said. "The butcher got some fresh beef from Cuba, so we're having steak tonight. You're cooking on the outside grill," Cook teased, and sat farther back in her chair, putting her feet up on the one abandoned by Richard.

Fresh beef was a rarity on the island, and he'd given Cook a standing order that anytime there was a shipment she should purchase some.

"I see." Ellis hoisted Richard up on his shoulders. "Come on, Son. It's our night to cook for the ladies."

At the back of the yard he lifted Richard off his shoulders and placed him on the ground beside him. In the sheltered work area, he loaded the brick grill with small chunks of wood for the fire.

Young Richard grabbed a bucket filled with blocks of hickory wood soaking in water. "Cook said you use these."

"Thanks. Do you know why?"

His blond curls swung with the swift movement of his head going up and down. "It's smelly wood."

Ellis chuckled. "Yes, you could say that. This hickory gives the food a great outdoors cooking taste." Ellis continued to pile the wood into the grill then lit the kindling. Flames climbed the small pile.

Richard clapped his hands.

Ellis bowed. "Thank you." Richard stood proud, encircling his right arm around Ellis's left leg. A storm of emotions caught in Ellis's throat. How could a child love so easily, so unconditionally?

"Uncle Ellis?"

Ellis poked the burning embers with an iron rod and placed a couple of water-soaked hickory chunks on the pile.

"Yes, Richard?"

"How come Nanna couldn't race me to the corner?"

Chapter 8

What?" Ellis's own voice echoed back at him of the shelter's tin roof. *Is that why she appeared so pale, so lethargic?*

Richard instantly released his clasp of Ellis's leg.

Ellis struggled to quell his uncharacteristic temper. "I'm sorry, I didn't mean to bellow. But I want to know what happened."

"Nanna doesn't yell," Richard whined.

"Son. . ." How could he explain this? It wasn't normal for him to yell either. He loved Richard and he was happy—no, honored to raise his brother's son. However, something—or rather someone—was getting the better of him. The constant fighting with himself not to think of a certain hazel-eyed nanny was wearing him down.

Ellis took a deep breath and went down to one knee, capturing the small boy's upper arms in his hands. "Normally, I don't yell either. I didn't mean to be so loud. Maybe I'm not used to having a lot of folks around me when I'm at home. Be patient with me, Son. I promise to try and not yell so often."

Richard scrunched his eyebrows together. "All right, Uncle Ellis. Nanna said some folks yell."

"Well, normally I don't. But I will try to be more careful. Deal?"

"Deal." Ellis held his hand out and Richard slipped his tiny hand into his. Such a good boy. A bright boy. And that was due to his nanny. His brother, if truth be told, had little to do with the raising of his own son.

"So tell me, why was Nanna racing you?"

"I asked her to."

"I see," he responded, carefully modulating his tone of voice. He could see the boy felt terribly guilty. "Then what happened, Richard?"

"I won. But Nanna didn't feel so good. We stopped at Mrs. Vivian's house. She gave me cookies. Nanna sat and had some lemonade."

So, Miss Smith overexerted herself. Hadn't the doctor given her firm orders to stay down, relax? Not only did she not stay down, she actually raced the child. And what's a woman doing racing a small boy down the street anyway? Ellis fought to keep his resurgent anger from surfacing again. "Richard, I think your Nanna needs to rest some more."

"I know. Nanna said we can't go shopping or exploring."

"Right, not for awhile."

"Nanna said she may never be able to."

What nonsense is this woman feeding the child? "I'm sure you'll be able to, real soon."

"Nanna said when she gets better, she'd be going home to New York."

So the woman doesn't want to stay in the area. Well, no sense asking her to stay on. He'd just have to find a nanny somewhere on the island. Until then, he would have to alter his work schedule, take the lad to work with him whenever possible. Take him fishing on the dock even. Yup, he'd better start doing what he needed to do to take care of his nephew. It was apparent Miss Smith was breaking her ties with Richard and would be traveling home on the next ship.

The back of Ellis's neck tightened from the tension. He would do what was necessary for Richard. He didn't regret that. But the boy loved and depended on Miss Smith in more ways than she obviously knew. Here she was ready to release Richard into his care with barely a moment's thought. Maybe Beatrice Smith wasn't the kind of person he had been building her to be in his mind. Maybe raising Richard had just been a matter of duty, of patronage to an old friend.

Ellis massaged the back of his neck with his right hand and sighed. *Guess it was good I hadn't offered her a permanent position as Richard's nanny.*

If looks could kill...

Beatrice swallowed hard and broke her gaze from Ellis's, who stood just outside the shelter glaring at her. What was he thinking? Those bluish-gray eyes of his, so dark beneath a deeply furrowed brow, bore into her. She had heard his outburst. Richard must have told him about their excursion.

"Excuse me, Cook. I believe I need to lie down. I don't think I'm up for dinner tonight."

"Nonsense, Child. You need to eat." Cook crossed her hefty arms across her rounded stomach.

Beatrice lifted herself up off the chair. "Perhaps Richard could bring a little something later." She closed her eyes and rubbed her temples for emphasis. "I feel a headache coming on."

"Uh-huh." Cook eyed her cautiously.

"I just need to lie down. I'll be fine." She didn't want to overemphasize her physical weakness. Truth was, a tension-filled headache was coming on, but more out of fear of dealing with Ellis Southard, who already thought her a coddling nanny. Now he was certain to think her a fool as well. Why on earth had she agreed to race Richard today anyway?

"Mr. Ellis, he cooks a great steak. Can't say I enjoy anything else the man puts his hand to, food-wise that is. But outside on the grill—umm-hmm, the man can cook."

"I'm quite certain he can, but I really must go lie down now."

"Sure, you go run along now. Just remember to stop running sometime."

Bea squinted hard at Cook. Was she implying something here? Sure, she was old enough not to be running down a street after a child like that, but. . .did she mean something else? Beatrice turned and headed toward her cottage. Whatever the old woman meant, she wasn't going to wait around to find out. She'd seen enough of Cook to know she was able to read her thoughts. A wise woman, her father would have said. A nosy one, her aunt Tilly would have said. In either case, Bea wasn't about to stick around to confirm Cook's suspicions that she might be running from Ellis Southard.

She opened the screen door and entered her cottage, letting the door slam behind her. It wasn't quite as cool as being outdoors under the banyan tree, but it was far cooler than earlier this afternoon. *Thank You, Lord, for this cool breeze tonight,* Bea silently prayed as she headed to the quiet sanctuary of her room.

Her bed, still rumpled from an earlier nap after her failed excursion with Richard, lay convictingly before her. Never would she have left a bed in that state back home.

Bea sighed and worked the wrinkles out of the bedding before collapsing on the rocker beside the bed. "O Lord, how long before I return home? I thought I would be happy with a few extra days with Richard. Instead I've gotten sick and I am miserable, Lord. I tried, Father, today I really tried to explain to him why I had to go home. I believe he understood. But I saw the pain in his eyes. Or was it fear, Father God? Please be with Richard; give him strength and bless his relationship with his uncle. Make it strong; give him the father he's never had. Amen."

Bea wiped tears off her cheeks with a delicate hand-laced handkerchief Elizabeth had made for her years ago. Embroidered on one corner were small purple violets, Bea's favorite flower. Bea sighed. "I've been a good mother to the child, just like you asked, Lizzy. But it hurts so much to let him go. I understand now why you held on so long, just one more day, one more hour to touch, to love that precious little boy. I grieve to be parting with him, but I know it is right, and I can't possibly live in this area with his uncle. I don't know if you ever met the man, Lizzy, but he is quite different from your Richard. Sometimes he terrifies me."

Bea stopped, realizing she'd been rambling aloud. It gave her some relief to think her dear friend was looking down from heaven, yet she knew that only God could answer her pain, that only He could give peace to the heart-wrenching grief she was going through. She needed to return home. She needed to return soon. Why wait until she was recovered? The ship would be sailing into a colder climate. Wouldn't that be better for her?

She lifted herself from the rocker, went to her garment bag, and pulled out a sheet of stationery. At the small desk in the farthest corner of the room she penned a letter to Mr. Ellis Southard.

"Are they done yet?" Richard asked for the third time.

"Just about, Son. Why don't you go tell Nanna her steak is ready?"

"All right." Richard ran off toward the cottage. Ellis had seen her leave, wondered if she was all right, but figured Cook would have alerted him to any problem.

It was odd how old Cook sat relaxed in the chair with her feet up. Eyeing her from a distance, he realized she was slowing down. Not that he'd ever say anything to her about it. But he would like to see her do less walking and live with him. Her family could manage just fine without her. Probably should too. The woman gave far too much to folks. She needed to slow down. Relax. Enjoy. . .

"Uncle Ellis!" Richard yelled.

Ellis smiled. At least outside it wasn't quite as piercing as in the house. He looked in the boy's direction but didn't answer.

"Nanna says she's not feeling up to dinner."

"Not up to dinner?" he mumbled.

"Cook?" he called as he brought the plates piled with mouth-watering steaks to the small table at her side.

"She said she needed to rest."

"Do you think she's all right?"

"I believe so. Think it's more her pride than heat."

"Ahh." Ellis would let that issue alone. He wasn't going to be baited by Cook into doing something he shouldn't. Like offering her the opportunity to stay on as Richard's nanny.

A quiet meal was eaten. Ellis grinned, reflecting. His father often said a quiet table meant the meal was exquisite. A small dinner plate was prepared for Miss Smith. Cook cleaned up, Richard delivered the meal, and Ellis retreated to his study.

The old wood floorboards shined from Cook's excellent housekeeping. She once told him it didn't need much fussin' 'cause he mostly sat in his chair at the desk. That had been true enough, but he'd begun pacing in recent days. Pacing and bellowing. "What a combination," he groaned.

"Uncle Ellis?"

A somber child stood in front of him.

"Yes, Richard."

"Nanna said to give you this."

Ellis reached for the thin piece of paper crumpled between the boy's chubby fingers. "Thank you, Son."

Not wanting to open the letter and be distracted from his nephew, he placed it in his trousers pocket. Whatever Miss Smith had to say could wait. The time before Richard went to bed was their private time, and Ellis cherished it.

"Would you like me to read a story for you tonight?" Ellis asked, combing the blond curls from Richard's face.

Richard beamed. "Can we play checkers?"

"Checkers it is. You get the pieces, I'll clear the table."

Richard scurried off.

Ellis lifted some papers he had brought home from his office and placed them on his desk.

"Good night, Mr. Ellis. Remember, I'll be comin' after breakfast tomorrow."

How could he forget? But he had. "Thanks for the reminder."

"You might ask Miss Smith to fix the morning meal," Cook suggested.

"I'll manage." After all, he would have to once Beatrice Smith moved back home. Until he found a suitable nanny or nurse, he would need to fend for himself and Richard.

"Oh, and one more thing, Mr. Ellis. I think the nanny is feeling somewhat useless," she added, tilting her head toward the cottage.

"Useless? What are you talking about, Cook?"

"I don't rightly know, but something is wrong with the dear gal. And I'm certain it isn't the heat."

Ellis snorted. "You call running wise?"

"That's nothing. I mean, yes, she shouldn't have pushed herself that way. But, well. . .I can't put my finger on it. But I knows something else is wandering around in that pretty little head."

Ellis shifted uneasily from one foot to the other. "She told Richard she was going home today."

"Mercy, no." Cook placed a hand over her heart.

"Afraid so. I'll talk with you tomorrow about this. Right now I don't want Richard hearing us."

"I can't figure what's going on. I knows she wants to be here with the child," Cook mumbled as she left the room.

Had Ellis heard her right? Beatrice Smith wants to be here? But why would she tell Richard. . . ? Ellis dropped his hand into his pocket that held her letter.

" 'Bye, Cook," Richard called out. Ellis heard the pattering of his shoes on the hardwood floors and released the letter back into his pocket.

"I got it, Uncle Ellis."

"Excellent." Ellis rubbed his hands together. "Tonight I'm certain I'm going to win."

"I don't think so." Richard giggled. "You're worse than Nanna."

Ellis chuckled. Guess he needs to work on his losing skills some. "I wouldn't be too confident there. I was practicing today."

"You were?"

"Yup, an old sea captain showed me some pointers."

Richard's eyes widened. When was the time to start winning, Ellis wondered, in order to challenge the child more? There was so much he still needed to learn about raising a boy.

O Lord, he said inwardly, *help me to know what's best.*

Ellis placed a white ivory checker in one hand and a black ivory checker in the other. He'd received the game as a gift from an old sailor who had carved it from whales' teeth. The board was of finely polished wood, with the black squares painted on. He put his hands behind his back, placing both checkers in his right hand. "Pick one."

Richard tapped his left arm. Ellis swung it around revealing his empty hand. Richard tapped the other and Ellis swung it around, after dropping the checkers in a back pocket, and revealed it was empty also.

"Hey!" Richard placed his hands on his hips. "That's not how you do it, Uncle Ellis."

"It's not?" he asked, feigning innocence. Ellis scratched his head. "I know I put them in my hand. . ."

Richard chuckled. "Where are they?"

"I don't know." Ellis winked.

"Yes, you do, you're trying to trick me."

"Am I? I know I put them in my hands; you saw me." Ellis turned around for effect and pretended to look for the missing checkers. Soon Richard was beside him searching.

"Where are they?" Richard asked.

"I don't know."

"Uncle Ellis, you're trying to trick me," Richard accused, his laughter growing louder by the moment.

Ellis roared in full-belly laughter, lunging across the table to tickle the boy.

Laughter floated on the evening wind through Bea's cottage window, as it had every previous night. How could such a joyous sound be so heart-wrenching? How come she wasn't happy with the joy Richard had found with his uncle? How could she be so jealous? So self-centered? Bea wept into her pillow. "Father God, I'm so terribly selfish."

Chapter 9

Ellis sat on the edge of his bed, the room dark, the house quiet. The gentle glow of candlelight beckoned his attention to the cottage below where Bea still placed the candle in her window for the boy. Ellis grinned briefly before pursing his lips in reflection. How could she truly love the child if she was so anxious to leave? Remembering the note, he reached into his pocket and pulled out what she had penned for him earlier.

Ellis lit the flame of his oil lamp beside the bed. The onion skin paper crinkled as he unfolded it. His eyes focused on the words flowing across the page in exquisite penmanship.

Dear Mr. Southard,

Would you be so kind as to procure my departure as soon as possible? I feel the trip home would do no further harm to my health in as much as Key West's climate is not agreeable at all.

I love Richard dearly and ask only to be able to correspond with him. I hope you will find that acceptable. In time, I imagine Richard will have only vague memories of me. But I suppose that is how it should be.

Sincerely,
Beatrice Smith

Ellis's hand trembled. She did love the child, there was no question. But why couldn't she wait and give her body a chance to adjust to this area? *Why is she in such a hurry to return home, Lord? I don't understand.*

A whispered thought flickered past his ears. "Perhaps you should ask."

Should he? The hour was late. Was it proper to call on someone this late? To call on a single woman?

But she isn't just a single woman. She is the child's nanny. *And this is a matter that concerns the child,* he argued with himself. Didn't he, as Richard's guardian, have the right to ask his nanny questions, no matter what the hour? Was there some law that forbade such things? He couldn't think of one.

Ellis turned down the lamp and headed out of his room. He straightened his shirt, removed some of the creases from his trousers, and headed down the stairs toward the front door, stopping to listen for Richard. He was sound asleep. He could leave him for a moment, he decided. Besides, the boy's bedroom window was open, and he was confident he could hear the child from the cottage.

A few long strides and he was at her door. He raised his hand to knock.

Then he lowered it.

He raised his hand again, but stopped short of tapping on the doorjamb.

He stepped back. Perhaps this should wait until morning.

He stood there undecided. Perhaps not. He stepped forward again.

Ellis muttered under his breath and rapped on the door. It protested in its frame, and instantly he regretted having knocked so hard.

"Hello?" a weak voice called from the bedroom.

"Miss Smith, I'm sorry to call on you so late. May I have a word with you?" *A bit formal, perhaps, but it got the point across.*

"Mr. Southard, did you receive my letter?" she asked, peering around her partially opened door.

She had taken her hair down for the evening, its silken strands cascading over her shoulders. Ellis swallowed and cleared his throat. "Yes. Can we talk?"

"All right."

Her chocolate curls enhanced her delicate features. Ellis caught himself sniffing her hair as he followed her into the living room. Perhaps it was a mistake to have come in the evening. His palms beaded with sweat. He rubbed them dry with his fingers, only to find they immediately started to perspire again. He sat in the single chair in the living room, leaving her the sofa.

"Is there a reason you need to return home so quickly?" he asked. *Remain on the subject. . . you can get yourself through this.*

"No, nothing of a pressing nature."

"Then why can't you remain a little longer? You should be feeling much better soon. Running was definitely not a wise undertaking, but it presents only a momentary setback."

"Is there a problem with procuring my return voyage?"

"No. I. . .I. . ."

Beatrice searched his blue-gray eyes. He seemed strangely vulnerable, and yet so formal.

"Richard. . ."

"Is something wrong with Richard?" Bea jumped up from the sofa.

"I'm sorry. No, he's fine. I'm just concerned that your immediate departure would be terribly hard on the child."

"I spoke with him this afternoon. He seemed to understand my need to return home."

"Understand, yes. But is he ready to break his emotional connection with you?"

"I don't believe I've coddled the child as much as you think."

"Coddled? What are you talking about?"

"Coddling. The first day we met, you said I coddled the child."

Ellis stood up and approached her. "I may have said that, but I've come to see you have not coddled the boy at all. I've never met a woman who could bait a hook. And to hear Richard say it, you're the best there is." Ellis winked.

Beatrice lowered her gaze and nervously rubbed her fingertips. "It took some practice."

"I can imagine. All the girls back home would scream and run away from me. Of course, I was threatening them with a fierce and mighty 'worm.' "

Bea giggled. "I can see Richard doing that one day."

Ellis chuckled. "Boys—we are different."

She sighed and relaxed. "I truly love him, and will miss him greatly, but my time in his life has come to an end."

"That may be, Miss Smith, but don't you see—a few more days or weeks won't hurt you, and those same days will help him tremendously."

"Perhaps. I just don't know how long I can survive in this heat."

"You're looking much better, and doing better. Granted, your little morning escapade was a supreme act of foolishness."

This man is some charmer. "Thanks."

"I'm sorry, I'm not your father. I have no right scolding you. But you do see the foolishness, don't you?"

"Of course I do. I saw it when I nearly passed out on Front Street. I thought I could handle the short distance. Richard and I did a lot of racing back home."

Ellis bobbed his head.

"I suppose you think a lady shouldn't do such things."

"Now don't go putting words into my mouth, Miss Smith." Ellis shook a finger in the air. "I've never seen a woman running before, that's all."

"I reckon. But you grew up on Richard's family farmstead. You know there are no children around for miles. The boy needed a playmate, as well as a mother, father, nurse, teacher, and whatever else needed doing at the time."

"True. I always had my brother Richard to play with. Granted, he was older, but it was still someone."

Bea sat back down on the sofa and Richard returned to his chair.

"Miss Smith, please tell me you'll stay for a few more days, perhaps a week or so."

"I would love to explore this island some. I've been trapped in this yard for days, and while you do have a charming yard and beautiful garden, I would like to see more."

Ellis grinned. "I understand. But. . ."

Bea watched his hesitancy, his hands folding and unfolding. "I need you to be spending your free time with the boy. I don't think courting would be proper."

"Courting? What on earth are you talking about?" She watched his eyes focus on his lap. Was he considering asking her to court him? Couldn't be, he'd hardly even looked at her since her arrival.

"Sorry. I had a gentleman caller today who asked for my permission to seek the pleasure of your company."

"He asked you?" She huffed. How dare the man. She wasn't Ellis Southard's ward. She wasn't anyone's ward. She had a free mind and a bright one at that, and she would determine whom she would or would not court.

"Now before you get yourself worked into a tizzy, let me explain that Mr. Dabny comes from the North. Where, as you probably know, in good society a man comes to the father before approaching the woman."

How could she possibly forget? She was born and bred in that society, and while Ellis Southard didn't have an inkling of her true social status, she shouldn't have been so offended.

"I see," she said, her voice controlled.

"I let Marc know he would have to ask you himself."

Well, that ended any lingering doubt she might have had that Ellis's intentions were to court her. No, while she had noticed how handsome Ellis was, obviously he didn't have any attraction toward her. On the other hand, hadn't she caught him staring at her when she first greeted him at the door?

Ellis appeared to be awaiting her answer. What was his question. . . ?

"Thank you."

"You're welcome." Ellis shifted in his chair and pulled at his collar with his right forefinger. "Do you agree you shouldn't be socializing?"

"Mr. Southard, whether I do or do not accept Mr. Dabny's offer has little or nothing to do with my care of Richard. Wouldn't you agree that once you are home for the evening, my time is my own?"

Ellis squirmed. "I reckon."

Bea smiled. "Then if I should accept an invitation from Mr. Dabny or anyone else, it would be when my duties as Richard's nanny are over for the day."

She couldn't believe her own ears. Was she really telling this man she was going to get on with her life, begin socializing again? Allow for the possibility of a courtship? A prickly feeling climbed her spine.

"Very well, Miss Smith." Ellis lifted himself from the chair.

She'd done it again. The man became an instant board around her. Straight, rigid, and totally unfeeling. "Why do you do that?"

"Do what?"

"Put up a wall of defense around me. Just when I think we are beginning to talk like normal people, you pull back into. . .into. . .a plank. Stiff, unbending, un—"

Fire ignited in Ellis's eyes. He closed them, and when he lifted his lids again his eyes were stone cold, dark, and piercing. "Good night, Miss Smith."

For a moment she thought she had reached him. But it was gone in a flash. With long strides to her door he made a hasty retreat. If the man had any appreciation for her as a woman, he sure kept it well hidden. No, she could never stay in Key West. Living under the same roof with a man she found so attractive she lost sleep over, yet who seemed almost repulsed by her, would be nerve-racking, to say the least. Still, he wasn't truly heartless. He had spoken words of appreciation for the fact that she would even bait a hook for the sake of his nephew. "I'm so confused," she huffed.

Ellis stomped back up to the house. How could she be so casual about courting? And why did he feel like a child caught with his hand in the cookie jar? Fact was, he would like to explore the option of courting the woman, but he was too afraid of himself, of his responses, of her beauty.

Ellis groaned. "Heather, I'm so sorry." His past, his mistake, would continue to haunt him when in the presence of someone as tempting as Beatrice Smith. Her beauty was only part of the attraction. Her strong, determined spirit. Her ability to reason. Her way with Richard. These traits and so many more formed the foundation of his attraction. An attraction he could never act upon.

No, he was not a man to be trusted.

Chapter 10

Beatrice saw nothing of Ellis Southard the following day. He even missed his evening meal with the family. "Is he still angry, Lord? And what is he so angry about, anyway?" she rambled in prayer, pacing the small cottage floor from the front room into her bedroom. "I only agreed it was my business if and when I accepted anyone's invitation."

Marc Dabny had been a perfect gentleman, but she had turned him down. For a moment she considered accepting his invitation just to get a rise out of Ellis Southard. But she saw the intensity of Mr. Dabny's interest as a wife-hunter, and she would not be the woman to break the man's heart. Better to leave a man before he's attached, she felt. Not to mention his intentions were totally self-motivated and had little to do with "love."

Given Ellis's recent behavior, all signs seemed to indicate that he was avoiding her. She'd never been so offensive to another individual and that bothered her. Of course, the other side of this meant that, by his absence, she wouldn't be led down the wrong path of temptation.

To Ellis's credit, he did manage to make time for Richard that evening. As she stayed within the confines of her cottage, laughter drifted across the yard once again, creating within her a longing to be in the middle of such joyous activity.

The candle on the windowsill remained unlit, as per young Richard's instructions. He had proclaimed during dinner that he was a big boy now and didn't need it. The unlit candle was now a solemn, cold reminder of her time to release Richard and give him to his uncle and new life.

"Nanna!" she heard Richard call. Bea raced to the window which faced Richard's room, lifted the screen in its wooden track, and waved. A wide smile filled his face, his small arms wiggling back and forth. Bea could see Ellis's strong arm wrapped around Richard's small waist. A proud smile softened Ellis's otherwise rigid stance.

"Good night, Nanna. I love you."

"Good night, Richard. I love you, too." With all the energy she could muster, she stepped back from the window and lowered the screen. Mosquitoes thrived on this island, in numbers she'd never seen before. Grateful for the mosquito netting draped around her bed, she checked its corners again to make certain it hung properly, then prepared for bed.

Sitting in front of the vanity, Bea let down her hair. As a child she had worn it loose. After her coming-out party she had taken to wearing it up in public, wrapped into a tight bun and generally hidden beneath a hat or scarf, in keeping with proper etiquette. A nightly custom of a hundred strokes kept her thick curls from snarling in her sleep. She loved the feel of her hair on her shoulders and back, sometimes feeling a little ashamed of her own vanity. She'd known many women who would curse their hair, wearing it in all kinds of unnatural styles, and fuss and fume when it didn't do what they wanted.

Her hair brushed, she sat down to read before retiring for the night. Lost in her loneliness, the comfort of her nightly ritual had a hollow feel.

"Uncle Ellis?" Richard looked up from his pillow.

"Yes, Richard." Ellis sat down on the edge of Richard's bed.

"Is Nanna going to always sleep over there?"

How could he tell the boy she would be leaving soon? Granted, Miss Smith had prepared him for her departure, but. . .

"No."

"Can she move into the big house?"

"I don't think so, Son. She'll be going back to New York."

"Will you be going to New York too?"

Ugh, Ellis inwardly groaned. For a child he sure did ask difficult questions. "Richard, it's late, and you need to get your sleep. Remember, we're going fishing in the morning."

Richard nodded his head and wiggled himself under the covers.

"Is Nanna coming fishing?"

"No, Son. Not tomorrow."

"When?" Richard lifted his head up off the pillow.

"I don't know. When she's well enough. Now, let's say your prayers."

"Yes, sir." Richard lay back down and clasped his tiny fingers together. "Dear Jesus, tell Mommy and Daddy I miss them. Help Nanna be happy again. And bless Uncle Ellis and Cook. Amen."

"Amen," Ellis echoed.

Help Nanna be happy again? Was she upset with the boy? he wondered. Truth be told, he had avoided her today. Was she still upset regarding their conversation last night? Did she regret her decision to postpone her departure even for a few days?

Ellis kissed Richard on the forehead. "Good night, Richard."

"Good night, Uncle Ellis."

Ellis closed the door to the child's room and headed down the stairs to his study. Invoices needed posting. Jedidiah Brighton had managed to load additional sponges to carry to New York. Pleased with the sales and the plentiful supply of natural sponges on the various reefs around the small island, his business would continue to grow. The Bahamian men he hired were naturals in the water and excellent sponge fishermen.

A parrot cawed, and Ellis looked out the window. The sky, a blanket of dark velvet with a silver pearl nestled on it, created a wonderful backdrop for his tropical garden. He lowered his glance to the cabin in his backyard. Scratching his beard, he wondered if it was wrong to separate the nanny from the boy. Should he offer her a permanent position to stay in Key West? He had assumed from the start she would want to get back to her life in New York. From their conversation last night, he finally understood that Richard was her life. She had poured her heart and soul into the child. And his brother had spoken highly of her competency. Maybe he should ask her to stay in charge of the boy's care.

Ellis leaned his chair back on its two hind legs and plopped his feet on his desk, a bad habit he never saw the need to break. Maybe he should pray about this. He'd been praying about how to be a good father to Richard, and reading every verse in Scripture he could find about children and disciplining them. But had he actually asked God if Miss Smith should remain on for a time as his nephew's nanny? Or was he simply allowing her to leave because of his attraction to her, not wanting to fight with temptation? Not wanting to deal with his past, his. . .

Yes, prayer was most definitely in order.

The next morning, Bea woke early and hurriedly dressed. She knew of Ellis's and Richard's fishing plans. She'd hoped for an invitation. Oddly enough, she'd gotten used to the sport. She'd done it simply to do "manly" things with Richard, and much to her surprise found she actually enjoyed it. The peaceful ripple of the water allowed one to think and pray. She'd never fished in an ocean before. In fact, until she boarded the *Justice* in New York harbor to come to Key West, she'd never even seen an ocean. The vast water contrasted dramatically with the mountain springs that fed the various farms she'd lived on in upstate New York. The smell of salt permeated the air. Low tide. . .well, low tide left something to be desired.

The movement of the water was different as well. In the springs it flowed in one constant direction; the ocean flowed in different directions depending on the tides. And the gentle roll of the surf as it lapped the shore was just as captivating as the constant movement of the water rushing downstream. While she found the two types of water very different, they both had the same soothing effect on her—gratitude to her heavenly Father. It gave her something to remind her of home.

Late last evening she had penned a letter to her parents, hoping there would be a boat heading to New York so she could hand it to the captain. She tapped her pocket in her long apron-covered shirt to be certain it was still there. . . . Perhaps the *Justice* would be coming back from Cuba soon, and she could send it that way.

The large front door opened and out stepped Richard with his pole in hand, immediately followed by Ellis Southard. Richard's bright smile filled his face. Ellis's eyes sparkled as he watched his nephew maneuver the fishing pole down the front steps.

Perhaps I shouldn't. . . Bea stepped forward from the trees' shadows. "Good morning, gentlemen."

"Nanna! Are you going fishing?" Richard ran up to her.

She glanced over to Ellis. His eyes no longer sparkled. He didn't want her along. "No, I have a letter I need to post."

Richard pouted. "Why don't you want to come fishing with me?"

I do, Child, I really do, she wanted to say but held back her emotions and her tongue.

"If you would like to come with us, Miss Smith," Ellis paused, "you are welcome."

"I would enjoy it, but I wouldn't want to intrude."

Ellis grinned and then sobered. "Come along then, and be quick about it."

Bea tucked the letter back into the apron over her skirt and placed her hands on her hips. "Ready when you are, Sir."

"Yeah! Nanna's coming." Richard pranced up and down.

Looking over at Ellis Southard, she noticed he stiffened and shut down his emotions. Why did the man keep doing that? Bea rolled the tension out of her shoulders. She didn't understand him, but she would have to accept the discomfort of the day. After all, she had wormed herself a place in this little fishing expedition.

"Let's go."

Ellis bolted ahead and walked a brisk pace through the streets to the harbor and down one of the large wooden docks that reached far into the ocean. Lined with sponges, nets, and a variety of ropes in different widths and sizes, she surmised that the dock belonged to Ellis and his sponging company. Afraid to ask, she held her tongue.

She worked up a sweat just keeping pace with Ellis Southard. Even Richard seemed a bit tired from the walk. She slowed her pace. She wasn't going to fall victim to heat exertion again. Little Richard's legs took three steps for every one of Ellis's.

As Bea and Richard started walking on the wooden planks, Ellis stood at the end of the pier. He turned to face her and muttered something to himself, muffled by the expansive ocean. Bea and Richard continued to plod on down the dock. Bea decided a word with Ellis Southard about his careless behavior was in order. But she would wait so that little Richard wouldn't be privy to their conversation.

Bea sat on the edge of the dock beside Richard and dangled her legs over the water. "It's a pleasant morning, Richard, don't you think?"

"Yup." Richard's head turned as he scanned the horizon.

"Nanna, see those clouds?"

Bea looked to where he pointed and nodded.

"Uncle Ellis says they are spinning around like a top."

She looked over to the horizon. Half a dozen small funnel clouds stood up from the sea. "Really?"

"Yup. And you see those clouds over there?" Richard pointed straight in front of them.

Bea nodded again.

"Those are new clouds being made."

"Do you know how clouds are made?" Bea inquired.

"Yup, Uncle Ellis says the sun makes the water hot and it 'vaporates, and when it gets high in the sky, it turns white and becomes a cloud."

"I see." For a four year old he really had quite an acute mind. Pleased and impressed that Ellis could talk with Richard in a way he could understand, she decided to acknowledge those things when she confronted him.

Beatrice Smith's presence this morning annoyed Ellis. She'd known he planned to take Richard fishing. And she obviously made herself available to come with them. Was he jealous of Richard's affection for her, or fighting his own attraction? He wasn't certain. Last night, in his stocking feet, he had buffed the floor to a high gloss from his continuous pacing. Successfully, he had resisted the urge to go to her cottage and speak to her, wanting, longing, to come up with any excuse just to see her smiling face.

Richard had thrived from Beatrice Smith's care. In his opinion, his brother had made a terrible error in judgment. How a man could avoid his own child because the mother died was beyond him. He understood his brother's deep love for his wife, but wasn't young Richard a part of her that continued to live?

Maybe he should let Beatrice and Richard return to the farm. But his brother's wishes were most emphatic that Ellis raise his son if anything should happen to him. And dealing with his own past would be at stake if he returned to New York, having been warned never to step foot again in the state, or Heather's father would press charges. He knew from Richard's letters that Heather had married. Perhaps enough time had passed.

"Nanna, Nanna, help!" Richard cried with excitement.

"Hold on tight, Richie."

Bea stood behind the boy, allowing him to work the fish and bring it in. Ellis smiled. Anxious to help, and yet proud to watch, he stationed himself beside the child.

Instinctively, they both reached for the line to help pull in the fish. Their hands grazed each other's, and Bea abruptly pulled hers away. Ellis held the line and pulled the fish up on the dock.

"It's blue and green!" proclaimed Richard.

"It's a snapper. Good eating, I think you'll like this fish," Ellis offered.

Richard jumped up and down around the fish. "Can I eat it for breakfast?"

Ellis placed his foot gently on the fish to keep it from flapping itself back into the water. "I imagine Cook would be happy to prepare it for you."

"Nanna can do it. Can't you, Nanna?"

Bea smiled and nodded her head.

"I'm sure she can, but Cook gets fussy about who she lets in her kitchen."

"Oh." Richard held Bea's hand. "Nanna, is it okay if Cook does it?"

"Yes, it's like Daisy in New York. She prefers to do all the cooking."

"Yeah, but not the fish. You had to clean the fish."

"I remember." Bea smiled. "That's a mighty fine catch, Richie."

She even cleans fish. Of course, if she wasn't too weak to put a worm on a hook, it only stood to reason she was capable of cleaning a fish, too. Even though Beatrice informed him she was the child's playmate, father, mother, nanny, etc., the other night, he realized he was just getting a glimmer of the real person. Beatrice Smith certainly was a unique woman. Aside from Cook, he had never met such a bold woman. But, Cook was another kind altogether.

"Can you remove the hook or should I?" Ellis asked.

"Nanna does that."

"Nanna." Ellis motioned her to take her place in the tradition of Richard's fishing. "Be aware of the spines on the dorsal fin."

Bea simply nodded and knelt on her skirt and gracefully removed the hook from the fish. "Looks like you shall have a big breakfast this morning, Richard."

Richard beamed. His smile ran from one side of his face to the next. Ellis loved the boy. He would be staying with him whether in New York or here, it didn't matter.

Bea placed the fish in the small bucket Ellis brought. The tropical fish flapped and fluttered, slapping the sides of the bucket with its tail.

"Can we go home now, Uncle Ellis?"

Ellis searched Bea's eyes for an answer to his silent, "Why?"

"Once Richard catches a fish, his only interest is his tummy." Bea chuckled.

Ellis smiled. "Sure, Son. I'm quite certain Cook will be happy to see your breakfast."

"Come on, Nanna. Let's get a head start on Uncle Ellis," Richard called out as he started down the pier toward shore.

Bea turned and whispered to Ellis. "Sir, you might want to remember, small boys have small legs and can't keep the pace of a full-grown man."

Ellis nodded and went in the opposite direction to pick up his pole and tackle. Bea carried the bucket and Richard's pole. The boy was determined to beat his uncle Ellis home.

Ellis sidled up beside her, tenderly removing the bucket from her hand. "Thank you for your admonition. However, Richard will need to learn to take care of his pole and catch."

"Generally he does. I believe he wishes to show you how much of a man he really is."

"A man, huh? He needs to enjoy being a boy longer. There's plenty of time for being a man."

"Perhaps, but he's had more losses than most my age. He's had to grow up fast. All of this," Bea spanned the area around them with her outstretched hand, "is an adventure. Soon he will need to mourn the loss of his father, his home and. . .me."

Chapter 11

Cook smothered Richard with praises for his fine catch and breakfast. After a simple fare of fresh poached eggs with toast, freshly squeezed orange juice, and Richard's catch of the day, Ellis slipped off to work with a single salutation.

If Bea wasn't careful, she would soon start daydreaming about Ellis. He was such an interesting character, with a kind and gentle side full of passion and warmth, as she'd witnessed in his interchanges with Richard. But there was this other darker side of him that held everyone at bay. His emotions seemed to run hot and cold. She had been too forward the other evening, addressing him on this part of his personality.

"What be on your pretty mind, Miss Bea?" Cook inquired as she helped her out of her corset at the end of another long day.

"Nothing."

"I don't know what it is with you young folks, always carrying on and saying nothing is on your mind when it's obvious there is plenty happenin' up there."

"I'm sorry, I'm not used to sharing my personal thoughts."

"I reckon it should be me apologizing for prying where I shouldn't be. Some say I have a problem with that. On the other hand, I tend to believe it's my duty to get beyond the surface and sink right down to the heart of the matter. You wouldn't be thinking about when you leave Master Richard, would you now?"

"Truth be told, it has been on my mind. But no, that wasn't what I was pondering. How well do you know Mr. Southard?"

"I suppose I've known him longer than most. He wasn't much of a man when he landed on this here rock. At the time he come, let me think, I believe it was 1850 or '51—sometime thereabouts—there weren't too many folks living here. I heard say there was around a thousand. Personally I never had a mind to count 'em."

"He's been here that long?"

"Wet behind the ears and carrying a heap of trouble on his back. He never did say what he was running from, but he's made his peace with it. At least I think he has."

Bea's curiosity rose a notch. Why had he left New York? If she recalled correctly, he was seventeen at the time. In all her talks with Elizabeth she'd never really been curious as to why he left. It simply hadn't seemed all that important.

"He seems to have a good heart."

"I see, you're worried about him being a good man to raise the child."

Bea nodded.

"There's few men with as fine a moral character as Mr. Southard. He works hard, cares for those around him, treats people fairly. He'll do right by the boy."

Bea's heart tightened. Soon she would be leaving Richard. And oddly enough, he would go on and hardly remember her, and yet, he had profoundly affected her for the rest of her life. "Cook, do you know if the *Justice* has come back from Cuba?"

"Come and gone. Why do you ask?" Cook was folding her corset and placing it on the chair beside the chest of drawers.

"I thought perhaps I should seek transport back home."

"But Mr. Ellis hasn't hired a nanny yet."

"I know but. . ."

"Ahh, I understand, Child. Your heart is breaking."

Gentle tears rolled out of her eyes. "Yes. It's so hard, Cook. I love Richard as if he were my own. But I have no rights to him. And Ellis is. . .well, he is his uncle." Bea sniffed and immediately she found herself engulfed in Cook's soft, loving arms.

"There, there, child. Trust the good Lord; He knows what is best."

"I'm trying, and He's been trying to teach me Ecclesiastes 3:5, 'a time to embrace, and a time to refrain from embracing.' "

"Personally I don't know what Mr. Ellis's problem is with having you continue on as the child's nanny, but I reckon men don't have an eye for maternal love."

"Cook, I. . .well, I am not a normal nanny. I was Richard's mother's best friend. I come from high society. I gave it all up just to help my friend. And now I love Richard not because he is Elizabeth's son, but because he has become so dear to me. He's as close as the air I breathe."

"I'm not surprised about your status in society, but what does that matter? You love the child, the child loves you. That should be the end of it."

"But it's not, and we both know Mr. Southard is not happy with me."

"Does he know? Your status, I mean."

"I can't imagine he does. I've not told him. Besides, I was eight when he left, and it's as you say, it doesn't matter."

"Maybe. If the man knew what you've given up for the child, perhaps he might think differently about you," Cook huffed. "I tell you, the man hasn't been right since you arrived. If I didn't know better, I'd think he fancies you."

"What? You can't be serious. He can barely stand to be in the same room with me."

"Precisely my point."

"Cook, you've been out in the sun too long. He can't possibly. . ." Bea couldn't even continue the thought. There was no way on God's green earth that Ellis Southard was attracted to her. However, if the tables were turned she would have to admit she was mighty attracted to him.

"Think what you will, Child, you might be right. I'm just an old woman who's lived too long."

"Nonsense."

Cook smiled. "I must be leaving your wonderful company, Miss Bea. My family needs me. They just love to tell me how their days went and to hear about mine. I must tell you, you coming from New York has made for some delightful stories these many days."

"Oh my." Bea blushed.

Cook hugged her again. "Trust the Lord, Child. He knows the desires of your heart."

Bea felt the heat on her cheeks deepen. God truly did know all her desires, which included the temptation that one Mr. Ellis Southard had caused since her arrival on Key West.

Ellis's ears still rang from the chastisement Cook gave him for not allowing Beatrice Smith to stay on as Richard's nanny. She had a point. Several in fact. And he had considered the idea. He just didn't know if it was the wisest thing for him to do. He couldn't deny his attraction to her. Yet, he knew better than to act on such impulses. Could he possibly allow her to live in his home and not react to her presence? Ellis paced his office floor.

A dim light still burned in Bea's cottage. Bea's cottage? When had he given her possession of the place? Beatrice Smith was like that. Whatever she touched, wherever she went was illuminated by her presence. She was an incredible woman. But he was a man not to be trusted around women.

Key West had been a perfect place to settle. So few women, so few temptations. It was easy to get lost in his work here and avoid the fairer sex. As the years passed and more women moved to the island, he had remained in control. He'd even escorted a few of the ladies to church and social functions from time to time, and had become the perfect gentleman.

Ellis snickered. Heather O'Donald and her father would never believe that.

What if Bea remained in the cottage? He could remodel the place to suit her needs. She probably came from a home about that size before she became Richard's nanny. Ellis scratched his beard and gently stroked it back in place with long, thoughtful strokes. He peeked out the window. A single lamp glowed. If he was going to ask her to stay on, he'd better do it now before reason won over.

Ellis's steps were fluid and fast as he made his way out of the house to the captain's quarters cabin. Taking a deep breath, he lifted his hand and paused. Should he? He held his knuckles suspended in the air. Perhaps he should pray about this, consider all the ramifications of how this woman would bring him to the brink of his self-control.

He turned around and stepped away. Only to be halted by Cook's words. "What are you afraid of?"

What indeed? Cook didn't know. No one knew. Well, Heather O'Donald and her father did. But his brother, the only other person who knew, was gone. A gentle voice whispered in his head. "It's been fifteen years."

Ellis knocked the doorjamb with his knuckle.

"Who is it?" Bea asked behind the still closed door.

"Miss Smith, it is me, Ellis. May I have a word with you?"

Bea slowly opened the door.

Ellis took in a sharp breath. She was lovely. She looked like a young girl rather than a grown woman with her long brown hair curled in spirals, cascading over her shoulders and framing her lily white neck. He swallowed and cleared his throat to speak. He'd seen her with her hair down before, but now the stark difference in their ages was once again made apparent. "May I come in?"

"Yes." Bea stepped back and allowed him to enter.

Ellis began to pace.

"What's the matter, Mr. Southard? Is Richard okay?"

"He's fine. Sorry. I. . .well I. . .I wanted to ask you something."

"Please sit, you're making me nervous," Bea pleaded.

"Sorry." Richard sat on the sofa. Bea sat a respectable distance away from him.

"I don't know how to say this other than to state my business straight out. Do you have obligations in New York?"

"No. Not really. Why do you ask?"

"What do you mean 'not really'?"

She hesitated, took in a deep breath, then looked him straight in his eyes. His heart stopped beating from the deep scrutiny he felt coming from her hazel-eyed gaze.

"My family wishes to have another coming-out party for me upon my return."

"Coming-out?"

"Mr. Southard, I come from a family such as your own. I took the job as Richard's nanny because of my deep love for Elizabeth. We all assumed she would get better shortly after she gave birth, but that simply wasn't the case. As you are well aware."

"You did all of that for the love of a friend?"

Bea nodded.

"I am in awe of you, Miss Smith. There are few who would sacrifice so much for the love of another."

"Thank you, but it hasn't been a sacrifice."

Ellis looked around the cottage. Such humble furnishings, and she was accustomed to the finer things in life, yet not once did she complain or voice her disapproval. Nor had she informed him who she was and his obligations to arrange proper housing for her stay.

"I am sorry, Miss Smith, if I had known. . ."

"Nonsense, I didn't need to tell you. I wanted to be with Richard. He's. . .he's special."

"He's more than special to you. You love him as if he were your own."

Bea looked away and whispered, "Yes."

"I came to ask you to stay on as his nanny, but I can't do that now. Knowing who you are, I can't ask you to give up your life again for Richard."

"I would love to stay on as Richard's nanny. Wealth isn't that important to me. Mind you, I'm not saying I don't appreciate some of the finer things. But Richard is of far more importance than wealth to me. I would be honored to stay on as his nanny."

"I can't allow you. It just wouldn't be right."

"Who is to know? If I don't care, why should you?" Bea reached over and touched his arm. "Ellis, please let me stay."

Bea was trembling from her contact with Ellis. "I've prayed, I've asked God for a way for me to continue to be a part of Richard's life. In six years he will be ten and I will still be young enough to marry."

"Beatrice. . .Bea. . .I–I just wouldn't feel right. You should be marrying a man and raising your own children."

"I don't want that as much as I want to be with Richard. Can't you understand? I love him that much." Bea swallowed back the tears that threatened to fall.

Ellis took her hand from his arm and held it tenderly within his own callused palm, massaging the tops of her fingers with the ball of his thumb. He glanced into her eyes and raised her chin with his left forefinger.

Bea's heart hammered in her chest. She was drawn to this man in a way she couldn't put into words.

Ellis touched the ringlets of her hair. "You're an incredibly beautiful woman, Bea."

Bea blushed. His eyes filled with passion. The realization excited her and frightened her at the same time. She removed her hand from his and rose from the sofa.

Ellis followed and stood behind her. "I'm sorry for being so forward, Beatrice. Please forgive me."

Bea nodded. She didn't trust herself to speak.

He placed his hands on her shoulders. "I would like to get to know you. May I call again tomorrow evening? After Richard is in bed."

"Yes," she whispered, her voice shaky, her body protesting. A driving need to turn to him and bury herself in his embrace threatened any sense of decency and proper behavior she had ever been taught.

He stepped back and removed his hands from her shoulders. As if instantly chilled, she shivered. What was the matter with her?

She turned to the gentle click of her door being shut. He was gone now. The cottage seemed darker. Lonelier. A somber air filled the empty space.

O Lord, what has come over me? Over us? She truly would have to admit Ellis's eyes spoke of his untold desire. She wondered if her own eyes revealed the same passion.

Chapter 12

All the next day, Ellis found himself as edgy as a land crab in search of shelter and protection. He had almost lost his self-control last night. He prayed long into the night, thanking the Lord for stepping in and pulling them apart at the moment He had. Granted, Bea had possessed the wisdom and strength to break the connection that drew them to each other. Bea had found the resolve to step away from him and their passion. And yes, she had the same desires as he.

What was it about him and his desires which brought a woman to a point of forgetting all propriety? He must be some kind of beast or animal, unable to control his desires.

On the other hand, they needed to talk. A physical attraction between them could not be denied. But could they live so close to one another and not succumb to temptation? Ellis was quite certain he would not stand the test. He hadn't in the past. What gave him a chance of withstanding it in the present? Especially since his desires for Beatrice far outweighed any desires he ever had for Heather.

Cook was exceptionally cold to him this morning. He didn't have the strength to tell her he had gone to ask Bea to stay on, only to find out that he couldn't allow her to take the position due to her social standing.

He felt grateful his parents were no longer alive. They would not be shamed once again by his actions. They had never known exactly what he had done, but they understood from Richard, Ellis had no choice but to leave, for the family's honor.

"Honor," Ellis sighed. "Father God, why did You do this to me? Why bring a woman into my path that I can never have? If we should ever marry, she would be a social outcast for marrying the likes of me. It wouldn't be fair to her, Lord. I couldn't put her through that."

"Through what?" Bea asked.

"Bea." Ellis fought every muscle in his body to stay in place. "Miss Smith, I was unaware of your presence."

"Apparently, and you do that quite well. How long have you been practicing the cold, standoffish man?"

"Long enough."

"Ellis, something happened between us last night. Don't you think we ought to talk about it?"

Ellis turned and faced the window looking over the gardens. "I was forward last evening, Miss Smith. It will never happen again."

"Oh, so if I came over to you right now and placed my fingers upon your chest, you would not respond?"

"Don't!"

"Don't what, Ellis? Admit that I'm attracted to you?" He heard the shuffle of her dress behind him.

"Yes. . .no. Bea, we can't."

"We can't, or you won't?" She placed her hand upon his left shoulder.

"I won't."

"Why?" she whispered.

"I am not an honorable man." Ellis walked away from her grasp.

"What?" Confusion knitted the features of her pretty face.

The sun was setting and the pinks and purples of the sunlight set a rose-colored haze across the garden.

"I have a past I'm ashamed of, Bea. I can never return to New York."

Never return to New York? What kind of crime had he committed? Is that why he left town and never returned so many years before?

"Fine. Be that way. I can't force you to explain. However, I think you're afraid. I certainly am. What we saw in each other's eyes last night was. . .was. . .well, I don't know what it was. But I know one thing, it scared the life out of me."

Bea retreated from Ellis's study. It had been a forward move to approach him in the house rather than to wait for him to come to her cottage later. But it seemed safer to speak with him there, while Cook was still in the house and with Richard running around.

She found Richard playing in his room. She now knew she couldn't stay, even if Ellis offered her the position. Whatever was going on between the two of them was unstoppable if she remained. And Bea wasn't all that certain she wanted to find out what it was. She had been known to speak her mind occasionally, but she prided herself on her ability to remain in control. Last night she was not in control. And neither was Ellis. If they had kissed at that moment it would have been. . . Bea shook the thought right out of her mind. She would not allow herself to ponder such things again.

All night she had tossed and turned, hoping that she and Ellis might have a future together. And that, through their union, the three of them would become a family. And Richard would legally become her son. *Such foolish thoughts,* she chided herself. Ellis had no intentions of giving into his feelings. Instead he erected a stone wall around himself that she was too afraid to climb.

"Richie."

"Yes, Nanna."

"I want you to know I love you very much." She fought for control of her emotions and continued. "I will always love you."

"I love you too, Nanna."

She balled her hands into fists and released them, working out her tension. "Like I mentioned the other day, I'm going home, Richie."

"Home? To my New York house?"

"No, to my parents' New York house. You remember visiting my parents' house, don't you?"

"Yes. But, Nanna, I want you to stay."

"I'd love to, but I can't. Your uncle Ellis loves you very much, and he will take good care of you. Perhaps when you are older and a man yourself you could come for a visit and see me in New York."

"I'll visit you, Nanna." Richard grabbed her legs through the loose-fitting Spanish-style skirt she had purchased the other day.

Bea pulled him up in her arms and hugged him hard, groaning and giving him a great big bear hug. "I don't know exactly when I'll be leaving. I have to wait for a ship. Hopefully, I'll have a few days to spend with you before I go."

"Can we go fishing?"

She grasped him more firmly. His bright blue-gray eyes darted back and forth imploring her to say yes. How could she not? "Sure, how about tomorrow morning?"

"Yippee."

Bea smiled. A child could shift his or her emotions as easily as the wind. One minute, sad about her leaving. The next, excited to go fishing. She set him back down on the floor. "I'll see you tomorrow morning. Good night, Richie."

" 'Night, Nanna." Richie continued to play with his blocks on the floor, his face intense as he worked on his next masterpiece.

Bea slipped into the hallway and tentatively approached the staircase. This was now the second time she broached the subject of her leaving to Richard, and it was getting easier, for him and for her. Perhaps she would be able to get over the tremendous loss in time.

At the foot of the stairs the darkened silhouette of Ellis Southard stood, waiting, his stance rigid, even more than before, if that were possible. Bea took in a deep breath and descended the stairs. "Good evening, Mr. Southard."

How could she be so casual? Ellis reached out to her and pulled her toward him. Fear blazed in her eyes. He paused, then released her. "Good night, Miss Smith."

The stunned woman stood in front of him. He stepped back. Timidly she reached her hand toward his forearm, but before it connected she pulled it back.

"I'm taking Richard fishing in the morning. Then I'll begin searching for a ship to make my departure. I think it would be best."

Ellis didn't want her to leave, but he didn't trust himself around her. The temptation he had felt with Heather was nothing compared to the pull of this woman. Unable to speak, he simply nodded his assent.

She turned and walked out the front door. She would be out of his life soon. The temptation would be gone. He could get back to living his quiet life. Ellis eased out a pent-up breath.

"Uncle Ellis," Richard hollered from up the stairs. Perhaps his life wouldn't be all that quiet. He mounted the stairs two at a time and hurried to the child.

Bea set out for town after cleaning up from her morning fishing expedition with Richard. Unlike the time before, Ellis had not joined them. There must be a ship going to New York. She fortified her resolve to go back home.

Most ships passed through the Key West seaport as they worked their way from the states to the Caribbean or vice versa. Disappointed to find all the ships sailing in the wrong direction, Bea headed toward a small shop she had passed earlier. Purchasing some gifts for her family might help her to focus on New York rather than on what she was leaving behind. A few more days on Key West would give her a few more days with Richard. Granted, the tension between Ellis and herself would probably mount, but. . .

Bea's heart caught in her chest. She saw Ellis working on his dock. He appeared to be washing the sponges. His well-groomed beard glistened in the sunlight. Its red highlights made him even more striking. Bea fought the urge to walk up to him. Again last night he had almost kissed her. Frightened by such raw emotion, she had pulled away from him. Yet, she couldn't stop thinking about what it would be like to kiss—and be kissed—by such a powerful man.

She walked into the small shop featuring handmade crafts from the area residents. There were figurines made from shells, carved coconut husks and a variety of other strange items.

"May I help you?" a medium-height, fortyish woman asked.

"I'm just browsing, thank you." Bea glanced at the shell figurines.

"Take all the time you'd like. My name is Peg; I own this little shop."

"Did you make these?" Bea pointed to the shell critters.

"Actually, those are made by someone else. My hobbies are over there." She motioned to the side wall where various cloth items lined the shelves.

Bea worked her way over. There were linen tablecloths with finely embroidered flowers on the corners, some matching napkins, napkin ring holders, and a variety of rag dolls. "These are wonderful."

"Thank you. I opened the shop during the war. I found the soldiers loved to purchase items to send home to their mothers, wives, and sisters. The island has a certain uniqueness, being so far south. And people seem to like to buy trinkets for loved ones when they travel."

Bea chuckled. "That's why I'm browsing."

"Where are you from, and how long are you here?" Peg sat down behind the counter and brushed back her long blond bangs.

"Came from New York. I'll be returning home as soon as I procure passage."

"New York, as in the city?"

"Oh no, I'm from way upstate, near the Canadian boarder. I brought Richard to his uncle Ellis."

"The nanny. I should have realized. Heard you had a bout with heatstroke."

Did everyone know her business? "Yes. Didn't know if I was going to make it at one point. The doctor said it was because I'm used to the very cold temperatures up North, in contrast to the heat here."

"Happens to a lot of folks—no shame in it. Has Mr. Southard found a new nanny for the child?"

"I don't believe he has, but Richard is a good boy. It shouldn't be difficult."

Peg laughed. "This is Ellis Southard we're talking about, right?"

Bea knitted her eyebrows. "Yes."

"You should have seen his list. The woman had to be a saint and fifty years old at least, according to what he put together. Of course, most of the young gals here were hoping to get the job in order to hook the man. He's just not interested in marriage. And it ain't from a lack of some gals trying, let me tell you."

Bea blushed.

"Sorry, I shouldn't be so forward. Comes from living here so long. People just learn to let their mouths flap a bit. Never did gossip much at home, but here. . . well, it's the favorite pastime."

"I understand."

"So, I take it Mr. Southard isn't interested in keeping you on as the child's nanny."

"I have responsibilities back home. My family is planning another coming-out party."

"Coming-out party! You best set yourself down, dear. We've got plenty to discuss." Peg beamed and pointed to a stool.

Ellis worked his shoulders back, easing out the tension. He watched Beatrice make her way around to the various docks and ships. He supposed he could have told her there were none immediately heading to New York, but he wondered if she would have believed him.

She looked wonderful this morning in her Spanish skirt and blouse. The style of clothing fit her and her more aggressive personality. He wondered what some of the high society ladies back home would think if they saw her dressed in such a casual style. "Probably collapse," Ellis chuckled.

She had slipped into Peg Martin's gift shop and seemed to be spending quite a bit of time inside. Peg was a great gal, but she could rattle on so. He wondered if he should go over to the store and rescue Bea from Peg's assault of questions.

" 'Morning, Ellis." Marc Dabny headed toward him.

" 'Morning."

"Heard the lady was leaving the island soon."

"Appears so."

"I asked her if she would like to go to dinner with me one night, but she let me know she would be leaving and was in no position to begin a relationship."

"Sounds wise." She'd given Ellis just the opposite impression. He reminded himself he wasn't interested in pursuing a relationship. She was leaving.

"She's quite a looker." Marc whistled.

"I guess. So tell me, what brings you over this morning, Marc?" He must have spent too much time in the sun; his head was pink from an obvious sunburn, Ellis observed. Why a man with so little hair on his head didn't wear a hat baffled him.

"Oh, right. I was wondering if you had room for a partner."

"Partner?"

"Yeah, I've got some money set aside and I think your business is going to be growing. I also have a couple ideas about expanding your market."

"Haven't given any thought to expanding." In fact, he was beginning to think about closing down the business and returning home to New York to raise Richard on the family farm. "Maybe we should talk, Marc."

Marc rubbed his hands together. "Great. With my investment we could hire a few more men, buy a few more boats, and begin shipping the sponges into other cities besides New York."

"I'm listening." And Ellis seriously was. If Marc bought into the business, maybe Ellis could return home and still maintain his business here in Key West.

"As you know, the railroad is expanding across the western frontier. And I was thinking, if we took the sponges to the cities where people connect with the trains, we would see the sponges move out West as well."

"Interesting. Do you have contacts in some of these cities?"

"Some. Men I served with in the war. But I could make a trip north, make some contacts, and line up initial sales."

Marc was a go-getter, and he seemed to have an eye for business. "Marc, I would need to see your books and how well you manage your assets before I agree."

"And I would like a look at yours as well."

"That's fair. All right, why don't you come over this evening and we'll discuss business in a more formal manner. I'd want a lawyer to draw up any agreement."

"Naturally."

"I must tell you, I might be interested in having someone else run the business so I can return to New York for awhile and take care of the farm."

"Either way, you stay and run it or I stay, doesn't much matter. I'll be over after dinner tonight."

"I'll have my books ready," Ellis said and took a step back toward his work.

Marc waved his salutation and left.

Should he move back to New York? Should he raise Richard there? Or should he just stay put and enjoy his life here? So many questions. So many changes in such a short span of time. Ellis sat on the edge of the dock and prayed. "Father, I'm confused. I see advantages to Marc coming on as a partner, but I want to be wise. I want to honor Richard's request to raise his son, and I know he wanted the boy to enjoy growing up on the farm. But can I really return home? And what about this attraction to Beatrice Smith? If I return to New York won't she be there also?" Ellis groaned.

He sprang up, peeled off his shirt, shoes, and socks, and jumped into the ocean. A long hard swim was in order. He needed some physical exercise. He needed to relax.

"Goodness, you did all that for a friend?" Peg asked.

"Yes, and I'd do it again." Bea sipped a cup of tea Peg had given her.

"That kind of friendship is hard to find. I'm pleased to know you, Bea."

Bea dabbed her mouth with the cloth napkin. "Thanks, I'm sure many folks would do what I did."

"I wouldn't be so sure.

"We have a dinner at the Presbyterian church tonight. Would you like to come?"

"Goodness, what time?"

"Six."

Ellis usually returned home at five. "Sure, I'd love to. Thanks."

"Tell you what, I'll have my brother, Danny, come by your place and escort you to the church."

"If you tell me where it is, I think I can manage it." Bea shifted on the stool.

Peg waved her hand with a quick flick of the wrist. "Nonsense, a woman should have an escort. You know that."

"But I thought such things weren't followed down here."

"True enough, but once the sun goes down and the sailors start to drinking, it's just wise to have a man escort you." Peg tapped her hand onto Bea's.

"I see your point. I'm staying in the cottage in back of Ellis Southard's home."

"The cottage?"

"Don't ask," Bea sighed.

Peg laughed. "Guess it has to do with you not being over fifty, right?"

"Possibly. . .I really don't know. But it is the cutest little cottage. I love it." Bea smiled. "I better get going. Cook will have my hide if I don't return soon. Thanks for the tea and the conversation." Bea slipped off the stool.

" 'Welcome. Next time I'll let you buy something." Peg winked.

Bea giggled and walked out the door. She glanced over at Ellis's dock and saw him jump in the ocean, half naked.

"Oh my!" she exclaimed and turned her head. Her face flushed. She quickened her pace. *Lying in a snow bank might be the best thing at the moment,* she thought. Snow was not to be found in Key West and likely never would be. Bea opened the fan she had brought with her and fanned herself as she walked up Front Street back to Ellis Southard's home.

Chapter 13

Ellis couldn't believe it. The first evening he was home for dinner in two nights and Beatrice Smith had accepted an invitation to dine at the Presbyterian church. Seeing Peg Martin's brother, Dan, come to escort Bea had him speculating that Peg might have other intentions besides dinner. Pacing back and forth down the hall, stroking his beard, he wondered why the thought bothered him so.

While Richard slept peacefully upstairs, Marc had come and gone, scrutinizing Ellis's books and finding them in order, just as Ellis had found Marc's. It seemed plausible that the two could become partners. Marc's bid to purchase half of the business was a fair market value. But before he moved on with this merger, Ellis wanted and needed references. Truth be told, harvesting and exporting sponges was the furthest thing from his mind.

Listening, waiting for Beatrice's return, drove him into a frenzy of worry. The late hour, along with his inability to go searching for her without waking up the child, left him feeling helpless. The rich mahogany grandfather's clock chimed once, noting it was half past the hour of ten. Perhaps he should wake the boy? He placed his foot on the first step, and then heard laughter. Ellis paused.

Yes, it was definitely laughter, feminine laughter. He eased his foot off the step and sauntered over to the front door. Leaning around the doorjamb, he could see the young couple. Beatrice removed her hand from Dan's arm. They were talking; she was smiling, a friendly banter exchanged between them.

Dan bowed slightly and kissed the top of her hand. Fire blazed up Ellis's spine. How dare he be so forward? And yet, Dan was being the perfect gentleman.

Ellis waited for Dan to leave before he opened the door.

"Hello, Ellis." Bea smiled.

Had she seen him behind the door? "I was wondering if we could talk?"

"I think that would be nice. Shall I come into the big house and we can share a cup of tea?"

"Sure." Ellis slipped back into the house and raised the lights. The warm glow pushed aside some of his earlier dark emotions.

Bea slipped through the open door, the swish of her skirt alerting him to her nearness. He turned. She was beautiful.

"You waited up for me?" she asked and walked past him toward the kitchen.

"Yes. We need to talk."

"Yes, we do." She placed the full teakettle on the lit stove, and then she moved swiftly to the cabinet where the cups were stored, removing two with their saucers. She must have spent more time with Cook than he imagined.

"I had an offer today to buy into my sponge business."

She paused for a moment and asked, "Was it a good offer?" She went back to her work.

"Respectable."

"Do you know and trust the man enough to join in a partnership with him?"

"Marc seems responsible."

"Marc Dabny?" She turned from the counter and faced him.

"Yes."

"And this is the same man that—"

"Yes." Ellis cut her off. He didn't want to be keelhauled all over again for that one.

"And you trust him?" She raised her cinnamon brown eyebrows.

"At this point. Is there something I don't know about him that you would question my judgment so?"

"Seems to me a couple days ago the man was hunting for a wife. Not an ordinary wife, a slave, with a pretty figure, mind you."

"He told you that?"

"Not in so many words, but yes, it was clear to me what the man's intentions were. If a man can treat a woman like that, what kind of a man would he be as a business partner? Would he want you to slave and do all the work while he sat back and enjoyed your profits?"

"I hadn't thought about that." Truth was he hadn't had much room for any thought which didn't revolve around her.

Bea poured the boiling water into the teapot and let it steep. "Why did he want to buy into your business, Ellis?"

"He said he saw room for expansion, and I think he has some valid ideas." There. He wasn't a total idiot when it came to business.

"Well, I don't know the first thing about your business and where it may or may not be expanded. Truth is, I've never heard of a sponge business before. But you seem to be doing well. Would this expansion need the help of another owner?"

"Possibly, possibly not."

Bea set the teapot on a tray with the cups. "Shall we sit in the living room or would you prefer to sit at the table?"

"Living room is fine." Ellis scooped up the tray and led the way.

Bea followed Ellis, noticing how his strong shoulders pressed his white cotton shirt. The man was in excellent shape.

Ellis poured her a cup.

Bea sat on the sofa in front of the cup of tea he had placed on the Queen Anne mahogany table. She smoothed her skirt and waited for Ellis to pour his own tea and sit down. He sat beside her on the sofa. "What do you want to talk about, Ellis?"

"Are you aware of the hour?"

"Yes, and you and I both know you don't want to talk with me about the time I've returned home."

Ellis tugged at his collar and nodded. He stood up and began to pace. *At least he is working out his thoughts,* she mused.

"Richard said you would be joining us tomorrow morning."

"Yes. After you so wonderfully put it back in my lap."

"What?"

"Richie said that you said to go ask me about fishing with the two of you."

"Oh. Well, I didn't know what to tell the boy, and I certainly wasn't going to be answering for you."

"Thank you."

"Bea, this is crazy. I'm so full of wild emotions I don't know what to think or do. Let alone make sense of anything."

"And you think I understand these emotions?"

He sat down beside her on the sofa. The warmth of him so close to her sent a warm glow radiating within her. *O Lord, help me now,* she silently pleaded.

"Ellis, tell me what happened." Without thought, she reached over and touched his sun-darkened hand, tenderly stroking it.

"I'll tell you, but please do not pass judgment on my family for my actions. They were mine and mine alone."

"Very well."

And Ellis began. He told her about Heather, their whirlwind romance, and about the night they stole a passionate kiss. How her hands went beneath his shirt, and how he was driven by desire to go beyond where a gentleman should. And about her father, finding them locked in each other's embrace, and his warning for Ellis to get out of town or he would ruin the reputation of the Southard family name.

"So, you created a stone wall and kept women at bay for all these years?"

"It was the only way. I was so out of control that night."

"I see. And it was all you, right?"

"Of course. I was the one who initiated the kiss."

Bea smiled. "Ellis, in my opinion, unless you force yourself upon us, by and large, women are the ones who send out the signals about wanting or not wanting to be kissed."

"But what about the other night? You and I both know we could have been lost in our passions."

"True, but we weren't. At the right moment, wisdom prevailed and we stopped. Emphasis on the word 'we,' Ellis. You and I both stopped.

"Can I ask you something even more personal?"

Ellis chuckled. "I don't think anything is more personal than what I just admitted to you about myself."

"Were you used to women putting their hands under your shirt?"

His eyebrows arched up into his forehead. "No, it was a completely new experience."

"Did you direct Heather's hands to go there?"

"No." He knitted his eyebrows together.

"Do you see my point yet?" Bea stroked her thumb over Ellis's firm grip.

"I'm not sure. Are you suggesting Heather was the more aggressive person?"

"Yes."

"But I didn't do anything to stop her. She was a sweet, innocent girl before I kissed her."

"Had you kissed many women before Heather?"

"No."

Bea knew Heather O'Donald's reputation, and obviously Ellis didn't. While still a young girl, Bea had heard the whispered news of Heather O'Donald's hurried wedding and soon-delivered first child. And this occurred a year after Ellis left. Obviously, Ellis never knew, or if he did, he probably blamed himself for that as well.

She reached up and stroked his bearded jaw. "Ellis, was it Heather O'Donald, by chance?"

"Yes. But for her sake, please don't repeat any of this."

"I won't. But what I'm going to tell you isn't pretty, and I'll be as gentle as I can. Heather O'Donald married quickly, a year after you left the area, and had a child six months later." Ellis lowered his head and wagged it back and forth.

"It's not your fault."

"Of course it is. Don't you see? If I hadn't kissed her so passionately, she never would have known. . ."

Bea took both of her hands and placed them on his face and lifted it to look at her. "Ellis, I think you were the innocent one. True, you had desires, and perhaps you would have acted upon them. But Heather had desires, too. She was bold, far bolder than you. Don't you see?"

"Maybe, but I'm the man. . ."

Bea chuckled. "And only men sin, right?"

He narrowed his gaze.

"Ellis, I always found that when two people sin, both are guilty. God will forgive you, and you can ask Him to forgive Heather. The hardest part is for you to forgive yourself."

"How did you become such a wise woman at such a young age?"

"I'm not. But I do pay attention, and I think what you and I are fighting is an attraction far deeper than your lustful moment with Heather."

Ellis pulled back from Bea's loving embrace. Her words made perfect sense. Had Heather already been exposed to such passions? He thought back on their few dates. She had been the aggressor. She seemed to. . . Ellis cleared his throat. "So, do you think you can trust me with these intense passions?"

Bea turned her head then looked back at him. "Can you trust me?" Her faint blush accented her beauty.

Ellis sat in the chair opposite the sofa. "You're an incredible woman, Beatrice Smith. Not only are you beautiful enough to take my breath away, your mind is quick, and you get to the heart of the matter with a forward resolve I've never seen before."

"Thank you—I think."

Ellis chuckled. "My words were meant as a compliment. Unlike Marc, I would never want a servant for a wife. I would want a companion, someone who would challenge me, someone with whom I could share my deepest thoughts and concerns. Someone I could trust with my heart."

"Is that a proposal?"

Ellis gulped.

Not giving him a chance to respond, she quipped, "And you say that I'm honest. I've never met a man like you, Ellis. And I must tell you, I like what I see."

Ellis grinned. Was she admitting she found him handsome? "What do we do now?"

"I have no idea." Bea lifted her teacup. It shook in her hand and she immediately nested it back on the saucer.

"You're afraid to be with me, aren't you?"

"Yes. . .no. It's not what you're thinking."

"Explain." Ellis lowered his chin onto his clasped hands with his elbows supported by the arms of the chair.

"Yes, I'm afraid of the attraction between us. No, I'm not afraid of you and your past. You were a boy bursting to be a man. I've heard that it is a difficult time for all young men."

Ellis's cheeks flamed. "It can be."

"I found out today that no ships will be leaving for New York for awhile."

"I know."

"You knew?" She knitted her eyebrows.

"I know the comings and goings of ships. It's all a part of my business. I need to find ships to carry my cargo."

"Oh, right. Well, I was going to say, why don't we slowly see what develops between us? You know, spend some time, talking like this."

Ellis smiled. "Yes, I think that would be in order. Shall I come to your cottage tomorrow night after Richard's gone to bed?"

"Why don't we start with some time in public?"

"In public? You want me to court you?"

Bea chuckled. "Is that a problem?"

"No, but—"

"But, since the woman is right here in my backyard, why do I need to fuss over her, right?"

She could be forward. He amended his words. "I didn't mean it that way. If you want me to court you, I'll do it." Ellis squirmed, working the tension out of his back.

"No, you don't have to court me. I was merely trying to suggest we spend time together. Like meal time, playing with Richard after dinner, those times. You've been avoiding coming home at dinner since the other night in the cottage."

"Work kept—"

"Ellis!"

"Oh, all right, yes. I was thinking up work that needed doing so I didn't have to face you. Better?"

Bea smiled. "Much."

"Oh, you can have a nasty side, I see," Ellis teased.

"Nasty? Me. . . ? Now, Ellis, whatever gave you that idea?" She winked.

Just what had he gotten himself into? Ellis's fingers tightened around the arms of the chair.

Chapter 14

Ellis lay in bed as the sun rose. The bright orange glow cast stark shadows over the room. He rubbed his face. "I can't believe I admitted everything to Beatrice last night," he groaned. Granted, she was easy to talk with, but. . . "Marriage? Did I really propose marriage?

"Lord, I'm certain I didn't. I was just saying if I was to marry. That isn't asking a woman, is it? Do I want to. . .to. . . I can't say it, Lord. The very thought sends shivers of fear up my spine. Although the conversations would be lively with Miss Smith."

Ellis pulled the covers off and sat up, swinging his feet over the edge. He stood and stretched his sore muscles. His bed looked like a battlefield. And a battle of emotions had been waged all night. Did he want to pursue a relationship with Miss Smith, or not? One thing was certain. It would solve the need for a nanny. And Beatrice does love the child. *She isn't an unpleasant woman for a man to get saddled with. . .if a man must be saddled,* he reasoned.

But a wife wasn't a saddle. She was to be cherished, loved, honored, and adored. Could he truly do those things with regard to Beatrice Smith? "I don't know, Lord. I'm so confused. And what's this sixth sense You've given her about Marc? Is there something I don't see?" Ellis paced back and forth in his room.

The gentle knock on his door stopped him midstride. "Who is it?"

"Me, Uncle Ellis."

"Come in, Son."

The door creaked open slowly. "Cook says to come to breakfast."

Ellis smiled, confident Cook would pronounce it as an order. "Tell her I'll be right down. I need to shave."

"Shave? You taking off your beard?" Richard questioned, his eyes opened wide, waiting for an answer.

"I may have a beard, Son. But I do still shave." Ellis pointed to the various places on his face and neck where he did shave. "Plus, I have to keep it trim."

"My daddy didn't wear a beard, just a 'stache."

Ellis grinned. "A 'stache, huh? Do you think I should take off my beard?"

"No, you look like Uncle Ellis with a beard."

Ellis chuckled. Children's logic could be so profound. "You better go tell Cook I'll be right down or she'll have both our hides."

Richard ran out of the room as if lightning would strike. Ellis grinned. The woman did have a way of putting fear into a person. He looked into the mirror. Would Bea prefer no beard? Ellis tried to imagine what his face would look like without it. He'd grown the beard when he was twenty and had never once shaved it off. He remembered her loving touch on his beard last night, cupping his face in her tender hands. Such compassion. Such honesty. No, he'd leave his beard. She certainly didn't seem to have a problem with it.

Ellis finished getting ready for the day and worked his way down the stairs. The lilt of Bea's laughter floated into the hall. He paused, enjoying its merriment, then continued on to the dining room. "Good morning, everyone." He caught a glimpse of Bea, and she flushed slightly. Goodness, she was beautiful in the morning. He sat down at the head of the table. Cook was in the kitchen. Richard was buttering his biscuit. Ellis caught Bea's glance and mouthed the words, "You're beautiful."

A deep crimson blush painted her high cheekbones. Ellis smiled and released his gaze. While questions abounded in her absence, in her presence all arguments, fears, and worries dissolved. For the first time in fifteen years he truly felt forgiven for his past, and he owed his inner release to this incredible woman. If only he had learned that lesson before his parents had passed. He would have gone home for a visit. Heather's family's threats were meaningless in the scope of her wedding a year later.

A peace settled within him regarding his parents. They were in heaven. They would know the truth, and one day he would meet them again.

"Uncle Ellis, where are we fishing today?"

"I thought we might go for a sail and fish for some deepwater fish, like kingfish." Ellis picked up the fork with his right hand.

"Fishing on a boat?" Richard bounced up and down with excitement on his chair.

"Yes, we have to sail out quite a distance before we can fish. Would you like that?"

Richard bobbed his head up and down with such vigor, his entire body shook.

"Miss Smith, do you think you can handle the sun for an entire day?" Ellis asked, scooping another forkful of eggs.

"I'm not sure. I've been feeling stronger." Bea's voice seemed uncertain. Was she afraid of being on a boat? No, that couldn't be. . .she had sailed here from New York. Was she afraid of being alone with him for an entire day? But Richard would be with them, he reasoned.

Ellis dabbed his mouth with his napkin then spread it over his lap again. "There's a small cabin on the boat where you can get some shade."

"I know you didn't ask my advice," Cook interrupted, "but I think a full day's sail might be a bit much for the lady." Cook sat herself down at the table.

"You think so, Cook?" Bea asked, fussing the edge of her napkin with her fingertips.

"I'd be waiting a bit more if it was myself." Cook lowered her head, clasped her hands, and silently prayed over her breakfast.

"I think I'll take Cook's advice and stay here. I'm sorry, Richard, but I won't be fishing with you today."

Ellis straightened in his chair. "We don't need to go deep-sea fishing. We could still use the boat and fish around the island."

"No, thank you. You and Richard go ahead. I'll browse some more through town. I barely scratched the surface yesterday."

Richard tattled. "Nanna didn't like the big waves on the boat from New York."

Ellis searched Bea's eyes. "Were you seasick?" he asked.

"A little," Bea admitted.

"Land sakes, child. No wonder the heat got you so bad." Cook tossed her head from side to side and ate some of her eggs.

"Did that matter?" Bea asked.

Ellis couldn't believe his ears. *Did it matter?* he grumbled to himself. "Of course it mattered. You were already a bit dehydrated from the seasickness. No wonder you were hit so hard. I want you to stay home today, and don't be spending too much time in town. We don't want you having a relapse."

"Is that an order or concern?" she rebuffed.

"Ew-wee, I'm not touching that one." Cook giggled and stood up, removing her plate from the table.

"Concern." Ellis held back his temper.

Richard's head bobbed back and forth between the two of them, then settled on Bea to wait for her response.

"Then I'll not be upset with your concern. And I'll do as you recommend."

Ellis reached over and cupped her hand under his own. "I am concerned, Bea," he whispered.

"Thank you."

Richard knitted his eyebrows together. Bea removed her hand from Richie's prying eyes. He was trying to figure out what had just happened, and Bea suspected Cook knew exactly what was going on between Ellis and her. "Richie, finish your breakfast so you can go fishing and sailing with your uncle."

"All right." He stabbed his fork into some eggs and gulped them down.

Ellis and she had agreed to take things one step at a time, but he had thrown her with his comment about how beautiful she was. On the other hand, she couldn't help but notice how handsome he was this morning, as well. They would have to decide fast if they were, or were not, going to court. She wasn't sure she could take too much of this.

"All done," Richard proclaimed, and took his empty plate to the kitchen.

"I'm sorry, Ellis," she whispered. "I should have known you were speaking with concern, not orders. I have a tendency to dislike being ordered about."

Ellis grinned. "I'm rather accustomed to women like that. I'll be more careful how I word my thoughts in the future."

"Can I have another offer for a gentle sail around the island?" Bea allowed her hand to travel in Ellis's direction.

He picked up on her cue and cupped her hand again. She breathed in deeply. His warmth and strength blended with his tenderness and found expression in the simple gesture. *Amazing,* she mused.

His voice lowered. "You feel it too?"

She nodded.

"We'll talk some more tonight." Ellis looked back to the kitchen. Cook seemed to have given Richard a chore. "Thank you for last night. I feel so at peace with my past."

"You're welcome."

He squeezed her hand slightly. "Later," he whispered.

Bea nodded and removed her hand. As much as she didn't want to, she knew she had to. Richard was bound to come racing through those doors any minute.

As if on cue, the door banged open. "Uncle Ellis?"

"Yes, Richard." Ellis winked at Bea.

"Cook says I need sailing clothes. What are they?"

"You'll need some oilcloth clothes to protect you from the rain. But we'll be okay today. Just gather a set of warm pants, a shirt, and a sweater or winter coat."

"It's too hot."

"It's in case of a storm on the water, Richard. You need to be prepared."

A storm? Could they run into a storm? Bea implored Ellis's gaze for some assurance.

"Truth be told, there aren't many storms down here in the winter months. Hurricane season is over."

"Hurricanes?"

Ellis chuckled. "An ugly Nor'easter—but these come from the south."

"Oh."

"Go get your change of clothes, Richard. We need to get going if we're going deep-sea fishing."

Richard scurried off.

"Is he safe out there?" Bea asked in Richard's absence.

"He'll be fine."

Bea tried not to worry. She didn't know anything about sailing. Her first sail was on the *Justice.*

"Trust me." Ellis now stood beside her and placed his hand on her shoulder. "We'll be fine."

Bea nodded.

She watched Ellis retreat from the dining room. Bea gathered up the few remaining dishes to take to the kitchen. Cook's remaining in the kitchen meant she was deliberately giving the two of them some privacy. But Cook being Cook, she would have plenty of questions when Bea entered the kitchen. Bea took in a deep breath and pushed the kitchen door open with her hip.

"Here's the rest of the dishes, Cook."

"Thank you. Put 'em by the sink."

"May I help?" Bea offered.

"I'd be a fool to turn down a good offer. Water's hot, you can start washing."

And Bea went straight to work.

"Nanna," Richard yelled.

"In the kitchen," she called back.

" 'Bye. Uncle Ellis said we'd be gone until supper."

Bea wrapped her damp arms around Richard and gave him a great big bear hug and groaned, "Have fun, Richie."

Richard ran out of the kitchen and grasped his uncle's hand.

"He sure took to his uncle," Cook said.

"There seems to be a connection." Bea went back to the dishes.

"Seems to be one between Mr. Ellis and you, too."

Ugh, here it comes. Bea continued to scrub. What could she say?

"I told the man to make peace with you, I didn't tell him to. . ."

Bea rewashed the plate for the second time. "Oh, for pity's sakes, Cook. We're just. . ."

"Just?"

"Oh, all right, we're attracted to each other."

"If you don't mind me saying so, I knew it." Cook's grin slipped up to her eyes, causing them to sparkle.

"What?"

Cook laughed. "I could tell the first time I saw you. You were smitten by Mr. Ellis. Thing is, I've seen that in other young ladies before. But I must say, you're the first one to ever have him return the interest."

"We're going to take it slow. Be friends. See if anything develops."

Cook continued to laugh as she cleaned her counter. "I say you'll be married before the end of the month."

The woman was crazy. The end of the month was next week. There was no way she and Ellis would. . .well, maybe it was possible. A flicker of desire stirred in Beatrice. She thanked the Lord she wasn't facing Cook and closed her eyes to calm her emotions.

"Do you love him?" Cook tenderly asked. Having come up beside her, she placed her firm hands on Bea's shoulders.

Bea turned and faced her. "I don't know. I can't say what it is I'm feeling for him."

"Give it time, Child. Give it time."

"I don't know what to do, Cook. I'm supposed to go home in a few days. I can't very well stay here in his house or even his cottage if we're courting. It wouldn't be right. And yet, I don't have a job to support myself and stay on the island. I have some funds saved, but they're back home in a bank."

"Like I said, give it time. The good Lord understands all your needs, desires, and confusion. He'll help you out."

Bea sighed. "I was up most of the night praying. I've never been so attracted to a man, and yet is that grounds to get married?"

Cook's eyebrows went up. "He asked you?"

"Well, no, not exactly, but the subject did come up."

"Land sakes, he's hit worse than I thought." Cook slipped her arm around Bea's back and led her to a chair at the kitchen table. "Mr. Ellis has been asking me to move in ever since he bought this place. Guess maybe the time's come."

"What about your family?" Bea asked.

"They could use my room for some of those young 'uns who's growing up. I'll start moving my things in today."

"Don't you think we ought to approach Ellis about this?"

"Fiddlesticks. I won't let silly town gossip compromise him or you. I'll move in, and you stay in the cottage."

Bea giggled. "That's an order, isn't it?"

"Yup, and I'll be watching you two. Don't you worry yourself none. With me and the good Lord, you'll be behaving yourselves."

Bea laughed and threw her arms around Cook. "Thank you. You don't know how much your being here will help."

"I believe I do, Child. I was young once, too."

Bea flushed.

Cook roared with laughter. "I say, you young folks have a terrible time realizing us older ones were ever your age."

"With you around, Cook, I don't think I'll be forgetting it."

"Good. Well, if I'm moving in today, you'll be giving me a hand."

Bea gave a mock salute. "Aye, aye, Captain."

Chapter 15

I like the waves, Uncle Ellis," Richard hollered, standing on the bench of the sailboat.

"Richard, get down, now!" Ellis roared. The surf rocked the boat and battered the hull as it crashed down on the waves.

Richard slipped back down on the bench. "But it's fun standing up," he pouted.

"It may be fun, Son, but it is dangerous. If you're going to sail with me, you have to obey the rules."

"Yes, Sir. I'm sorry." Richard lowered his head and looked at his dangling feet.

"Thank you. Now, it's time to go back home. The sun is low on the horizon.

"But I didn't catch a big one, like you."

"Next time." If there was a next time. He had had no idea how hard it would be to keep a four year old contained on a boat. And it wasn't that big a boat. Yet he still managed to get into everything. Ellis's nerves were shot. Not with the child, but with the fear that something might happen to him. He would take him again only if he brought Bea along. She could help watch Richard.

Ellis turned the bow toward Key West and began the long sail back to the island.

"Richard, cast your rod. Let's see if you catch anything on the way home."

His head bobbed up and down as he picked up his rod and placed it over the side, letting the line go out farther and farther.

"That's enough, Son."

Richard secured his rod and placed it in the mounts Ellis had put into the boat long ago. Richard lay back on the bench and watched the top of the rod to see if he snagged a fish.

"Uncle Ellis?"

"What, Son?"

"Do you like Nanna?"

Oh dear, the child had caught him placing his hand upon Bea's. "Yes, she's a nice lady." There. *That's honest, and not too leading.* He hoped.

Placing his hands behind his head, Richard leaned back and said, "Are you going to marry Nanna?"

Ellis held back an audible groan. "I don't know. Why do you ask, Son?"

"Billy's mommy and daddy hold hands, and they're married."

"Holding hands doesn't mean a man and woman are married."

"Oh." Richard sat up. "What makes a man and woman married?"

"First, they have to love each other."

"Do you love Nanna?"

Ellis closed his eyes and whispered a silent prayer for guidance. "I don't know. Nanna and I just met. We need to get to know one another. Love has to develop; it doesn't just happen overnight." While he had felt an instant attraction to Bea the first time he met her, he wouldn't call such an attraction love. On the other hand, his feelings for her today were far stronger and closer to love than attraction.

"So if a man and woman love each other, they're married?"

"No, they have to decide they want to get married."

Richard knitted his eyebrows.

Ellis continued. "A man and a woman have to go to a preacher to 'get' married. When they do that the preacher declares them married, and they kiss."

"Have you kissed Nanna?"

The sudden intense heat on Ellis's cheeks made him acutely aware he was blushing. "No, Son. I haven't."

"I love you, Uncle Ellis. And I love Nanna. If you get married, we'll be a family, like Billy's."

Ellis couldn't respond. The child longed for a family like his friend's back home. A part of Ellis would love to jump in and marry Bea just to give the child some security. But marriage was far too serious a venture to jump into for the wrong reasons. What would happen after Richard was grown? Would they separate, no longer needing to be together, or would they slowly grow in love with each other? No, Ellis resolved. The child needed stability, and he wasn't going to jump into a marriage unless love, friendship, and honesty were a part of it right from the very start.

"Richie, look—a porpoise jumping in the waves." Ellis pointed to the gray bottle-nosed dolphin near the bow of the boat. "They're swimming with us."

"Wow." Richie leaned over the side. Ellis grabbed the boy by his britches and held him fast. *Thank You, Lord, for dolphins.*

Bea couldn't believe the pack of children gathered at Cook's home. It was a simple home, clean and well-kept. Several bedrooms ran along the left side of the house, while a large living area, dining area, and small kitchen ran along the right side. Little brown children of all shapes and sizes looked at Bea. *No wonder Cook runs things with a firm hand.*

"Grandma, can I have your room?" a young girl with braided hair pleaded.

"It'll be up to your parents. But you can't move in until I move my things to Mr. Ellis's house."

The young girl nodded and walked off.

"That's Darlene. She's the oldest of my son George's children. That's Ben, he's eight, and my daughter Lizzy's oldest." Cook pointed to a thin boy with a wide grin.

"How many live here?" Bea questioned.

"Let me see. . .George, his wife and their three children, Lizzy and her four children. Lizzy's husband died fighting in the war. And myself, so I guess that makes eleven."

More than seven children filled the house. Bea slowly scanned and counted the children. Cook laughed. "Kids from around the island come here for Lizzy to teach 'em some math and reading."

"Oh."

"We try to pass on to the children things they'll need in the future." Cook walked down the hall to the back bedroom.

"I might have some books Lizzy could use," Bea volunteered. "I bought them for Richard."

"That'd be nice, Dear. Let's get to packing my clothes. We've got a heap of work to do."

"Grandma, can I help?" Ben asked.

"Sure can. I'll be needing your strong arms to help me carry some of my things to Mr. Southard's house."

"Mother, are you certain?" the tall, thin, elegant woman asked.

"Quite. Lizzy, you know I'll still be over here pestering you. Don't you worry none."

Lizzy laughed. "I'm sure."

"Forgive me my manners. Bea, this is my daughter, Lizzy. Lizzy, this is Bea Smith."

"Hello." Bea reached out to shake Lizzy's hand.

Hesitantly Lizzy reached hers out. When Bea gave her a firm handshake, Lizzy smiled. "A white woman who's not afraid. I like you."

Bea laughed. "Your mom's a gem, but I'm sure you know that."

"She certainly can be. Other times she can be a real nag. Don't try and keep a secret from her."

Bea continued in her laughter. "I've already discovered that."

The three women wrapped some of Cook's clothes into a quilt. With the three of them it didn't take long to pack everything. Soon Bea found herself and Cook unpacking everything in Cook's new room.

"Sure takes longer to unpack," Bea commented, placing a dress on a hanger in Cook's closet.

"Mr. Ellis will sure be surprised." Cook giggled. "He'll think I got a touch of the heat."

Bea laughed. Having Cook around would be a blessing in more ways than one. "I like your family."

"Lizzy seemed impressed with you. You being from the North you might not be aware, but a lot of white folks don't touch colored folks."

"Oh, I'm aware. I'm afraid that's a problem in the North as well. Even with the war being fought."

"Sin is a pretty hard thing to rid from a man's heart," Cook wisely proposed.

"You know, I hadn't thought it was sin, just man being foolish and proud in ways he ought not. But you're right, it is sin. The Bible does say we're all from Adam and Eve, so we all have the same parents." Bea folded the quilt and placed it at the foot of the four-poster bed.

"I believe it's goin' ta take people some time to change, but one day I think most folks will realize that, like President Lincoln said at the Gettysburg Address, 'all men are created equal.' "

"It was a sad day when he was shot," Bea whispered. It had been seven months since the president's assassination.

"That be true, a lot of people still mourn his death." Cook paused and took a deep breath.

Three chimes rang out from the grandfather clock down the hall. "Goodness, Child. I better be fixin' dinner."

"You don't think they'll catch anything?"

"Oh, I reckon they'll catch some. But Mr. Ellis likes more than fish for his supper. I may just fix him some black beans and rice. I canned up some beans this summer."

"I don't believe I've ever had black beans."

"Ewww, Child, are you in for a treat. Could you fetch me a few tangerines for a sauce for the fish? If'n I know Mr. Ellis, he's caught some kingfish, and he loves this tangerine sauce I make as a marinade for the fish."

"Sounds wonderful. How many?" Bea headed for the door.

"Fetch me a half a dozen," Cook said, brushing the dust off her hands.

The evening breeze brought the sailboat gently into the harbor. Richard was asleep. The porpoises had followed the boat, playing for at least an hour before turning back to the sea. Ellis loved hearing Richard's laughter. And he enjoyed the contentment on the child's face as he slept. The sailboat slowly slid into place alongside the dock. Ellis captured a piling and held the boat fast while he draped a line around it.

In short order he lowered the sails, wrapped the mainsail around the boom, and put the jib into a sack, tossing it through the hold into the bow.

Should I wake the child or let him sleep?

"Richard." He sat down on the bench beside the small boy. "Wake up, Son."

Richard groaned and rolled to his side.

Ellis smiled. The ocean had a way of relaxing a person. Often he would end up taking a nap after a good sail. He hoisted Richard up and held him firmly, the boy's head resting on his shoulder. Ellis kissed him tenderly on his soft curls. It was hard to believe how much love he had for this child in only a few short days.

With his free hand, he lifted the fish for the evening's dinner. Taking a giant step from the boat's deck to the dock, he steadied his feet on land once again.

Ellis soon found himself a bit winded as he carried the child the entire distance to the house.

Bea greeted him at the door. A warmth spiraled down his back to the tip of his toes. She was a welcome sight to return home to. "Hi." He smiled.

"Hi. Is Richie all right?" Bea tenderly touched Richard's back.

"Fine, just exhausted and relaxed." Ellis handed her the fish. "Take these, and I'll put him to bed."

"All right. Don't forget to remove his shoes."

"Yes, Ma'am." Ellis winked.

"Sorry—habit." Bea grabbed the fish.

"By the way, I look forward to our time alone tonight," Ellis whispered.

A soft pink rose on Bea's cheeks. "We have a lot to talk about. Come to the kitchen after you put Richard down on his bed and wash up."

Something in the tone of her voice made him question what else had transpired today. He wasn't certain what it meant. "All right," Ellis said with apprehension.

Slowly he worked his way up the stairs, skipping his normal pattern of taking two steps at a time. He didn't want to jostle Richard and possibly wake him up.

Ellis tenderly placed Richard on his bed, pulled off his shoes, and unbuttoned the top button of his shirt. Richard stirred slightly and rolled himself into a curled position. Silently Ellis departed.

In his room he made quick work of changing his shirt and washing the fishy smell from his hands. He sniffed his clean hands, but a pungent odor still remained. His nose crinkled. A desire to smell fresh and clean for Bea encouraged a second washing.

Downstairs he found Bea and Cook working side by side. " 'Evening, ladies."

" 'Evenin', Mr. Ellis." Cook continued to fillet the fish. "I've done what you asked me to do."

"And what is that, Cook?" Ellis leaned against the counter.

"I've moved in."

"What? I mean, that's wonderful. But what brought the sudden change?" Ellis looked at Bea. Bea's face crimsoned.

Ellis shifted his gaze back to Cook.

"Miss Smith and I were talkin'—"

"And?" Ellis cut her off.

"I'll be gettin' to it, now hold on." Cook smiled. "As I said, we were talkin', and we decided it would be best for you to have me in the house."

"I see." Ellis looked at Bea.

"Ellis, you aren't truly upset about this, are you?" Bea implored.

"No, I've been asking Cook to move in with me ever since I bought the house. Far too much room here for one man, and her home could use another open bed." Ellis smoothed his beard. "I'm just surprised."

But why was he surprised, really? Cook could get anything out of anyone. And he had openly touched Bea's hand this morning.

"Do you need me to haul over your belongings, Cook?"

"No, Sir, we moved 'most everything this afternoon. I don't see no need to take my linens, fine china, and stuff. The family will need it, and you have plenty here."

"True. But I would've moved your belongings." Ellis pushed himself away from the counter and sauntered over to the table where he saw the kingfish fillets marinating in Cook's tangerine sauce. "My favorite, thanks."

"You're welcome." Cook smiled.

Bea remained quiet and continued to work. Besides the need to report on his conversation with Richard, they needed to discuss her conversation with Cook.

Ellis rubbed his hands together and asked, "What can I do to help?"

Bea sat pensively still throughout dinner. She wasn't certain how to read Ellis. He seemed glad that Cook had moved in, but it appeared as if he had something on his mind. He left obvious holes in his description of the fishing excursion with Richard.

Richard woke as everyone was finishing up their meal. Bea sat with Richie as Cook and Ellis went off for an inspection of Cook's new room.

"Nanna, you should have seen 'em. They jump in the waves and swim really fast," Richie excitedly explained about the porpoises. "Uncle Ellis says they breathe air like we do. They have a hole on top of their heads and everything."

"Wow, you had quite a trip." Bea smiled.

"I didn't catch any fish, but Uncle Ellis said sometimes deep-sea fishing is like that." Richard scooped another forkful of his fish dinner. "Isn't this good, Nanna?"

"Yes. Now don't talk with your mouth full, please."

"Sorry," he mumbled through a mouthful of fish.

Bea stifled a chuckle, especially when Richard took up the linen napkin and wiped his mouth, trying to be so grown up.

"Nanna, do you like Uncle Ellis?"

Oh dear, nothing like the direct approach. "Yes."

"Are you going to marry him?"

Bea shifted nervously in her seat. *This isn't conversation for a four year old.* "I don't know if I like him that way yet."

"What way?"

Bea eased out a pensive breath. "Richie, there are many kinds of love. For example, I love you and I love my parents, but it's not the same kind of love a man and woman need to share to get married."

"When will you know?"

Bea smiled. "I don't know. I suppose when the Lord tells me so."

"Is that when you'll go to church and get married?"

Church? Getting married? What was going on in this little one's mind? "Where are all these questions coming from, Richie?"

"I saw you hold hands with Uncle Ellis, and Billy's parents hold hands."

"I see. Do I hold hands with you?"

Richie nodded.

"Are we going to get married?"

Richie's eyebrows knitted.

"Do you see, Richie? Not everyone who holds hands is getting married."

"Oh. But Uncle Ellis said he likes you."

So, he had spoken with Ellis about this too. "Richie, am I good about doing what's best for you?"

"Uh-huh."

"Then trust me to take care of marriage and other grown-up kinds of things."

"All right." Richie went back to eating his supper. The child was far too observant.

A warm feeling of being watched flowed over the back of her neck. She turned and saw Ellis's handsome figure casually leaning against the doorjamb. A mischievous smile and a wink sent her heart racing in anticipation of their evening's conversation. A lot had transpired since last night, and her desire to get to know him had increased a hundredfold. Was it possible to fall in love at the mere sight of a man?

Bea broke her gaze and fixed it back on Richie, who was finishing his rice and beans. "After you're done, Richie, do you want to play a game, perhaps checkers?"

"I beat Uncle Ellis."

"Oh really? Perhaps I'll challenge him to a game later." Bea turned to Ellis, softly lowered her eyelids, and slowly opened them. Flirting. At her age. She could hardly believe it, and yet it felt so right.

Ellis cleared his throat and slipped into the darkened hallway.

Chapter 16

Is he asleep?" Bea asked as Ellis descended the stairs.

"Soon. He's exhausted. Three checker games plus all those questions would wear anyone out. Have you encouraged him to ask so many questions?" Ellis sat on the chair opposite the sofa.

"He seemed to come by his curiosity naturally. I was going to ask if you or your brother were inquisitive children."

"Not that I'm aware, but I've been gaining a new perspective since Richard moved in here. I used to think I was a well-behaved child, but as I've questioned some of Richard's behavior, I remember being scolded in some of the same ways." Ellis reclined in the chair, stretched his legs, and crossed them at the ankles.

"Richie seemed to have had the 'love and marriage' question discussion with you earlier," Bea started.

"I think sitting on a hundred tacks would have been easier than dealing with his questions. By the way, you handled it better than I."

Bea laughed. "I've had a bit more experience. I found you don't have to give all the details to the innocent questions he's asking."

"I've got so much to learn." Ellis wrung his hands. "I thought I handled it well, but we ended up talking about church weddings, and other unnecessary details."

"Speaking of church, are we going in the morning?" Bea intended to go to the Presbyterian church with her newfound friends, if Ellis wasn't planning to attend a morning service.

"I was planning on going. Would you like to accompany us?"

"As in a date?" Bea teased.

"You realize things are happening fast between us," Ellis said.

"Things will slow down now that we have admitted to each other what we're feeling." Bea hoped her words were true. She certainly hadn't told him all of her thoughts, and suspected he hadn't told her all of his.

"Maybe." Ellis sat up straight in the chair. "Is Cook intending to be our chaperone?"

"In a manner of speaking, yes. Ellis, I couldn't have stayed in the cottage if we do start courting. It wouldn't be right. And gossip spreads faster on this island than a hailstorm covers the cornfields back home."

Ellis laughed. "That's true enough. I'm glad she moved in. I planned to have her stop coming for breakfast if she didn't. I didn't want her walking the streets before dawn. The island is pretty safe, but we get all kinds of ships in port from time to time, so you never know what sort of sailors will come ashore."

"You've a good heart, Ellis."

"Thank you. Yours isn't so bad either. I've never known Cook to let anyone into her kitchen, and yet you seem so at home there."

Bea enjoyed working in the kitchen, and Cook was fun to work with. "I like her. She's unique."

Ellis roared. "That she is. So, how long did it take for Cook to get the details from last night out of you?"

Bea felt the heat rise on her cheeks. "Maybe five minutes."

"She's slipping."

"I heard that, Mr. Ellis," Cook called from down the hall.

"Then come and join us so you can hear it all without straining." Ellis stood to await Cook's entrance into the room. He leaned over to Bea and whispered, "I want her to feel comfortable in my home."

Bea nodded.

Ellis pulled away quickly. The smell of lilac in her hair, so soft, so feminine, stirred a desire to kiss her behind her right ear. Thankfully, he constrained himself before he acted on his impulses.

"Are you certain, Mr. Ellis?" Cook slowly entered the room.

"Cook. . .Francine. . .this is your home now. You're always welcome."

Ellis watched Cook's imploring gaze. "Come, sit beside Bea. You've worked hard today." He held her by the hand and led her to the sofa.

"Good thing Master Richard be in bed; he'd have us married." Cook giggled.

The room erupted in laughter. The rest of the evening was spent enjoying each other's company—getting to know one another. At ten, Bea stood.

"I don't know when I've enjoyed myself more. It's been a wonderful night, but I must get some rest." Bea bid the others a good night.

"Land sakes, I don't believe the hour. I would have been in bed for an hour if I was home." Cook lifted her ample body off the sofa.

Ellis rose. "May I escort you to your door, Bea?"

"That would be nice, thank you."

"I'll see you young folks in the morning. Behave yourselves." Cook winked and headed down the hall to her room.

Ellis wrapped his arm around Bea's narrow waist. It felt right. Bea leaned into his shoulder and sighed.

I could grow accustomed to this, Ellis thought. *Quite accustomed.*

"Take me home, Ellis, before I fall asleep standing up," Bea whispered.

Ellis squeezed her tightly and led her through the front door, down the steps, and to her front door. "I would like to court you, Bea. May I?"

"Will courting be enough? It seems so shallow to what we are already experiencing."

"Perhaps, but you deserve to be treated like a lady. I'll speak with Cook to arrange an evening when I can take you out on the town and she can watch Richard." Ellis didn't release his grasp of her waist. She turned in his arm to face him.

"I'd like to go out with you." Bea's smile affected him so that his own smile swelled. "You're an incredible woman, Beatrice Smith. I think I'm falling in love with you."

"Oh, Ellis." Bea buried her head in his chest.

Ellis wrapped her tenderly in his arms.

"How can this be happening so quickly?" Bea mumbled into his thick cotton shirt.

"I don't have a clue, Darling. But I'm not inclined to fight it any longer, are you?"

"No. I'm scared."

"Me too."

Ellis held her as she trembled in his arms. How is it that love, if this was love, could be so frightening? Was it merely the fact he was ready to throw all his plans aside to pursue a relationship with a person he barely knew? Yes, that's what terrified him so. The thought of being with Beatrice the rest of his life wasn't scary, that was comforting. Yet the ramifications of it were a bit daunting.

Bea placed her hands on his chest and pushed herself back from his grasp. "I should go to bed."

"Good night, Bea." Ellis lifted her right hand and placed a gentle kiss upon it.

"Sleep well, Ellis." Bea gently removed her hand from his embrace and reached for the latch. But Ellis was faster. His hands already set on the latch, he opened the door for her. Reluctantly, she placed one foot in front of the other and entered her darkened cabin.

The door closed behind her. She listened as Ellis's footsteps disappeared into the distance.

"Father, I think I love him. How is it possible?" she called out to God. Not bothering to light her lanterns, she made her way in the dark to her room. "And how can I feel so differently about him than when I first met him a little over a week ago? I don't know how, Lord, but I do. And I know I'm wanting to be with him night and day, wrapped in his arms. Is love like this possible?"

Bea readied herself for sleep. She lit the lamp beside her bed and opened her Bible. In spite of the late hour, she needed to go to bed with the Word of the Lord on her mind. She absentmindedly opened the Bible, and it opened to Ecclesiastes 3:5: "A time to embrace, and a time to refrain from embracing." Had her time for embracing come? Was Ellis the man God had chosen for her life partner?

The Lord's Day had come, and church with Ellis and Richard gave Bea a hope that maybe they would become a family. The afternoon was spent reading and playing with Richard. Cook spent the day with her family, so Bea prepared the evening meal. It was the first full meal she had made since her departure from the Southard farmstead. A roasted chicken with cornbread stuffing, mashed potatoes, and carrots rounded out the fare.

Cook returned soon after they finished their dinner. "Smells good in here, Child."

"Thank you. How was your visit home?"

"Just fine. The older girls were given my room. They had to show me. They were so excited." Cook grinned.

"Do you miss them?" Bea asked, with her arms up to the elbows in dishwater.

"Sure enough do, but this is best. Now they can come and visit me. I told 'em all about sitting in Mr. Ellis's fancy parlor last night, and they can't wait to come see it."

"I'm sure Ellis won't mind." Bea reached for another plate and placed it in the hot soapy water.

"He's the one who told me to invite 'em. Fact is, he wants them here for dinner on Tuesday."

"Tuesday? The whole family?" Bea wondered where they would put everyone.

Cook chuckled. "The whole family. He said he was going to do a barbecue, and you know what that means."

"He's cooking?"

"Yes'm, for the whole lot of 'em. I thought Lizzy was going to fall off her chair when I made the announcement."

Bea laughed.

"I'm used to Mr. Ellis cooking for me a time or two, but my family, well, let's just say it'll be a new experience."

"I can imagine." Bea wondered what was going on in Lizzy's mind.

"How was church?" Cook asked, putting on her apron.

"It was fine. Cook, I can handle the dishes. You relax."

"I'm sure you can, but my family waited on me hand and foot like I was the Queen Mother. I need to do something useful today or I think I'll burst."

Bea removed her hands from the water and stepped back from the sink. "I never liked doing dishes." Bea dried off her hands.

Cook chuckled and plunged her hands into the soapy water. "I think we're going to get along real fine, Miss Smith, real fine."

And Bea could picture herself as the woman of this household working alongside Cook. It was a pleasant picture. Her heart warmed, her lips turning up in a smile.

Ellis caught a glimpse of Bea working in the kitchen with Cook. She fit right in, and she looked mighty pretty today. Her hair was up in a bun, but she allowed a few wisps of hair to come down in ringlets alongside her cheeks. One day he was going to run his fingers through that wonderful crown she wore.

"Uncle Ellis?" Richard tugged on his pant leg.

Ellis turned to see the imploring gaze of his nephew, who jumped up and down, wiggling like he had to go to the bathroom.

"Is there a problem, Richard?"

"There's a monster in the outhouse."

"A monster?"

Richard nodded and continued the wiggling.

"Let's go check it out." Ellis grabbed a lantern. He'd found large iguanas in the outhouse before. To a four year old, a two-to three-foot iguana could be pretty scary. On the other hand, he was proud that Richard hadn't yelled upon first spotting the creature.

Richard's grasp of Ellis's hand tightened the closer they came to the outhouse. "Stand behind me, Son." Ellis waited until Richard was behind him before he pulled the door open. The bright flash of light caused the iguana to scurry away.

"What was that?" Richard cried.

"An iguana, an overgrown lizard." Ellis encouraged the child to make use of the outhouse. "I'll wait for you."

Richard nodded and stepped inside. Moments later the door swung open and Richard reappeared.

"Uncle Ellis?"

"Yes, Son?"

"Do iganas hurt people?"

"Iguanas," he corrected. "And no, they don't. Some folks keep them as pets, others eat 'em."

Richard's eyes grew wide. "They eat 'em?"

"Uh-huh." Ellis grinned. "Some say it tastes like chicken."

"Chicken? That's silly. It didn't have feathers."

Ellis grabbed the boy and tossed him into the air. "That's right, Son, they don't have feathers."

Ellis removed the lantern he had hung on the hook to the left of the door. He couldn't imagine what Bea would have done if she had seen the iguana. Most women would scream, but he'd seen enough of Beatrice to doubt what her immediate response would have been.

"Come on, Son. Let's go play a game of checkers before you go to bed."

"I'll beat you." Richard beamed.

Maybe it was time for Ellis to win a game. He placed Richard on his shoulders and ran to the front of the house, bouncing and jumping. Richard squealed with laughter. Ellis loved children, and he wondered what it would be like to have some of his own. An image of Bea swollen with child burned a desire within him. *Could it be possible, Lord?*

Ellis watched as Bea descended the stairs, having put Richard to bed for the evening. Pleasure radiated from her. "Thank you, Ellis. It meant a lot to me to be able to put him down for the night."

"I know. I cherish my time with him also." He patted the sofa for her to sit down beside him. "Cook's retired early tonight."

"Then maybe I should sit on the chair," Bea suggested, and paused in the center of the room.

"I promise to be the perfect gentleman," Ellis implored. He wanted her close tonight. So much had developed between them in such a short span of time. "Please."

"Ellis." Bea sat down beside him. "Don't you understand? I want this too much."

"Trust me, Bea. I'll be strong for the both of us."

She sat back and he placed his left arm around her shoulders, encouraging her to rest her head on his shoulder. He breathed in the sweet gentle scent of lilac.

"I enjoyed the message from Pastor Williams today. Can you believe he has all those children?"

Ellis chuckled. "Eight is a handful. Do you want children?"

"Yes. I don't think I'd want eight, though." Bea folded her hands in her lap.

"I'm not sure I want eight either, but I'd like a few. How many do you want?" Ellis raised his hand and captured a ringlet of hair which rested on her cheek. Chocolate silk best described the sensation.

"Truthfully, I'll take as many as the Lord gives. But I think four is a good number."

"Hmm, four, huh?" Ellis whispered.

Bea lifted her head from his shoulder and looked into his blue-gray eyes. They were dark, yet as open and revealing as his soul. "Ellis, what's behind these questions?"

"If you and I should decide to. . .uh, hmm. . .tie the knot, I thought maybe we ought to find out how we feel about children, raising them, our goals, desires, plans, and all that sort of stuff. Like what Pastor Williams spoke about this morning, being prepared in season and out of season."

Bea sat up straight and grasped his hand. "I love children, as you can tell. I believe in being firm with discipline, but I also believe a child should have time to play, enjoy life.

"And you?"

"The same. What about planning for their futures?" Ellis moved his thumbs gently over her fingers.

"I think children should decide their careers. My parents encouraged me in some of my talents even though they're traditionally more male."

"Such as?"

"I have a mind for numbers, business. Father allowed me to learn some of his business and keeping records and such. He said any man would be proud to have a wife who could keep a budget. Truthfully, the skill was handy with your brother being off to war."

"I can well imagine." Ellis shifted and faced her. "Why is it that the more I get to know you, the more I like who you are, Beatrice?"

"Probably because it is the same with me. I thought you were an uncaring, rigid man the first day I met you." Bea paused. Seeing he wasn't offended, she continued. "I soon learned that it was me who you were rigid around. Little did I know you were fighting the same attraction I was."

"And we fought it so well," Ellis chuckled.

Bea struggled for neutral territory. "So we're agreed on children, what about foods?"

Chapter 17

Monday came and went with an odd sensation of normalcy. Tuesday, Bea found herself immersed in the preparations for the barbecue for Cook's family. "Where are we going to get all the tables and chairs?" Bea inquired of Cook. "I can't believe he invited his crew and their families, too."

"I think Mr. Ellis has done freed his heart." Cook laughed.

"Well, I think he's lost his head," Bea proclaimed.

"Same thing." Cook waddled over to the stove. As she lifted the lid, steam billowed into the air.

"What did you call that again? Yucka?"

Cook wagged her head. "No, Dear. Yucca. It's a root like your potatoes, but we serve it the Cuban way with a garlic sauce poured on top." A fresh aroma of garlic permeated the room as Cook opened the lid of a small pot on the stove.

The food, the trees, everything is so different here—even the fruit, Bea reflected. She loved the passion fruit Cook had been serving for breakfast, but had been avoiding it for fear there was something to its name. "I thought Ellis was going to be doing all the cooking?" Bea pushed back a stray wisp of her hair.

"He's paying and he's doing the barbecue. The men don't think in terms of the whole meal. Unless of course it's missing on his plate."

Bea laughed. "I'm just grateful that the other families are bringing some side dishes as well. We should've started cooking a week ago for such a big crowd." Bea shaped the bread dough into rolls and placed them on the baking pan. She wiped the sweat from her brow. "I can see why the original owners put a kitchen outside—it gets downright exhausting in here."

Cook's worried gaze searched her own eyes.

"I'm fine," Bea responded.

"Nonsense, Child. Drink some water."

Obediently, Bea downed a glass of water and poured herself another to slowly sip.

"We'll have some time after the food is ready to freshen up. I want you to strip right down and cool yourself off, you hear me?" Cook wagged her finger.

"Yes, Ma'am."

"Don't need you getting all faint, no siree," Cook mumbled.

"I'm fine, Cook, really." A simple nod of Cook's head for a response was all that Bea received. She was fine. She caught a glimpse of herself in the glass, her color normal. Sweating was natural from the heat, she reminded herself. Cook was just being overly cautious.

Bea finished shaping the rolls and placed a clean cloth over them to let them rise. Wiping her hands on her apron, she began rolling piecrusts, placing them in the tins. "Where'd you get all these pie tins?" Bea asked.

"Oh, I asked around. A few from my home, and Mrs. Matlin, you remember her?"

"Yes." How could she forget the woman and the tender mercy she'd shown to her last week when she had pushed herself too soon after being sick?

"Oh, by the way, she'll be joining us, too."

Bea threw up her hands. "Is there anyone on the island not coming?"

"Not used to crowds, are you, Dear?"

"No."

"Well, here on the island things kinda have a way of growing like this." Cook lifted the large pot of boiling yucca from the stove and brought it to the sink.

"I see." Bea encouraged the pie dough into a circle.

"You'll get used to it. Island folk, we all know each other and depend on each other. It's a matter of survival. Nowadays, it doesn't seem as much so. But wait 'til we have a storm. Then you'll see how we all pull together."

Like a real community, Bea mused. Being so far out with Richard's homestead, she hadn't been a part of a community for a long time.

"Don't be surprised if'n you see some folks here that we didn't invite. They'll be bringing some of their own food."

Bea closed her eyes and rubbed her palms on her shirt. To go to someone's house uninvited broke all the rules of social graces. Bea couldn't imagine such an impropriety. "What's Ellis doing out there?"

"Roasting the pig. He started it last night."

Ellis turned the pig on the spit once more. He still had enough time to run to town and order the fresh fish. One of his men was bringing conch chowder. At last count, he figured there would be close to thirty coming to dinner. But he'd been to enough occasions on the island to know that number could double in an hour.

He locked the spit in place and hurried to town. Across the street was a teenaged boy he knew. "Hey, Brian, do you have a minute?"

"Sure, what do you need, Mr. Southard?"

The lean boy with a crop of long, black hair walked across the street.

"Can you run an errand for me?"

"Sure."

"Could you fetch a twenty-five-pound bag of rice and a mess of fresh vegetables from the store and bring them to my house?"

"It'd be my pleasure." The lad smiled. "Party?"

Ellis chuckled. "Yup. Wanna come?"

"Sure."

"Tell you what, if you can get your mom to cook a couple pies and a mess of that rice for me, your whole family is invited. I'm roasting a pig, picking up a mess of fresh fish and possibly some steaks if the butcher has some."

"I'll let Mom know."

Ellis handed Brian some money and proceeded to the docks. He spoke with a couple of the local fishermen. After he had purchased some fresh fish, he noticed Gerry Halstead cleaning his boat.

" 'Morning, Gerry. How's the fishing?"

" 'Mornin'." Gerry removed his glove to shake Ellis's hand.

"Looks like a good catch. Is it taken?" Ellis peered into a basket crawling with lobsters.

"Not yet, you buying?"

"I'll take the lot. How much?"

"I was hoping to make ten dollars." Gerry raked his thinning brown hair.

"Ten it is." Ellis pealed off a ten-dollar bill. "Here you go."

"Wow, thanks." Gerry lifted the basket of lobsters. "You throwing a party?"

"Sure enough. Wanna come?" Ellis invited.

Gerry chuckled. "I'm afraid I wouldn't have any lobsters to bring."

"Not a problem. Bring a salad, rice and beans, or something to drink."

"All right, what time?"

"Six, my place. If you recall, I bought the Captain Curtis house."

"I'll be there. Thanks. What's the special occasion? Getting hitched to that pretty nanny?"

Ellis's cheeks burned. "No. It started as a meal for Cook's family. It's kinda grown."

"That tends to happen around here. I'll get the wife to cook up something. See you at six."

"*Adios.*" Ellis waved and headed home. The fish purchased and several more families invited, he needed to stop by the church next and get some tables and chairs. Naturally, Pastor Williams and his family would be coming. Ellis laughed and quickened his pace toward the church.

"You what?" Bea couldn't believe her ears. "You've invited more?"

Ellis chuckled and pulled her into his embrace. "Shh, Dear, it's going to be all right. Trust me."

A shiver slithered down her spine from Ellis's warm breath on her ear. "Ellis, we don't have food for fifty people."

"Sure we do. And other folks are bringing stuff, too."

"I've never given a party like this." And never would she plan one this way either. Her mother had taught her well. Occasions of this magnitude took months of planning.

"It's the island way. Trust me." Ellis's firm hand rested on the back of her neck. His thumb slowly worked its way across her cheek. Bea's knees started to tremble. He held her steady. "Do you trust me, Bea?" he whispered in her ear.

What could she do? He exuded confidence, and in his arms she did believe him. It made no logical sense, but she did trust him to pull this party off. "We'll need to make some more. . ." She was at a loss as to what to make. "Something."

"Shh, come here, Honey." Ellis led her to the parlor. "Sit down."

Ellis knelt before her. His blue-gray eyes steeled with confidence. "I've been out of proper society for a long time. But I do recall some things, and I know my mother would be in a tizzy if a party this size was suddenly thrust upon her. So I understand your fears. But, Darling, on the island things are done differently. You don't need to make any more food. There's plenty coming. Pastor Williams is bringing the tables and chairs. . . ."

"Pastor Williams is coming?" Bea was in shock. The house wasn't ready for a visit from the clergy. "Oh my. We need to get the house ready."

"No, we don't. Bea, look at me." He gently took her chin in his hand and nudged it so it was face-to-face with his. Bea quieted her soul and concentrated on the handsome man before her. His thumb touched her lips. "Oh, Ellis."

Ellis leaned into her and lifted slightly, kissing her forehead. Bea's eyes closed and soaked in the nearness, the soft touch of his lips upon her forehead. His whispered words brought her back to reality.

"We have an audience."

Bea's cheeks flamed. Ellis leaned away from her.

"Excuse me, Mr. Ellis, Miss Bea. Brian Fairfield is here." Cook departed after her announcement. Ellis stood up and went to the front hall. Bea could hear his conversation. "Thank you, Brian, you did great. Bring them to the kitchen for Cook."

"Yes, Sir. Oh, Mom said we'd be coming, and she's fixing a few pies and the Spanish rice."

"Great. Pastor Williams will be here shortly with the tables and chairs. Do you think you can lend him a hand?"

"Certainly, Mr. Southard."

Bea clasped her hands, closed her eyes, and silently prayed. *Father, give me understanding regarding this "party," and give me strength regarding Ellis and my attraction to him.*

Lord, the woman is incredible. Thank You for putting her in my path, Ellis silently prayed, walking back into the parlor. "Bea," he whispered. "I'm sorry, I shouldn't have been so forward. You were so worked up about the party I didn't know what else to do."

Her eyes fluttered open. "So, you get me flustered in another way?"

"No, the kiss was an impulse and for that I apologize."

Bea smiled. "You're forgiven."

"Good. Now I want you to go to your cottage. Relax. Take a nap, perhaps, and freshen up for this evening."

She narrowed her gaze. "Mr. Southard, are you suggesting I'm not presentable?"

Ellis prayed she was teasing. "Precisely," he teased back.

Bea's mouth gaped open.

"I can tease, too, my dear." Ellis grinned. "Besides, would I have kissed you if I found you so unattractive?"

"You did miss," she coyly replied, and rose from the sofa.

"Touché." Whatever possessed him to think he could battle wits with this woman? "If you'll excuse me, Beautiful, the swine needs turning."

Bea laughed and headed toward the kitchen. "Bea, your cottage is that way." Ellis pointed to the front door.

"But. . ."

"But, nothing. I want you well tonight. Now go." He smiled to tame the intensity of his order.

She mocked a salute. "Aye, Captain."

Ellis groaned inwardly. He'd done it again. Delegating—giving orders and expecting them to be followed—came with being the boss. Bea, however, was not his employee.

Once outside, he turned the pig, added some wood to the fire, and began raking the lawn free of debris. Folks would begin arriving in a couple of hours. Pastor Williams pulled in with his wagon loaded with tables and chairs. The fishermen delivered their fish. The house was alive with activity. Every so often he saw Bea peeking out a window. *This isn't right,* he chided himself and dropped his rake. A few long strides and he was rounding the corner of Bea's cottage. "Bea!" he hollered.

"Ellis, don't come in!" Bea cried out.

"I won't. Forgive me. If you want to help or even be a part of greeting everyone, please come out."

"In a minute," Bea whispered behind the closed door. "Ellis, would you send Cook over please?"

"Are you all right?"

"I'm fine, I just need a woman's assistance."

Of course, a corset. Personally he'd prefer the woman to not be so tied up, but this being a social occasion, and Beatrice wanting to impress, he understood her need. "I'll fetch her. And, Honey, I'm sorry, I didn't mean to order you."

"I understand, Ellis, and I did need the rest, but I like being in the midst of things. It's been driving me crazy sitting in this cottage."

Ellis chuckled. "I want you in the midst of things," he mumbled.

"What? Speak up, Ellis, I can't hear you through the door."

"Never mind, I'll tell you later."

Bea heard the gravel under Ellis's feet protest his weight as he walked away from her cottage. "Did he say what I think I heard, Lord?" Bea moved to her bedroom in the back of the cottage. On the bed she had laid out her lilac summer dress with a white laced collar and pearl buttons down the bodice. The skirt of the dress gathered at the waist and descended into a V shape in the front.

The door creaked open and Cook called out, "It's me, Bea, what do you need me for?"

"My corset."

Cook entered the bedroom. "The light one, I hope. Goodness, Child, that is a pretty dress."

"Thank you and, yes, the light one. I want to be comfortable."

"Turn around," Cook ordered.

Bea turned. "How's it going in the kitchen?"

"All done, just been cleaning up. Gonna wash and change after I get you hooked up here." Cook groaned straining at the laces.

"Ouch, that's tight enough. I'm not that vain." Bea giggled.

"Sorry. Want me to help you slip the dress over your head?"

"Yes, thanks."

"I used a slip-knot. Just pull your right-hand string and it should unfasten. If not, holler and I'll come over."

Bea reached back and found the right-hand string Cook mentioned. Soon they had her dress slipped over her head and flowing down to the floor.

"Mercy, Child, you are beautiful. Mr. Ellis gonna have a time keeping his mind on his company and not on you." Cook grinned.

"I hope so." Bea winked.

"You know, with Pastor Williams coming over tonight, we could make this into a wedding."

"Hush. We're not ready," Bea admonished.

"Don't take much more than what I saw in the living room. Admit it, Child, you love him."

"Cook, I think I do, but how can you love someone so quickly?"

"It's a mystery, but some folks just get hit like that. George and I did. Once I met him, my heart was aflutter. I couldn't think of anything but George. Of course, my parents had a thing to say about that, but in the end we were married inside a year."

"A year?" Bea didn't think she could wait that long. On the other hand, a year's formal engagement period would be expected back home.

"Yes'm. 'Course, George was away most of that year. If'n he was at home, I imagine we would have been married much sooner."

Bea felt her cheeks flush.

"Truth, is all. Of course, we never told the children that until they were older, much older." Cook winked.

Bea reached out and hugged Cook. "Thank you, Francine, you're a good friend."

"I'm honored to be yours, Miss Bea." Cook patted Bea on her back. "Do you need help with your hair?"

"No, thank you. Ellis likes it down, but that's not really proper, so I thought I'd put it in a French braid."

"Sounds beautiful. Well, if'n you don't need me, I best get cleaned up. I smell like fish. You wouldn't believe how much Mr. Ellis bought."

Bea closed her eyes and let out a small sigh. "No, I'm sure I wouldn't."

Cook departed and Bea sat down at her vanity. She took down her tight bun and began combing out her hundred strokes.

A sudden knock and crash at her front door startled her.

Chapter 18

Nanna!" Richard cried with excitement.

"Richard, you frightened me." Bea placed her brush down on the vanity.

"Sorry." Richard jumped up on her bed and bounced. "I'm so excited. Uncle Ellis said everybody is coming."

Bea chuckled. "I can see you're excited. What have you been doing? You're filthy."

"Helping."

"Helping with what, dirt?"

"No, silly, raking the leaves and broken trees and stuff."

"Oh." Bea smiled. "I'm sure you've been a big help."

"Uncle Ellis said I needed to get washed up."

Oh dear, Bea had forgotten about getting Richard ready first. Dirt would attach to this dress like a moth to a light. "Can you wash up by yourself?"

Richie nodded his head.

"You wash up, and I'll help you put on your Sunday clothes."

"Can I play in them?"

"Of course not," Bea lightly scolded. "You know that."

"I wanna play the games with the other kids. Can I wear something else?"

Naturally he would want to play.

"Of course." Bea wondered if she had made the wrong choice in her dress.

"Richard," Ellis called from outside Bea's door. "I told you to go clean up."

"Nanna always helps me," Richard called back.

When Richie came barreling in, Bea had completed twenty brush strokes on her hair. "Ellis, you may come in."

The door creaked open. "Richard, go to the house, Son. I. . .I'll. . . Bea, you're beautiful," Ellis proclaimed.

"Thank you. Richie, you go on. I'll be right up there to help you pick out your clothes," Bea encouraged.

"I can do it, if I can wear play clothes."

The boy was growing up, Bea thought with a smile. "All right."

Richard slipped off the bed, leaving a streak of dirt behind him. "I'll see you at the big house, Uncle Ellis."

Ellis stood there motionless, speechless. "Please stand up," he finally spoke.

Bea trembled and stood. "Do you approve?"

"Goodness, do you have to ask? I've never seen anyone as beautiful."

Heat fused with joy and painted a faint blush on her cheeks.

"Thank you."

The intensity of his attraction forced her to restrain an urge to jump into his arms. She needed to break the tension between them. "You're a handsome man, Ellis Southard, but I've seen you look much better." She winked.

Ellis looked at his blackened hands. Amused by her ability to understate the obvious, he smiled. "I'm in need of a good scrubbing."

"At the very least."

"I. . .I need to go. If I don't, I'll soil that dress." A desire to wrap her in his arms fought to have its way. Ellis thought of the Lord and how He would behave given this situation, and swallowed hard, silently thanking God for His grace.

Bea giggled. "You do and you'll not hear the end of it."

"Later, my love." Ellis wiggled his reddish brown eyebrows and turned to leave.

A faint whisper tickled his ears. "I'm looking forward to it."

"I heard that, Beatrice Smith. You're a siren for certain, here to test me."

His hand reached the latch of her front door.

"Or vice versa," she replied.

He didn't have time for this playful banter, although he fought a tremendous desire to continue it. As if working his way through a thick marsh, he pushed himself toward the house. Guests would be arriving shortly.

Mounting the stairs two at a time, he arrived at his room in short order. He grimaced at the sight of his filthy face in the mirror. Sweat mingled with black soil and small bits of decaying leaves plastered his face and beard. Looking at the amount of dirt in his hair and on his body, Ellis slipped on a robe and headed for the outside shower, an ingenious contraption of a fifty-gallon barrel with a spigot. When one pulled on the string attached to the spigot, water sprayed down on him.

Showered and dressed, Ellis entered the parlor. Bea stood at the far wall examining a hand-painted vase from the Far East. "Am I more presentable now, Miss Smith?"

Bea turned with the grace of a dove floating on the wind. Scanning him from head to toe, she spoke. "Mr. Southard, you are most handsome indeed."

Ellis stepped farther into the room. "Come here, Love."

Bea placed the vase back on the shelf and walked toward him with elegant poise.

"Your hair, it's beautiful. What style is this?"

"It's a French braid. I know you like my hair worn down, yet a woman should always wear it up. So this braid allows it to be tied neatly in the back."

"Bea, you're incredible. . . ." Ellis reached for her delicate fingers. She slipped her hands into his. "I. . ."

"Uncle Ellis!" Richard yelled. "They're here."

"Later, my love," Ellis whispered in her ear. Then he took in a deep breath and released her.

He turned toward the doorway and marched to the front door. Pulling it open, he greeted everyone. "Welcome, come on in." Members of Cook's family started pouring in. As the door was about to close, another group, and then another, entered as well. The house was soon brimming with people.

Ellis encouraged the men to join him outside at the pit. The ladies began carrying out the food to the tables in the backyard. The children followed Richard as he first showed them his room then the various nooks and crannies of the house.

Bea mingled well, Ellis noted. She spoke with loving grace. Constantly throughout the evening he watched her. Occasionally he would catch her watching him. All different ages and races mingled together, the house and yard overflowing with people.

Key West is a good place to raise a child, Ellis decided. *But what about the homestead—my brother's wishes? I must make a decision regarding that property someday,* he mused. *But today is not that day.*

Pastor Williams, in his black and white preacher's suit, walked up to him with a hand outstretched. "Quite a feast, Ellis. Thank you for inviting us."

"My pleasure, Pastor. Thank you for the use of the tables and chairs."

"They're always available. So, tell me about this Miss Smith. . .will she be staying on?"

"That's hard to say, Pastor." How could he admit his feelings for Bea when they hadn't yet discussed them?

"Does she have a commitment back North?" Pastor Williams inquired, searching Ellis for an answer.

"No, but I can't ask her to stay on as the child's nanny."

Pastor Williams lowered his voice. "Why not?"

Ellis looked at Bea. Pastor Williams caught his glance. "I see." Pastor Williams smiled. "If you don't mind me making a suggestion, totally unasked for, I wouldn't let that one slip from my hands, if I were you." Pastor Williams slapped Ellis on the back. "God's blessings, Son. You're going to need it."

Ellis swore he heard the pastor chuckling under his breath as he walked away. Was it that obvious? Heat blazed on his high cheekbones.

" 'Evening, Ellis." Marc Dabny sidled up beside him, his swollen belly lined with a gold chain. "Quite a crowd here tonight. Anything special going on?"

"Just invited a few friends, and it kinda grew." Ellis smiled, grateful for the distraction.

Marc whistled for Lizzy, Cook's daughter, as she walked past. "Hey, get me a drink."

Lizzy turned to face Marc, but held her tongue.

"She's a guest, Marc. You can get your own drink, like everyone else here." Ellis held back his emotions.

"Excuse me?" Marc confronted Ellis face-to-face. "I can understand you throwing a party for your workers, but to consider them guests. . . Are you daft?"

"Forgive my friend, Lizzy. He seems to have forgotten his manners." Ellis stood toe-to-toe with Marc, towering over the balding man. "Lizzy is my guest. Her mother works for me, but she is not my employee. May I suggest you apologize?"

"You're daft, I'm not apologizing to no n. . ."

Ellis grabbed Marc by the collar and lifted him to his toes. "Not in my house. No one, not anyone, uses that word in my house. Do you understand, Marc?"

Marc's bulging eyes blazed with anger as he nodded his assent.

Ellis eased him back to the ground. "I believe our business partnership will not be pursued, Mr. Dabny."

"You'd throw away a solid offer for the likes. . ."

Ellis knitted his eyebrows.

". . .for. . ."

Ellis leaned closer and set his jaw.

". . .those. . .those. . .people?" Marc spat on the ground.

"Any day. I believe you've worn out your welcome, Mr. Dabny. Have a good evening." Ellis turned his back to Marc and stepped back into the crowd which had gathered behind him.

Marc spat at Ellis's feet. "You're a fool, Ellis Southard, an absolute fool."

Ellis refused to bait the man, but simply ignored him and walked up to Lizzy. "My apologies, Lizzy." He reached for her hand and bowed. "You're welcome in my home anytime."

Bea watched as Lizzy's eyes pooled with tears. Bea's own eyes threatened to stream. She bit the inside of her cheek to hold back the tears. Ellis had handled Marc with absolute authority. She was so proud of him. By the looks of the folks gathered around him, they were proud of him as well.

Bea worked her way to one of the tables. On its far corner a lantern glowed. She sat down and waited. She'd been on her feet all evening greeting folks, learning people's names and their relationship to Ellis. She rubbed the back of her calves. She hadn't been in high heels since she arrived, apart from the short outing to church the other day.

"Care if I sit down?" Mrs. Williams, the pastor's wife, asked, holding a bald baby with a toothless grin.

"Of course not." Bea placed her hands in front of her on the table.

"Are your feet hurting?"

"I'm afraid so. I haven't been in high heels much."

"Hardly wear them myself. Can't go chasing eight children in high heels." Mrs. Williams bounced the little one on her lap.

"I can't imagine. Chasing one child keeps me busy."

Mrs. Williams chuckled.

"Will you be staying, Beatrice?"

Bea didn't know what to say. To respond that she had fallen madly in love with Ellis and prayed she would be staying at his side forever was not an option. "I'm waiting on a ship bound for New York."

"So, Mr. Southard doesn't want to hire you on as Richard's nanny? Or do you have obligations back home?"

"Truth be told, I have no obligations. But Mr. Southard doesn't believe he can hire me to stay on as Richard's nanny."

Mrs. Williams's pleasant face contorted with confusion.

"It's complicated."

Mrs. Williams's brown eyes softened. "I'm sorry, I didn't mean to pry."

"It's hard to explain. Ellis—I mean Mr. Southard—learned of my social status and he feels it is improper for me to continue on, especially since he is quite capable of hiring someone."

"That doesn't sound like the man who just. . ." Mrs. Williams caught herself and stopped. "I'm sorry, I have a tendency to rattle off my thoughts before thinking them through."

"Mrs. Williams. . ."

"Edith, please."

"All right. Edith. Please don't think poorly of Mr. Southard. In our community back home I already created quite a scandal by staying on as Richard's nanny. But over time, many came to realize I deeply loved Richard's mother and would honor my commitment to her."

"There seems to be a lot in that pretty head of yours, Dear. Is it your prayer to stay with Richard?"

Bea placed her hands in her lap.

Edith's black hair sparkled from the light—or was it tears threading her eyelids? Bea wasn't certain. The baby cooed at a moth flying around the lantern.

Edith reached her hand and placed it upon Bea's. "The Lord will give you the desires of your heart. Trust Him."

Bea nodded her head, afraid to speak. The desires of her heart had shifted drastically since the day she first arrived on the island. No longer did she simply want to not separate from Richard. Now, she no longer wanted to part from the man who had captured her heart.

She glanced up and saw Ellis saying good night to a few families with younger children. He lifted a small child and tossed him in the air. *He's so good with children, Lord.*

"There's something more than your social status keeping you from being Richard's nanny," Edith whispered.

Bea nodded. She couldn't deny it any longer. Of course Cook knew, but was Ellis ready to have the town, the pastor and his wife, know of their budding relationship? "Please don't think poorly of Ellis, Mrs. . . .I mean, Edith. Cook has moved into the house, and I am remaining in the cottage."

"I do not thinking badly of you or Ellis. Go with your heart, Dear. Trust God to work out thc details."

"Thank you."

"Forgive me for leaving so, but I'll never get these children to bed if I don't start rounding them up now." Edith smiled. "Good night, Beatrice. It's a pleasure meeting you. I'll be praying."

Bea started to get up.

"No, Dear, sit. . .relax. You've done enough."

"Good night, Edith, and thank you."

"You're welcome. Stop by the parsonage anytime if you need to talk or just want to visit." Edith slipped back into the darkness, calling her children.

A parade of lanterns exited Ellis's home and worked their way down the street. *What a truly different place this is, Lord,* she pondered.

Ellis said good-bye to Pastor Williams and his family. Some of Cook's family members were helping with the cleanup. Most folks were gone, and Bea sat alone at a table. He longed to be next to her. But one person after another kept them apart.

Ellis looked to the right and left. No one. He grinned and hurried over to Bea's table. "Finally, we can be together." He sat down beside her. Tears edged her eyelids. "Bea, have you been crying?"

She smiled and shook her head, no.

Ellis brushed his thumb up to her eye. A tiny droplet of water sat on his thumb. "Then what's this?"

"I've been holding them back," she whispered.

"What's the matter?"

"Nothing."

"Nothing?" Do women cry at nothing? He thought back to his mother. There were a few times when he found her with tears in her eyes.

Ellis scooted closer on the wooden bench and leaned toward her ear. "I've longed to be this close to you all night."

"Oh, Ellis." Bea reached her arms around his shoulders.

Ellis completed their embrace, pulling her closer.

"I'm so proud of you, the way you stood up to Mr. Dabny tonight."

Ellis squeezed her gently. "Thank you. The man is a. . .I won't say it."

Bea giggled. "I think I know what you were going to say."

"Hmm, you're dangerous, do you know that?"

"Me, dangerous?" She pulled back and looked him straight in the eye. "You, Sir, with your gallant behavior. . . And tonight—this entire evening—I can't believe you pulled it off with no planning. It was just like you said it would be. Folks brought plenty of food. Everyone enjoyed themselves. I'm amazed, Mr. Southard, truly amazed."

"Amazed enough to. . ." Ellis trailed her lips with his thumb.

Bea's eyes closed in anticipation.

Did he dare? If he kissed her there would be no turning back. He wouldn't be able to let her leave. Everything shouted she was the one for him. His soulmate, his gift from God. But for so long he had given up on the possibility of having a wife, a woman who could love him, accept him, forgive him.

But how could he resist her? No, he would not resist. "I love you, Bea," he whispered before her velvet lips touched his.

She kissed him back. He tightened his hold of her. She tightened her hold on him.

Time dissolved into a blanket of tranquillity. Slowly he pulled away. He opened his eyes. A blush, the shade of a pale pink rose, accented her delicate nose.

Bea's eyes fluttered open. They were wide with passion and honesty. "I love you, Ellis." Her fingers trailed his swollen lips.

Ellis felt a tug on his pant leg. "Uncle Ellis, are you and Nanna married now?"

Ellis groaned.

Bea coughed out, "No."

"But Uncle Ellis said that when you kissed you were married!" Richard whined.

"Richard, I said after the pastor says the man and woman are married they can kiss."

"And you were kissing."

"Honey, your uncle Ellis and I were kissing, but we aren't married. We like each other," Bea pleaded. *How do you make a four year old understand?*

"But. . . ," Richard pouted, "don't you have to marry Nanna now?"

Ellis left her side and squatted next to Richard. "Son, a man has to ask a woman first if she would like to be his wife."

"Did you ask her?" Richard held his mouth firm.

"No, Son."

"Are you gonna?" Richard folded his arms over his chest.

"I'm thinking about it." Ellis squirmed.

Bea smiled. Was he really? She'd been thinking about it forever, or so it seemed. And yet it had only been a little over a week.

"Then ask her."

"Richie. . . ," Bea admonished. She hoped Ellis wouldn't think she put Richard up to such nonsense.

"I might just do that, Son." Ellis turned to Bea.

"Ellis, you don't have to do this." Bea squirmed on the bench. Was he really going to ask her? Now? Here? In Richard's presence?

Ellis smiled a wicked grin and took her by the hand. "If I ask you, Bea, it's because I want to do this, not because of Richard's pleading."

"Oh, my!" Bea needed a cool cloth, her cheeks were on fire.

"Beatrice Smith, you are the most incredible woman I've ever known. First, you've raised my nephew through all sorts of perils, and all because of a love for a friend. Second, you showed me how to release myself from my past and to allow God's forgiveness in my life. Third, you're profoundly beautiful inside and out, and I would deeply be honored if you would consent to become my wife."

Bea trembled. Her hands shook as they nested inside of Ellis's larger ones and she noticed his were trembling, too.

"Are you married now?" Richard said impatiently.

"No, Son. You have to let the woman answer first."

"Oh. Answer, Nanna."

Bea chuckled. This had to be a first, being coached by a four year old for a proposal of marriage. "I'm going to answer your uncle Ellis."

"When?" Richard placed his hands on his hips and tapped his foot.

Ellis bit his lips. Bea did the same and composed herself. "As soon as someone stops interrupting me."

"Me?" Richard asked.

Bea nodded. "Yes, you. Now hush for a minute."

"Ellis, I love you with all my heart and soul, and I would be truly honored to be your wife."

"Is that a 'yes'?" Richard asked.

Bea and Ellis roared in laughter. Ellis composed himself first. "Yes, Son, that was a yes."

"Yippee! Nanna has married Uncle Ellis!" Richie ran into the house screaming.

"Are you certain, Ellis?"

Ellis climbed up off the ground, brushing the sand off his pant knee. He sat down beside her on the bench again. "Quite, my love." He reached his arm across her shoulders. "I wasn't going to ask you so soon, or with an audience, but I was going to ask."

Bea combed his beard with her fingers. Soft warmth coiled around her fingertips.

"Would you be needing a year's engagement period before we marry?" Ellis asked.

"Not if I can help it," Bea blurted out.

"Good, I was hoping you wouldn't want to wait. How's next week?"

Bea chuckled. "Too soon. Although Cook said we'd be married by the end of next week."

"I always did like Cook." Ellis nuzzled into her neck.

"Ellis, could we wait until my parents can come, or reply if they can't?"

"Of course. I don't want to wait forever, but I'll wait as long as it takes."

Bea wrapped her arms around his neck and gave him a quick kiss.

"Now you two better stop that. Unless what the boy said is true and you're already married." Cook chuckled.

"Oh dear." Bea blushed. "He said that?"

"Yup, the entire house knows you were kissin' and are married."

Bea groaned.

"Well, he got part of it right. We're getting married, Cook. Bea's honored me by saying she'd be my wife."

"Well, praise the good Lord in heaven. It's about time the two of you got it straight."

Bea and Ellis chuckled.

"Suppose we ought to go in the house and correct the rumors our son has been spreading?" Ellis asked.

"Our son," she whispered. *Our son.* Richard would finally be her son.

"Yes, our son." Ellis squeezed her gently.

"I suppose so." Bea hated the thought of being out of Ellis's arms. Perhaps her parents would understand if she were to just write them and tell them her happy news.

No, she reasoned. They'd be fit to be tied. She and Ellis would have to wait. And waiting wouldn't be such a bad thing. They still needed to get to know one another better.

Ellis stood and held his hand out for her to grasp. He curled her arm into the crook of his elbow and he led her to the house. "Come on, Cook, they're your family. Help us straighten this mess out."

Cook chuckled. "You has got yourselves into this mess, you can get yourselves out. I'm goin' to enjoy watching ya."

Epilogue

Three months later

"Mom, help me?" Bea pleaded. "I'm so nervous I can't clasp this pearl necklace."

"Relax, Bea." Joanna Smith eased the necklace from her daughter's hands.

"I can't believe my wedding day is finally here." Bea looked at the high-collared, French-laced wedding gown that she, her mother, Cook, and Lizzy had sewn. Every day and evening for the past month, they had worked on the gown, the train, the headpiece, Lizzy's gown, Cook's dress, and her mom's dress. Bea often thought Ellis had it easy. He simply went into town and hired a tailor.

She put her hair in a French braid, interwoven with pearls.

Joanna's eyes teared. "You're so beautiful, Bea."

"Thanks, Mom. I hope Ellis is pleased."

Lizzy laughed. "The man would have to be dead not to notice how beautiful you are." Bea smiled at the woman who had quickly become her closest friend.

"Thank you, Lizzy."

Although Lizzy still mourned her husband's death, she was free from the anger toward the white man who had killed him. Prejudice still existed in the world, even on Key West, but Bea and Lizzy learned the only way to battle it was one person at a time. And to hate an entire race because of the actions of others was foolishness to God.

A gentle knock on the door caused Bea to stiffen.

Her mother opened the door and smiled. "You're looking mighty handsome today, Dear."

Bea watched her father enter the room, his sideburns laced with gray, his mustache completely gray, and his receding hairline glowing with maturity. His eyes sparkled. "You're beautiful, Beatrice. Almost as pretty as your mother."

"Thanks, Daddy."

"Are you ready?"

"Yes." Bea stepped forward and captured her father's elbow. It was firm and comforting. Today she needed his confidence.

"Thank you for coming, Dad."

"I wouldn't have missed this for the world. Come on, Precious, let's go meet your groom."

Bea took in a deep breath and stepped to the edge of the doorway.

The music began. Ellis stepped out with Pastor Williams and Richard. Richard looked so handsome in his junior-sized black tails with a white shirt and black bow tie. Beatrice didn't know he had Richard fitted; it was one of many surprises he had planned for her today.

Ellis watched as Lizzy came down the aisle, followed by Ruth Williams, Pastor Williams' four-year-old daughter. She tossed the flower petals in front of her with precision, stopping to make certain the area was properly covered before moving on. Ellis grinned and spied Pastor Williams enjoying his daughter's performance.

The music shifted and the congregation stood. Ellis watched as Bea's father rounded the corner and a billow of white followed. His heart raced, his palms instantly dampened. "O Lord, she's beautiful," he whispered.

Richard tugged on Ellis's pant leg. "Nanna's pretty."

Ellis smiled. "Yes, she is."

It had taken awhile, but Richard finally understood that marriage was more than kissing and holding hands, that it was a pledge between a man and a woman with God and others watching.

Bea was so close he wanted to reach out and take her hand. Instead, Ellis held himself back and waited for the pastor's cue.

"And who gives this woman to be married to this man?"

"Her mother and I do," Jamison Smith answered in a strained voice.

Ellis reached out his hand to his bride. Jamison slipped her hand into his. Ellis's strong hand encircled hers. They turned and faced Pastor Williams.

"Dearly beloved. . ." Pastor Williams continued with the service. When he reached the pronouncement that they were husband and wife, he proclaimed, "You may now kiss the bride."

Ellis lifted her veil and cherished the sweet kiss of his new wife, then felt the all too familiar tug on his pant leg. "Are we married now?" Richard asked.

Bea and Ellis started to bubble with giggles. Soon the entire congregation was laughing.

"Yes, Richie, Bea and I are married," Ellis replied.

"Yippee!" Richard screamed, then cupped his mouth with his hands. "I'm sorry." He stood up straight and placed his hands by his side.

Bea smiled. "It's okay, Son. We're a family now; you can relax."

Bea embraced her new husband and was reminded of Ecclesiastes 3:5 once again. Her time of embracing had come. She held Ellis even tighter.

THE CAPTAIN'S WIFE

by Mary Davis

In loving memory of my stepdad, Allen Basart.
Thanks for the history lesson, Dad.

Chapter 1

Port Townsend, September 22, 1898

Leaning against the ornately carved mahogany mantel, Conner Jackson stared into the fire. The flames danced and licked at the logs like his guilt licked at his conscience. How could he have fallen for the wrong woman? In all his twenty-seven years of waiting, he thought he was smarter than that. He thought he could control his heart. Long ago, he told himself that he would leave town before coming between a friend and his lady. It was time to pull foot. Or as he'd once told his friend Ian MacGregor, he'd kick himself in the head. If he could figure out how, he'd do it.

"Here's your cider, Conner."

He turned to Mrs. Randolph Carlyle and took the amber liquid. "Thank you, Vivian." Guilt caused him to avoid her gaze lest his secret be revealed—he was in love with his best friend's new wife. His revelation twisted his gut.

Before Randolph had married, Conner had spent most of his time away from his store here at Randolph's house. He'd attempted to stay away after Vivian arrived to give the newlyweds some privacy, but Randolph wouldn't hear of it, insisting Conner spend time with him and his bride. Randolph seemed to need Conner to approve of his new wife, so he worked hard at getting to know her to give his friend an honest assessment. She was good for Randolph: a sweet, caring woman. Vivian had given Conner a warm welcome, treating him as a longtime friend she hadn't seen in years. He began to envy his friend's good fortune, wishing he'd met Vivian first.

Randolph clamped a hand on his shoulder. "Won't you have something stronger? I have some fine brandy."

"I prefer the cider. It's fine, as well. You should try it."

Conner's longtime friend stood two inches shorter than his six-foot frame but was stockier and had a booming voice. For twenty years, they had looked after each other, seen each other through difficult times and good. Randolph was his best friend.

"Too sweet for my taste." Randolph stared into his glass but didn't take a drink.

Conner hoped his friend was reconsidering his drinking habits. He'd already cut back quite a bit since marrying Vivian. Conner was praying Randolph would quit altogether.

Vivian sat like a regal princess, the epitome of decorum with porcelain skin, violet eyes, and raven-black hair. A rare beauty, but her real beauty came from within. She was kind and generous and always had something good to say about everyone, including the riffraff in town.

The ripping ache in Conner's heart helped him with his difficult decision. He would make arrangements to leave town while Randolph was away. His store had done well with miners heading up to the Alaska gold rush, and he had plenty of money to start over someplace else. Maybe he would head south to Olympia.

"Randolph, you know what Conner needs?" Vivian's sweet voice drew him back. "A wife."

Dread clutched his gut. Did she suspect his affections for her? He groaned mentally.

Randolph took a drink of his brandy. "I believe if Conner wanted a wife, he could have any single lady in town to choose from. Isn't that right, Conner?"

He grimaced at the truth in the crass remark. Ladies had always thrown themselves at him and made it very clear that they were available to him, married or not. Those kinds of women held no appeal. "The women around here are a bit too bold for my taste."

"My point, exactly, Randolph. We need new blood in town. Do see what you can do about bringing him back a suitable lady."

Randolph guffawed. "You don't just land in port and pick up a lady."

"You did." She smiled at her husband, and Conner's heart tripled its beat. She was always generous with her smile and made anyone feel welcomed.

Randolph smiled back at his wife and raised his glass to Conner. "What do you say? Shall I bring you back a bride?"

"No, thank you." He wanted to tell his friend that he wouldn't be around when he returned but knew Randolph would try to talk him out of leaving and would insist on knowing why he was pulling foot. He would never tell Randolph that he fancied his wife. It was just plain wrong. The only way to stop this, or at least to control it, was to vamoose. Randolph had been the one to talk him into starting his general store in Port Townsend and would be disappointed when he was gone.

Vivian sat forward. "Oh, Conner, please. It would be so much fun if you had a wife; then she and I could be friends, and the four of us could dine together and throw parties." Vivian had had trouble making friends in town. She didn't behave like the other women of the town's proper society. She didn't value people based on how much money they had. She valued people simply for being people. Consequently, the members of the town's elite hadn't given her a warm welcome.

She made solving his problem sound simple. Get a wife and live happily ever after. But not if he didn't love the woman and he was in love with another man's wife. Maybe he wasn't so much in love with Vivian as he coveted Randolph's happiness. Either way, leaving town was the best option. "I should be going." And not just from Randolph's house. He set his cider aside and stood.

"A toast first." Randolph held his glass high. "To Vivian, my lovely wife, a more virtuous wife you will never find." He drank down the last of his brandy.

A hint of sadness in Vivian's eyes twisted Conner's heart. What could possibly cause her sorrow? She had everything she could want. Couldn't Randolph see her distress?

It wasn't his place to bring it up or to comfort.

Vivian sat at her dressing table, removing the pins from her hair. Randolph hadn't said his loving wife or the wife he loved and adored, but his lovely wife. Once again it was her beauty he saw, her body he desired. Could he ever truly love her? Not if he thought she was his virtuous wife but found out she was once one of the lowliest of sinners.

Randolph caressed her hair and held it in his fingers. "I never imagined hair could be this silky." He looked over her shoulder and gazed at her reflection. "You are so beautiful."

Though the compliment saddened her, she gave him a small smile. What she knew he expected. "Thank you, Randolph."

She pulled her hair over her shoulder and stroked it with her sterling silver brush. Married only three months, she didn't know her husband well. They had married two days after they had met in Coos Bay, Oregon. Then they arrived in Port Townsend, and he'd been out to sea much of the time. He was a good man but haunted by his childhood. She realized now her error in her haste to latch onto the security of marriage. Her secret would eventually tear them apart. How could they love each other with her past standing between them? William had sternly warned her never to tell his brother what she had done.

When William and Randolph's father had died, their mother had turned to prostitution for a while to feed and clothe her two boys. Randolph had never forgiven her.

She gazed at her reflection. Only twenty-five, she felt as though she'd lived two lifetimes. She shifted her gaze to Randolph's reflection. "When do you head down to your ship?"

"In a few hours, but I want to spend some time with my wife before I leave." Randolph raised her to her feet and turned her to him. "My exotic beauty." He captured her mouth.

Is that all he could see? Her heart cried out for more. For love.

His lips traveled across her cheek, and he stopped. "What is this, tears?" He caressed them away with his thumbs.

She hadn't realized her tears had escaped. She turned away from him and dried the rest of her face with her hands. "I'm going to miss you."

He turned her back. "These aren't the tears of a wife missing her husband before he leaves. What's upsetting you?"

She should tell him. William's warning rushed back to her. *He will never accept your past. Never!* "Nothing, really."

His expression hardened as did his grip on her arms. "Tell me."

"Randolph, that hurts."

He jerked his hands away, horror twisting his face. "I'm sorry." He knelt in front of her and took her hand, kissing it. "Forgive me."

"Please get up." She hated seeing him grovel. Not to her. Never to her.

He stood. "I promised myself I would never hurt a woman or child. I don't know what came over me. I'll never do it again. You have my word."

"Sometimes we find ourselves doing things we never thought we would." *Becoming a person we don't want looking back at us in the mirror.*

"Not you. You are a perfect wife, a perfect lady."

She turned away from him to hide her shame. "I am far from perfect."

He stepped in front of her. "Look at you. Everything about you is perfect. Every lady would want to look as you do. What small imperfection do you think you have?"

See more in me than physical beauty, her heart cried. "I am more than outward appearance."

With a finger under her chin, he lifted her face. "Why the tears tonight?"

He blurred in front of her.

"Have I done something to upset you?"

She blinked the tears back. "I don't want to spoil things before you leave."

His mouth turned up in a kind smile through his whiskers. "You are too good for me."

She couldn't stand his misconceptions any longer and stepped back from him. Her red taffeta dress rustled. "No, Randolph. It is you who are too good for me. I am not worthy to be your wife. I'm not worthy of you at all." She couldn't harbor this secret any longer. Like a slow-burning ember, it was consuming her newfound faith a little at a time. Even if it destroyed them both, he had a right to know. "I am not the lady you think I am. I'm a harlot. Or at least I was." She let the words rush out before she could change her mind, then held her breath.

He took a step back and frowned. "That isn't true. You can't be."

She reached out to him as a child would for understanding, but he moved out of her reach. "I was a widow and had nothing. I was hungry and cold and had no place to live. A man was kind to me. I didn't know the Lord Jesus. I didn't know it was so wrong. But Jesus changed me. I no longer lived like that when you met me. Friends helped me. Believe me, I would never go back to that. Never."

He gritted his teeth and his face flamed red. "Friends? What friends?"

She shrunk away from his booming voice. "It doesn't matter."

His features hardened even more, and his tone turned accusatory. "My brother and his wife."

A tear slipped down her cheek. "I want to be a good wife to you. What does my past matter? I am a new creation in the Lord Jesus Christ."

His face twisted into a snarl. "You deceived me. Made me believe you were a proper lady. Was marrying me just another harlot trick?"

"No, Randolph. I truly was trying to make a new start. I never meant to hurt you. I want to be a good wife to you. I want you to really love me, but it wasn't going to be possible with my secret between us."

"Love a harlot? Not likely." He strode out of their bedroom, slamming the door behind him.

She jerked it open, refusing to be dismissed. She caught up to him by the front door. "Please forgive me. Please." There had to be a way to salvage the remains of her short marriage. "I am the lady you married and a new creation. God has forgiven my past. Can't you?"

"A lady would never sell herself. Never. You deceived me to get me to marry you." He swung on his captain's overcoat and hat. "I'll deal with you when I return."

She reached out for his arm. "Please, Randolph, forgive me."

He pulled from her grasp. "Don't touch me." He slammed the door on his way out.

She covered her eyes and cried. *Sweet Lord Jesus, please let him forgive me.*

An arm wrapped around her shoulder. "Come, dear. He'll return soon." Maggie, the cook and housekeeper, guided her back upstairs and helped her change for bed.

Conner woke in the middle of the night to the slurred bellowing song of a drunk out on the street. He wanted to ignore it, but he recognized that song and the singer's voice. He pulled on his pants and a shirt. "Come on, Fred."

Fred cocked one brown scruffy ear from where she lay in a circle on the end of his bed.

"Come on, girl."

The little terrier stood and stretched from her nose all the way down to her hind legs then jumped off the bed.

People often wondered about giving a boy name to a girl dog, but it was just one of those things that happens. When he'd seen the cold, dirty, wet stray wandering the streets of Seattle, the name Fred immediately popped into his head and fit. He'd soon realized Fred was a girl but kept the name. At least that's what he told people. The story of how as a lonely little boy he had been refused the comfort of a pet by a mother who hadn't wanted her own son, let alone a dog named Fred, was not a good tale. His mother had kicked the dog and sent it away. Conner never saw Fred again. Over the years, he'd wondered what had happened to that dog. So when another stray entered his life, it only seemed natural to name her Fred.

He headed downstairs and through his store, with Fred on his heels.

Randolph sat on the boardwalk step outside. Drunk as a skunk. This had been his normal pattern when he was in port: to get drunk at least one night and end up here. But since he'd married Vivian, he'd not spent one night sleeping off a drinking binge in Conner's back room. What had changed things tonight? Had he fought with Vivian? Conner looked toward uptown. Was she in as bad shape as Randolph?

He'd been friends with Randolph since he was seven, Randolph was ten, and Randolph's brother was five. The three had run barefoot around the streets of San Francisco together. Or at least the streets of their block. Randolph's mother had combed their hair and made them go to church every Sunday. Conner's mother had done her best to ignore the fact that she'd produced a child. "Come inside, old friend."

Randolph turned toward Conner's voice and waved his bottle at him. "Sit down. Have a drink. 'S good whiskey."

Both Randolph and Conner had accepted Jesus Christ as their Savior when they were boys. But unlike Conner, who had pressed harder toward the Lord when trouble came, Randolph had turned his back and had been running ever since. No matter what Randolph said or did, Conner knew that the Lord had not turned His back on the crusty sea captain. When Randolph was ready, he would see that God had been waiting with open arms the whole time to welcome back His prodigal child. And Randolph wasn't so far away; he'd gone to church twice with Vivian. The only two Sundays he'd been in town.

Conner sat but refused the whiskey. "You should come inside so you don't disturb those trying to sleep."

Randolph groped the railing and awning post to pull himself to his feet and started staggering. "I have to be on my ship. I'm the captain. My men need me."

Heading in his current direction, Randolph wasn't going to make it to his ship, so Conner turned his friend toward the dock. "This way."

Randolph poked him in the chest. "Don't ever trust women. Not ever. You can't trust 'em. They're all bad." He waved his bottle in the air. "All of them." He sighed and quieted.

What had happened tonight after he'd left? Randolph must have fought with Vivian. Conner hoped it wasn't over finding him a wife. He didn't want to come between the two of them, not ever. It was good that he'd be leaving town. "Wait here while I lock up, and I'll walk you to your ship." He locked his store door and quickly returned to his swaying friend.

"You're a good friend, Conner. You always were." Randolph patted him on the chest with his palm. "Promise me you'll look after her until I return. Look after Vivian."

That was the last thing he should do. The fox guarding the henhouse? Oh, what trouble could be had. He looped his arm around his friend to help him walk.

"Look after her, but don't get any ideas about her. Don't you touch her. I should have known she was too beautiful to trust. Don't you ever touch her."

"I promise not to touch her." That was one promise he could make and vow to keep. Vivian was another man's wife—his friend's wife. He could never touch her.

"And you'll guard her while I'm gone."

Guard? He struggled to keep Randolph on his feet.

"Promise me."

"I promise, Randolph." If Vivian stayed uptown and he remained downtown, that should be easy enough to keep.

Randolph seemed to sober and spoke clearly. "If anything happens to me, you'll see that she's all right."

"Nothing's going to happen to you." Conner staggered under the weight of his friend. "You're the finest captain on the sound and all the West Coast."

Randolph stopped in the middle of the dock and grabbed Conner by the front of his coat. "Promise."

He wanted to shout no, but what reason could he give his friend for not being willing to honor this simple request? He gritted his teeth. "I promise." As soon as Randolph's ship was spotted on the horizon, Conner would pull foot.

He loosened Randolph's grip on his coat and hailed the first mate. "Help me get your captain to his cabin." He and the first mate supported Randolph to his cabin and laid him on his bed. Conner said nothing more to the first mate as nothing needed to be said. He patted his leg to the scruffy brown terrier at his feet. "Come on, Fred, let's go home."

At his store, he went upstairs to his living quarters and gazed out the back window at the sparkling water in the moonlight and laid his head upon the cold glass. It was not good to test temptation. "Lord, what have I done making such promises? I will leave as soon as Randolph sets foot back in Port Townsend. Help me to honor my promises to an old friend while still honoring You."

Chapter 2

Thunder cracked and rolled across the sky, startling Vivian awake. A storm. Good. They could use the rain. It had been three weeks since they'd gotten a drop. And a week since Randolph had left. He would be pleased if his roses got the water they needed. Maybe it would soften his mood when he faced her. She climbed from bed, slipping on her dressing robe before stepping out onto her balcony. Most people called it a widow's walk, but it was only that if a widow was on it, in her opinion. The air was heavy with humidity, but no rain fell yet, the rolling black clouds begging for release.

She shouldn't have told Randolph the truth. William had warned her. But her secret had weighed so heavily on her; she couldn't stand it. What would he do to her when he returned? Would he beat her? Send her away? A tear slipped down her cheek as she remembered Randolph's disgust with her before he left. Would she get a chance to make amends with him?

Lord, please let Randolph see that I can be a good wife to him. Forgive me for keeping this secret from him. I just wanted to start over. I wanted to be the person Randolph thought I was.

The first huge drop of rain splashed onto her hand. She gripped the cold metal railing and turned her face to the sky as the clouds gave up their bounty, washing her in refreshing cool water. But the rain that watered and gave life would also turn the streets to mud, and people would grumble about the lack of sunshine. She let the rain cleanse her, but it couldn't touch her inside. Jesus had forgiven her and cleansed her soul. Could Randolph forgive her, as well?

Vivian cut the quarter chunk of the ten-inch Colby cheese wheel into five pieces, wrapped the bundle in a cheesecloth, and put it in her basket along with five apples and five biscuits. "Maggie, would you hand me those stale bread crusts for the seagulls?"

The cook held out the paper sack Vivian had been collecting the bread in; then she peered into Vivian's nearly full basket. "Those are mighty hungry birds."

Vivian put the sack into her basket and covered it with a yellow checkered cloth. "That they are."

"We got a couple of young roosters in this last batch of laying hens. They're causing a fuss chasing around my hens. Maybe I'll just butcher them and fry them up. You think those birds of yours like fried chicken?"

Vivian kissed Maggie on the cheek. "They would love it."

"You be careful now. Anything happens to you, and the captain will be butchering me."

That might have been true two weeks ago before Randolph left, but now if something were to happen to her, Randolph might be relieved. He could be the grieving widower captain, and no one would ever find out about his poor choice in a wife. How would he choose to "deal with her"? Maybe it would be best if she weren't here when he returned.

She gazed at Maggie's concerned face and, remembering the cook had admonished her to be careful, patted her skirt pocket. "I have my Derringer. I'll be fine." After all, she was going downtown in the middle of the day. Unfortunately, she had experience in handling unruly men.

She walked the blocks to the steep, narrow stairs that connected uptown with its respectable residents and her new station in life to downtown and a reminder of her old life. She descended to the bustling streets below past people who did hard physical labor to put food on their family's table, miners who were passing through on their way to Alaska to make their fortune, sea dogs who were grateful to be on land for a few hours, and the dozens of other good people trying to make their way. The common people of downtown stared at her, and she smiled back. She traveled along the main street and climbed down the wooden steps to the beach, where the air became even saltier. She stepped carefully over the uneven rocks to the drift log and sat.

With her basket beside her, she began throwing bread crumbs to the gathering seagulls. Through the squawks of the gulls, she heard crunching in the rocks behind her and smiled. It never took them long. They didn't have much else to do but wait for her to come. Five dirt-smudged faces stared expectantly at her. All the children had tears in their clothing, and none of them had bathed or combed their hair in a long time.

She had discovered these homeless orphans a week ago when she'd come down to the beach to contemplate her future after Randolph's return. With no local orphanage, these children were left to fend for themselves. The good people of uptown had no idea there were any needy children or any needy people at all. They preferred to remain on their safe streets away from the harsh realities of life, thinking everyone lived in the same kind of proper, perfect world they'd sequestered themselves to. They thought that only rough miners heading north to the Alaska gold fields were on the streets below. They didn't want to know about needy families, women, and children. They preferred to live in their utopian world, looking to the salty water beyond without seeing the riffraff below.

She held out her hands to Samuel on one end and Peter on the other, forming a circle. Together they all recited, "Thank You, Jesus, for this food. Amen."

"What did you bring uth?" Peter, five years old and the youngest of the bunch, had brown loopy curls and a smile that would one day melt hearts. And, she noticed, he had developed a lisp.

Betsy shook Peter by the shoulder. "Pipe down. That ain't polite." At ten and the only girl in the bunch, she'd taken on mothering all four boys—even the two older ones.

"Oh, she don't mind." Peter jumped up onto the log next to her. "Do you, Mith Vivian?"

"Betsy is right. If you want to find a good home, you need to have proper manners." She smiled at the boy. "But I don't mind." She put her basket on her lap and pulled back the yellow cloth.

All five children sucked in an audible breath. She handed them each a chunk of cheese, a red apple, and a biscuit. They took the food greedily.

Peter handed back the apple. "I cain't eat no apple." The boy turned to her, bared his teeth, and pushed one of his front teeth straight out with his tongue.

It wasn't hanging on by much and was the reason for his newly acquired lisp.

George, the oldest at fourteen, held out his biscuit to Peter. "Trade?" These kids looked out for each other. They were all each other had.

Peter eagerly swapped his shiny red apple for the fluffy biscuit. If Peter worried about eating the apple with his loose tooth, he'd also have a hard time with the cheese.

She didn't want him to go hungry on account of his fear over a loose tooth. "Why don't you let me pull that tooth for you?"

Peter pinched his mouth shut and spoke through pursed lips. "No, ma'am."

"It will be easier to eat."

He shook his head hard, brown curls flopping back and forth.

She reached in her skirt pocket past her little gun and pulled out a penny. "I'll trade you this penny for your tooth."

Peter's eyes widened as he stared at the copper coin. He reached into his mouth and pinched his eyes closed as tight as he could get them. He pulled just a bit and held up the tooth in triumph. "Hey, that didn't hurt." Then he quickly swapped it for the penny.

"You're a brave little boy."

Peter danced around, holding up his prize. "I goth a penny. I goth a penny."

She noticed George, Samuel, and Tommy staring at the penny. She pulled out five more pennies, leaving four in her pocket, and gave them each one, with Peter getting a second one. She would get another penny from home and give them each another one tomorrow when she brought them Maggie's fried chicken. The children scattered on the beach to eat.

She looked around at the four older children sitting on the smooth sand that was closer to the water's edge. George was fourteen and nearly a man. Samuel was twelve, Betsy ten, and Tommy nine. Samuel and Tommy were the only two who were related. She worried about Betsy the most. The boys would eventually find jobs as George had done. Girls had a harder time finding a decent job at a young age. There were two options for Betsy when she got older: find a husband while she was still a girl or become a. . . Vivian had to do something to help these children. Food was fine for now, but what would they do when the weather turned cold?

The days were already getting cooler. She wanted to take them home but knew Randolph would never approve of orphans running loose in his house. She didn't even know what would become of her when her husband returned to "deal" with her. She'd liked the idea of having a husband to care for and protect her, but now it was a bit scary having her fate in the hands of someone else.

She stood and went to Betsy, draping the yellow gingham cloth from the basket over the girl's shoulders. "That's for you."

"Thank you, Miss Vivian."

"Do you know how to sew?" Not that her sewing ability was very good nor had helped her when she was in need those years ago, but maybe Betsy would have better luck, and she would be praying for the girl to get a respectable job. Maybe if someone had been praying for her, things would have turned out differently.

Betsy tipped her head up and shook it. "I never had a mama to show me."

"I'll bring some dry good squares tomorrow and teach you." If the girl took to it, well, maybe she could get a job sewing or mending when she was a little older.

When the children had finished their cheese and tucked their apples and biscuits into their pockets for later, they headed back to wherever they had come from. Vivian wished she could do more for them, but when Randolph returned, she might not be able to do anything for them anymore. Would she be as destitute as they? She knew what that was like.

She headed back up through town, and as she walked, she noticed a man in a Stetson. He tipped his hat back, staring at her openly. She crossed to the other side of the street. He followed and stepped in her path. "Well, aren't you a purdy thing."

She tried to sidestep the man, but he blocked her.

Heavy footsteps rushed up behind her. Her heart thumped hard in her chest. His friend, perhaps? Reaching into her pocket, she wrapped her fingers around her Derringer. Only one bullet. Maybe she could scare them off with it.

A sinister voice came from behind her. "You lay one hand on Mrs. Carlyle, and I'll have to kill you."

The cowboy held up his hands and backed away. "I'm sorry, mister. Didn't mean no harm to your missus."

She turned and smiled at Conner.

Conner's gaze and pistol remained on the retreating man. When the man was a safe distance away, Conner lowered his gun and turned his glare on her. "What are you doing down here? It's not safe for a lady to be downtown. Do you know the kind of people who are down here? Miners and strumpets and people like that man and worse."

If he knew she had been one of those kinds of people he'd just described, he'd be just as disgusted as Randolph. She released her grip on her gun. "I came to see you." He would only scold her further if he knew she had been down at the water alone. Well, not exactly alone.

The V between his eyebrows deepened. "You shouldn't have come. If you needed something, you should have sent someone to get me."

"Let's get you off the street." Conner guided Vivian back to his general store, careful not to touch her.

"How did you know to come to my rescue?"

The lilt in her voice tickled his ears. "I saw him follow you across the street." He'd grabbed his gun from his holster behind the counter and left. "Martin went out to get himself lunch." Martin Zahn had worked for him for eighteen months. Before that, Conner had had a slew of dishonest men work for him. He had a couple of other all right fellows who worked for him on occasion. "When he returns, I'll see you home safely."

"That's not necessary. I can walk by myself."

"You walked down here?" Was she crazy? "That cowboy wasn't going to stop at 'How do you do?'" Was she so innocent that she didn't realize some people had ill intentions? Her acceptance of all people regardless of their background was one of the things that drew him to her.

"Can I get a little help here?" A customer called.

He resisted the urge to growl. "I'll be right with you." He turned to Vivian. "You'll be safer waiting in the back."

"I don't want to go in the back."

He did growl now. "Then sit on that stool behind the counter." He walked her over then looked down at his dog. "You keep an eye on her, Fred." The dog sat next to the stool. He went to attend to his customer. He waited on several more people before Martin returned. When he reached Vivian, she had Fred on her lap and the Sears and Roebuck catalog open on the counter in front of her.

"I'll walk you home now."

She turned to him. "I want to order from the catalog."

His heart hammered hard at her smile. "You can shop at plenty of places uptown, and I'm sure one of them has a catalog."

"But I want to order from you, my husband's dear old friend."

If Randolph knew the feelings he had for his wife, Conner wouldn't be his friend anymore. He pulled out a sheet of paper. "What do you want?" The sooner he got this over with, the sooner he could get her home and away from his temptation.

Vivian named several things. "Let me know when those come in."

"I'll have them delivered to your house. Can we go now?" He needed to get away from her, and to do that, he had to get her back uptown where she belonged.

Vivian held out her hand for him to assist her off the stool. He took it grudgingly, soft and delicate, then dislodged his hand from hers and turned to Martin. "Would you prepare this order and send it?"

On the walk to uptown, Conner kept his hands clasped tightly behind his back and took in slow, controlled breaths. Randolph would be back soon, and then Conner would leave for good. Just a little longer, and he'd be free.

When they reached Randolph and Vivian's blue Victorian house, she said, "You must be parched. Won't you come in and have a cup of tea with me?"

His mouth was drier than all get-out, but the last thing he needed to do was socialize with his friend's wife, who made him wish for things he had no business pining for. Trouble, that's what it all was, downright heart-wrenching grief any way you sliced it. "I have to get back to my store. Stay uptown," he ordered.

"Conner, you worry too much." She touched his arm, and he flinched.

Better to be on his guard and worry too much than not enough and get himself in a heap of trouble. He tipped his hat to her, patted his leg for Fred, who seemed a little confused about who to go with, and left. Once back on the street, he could breathe again. He had to maintain control and distance.

Vivian's gentle smile and kindness had lassoed his heart as proficiently as if she were an experienced cowhand. And she didn't realize it. He'd seen so many men who would cut off their right arm for a lady who was nice to them. He hadn't thought he was one, but Vivian's sweet nature and acceptance of him without question had dragged him down to a place he didn't want to be. In love with his best friend's wife. She didn't mean to make him fall in love with her, but here he was, the worst kind of man. He would be leaving soon, and it would all get a lot easier.

Chapter 3

Shortly after Conner returned from Vivian's, Finn came into his store, scratched his whiskers, made eye contact, and headed to the back room. Finn was a strange character in his late fifties with well-worn clothes that bordered on rags.

Conner finished the customer's purchase and found the old drifter with a cup, drinking the dregs from the coffeepot. "Why the long face?"

Finn had come with Conner over from Seattle two years ago. The old codger helped out when he needed money or food but mostly just hung around to jaw with the miners as they came through. "I have news."

Finn heard the strangest stories. Conner only believed about half of them. Tall tales were common in port towns. He didn't think Finn believed most of the stories either, but the older man liked to tell them anyway. "What news?"

Finn swiped his mouth with his shirtsleeve. "About your friend, the captain."

Finally, Randolph was back, and Conner could pull foot. "When does he dock?"

"He don't."

"What?" That didn't make sense. Randolph should have returned two days ago.

"He was making a run up to Alaska with keg powder and dynamite. The story goes that he was just off the coast when a storm come up. Lightning struck the ship. They say the captain ordered his men to abandon ship. Some of 'em did, but some of 'em stayed and helped the captain try to put out the fire before it reached the cargo hold. It lit up the western sky when it blew, the people on land said."

"Randolph?"

Finn nodded. "Men say he was still working the fire when it went up."

"No." Conner raked his hand through his hair. "Are you sure?"

Finn handed him an Alaskan newspaper. The front-page picture showed something burning on the horizon of the water with a lightning bolt streaking across the sky.

Finn's story wasn't just hearsay from the sailors but news. Conner blinked back tears as he read. There was no hope of Randolph making it. "I have to tell Vivian. Can I take this?"

Vivian turned the apple in her hand, spiraling off the peel with a paring knife as she created one long strip. Maggie was making applesauce to can. She hadn't tasted Maggie's applesauce before, but if it was anything like her other cooking, it would be delicious.

Scotty, their handyman, entered the kitchen with his old hat pressed to his chest. He acted as butler when he was near, groundskeeper, stableman, and anything else Randolph or Vivian needed him for. But mostly, Randolph let the old man live out his remaining years doing only the jobs he chose to do.

Scotty was stoop-shouldered and had a weathered face. If she had to guess, Vivian would say he was in his seventies. "Mr. Jackson's here to see you, ma'am. I put him in the parlor."

Had he come to scold her again? She stood to walk out of the kitchen.

"Where do you think you're going?" Maggie wiped her hands on her apron.

"To see Conner."

"Not like that." Maggie untied Vivian's apron.

"It's only Conner, my husband's dearest friend, who doesn't care what I look like."

"You are the wife of Captain Carlyle." Maggie rolled down the sleeves of Vivian's white blouse and buttoned the cuffs. "You must always look proper. It would be no good if word got back to the captain that you were working in the kitchen. He'd turn me out on the street."

Randolph would never get rid of Maggie, but since he already had enough to hold against her, Vivian let Maggie fuss over her and tuck in a hair or two. Maybe if she showed her husband she could be a proper wife to him despite her background, he wouldn't turn her out and would one day come to love her. She stepped away from Maggie and held out her hands. "That's quite enough. I'm sure I'm presentable."

She went straight to the parlor. "Conner, so good to see you."

Conner turned from where he stood by the window, ashen faced, his expression bleak. "Sit, Vivian."

Her stomach constricted. "What is it?"

He came around the sofa with a newspaper tucked under his arm. "Sit."

She didn't want to sit. Conner loomed six inches taller over her, and she sank back onto the sofa. "Tell me." Her stomach pinched into a tight ball, and her heart struggled to beat at the sight of Conner's serious countenance.

❧

Conner hated being the one to break Vivian's heart with bad news, but better him than a stranger. "It's Randolph." He swallowed hard. "His ship went down."

She gasped. "No. Is he all right?" She stood. "Take me to him."

He took her elbow and lowered her back to the sofa. "He didn't make it."

Her hand flew to her mouth.

He unfolded the paper.

She gasped. "Is that. . . ?"

"His ship? I'm afraid so." He wished it weren't.

She took the paper in a shaky hand and stared at the grainy photo taking up most of the front page. "It shouldn't have been him. It should have been me."

What was she saying? The shock must be confusing her. Conner fisted his hands as he watched the agony play on her face. "Maggie." He wanted to hold her and comfort her, but he knew he couldn't. "Maggie!"

Maggie entered and looked from Vivian to him. "What have you done to her?" She sat next to Vivian and wrapped an arm around her.

He stared at the woman sitting where he wanted to be. "Captain Carlyle is dead."

Vivian's gaze remained on the photo.

Maggie glared at the paper then up at him. "Take that away."

He folded the paper and slipped it back under his arm.

Vivian's confused gaze followed the paper then traveled up to his face. "It shouldn't be this way. He shouldn't be dead. Maybe he got off."

Maggie looked to him.

He shook his head.

"Let's get you up to bed." She helped Vivian stand and ushered her out of the room.

He turned to Scotty, who stood silently near the doorway. "If she needs anything, come get me. If any of you need anything. I'll come by tomorrow and see how she's doing."

❧

The next morning, Conner shuffled around the kitchen area of the small living quarters above his store. He still couldn't believe that Randolph wasn't coming back. Was there any way he could have survived? He unfolded the newspaper and stared at the photograph then shook his head. Anyone on that ship when the powder went up hadn't had a chance. The concussion from the explosion alone would have rendered anyone nearby unconscious. If they had lived through the blast—whether they were thrown from the ship or not—they would have drowned. His friend was gone, and he had to accept that.

He rubbed his face as he headed downstairs and to the front where Fred sat. "So that's where you went." After he'd let the dog out the back this morning and inside again, Fred had remained downstairs. Conner raised the shade and froze in the middle of unlocking the door. Scotty stood leaning against the awning post. Conner quickly opened the door. "Scotty, what is it?"

"Miss Maggie's in a terrible state. She doesn't know what to do with Mrs. Carlyle. She's been out on that widow's walk all night. Wouldn't let Maggie bring her in. All Maggie could do was wrap a quilt about her."

"My assistant will arrive soon; then I'll come straightaway. You return and let Maggie know I'm coming." He wasn't sure what he was going to be able to do. If Vivian wouldn't come inside for Maggie, she wasn't likely to for him, either. But he would do something neither Maggie nor Scotty would; he'd physically carry her inside if he had to.

As he strode up to the house a half hour later, he could see Vivian on the widow's walk in the same green skirt and white blouse she had worn yesterday, her gaze firmly fixed on the water's horizon. What must she be thinking? He hoped nothing dire.

The door opened before he reached it. Maggie clutched her hands to her chest. "Mr. Jackson, it's good that you're here. I fear Mrs. Carlyle has lost her mind. She won't speak, and she won't come inside. I fear for her."

He swept past Maggie and took the stairs two at a time. He didn't bother to knock on Vivian's door, went straight through the room to the balcony, and stopped.

"I've been praying all night that he's still alive." Her voice was as limp as her raven hair hanging around her face.

It tore at his heart. "I'm sorry, Vivian."

"Me, too. For so many things. Life seems to be full of regrets. He was a good man. He deserved to live—not me."

He didn't like the sound of that comment. She was just as deserving of life as anyone else. "Vivian, let's go inside."

She turned her gaze on him. "I won't do it, Conner."

Won't come inside?

"I know that's what everyone is afraid of."

That comment didn't make sense. Was she talking about something else?

"I'm not planning to jump. I know that's what Maggie thinks I'll do."

Was she speaking the truth? He had no way of telling.

She took a step closer to him. "You believe me, don't you?"

He studied her, trying to discern the truth. "Let's go inside."

"Conner, it's important you believe me."

He wanted to, but he couldn't see past his heart. Any possible threat to her life, even from herself, was blurred by his love for her. "Prove it to me by coming inside."

She gave him a slight nod and walked back into her room. "Maggie, Conner and I will take tea in the parlor."

"You should go to bed, ma'am." Maggie shot him a worried look.

"Later. Mr. Jackson has come all this way to see that I am well. It would be improper to send him on his way without serving him tea." Vivian swept through the open doorway and headed down the stairs.

He gave Maggie a reassuring nod then followed after Vivian down to the parlor, where she stood at the window once again looking toward the water. He stood for several minutes, staring at her back, wondering what to say.

"I thought I knew what God wanted, but now it's all so unclear." Vivian's voice was soft. "Like a compass with its needle spinning round and round. I don't know what to do. I just wanted to be a good wife."

Maggie entered with the tea tray. He motioned for her to leave it, grateful to have a distraction. "Tea?"

Vivian turned quickly. "I'll serve."

He studied her as she poured him tea. Was she putting on a face of doing well? Or was it for his benefit so he would leave her be and she could do whatever was swirling around in her head?

"Sugar? Cream?"

"No, thank you." He took the dainty china cup she held out to him. *Lord, help me assess her mental state accurately.*

She prepared her own and took a sip. "I know you hold concern for me, but I will be fine."

Was she really fine?

"I survived the death of my first husband, and I will survive this, too." She stared straight into his eyes. "I promise you that I will do myself no harm."

He held her gaze. Could he believe her? He wanted to believe her. But more than believe in her, he wanted her to remain safe. He'd promised Randolph that he'd look after her while he was away, but what did that promise mean now? Was he still to look after her? Should he leave town? Should he stay? What was the *right* thing to do? It had all been so clear when Randolph was coming back and Conner would be leaving.

He, too, felt like a compass needle spinning without direction. *What do I do, Lord?*

Conner woke two mornings later to his dog, Fred, standing on his chest, licking his face. Fred was a scruffy brown dog with a strong line of terrier in her. She'd ridded his previous employer's store of a rat problem in Seattle, and she'd kept Conner's store rat-free for the past two years. "I'm awake." He lifted Fred up into the air, but her tongue continued to lap in and out, trying to reach his face. He shifted her to one hand and lowered her to the floor before sitting and swinging his legs over the side of the bed.

The light coming in his window was brighter than it should be. What time was it? He plucked his pocket watch off the bedside table. Seven? He never slept that late. He put it up to his ear. The soft ticking of the inside works filtered into his ear.

Fred wiggled from the middle of her back down to the tip of her tail, shaking off whatever it was that dogs tried to get rid of.

"You have to go out, don't you, girl?" He pulled on his pants, swung on a shirt, and patted his leg. "Come on, girl." He headed downstairs and let Fred out the back door to the beach.

When he came back in with Fred, someone was banging furiously on his front door. Fred barked as she ran for the front of the store. He followed close behind. Scotty again. *Please, Lord, don't let anything have happened to Vivian.* He opened the door.

The old man huffed and puffed. "It's Mrs. Carlyle. She's gone."

Conner felt as though his rib cage were pressing in on his lungs. "What do you mean, gone? She didn't. . . ?"

Scotty shook his head. "We can't find her anywhere. Maggie searched the house three times. I searched the grounds and the stable. She's nowhere."

He raked his hands through his hair. "She can't have just disappeared. She has to be somewhere."

"Maggie says Mrs. Carlyle's red gown is gone and her black-hooded mantle."

"You head south and look on those streets, then head back to the house. I'll finish getting dressed, get my horse, then head north. I won't stop until I find her." He closed his door and rushed upstairs.

Chapter 4

Vivian stared at the churning dark waters and the boiling sky. It wasn't so long ago that she'd enjoyed a storm like the one coming in, the storm that had likely killed her husband. If she'd known it had come from where Randolph was and had been a threat to him and his men, she would have viewed it differently. She had much to learn about ship travel and the dangers of the sea. What men might be out in this storm, scared? Terrified that they may never again see their loved ones. What wives, mothers, sisters, and daughters waited on the shore, hoping for their safe return?

Sailors milled around the dock. Most knew Randolph and respected her as his wife and left her alone. One seaman had approached her with ill will on his mind, but before she could pull out her Derringer, three sailors had threatened him and dragged him away with a warning never to go near her again. She heard slow, heavy footsteps approaching and slipped her hand into her pocket, wrapping her fingers around the pearl handle hidden there. The man stopped directly behind her. Should she pull out her Derringer and confront him? Or wait?

"Vivian," a man said in a hoarse whisper.

She turned to face Conner, anguish and relief etched on his face.

"What are you doing down here? Maggie's very worried about you."

"I didn't mean to worry anyone. I couldn't sleep. I want to say good-bye, but I don't know how."

"I know this is hard. A love like yours and Randolph's comes once in a lifetime."

A love like hers and Randolph's? She turned back to the water. How wrong outward impressions could be. In time, the ruse would have become reality. . .if Randolph had been able to forgive her. She sighed. "I didn't love him."

"What?"

She swung her gaze back to Conner. "I never loved him. Nor did he me. We married in haste. I was in need and took advantage of his attraction to me." Her looks had been a blessing as well as a curse. Had her first husband really loved her? Had any man? "I should have said no when he insisted we marry the day after we met, but I wanted the security of marriage. I was completely committed to Randolph. I was going to be the best wife I could for him, and I hoped to fall in love with him. There just wasn't time."

His silent stare unnerved her, so she went on, her voice thick with emotion. "Maybe if I hadn't married him until I was in love with him, he wouldn't have died. Maybe I shouldn't have married him at all. Maybe he would still be alive if he had never met me."

Conner took her shoulders in his hands. "Stop it. There was a freak accident. You had no control over the weather."

"But he might have been in a different place, and the lightning wouldn't have struck the ship." One small change might have made the difference.

"He was on the water. Lightning strikes the high point. Five miles this way or that, his ship still would have been the attraction for the bolts. It's not your fault."

He was right, but she wanted to blame herself. She looked back to the rolling water. "We fought the night he left."

"I know."

She jerked her gaze back to him.

"He had a few drinks and came to my store. That had been his habit when he was in port before he married you. In the three months you were married, he never once came, so I figured you must have fought. Why else would he come on his last night in port?"

She dipped her gaze away. "Did he tell you what we fought about?"

He shook his head. "I didn't think it was any of my business."

"What did he say?"

"He made me promise to look out for you while he was away."

Even after their fight, Randolph had been concerned for her well-being.

"Then I saw that he got to his ship."

Conner had always been there for her husband, and now he was here for her. He was a loyal and trustworthy friend. Randolph couldn't say enough good things about him. She'd felt as if she'd known him before they ever met, and she wanted to rely on him now. Always. Her future was so uncertain. She'd been on a road for her life, and in marrying Randolph, she knew where it was going and what it would look like, even if Randolph threw her out. But now as the respectable widow of a favored captain, she didn't know what to do. Where to turn. Conner seemed like the only stable thing the Lord had placed in her life. She leaned into his chest.

He pushed her away after only a moment. "What are you doing?" His gaze darted around the dock. "There are sailors all around."

They wouldn't care. They'd probably cheer. "I'm sorry." An emptiness opened up inside her at his rebuff.

He looked up to the darkening sky. "Let's get you home."

She felt a raindrop land on her hand and let him lead her away.

Conner lifted Vivian up onto Dakota's saddle sideways. The rain started coming harder, so he swung up behind her. "Hold on."

When she gripped the saddle horn instead of turning to him, disappointment sank in his gut like lead. He goaded his horse into a trot. He shouldn't have pushed her away on the dock. He'd just been so shocked. The sailors wouldn't have minded, but she was the widow of a respected captain.

She never loved Randolph. He couldn't shake that thought. He would not do anything to tarnish her reputation nor Randolph's memory. It was still best if he left town, wasn't it? He didn't want to.

Dakota made short work of the trip and stopped in a puddle in front of Vivian's house. He nudged the horse forward to drier ground when Maggie flung open the door.

Maggie clutched her hands to her chest. "Thank the Lord, you found her."

He swung down then lifted Vivian, carrying her up the steps and into the house. "She's fine."

Scotty pulled on his coat and hat. "I'll see to Dakota."

"Thank you, Scotty." He set Vivian down in the foyer. He didn't want to. He wanted to hold her. "Maggie, would you make Mrs. Carlyle some tea? I'm sure she's cold."

"The water's hot. It'll only take a moment." Maggie hastened away.

He took Vivian's cape then guided her into the parlor and near the fireplace. "I'll build this up nice and warm for you."

Vivian didn't move as he worked, and soon Maggie came in and gave them both a cup of hot tea. "Mercy me, we have to get you out of that dress and into something proper."

"I'm fine, Maggie." Vivian's voice was soft, almost shy. "My dress isn't even wet."

"It's red! You should be wearing black. I took the liberty of dyeing that orange dress you never liked. It should be dry. We'll put that on you until we can have some proper mourning clothes made for you."

"Very well, I'll change later. But I won't have any other black dresses made. One will be sufficient. Is that clear? I'll not waste the money."

Maggie nodded.

Vivian waved a hand. "You may go."

Maggie dipped her head and turned to leave.

"And, Maggie, thank you."

Maggie beamed and left.

Conner took a swallow of his tea. "Is the fire all right?"

"It's lovely, but you're soaked."

"I'm not so bad. My coat in the foyer took most of it." He set his tea on the mantel. "Out on the dock, when I pushed you away—"

"Please, Conner, don't. I was overcome and wanted a little comfort. I shouldn't have imposed. I'm fine now."

"I know you said you weren't in love with Randolph, but you're still grieving a loss. He was my friend, too." He held his hands from his side. "I could use a little comfort, too."

"Oh, Conner, I never thought about how this was your loss, as well." She stepped to him.

He wrapped his arms around her. He wanted to hold her forever. Just because he was in love with her didn't mean she would ever have feelings for him. He wanted to kiss her but stepped away before he felt the embrace had crossed the line of impropriety. Maybe it already had. His friend was barely dead, and he was thinking about kissing his widow. What kind of man was he? He should give up on Vivian while he still could and leave town as planned.

She studied him a moment as if he were a new face to her. "Do you remember what I said the other day about the compass?"

He nodded. "You felt like you were the needle spinning around."

She took a sip of tea. "Do you know that a ballerina fixes her gaze on a stationary object as she twirls around and around? When she stops, she's not dizzy because she kept her eyes fixed on one thing. I'm trying to keep fixed on the Lord and know that He will take care of me. I don't feel so dizzy. But when I look at you, I don't feel dizzy, either. The Lord and you are both stationary objects for me. He in heaven, and you in the flesh."

He wasn't sure how to feel about that.

"I don't mean to occupy all your time or take you away from your duties or your store. But for now, until the Lord helps me figure things out, if I can look to you, I know I won't get so dizzy I fall down."

"I don't know what to say."

"I believe He has placed you in my path to help me through all this. I promise not to be a burden to you, but if you'd rather not. . ."

"You could never be a burden. I'm glad to help in any way I can."

"Thank you. You always were a good friend to Randolph."

Not as good as she might think or he wouldn't have had feelings for her. "Have you thought about a service for Randolph?"

She sucked in a breath. "But there is no body to bury."

"Men are lost at sea all the time, bodies rarely recovered." He couldn't tell her that whatever was left after the explosion was probably eaten by a shark or other sea creature. "It'll give you closure."

Her brow furrowed. "It would be the proper thing to do, wouldn't it?"

He nodded.

"What do I need to do?"

"I'll talk to Minister Sciuto and make all the arrangements. You don't have to worry about anything." He wanted to take care of everything for her. Take care of her, too.

He left shortly after that to the clouds' steady offering of rain. How could he leave town now after promising Vivian to be her anchor through this? *Lord, I guess I'm staying if that's what You want. Please help me show proper decorum and not dishonor You, Vivian, or Randolph's memory.*

After Conner left, Vivian stood in her room and inhaled as Maggie cinched her corset a wee bit tighter to fit her into her mourning dress. The dress wasn't nearly as bad in black as it had been in peach. Any orangish colors made her look as though she were recovering from a long illness.

"You must've gained a little weight since the captain commissioned this dress for you." Maggie huffed with exertion behind her.

"It's all your fine cooking. You spoil me."

Maggie held out the bodice. "It might not be the fixin's."

Vivian slipped her arms into the sleeves. "What's that supposed to mean?"

Maggie stepped behind her and started hooking up the back. "You've been married three months. You could be carrying a little one."

The breath froze inside her lungs, and she put a hand on her belly. Did she want to have a baby, Randolph's baby? It would be a fitting tribute to him, but she knew he wouldn't want her to be the mother of his only heir. *Lord, Your will be done in this. If I am to be the mother of Randolph's child, let it be a son. He would have liked that. And help me to train him up to be an honorable man who follows closely after You.*

"All done." Maggie nodded at her. "Now you look the proper widow and very becoming in black."

She gazed at her reflection. "But black is so dreary. Do you know that in Mississippi the governor tried to pass a law banning mourning clothes after the War Between the States? Everyone had lost someone, and it was depressing to have the whole state in black."

"Now we aren't in Mississippi, are we? We're in Washington State. And that war was over long before you were born."

Randolph hadn't had the wife he wanted, but maybe she could be the kind of widow he would have been proud of. "Maggie, what do we have to fill my basket?"

"You aren't going to feed the birds? Today?"

"It stopped raining. They have to eat. They were expecting me yesterday."

Maggie took a deep breath. "I'll have Scotty hitch up the carriage."

She opened her mouth to protest, but Maggie held up her hand and went on quickly. "I don't want no fuss from you. You're a widow now, and I won't have you walking around when you are in black."

She opened her mouth to object.

"One word of fuss from you and I'll have Scotty bolt this door shut. I'll talk to Scotty and meet you in the kitchen."

"Maggie."

The housekeeper turned in the doorway with a look of determination. She was a feisty woman, and she was just trying to look after her mistress.

"Thank you."

Vivian had the basket half full by the time Maggie entered the kitchen.

"The carriage will be around front in a jiffy." Maggie walked into the pantry and came out with a paper sack. "I was so upset yesterday that I had to bake. I think those birds will like these gingersnaps."

"You're a peach." She put them into her basket, and she walked out front with Maggie as Scotty drove up in the carriage. Scotty helped her into the carriage then assisted Maggie with her own basket for shopping.

Maggie insisted that she be dropped off at the fish market first, and Scotty stayed with Vivian. She didn't object, because she knew that Maggie would win. She left Scotty in the carriage and went down to the beach. She barely sat when Peter came running with the others close behind.

"Where were you yesterday? We couldn't find you." Peter jumped up onto the log next to her.

"I'm sorry I couldn't make it." She didn't want to explain her troubles to them. They had enough of their own. "Let's thank the Lord for this food."

They joined hands and all said, "Thank You, Jesus, for this food. Amen."

She handed out the food. "How is that other loose tooth of yours?"

Peter bared his teeth, or at least what was left of them, then fished in his pocket, pulling out a white baby tooth.

She smiled. "It came out."

"He kept pulling at it until it came out," Tommy said, looking half jealous that Peter would be getting another penny. "There was blood all over his face."

"Can I have another penny?"

Betsy looked up. "That's not polite. You don't ask people for money."

"But she gave me one last time."

She had forgotten the pennies. "I haven't any. I'll bring you one next time. One for each of you."

Peter wiped his mouth with his sleeve. "Why're you wearing black?"

"Peter! That's not nice," Betsy piped up.

"Well, I don't like black. It makes me sad."

It made her sad, too, but out of respect for Randolph she was almost glad she was wearing it.

Betsy put her hand on Peter's arm. "It means she knows someone who died."

Peter looked at Vivian with big brown eyes. Eyes that could melt any girl's heart. "Who died?"

Betsy huffed and shook her head.

"It's all right, Betsy." There was no reason not to tell them. "Have you ever heard of Captain Carlyle?"

They all shook their heads except George. "He's your husband, and a mighty fine captain, from what I hear."

"That's right, but his ship sank."

"Did he swim to shore?" Peter's eyes rounded even more.

She wrapped her arm around the boy. "No. He didn't."

"He's the one who died, silly," Betsy said.

Peter sat up straighter and frowned. "He shouldn't have died. Didn't he know you would be sad for him?"

She hugged Peter. His simple comment warmed her heart. "He didn't have a choice. He was on his ship when it got struck by lightning."

When Betsy had eaten part of her food and put the rest in her pocket, Vivian took out the yard goods scraps, needle, and thread. "First, I'll show you how to thread a needle and sew two pieces of fabric together." If Betsy could learn simple sewing skills, maybe she could apprentice with a real seamstress and not live her life on the streets or in some seedy back room.

Vivian was tired by the time she returned from visiting the children. She stared up at the two-story blue Victorian house. She didn't feel as though she belonged here, but where else should she go? Wasn't the house hers now? She entered and walked around, slowly surveying everything in it. Nothing of hers was there. It was all Randolph's. He wouldn't like for her to start changing things, but she didn't feel comfortable here knowing Randolph disapproved of her. Would he want her out of his house?

A throat cleared behind her. "Ma'am."

"Yes, Maggie."

Maggie looked a bit nervous but squared her shoulders. "I know you said not to, but there will be a seamstress arriving momentarily to measure you for a new mourning dress."

She thinned her lips. Just because she had money didn't mean she should waste it. "You have wasted her time then, because I'm not commissioning another mourning dress. This one will do fine, and if I need another, we can dye one of the many other dresses Randolph bought me." Randolph had spared no expense on her wardrobe.

"She's a widow."

Vivian relaxed her mouth.

"She has a small son to provide for."

Maggie knew just how to pull at her heartstrings. "Is she bad off?"

"She's going to lose her home soon."

"When will she arrive?"

Maggie went to the window. "I think that's her walking up the street."

"Hurry. Help me get out of this dress." She headed for the stairs.

Maggie trailed after her. "Why?"

"I'll wear the gray dress or another one. If I'm wearing black, she might think I don't really need a mourning dress."

"You're a wealthy woman. You don't need a reason to purchase another dress."

"Just help me out of this." She knew that this woman would want meaningful work and not just charity handouts.

Maggie unhooked the back of the bodice. The doorbell chimed.

"Put her in the parlor and then come back up to help me."

As Maggie hurried from the room, Vivian shucked out of the rest of the dress. She got her gray dress and had the skirt on and fastened and the bodice pulled on when Maggie returned.

"She's in the parlor. I served her tea and gingersnaps. Her son is a little cutie. He'll steal your heart."

She put her hand on her stomach as Maggie hooked up the back of her bodice. Would she be having a son?

She wanted to rush down the stairs and greet this poor widow, but she took the stairs slowly and entered the parlor to see a sunny-faced woman smiling at her four-year-old son.

Maggie cleared her throat. "Mrs. Parker, this is Mrs. Carlyle."

The woman stood, straightening her blue dress and schooling her smile. "I'm sorry, ma'am." She put her hand on her son's shoulder. "Harry won't be any trouble; I promise. He's a good boy." The poor woman looked so nervous.

Vivian smiled at the blond woman. "It's no problem. Please sit." Mrs. Parker didn't look like a widow. She hadn't really expected the woman to be dressed in black, but without it, she looked like any other woman. How long a widow? How long would she herself be required to wear mourning garb?

She turned to the boy and held out the plate of gingersnaps. "Would you like a cookie?"

The boy looked up at her with big brown eyes. When he nodded his head, his blond curls danced. He reminded her of Peter with blond hair. He didn't take a cookie; instead, he looked to his mother, who nodded. Mrs. Parker held up one finger, and he reached out a chubby hand and took just one.

"What do you say, Harry?" Mrs. Parker prodded.

The cookie hovered between his lips, but he managed to say, "Thank you."

Mrs. Parker turned her blue eyes on her. "Thank you, Mrs. Carlyle, for the cookie as well as the opportunity to interview with you. I wore my best dress so you could see my sewing. I also made Harry's clothes." She held out her arm for Vivian to inspect her work.

"Please call me Vivian." She made a show of studying the dress then looking at Harry's clothes. She wanted the woman to think she'd given it thought and wasn't just handing out charity. Some people were proud. *But if you got hungry enough, or your son got hungry enough, even a proud person would stoop to accepting charity. . .and even lower.*

"Please call me Abigail." Abigail handed her a small patchwork of fabrics. "I brought this so you could see my stitches."

The stitching was even and smooth, better than Vivian had ever done. "Abigail, as you can see, I'm in need of a mourning dress, and rather quickly so. How soon would you be able to complete it?"

"If I work very hard, a week."

"Fine. I'll have Scotty bring round the carriage while you take my measurements, and we can go choose a pattern and fabric right now, if that suits you."

Abigail smiled. "The sooner I have all the materials, the sooner I can have your dress completed."

Vivian took Abigail and Harry to an uptown shop, purchased everything needed to make the dress, and dropped them off at their little house with a For Sale sign in the front yard. It warmed her inside to know she was helping a woman in need. A side benefit was that Maggie wouldn't harp on her for having only one appropriate mourning dress.

When she returned home, Maggie met her at the front door and handed her an envelope. "This came by special messenger."

She turned it over. Benton, Attorney at Law. Randolph's lawyer. She broke the seal.

"Mr. Jackson is waiting for you in the back garden."

What was Conner doing here in the middle of the day? It must be important. He had a store to run. She thanked Maggie and went out back. Conner stood in the yard by her lilac bushes, whose leaves were beginning to turn color. "Conner, is everything all right?"

He turned and met her on the stone patio. "How are you doing?"

"You left your store and came here in the middle of the day to ask me how I am?" But then why shouldn't he? Scotty had been at his store first thing two mornings on her behalf. "I'm fine."

Maggie came out and set a tea tray on the patio table. "Shall I serve?"

"I'll do it. Thank you, Maggie." She sat at the table, setting down her envelope, and gave Conner a cup of tea.

"Thank you." Conner took a sip then set his cup down before reaching into his coat pocket and pulling out an envelope similar to hers. "I came about this. I'll come and get you and take you. You shouldn't have to go alone."

She picked up her envelope. "I just received one, too. I haven't read it yet. Maggie told me you were waiting for me. What does it say?"

"It's about Randolph's will."

Her breath stilled in her chest for a moment before she could breathe again. "I hadn't thought about a will."

"I'm sure he left you everything."

If Randolph had had time before he sailed, he wouldn't have left her anything. "Then why would you have received a notice?"

He looked at her, concerned for a moment. "We're old friends."

She hoped Randolph did leave Conner something of value. He'd always been a good friend to her husband. He deserved something for his friendship and loyalty all these years. "I would appreciate the company."

"The reading is in three days, the day after the funeral, at two. I'll come for you at one thirty." He stood, gave her a small bow, and left.

She put her hand on her belly. If a baby was growing inside her, it would be good to know what Randolph had left his child. She opened the envelope and read it briefly. She was to be at the attorney's office at one thirty, not two. It also said that if that was inconvenient or she would prefer he come to the house, he would make those arrangements.

She went into the parlor and sat at the writing desk. She penned one letter to the attorney saying she would be at his office at one thirty in three days and penned a second informing Conner she would meet him at the attorney's. Then she sent Scotty to deliver them. Conner came that evening to tell her he would arrive at one and still accompany her; then he stayed for supper.

Chapter 5

Two days later, Vivian sat in the front pew of the church with a multitude of Randolph's mourners gathered behind her. Most of them likely attended as a social obligation. She wished all but his true friends had stayed home; that would be the best way to honor the dead.

She turned her focus to the wreath of fall flowers with a sash of black crepe. All that there was to represent a life. How sad. *I'm sorry it wasn't me, Randolph. You were a good man, better than me. I might be carrying your son. I'll raise him well and tell him all about his brave sea captain father.*

She was as much a hypocrite as some of the others in attendance. A tear trickled down her cheek. She went to wipe it away with her gloved hand when a black handkerchief dangled in front of her. She took it and looked up at Conner. "Thank you." She dabbed at her face.

He stood tall and lean and was quite handsome in his black suit. "It'll be starting soon." He sat next to her.

Maggie and Scotty sat at the other end of her pew. They were going to sit in the back, but she insisted that they sit up front with her. She didn't want to sit alone, and they were as close to Randolph as she—probably closer. They had known him longer, and Randolph always regarded them highly. She'd appreciated that Randolph treated them well and spoke to them with respect, from one human being to another.

Minister Sciuto's words about her husband were beautiful. Then Conner stood up front and shared about his childhood friend.

"I met Randolph twenty years ago. He was ten and I was seven and his brother, William, was five. At a time in my life when the whole human race looked hopeless to me, I admired and respected Randolph. He always looked out for me and William. He was a friend and claimed me as a brother."

Vivian choked up. In her own troubles, she'd forgotten just how close Conner had been to her husband all his life. He must be grieving terribly. It was a far greater loss for him than it was for her, and that saddened her further. She cried for Conner's loss. Conner ended by reading a lengthy poem called *The Rime of the Ancient Mariner*, Randolph's favorite. Since she'd become a Christian, she'd been plagued with the question of God really loving her with her past. So when Randolph had recited this poem for her, she'd latched on to the third stanza from the end. Now she listened for it:

> *He prayeth best, who loveth best*
> *All things both great and small;*
> *For the dear God who loveth us,*
> *He made and loveth all.*

It once again comforted her to know that God made her and that He loved her in spite of herself.

When Conner finished, he sat back down next to her. She gripped his hand to comfort him. He squeezed back. The remainder of the service, she sat with her hand in his, afraid to take the comfort from him; he'd suffered such a deep loss.

At the conclusion of the service, she was ushered out a side door to a waiting carriage. The carriage she shared with Conner came immediately after the minister's carriage. There were no pallbearers to keep him company, and there was no hearse between that carriage and hers. There was no need. There was no body. It bothered her that she couldn't put Randolph's body to rest in the ground. But he was a seaman through and through and probably preferred to die at sea rather than on land.

She stood beside an empty grave. Not even a grave. A stone marker to remember the passing of a life. Conner had had an image of Randolph's ship engraved in the stone:

Captain Randolph Carlyle
Devoted Husband
May he rest at peace in God's loving arms
March 1, 1868–September 29, 1898

Devoted husband. Conner had suggested putting *loving husband* on the marker, but Vivian knew that wouldn't be accurate. Loathing had filled Randolph's eyes the night he left. Yet she could concede that he might have been devoted to her, at least for a time. If she could only go back and change it all. She knew he wanted to marry her because of her beauty, and she wanted the security of marriage. She would never make that mistake again. She would only marry for love. Someone who could love her in spite of her past.

She gripped the white roses in her hands. Maggie had cut them from Randolph's own garden and lovingly removed all the thorns for her. A last remembrance of a man who loved the sea and loved his roses. If he could have taken his rosebushes on the ship with him, he would have had no reason to step foot on land.

Minister Sciuto began speaking: "Randolph John Carlyle. Captain. Husband. Friend."

The minister's voice faded away as she lowered her head. Tears gathered in her eyes but not for the reason that other widows had tears at their husband's funeral. So many regrets.

Chapter 6

The day following the funeral, Maggie helped Vivian into her dyed mourning dress once again. She wasn't with child. She knew that now. Her time had come. She had been looking forward to the challenge of motherhood and raising Randolph's son to be an honorable man whom Randolph would have been proud to call his son. It would have given her a purpose—direction—and somehow redeemed her. Now all she had was herself.

Conner rode up on Dakota, and Scotty had the carriage waiting out front. Conner gave Dakota's reins to Scotty and took the carriage with Vivian. They arrived at the attorney's office just before one thirty and were ushered into his office precisely at the appointed time.

Mr. Benton was a plump man in his sixties with a welcoming smile. "Please sit down." After Vivian had taken a seat, Conner and Mr. Benton also sat down. Mr. Benton looked over his glasses from her to Conner. "Mr. Jackson, I was not expecting you until two."

Conner nodded. "I didn't want Mrs. Carlyle to have to face any of this alone."

Mr. Benton shuffled some papers. "This puts me in a bit of an awkward position. I have a private matter I wish to speak about to Mrs. Carlyle before I read the terms of the will."

Conner stood immediately. "I'll wait in the reception area."

Mr. Benton stood as well. "Thank you. We won't be long."

Her stomach knotted. She'd wanted Conner here with her, but what if the attorney knew something of her past. She didn't want that revealed to Conner. Mr. Benton had said a private matter.

When the door closed behind Conner, the lawyer sat back down behind his mahogany desk and smiled at her. "There is a matter concerning your husband's will."

Her insides twisted tighter. "What is it?"

"Captain Carlyle came to me about changing his will."

When had he had time after their fight?

"He'd said he'd been lax in making arrangements since marrying. His intent was to add you to his will. I prepared the document, but he hadn't come in yet to sign it."

"I don't understand."

"You are not mentioned in your husband's legal will."

She would get nothing. Had a part of Randolph known she hadn't been honest with him, and was that why he'd put off changing his will? "Then there's no need for me to be here."

"On the contrary. I have his revised will that includes you."

"But it's not signed and therefore not legal." She still got nothing. That's how Randolph would have wanted it in the end. Her just reward.

"And that's why I didn't want Mr. Jackson in here. We can petition the court to consider this new will, though unsigned. I will testify on your behalf and inform the court of Captain Carlyle's intent. If the other parties listed in your husband's will don't object, you should get your share."

"And if they do?"

"We might be able to get you something. You were, after all, Captain Carlyle's legal wife. I was your husband's attorney, and now I'll be yours."

She studied the man. "Mr. Jackson is in my husband's will, isn't he? That's why you've summoned him."

Mr. Benton nodded. "And why I didn't want him present during this meeting with you. If you choose to pursue this, we would be petitioning against Mr. Conner Jackson and Mr. William Carlyle."

She'd kept a secret from Randolph that she knew he never would have approved of. William had warned her. When Randolph returned, he wouldn't have signed the new will that included her. A will was to carry out a person's wishes, and she was sure that Randolph's wishes didn't include leaving her anything. "Leave his will as it is. We weren't married very long. Mr. Jackson and Randolph's brother are more deserving."

"Mrs. Carlyle, please reconsider. The length of time you were married has no bearing on whether or not you're deserving."

No, but her secret was. She'd married Randolph with a lie between them that she knew he would never accept. She didn't deserve any of Randolph's money or possessions. "I've made up my mind."

Mr. Benton shook his head. "I'll give you a week to reconsider the ramifications of your actions, and then we'll talk again on this matter. I would be doing Randolph a disservice if I didn't at least try to persuade you to take action."

If he knew what she knew about how Randolph felt about her past, he wouldn't insist, so she simply nodded. "I'll wait out in the lobby while you speak with Mr. Jackson."

Conner stood when he saw Vivian exit Mr. Benton's office. She looked neither unduly upset nor pleased. What had Randolph left her?

"Mr. Jackson, won't you come in?"

"What about Mrs. Carlyle?"

"I'll wait out here."

"Why?" He looked from her to the attorney and back.

"The reading is just for you."

He turned back to Mr. Benton. "Shouldn't she be there for the reading?"

"There are extenuating circumstances that don't require Mrs. Carlyle to be present." Mr. Benton motioned for Conner to enter his office.

This was all very odd. "Can Mrs. Carlyle be present if I want her to be?"

Mr. Benton nodded.

He turned to Vivian and held out his hand to her. "Please come."

She glanced at Mr. Benton then took Conner's hand. Why had she hesitated?

When Mr. Benton finished reading the will, Conner stared at the man. There had to be more. There had to be something for Vivian. William inherited the house and half of Carlyle Shipping, and he'd inherited the other half of the shipping enterprise. What was left for Vivian? "There has to be more. What about Mrs. Carlyle?"

"As I explained to Mrs. Carlyle, Captain Carlyle hadn't signed his new will that named her as a beneficiary. The will he had in place before he married is legal and binding."

"But she should get something. She was his wife."

"I'm not going to pursue it," Vivian said.

"Pursue what?"

Mr. Benton took a deep breath. "I have counseled Mrs. Carlyle to petition the courts to consider the intent of Captain Carlyle's new will that he had not yet signed."

"Then do it. What will she get?"

"Half the house and one-third of the shipping business. It's in your best interest to find yourself an attorney."

Mr. Benton had no idea what was in Conner's best interest. "I won't fight." Vivian's well-being was in his best interest.

"It's okay. I'll write to William, and as soon as he can come and take possession of the house, I'll leave."

His gut clenched. She couldn't leave. He wouldn't let her. "This is wrong."

She turned soulful eyes on him. "This is the way Randolph left his affairs. I will honor that."

Why? He wanted to fight for her. "Randolph would want you taken care of. He asked me to see that you were taken care of if anything should happen to him." Had Randolph sensed something? "I made a promise."

"Please let it be."

He didn't want to, but because she asked, he would. . .for now.

On the carriage ride back to her house, she said, "I'll write to William and ask him what he'd like to do about the house. Maybe he and Sarah will move up here. I think they'd like it here, don't you?"

What did it matter if William and his wife would like it here? "I'll write to William, as well, and tell him Randolph died before he could change his will. I know he will insist on honoring the new will, even unsigned."

"Don't. I won't accept it. Promise me you won't ask anything of William on my behalf."

"Why not?"

"I have my reasons. Please, Conner."

He couldn't refuse her and nodded, but he could still tell William what he thought without asking anything of him. William was an honorable man like Randolph; he would do the right thing. And from what Conner understood, William's wife was a friend of Vivian's. Certainly she wouldn't stop William from doing what was right and fair.

"Would you like to come inside, or do you need to get back to your store?"

If he stayed, he'd probably just make her mad trying to convince her to take action. "I should get back. Martin might be overwhelmed." He should head over to Randolph's shipping business and see what state his affairs were in.

Vivian entered her foyer, and Maggie took her cape. "Mrs. Parker and her son are in the parlor."

When Vivian strode through the doorway, Abigail was once again smiling at her son. An emptiness opened in her belly; she wouldn't be having a son.

"Abigail, it's so good to see you again."

Abigail turned, her gaze flickered down Vivian's dress, and her smile dipped slightly. "I wanted to fit the bodice on you and size the waist of the skirt."

Vivian looked down at the dress she had on, her black mourning dress. Should she say something about it or let it pass? Abigail had obviously noticed. "I'm sure you are wondering about my dress."

"Your wardrobe is none of my concern, except for the dress you have commissioned from me."

She sat. "I'll tell you anyway. This was a dress I already owned that I never liked. It was peach, which is a dreadful color on me. Maggie dyed it so I would have something appropriate to wear until I could have a dress made. It's better in black, but I still don't like it much. I've never been fond of black."

"Sad," Harry said from his seat next to his mother.

Abigail patted her son's leg. "That's right." Then she turned to Vivian. "Harry thinks black is sad and refused to wear it after a time."

"If you don't mind my asking, how long did you wear mourning clothes?"

"Three months to the day. It was as if something inside Harry said enough mourning. It's time to get on with living. I still grieve my loss, but I try to be happy as much as I can in front of Harry."

"How long since your husband passed away?"

"Six months next week." Tears welled in Abigail's eyes. "We've almost run out of the money my husband saved. I don't know where we will go when we lose the house."

"You're young. You'll find another husband."

"I hope not. I don't know if I could handle another loss." A tear slipped down Abigail's cheek. She quickly swiped it away and stole a glance at her son. Harry hadn't noticed as he was busy picking cookie crumbs off his jacket.

An ache welled up inside Vivian to have a love like that. She hadn't had that with her first husband and certainly not with Randolph.

After Abigail left, Vivian prayed for Abigail and her small son. She also prayed to find a love like the one Abigail had had with her husband. Then she sat down and wrote a letter to William, telling him about Randolph's death, what he'd been left in the will, and asking him what he wanted her to do about his newly inherited house. After that, she went to bed without supper. It had been a long day, and she was exhausted. Tomorrow she would consider what she was to do with the rest of her life.

Chapter 7

Conner entered Carlyle Shipping. The sandy-haired clerk was leaning back in his chair with his feet up on his desk, eyes closed.

Conner cleared his throat.

The man looked up at him with sleepy eyes then suddenly came alert, dropping his feet to the floor. "What can I do for you, sir?"

"I want to talk to whoever is in charge here."

"Captain Carlyle owns Carlyle Shipping, but Mr. Abernathy manages the office."

"Are you aware that Captain Carlyle recently died?"

The man sat straighter and swallowed hard. "Yes, sir. We've been running things as usual. Mr. Abernathy says he still has a business to run, orders and shipping to provide and schedule."

"It sounds like Mr. Abernathy thinks he's inherited the captain's business."

"I don't know, sir. I'm just a clerk."

"What's your name?"

"Jonathan Kirkide, sir."

"Please stop calling me sir. My name is Conner Jackson, and I'm one of the new owners of Carlyle Shipping."

The young man's eyes grew wide. "Yes, sir, Mr. Jackson, sir. Oops. Sorry, sir. I mean, Mr. Jackson."

He wasn't going to discuss the future of Carlyle Shipping with a clerk. "I need to see Mr. Abernathy now."

"Yes, sir." Jonathan stood so fast that his chair tipped back to the wall behind him. "Right this way." Jonathan guided him down a hallway and through a door to the warehouse where men were busy moving crates.

Conner followed Jonathan up a flight of stairs to an office that overlooked the warehouse floor.

Jonathan knocked then opened the door. "Mr. Abernathy, Mr. Jackson to see you."

Mr. Abernathy, a middle-aged man with a handlebar mustache, sat at ease behind the large mahogany desk. "I'm busy right now. Make an appointment with Mr. Kirkide, and I'll see you later in the week."

Conner stepped into the room and up to the desk. "Mr. Abernathy, let me introduce myself: Conner Jackson, one of the new owners of Carlyle Shipping."

Mr. Abernathy's gaze shifted up but his head did not move. "Is that so?"

Conner reached into his inside coat pocket and pulled out a letter. "This is from Captain Carlyle's attorney."

Mr. Abernathy made a point of reading the letter carefully and slowly before refolding it and handing it back. Then he stood and held out his hand. "It's good to meet you. Please have a seat."

There was something in the hardness of the man's face that belied his pleasant-sounding words. Conner shook the man's hand and sat.

Mr. Abernathy steepled his fingers. "We all speculated that the captain's new wife would get the business. Of course I planned to run the business as usual for her. No need to worry the poor widow with business affairs."

Conner didn't like the slightly demeaning tone in the manager's voice. "There is some dispute as to Mrs. Carlyle's portion of the business, but I'm taking charge until the other owners and I, along with the attorneys, can decide just how to distribute this asset. Until then, I'll be making all decisions."

Mr. Abernathy's eyes narrowed ever so slightly. If he hadn't been looking, Conner would have missed it. "Of course. I'm at your service. The captain trusted me with all aspects of this business, so I can answer any questions you have."

"What is the state of the business?"

"Business has not been so good lately, but we're in the black, barely."

He didn't like Mr. Abernathy speaking of Randolph's business with so much possessiveness. "I would like to see the account books if you don't mind."

"Why should I mind? You're part owner now." Mr. Abernathy stood a little too eagerly. "Right this way." He walked through a door at the side of his office into an adjoining office where a brunette woman in her thirties sat behind the desk.

"Miss Demarco, this is Mr. Jackson, one of the new owners."

Her eyes widened slightly. "Is that so?" She gave him a tip of her head. "It's nice to meet you."

Conner noted a bit of insincerity in her greeting.

"Mr. Jackson would like to see the books."

"I can assure you they're all in order."

He hoped they were. "I appreciate you keeping the books so well. If I can just look through them to get an overall view of Carlyle Shipping so I can let the other owners know how the business is faring..."

Miss Demarco seemed reluctant to give up her books but finally said, "Certainly. How far back would you like to go?"

"Let me start with the most recent and go back a year to start."

Miss Demarco pulled several ledger books and placed them on her well-ordered desk. "I'll finish recording today's totals in the morning if that is all right with you, Mr. Abernathy."

"That will be fine. Come to my office. I have some other work for you."

Conner determined to be at this office more often than Randolph would have had time for. The people here had an air about them that this was their company and not Randolph's. He poured over the books for three hours until he was starting to see cross-eyed.

Conner's head was pounding by the time he left the shipping office. It would be a sweet relief to see Vivian.

First, he stopped by his store. It was late. Martin should have closed up by now. The Closed sign was in place and the door locked. He unlocked and opened the door to find Martin sitting on a stool behind the counter looking guilty with an open can of beans in his hand and his mouth full. He chewed quickly and swallowed. "I was really hungry."

Martin deserved more than a measly can of beans for all he did. He waved the younger man off. "Why haven't you gone home?" Fred trotted over and stood on her haunches. He picked her up.

Martin dropped his spoon into the can. "I wasn't sure what to do when you didn't come back from the attorney's. I knew you'd be back eventually and thought I should wait...but I got hungry." Martin dipped his head as though guilty of some great crime.

Martin was young, only twenty-three, but he was reliable. Conner couldn't say that about his other transient employees. Now he understood how Ian, his own former boss, had felt about him. Conner had just done his job as well as he could, always a fear in the back of his mind that Ian would terminate his employ or find someone else to do his job better. But now that he had employees of his own, he understood the value of reliable help. He grabbed a bag of Saratoga chips and tossed them to Martin. "Enjoy, and don't worry about the beans." He would have to reward Martin in some other way, as well. With so many dishonorable people around, Martin needed to know that he was appreciated. "Go home. I'll see you tomorrow."

Martin swung on his coat and grabbed the bag of chips.

As Martin opened the door and prepared to step outside, Conner said, "Thanks."

Martin shot him a smile and a nod then was gone into the night.

Conner looked at his pocket watch. Vivian would be sitting down to supper any minute. If he hurried, he might garner an invitation to join her. He locked up the shop and rode Dakota at a gallop uptown.

The black crepe on Vivian's door weighed heavily on him. He wished Randolph were coming back, but at the same time, there was Vivian. He was being torn apart by this conflict and didn't know how to resolve it. He could still leave town.

He knocked softly. Maggie opened the door to let him in. "Good evening, Mr. Jackson."

He smiled at the plump older woman. "I wish you'd call me Conner."

"You know I can't do that."

He nodded. "Is Mrs. Carlyle in the dining room?" He hoped she hadn't eaten early and he was too late.

"She went to bed an hour ago and fell right asleep."

"It's only suppertime. She can't be sleeping." Conner couldn't believe it. Something had to be wrong.

"She was very tired from the day." Maggie tried to placate him. "She will feel better tomorrow."

"I want to see her."

Maggie squared her shoulders. "I'm sorry, Mr. Jackson. You'll have to come back tomorrow."

"I need to know she's all right."

"She was fine when she went to bed."

"That was an hour ago. Please go check on her for me."

Maggie seemed reluctant but finally conceded. "You wait here." She headed up the stairs one slow step at a time.

When she was halfway up, a scream came from above. He took the stairs three at a time, overtaking Maggie quickly, who sped up. He burst through Vivian's door and stared at her thrashing the covers around with her hands and feet.

Maggie hurried past him. "Just a bad dream." She braced her hands on his chest and pushed him out into the hall. "You stay out here." She went to Vivian's side and soothed her with a gentle hand on her forehead, apparently without waking her.

Vivian calmed, and Maggie smoothed the covers back into place before returning to the hall and closing the door. "The past week has been very hard on her. She hasn't slept well."

It had been a long week, and Conner hadn't had the comfort of a good night's sleep, either. He went home to bed and flopped most of the night like a dying fish cast upon the shore.

Chapter 8

Conner sat in the chair opposite Mr. Benton. "Do you have the papers for me to sign?"

"Are you sure you want to do this? Even if Mrs. Carlyle chooses to petition the courts, it doesn't mean she will win."

"Randolph was my best friend. I would be dishonoring him to cheat his widow. Before Randolph left, he asked me to take care of Mrs. Carlyle should anything happen to him."

Mr. Benton opened a folder. "This document turns over one quarter of Carlyle Shipping to Mrs. Carlyle, half of what you inherited. That is very generous of you."

"I have my own business that is doing well. I don't need half of Carlyle Shipping." He didn't need any of it. The gold rush had been a huge boon to his business with miners pouring through town to head north to Alaska. He was wealthier than he ever thought he would be. But his gift to Vivian wasn't all that unselfish. As long as both he and she were part owners, she would be a part of his life. That's the way he wanted it. If he stayed close to her during her time of mourning, he'd be aware if any other man began to show an interest in her before he could tell her his feelings and court her. No, he wasn't being generous; he was being cautious and looking out for his own interests.

He took the pen and dipped it into the inkwell. Satisfaction wrapped around his heart as he scratched his name on the line, binding his life with Vivian's.

Mr. Benton blotted the signature and blew on it before setting it aside. "These next documents give me the right to transfer funds from Carlyle Shipping to a new account in Mrs. Carlyle's name."

"She doesn't have to know I set this up, does she?"

Mr. Benton shook his head. "She's coming into my office in two days. I'll suggest that it must have been Captain Carlyle."

"It'll be six months' worth of her share of the profits from Carlyle Shipping?" He didn't want her to get suspicious with regular deposits. It would put him in a bit of a pinch, but he figured he'd be all right.

"I don't think the business can handle that amount all at once. I'll have just part of one month's profits to start with put into the account. That should be plenty for her needs. I'll talk to the banker, so when I take Mrs. Carlyle to the bank to sign over the account to her, he will tell her that arrangements have been made for a monthly allotment to be deposited into her personal account from Carlyle Shipping." Mr. Benton turned the document to face him. "If those terms suit you, sign all three pages."

As long as Vivian thought Randolph had set this up and she would have money enough, that was all he was concerned with. He scratched his name on all the lines.

"Now if you will accompany me to the bank, we'll get the account set up in her name."

On Thursday, Vivian sat in Mr. Benton's reception area. She'd purposefully not told Conner that she was seeing Randolph's attorney again. She didn't want him to come and try to talk her into taking part of his and William's inheritances. She knew that somehow the Lord would see to her needs. She would not go back to the old life she'd left only ten months ago. She would starve to death first. Death didn't scare her as it once had. If she died, she knew she'd go to heaven and see Jesus. No one would miss her here on earth.

The door to Mr. Benton's office opened. A man exited with Mr. Benton. They shook hands, and the man left. Mr. Benton turned to her. "Sorry for keeping you waiting, Mrs. Carlyle. Please come in."

She entered and sat in the offered chair.

Mr. Benton rounded his desk and sat. "How are you doing today?"

"Fine, thank you."

"Have you considered my proposal to petition the court to uphold Randolph's unsigned will?"

"I have, and I still decline." She felt bad enough deceiving Randolph without trying to steal from Conner and William. They were both good men, very good men, and both deserved every penny Randolph had left them. She'd prayed and didn't believe the Lord wanted her to pursue action against the will.

"Very well."

That was it? He wasn't going to try to persuade her? "If you were going to so easily accept my refusal, why have me come down to your office?"

"I have other business to discuss with you. It is that other business that allows me to accept your decision so readily." Mr. Benton shuffled papers on his desk. "Which to cover first?"

First? What was going on?

"It has come to my attention that a bank account has been left in your name. This letter came from Northwest Bank." Mr. Benton handed her a letter.

She read the letter that indeed detailed she had an account in her name. "Why send this to you instead of me?"

"It's much easier to deal with me than a distraught widow."

She was far from distraught. Guilty, yes, but the banker didn't know that. "Who would set up an account for me?" She also wondered how much was in the account but didn't want to ask.

"The letter doesn't say. When we are finished here, I'll take you over to the bank and help you get everything settled. I made an appointment with the bank's manager."

Mr. Benton took the letter back, set it aside, and picked up another paper. "I sent word to Mr. William Carlyle on his inheritance. I received this telegram this morning."

> *Tell Mrs. Randolph Carlyle to stay in the house. Make arrangements for her to use any money needed for household expenses until my arrival. Sending letter with further details.*

"Your husband's brother is putting you in charge of his estate for the time being." Mr. Benton took back the telegram. "We'll take this to the banker, as well. It seems you are being taken care of, so I'll not worry about you for now." He stood. "Shall we go to the bank?"

She nodded and stood. "We can both travel in my carriage. It's right outside."

Once at the bank, she and Mr. Benton were ushered into Mr. Olsen's office.

"I just have a couple of papers for you to sign." Mr. Olsen held out a piece of paper. "This one completes the transfer of the account into your name so you will have complete access to it. I just need your signature at the bottom."

Mr. Benton took the paper.

She scooted slightly forward in her seat as Mr. Benton read. "Who set up this account? Did Randolph?"

"I'm not at liberty to disclose that information, but who else would?" Mr. Olsen kept his nose crinkled to hold up his glasses, which caused him to wear a perpetual frown.

Mr. Benton handed her the paper. "It's okay to sign."

She signed and handed it back to Mr. Olsen.

"How much money is in the account?" Mr. Benton asked.

That was the question she was hesitant to ask because she didn't want to seem greedy. She just wanted to know how long it would sustain her after William and Sarah came and she moved out of their house.

Mr. Olsen handed her another sheet. "This is the amount of money currently in the account. Each month an undetermined amount will be deposited from Carlyle Shipping."

That was a significant amount. She could live on that if she lived frugally. So Randolph had set in place a means to take care of her even if he hadn't gotten around to signing his will. She didn't mind using this money, because she wouldn't be taking money from Conner or William. "May I draw on this account today?"

"Certainly. How much would you like?"

She gave him the figure. She wanted to have money to pay Abigail when she brought her finished dress, and that sum would pay her well for her services.

"I'll get that and be right back."

"Before you go, we have another matter," Mr. Benton said. He handed Mr. Olsen the telegram. "I took the liberty to draw up a temporary agreement for both you and Mrs. Carlyle to sign as to how much money she may withdraw to take care of household expenses. If this agreement suits you, she'll also need money to pay the salaries of the two domestic servants who were in Captain Carlyle's employ at the time of his death as well as other household needs." He handed Mr. Olsen another paper. "As you can see, the amount is rather conservative, bare essentials for the house. Mrs. Carlyle has her own money now for her personal needs. When I hear more from Mr. William Carlyle or his attorney, I'll have a more complete document to sign if Mr. Carlyle isn't present to retain possession of his affairs."

"This seems reasonable." Mr. Olsen signed, and she signed; then Mr. Olsen retrieved the money requested.

She had Scotty return Mr. Benton to his office. "Mr. Benton, thank you for everything."

"You're welcome. I'll let you know when I hear from Mr. Carlyle. In the meantime, be wise with that money."

"I will."

She arrived home to find Abigail waiting for her.

"Hello, Harry." She bent down to the boy's level. "What kind of cookies does Miss Maggie have for you today?"

He pointed a chubby finger at a dark spot on the oatmeal cookie. "Dat's a waisin. I love waisins."

"You eat as many as you like." She straightened and sat on the sofa with Abigail. "You have a very sweet boy."

Abigail smiled. "That I do. I don't know what I'd do if I didn't have him." She stood and walked over to one of the side chairs. "I finished your dress."

She patted the cushion. "I just arrived and would like to rest a bit before I try it on. Do you have time for a short visit?"

Abigail nodded and sat. Vivian figured that Abigail kept busy to provide for her and Harry and that her schedule afforded her little time to rest. She felt a bond with Abigail, and they spoke easily for nearly an hour. Then she put on the dress and came back downstairs.

"I love it. I would love it more if it weren't black. When I'm not in mourning any longer, I'll have you make me another dress." If she could afford it. The money in the bank account was limited, but she would survive on it. The Lord had provided for her, and the least she could do was share with someone else in need. She took the money she had gotten to pay Abigail from her handbag and gave it to her.

"Mrs. Carlyle, this is too much. I can't accept it." Abigail held the money back out to her.

She put her hands around Abigail's, tucking the money into her palm. "Please take it." She glanced at Harry who had curled himself into the chair and fallen asleep. "The workmanship is worth every penny."

Abigail threw her arms around her. "Thank you. I didn't know what I was going to do. May the Lord bless you for your generosity and kindness."

"He already has."

Chapter 9

On Friday, Conner pulled the shade up and flipped his CLOSED sign to OPEN. A young man about seventeen stopped his pacing on Conner's boardwalk and stared at him through the window. What was it with people on the store's doorstep? First Randolph drunk, then Scotty twice, and now this young man. He unlocked the door. "You're an eager fellow. Are you heading to the goldfields up north?"

"Nope. I just came from Alaska, and if I never return, it'll be too soon." The lad wasn't particularly handsome, with a pockmarked face and red blotches.

"You didn't find gold?"

"I wasn't looking for gold." He cinched a brown leather satchel up higher on his shoulder. "I was on board a ship. I came back by land."

"Ship would've been faster."

"I won't step foot on another ship for as long as I live." His voice was hard and determined.

"What can I do for you? Are you looking for something in particular?"

"I'm looking for Conner Jackson. Is that you?"

He nodded and studied the lad a moment. "What's this about?"

"I was a cabin boy on Captain Carlyle's ship."

No wonder the boy didn't want to sail again. He probably barely got off with his life. Randolph would have seen to the lad's safety and that of his crew before his own.

The lad took the satchel from his shoulder. "He told me to find you and to give this to you." His jaw worked back and forth.

"You were on the ship when it sank?"

"No, sir. The captain put this satchel over my head and shoved me into a dingy." Moisture filled the boy's eyes. "Said I had to live and find you. That it was an order. He told the others in the dingy to get as far from the ship as possible and paddle for land as fast as they could. I thought he and the other men would make it. It just all exploded."

A tear escaped and trickled down the lad's face. Conner averted his gaze and choked back some tears of his own.

"Mr. Jackson, the captain said you'd pay me back for the cost to get from Alaska to here."

He doubted Randolph was thinking about money for the lad when his ship was on fire, but the boy had been honorable in seeing that his captain's last wishes were carried out. If this really were from Randolph, he would pay the lad well. "Let me see what you brought." He pulled out the ship's log and a ledger book as well as a flat pouch with cash in it. There was no way to know how much had been in there, but the lad had to have brought at least most of it. The ledger was a copy of Randolph's shipping business's finances. He would take this over to his accountant right away and have him compare it to the ones from the shipping office.

Tears welled in his eyes. Randolph had known he wasn't going to make it, or why else would he have sent the lad off with this satchel? He took a deep breath and blinked several times before turning back. "Have you eaten breakfast?"

The lad shook his head.

"You like peaches?"

The lad nodded.

Conner took a can off the shelf and opened it with an opener from behind the counter.

He handed it to the lad, along with a fork from a small stash he kept behind the counter. "I'll get you something more after my assistant arrives."

The lad was shoving the peach sections into his mouth as fast as he could get them out of the can. He better get this boy something else, or he might start eating the can. Conner ran upstairs for a bowl, spoon, and a bottle of milk. When he came back, Martin was glaring at the boy, whose name he didn't know. "Martin, it's all right."

Martin nodded and walked to the back to hang up his coat.

"What's your name?"

"Todd Major."

"Do you like shredded wheat?"

"Heard of it, but I never had it."

He poured the boy a bowl full. "You'll like it."

The lad had downed one bowl and started on his next before the first customer crossed the threshold. Martin assisted the man in the pale blue coat. Conner went to Todd. "Do you have a place to stay?"

"No, sir." A drop of milk sat contentedly on Todd's chin.

This lad was trustworthy, or he wouldn't have bothered to come all this way on his dead captain's mission half starved with a pouch of cash. "You looking for a job?"

Todd shrugged. "It depends on how much it's worth to you what I brought you."

"Depends on what?"

"If it's enough to make it down to California. If not, I'll go as far as I can and pick up odd jobs along the way. People can always use a strong back."

"Is that how you came down from Alaska? Odd jobs?"

"Yes, sir. I hear California is a sunny place. No snow, either."

Conner handed Todd a piece of paper and pencil. "Write down how much money you spent to get from Alaska to here."

Todd pushed the paper away. "I don't know no reading or writing."

But he spoke well enough. "Can you tell me what you spent?"

Todd listed off every place he worked, how much they paid him, and every place he spent money along with how much. The boy had a good memory. With a little tutoring, he could learn to read and write easily enough.

Conner filled a knapsack with food, gave the boy a new pair of blue jeans and a shirt, reimbursed him for his trip from Alaska, and paid him well enough that he shouldn't have any trouble reaching California. "If you decide to stay in town or come back this way, let me know."

Todd nodded, slung the pack onto his back, thanked him, and walked out the door.

Martin said, "Who was that?"

"Someone I wouldn't mind hiring. He was on Randolph's ship and brought me his logbook and a few other things. I'm going to go in the back and look through this. Let me know if we get busy and you need me out front. Owen and Hansel said they'd be in to work. We'll see if they show."

He first read the last entry in Randolph's log:

29 September

I don't like the looks of the clouds boiling in the northwestern sky. The wind blew all night, rocking the ship. Hardened sailors who never fell ill were heaving over the side but stayed at their duty. We are in for a rough day and night before we dock. If we dock. I hope we survive.

Tears welled. Randolph had known he likely wouldn't make it. A seasoned sailor could read the sky, the clouds, and the water. Randolph had been at sea for nearly sixteen years—since he was fifteen. He knew all too well what he was up against. Conner would give up the chance he now had to have a relationship with Vivian if he could have Randolph back. He missed his friend.

That night after a pleasant evening with Vivian, Conner worked for two and a half hours at the shipping office, sorting through invoices and scheduling shipments, trying to make sense of the paperwork with the ledger from Randolph. His head bobbed forward and he jerked awake, causing a muscle in his neck to twinge. He needed more sleep than he was getting lately, but what could he do? He had his own business to run, and he had to keep Carlyle Shipping afloat until William could come and oversee the business—whenever that would be. And then there was Vivian. He wanted to spend every waking moment with her. But if he did that, both businesses would go under.

He looked at his watch as a yawn overtook him, so he stood and stretched. He would get up early, come back, and finish the invoices before he opened his store. Rubbing his face, he shook off another yawn. The night air would revive him.

He locked up and left. Drinking deeply of the cool air, he felt more alert as he began the walk home, but he knew he'd fall asleep the moment his head sank into the pillow.

He heard a scuffle up ahead and stepped into the shadows of the nearest building.

Someone said, "No! Let me go!"

"You're coming with us," a gruffer deeper voice said. "Tie his feet."

Don't get involved. Just go home. He knew what was likely going on. Men were often shanghaied and taken on board ships as unwilling crew. Usually they were too drunk to realize what was happening and just woke up the next morning at sea. But this was different. This man sounded stone sober, and he definitely didn't want to go. *Lord?* As soon as Conner opened his thoughts to his Savior, he knew he'd help the poor soul if he could. But how?

"No! No! No!" the frightened, young first voice said.

He recognized that voice, but from where?

"Shut him up!"

"Not on a ship!"

Todd! Todd Major. He definitely couldn't let them put that poor boy back on a ship, not after what he'd been through. He peeked around the corner and saw them carry Todd bound hand and foot into the saloon. They would take him through the tunnel under the street and to the dock.

He couldn't confront them in the saloon or the tunnel unless he wanted to end up hundreds of miles from home at sea. He had to hurry if he was going to get a gun and reach the dock in time to rescue Todd. Martin lived a block away in an apartment. He ran there and knocked several times before he got Martin to come to the door.

"Do you have a gun?"

Martin nodded. "What's up?"

"Todd Major, the boy from this morning, was just shanghaied. I can't let them take him back out to sea."

Martin crossed the small room to a bedside table and retrieved a six-shooter. "I'm going with you." He pulled on a shirt and his boots.

"Martin, I can't ask you to come. It might get ugly."

"Because it might get ugly is exactly why I should come. And you didn't ask; I volunteered." Martin grabbed his coat. "Let's go."

Conner had to smile at Martin, only four years younger than himself, so full of virtue and gumption. He didn't want to endanger Martin, but he didn't have time to argue if he was going to save Todd from going to sea. A seaman's life was suited for a bold few like Randolph. Others chose it out of necessity or because it was thrust upon them.

"Three men took him into Barter Saloon. I figure our best chance will be to follow them when they come out the other end and free him before they put him on the ship."

Martin nodded and followed close behind. They moved through the shadows and arrived at the dock as Todd and another man were being carried over the shoulders of two men up the gangplank. They were too late. Conner wanted to curse but refrained. He ducked into the shadows and leaned against a shed wall.

Martin followed suit. "Is that him squirming?"

"Yes."

Martin sighed. "We're too late."

He could hear the regret in Martin's words. "They haven't sailed."

"We're not going to go on board?" A bit of panic crept into Martin's voice.

"I can't let them take him like this." It was one thing to go voluntarily as Conner had done as a boy, but to be forced. . . He had to think of a way to get on board without being noticed.

"Conner?"

"What?"

"I have to confess that I'm a mite scared."

Martin seemed to realize that if they failed, they, too, could be sailing for the unknown. *Lord, don't let us fail.* "I'll take the gun. You go home."

Martin shook his head. "Tell me what you want me to do."

He clasped Martin on the shoulder. "Thank you." He stared at him a moment. "I'm scared, too." He wasn't sure if he should admit that, but it seemed to encourage Martin. "I'll get aboard. You stay here."

"Shouldn't I come with you?"

"I think it will be easier for just one of us to board unnoticed. Two would look suspicious." He was pretty sure he could get on the ship. After that, he'd have to improvise as he went.

"How are you going to get aboard?"

Conner thumbed toward the supplies that would soon be loaded. "I'll hoist a sack of flour over my shoulder and walk up the plank like I belong there."

"What do you want me to do?"

"Keep a lookout." For what he wasn't sure, but it was comforting to know that someone would know what happened to him if everything went wrong. And he wouldn't be worrying about Martin's safety.

Martin held out the gun. "You might need this."

"You keep it. If things get messy, shoot it into the air. That should bring the sheriff and a few other folks."

Martin shoved the gun back into the waist of his pants. "Do you want me to go get the sheriff?"

"He won't likely do anything. If it was a matter of the captain's word against mine, it would be easier to side with the captain and let a boy no one knows sail."

"Then why shoot to get the sheriff to come?"

"Just a diversion. If we get separated, meet back at my store." He didn't wait for Martin to acknowledge his order but trudged out toward the supplies and hoisted a sack of what felt like potatoes onto his shoulder. Sailors moved around the dock and up and down from the ship, so he strode up the gangplank, half holding his breath. No one stopped him.

When he stepped on deck, someone said, "You, there. Captain's itchin' to get under way. Pile the supplies over there. We'll carry them to the galley after we set sail."

Conner acknowledged him with a grunt, crossed the deck, and set the sack down, all while scanning the ship to decide his next move and discover where Todd might be. Near the forward hold, four bodies lay. Three looked passed-out drunk; one, bound and gagged and squirming. He strolled over, pulling out his knife, trying not to draw attention to himself. When he was sure no one was looking, he knelt down. "Shhh."

Todd's eyes widened in recognition.

He slid his knife under the rope around the boy's wrists and sliced it, then did the same with the ankles while Todd yanked the gag from his mouth. Conner glanced at the other three men. There was no way to help them while they were unconscious.

Another sailor joined the one at the top of the gangplank and began surveying the deck. Conner grabbed Todd's arm and pulled him into the shadows under the stairs leading to the smaller deck above.

"Where's the boy?" the new sailor bellowed as he strode over to the three sleeping men.

Conner could see the feet of two more sailors join the first, who picked up a piece of cut rope.

"He had help. Find them."

Men scurried around the deck. Conner leaned close to Todd's ear and whispered, "I'm afraid there is only one way off this ship now."

"Dead?" Todd's voice was small and scared. "I'd rather die than sail."

Conner wasn't planning on dying tonight, but that was one option. He immediately thought of Vivian. If he died or was forced to sail, he wished he'd told her how he felt about her, but there was no time for regrets now. "Do you swim?"

"A little."

"When I start moving, we'll only have a few seconds to run for the side and jump."

"Will they shoot at us?"

He hoped not. "We won't be worth the effort." *Lord, give us an opening to get off this ship.*

Todd shimmied into his canvas pack. When had he grabbed that? He didn't want to fight the boy over it now, but once they were in the water, it would only weigh him down.

Two rapid gunshots on shore caused him to instinctually duck. Martin. The sailors momentarily turned their attention, and Conner grabbed Todd by the coat and dragged him to the railing; then he grabbed the boy by the pack and helped him up and over the railing. *Splash!* Shouts came from the sailors as they headed toward him. He dove over the side into the frigid black water. His skin tingled from the cold and nearly rendered him immobile.

He broke the surface to shouts from the sailors above. He heard four more shots coming from the shore. It was time for him and Todd to get as far from there as possible before the sailors decided to start shooting back.

Todd struggled to keep his head above water, flailing like. . . like a drowning man.

"Give me your pack."

"No. It's everything I own."

It was filled with the food and supplies Conner had given him that morning. "It's pulling you down. I'll take it. I'm a better swimmer."

"You won't let it go?"

"I'll get it to shore. I promise." He wrestled the pack off the boy's back.

Todd was able to maneuver better.

"Head for shore." Conner swam with one arm and pulled the pack behind him.

When Todd said he swam a little, he meant a very little. Even with the pack, Conner beat the boy to shore. In waist deep water he tossed the pack onto the beach and reached back to help Todd wade to dry land. Todd collapsed on the ground. Conner knelt beside him. "You okay?"

Todd nodded. "Mr. Jackson, I have a confession to make. I can't swim."

This lad had more determination than stampeding cattle. Conner had to admire that. "Well, you did pretty well. Let's get going in case they decide to come find us." He hoisted the boy up, and the two staggered down the beach all the way to the back of the store.

Conner dropped the dripping pack inside the door and opened the potbelly stove. Embers still glowed. He added wood and blew on it until flames jumped to life.

Todd bent down and petted Fred, who was sniffing him. "It's real fortunate about those gunshots. They helped us get away."

"They weren't fortunate; they were Martin. He should be at the front." He started walking. "Come along, and we'll find you some dry clothes to wear."

He opened the front door, but Martin wasn't waiting for him. Martin should have beaten them here. Unless Martin didn't realize he'd gotten off the ship already.

He turned to Todd. "Look through the Levis and shirts and find yourself something that fits. You stay here."

"Where are you going?"

"Those gunshots were from my assistant. I'm going to find him." He wasn't going to save Todd just to lose Martin.

He got to the building he'd hid behind with Martin and watched the scurry of men on the dock and ship. Had they caught Martin? He raked a hand through his hair. He loathed the thought of going back aboard. Escaping once had been a miracle. Escaping twice? Impossible.

"Conner," a voice whispered from the deepest shadow.

"Martin?" When he saw Martin stand and could make out a few dim features, relief filled him. "I was afraid they got you."

"They almost did. I scared a cat out of the corner, and they thought that was all that was back here. Did you find him?"

"He's back at the store. Let's go."

"You're all wet."

"We had to jump ship."

Once he got Todd settled in his own bed, sent Martin home, and got into some dry clothes, Conner walked uptown and stood outside Vivian's house. He could see her kneeling on the widow's walk, so he stayed in the shadows. What was she doing?

She stood and went back inside.

"I love you," he whispered into the night. Even though he knew she couldn't hear him, he felt better for having voiced it. Now he could go back and sleep.

Chapter 10

A week after receiving Randolph's satchel, Conner had read through the log. It spoke of nothing personal, only business about the ship and crew, but as he closed it, he noticed the corner of a paper sticking out from the back cover. He pulled it out. An envelope with Vivian's name on it. His heart skipped a beat. Randolph's last words to Vivian. His wife.

He couldn't forget that. She'd been Randolph's wife and still was while she wore mourning clothes for him.

He turned the letter over and over in his hands. What had Randolph said to her? Should he give it to her? It was in the back of the ship's logbook. Did Randolph mean for it to be there? The boy hadn't given him any message to pass on to Vivian. He did know two things: He desperately wanted to know what was in this letter, and he didn't want to give it to Vivian.

After he closed up shop the next day, Conner felt awful from lack of sleep. He'd waffled in his decision about giving Vivian the letter. When he finally had fallen off to sleep, Fred had spent half the night chasing a rat, which she caught and killed.

He saddled Dakota and rode up to Vivian's. The letter was none of his business. Whether Randolph knew it was there or not and whether he intended for Vivian to have it or not, it belonged to her. He believed that God had made sure it reached him so he could give it to Vivian.

Scotty was in front of the house pulling weeds when Conner rode up. "I figured it was about time for you to be arriving."

Was he becoming that predictable? "How's she doing today?" He swung down off his horse.

"Maggie's not fussing, so Mrs. Carlyle must be fine." Scotty took Dakota's reins. "Go on in. Maggie's expecting you."

Very predictable, but as long as no one minded, he wasn't going to change.

Maggie met him in the foyer and took his overcoat. "Mrs. Carlyle's in the parlor. Go right in. Supper will be ready shortly."

"Maggie? Should I not come over every evening?" He held his breath for fear of the answer. Why had he even asked?

"You always came before the captain was married and then after he married, so why not now? He would like that you are looking after Miss Vivian. You were a brother to him. She has no other visitors because of the mourning time. It does her good to have daily company. It does us all good." Maggie hung his coat on the entry rack. "I feel better knowing you are aware of her daily moods. She's been doing real well since those first few days."

"Maggie, I believe her mental state is fine." Except for maybe not minding that she wasn't included in her husband's will—that still bothered him—but he'd taken care of it.

"Sometimes a widow looks fine but something's brewing inside, and one day she just snaps. I don't want nothing to happen to Mrs. Carlyle. She's a good woman."

That she was. "I'll tell her that supper is almost ready."

"Thank you." Maggie nodded and headed back toward the kitchen.

When he entered, Vivian sat on the settee, working blue spun truck into a mitten with four thin knitting needles. "Maggie says supper will be soon."

Vivian looked up through sorrow-filled eyes. "Thank you. It's so good of you to come. Please sit down."

How had he not noticed her downhearted countenance? Was it the will or something else? "Are you feeling all right?"

She tried to smile, but it didn't reach her eyes. "I'm fine."

Something was troubling her. "Have you spoken to Mr. Benton about petitioning the courts to initiate the unsigned will?"

"Yes." She set her knitting aside and stood. "I told him to destroy it."

He turned her around by the shoulders and heard Randolph's voice in his head. *Don't touch her. Don't ever touch her.* He took his hands away. "Why?"

"I can't explain it. I just know that things are the way they are as God has ordered them."

"Is that why you're sad?"

"I'm not sad."

"It's in your eyes."

"I'm tired of being cooped up, and when I do go out, being expected to behave the grieving widow. I am very sorry Randolph died, but I hardly knew him. I know more about you than I did my own husband. I hope you don't tire of my somber mood. I need your friendship even if it's only because of your loyalty to my husband."

"I'm your friend, too."

"I hope you don't think me a terrible person because I didn't love Randolph."

He couldn't tell her he felt a measure of relief knowing her heart wasn't broken. "I could never think you terrible. Speaking of Randolph, you know the young man I told you about from his ship?"

"The one you rescued, hired, and is now living above your store?" She gave him a genuine smile.

That's right, he'd told her. . .more than once. He needed more sleep so he could think more clearly. "I found this in the back of the ship's log." He pulled the envelope from his jacket pocket and handed it to her.

She seemed to pale slightly. "Thank you." She took it over to the writing desk and set it there.

"Aren't you going to read it?"

"I'll read it later." She put on a smile.

Of course, in private. She wouldn't want to read it in front of him even if he wanted her to read it aloud so he would know what it said and could see her reaction.

Maggie came in announcing supper was ready and breaking the tension that had shot between them.

He seated Vivian at the far end of the table, and took the seat across from her, leaving Randolph's seat on the end empty. . .between them, a reminder of who they each were and who they were to each other. He said grace, and they ate in silence for a while.

"Conner, I have made acquaintance with a widow in need. If I send her to your store, will you reduce the price on the food and other items she needs?" Then she added quickly, "I'll pay the difference."

When had she had an opportunity to meet someone? "No need. Give me her name, and I'll sell her whatever she needs at my cost." There it was again. In her time of loss, Vivian was thinking of others.

"So where did you meet this widow?" He took a bite of his roast meat, hoping the action would make his question seem more casual.

"Maggie found her, and I commissioned this dress. She's a wonderful seamstress.

Her name is Abigail Parker."

So Maggie had met this woman. It would still be only a matter of time before Vivian met others or renewed old acquaintances. Some possible suitors. In a town comprised of so many unmarried men, she would have her pick of several eligible bachelors. He needed to make sure he was always close at hand to size up his competition. He needed to make sure Vivian continued to look to him for support.

The next day, Sunday, Conner escorted Vivian to church. She hadn't been in nearly a month since hearing about Randolph's death. It was time to return, though she both longed for the fellowship and dreaded the false well-wishers. It was customary for society folks to leave their cards at the house of a family in mourning to let them know they were thinking of them. When she was up to receiving visitors, she only had to send word and the visitors would flood in. . .out of proper etiquette and not real concern. She wasn't up for their false niceties. She could put them off for at least six months. They would probably prefer it.

Conner had dinner with her and spent the afternoon. She was grateful for his company. He alone knew she hadn't been in love with Randolph and seemed to accept it well. She didn't have to pretend grieving more deeply than she felt. And she didn't have to feign politeness.

Conner stayed for supper, as well, and retired in the parlor afterward with her. He seemed hesitant to leave. She wasn't eager for him to leave, either. She was sure he had better things to do than look after her all day, his only day of rest. He worked too hard and looked tired.

"I've been meaning to ask you something. Actually, it's more of a curiosity. Randolph's letter to you—I'm not asking to read it, but I was wondering if it was a comfort to you."

"Oh that." She would like to say she'd forgotten about it, but the truth was she was avoiding it. "Um, I haven't read it yet."

He pointed toward the writing desk. "You set it aside. I'm not surprised you forgot about it."

Did he really believe a wife, even one not in love with her husband, could forget about such a letter? It haunted her. A voice from the grave calling to her. Condemning her.

"Would you like me to leave now so you can read it?"

"That's not necessary." She didn't want him to leave. This big house was lonely. She wasn't ready to step back into society. The only people she really felt comfortable with were Maggie, Scotty, her new friend Abigail, and, of course, Conner.

Conner left at the stroke of nine as was his habit. She stared at the letter on the writing desk, wanting to pass it by and continue ignoring it. She wasn't anxious to find out what Randolph's last words were to her, but she knew that Conner would ask her again. She couldn't feign forgetfulness again. She took the letter, went up to her room, and turned it over in her hands. *What do you have to say to me, Randolph?*

A knock on her door startled her. She shoved the letter under her pillow. "Come in."

Maggie entered. "I came to help you out of your dress."

She smiled. "I don't know what I'd do without you. Thank you for everything you do around the house and for me."

"It's my job," Maggie said matter-of-factly as she unhooked the back of Vivian's bodice.

"It's more than that. When William and Sarah get here, I'll highly recommend that they keep you on."

"You won't be staying in the house?"

She inhaled deeply so Maggie could unhook her corset. When she was freed, she could speak. "Captain Carlyle left the house to his brother."

"What about you? Where will you to live?" Maggie sucked in a deep breath. "I'm sorry.

That's not my place."

"Randolph left me some money." She stepped out of the skirt and handed it to Maggie. "I'll be fine."

Maggie hung the dress in the closet. "This is a beautiful dress Widow Parker made."

"She does very fine work."

"Would you like me to turn down the bed?"

"No," she said too sharply, then schooled herself. "You've done enough. Go off to bed yourself." She didn't want Maggie to find the letter from Randolph.

Maggie nodded and opened the door. "I'll see you in the morning."

"Good night, Maggie."

Maggie closed the door behind her.

Vivian slipped off her undergarments and into her nightgown and dressing robe. She took the letter from beneath her pillow and sat on the red velvet fainting couch. Her hands shook, and she was suddenly cold. Determined to get this over with, she broke Randolph's blue wax seal.

Vivian,

I am a man torn in two. I long to be with you and hold you, but when I think of what you have done, what you were, I can't stand the thought of you. I have tried to tell myself you are not that other person, but I can only see you in the arms of other men. My mother was a harlot as you were. I could see no excuse then for her to do that, and I can see no excuse now why you should have done it.

I cannot reconcile this. You are not the woman I thought I was marrying. I can't live with you, but I fear that neither can I live without you. I have tried to come to terms with it, but I'm struggling. You have given me a weight that is too much for me to bear. What you told me broke me.

I will divorce you quietly and give you passage to anywhere. I will also provide you with a small stipend as long as you don't return to your former life.

R

Vivian set the letter down and let the tears well in her eyes. Had Randolph stayed on his ship knowing it would likely sink because her secret had been too much for him to bear? She shook her head. He was a good man and a good captain. He would never abandon his ship, just as he wouldn't completely abandon her even though he couldn't forgive her.

She felt the weight of her secret lift from her. Randolph had released her, and she could tell Conner that Randolph's letter had brought her comfort, a sad sort of comfort. She could finally put her past behind her and remember it no more. Or at least try.

Chapter 11

On Monday, Conner took Randolph's ledger over to Carlyle Shipping. Jonathan Kirkide once again showed him to Mr. Abernathy's office.

Mr. Abernathy stood when he entered. "Back so soon?"

"I just received some things from Captain Carlyle's ship. I wanted to compare this to the ones here." He held up the ledger. "Will Miss Demarco mind me interrupting her?"

"She's out sick today. Go right on in." Mr. Abernathy opened the adjoining door for him. "I have to go out. I'll be back later this afternoon if you need anything."

Conner sat at Miss Demarco's desk and found the most recent ledger. He tried to match up entries. After a half hour, he wasn't so sure that Randolph's ship ledger was a record of the shipping business. He needed to get back to his store, so he took both ledgers. Mr. Abernathy wasn't back yet. He stopped at Jonathan Kirkide's desk on his way out. "Tell Mr. Abernathy I have one of the ledgers."

The young man nodded.

He stopped by the accounting office that took care of his store's books. "Paul, would you look at these two ledgers and tell me if you think they cover the same entries?"

"I can't today, but I'll look at them later this week."

"That will be fine."

Maggie was boiling laundry in a large kettle over the fire when Vivian stepped into the kitchen.

Maggie pushed damp tendrils of hair off her moist forehead with her forearm. "It was awful nice of you to pay Mrs. Parker so generously."

"She did excellent work. She deserved it."

Maggie raised her eyebrows but didn't voice an opinion.

"Sometimes a person just needs a little help before they can get back on their feet. I don't want Abigail to despair." She took her basket out of the cupboard.

"With a friend like you, how could she?" Maggie stepped away from the steaming water. "I made extra scones this morning. The ones with sausage and cheese in them. I have some oatmeal cookies. Here is a pint of milk and some butter for the scones."

"Maggie, you're spoiling those children."

"Humph. I don't see how you can spoil children who have no home. You could bring them back here to live."

She'd thought of that. "They are good children, but what if they accidentally do something to the house? It belongs to William. I couldn't in good conscience do anything that might result in damage to his property. I'll just have to think of something else." She added some cheese to her basket and headed over to Abigail's home before going down to the water.

Abigail welcomed her warmly. "I'll make us some tea. I have some dried spearmint and rose hip from my garden." She headed through the living room with only a rocking chair in it toward the kitchen. "I've had to sell some of the furniture."

Vivian followed Abigail into the kitchen. "I'll help." It looked as though Abigail had had to sell more than some furniture.

"I'm sorry I don't have any baked goods today, but I do have some applesauce I canned."

She took a jar from her sparse cupboard. "I could quickly mix some of this up into apple cinnamon muffins."

"The applesauce will be fine." She hadn't realized Abigail had so very little.

Abigail prepared the tea then brought two cups over to the table and sat. "I haven't had a visitor since before Harrison died."

How sad.

"No one quite knows what to say to a widow, so they say nothing at all. They give you a sad look and a wan smile."

Yes, she'd experienced a little of that the few times she'd encountered people. She was grateful they stayed at bay. She didn't know what to say to them, either. She'd thought she'd been successfully avoiding people. It seemed to go both ways. She took a sip of her tea. "I spoke with my friend at Jackson's General Store in town. He will give you a reduced price on everything you buy."

"Can he do that?"

"He's the owner. Just ask for Conner Jackson and tell him you're my friend."

Tears glistened in Abigail's blue eyes. "Thank you. It's plain to see that we are at the end of our means. To have my few pennies buy more food for Harry means more to me than I can put into words."

Vivian knew all too well how far a small bit of help went toward strengthening one's hope. She would have to think of a way to do more to help Abigail help herself. Maybe find her a permanent job. "How soon do you have to move from your house?"

Abigail looked away then said, "About a month. I'm hopeful the Lord will provide a place for us."

Which she would guess meant it was probably less than a month. Abigail was trying to look at things in the best light so they didn't appear so bleak. Vivian knew how that was. She wanted to invite Abigail and Harry home with her, but she didn't feel that would be right considering it was William's house now. What would Abigail and her son do when William arrived and Vivian had to leave? Abigail coming to live with her wasn't the right solution, but she'd take them in before she'd let them be booted out on the streets like the orphans she was on her way to see. "I have something for you. I'll be right back." She went out to the carriage where Scotty waited, brushing Honey. "I'll be ready to leave in a minute."

Scotty nodded.

She took out the five cheese wedges and went back inside the house. "Here. I know it's not much, but it will help."

Abigail took the wrapped cheese. "Thank you."

"I need to be going, but I'll pray for you and Harry."

"Thank you. That means more to me than the food."

She took her leave and headed straight down to the rocky beach. Everyone came but George. He was getting steady work at the dock, unloading ship's cargo. He was a good boy, and she prayed he would be satisfied with the work and not get into trouble.

Peter stood directly in front of her as she handed out scones and cookies. While the others went a few feet away to sit and eat, Peter stood, staring at her. "I don't got a tooth for you. I tried and tried, but none of 'em would come loose."

She smiled at him. "That's okay. I have something for you."

The others looked up expectantly.

She pulled out a penny for each of them. "And, Peter, I want you to give George his penny."

"Why? He gots a job. They give him lots of pennies, and nickels and dimes, too."

"Because one of those pennies is his. If you keep it, you'll be stealing."

He nodded sadly, staring down at the two coppery coins in his hand. "I'll give him the not so shiny one, on account he has so many."

She knew George didn't just keep the money he earned. She wondered if he spent it all on himself or if he shared with the others. Maybe with her bringing food for them all, George would be generous, too. Then it made her mad. George was just a boy; he shouldn't have to be trying to provide for the other four.

Betsy brought over her fabric pieces. "I sewed them together just like you showed me."

The stitches were uneven, loose in some places and tight in others. "Very good."

"I even sewed a button back on Tommy's shirt." Betsy pulled Tommy over to show off her handiwork.

Threads stuck out from under the button, and the fabric was puckered where some of the stitches were too wide and pulled too tight. "That was very ingenious of you to try that without being shown." Vivian pulled out more fabric pieces. "When you are sewing these together, I want you to concentrate on making all your stitches the same size. Then sew these pieces to the ones you sewed before."

Betsy seemed eager to try, and soon the children scattered.

Chapter 12

Conner stood in the middle of his store with Martin. It was nearing closing on Wednesday and unusually quiet, but he knew he'd likely get a last-minute rush. "I want to move all these center displays a little closer together so we can squeeze in more supplies for the miners heading to Alaska. I have a large shipment coming in tomorrow, and I want to get as much of it inside the store as possible."

Martin's gaze shifted from him and was clearly focused on the door.

He turned to see what had captured Martin's attention. A pretty young blond lady stood near the door, the reason for Martin's dumb smile. "Would you go see to that customer?"

Martin looked at him. "What? I'm sorry. What did you say?"

Conner smiled. "We have a customer. Would you go see what she needs?"

Martin's smile broadened. "Yes, sir." He hastened to the front and the beautiful lady.

Conner took a measuring stick from behind the counter and began measuring the floor space between displays. He wrote the numbers on the sketch of the store's floor plan that he'd attached to his clipboard.

"She asked for you by name." Martin looked downtrodden.

That wasn't his fault. He strode toward the woman, who now had five miners hovering around her. What a pretty woman did for business. "I'm Conner Jackson. May I help you?" He guided her away from the men.

"I'm Abigail Parker. Mrs. Carlyle said you were a generous man and wouldn't charge me as high prices as some of the other stores."

Ah, so this was the widow Vivian had asked him to help. "I would be more than happy to accommodate you. I'm going to have my assistant help you while I see to these men."

He went back to Martin, who was sulking where he'd left him. "Widow Parker is to have everything she needs, and only charge her my cost for the items, but don't tell her that."

Martin nodded lethargically.

He snapped his fingers in front of Martin. "I want you to help her."

Martin stood up straighter.

"Any time she comes into the store, either you or I will assist her."

Martin's smile returned, and he swaggered back to Mrs. Parker.

That evening when Conner arrived, Vivian opened the door, glad to see him.

He held a box in his arms. "Your order. Most of it is here. The rest will be coming soon."

"I'd nearly forgotten about that. Just set it here in the foyer." She didn't want to open it now. She'd bought a pocket watch as a Christmas present for Randolph among other things for him. Maybe she'd give them to William when he arrived. "Supper is almost ready. Shall we go directly into the dining room?"

He nodded, looking so tired.

He sat across the table from her. Even after Randolph's death, Conner had continued his habit of stopping by every evening to check up on her. She made Maggie hold supper until he arrived so she could invite him to stay. Being in mourning didn't afford her much company, and for that she was glad. She didn't want to start socializing any sooner than was necessary.

"How is your business doing? There seems to be a steady stream of miners flowing through town."

Conner's eyebrows tightened. "You could only know that if *you've* been downtown again. I told you to stay up here where you're safer."

"I could have heard it from someone."

"You haven't been accepting visitors yet, so you could only know if you've gone downtown."

She squared her shoulders. "I could have heard from Scotty or Maggie."

He narrowed his eyes. "But you didn't. You've been downtown recently."

"Don't scold me." Let him believe it was just once, recently. He would really scold her if he knew it was most days.

"I hope you at least let Scotty drive you in the carriage."

She nodded. "Maggie insisted." She wanted to get the focus off her. "So, your business is doing well."

He looked at her over the rim of his water goblet while he took a long slow drink. She could tell he was making her wait. Probably considering whether to answer her question or scold her. She was a grown woman of twenty-five, and she could go downtown if she wanted. She didn't need his permission, but for some reason, she wanted his approval. Maybe by having Conner's approval, she somehow gained Randolph's.

Conner finally and carefully set his glass back down. "Business is very good. Your friend made quite a stir at my store today."

She raised her eyebrows. "My friend?"

"Your widow friend, Mrs. Parker."

She couldn't imagine Abigail causing any kind of fuss. "How on earth could she have caused you trouble? She is the sweetest thing."

"A beautiful young woman like that? All she had to do was walk through my door." A smile played at the corners of his mouth.

Her insides twisted. Was Conner attracted to Abigail? No, he wouldn't be. He couldn't be. Conner took a bite of his chicken, still smiling.

Something curled up inside her. It couldn't be. But it was. She was jealous that another woman had caught Conner's eye. She lost her appetite and dropped her gaze to her plate, moving her peas around with her fork. "So..." She didn't know what to say without sounding jealous. "You were able to help her?"

"Once I got her away from the gawking miners and had Martin assist her. I told Martin to discount all her purchases."

She looked up. "Martin?"

He nodded. "You should have seen the way he looked at her. That man is smitten with Widow Parker. I hope she doesn't come by very often. I'll not get a lick of work out of him when she's around."

She smiled. "Martin."

He frowned. "I hope you don't mind me handing her off to him."

"No." She took a bite of peas. Her appetite returned as quickly as it had vanished.

"Good, because I haven't seen Martin this interested in a lady before."

"Oh no. He can't be sweet on her."

"Why?"

"He'll get his heart broken. Abigail doesn't want a suitor. She's still grieving her loss and never wants to marry again." She felt bad for Martin pining for a woman who wouldn't be interested.

"I'll let Martin know to give her some time. Maybe he can change her mind about marriage." His words almost seemed to have a twofold meaning, but she didn't know why.

"I'm not so sure."

"Don't you think widows should marry again?" The intensity with which he asked took her back a little. He was a bit eager for Martin.

"It's not that. She was pretty sure of herself. And I was married before Randolph and widowed, so I obviously approve of marrying again."

Conner stabbed a piece of chicken. "Will you marry again?" He quickly put the bite into his mouth.

She couldn't tell what his interest was in asking that question. Was it simply because she was the wife of his good friend, or was it personal? "If the right man stole my heart. I wouldn't rush into it as I did with Randolph just for the security of being married." Would Conner protest if she decided to marry again?

He nodded but kept his focus on his plate.

For the first time, she felt awkward with Conner. "Did Martin get on well with Harry?"

He looked up then. "Who's Harry?"

"Abigail's son. He wasn't with her?"

He shook his head. "He can't be very old."

"He's about four. Will Martin care if she has a child?"

He shrugged. "I don't know, but I'll tell him so he's prepared."

"If Martin really wants to win Abigail's heart, he has to accept her son. If a woman has to choose between her child and a new man, she will choose her child."

"It sounds like finding a husband when you already have children has its challenges. But you won't have that worry."

She didn't need that reminder and wanted to talk about something else. "I received a letter from William."

Conner finally looked up from his plate. "What does he have to say?"

"He told me to stay in the house until he and Sarah can visit in the spring."

"Why so long?"

A smile forced its way to her mouth. "They're going to wait until after the baby is born."

"I'm happy for them." He pushed his empty plate forward and crossed his forearms in front of him on the table. "I know you asked me not to, but I wrote to William and told him about your being left out of Randolph's will. I know he'll give you what's due to you, as I will."

"Randolph left his wealth to you and William, and that's where it'll stay. I won't accept it." She had guilt enough over deceiving Randolph. His money and possessions would only be a reminder of her deception.

"I promised Randolph before he left that I'd look out for you. Seeing that you get your share of what was his is what he'd want me to do."

She raised her voice slightly. "You have no idea what he would have wanted." She didn't need Conner to force more guilt upon her.

"I don't want to fight with you, but if it's the only way to make you see reason, then I will. I will see that you are taken care of whether you like it or not."

"I have a headache. Good evening." She stood and left the room.

Vivian climbed the steps back up to the street level from the beach. Only Betsy and Peter had come today. Scotty stood next to the carriage ready to help her inside. She had another errand she wanted to accomplish while she was downtown. Not really an errand, but someone to see.

"I'm going into Mr. Jackson's mercantile." Since Conner already knew she came downtown, he couldn't be any more upset at her.

"I'll drive you."

"I'll walk." It was only a block down, but Scotty drove the carriage on the street next to her the whole way. She smiled at him before entering the store.

A short dark-haired man with deep-set black eyes approached her. "May I help you?" He openly gawked at her from head to toe.

"Owen, finish unloading that crate over there." Martin glared at the shorter man then turned back to her. "I'm sorry about that. Owen is only supposed to be stocking the shelves. How may I help you, Mrs. Carlyle?"

"I'm looking for Mr. Jackson."

"He's in the back disposing of some spoiled produce." Martin glanced at the three men who just entered the store. "I need to see to these customers. If you go straight back, you should find him."

"Thank you. I'll manage." Martin was a good man.

She found Conner hoisting a small crate and headed for the open back door.

"Hello."

He turned to her and smiled. "Hello."

That same feeling about him that she'd had last night warmed her insides. Last night it had come in the form of jealousy; today it was more of a satisfying comfort. "What are you doing?"

"Bad fruit and vegetables. I can't sell them, so I'm disposing of them."

She picked up one of the apples. It had a large bruise on one side but the rest was still good. "Some of this isn't so bad." She knew five children who would love to have all this wasted food, but how could she get it away from Conner without telling him about her almost daily visits to the beach? "There are needy people who wouldn't mind a bruise or two."

He set the box outside the back door and closed it then went to the window. "Watch."

It was hard to lean over far enough to see out the window.

Conner grabbed her hand. "This isn't going to work. We have to hurry." He pulled her behind him up the stairs to his apartment and over to the window. He pointed. "There. They're coming already."

She smiled when she saw Samuel and Tommy running across the beach behind Conner's store. She lost sight of them when they were right up next to the building, but in a moment, they each had a side of the crate and were carrying it off. Were they waiting for Conner to leave the food? Is that why they hadn't shown up on the other beach for her today?

"I don't know who they are, but sometimes there is a smaller boy and sometimes a girl."

Peter and Betsy. She knew who they were but thought it best not to reveal that to Conner. "That's very sweet of you to help out those children."

"I wish I could do more."

"To someone who is homeless, offering a bite to eat can mean everything." When Conner raised an eyebrow in question, she quickly added. "Or so I'd think." She did not want to explain how she knew that food was very important to the homeless and hungry.

Conner continued to look at her with one eyebrow raised. "What are you doing downtown?"

"Don't scold me. I wanted to see you." She wanted to see if the feelings of affection she'd felt last night were still with her today. And they were. That made her happy.

"I'll come by around supper. You shouldn't be down here."

"I have Scotty with me. I wanted to see if the rest of my catalog order came in."

"Since last night? I'll personally deliver it to you." Conner went to the stairs to take her back down.

She glanced around Conner's small space: a table with two chairs, a narrow bed, a braided rug on the floor. It was homey and had a warmth that her large house didn't have.

He led her outside and helped her into the carriage. "Please stay uptown so I don't worry over your well-being."

"I'm bored up there. I want something useful to do. I promise if I come downtown, I won't come without Scotty, so you needn't worry." But she could tell by the look on his face that he would still worry, and she liked the idea of Conner caring about her well-being.

Chapter 13

On Friday morning soon after Martin arrived at Conner's store, Conner went over to his accountant's office at Paul's request. "Something isn't right with these two sets of books," Paul explained. "I'd like to go over to the shipping office and look at the rest of the records."

"I'll take you over any time you want."

"I have the rest of the day to devote to this, so I can go now."

Conner put both ledgers in the satchel Todd Major had used to deliver the one ledger. He and Paul went across the street to the livery to get their horses then rode to Carlyle Shipping.

"Paul, this is Jonathan Kirkide. Jonathan, we need to see Mr. Abernathy."

Jonathan's gaze darted from him to Paul and back again. "Mr. Abernathy's not here."

"Where did he go?"

"I don't know. He was here Wednesday morning when I arrived but left shortly afterward. I haven't seen him since."

"He's been gone since Wednesday and no one told me?"

"I didn't know what to do." Jonathan looked down nervously. "He's only been out one full day. Is something wrong? Is he all right?"

Conner had a gut feeling something was decidedly wrong. "Is Miss Demarco here?"

"She was here on Tuesday, but that's the only day I saw her."

"Come on, Paul. I smell a skunk." He strode down the hallway to the warehouse.

"Am I still going to get paid?" Jonathan called after him.

He ignored the young man for now. He needed to find out if his suspicions were true. Taking the stairs up to the manager's office two at a time, Conner went straight to the safe. The door was closed tight. Paul came in with Jonathan right behind him.

"I'm sorry I didn't tell you about Mr. Abernathy. I didn't know anything was wrong." Jonathan's voice quavered with worry.

"Do you know the combination to this safe?"

Jonathan shook his head vigorously as though he'd been accused of stealing from it.

"Go back to your desk." When Jonathan just stood there, he added, "Yes, you'll get paid." *Provided you had nothing to do with whatever went on here.*

"Paul, the ledgers and other records are in this room." He showed Paul to Miss Demarco's office. "Here are the two you've already looked at." He took them from the satchel and handed them to him.

Paul sat behind the desk and began sorting through the mess.

Conner went down to the warehouse floor and spoke to the first man he met. "Who's the foreman?"

The man pointed to a broad-shouldered, squat man who couldn't have been more than five feet six inches but had muscles enough for three men. "You the foreman?"

"Aye, Collin O'Keefe." He had a strong Irish accent.

"Conner Jackson, one of the new owners."

"I heard we had a new boss. I was sorry to hear about the captain. He was a good man."

"Thank you. You look like you're still working orders."

"No thanks to the dandy." He thumbed up toward the office. "I've been going up there to find the orders. If you ask me, I don't think he's coming back."

"Why do you say that?"

"I haven't seen him since the other morning. He was acting real squirrelly since Monday, like someone put clinkers in his drawers and he didn't want no one to know about it."

Conner had brought the ship's ledger over on Monday morning. "Do you know the combination to the safe in Mr. Abernathy's office?"

O'Keefe shook his head. "As far as I know, *Mr.* Dandy and the captain were the only two who knew that."

Conner turned away frustrated.

"But I could get a couple of my men, and we could blow it open."

He smiled. He liked O'Keefe. "Let me check with the captain's widow. Maybe she has the combination." He went back up to the office. "Paul, I'm going over to Mrs. Carlyle's house to see if she has the combination to this safe." He heard a rush of footsteps on the stairs and went to meet the men in the other office, the crowd of men.

O'Keefe had his hand on the shoulder of a beanpole of a man who was nearly a foot taller. "Tim here says he can crack the safe without dynamite."

Tim straightened his shoulders. "I always had real good hearing."

Conner nodded for the man to go ahead.

Tim knelt down by the safe and put his ear to it, slowly turning the knob, then looked back at the crowd. "Shhh." The full room fell dead silent. He went back to work.

Paul entered from the other office. "Conner."

The whole room turned to Paul. "Shhh!"

Paul closed his mouth.

Tim frowned then continued. He pulled his head away from the safe and turned the handle, but the safe didn't open. He tried several more times, and the crowd started murmuring restlessly.

O'Keefe waved his hand. "All right. Show's over. Back to work."

Conner shook Tim's hand before he left. "Thanks for trying."

O'Keefe was the last to leave. "Let me know if you want my men and me to blow it." He walked out.

Conner needed to get the combination and see inside the safe but turned to Paul. "What did you need?"

Paul opened the ledger. "Look here in the binding. See that number?"

He saw the number eight crammed in the centerfold of the pages. "What's it mean?"

"I noticed them when I was looking at this ledger earlier this week." Paul flipped a few pages and showed him a number eleven in the crack then several pages later a twenty-six. "Those are the only three, and they don't seem to have a purpose."

"Unless. . ."

Paul smiled. "Exactly."

Conner knelt down and tried a few different sequences of the numbers in the ledger's centerfold until the safe opened. As he suspected, no cash. He pulled out a pile of papers and receipts and put them on the desk. "Let me know what you make of these."

"I'll come by your store at the end of the day and report what I find."

He shook Paul's hand. "Thank you."

The day dragged with few customers. Conner wanted to go back to the shipping warehouse but was afraid the store might get busy and overwhelm Martin and Todd. Owen and Hansel had signed on with a ship and left a week ago. Paul showed up at closing as promised.

Conner sent Martin home, locked up, and showed Paul to his office.

"I haven't been able to go through everything, but it looks like it's as we suspected. According to the receipts, there should have been over five hundred dollars in the safe. I think there is normally more, but a large sum of cash was paid out for an order. I'm going to compare some of the figures with the bank on Monday. I think we'll find that Mr. Abernathy and Miss Demarco were taking advantage of the owner being out to sea much of the time."

"Thanks, Paul. O'Keefe seemed like a decent fellow. I'll put him in charge for now, and I'll be spending more time over there."

Paul left for home, and a short while later, Conner headed to Vivian's.

Chapter 14

Conner looked up just as Vivian glided through the doorway of his store. Was she trying to drive him crazy? *Stay uptown.* What was so hard about that? He would just have to be sterner with her. He would forbid her from coming downtown. It was for her own safety. With his resolve bolstered, he strode toward her. "Vivian."

"Conner." She smiled up at him, and his resolve melted.

It was so very pleasant to see her in the middle of the day. His voice softened. "What are you doing here?"

"I need your help."

He folded his arms. He couldn't look like the pushover he was around her. "With what?"

"I'm looking for a house."

He smiled. "You have a house."

"Technically, until William and Sarah come. I'm looking for a different house. Well, actually I found one. I want you to take a look at it and tell me what you think."

He leaned a little closer, and his heartbeat quickened. "I can tell you what I think: Stay in the house you have."

"Oh." She looked a little flustered.

Good. Maybe she'd stay where she was safe.

She straightened and seemed to pull her thoughts together. "This house isn't for me. I've sent a telegram to William to see if I can use some of the money Randolph left him to open an orphanage. The Randolph Carlyle Home for Children. I haven't heard back from him yet, but I'm sure he'll say yes."

"You want to run an orphanage?" She couldn't be serious.

"Not me. I want to open it and have someone else run it."

She better not be thinking of him for the job. He was already juggling two, and not very well at that. "Do you realize what kind of undertaking that will be?"

"That's why I'm asking you for help. I know you have your store and the shipping company, but I was hoping you'd have a little time for this."

Time was one thing he needed more of not less of. "When you find someone respectable to run it, I'll help you." That ought to hold her off for a little while. Hopefully months, until William arrived.

"Mrs. Parker. She has a son to care for and is about to be evicted from her house. I've seen her with her own child, so I know she'll be caring to the children."

"Children? Are you thinking about those two boys who took the food from my back porch?" It had evidently been a bad idea to let her see the needy children.

She nodded. "Sam and Tommy, but also Betsy, Peter, and George."

He couldn't believe she knew their names. "After I told you about them, you went out and found them?"

She opened her mouth, closed it, opened it, then pursed her lips shut.

"Vivian, what have you done?"

"I met them about a month before I knew you were feeding them." She gave him an "I'm sorry but not really sorry" sort of smile.

"Met?" There was more to this than what she was telling him.

"I've been taking food to them down at the beach. They're hungry. Someone has to feed them."

"You've been going down to the beach? Alone? How often?"

"At first it was just once or twice a week."

"At first?" He rubbed his temples. "Please don't tell me you go every day."

"Okay." She bit her bottom lip.

It was every day. He groaned. She *was* trying to drive him crazy. And doing a good job of it. "Let's wait until spring. I'll have more time after William gets here to help with the shipping company. In the meantime, let me feed those children."

"They can't stay out all winter. They'll freeze and get sick."

He rubbed the back of his neck. "Fine. Get the house, and if William doesn't want to spend the money, I'll back you."

"I want you to come look at the house."

"Why, if it's the one you want?"

"I want you to look it over and tell me if it's worth the price they're asking."

He took a deep breath. She'd succeeded. He was crazy. "Tomorrow morning, first thing before I open."

"Thank you, Conner."

"Now will you go back uptown where you belong?"

She smiled and nodded.

So much for being stern.

Conner pushed on the stair railing going up to the porch of the house Vivian wanted for her orphanage. It was loose. The wood of the bottom step bowed under his weight. The front door stuck. Several windows were broken out.

"I know it needs a little paint, but Abigail, the children, and I can do most of it."

It needed more than a little paint. It probably needed a new roof. He didn't have time for this. "Why this house?"

She took his arm and pulled him through the house and out to the back. "It has a barn to put a milking cow, a chicken coop, a vegetable garden, and plenty of room for the children to run and play."

He could hardly think for her hand on his arm. He worked hard to focus on the building before him. The barn had no door, several boards were missing on the front, and who knew what kind of shape the inside was in. The chicken coop was broken down, and the garden hosted a variety of thick, prickly weeds. "This place needs a lot of work." And he'd likely be the one doing it.

"As long as the roof doesn't leak, Abigail and the children can move in and work on the rest later."

"And if the roof does leak?" Which he assumed it did.

"We can get a better price and have it fixed."

She meant he could fix it. "Fine. Negotiate a price."

"Me?"

"You're the one who wants the house." Vivian was a smart woman. He knew she could do this. She just needed a little confidence.

"But he'll give you a better price. He'll respect you because you're a man."

Unfortunately, she was right. And right now, the way she was looking at him with hope, biting her bottom lip, he could refuse her nothing. If he didn't start talking soon, his temptation to kiss her would overtake him. But then her black dress reminded him she was recently widowed, so he cleared his throat. "I'll go with you, but you make the deal. I'll fold my arms. When I think the price is fair, I'll unfold them."

She nodded reluctantly.

He strode back through the house. "Let's go." The sooner he was no longer alone with her and away from temptation, the safer he'd be.

Vivian stole a sideways glance at Conner as she stepped up onto the boardwalk across the street from the livery. He'd left her carriage and horse there for safekeeping while they were at the bank. Walking down the street with him was quite an education. She'd always thought Conner a handsome man, but every woman they passed assessed him. Some boldly turned their heads to get a better look. Others simply gave a dart of their gaze. It didn't seem to matter whether they were in the company of a man or not. Conner didn't seem to notice any of them. Why hadn't Conner ever married? He'd told Randolph not to bring him back a bride. Was there a special lady who was unreachable to him? Or had someone broken his heart, and had he then vowed never to love again? If she wasn't wearing black, maybe he could see her as more than just Randolph's widow. She hoped no one stole his heart before she could shed her mourning garb. She slipped her hand in the crook of his elbow to let the other ladies know that he might be taken.

She stopped short outside the bank door and took a deep breath. "What if William won't agree to the children's home?"

"Then I'll cover it."

She tilted her head back to get a better look at him. Just like that? He'd "cover it"? Did he have that kind of money?

He motioned for her to go through the open doorway as he held the door for her.

The clerk behind the cage window adjusted his glasses. "May I help you?"

She looked to Conner to answer. He raised his eyebrows, waiting for her to speak. She turned back to the clerk and took another deep breath. "I would like to see Mr. Olsen, the bank manager." She didn't know if she could do this. Mr. Olsen scared her. He always seemed to be frowning.

"Do you have an appointment?"

"No."

He left and came back a minute later. "Mr. Olsen has an opening tomorrow at one."

She looked up at Conner to see if that time was fine with him. His eyes were narrowed at the clerk, and he folded his arms. Did that mean she wasn't supposed to accept that? "I'd really like to see him today?" Her nerves made her words come out like a question. She wished she could take them back and try again.

The clerk seemed intimidated by Conner and left again. When he returned a moment later, he was on their side of the cage windows. "Right this way." He led them into the manager's office.

Frowning, Mr. Olsen stood, pressing the bridge of his glasses higher on his wrinkled nose. "Mrs. Carlyle, please do have a seat."

She sat.

"Mr. Jackson, won't you have a seat?"

"I'll stand. We haven't much time and need to get down to business."

Mr. Olsen kept his gaze on Conner. "What can I do for you?"

"It's Mrs. Carlyle who has come to do business."

Mr. Olsen raised his eyebrows but turned to her. "How may I help you?"

"How much is the house on Cherry Street?"

"You already own a house. Why would you want another?"

"I'm going to open a children's home."

Mr. Olsen narrowed his eyes in disapproval then quoted a price that was twice what Conner had told her would be fair.

She wasn't sure what to do. "Isn't that a bit high?"

"It sits on five acres, but for you, Mrs. Carlyle, I can come down." He quoted a price that was still high.

Conner's arms remained locked across his chest.

She took yet another deep breath. "Windows need to be replaced, the outbuildings are in disrepair. . .the whole house is in disrepair."

"I'm sorry. That's as low as I can go."

Conner put his hands on the desk and leaned forward. "Randolph Carlyle has done business at your bank for years, and this is the way you treat his widow, cheating her out of money for a rundown house that has been vacant for years?" He turned to her and held out his hand. "Let's go. This is a waste of your time."

She gave him a quizzical look but took his hand and stood. She wanted that house for the children. She would pay what Mr. Olsen was asking.

Conner opened the door for her.

"Wait."

She and Conner turned back to Mr. Olsen.

Mr. Olsen's frown had deepened. "How much are you willing to pay?"

She quoted in the middle of the range Conner had told her. He'd said to start at the bottom and work up, but she didn't want Mr. Olsen to laugh at her. Mr. Olsen countered. Conner finally unfolded his arms, and they settled on a price at the high end of the range Conner had given her.

"You drive a hard bargain, Mrs. Carlyle." Mr. Olsen almost smiled.

She couldn't have done it without Conner. They left. "Thank you, Conner. I have never done anything like that before."

"You did well. You were at a disadvantage. Mr. Olsen knows exactly what's in your bank account."

"But it's not my money. It's William's."

"He gave you power of attorney over it. And agrees with me that Randolph's unsigned will should be the legal one."

"Well, it's not."

Conner retrieved her carriage from the livery and drove her to his store. "You go straight home."

"I can't. I'm going over to Abigail's to tell her about the children's home."

Conner shook his head as he set the brake. "Did Mrs. Parker agree to run the children's home?"

"Not yet."

"How do you know she will accept the position?"

"Why wouldn't she? She's about to be thrown out of her house and has no family to go to."

Conner shook his head again. "I suppose there's no talking you into staying uptown, is there?"

She shook her head.

"Do you at least know how to handle a gun?"

She nodded.

"I'm going to give you one. Use it if you need to."

"I have one." She pulled her Derringer out of her skirt pocket.

He frowned at it. "That's only got one shot."

"The threat of one well-placed shot can deter any man."

He waggled his head back and forth. "Be careful."

"I always am."

Moments later, she pulled up in front of Abigail's house. A sign nailed over the For Sale sign read Sold. She knocked on the door.

Abigail's eyes were red rimmed and swollen when she answered.

Vivian immediately pulled her into a hug. "How long do you have?"

"Three days. I don't know where I'll go."

"Get Harry. I have something I want to show you." She drove Abigail to the house she'd just purchased.

"What do you say to being the headmistress at the Randolph Carlyle Children's Home?"

Abigail stared at her, then gaped openmouthed at the house. "You're opening an orphanage?"

"If you'll run it."

"Where are the children?"

"I don't exactly know. But I visit them at the beach. They must stay somewhere around there, but they can't stay out all winter. Please say you'll do it. Those children need you."

"Can I see the place?"

"Of course. It needs a few repairs, but I got a good price on it."

They walked around the two-story house: a parlor, dining room, kitchen, and bedroom on the first floor, and four bedrooms upstairs. When Abigail stepped out onto the back porch, which needed a whole railing replaced, she clapped her hands together. "Look, Harry, a barn, and we can put in a nice big vegetable garden to feed everyone."

Vivian smiled at Abigail's enthusiasm. "You and Harry can move in immediately, and as soon as I talk to the children, I'll bring them here, as well. The children may have to start out sleeping on the floor, but at least they will have a roof over their heads. And I'm sure the children will help clean up the place. I'll see that the windows get boarded up for now and replaced soon."

Abigail suddenly hugged her. "Thank you. This is the answer to all of my prayers, a place to live and meaningful work where I can keep Harry with me." Tears trickled down her face.

"This answers my prayers, too, for those children. How soon can you move in?"

"We don't have much anymore. With some help to move the beds and bureaus and kitchen table, we could be packed and moved in a day."

"That will be perfect. The children will have a place to live for Thanksgiving. I'll take you home to pack and make arrangements for the furniture."

Vivian left Abigail and Harry at their house to begin packing and headed to the beach. She sat there for half an hour before Betsy came with Peter.

"Where are the others?"

Peter held his hands in his armpits to keep them warm. "George is working. Sam and Tommy went up the beach."

She handed Peter the blue mittens she'd knitted. "I made these myself."

"Gee, thanks." Peter put them on.

"Betsy, I'll make your pair next."

Betsy nodded as she held a thin blanket tight around herself. "I'll see to it the others get the food you brought for them."

These poor, freezing children. She'd gotten the home just in time.

Peter stared at her basket. "Are we gonna pray or what?"

The three of them recited the short prayer, and she handed out the food. "How would you like to live in a house?"

"Don't got one," Peter said with crumbs tumbling from his mouth. He tried to catch them and eat them off his mitten.

"Would you like to live in one?"

"Your house? I know'd what it looks like on account of George took me there. He said a rich lady like you wouldn't never want a poor boy like me."

Her heart ached for these unwanted children. "I'm going to open a children's home, and all of you are invited to live there."

"You mean an orphanage?" Betsy asked.

She nodded.

"Are you going to be there?" Peter asked.

"No, but I found a really nice lady to take care of all of you."

"I don't like no orphanage ladies." Peter shoved his hands, mittens and all, into his pockets.

"Why? Have you lived in an orphanage before?"

"Nope, but George told me all about mean people at orphanages. I don't want to be chained in the root cellar with the rats and fed only bread and water if they remember to feed me at all."

Apparently, quiet George was quite the storyteller. "Mrs. Parker isn't like that. She's very kind. I promise she won't chain you in the cellar. She may make you scrub behind your ears."

Peter scrunched up his face.

"She has a son just about your age."

He widened his big brown eyes in interest.

These children needed more, so much more than just a roof over their heads.

Conner felt a tap on his shoulder. He turned from his customer to Martin.

"I'll help Mr. Fink. You're needed over there." Martin thumbed toward the front of the store.

Vivian stood with a young girl of about ten with a dirt-smudged face and dressed in ragged clothes. He recognized her as one of the children who had come to get food from his back porch on occasion and walked over to them. "Who is this lovely lady?"

The girl looked away, turning pink in the cheeks.

Vivian put an arm around her shoulders. "This is Betsy. She's going to live at the children's home."

Was she the only one? He'd thought Vivian said there were five children. Before he could ask how he could help them, Vivian spoke again.

"I need your help. The boys won't come. They would rather freeze to death this winter." Vivian's eyes were wide with concern.

"What do you think I can do?" He raked a hand through his hair. She was the one who knew the children; he'd only left food for them on his back porch.

"Talk to them. Maybe they'll listen to you."

If all the children didn't go to the home, Vivian would go back to the beach every day to feed them. It was in his best interest to see she didn't feel like she had to. He couldn't believe it when she had told him she'd been going down almost daily to the beach. . .by herself.

"I need to wait for Finn to get back from a delivery, then Martin and Todd can handle the store for a little while with Finn here to help." A warmth wrapped around his heart at her look of appreciation and relief.

"I'll take Betsy over to the home and come back."

He could read in her eyes that she didn't want Betsy to change her mind. He watched the door long after she'd left.

An hour or so later, Finn was back, business was slow, and Vivian walked back through his door. He called, "Let me grab my coat." He got it from the back and headed out the door with her.

When they arrived on the beach, Vivian sat on a drift log, and he stood next to her. "Do you think they will come?"

"I told Peter I would be back and that he should bring the other boys." Her eyes widened. "Oh look, here he comes." Disappointment crossed her fine features. "He's alone."

He turned and watched the boy approach slowly.

Peter stopped twenty feet away. "Who's he?"

"He's a friend of mine," Vivian said. "You can come closer."

Peter shook his head. "He might grab me and take me away."

Someone must have told this small tyke tales, so Conner sat on the log next to Vivian. "I promise not to grab you."

Peter stayed where he was. "What do you want?"

He could understand Peter's lack of trust all too well. The image of his mother's painted face popped into his thoughts. He pushed it away immediately. "I know you. Did you know that?"

Peter scrunched up his face and shook his head.

"I own the general store. You are one of the children who comes and takes food from my back steps."

Peter backed up a few steps. "We didn't steal nothing."

"I know. I left that food for you." He remembered what it was like to always have that empty, hungry pain in the pit of his stomach, wondering if it would ever go away. Pain so bad he had wondered if his gut was eating him from the inside out.

"You gived it to us on purpose?"

"I did."

Peter walked over and sat on the log next to Conner. "I liked the sweetbread best." Peter hadn't been an orphan so long that he was incapable of trusting adults.

"Where are Sam, Tommy, and George?" Vivian asked.

"Sam and Tommy are under the dock." He pointed to the shadows under the dock on the other end of the beach. "They won't come on account he's here. George said he ain't never going to an orphanage again, so there ain't no point."

So George was the leader of this little band of wayward children and the one who'd told them tales. "Will you go tell Sam and Tommy I'd like to talk to them?"

"Won't do no good. They won't go to an orphanage, neither." Peter leaned closer to him. "I like you. You didn't grab me or nothing."

He stifled a chuckle and reached into his pocket, pulled out a nickel, and handed it to Peter. "You tell Sam and Tommy I'll give them each one if they come over and talk to me."

Peter looked up at him with one eye squinted shut. "You got more of these?"

He pulled out two more nickels.

Peter's eyes rounded. He scooted off the log and ran across the sand shouting. "Sam, Tommy, you gotta come! Look what I got!"

Two boys came out from the shadows and gawked at Peter's nickel. The threesome started walking in their direction, Peter in front and Tommy and Sam cautiously behind.

"You sure know how to get to those boys. I knew you'd be able to make them come."

Conner was bolstered by Vivian's confidence in him but wouldn't kid himself. "They're only coming over to get money." He wanted so very much to please Vivian and to help these poor children.

She nodded. "But once they are here, you'll win them over." She smiled at him, and his heart tripled its beat.

Sam and Tommy stopped at the same place Peter had stopped when he first arrived, but Peter came over and sat next to him. "They don't believe you got another nickel. I told them you had two."

Conner opened his hand to reveal two nickels on his palm, then closed it. "First, I want to tell you about the children's home. It's a two-story house and has room for all of you. Widow Parker will look after you and cook for you."

The younger of the two boys licked his lips. "Every day?"

"Every day. Three meals a day. Would you like that?"

The younger one nodded, and the older one shook his shoulder. "We ain't going there, Tommy."

"I want to eat every day," Tommy whined.

"We ain't going. He could be lying to us. George said not to trust no growed-up people."

Conner needed to talk to George. He obviously had filled their heads with terrible stories of orphanages, stories that he himself knew were probably true.

"Come on, Tommy." Sam turned to leave.

"But I didn't get my nickel."

"He ain't gonna give us nothing."

"I will, too." He flipped one nickel into the air toward Tommy. The boy missed it but plucked it out of the sand. Conner flipped the second one to Sam. Sam caught it and stared at him. "I have another nickel for each of you if you talk George into coming to my store and talking to me."

They exchanged glances and ran off.

Peter jumped off the log and faced him. "Me, too, mister? Me, too?"

He smiled. "Of course you, too."

Peter ran off across the beach as fast as his little feet would plow through the loose sand. "Wait. I'm comin'."

After the three boys were out of sight, Conner turned to Vivian. A tear trickled down her cheek. He brushed it away. "Don't give up. George is the key. I'll talk to him. I'll convince him everything will be okay."

She sniffled. "I know it will be. George will listen to you. I just know it."

He mentally kicked himself. How was he ever going to convince this boy who was set against it? *Lord, You and I both know I'm doing this mostly to win Vivian's heart, but I do want to help these children, too. I just never would have thought to do anything more than set food out for them. Soften George's heart for the sake of the other children.*

Chapter 15

The next day, Conner's store was teeming with customers when he saw an unkempt boy of about fourteen enter, looking quite uncomfortable. He hoped this was George and didn't want the boy to get away, so he quickly finished ringing up his current customer and hurried over to the boy. "Are you George?"

George nodded.

"I'm Conner Jackson." He held out his hand to the boy.

George stared at his hand a moment before he shook it. "I'm not going to no orphanage. I only came so the others can get their nickels."

As he suspected, George looked out for the others. He could use that to sway him. "Winter is coming on. I think this might be a cold one. We might even get a little snow. It won't be good for those kids to be out in the cold."

"We'll manage."

"Have you been in an orphanage where you were treated poorly?"

George looked down shyly. "I don't want that to happen to the others what happened to me."

"That's very responsible of you. But Widow Parker is not going to treat anyone poorly. She is a very nice woman who is as much in need as all of you. She has a son and she loves children."

"You could just be saying that. Grown-ups say a lot of things they don't mean."

True, but he had to win George over to get the others. "If Widow Parker and the children's home isn't everything I've told you, you and the others can leave."

"You don't leave no orphanage once they got you. You have to escape like I did."

"There are no bars on the windows, no fence around the grounds. You and the others can leave anytime you like."

George just stared at him.

Conner reached into his pocket and handed the boy three nickels. "For the boys." Then he gave George two bits. "That's for you." He shook George's hand. "Thanks for coming. I know you'll do the right thing."

George seemed to consider that, gave a small nod, and walked out.

Conner had a feeling that George would make the right decision and talk the others into giving the children's home a try.

Vivian looked out the front window of the new children's home again. Where was Conner? He said he'd be there for Thanksgiving dinner. Everyone else was gathered at the children's home: Abigail; her son, Harry; Betsy; Sam; Tommy; Peter; Martin, who couldn't pay Abigail enough attention; Maggie, who helped prepare the meal; and Scotty. Even George was there. The only one missing was Conner. As she turned from the window, Conner came in through the kitchen door.

"Mrs. Parker, I have a surprise for you. Come with me."

Abigail put on her coat, as did everyone else, following in a cluster behind Conner and Abigail out to the barn. In the middle stall stood a black-and-white milking cow. Abigail squealed like a schoolgirl. "Thank you, Mr. Jackson."

"The children need fresh milk."

Vivian saw Martin scowl at Conner's back.

If she didn't know that Conner wasn't interested in Abigail, she might be jealous, too. But what if he had developed feelings for her? She would have to talk to Abigail about Martin and see if she had any interest at all in him.

They all headed back inside as a pack, and soon Maggie, Abigail, and Vivian had Thanksgiving dinner on the table. After everyone had eaten their fill, Vivian offered to do the evening milking. Conner accompanied her, saying she shouldn't have to carry the milk bucket. Now she found herself alone in the barn with Conner.

"I think I made a big mistake." Conner sat on the milking stool, squirting milk into the pail. He'd taken over the job she had volunteered for.

Was he trying to win more favors with Abigail? "What would that be?"

"I should have had Martin present the cow to Mrs. Parker."

"Why?"

"Did you see the look on her face?" He shivered.

Yes, she had. It had been the look of deep gratitude. "Are you afraid of Abigail or of all women?" She hoped he wasn't one of those men who chose to remain a bachelor all his life. After all, he was twenty-seven, had never married, and had turned down her offer to have Randolph bring him back a bride. Now she was glad he'd turned it down.

"Only women who look at me with that glimmer in their eye of cornering prey."

"Are you against marriage?"

"No," he said quickly.

That was a relief. "Will you ever marry?"

He stroked the side of the cow and stood, picking up the pail. "If the right woman falls in love with me."

"She need only to fall in love with you, and she'd be the right woman?"

He cocked his head a little to the right. "The right woman would be the woman I'm in love with." He walked away, milk sloshing to the rim of the pail.

She stood staring after him. She wanted to be the right woman. But how did she make sure she was? *For one thing, don't look at him like cornered prey.*

Nearly two weeks later, Vivian headed to the children's home one afternoon. The roof was being repaired, and she looked forward to seeing Conner for more than just the evening. When Scotty drove her carriage into the yard, she saw Martin Zahn climbing down a ladder from the roof.

She took Scotty's hand as she stepped down. "Mr. Zahn."

He came over to her. "Mrs. Carlyle."

"I see you and Mr. Jackson are fixing the roof. Thank you so much."

"Just me and the boys." He waved his hand toward Tommy, Samuel, and Peter.

"Conner's not here?"

He raised an eyebrow at her use of Conner's first name.

She would pretend not to notice. . .either her slipup or Mr. Zahn's observation of it.

"He's at the store. Sent me over to do this job. My uncle was a carpenter in Port Angeles. I worked for him when I was a boy. I didn't much care for the work and came here. But I'm rather enjoying it today."

That was because he was sweet on the recipient of his labor. She would have to encourage Abigail to consider Mr. Zahn as a suitor. Vivian took off her hat as she went inside, then sat at the kitchen table and had tea with Abigail. "I didn't see George outside helping

Mr. Zahn." She was hoping to start a conversation about Mr. Zahn to gauge Abigail's interest in him.

"George left three days ago." Abigail took a sip of her tea.

"No." The boy needed a roof over his head.

Abigail's teacup clinked on the saucer as she set it down. "He signed on a ship. I got up when I heard someone stirring during the night. George was packed and preparing to walk out the door."

"Did you try to stop him?" She'd worked so hard to put a roof over all these children's heads.

Abigail shook her head. "His mind was made up. I cooked him some eggs. I didn't want him going off on an empty stomach."

Tears stung the back of her eyes. "Who will leave next?"

Abigail covered one of Vivian's hands with her own. "George told me this was a fine home, but he just didn't have a mind to stay. He told the others that this was a good place, and they were to stay here. They all seem content."

"I'm glad to hear that." Vivian took a drink of tea and heard banging on the roof. "Mr. Zahn sure is working hard."

Abigail stood. "Come look what he's done for us."

She followed Abigail upstairs to the large room the boys shared. Four wood-framed beds lined the walls.

"Every couple of days he brings another bed he's made. He started with one for Betsy. Now she's in love with him. He also brought yards and yards of mattress ticking. Betsy and I have been sewing mattresses and stuffing them with hay. He also brought two hens and ten chicks the day after Thanksgiving, all laying hens. Come summer, and we have a producing garden, we'll have food enough."

It sounded like Mr. Zahn was doing everything he could to win Abigail's heart, and Conner was staying away. Both thoughts eased Vivian's mind and heart.

They went back to the kitchen and found Mr. Zahn waiting there. "I've taken care of the roof. You shouldn't have any more leaks. I'll come by after work and fix the railing and step out front, then get started on the other work, but Conner needs me back at the store so he can go over to the shipping office."

Vivian picked up her hat and pinned it to her hair. "Mr. Jackson is going over to Carlyle Shipping?"

"He goes over there at least twice a day and then in the evenings."

"Evenings?" He couldn't go in the evenings; he spent evenings with her.

"I think he goes over late at night. Stays until midnight or so."

So he went after his visits with her. No wonder he was looking so tired. He was going to drive himself into an early grave. "I'm going to Mr. Jackson's store. Would you like a ride?"

"I have his delivery wagon. I'll let him know you're coming so he doesn't leave before you get there." Mr. Zahn tipped an imaginary hat to Abigail and left.

"I'd better hurry so I can catch Mr. Jackson." She hugged Abigail good-bye and went to Conner's store, which was teeming with customers.

She directed a couple of customers to what they were looking for, then went behind the counter, where she knew Conner would want her. She watched Mr. Zahn ring up a sale. The cash register didn't look too hard to operate. "Mr. Zahn, if you would give me a little instruction on how to use that, I could ring up sales while you and Mr. Jackson help the customers."

Mr. Zahn looked unsure but showed her, then went about the store.

Conner did a double take at Martin helping a customer. Hadn't he asked him to mind the cash register? He looked to the counter. His heart stopped for a moment. Vivian stood at the register, smiling at a customer. He strode over behind the counter. "What are you doing?"

"I'm helping," she said to him as she handed change to the customer. "Thank you, and come again."

"I didn't ask you to help."

"You didn't need to. You were quite busy. I asked Mr. Zahn to show me how the cash register works so he could help you out on the floor." She turned, smiled at the next customer, and began ringing up the sale.

When she was through, he said, "I want you to go home. It's not—"

"Safe. I know, I know, but you need help. Mr. Zahn told me you've been working here at the store and at Carlyle Shipping."

He shot a glare at Martin's back. He didn't need Vivian coming down here because he was busy. "I'm doing fine. When William gets here, he will share the work."

"Which isn't until spring. At the rate you're going, you'll be dead by then. I've decided to come down and help in your store every day."

"No, you won't. I won't allow it."

"If you're at the shipping office, you won't know. Excuse me, I have a customer." She smiled at the blond-haired man who eyed her with interest.

Conner raked a hand through his hair. If she were going to be here, he'd never be able to leave or work at the shipping office. A customer across the store caught his gaze and held up a can of beans. "Don't move from behind this counter."

She smiled at him, and his heart melted all over again.

When the crowd thinned to but a couple of customers, he went back to her. "Go home, and don't come back."

"When do you open in the morning?"

"Vivian, stay home. I don't want to worry about you."

"You're working too hard. Until William gets here, I'll help."

He raked his hand through his hair again. "If I hire someone, will you stay at home?"

She turned and faced him with a look of determination. He wanted to kiss her. Her lips moved, and she'd said something. He wasn't sure of it, so he swallowed hard and took a step back. "What?"

"I said yes. If you hire someone so you aren't working yourself ragged, I won't come down here and work for you."

He hired Finn that afternoon to look out for things at the shipping office and sent Vivian home. And although he hated to admit it, he did feel lighter knowing he didn't have to be at the warehouse all the time as well as at his store.

Chapter 16

Conner stood in Vivian's parlor, looking out the window at the budding bushes and trees. Winter had come and gone the same as the fall: cold and rainy. Spring was a nice relief with warmer rains and budding flowers.

He'd managed to keep both his store and the shipping business running smoothly over the winter months, as well as seeing to it that Martin had time to get the children's home fixed up. Mrs. Parker seemed grateful to Martin for all his work. Vivian had done her best to stay uptown at Conner's insistence, but when she had ventured down, he was always glad to see her. She'd started taking visitors but hated the falsehood in herself and the other ladies; everyone pretending to be friends and being glad to see each other when the society ladies didn't think her socially worthy any more than Vivian wanted to be their socially snobbish equal.

"You're so introspective, Conner."

Vivian stood very near to him, smiling. He tried not to think about how it would be to kiss her and tore his gaze away from her lips.

"I have a lot on my mind with William arriving in a couple of weeks. I want to make sure the shipping office is in order."

"I can't wait to see Sarah and the baby. She wrote in her letter that she'd had a girl but didn't tell me her name."

It would be good for Vivian to have a friend her social equal. He should comment but was struggling not to take her into his arms. He flexed his fingers then made fists again. He should leave now but found himself powerless to move.

"You'll like William." She shook her head. "I forgot you've known him longer than I have."

"I haven't seen him since he was twelve." But he'd known everything William had been doing over the years through Randolph.

"Oh, I didn't realize. That's a long time. He's grown into a godly man. And like Randolph, he's handsome. William, Sarah, you, and I can all socialize together." She stopped short and looked embarrassed. "I didn't mean to be presumptuous."

"It's not presumptuous." He wanted to say more but found his mouth unwilling to form words. Vivian's presence seemed to draw him closer. He should walk away into the night before he crossed a line that there was no turning back from and did something he shouldn't. She was still in black after all, a symbol of being Randolph's widow.

Instead, he took a step closer. Vivian tilted her head back and smiled up at him. That was his undoing. He leaned into her and pressed his lips gently to hers. When she didn't back away, he cupped her face in his hands.

He pulled away when the doorbell chimed. What had he done? She was still in mourning. He couldn't read her expression, and before he could say anything, Martin stormed into the room.

"What is it?"

Martin breathed heavily. "It's Finn. He got himself in a lick of trouble and is in jail."

Conner raked a hand through his hair then turned to Vivian. "I have to go."

She smiled and nodded.

He left with Martin. They arrived at the jail to find Finn lying on the cot in the cell, snoring. "Finn, what have you done?"

"He drank half the tavern then started a fight with three others." The sheriff stood beside him. "The doctor has looked after him. When someone pays the good doctor, I'll let him out, but not before morning, so don't bother coming back tonight. He'll be sleeping it off all night, anyhow."

"I'll be back in the morning."

Outside Martin said, "I'm sorry for disturbing your evening."

"Don't be. I'm glad you came to get me."

"But I spoiled your evening with Mrs. Carlyle. Are you going to head back over to her place?"

"Not tonight." The timing had actually been good. He had needed the interruption. He needed time to decide what to do.

"I know you care for her deeply."

"How do you know that?"

"The way you talk about her. The way you look at her when she comes into the store. The way you look at closing time when you're anticipating seeing her. It's the way I feel about Abigail."

"I can't hide much from you." He smiled. "How is Mrs. Parker?"

"She's doing well." Martin smiled now. "Those chicks I got her at the end of November have started laying, and I have the garden all tilled up. I'm going to see if she needs more seeds."

"It sounds like she might have softened toward you."

"She's started to think of me as more than just a handyman. She's invited me to supper a couple of times for no reason at all."

"Oh, there's a reason. How do you get on with her son?"

"He's been real shy. He sits off and watches me. I try to get him to help me, but he won't. He'll help the boys. Then last week when I was in the barn, he came up to me and said, 'My papa died.' I said, 'I know.' Then he took my hand."

"Sounds like he might have accepted you."

"I hope so. And Mrs. Carlyle? When does she come out of mourning?"

"I don't know." Conner rubbed the back of his neck. "I hope I didn't ruin things tonight. I may have been a might too forward."

"I thought I interrupted something. Maybe you should go back."

"I need time to think and sort things out." He parted ways with Martin and pointed his feet toward home.

Vivian hadn't seemed mad at him for kissing her—at least she hadn't slapped him—but neither did she seem pleased. It was as though she were stunned by his action. Had he ruined everything? He would apologize tomorrow and tell her he didn't know what came over him. She would forgive him.

The next evening, Vivian stood in her parlor, unfolded Conner's note, and read it again. She'd lost count of how many times.

Vivian,

We need to talk. I'll come by at 7:30.

Conner

Conner had never before sent her a note to announce his arrival. He didn't need to. *We need to talk.* Four words never sounded so ominous. She knew he wanted to talk about kissing her last night. Did he regret it? She'd been in high spirits all day until his note had stolen her joy.

Lord, please let Conner have meant that kiss. If the kiss was a mistake, please protect my heart.

The mantel clock struck the half hour. She sucked in a hasty breath, and her stomach tightened. The doorbell chimed a moment later. Maggie would get it. She walked to the window and stared out at the darkening sky.

"Vivian."

She couldn't turn around, dreading what he might say. *Protect my heart.* Conner was the one person she wanted to see most right now and the only person she dreaded seeing.

"Vivian." He stood right behind her.

She turned and looked up at him. *Protect my heart.* "Conner." She walked around him. "Won't you sit down?"

He took her arm and turned her to face him, then studied her face. "I've upset you."

She forced a smile. "Don't be silly. You just arrived. How could you have upset me?"

"Last night. I don't want you to be uncomfortable with me. I wasn't thinking. You're still in mourning." The lines around Conner's slightly squinted eyes belied his anguish.

Maggie entered with a tea tray. Vivian turned, grateful for the distraction. "Thank you, Maggie."

Maggie set the tray down on the table in front of the couch. "Would you like me to pour?"

Vivian was about to say yes so she wouldn't have to endure the awkwardness of being alone with Conner when Conner spoke up.

"We'll manage. Thank you, Maggie."

Maggie nodded and left the room.

Vivian wanted to call the older woman back but instead sat on the edge of the settee. "I'll pour you a cup." She tipped over one of the teacups reaching for the teapot. The cup rattled excessively as she tried to right it.

"I don't want any tea." Conner took her hand and brought her to her feet.

She forced her gaze to his. "Please don't say it," she barely whispered.

The V between his eyebrows sharpened. "Say what?"

Maybe if she kept it to herself, they could pretend nothing happened. "Nothing. The tea's getting cold."

"Vivian, I don't want to say anything to hurt you. Tell me."

She might as well, or she'd fuss over it in her mind until she made herself sick. "Don't say that you're sorry for kissing me last night."

He gazed at her. "What do you want me to say?"

She turned away from him. "I'm not sure."

He turned her back. "Tell me what it is."

Should she tell him what was in her heart? Did he feel anything for her? Would he think her an awful person for falling in love with her deceased husband's best friend while she was still in widow's garb? She should wait. "Conner, really, it's nothing."

He stared at her for a long moment then took her hand and held it. "Come, sit." He sat with her on the settee.

Her stomach tightened even more. She could barely breathe. He wasn't going to let this go. *Protect my heart.*

"When Randolph first introduced me to his new wife, I was happy for him and felt he'd found himself a good wife. As I heard him talk about you and I spent time around you…" He hesitated, looked down at his hands, then gazed directly at her, "I began developing feelings for you. I know it was wrong," he hurried to say. "That's why I had decided to leave town. But then Randolph asked me to look out for you while he was gone. I tried to turn him down but couldn't. Please don't hate me for falling in love with a married woman."

"Never, Conner. I could never hate you. You have proved yourself to be a loyal friend and honorable man. You never in word or deed did anything to betray your friendship with Randolph or to go against God's teachings." To love her all these months and do nothing about it. Her heart leapt for joy. She reached up and touched his cheek with her fingers. "I've fallen in love with you, too."

He gave her a lopsided grin and just stared at her.

"Well?"

"Well, what?"

"Say something. Do something." She was suddenly nervous he'd think poorly of her. Why wasn't he saying anything?

He opened his mouth to say something then closed it. He leaned forward and kissed her as she'd never been kissed before. This was the kiss of a man who truly loved her. Her heart exploded with thanksgiving to God for a love like this. *Thank You.*

Vivian stood in the carriage and let Scotty help her down. "Come back for me in an hour." When she entered Conner's store, he was ringing up a customer's order and handing back change.

Conner came over to her immediately. "What are you doing downtown?"

"Maggie needs a few things for the kitchen." She smiled up at him. "And I wanted to see you."

His frown melted to a smile. "I'm glad to see you, too." He guided her around behind the counter and lifted her with ease up onto the stool. He kept his voice low. "I got to thinking last night that maybe I'd dreamed I kissed you and you said you loved me."

"You didn't dream it."

"You shouldn't have come down here."

"Scotty drove me, and I'm with you now. I'm perfectly safe."

He shook his head. "Not that. I've held my feelings in for you so long, now that you know how I feel about you and you feel the same, I'm not going to be able to hide them from everyone."

"You shouldn't have to hide them. Besides, there has been some talk about town. People wondering if you've become more than Randolph's friend to me. Most people really believe you are Randolph's brother and that you only come around because you are family."

"But isn't it too soon for you to be openly courted? You're still wearing black. How much longer?"

He was as eager as she for her to no longer look the widow. "It depends. Some say a year, others eighteen months, while still others wear mourning clothes for two years. Abigail Parker wore her mourning clothes for only three months. They made her son sad. I think most people think six months is respectable enough. It's been about six months. I'll come out of mourning."

"Don't. Not just yet. Wait until after William comes. Let him see you are honoring his brother's memory."

"William knows I didn't love Randolph."

"Even so, for me, wear your mourning clothes until after William's visit."

She could wear black that much longer now that she knew how Conner felt about her. She'd been afraid that the black was keeping him away. "Anything for you."

He knit his brow slightly. "Except staying uptown."

She smiled. "You can't expect to keep a woman in love away from the object of her affection."

He thinned his lips. "See, it's things like that that will let everyone in town know there is something between us."

She glanced about. "No one heard me."

"Yes, but they could see that smile across the room, and they'll wonder why I'm smiling all day."

"I can't help it if I want to see you more."

"We'll talk about our future tonight."

Future. She liked the sound of that. She wanted him to take her in his arms and kiss her, but instead she held out a slip of paper. "This is what Maggie needs."

He took it. "Good. I need to keep busy while you're here." He walked off and started gathering her order.

Vivian picked up the Sears and Roebuck catalog and started flipping through it. The hour quickly passed as she pretended to look at the catalog but really watched Conner work around his store and help customers. She was fortunate to have a good and generous man love her. *Thank You, Lord.*

Scotty entered the store and came over to her. "You ready to leave?"

She wanted to say no but knew she should leave. "Con—Mr. Jackson has Maggie's order here behind the counter."

Conner came over to help carry it out to the carriage. "Do you have room for Mrs. Parker's order?"

"I didn't bring the wagon." Scotty hefted a sack of flour onto his shoulder.

If Conner had something for Abigail, then they would certainly take it. Vivian turned to Scotty. "Can't we fit it on the luggage rack in the back? We're heading over to see her anyway."

"Then where will I put Miss Maggie's things?"

She sighed. "We can't fit it all?"

"Finn should be back from a delivery with my wagon soon. I'll send him over with the food for the orphanage before I send him out for the next delivery," Conner said.

Scotty set the sack of flour back onto the floor and eyed Conner. "I'll tell you what. We can load the food for those children and take it over now. Then while Mrs. Carlyle is visiting, I'll come back to get Maggie's order and take it to the house, then pick Mrs. Carlyle up." Scotty turned to her. "Will that give you enough time to catch up with Mrs. Parker?"

"Scotty, that's perfect."

Conner and Scotty made short work of loading and tying down the supplies on the luggage rack in the back.

A bawdy-looking woman stopped at the store window and peered in. Conner frowned and headed over to her. "I'm afraid you'll have to shop elsewhere."

The woman smiled coyly with her red-painted lips. "I'm only here to shop."

"I don't serve your kind."

"Too bad for you." The woman winked at him and left.

Vivian felt no twinge of jealousy, because Conner wasn't at all interested in the woman. He almost seemed disgusted. At the same time she felt pity for the woman.

Conner was still frowning when he helped her up into the carriage. "I'll see you tonight."

"What was wrong? Didn't that woman have money?"

"I run a respectable business. I'll not have strumpets loitering outside my store."

"But she just wanted to shop. Isn't her money the same as everyone else's?"

Conner gritted his teeth. "No, it's not."

"But—"

"I don't want to talk about this any further." He walked into his store.

That wasn't like Conner. He was always kind and caring. How could he be so cold to that woman just because of her profession? She had feelings like everyone else. He had to have a reason for his strong reaction to that kind of woman. The kind of woman Vivian used to be. Would he hate her for her past? Or did he just hate women who were currently in the world's oldest profession? She needed to talk to him about it tonight, even though it saddened her to think his love for her might instantly die.

She tried to put Conner's reaction to the woman of ill repute out of her mind by the time she reached the Randolph Carlyle Home for Children. She was glad that Randolph would be remembered in this way.

Peter came running out before Scotty got the carriage stopped. "Miss Vivian!"

When Scotty set the brake, she held out her hand to the boy. "Hello, Peter."

Peter took her hand like a gentleman while she climbed out of the carriage.

"You have learned that very well."

"Mrs. Parker says being a gentleman is the most important thing next to going to church and knowing God." Peter scrunched up his face. "What's a gentleman?"

"Being a gentleman is being a good person. Treating people kindly and being fair." She paused to think. "A gentleman always helps a lady and never does anything to hurt a lady. A gentleman is always honorable. And a gentleman always lets a lady go first."

Peter frowned. "That's a lot to remember."

Abigail stood on the porch of the two-story house holding a year-old girl on her hip. "Vivian, I'm so glad you came."

She touched the girl's hand. "Who is this?"

"Sadie. She was dropped off two days ago." Abigail rubbed the baby's back. "Her mother died, and the woman who ran the boardinghouse they lived in won't care for the baby until the father returns. She doesn't think he will return."

Scotty walked up. "Mr. Jackson sent over a few things. I'll take the carriage around to the kitchen door and unload them."

"I'll get the boys to help," Abigail said to Scotty, then turned to Peter. "Get the other boys and help Mr. Scotty unload the supplies." When Peter ran off, Abigail turned to Vivian. "It's so sweet of Mr. Jackson to remember us and send food. Without it, I don't know what we'd do."

"He's glad to help. I know if he weren't so busy with his store and the shipping business, he'd do more." And busy coming over to see her. She felt her mouth turn up slightly.

"We've put in a garden, and when it starts producing, we won't need so much help." Abigail walked inside and motioned for her to have a seat on the sofa.

Betsy walked in from the kitchen. "Miss Vivian." She ran over and gave her a hug; then she pulled some fabric scraps from a basket at the end of the sofa. "Look at what Miss Abigail is teaching me."

It was a nine-patch quilt square. She turned it over. "Very nice. Your stitches are so much more even."

"I have seven squares so far." Betsy's face glowed with pride. "When I have twenty, Miss Abigail is going to show me how to sew them all together and make my own quilt."

"Betsy, would you go make some tea for our guest?" Abigail asked.

"Sure." Betsy put her sewing back and ran off to the kitchen.

"I'm teaching her how to run a household so she can find a good husband someday."

This is what she'd wanted for Betsy all those months ago when she'd met the girl on the beach. "I'm glad she's a help to you."

"I don't think I could do it all by myself, and I do enjoy having the company of another female in the house." Abigail caressed the baby's cheek. "And Sadie here makes three ladies in the house."

"Do you think her father will come back?"

"I don't know anything about him or where he went, when he's expected back, or if he's even a good man and father. We'll have to wait and see."

Sadie rubbed her face on Abigail's shoulder. "Someone's getting tired." Abigail shifted Sadie to her lap, holding her close and rubbing her back.

"How are all the children doing?"

Abigail smiled. "You'll be happy to know that George came back two weeks ago. I was about to go milk the cow when he waltzed into the kitchen with a full pail. He'd slept in the barn. He asked if I wouldn't mind him sleeping out there and having a few eggs if he did some chores around here."

"That's wonderful news. What did you tell him?"

"We fixed up a pallet in the little spare room. I told him since he behaved like a man, I wouldn't treat him like one of the orphans but like a live-in workhand. He liked that even though he knows I can't pay him. He's so opposed to orphanages. He's taken real well to the farm chores. He likes tending the animals and working in the dirt. He's dug irrigation ditches around and through the garden and built a trough to carry the water from the outside pump to the garden. Now if we don't get rain for a week, the garden can still get watered."

"I never really knew what he was like. He was always quiet and didn't say much."

"He still is."

Vivian was so happy for George. This might be the first time in his life that he had a stable place to live. "How are the others?"

"I've been inquiring after each of the children's families. I think I found an aunt of Peter's in Spokane. I'm going to write Miss Garfield a letter."

"How does Peter feel about leaving?"

"I haven't told him. Mr. Zahn promised the children one of Mr. Jackson's puppies. Peter won't be so happy to leave, and with a dog around here, I think it will be even harder."

"I'll ask Mr. Jackson if Peter can take one of the other puppies with him."

"What if the aunt doesn't want a dog?"

"If she's willing to take an orphan, don't you think she'd take the dog, too?"

Abigail nodded.

Vivian would be sad to see Peter go but glad at least one of the children might have a home with family. "How about Samuel and Tommy?"

"Samuel can be a bit of a troublemaker, and Tommy follows his brother's lead. George's presence helps keep them in line."

Betsy came in with the tea tray. She walked very slowly, staring hard at the tray, and set it successfully on the table in front of the sofa. "Shall I pour?"

"Thank you. That would be nice. You can leave mine on the tray for now."

Betsy seemed so much happier here where she didn't have to worry about where her next meal was coming from.

Betsy handed her a cup of tea. "Miss Vivian, I'm making mashed potatoes. Are you staying for supper?"

"No, I can't stay that long."

Betsy turned to Abigail. "Are we going to have an extra for supper?" Abigail nodded, and Betsy ran off.

"An extra?" Vivian took a sip of tea.

Abigail's cheeks turned pink, and she turned away, moving Sadie from her lap to the end of the sofa. "Mr. Zahn is coming over for supper."

"Martin Zahn?"

Abigail nodded and picked up her teacup.

"I thought you weren't interested in having a man court you."

Abigail smiled. "He wore me down."

"You seem glad for that."

"He's a very nice man and God-fearing. I don't think Mr. Parker would want me to be alone for the rest of my life."

"What does Martin think about you running this children's home?"

"He doesn't mind. Enough about me. How have you been doing?"

Vivian's mouth stretched into an involuntary smile. "I'm doing well."

"What else?"

"I'm in love. I think for the first time in my life."

"Mr. Jackson?"

"How did you know?"

"Is there any other man in your life?"

She shook her head. "He loves me, too. He's coming over this evening to discuss our future." It felt good to share her news with a friend.

"Futures are good." Abigail squeezed her arm. "I'm so happy for you."

She was happy, too, but something nagged at the back of her mind. Something she didn't want to address.

Chapter 17

Conner stood staring into Vivian's fire. It helped him think. Today had started out perfect. The woman he loved, loved him back, and while he was thinking of her, she walked through his door. Then his past had reared its ugly head, threatening to devour his happiness.

"Is everything all right?"

Vivian's lilting voice drew him back from his haunting memories.

"I'm fine." He turned to her. "I'm sorry. I'm not very good company tonight."

"Come, sit with me."

"I'm too restless to sit." He rubbed the back of his neck. He had to tell her. "That strumpet stirred up memories."

"Did something bad happen?"

Something bad? His whole childhood. "Did Randolph ever tell you about his mother?"

"William did."

He should just say it. "My mother was worse, and I loathed her for it."

Vivian went pale.

He shouldn't have told her. It upset her. But he had to.

Vivian clasped her hands in her lap. "But she was your mother."

His anger at his mother leapt to life anew. "That didn't stop her from sleeping with any man who had a buck in his pocket."

"She had a child to support."

"That's no excuse. There *is* no excuse. From the time I was eight years old, I was sweeping floors and cleaning spittoons to feed myself. All she ever did for me was keep a roof over my head because she needed a place to bring men home to. When I was fourteen, Randolph got me a job on the ship he was working, and I never went back." He wouldn't go into all the horrid details of his departure.

"You haven't seen your mother since you were fourteen?"

"And better for it." He fisted his hands.

"Is she still alive?"

"I don't know, and I don't care."

"But she's your mother."

He shook his head. "She was just another tramp." He turned back to the fire.

"What about your father?"

"Never met him. I don't even know if she knew who he was. I was an accident and a liability to her."

Vivian came up beside him. "Conner, don't say that. She must have loved you."

"She didn't. She tried to kill me twice. I don't want to talk about her anymore or ever again."

"But—"

He didn't want to hear it, so he drew her close and kissed her. She fit well in his arms. He hoped Vivian didn't hate him for what his mother was. "Marry me, Vivian."

"Conner." His name came out breathy.

"You want to marry me, don't you?" He held his breath. Did his lineage make a difference to her?

"Yes, I want to."

He kissed her again, relieved she hadn't turned him down because of his mother. He would spend the rest of his life proving to her that she made the right decision and that one's parentage didn't determine the man.

Vivian didn't visit Conner's store again during the day and stewed for a week over Conner's reaction to the strumpet and what he'd told her about his mother. Her stomach felt like she'd eaten rotten fish, though she'd hardly eaten all week. She had to tell him the truth, but how? He would turn his back on her for sure. But if she didn't tell him and they married and he found out later, he would hate her forever. She'd tried to tell him after his confession, but the words stuck in her throat.

In her naïveté, she'd thought marrying Randolph would make her respectable. Only the truth would make her respectable now.

"Maggie, do you know where Scotty is?"

"I believe he's in the barn this time of day. I can go get him. What do you need?"

"I'm going to take the carriage into town. I'll find him. Thank you." She went out to the barn but didn't see Scotty anywhere. The horse poked his head out of the stall and whinnied a greeting by bobbing her head.

She looked from the horse to the carriage parked on the opposite side of the barn and back again. "We can do this, can't we?" She walked toward the horse.

The horse nodded and flapped her lips. She went into the tack room and took the nearest harness off the peg on the wall, then went back to the stall and opened the door. She held the bit in front of the horse's mouth; then she turned it over. Which way was up? "Do you know?"

"May I help you?"

She jumped, sucking in a breath and spinning around to face Scotty, stoop-shouldered. "I want to hitch the carriage and go into town." She held out the harness to him.

Scotty took it. "Honey don't like this bit." He disappeared into the tack room and came out with another harness that looked the same to her. When he got the horse all hooked up and hitched to the carriage, he said, "I'll change my clothes into something more suitable for town."

"No need, Scotty. I'll drive myself."

"Mr. Jackson isn't going to like that."

Mr. Jackson wasn't going to like much of today where she was concerned. "I'll be fine. I'll tell him that you protested and I gave you no choice." She let Scotty help her up into the seat and drove off. A few minutes later, she pulled up in front of Conner's store.

Conner came out smiling before she could get the brake set. "What are you doing here? I thought I finally got you to stay uptown." He put his hands around her waist and lifted her down.

She put her hands on his shoulders as he gently set her on the boardwalk. "I need to talk to you. Are you busy? Can you get away?"

"I'll come by this evening, and we can talk then."

She didn't want him coming by unless he wanted to after knowing the truth. "Since I'm here, we can talk now."

"I have a few customers to help; then I think Martin and Todd can handle things here for a little while." He guided her inside and started to show her to the stool he usually made her sit on.

She couldn't be stagnant. "I'm going to look around a bit." She picked up a can of this and a box of that without really seeing what she was doing.

"I know you."

She turned to a man with a long, curled handlebar mustache. She couldn't say anything. She indeed knew the man from her days in Coos Bay but didn't know his name. She took a slow, deep breath. "You must have me mistaken with someone else." That was a lie, but she couldn't admit to her past like this. She'd thought her past wouldn't find her here. She was a new creation; her sins remembered no more.

"I remember that face." His gaze scanned the length of her. "And that body."

Why couldn't people be as forgetful as God chose to be? "No." Her voice came out small. This couldn't be happening.

The man shifted his gaze to just behind her. "Did you get yourself a respectable man?"

She looked back at Conner. The fury on his face said he wanted to rip the man's throat out. "Apologize to the lady."

The man laughed. "She's no lady."

"Conner, it's all right. Let's just go."

Conner stepped in front of her, his jaw set. "You have made a mistake."

"I've made no mistake. This is Vivian Miller. I've paid for her services before."

Conner squared his shoulders and stepped within inches of the man. "You will apologize to the lady, or I'll throw you out of my store."

The smaller man finally registered the potential danger he might be in from Conner. "Sorry, ma'am." The man hastily left.

"Conner, I can explain."

Conner pulled her by her arm outside and lifted her into her carriage. "Go home, and stay there."

"Conner, please."

He wouldn't look at her. "Don't come back downtown." He slapped Honey on her rump, and the horse stepped into motion.

Maybe Conner hadn't heard the man right. No, it was all too clear. Maybe he hadn't believed what the man was accusing her of. But the look on his face was so horrible. *Lord, give me the opportunity to explain to Conner. Please, please, please let him forgive me.*

By the time she reached her house, her vision was clouded and tears stained her cheeks. Good thing Honey knew her way home.

She waited all evening. Conner never came. She'd hoped he would but wasn't surprised. She went to her room and out onto her widow's walk. She'd never felt worse in her entire life.

Conner stalked the streets and ducked into every saloon until he located the man who'd come into his store earlier. The man sat at a table in a smoke-filled room, holding a fist full of cards. Conner walked over.

The man folded his cards and excused himself from the table. "I apologized to the *lady* as you asked."

"I want you to never repeat what you said and to leave town. Tonight."

"I'm heading up to Alaska. Won't let no one in the Yukon without a year's supply of food and such. I have to wait my turn."

"I'll have your supplies ready for you in the morning. You be gone by the afternoon."

"Vivian must be something important to you for you to be behaving this way."

He fisted his hands at his side. He wanted to hit the man real bad, but he wouldn't be goaded into a fight. This man was spewing nothing but filthy lies.

Conner tried to ignore Scotty when he entered his store. Vivian had sent him every day for the past five days to see when he was coming by her house. He didn't know how to face her. He didn't want her explanation for what the man had said to her. He didn't want to believe what he'd implied. "Scotty, tell her I've got trouble at the shipping office. I just can't come by."

"That's not going to work this time. Mrs. Carlyle says if she doesn't see you tonight, she's coming down here tomorrow."

"Tell her that I really can't come tonight, but I'll definitely be there tomorrow night. I have a big shipment coming in to Carlyle Shipping that demands my attention. I will come tomorrow night." That should give him more time to. . .to what? Avoid the truth?

He sent Martin home, or rather over to Mrs. Parker at the orphanage; then he locked up and headed over to Carlyle Shipping. He skipped supper and was still entering numbers into the ledger when someone knocked on the office door. "Come in."

Finn poked his head in. "You have a visitor."

He stood and stretched. "At this hour? Send him in."

"It's a her."

His gut flinched. She wouldn't come down here? This was worse than his store.

Vivian crossed his threshold looking like an elegant china doll.

He wanted to go to her and hold her and kiss her. Yet she repulsed him. "I told Scotty I'd see you tomorrow night."

"We need to talk." Her voice quavered a little.

"Tomorrow. I have a lot of work to do." He needed one more day of believing she was Randolph's respectable widow. But he knew the truth. In his gut. Her face told it, too.

She sat in the chair opposite his desk. She wasn't leaving. He had to face this now.

He sank back down into his chair. "Vivian, please don't say it's true."

"I wish I could. I wish I could change many things about my past, but I can't. That's not the way I wanted to live my life." Her voice shook more.

He swallowed hard. "But you were a. . .a. . . ?" He couldn't say it. "Like my mother?"

She nodded. "A prostitute. I'm not proud of it. I never wanted to live that way."

Disgust and anger rose in him, and he stood. "But you did."

"Let me explain."

"I don't want to hear it. Leave." He strode around his desk and grabbed the doorknob, but when she continued to speak, he froze with his hand in place, unable to look at her.

"I had no money and no place to live. I was hungry and sick. A man, a doctor, took me in. He was nice to me and took care of me."

He wrenched open the door and turned on her. "And for that you sold yourself?"

"I didn't have any other choice."

He clenched his teeth. "There are always choices."

"I didn't know the Lord. I didn't know the depth of my sin."

Tears flooded her eyes, but he wasn't going to let them sway him. She was no different than his mother. If he could walk away from his mother, he could walk away from her. "I never want to see you again."

"I'm not leaving until I make you understand."

Then he'd leave. He grabbed the railings and took the stairs three at a time.

"I love you," she said behind him.

He tried to block it out but couldn't. He ran all the way to Admiralty Inlet, trying to outrun her words and his feelings for her. He reached the beach exhausted and fell to his knees. He cried out as his heart ripped in two.

Chapter 18

Vivian wrapped herself in a quilt and sat out on her widow's walk all night with her unopened letters to Conner in her hand. She'd hoped when Conner's anger cooled he would at least read one of them, but every letter came back to her unread like a slap in the face. This was the eighth night in a row that she had watched the dark waters by night and slept by day. Now she felt like a widow. Why couldn't Conner see she had changed? She wasn't a strumpet anymore. She was a new creation. Why couldn't he forgive her?

The eastern sky began to gray as dawn approached. William and Sarah had sent word that they would arrive today but not until the afternoon. She would sleep until then, so she went inside and curled up in her bed.

She woke to Maggie shaking her. "Time to get up."

"What time is it?"

"Three o'clock. Your company will be here in a couple of hours. We have to get you presentable."

She didn't care if she was presentable or not, but it would be good to see Sarah and William again. They would lighten her heart.

As Maggie helped her bathe and dress, she did feel better. She didn't even mind putting on the black mourning dress. It seemed to suit her now. Or at least her mood. She would have Maggie dye all her dresses black.

"Scotty has gone to the dock to pick them up as soon as they get off the ship; and I've fixed you a little something to eat, and I don't want to hear no fuss about it."

"I'm not hungry."

"Hungry or not, you're going to eat. You haven't eaten hardly a thing in a week. It won't do you no good to be fainting as soon as your guests arrive."

She nodded and followed Maggie downstairs, but she was the one who would be the guest now. The house was William and Sarah's. She would need to move. But where? Seattle? She could find a job as a housekeeper there.

Vivian hurried outside when she saw Scotty arriving with the carriage. "Sarah!"

"Vivian!"

William, looking dapper in his suit, jumped down and took the baby from Sarah, then gave his wife a hand to help her down. Sarah gave her a hug then turned and took the baby from her husband. "I'd like you to meet our daughter, Vivian."

She caressed the sleeping baby's cheek. "What's her name?"

Sarah giggled. "I just told you. Vivian."

"You named her after me?"

Sarah nodded. "William insisted. We have some other good news."

"You're having another baby?"

"No. We're staying in Port Townsend."

"That's wonderful. Come inside."

They sat in the parlor, and Maggie served them tea.

"It only makes sense for you two—I mean three—to move here. You have this beautiful house." She almost wanted to cry at the thought of leaving it.

Sarah put her hand on Vivian's arm. "We're staying to be close to you and to Conner. We know there are no blood ties, but you're the only family that either of us has. William can't say enough about Conner."

At the mention of his name, the breath froze in her lungs.

"Speaking of Conner, he wrote to me several times about Randolph not updating his will before he died." William took a sip of tea. "I agree with Conner that you should have a full third of Carlyle Shipping, and Sarah and I have discussed it and think you should have half the house, as well. We want to uphold the will that Randolph never signed."

Tears stung the back of her eyes. She had to tell William what she'd done. "I can't accept it. Randolph was right in not putting me in his will. I never should have married him when I harbored such a dark secret. I know you warned me not to, but I told him the truth just before he died. He was furious with me. He wouldn't want me to have anything." And Conner certainly wouldn't want her for a business partner.

"Nonsense. You're my brother's legal widow, and I'll see to it that you are taken care of. If my brother hadn't been so greedy to marry you, you wouldn't have had to keep your secret from him."

"I kept it from Conner, too, but he knows now."

William grimaced.

Sarah squeezed her arm. "How did he take it?"

"Worse than Randolph. He never wants to see me again." She turned to William. "William, you have never held my past against me. Why are you so forgiving and accepting when your brother and Conner aren't?"

" 'All have sinned, and come short of the glory of God.' 'While we were yet sinners, Christ died for us.' Randolph and Conner could never separate the person from the sin. They couldn't see that our mother and Conner's mother were wounded, sinning people like the rest of us. To them, our mothers were their sin. But God loves us all in spite of our sin. He doesn't rank our sins on severity. They are all putrid to Him, but He covered them with Christ's blood."

That's what she believed. "Conner told me about his mother being a prostitute, too. Why can't he understand that sometimes a woman has few choices?"

"His mother did have a choice. Our mother only did it for a while to feed and clothe us. Conner's mother chose it over honest work. She worked as a maid in the same house as our mother and quit to go back to prostitution because the honest work was too hard. She was mean and vile. I don't know if Conner has ever forgiven her."

"He hasn't. If he can't forgive his own mother, then he'll never be able to forgive me."

"I'll speak to him," William said.

"He won't listen."

"He'll listen to me. I'll make him listen. I've known him since childhood."

Could William really make the difference? She desperately hoped so.

Conner sat in the Carlyle Shipping manager's office and held his head in his hands. It was getting late, and he had a headache again. He hadn't slept well since he had sent Vivian away—no—since he'd learned of her scarlet past. A knock mercifully interrupted his thoughts. "Come in."

A young Randolph filled the doorway of the shipping office.

He stood. "William?"

The man nodded and broke into a wide smile.

"You grew up." He came around his desk and hugged his oldest friend. Though he hadn't seen William since they were children, he'd learned all about what he was doing through Randolph; and since Randolph's death, he'd corresponded regularly with him. "You look good."

"You look like something the dog dragged in."

Conner raked his hand through his hair. "I'm having quite a time keeping up with my store and Carlyle Shipping."

"Where's Randolph's manager? Don't tell me you fired him?"

He shook his head. "I didn't have a chance. He and the bookkeeper ran off with the money in the safe months ago. Fortunately, there wasn't much there at the time. I'd taken most of it to the bank. I don't know for how long they were pinching from Randolph. I wrote you about that."

William nodded. "You didn't hire a new manager?"

Conner shook his head. "I didn't know who I could trust."

William took a deep breath. "Me. I'm staying in town. I'll run the shipping company for the three of us."

"Three?"

"You, me, and Vivian."

He'd forgotten about her being part owner. "I'd rather just sell you my share."

"I don't have the money to buy you out."

"Then I'll turn it over to you."

William narrowed his eyes and studied him. "Have you eaten?"

He shook his head.

"Let's go get something and talk."

Conner locked up the shipping office and took William back to his store, where he made some scrambled eggs and bacon. William didn't eat much. He'd probably already eaten.

"You have to forgive her, Conner."

"Forgive who?" He knew whom.

"Vivian. Your mother. The world. I can see that it's eating you up inside."

"Vivian was a prostitute." The word felt like poison in his mouth. "But you knew that, didn't you? Why didn't you tell me?"

"Because she's completely turned her back on that life. She's a good person."

"How can you say that?"

William picked up Conner's Bible from his bedside table and flipped through it. " 'For if ye forgive men their trespasses, your heavenly Father will also forgive you: But if ye forgive not men their trespasses, neither will your Father forgive your trespasses.' " He flipped a page. " 'And why beholdest thou the mote that is in thy brother's eye, but considerest not the beam that is in thine own eye?' " More pages rustled. " 'Judge not, and ye shall not be judged: condemn not, and ye shall not be condemned: forgive, and ye shall be forgiven.' Refusing to forgive is just as much a sin. When are you going to let go?"

Conner wanted to say never but knew that wasn't right. He didn't like William beating him over the head with scripture verses. "I can forgive, but that doesn't mean I have to see her or talk to her."

"But you haven't. You haven't forgiven your mother for being the person she was, so you can't forgive Vivian for being the person she was forced to be."

"She had choices just like we all have."

"But sometimes you get pushed so far you can only see one choice."

"There is always a right choice, always."

"Randolph told me something once I refused to believe, but now, seeing the hatred in your eyes, it might be true. He told me that you hated your mother so much that you thought about killing her. He wanted to save you from that and so got you that job on the ship to take you away."

Conner clenched his hands into fists. "I wouldn't have done it."

"Are you sure? If you were pushed to the point you thought you had no other choice?"

Defeated, he sagged in his chair. "Yes, I'm sure." A man his mother brought home had been slapping her around. He'd stepped in to protect her. The man left and his mother had been furious with him for losing her the money that man would have paid. She'd said it was all part of it and started hitting him. He'd found his hands around her throat but couldn't squeeze. He just held his hands there, and she laughed at him. He'd left and gone to Randolph, who smuggled him on board the ship he worked on. No, as much as he hated his mother, he could never kill her. The years had cooled his anger, and his hatred had turned to loathing pity, then apathy. But never forgiveness.

"Vivian's choices were to become a prostitute or to die not knowing the Lord. I'm not condoning what she did, but becoming a prostitute afforded her the time to meet her Lord and Savior, thus saving her soul from eternal damnation. She would rather die now than go back to that life. Separate the sin from the sinner."

"I don't want to talk about Vivian or my mother."

"You have to forgive them sometime."

Did he? "Tell me about your wife and child."

Thankfully, William allowed the change in conversation. It was almost like having Randolph back, at least in his looks. It was very late before William left, and Conner spent the remainder of the night tossing in his bed. If he'd gone back, would he have tried to kill his mother again? He didn't know. How could a son come so close to doing something like that?

He raked his hands into his hair. *Heavenly Father, forgive my unforgiving spirit.* He felt no relief in that prayer.

At breakfast, Sarah was incensed. "He won't forgive her at all?"

William wiped the last of his egg yolks up with his toast. "Give him time."

"You said that five days ago when you went to talk to him that first night."

"His wounds go back to when he was a little boy."

"So do yours."

William pulled his eyebrows down but didn't counter.

Vivian sat quietly. She had allowed a small portion of hope to seep into her heart that William would be able to change Conner's mind. "I'm going to move to Seattle or Port Angeles and get a job." Her voice came out as small as a little child's.

"You can't." Tears immediately filled Sarah's eyes.

She wanted to cry, too, but no tears came. She felt numb inside. "I can't stay here. It hurts too much to be this near him and know he hates me." She stood and left the room. She didn't want to hear any arguments for why she should stay. She'd thought Sarah and William being here would bring her joy, but knowing she would lose them, too, by moving away just deepened her sorrow.

A young brunette woman entered Conner's store and approached Martin behind the counter. "I'm looking for Mr. Jackson."

He was near enough, so he answered. "I'm Conner Jackson."

She gave him a smile that didn't reach her eyes. This stranger seemed to be mad at him, but he didn't know why. "I'm Mrs. William Carlyle."

"It's a pleasure to meet you." William had chosen well.

"I wanted to meet the unforgiving cad who broke Vivian's heart."

So it wasn't going to be a pleasure meeting her. "Would you like to come into the back?" If this woman was going to give him an earful, he didn't want it to be in front of Martin, Todd, and his customers.

"I just came to give you this." She opened her reticule and pulled out a rock.

He flinched, not knowing if she was going to throw it at him.

She handed it to him.

"What's this for?"

"It's the first stone." She turned and walked out.

He stared at the rock in his hand, still asking himself the same question, what was it for?

"What did she give you?" Martin asked.

"A rock." He turned the rock over into his other hand. On the back side was written, "St. John 8:1–11." He tucked it into his pocket.

That night after he'd gotten ready for bed, he took the rock along with his Bible and sat on the edge of his bed. He'd been curious all day about the one passage from God's Word she'd chosen. Fred jumped out of the box with her three sleeping pups and crawled up next to him. What one passage had Mrs. Carlyle thought would make a difference? He'd read the whole Bible. If this passage hadn't made a difference before, why would it now? He opened his Bible and began to read:

> *Jesus went unto the mount of Olives. And early in the morning he came again into the temple, and all the people came unto him; and he sat down, and taught them. And the scribes and Pharisees brought unto him a woman taken in adultery; and when they had set her in the midst, they say unto him, Master, this woman was taken in adultery, in the very act. Now Moses in the law commanded us, that such should be stoned.*

Conner slammed his Bible shut and stared at the cover. He didn't want to read any more. A stirring in his spirit told him this would change his life. It *would* make a difference. If he finished the passage, he could never go back to his old way of thinking, his old way of not forgiving.

Fred pawed his arm and whined.

"I don't want to read it." He didn't want to forgive. Forgiveness was for those who deserved it.

Fred tilted her head sideways.

He tossed his Bible onto his bed and strode across the room to the window. The dark, moonless night reflected his empty soul. After a while, he went back to his bed, compelled to open the Bible again:

> *Now Moses in the law commanded us, that such should be stoned: but what sayest thou? This they said, tempting him, that they might have to accuse him. But Jesus stooped down, and with his finger wrote on the ground, as though he heard them not. So when they continued asking him, he lifted up himself, and said unto them, He that is without sin among you. . .*

Conner choked on these words.

> *Let him first cast a stone at her.*

Conner squeezed his eyes shut for a moment then continued:

And again he stooped down, and wrote on the ground. And they which heard it, being convicted by their own conscience, went out one by one, beginning at the eldest, even unto the last: and Jesus was left alone, and the woman standing in the midst. When Jesus had lifted up himself, and saw none but the woman, he said unto her, Woman, where are those thine accusers?

"Right here," Conner said aloud.

Hath no man condemned thee? She said, No man, Lord.

"I have," Conner whispered.

And Jesus said unto her, Neither do I condemn thee: go, and sin no more.

Conner took a deep cleansing breath. " 'He that is without sin among you, let him first cast a stone at her.'" Jesus was the only one who had the right to condemn and stone that woman, but He didn't. Instead, He released her from her burden of sin; He sent her away to start her life anew. He didn't wait for her to confess her sin or ask for forgiveness. He just gave her a new start.

Conner thought of the men eager to condemn her. "'And they which heard it, being convicted by their own conscience, went out one by one.'"

He looked at the rock, then read again, " 'He that is without sin among you, let him first cast a stone at her.'" He squeezed the rock in his hand. Sarah had given him the first stone to throw at Vivian. He was only permitted to throw it if he were without sin. He let the rock fall to the floor, dropped his head into his hands, and cried.

He wept for the loving mother he'd always wanted but had never had. He wept for hating the mother he did have. He wept for Vivian. And he wept for disappointing his Savior. Jesus had died for his sins. Jesus had died for Vivian's sins. And Jesus had died for his mother's sins. He was just as unworthy of the Lord's forgiveness as his mother. Perpetual sinners.

But Vivian was worthier than them all. She had done as the Lord commanded and gone and sinned no more.

"Forgive me, Jesus."

"*Neither do I condemn thee: go, and sin no more.*"

"Thank You, Lord."

"*Go.*"

Chapter 19

The next day, Vivian sat in a chair on the back lawn with baby Vivian in her arms. "She's so precious."

Sarah beamed at her daughter. "I'm hoping we have a boy next."

"Are you in a family way?"

"You asked me that a week ago when we arrived. No. At least not yet. But we have this big house to fill now."

"I can see you running all over this yard, chasing after a dozen children." Her heart ached for the same future.

"I can't do it without you. You have to stay."

"Sarah, I can't." It would be easier on her and easier on Conner. He shouldn't have to live every day wondering if he was going to run into her. And he shouldn't have to avoid visiting his old friend because of her presence.

She would write and make a few inquiries about domestic positions in Port Angeles. It wasn't too far away, but far enough, and she could visit more easily. William had gone to her attorney and deeded her half the house. He said he would pay her for her share when he could. So she had gone down and deeded her share to baby Vivian. William shook his head and gave up.

William told her she was being silly. Maybe she was, but she didn't want anything to tie her to Port Townsend. . .and keep her near Conner.

"Vivian, you have a visitor," William said as he strode across the lawn with Conner.

She sucked in her breath at the sight of him. Conner looked neither happy nor mad. She wished she could read his intention. His coat hung heavy on him, pulling down at the shoulder seams as though under a great weight, and his pockets bulged.

Conner nodded to Sarah. "Mrs. Carlyle." Then he turned to her. "Vivian."

"Conner." She could see a rock clenched in his right hand. What was he going to do? She handed baby Vivian back to Sarah.

William held out his hand to his wife. "Let's go inside and give them some privacy."

Sarah's eyes widened. "But—"

William took the baby and helped his wife to her feet. The three left, and Vivian was alone with Conner. . .and the rock.

Conner stood no more than a foot in front of her. "Mrs. Carlyle came to me yesterday and gave me this." He opened his hand to reveal a rock the size of a fat plum. "She wrote, 'St. John 8:1–11,' on it. That's the story of the woman caught in adultery, and this is to be the first stone cast."

She glanced toward the house where Sarah had gone. What had Sarah been up to? Why give Conner a rock to stone her? She heard a thump. He'd dropped the rock on the ground at her feet.

"That was for treating you poorly these last few weeks." He pulled a rock from one of his bulging pockets. "This one is for not forgiving you." It fell to the ground, and he pulled out another rock. "This one is for hating you. I don't hate you anymore."

Forgiveness was one thing, but could he accept her back into his life? Would he still want to marry her? "Conner."

"Let me finish. Please. I have my pockets full." He pulled his coat front aside to reveal bulging pants pockets.

He went through a long list of foolish childhood sins. Rocks of various sizes littered the small patch of grass between their feet. Conner's accumulated sins lay discarded at her feet. But how did he feel about her?

He pulled out a particularly heavy rock the size of an apple. "This one is for my mother. For everything she is and everything she's not." The stone hit the toe of his boot and rolled toward her.

Tears welled in her eyes. She knew that that one was hardest for him. His mother had wounded him as a little boy, a wound that had never healed over the years. Now maybe it could.

Conner moved the stones aside from in front of her with his feet then knelt on the ground. He took her hand and put one last rock into it, a rock the size of the one he'd used for his mother. "This one is for you to use. I have been so wrong. My heart was hardened. Please forgive me for being unforgiving. For not forgiving you." Agony etched every line of his face.

She dropped the rock. It thudded onto the grass. "Of course I forgive you."

"Thank you."

Was there more? Would he say it? "Do you still love me?" She heard herself say, her heart aching to know.

He smiled wide. "More than ever. When I came here, I wasn't sure I could say that, but when I looked at you across the yard, I knew I'd spend the rest of my life loving you whether you loved me back or not."

She scooted forward in her chair and threw her arms around his neck, knocking him off balance and her, as well. His arms came around her as they both tumbled to the lawn.

She started laughing. "I'm sorry." She tried to get up.

"I'm not." He kept his arms securely around her. "I'm not letting you get away." He put his hand behind her head and lowered it until he could kiss her. Then he rolled her onto her back. "I'm not perfect and I'm doomed to make more mistakes." His head was framed by the clear blue sky.

"We all make mistakes."

"I'm going to San Francisco. I'm going to find my mother. When I get back, I'm going to propose to you again."

"I'll say yes."

He smiled. "You aren't supposed to answer yet."

"I didn't want you to have any doubt I'd be here when you got back. What are you going to say to your mother?"

"I'm not sure. I'll tell her that I forgive her."

"Are you expecting her to have changed?"

He shook his head. "But I need to see her face-to-face and tell her I forgive her. If I can do that, then I believe I can be a good husband to you."

"And if you can't?"

"I have to. I don't want to live without you."

"We could marry first, and I could go with you." She didn't want to chance losing him.

"This is something I have to do on my own."

"I'll start making wedding plans while you're gone. Shall we plan for the day after you return?"

"You're still in mourning clothes."

"I won't be starting this afternoon." She'd been in mourning garb long enough to honor

Randolph. It was time to put the past to rest once and for all. "If you'll let me up, I have something I want to show you."

Conner stood and helped her to her feet but kept his arms around her. "I know this is going to sound bold, but I always knew I could have just about any lady I desired. I have prayed every day that the Lord would keep that temptation from me. Then I met my best friend's wife, and my heart started on an impossible journey. I never thought I'd have you in my arms, and now I'm reluctant to let you go."

Vivian laid her head on his chest, and he felt complete at last. His other half. The Lord had given him another chance and blessed him with love. He released her and helped her back into her chair, then sat in one next to it. "You wanted to show me something."

"It may change everything."

"Only God can change *everything*."

She took a letter from her pocket and handed it to him.

"Randolph's letter to you?"

She nodded. "You may read it."

Both the envelope and letter inside were a bit rumpled. Had she read this often? He unfolded it and read the first paragraph. "You told Randolph about your past?"

"It's why we fought the night he left."

He nodded and continued reading. When he finished, he folded it but didn't say anything. How did she think this would change everything? "What does this change?"

"He couldn't forgive me. He was going to send me away."

"That was Randolph. I have already forgiven you. I would like to think in time Randolph would have come around, but I don't know."

"Something else, too." She looked away as though nervous. "I have been married twice without having any children. I might be barren. What if I can't give you children?"

He took her by the upper arms and turned her back to face him. "I don't need children as long as I have you."

"Are you sure?"

"Yes. We'll just have to see what the Lord brings." He didn't want to hear further excuses, so he kissed her.

Conner spent a week in San Francisco following leads to find his mother. His search ended at the Place of Hope Asylum. He was ushered into the administrator's office by a woman in full black nun's habit. He shook hands with a Mr. Clark and sat across the desk from the small man in a wrinkled blue suit. Suspicion squinted through the thick lenses of Mr. Clark's spectacles, making Conner feel as if he were being assessed for signs of mental illness.

Mr. Clark dipped the end of his pen into an inkwell. "Name of patient?"

"Bertha Jackson."

Mr. Clark wrote on the paper in front of him. "Symptoms?"

"I don't know."

"How am I to know if our facility is right for"—he looked down at his paper—"Bertha, if you don't tell me anything about her?"

"I was hoping you could tell me. I was told she might be here."

Mr. Clark lowered his glasses on his nose. "You're looking for someone who's already been committed here? Incredible. Rarely does anyone visit. Once the insane are dumped off here by either the state, a family member, or anonymously, they are forgotten by the outside world."

"Is she here?"

Mr. Clark removed his glasses and pinched the bridge of his nose as though gaining patience to answer. "We have over two hundred patients. I don't know every name. It'll take a search of our files. It takes a lot of time to run this facility." He stood and showed Conner to the door. "Sister Mary Agnes, would you help Mr. Jackson find out if we have the patient he is inquiring about?"

The stoop-shouldered nun smiled. "Come this way." She stopped at a door with a small pane of glass in it. "This is one of our women's wards." She motioned for him to look through the window.

Iron beds lined both sides of the room and ran down the middle. There was barely room to move between them. The women wore plain gray dresses that hung straight and loose. He searched for a woman who could be his mother. "Is she in there?"

"We have four more women's wards and two men's wards. Give me a name, and I'll know which ward. I know every person ever committed to this asylum."

"Bertha Jackson."

Sister Mary Agnes smiled. "I remember Bertha May. Come with me."

He was both nervous and relieved. *Lord, help me forgive her.* He had no choice. No matter how vile she still was or what insults she might fling at him, he *had* to forgive.

Sister Mary Agnes led him to a small office with a desk and filing cabinets. Along the opposite wall was an iron bed like that in the ward. She offered the chair to him. He remained standing. How could he sit while an old woman stood? Was this the sister's room? Did she live here?

She pulled a file from the middle drawer of one of the cabinets. "I am good with names and faces but terrible with dates." She opened the file. "Bertha was with us from January of 1884 until December 5, 1893."

His mother had come to this place a few months after he'd run away, and left more than six years ago. This wasn't the end of his search, just a bend in his journey. "She was here for ten years? Why was she here? Where did she go?"

"I'm sure you have many questions. Where to begin?" Sister Mary Agnes returned the file to the drawer. "Shall we walk the grounds?" She guided him outside.

A small fenced courtyard contained several patients walking around or sitting. His mother had once been in that courtyard.

"Bertha was brought to us by city officials. She'd been badly beaten and was at the hospital first. She wouldn't tell anyone her name. For days all she would do was cry and rock. They kept her in a hospital ward until she attacked a nurse. Then they took her to the jail. The jail staff didn't want to deal with her, so they brought her to us."

His mother was insane. Had she always been so? She would tell him how useless and what a burden he was one day, and the next, she'd buy him a useless gift instead of food to fill his empty belly. He never knew what mood she was going to be in. One time she'd looked at him with this blank stare and asked him who he was.

"When she first arrived, we didn't know her name and kept her separate from the other patients. She would spend most of the day crawling around the room and under her bed looking for something, muttering, 'My baby. I have to find my baby.' I made her a doll out of strips of cloth. I wouldn't give it to her until she told me her name. After that, she sat in the corner and rocked her baby. We slowly integrated her into the main ward. The only time we had any trouble with her was when someone would take her doll."

Sister Mary Agnes stopped at a wrought iron fence on the far side of the grounds and pinned him with a stare. "She named her doll Conner."

He widened his eyes. "How did you know my given name?"

The nun smiled. "I didn't. Conner is the name she gave her doll."

Did this mean that in some strange way his mother had loved him? "Where did she go?"

"I'm afraid she didn't leave." Sister Mary Agnes pointed beyond the fence. "She passed on from this life. She's in row three, plot seven."

He struggled to take in a breath as though someone had punched him in the gut. His mother was dead? He'd never considered that his search would conclude with news of her death. He stared over the fence to the grass beyond but could see no markers. He turned to Sister Mary Agnes, but she was halfway back to the building.

He made his way along the fence to the gate and entered. Small plaques in the ground marked burial sites. He turned at row three and stopped halfway down:

Bertha May Jackson
1850–December 5, 1893

"I wasn't expecting this. I really thought you'd still be alive. I always hated you for who you were and for your cruelty to me." He stared at the plaque for a long time. Then Vivian's face came to his mind. He had to do it. "I forgive you, Mother, for all the bad things you did." He laid a fist-sized stone on the marker. Written on the stone was St. John 8:1–7. Even though he now knew his mother had been insane, he still couldn't bring himself to tell her that he loved her. His forgiveness would have to be enough.

Vivian watched from her bedroom window as she waited for Conner to ride up. He would be discussing business again with William. Since he'd returned from California nearly a week ago, he'd hardly talked to her, too busy with his store and working with William on the shipping business. He wouldn't talk about his visit with his mother. It couldn't have gone well, or he'd be in better spirits. It felt as though he was more distant from her now than when he'd found out about her past.

She'd moved into one of the smaller bedrooms so William and Sarah could have the larger suite. William had told her that Conner gave her half of his portion of the shipping business, and that was where the money was coming from that was put into her bank account each month. The money didn't matter if Conner wouldn't speak to her.

She watched him ride up and dismount from his horse. She took a deep breath and smoothed her dress before descending the staircase in a ladylike glide. Maggie stood by the door, but Conner wasn't there.

"Where's Conner?"

"He's waiting for you in the parlor." Maggie returned to the kitchen.

Vivian entered the parlor. "Conner."

His gaze drifted from the fireplace to her. "You asked to see me?"

He stood stiff and aloof. Why was he being so distant? There was so much to say and ask. She didn't know where to begin. "Why are you avoiding me?" The question came out without her actually choosing it.

"I'm not avoiding you." His expression was flat, as though someone had taken the life out of him.

Her emotions were all a jumble. "You are, too," she blurted out. "You come and talk to William but not me." She didn't want to be angry with him, but her words came out that way.

"I've been busy."

Busy staying away from her. "Is our wedding off?"

He raked a hand through his hair. "I think that would be best."

Her heart struggled to beat. He couldn't mean that. He'd forgiven her. "My sins are too much for you to bear."

A shadow of grief crossed his features, and he crossed the room to take her hand. "No. It's not you."

"Then what?"

"It's my mother."

"You found her, then?"

He released her and turned back to the empty fireplace. "Sort of. She's dead."

She put a hand on his arm. "I'm so sorry."

He looked down at her hand, then pulled away. "She died in an insane asylum. She was touched in the head."

"Conner, I'm so sorry." Facing his back, she touched his shoulder.

He jumped away from her. "They say insanity runs in families. I could go insane, too. I'm trusting the Lord to spare me, but I won't burden you with that."

She took three steps forward to stand as close to Conner as she could without touching him, tilted her head back, and looked up at him. "You are not insane."

"How can you have such confidence?"

She touched her chest. "I know it in here. You have Christ in you. You wrestle daily with trying to make right decisions. You are an honorable man who humbled yourself to forgive the mother who hurt you terribly."

"But there is still a chance I could go crazy, just like her."

She put her fingers to his lips. "You won't. You are the most levelheaded, sane person I've ever met. We will trust in God to help us handle whatever circumstances we might be faced with. The only crazy thing I can think of that you might do is not marry the woman you love. You do still love me?"

A smile tugged at his mouth. "Every minute of every day." He pulled her close and kissed her.

Chapter 20

June 1 was a beautiful, sunny day. The rhododendrons were in full bloom. The small wedding took place in the backyard of the Carlyle House. Guests included Sarah and William and baby Vivian; Maggie and Scotty; Martin Zahn; Abigail Parker and her son, Harry; Peter and the other children from the orphanage; Finn; and a handful of other guests. Peter's aunt agreed to take him with the dog, and Finn had volunteered to accompany the five-year-old to the other side of the state. Finn said it was time for him to be moving on. He and Peter would leave the following day for Spokane.

Vivian waited anxiously to be signaled forward. She wore a cream dress with lavender flowers embroidered on it. William held out his elbow for her. "It's time."

She looped her hand through the crook in his arm and walked with him down the short aisle to where Conner stood. She could hardly believe this day was finally here and she was a June bride. After they had said their vows and exchanged rings, the minister gave Conner and Vivian a moment for another exchange they had requested. Conner handed her a white rock. "To always remember I'm a sinner and need to be forgiven daily."

She smiled. He'd found a truly white rock and had been thinking like she had. She pulled out a stone she'd painted white to show that they were cleaned white as snow by Jesus' blood. She handed the rock to Conner. "To always remember that I have been forgiven."

The minister pronounced them man and wife, and Conner kissed her.

The reception was held in the backyard, too, and the children had fun running around. After all the guests had left, only Vivian and Conner, Sarah and William remained.

Conner dangled a key in front of her face. She spun to face him and reached for the key. "What's this for?"

He snatched the key out of her reach and pocketed it. "Close your eyes, and I'll show you."

She closed them and covered them with her hand.

He put his hand over hers and guided her around the yard.

She trusted him not to let her fall or get hurt. She was trying to figure out where in the yard she was but finally gave up.

He kept turning her around and making her walk in different directions. He finally stopped her on what felt like a paving stone and turned her to face something. "Open your eyes."

Before her stood the white house next door to Sarah and William's blue one.

"I didn't want you to have to live above the store, so I bought you a house."

"We'll be neighbors and can spend our days together raising our children." Sarah stood next to her.

Conner scooped Vivian up into his arms and carried her across the threshold. "Welcome home." He set her down inside, kicked the door closed, and kissed her.

Her brand-new life had begun.

THE CASTAWAY'S BRIDE

by Susan Page Davis

Dedication

To my sister Pam, always supportive, never predictable.
You were brave enough to sleep alone in the Hired Man's Room for years.
You brought us Moon Man and Ambercrombie Benson.
Without you we'd all be a little more melancholy and provincial.
Sisters forever!

Chapter 1

Portland, Maine, 1820

Edward Hunter hurried down the gangplank to the wharf, taking a deep breath as he viewed the city before him. In the five years he'd been gone, the docks of Portland had grown more crowded, and they bustled with business. Since the end of the war with England, commerce was good, and merchants in the brand-new state of Maine prospered. So many changes! Maine was no longer part of Massachusetts. What else would he discover today?

When he gained the street, he glanced south toward where his father's shipping company had its offices and docks, but he squared his shoulders and turned inland instead. Abigail first, then home.

As he rounded the corner onto Free Street, he felt the tug of his heart stronger than ever and picked up his pace. At last he would be with her again. His pulse quickened as he thought of Abigail. She'd been so young when he'd left. Had she changed?

He chided himself. Of course she had.

For the last five years, that question had plagued him. His fiancée no doubt believed him dead for most of the time he'd been away. Anything could have happened during that period. She would have matured, which was a good thing. When Edward first approached him, her father had considered her too young at seventeen for an engagement. Several months later, after many evenings spent in the Bowman parlor under the watchful eyes of Abigail's parents, the betrothal had been allowed.

Age would not be a problem now; she must be two and twenty. But how else had she changed? He didn't like to think she had pined for him, grief stricken all this time, but neither did he like to think she might have forgotten him. She could have fallen in love with another man by now. She could even be married.

That thought slowed his steps as he walked up the path to the Bowman house. He had tried to avoid thinking about such possibilities during his years of isolation and loneliness on a desolate island in the Pacific Ocean. In all those lonely days and nights, his worst fear had not been death. He had faced that and come so close it no longer frightened him. What he dreaded most was learning that Abigail had forsaken his memory and married another man.

Edward stood before the door for a moment in silent prayer. *Dear Father in heaven, You alone know what is to come, and You know what is best for me. You saw fit to bring me back from near death in the deep, for what purpose I do not know. But now I trust my future to You, Lord.*

He squared his shoulders and lifted the knocker.

Deborah Bowman broke off her humming as the door knocker's distinct thud resounded through the lower rooms of the house.

"Can you get that, Debbie?" Her mother's voice reached her from the kitchen, where preparation of the evening meal was underway.

"Yes, Mother!" Deborah laid down the stack of linen napkins she'd been distributing on the long walnut dining table and headed into the front hall. It couldn't be Jacob Price, her sister's fiancé. He was due in an hour and a half for dinner, and his business usually kept him until the last minute.

The hymn she had been humming stuck in her mind, and she resumed the melody, tucking an errant strand of hair behind her ear as she crossed the hall. She turned the knob and pulled back the heavy oak door. A tall, slender man stood on the doorstep, taller even than Jacob. Almost as tall as. . .

She stared at his sun-browned face and swallowed the blithe greeting she'd prepared to deliver.

"Ab—" He stopped and frowned as he studied her.

The air Deborah sucked in felt heavy in her lungs. She must be mistaken. Again she surveyed the man's handsome but anxious face. A new scar dipped from the corner of his right eye down and back toward his earlobe, and he was thin almost to the point of gauntness. But his dark hair and eyes, his firm chin, even the tilt of his head were the same. It must be him.

"Edward? It can't be!" Her words were barely audible, but the flickering response in his eyes told her she was not mistaken.

"Not little Deborah!"

Her cheeks burned as she felt blood rushing into her face.

"Yes, it's me. But. . .Edward, how. . . ? You can't. . . ." She gave it up and shook her head.

"It's me." A glint stole into his eyes that assured her he was indeed the Edward Hunter she'd known and admired since childhood. The merry demeanor he'd sported as a youth was replaced by something more grave, but there was no doubt in her mind. Somehow Edward had returned from the dead.

"Praise God!" She seized his hands, then dropped them in a rush of embarrassment and stood aside. "Come in. I can hardly believe it's you. Am I dreaming?"

"If you are, then your mother is baking apple tart in your dreams."

Delight bubbled up inside her, and she grasped his sleeve. "Oh, Edward, do come into the parlor. I'll run up and tell Abby you're here."

"She's. . .she's here, then."

"Yes, of course." Deborah halted, anticipating the shock this revelation would bring her older sister. "I expect she'll need a moment to absorb the news." The thought of Jacob Price danced at the edge of Deborah's mind, and she firmly shoved it into oblivion. Edward was home! He was alive! Nothing else must get in the way of the joy his return brought.

She slipped her hand through the crook of his elbow and guided him across the hall into the snug parlor where her mother received guests.

"There, now. You just wait here."

"Thank you."

His strained smile sent a pang of apprehension through her. She longed to sit down beside him on the sofa and hear his tale, but that privilege belonged to Abigail. The pain and anxiety in his face transferred to her own heart. Should she tell him? No, that obligation, too, belonged to her sister.

There was one thing she, as the hostess greeting him, should ask.

"Your mother?"

"I haven't seen her yet." Edward's mouth tightened. "I heard about Father on the ship I took up here from Boston."

Deborah nodded, feeling tears spring into her eyes as she noted his deep sorrow. "I'm sorry, Edward."

"Thank you."

She took a deep breath. "Sit and relax for a few minutes. I'll tell Abby."

At the parlor door, she paused and looked back. Edward sank into a chair and sat immobile, staring toward the front windows. What was going through his mind? Five years! What had happened to him in that time? And how would his return affect Abigail?

She turned, lifted her skirt, and dashed up the stairs.

"Abby?" She careened to a stop in the doorway to her sister's room. Abigail was brushing her long, golden hair, arranging it just so.

"You shouldn't tear around so, Debbie." Abigail turned her attention back to the mirror.

"Abby, I have something to tell you." Deborah took two steps into the room. At least her sister was sitting down. "Something's happened."

Abigail's gaze caught hers in the mirror, and her hands stilled, holding a lock of hair out away from her head, with her brush poised to style it.

"Not Father?"

"Oh no, nothing like that. It's good news. Very good."

Abigail laid the brush down and swiveled on her stool to face Deborah. "What is it?"

"It's. . . Oh dear, I'm not sure how to say this."

"Just say it."

Deborah gazed into her sister's eyes, blue and dreamy like their mother's. For such a long time, those eyes had been red-rimmed from weeping. But recently Abigail had overcome her grief and taken an interest in life once more. Her family had encouraged her to leave off grieving for the man she'd loved. He was dead and gone, and it was all right for her to go on with her life. That's what they'd all told her.

But what would happen now? Deborah didn't want to be the one to shatter her sister's peaceful world again. She ought to have told Mother first and let her break the news to Abigail.

"Debbie." Abigail rose and stepped toward her, clearly annoyed. "Would you just tell me, please? You're driving me wild."

"All right. It's. . .it's Edward."

"Edward?" Abigail's face went white, and she swayed. Deborah rushed to her side and eased her gently toward the side of her four-poster bed. Abigail sat slowly on the edge, staring off into space, then suddenly jerked around to stare at Deborah. "What about him? Tell me."

"He's. . . Oh, Abby, he's alive."

Edward stood and paced the parlor to the fireplace of granite blocks. Turn. To the wide bay window that fronted the street. Outside was the Bowmans' garden and, beyond it, people passing by, bustling toward home and dinner, no doubt. So ordinary. So common. But to his eyes, painfully odd.

Five years! Dear God, everything is so strange here. How can I come back and pick up my life again?

He jerked away from the scene and paced to the fireplace once more.

He'd left the ship determined that the first woman he set eyes on in five years would be the woman he loved. Of course, he'd seen a few ladies from a distance as he walked from the dock to the Bowman house, but none whom he recognized. The city had grown in his absence, and new houses and businesses crowded the peninsula between the Fore River and Casco Bay.

His thoughts had skimmed over the surface of what he'd seen: a multitude of sailing vessels floating in the harbor, scores of people crowding the streets, freight wagons and carts, hawkers preparing to close business for the evening, and housewives hurrying home to start supper. He'd been thinking only of Abigail.

But the woman who opened the door to him had not been Abigail but her little sister,

Deborah. Debbie had grown strangely mature and womanly. She was not the child—with the gawky limbs, bushy dark hair, and big, brown eyes so unlike Abigail's—that Edward recalled. Deborah favored Dr. Bowman's side of the family, no question about that.

She was no longer the awkward tomboy. She had moved with grace as she ushered him to the parlor. Her hair had tempered to a smooth, rich chestnut, neatly confined in an upswept coiffure. Her green gown edged with creamy lace was the attire of a lady, not a rambunctious adolescent.

He turned and walked toward the window once more. Abigail. She was the one he longed to see. His thoughts should be focused on her. It was only the strangeness of seeing Deborah grown up that had pulled his mind in a different direction. He tried, as he had so many times in the past five years, to conjure up the image of Abigail's face: her creamy skin, her golden hair, her blue eyes. He sighed and stopped before the window seat.

He would have sent a letter before him at the first opportunity, but as it turned out, he traveled back to civilization by the fastest means he could find. The ship that rescued him conveyed him directly to Boston, and there he'd found a schooner heading north and east the next day for Portland. No letter could have winged its way to his beloved any faster than he had arrived himself.

Would the shock of his appearance endanger her health? Deborah recovered quickly and welcomed him with joy. Still, Abigail had always been less robust than Debbie. Was he inconsiderate to come here first? Perhaps he should have gone to his mother first and sent advance notice to Abigail, then come round to see her in the evening.

He glanced out the window and saw that the shadows were lengthening. He'd lost his pocket watch four years ago in the roiling storm that shipwrecked him, but he could tell by the angle of the sun that late afternoon had reached the coast of Maine. His gaze roved over the lush trees shielding the house from the street. The full foliage welcomed him like the face of an old friend. How he'd longed for the shade of the maples in his parents' yard during the searing summers of the island, where the seasons were turned about and the hottest time of year was in January and February.

He'd kept meticulous count of the days, as nearly as he could reckon, and consoled himself in the hottest times by recalling the ice and snow of Maine winters. He'd tried to picture what Abigail was doing as he sweltered in exile. Ice-skating with Debbie? Riding to church in her father's sleigh? He would imagine her wearing a fur hat and muff, romping through falling snow.

He walked once more to the fireplace, where he leaned one arm against the mantel.

How would she receive him? What would she say? It seemed like he had been waiting for hours. What could possibly be keeping her? She ought to be tearing down the stairs and into his arms. Shouldn't she? Edward offered another silent plea for serenity, knowing that the next few minutes would determine the course of his life.

"How can I face him, Mother?" Abigail sat on the bed, twisting the ends of her sash between her hands.

Deborah stood by, panting a little after her dash down the back stairs and up again with her mother.

"My dear, think of all he's been through. You must see him. You cannot send him away without hearing his story. Furthermore, you must explain your current state to him."

"Oh, Mother, must I?"

"Yes, I'm afraid you must. Break the news to him gently. He will understand, I'm sure, that you've grieved him properly and moved slowly in pinning your affections elsewhere.

Your father and I watched you mourn and weep over that young man for three years. No one can fault you in your devotion to him. But now you've got beyond that."

"But, Mother, it's Edward." Deborah grasped her mother's arm, fighting the unbearable confusion that swirled inside her.

"Well, yes, dear." Her mother glanced at her, then back at Abigail. "Of course we're thrilled that he has returned, but your sister hasn't entered into this betrothal with Jacob lightly. It's not something to cast aside—"

"But she loved Edward first." Deborah saw the agony in her sister's eyes as she spoke and clamped her lips together, determined to say no more on the matter. This was Abigail's dilemma, not hers. Still, she couldn't imagine a better surprise than to learn that Edward, whom she'd always adored, was still alive. Deborah had been only fifteen when the news of Edward's death came, but she had felt her heart would break along with Abby's. He was such a fine young man. Deborah knew that if she ever gave her love to a man, he would be a man much like Edward Hunter.

"Couldn't Father just tell him?" Abigail pleaded.

Mother frowned. "Really, Abby! I sent Elizabeth around to ask your father to come home as soon as he can, but he has no inkling of the situation. And he might not be able to leave his office for some time if there are a lot of patients. You mustn't keep that young man waiting."

Abigail stood and walked with wooden steps toward the looking glass.

"Your face is pale," Mother murmured. "Let me help you freshen up. Debbie—" She turned, and Deborah looked toward her. Mother's usual calm expression had fled, and her agitation was nearly as marked as Abigail's dismay.

"Debbie, go down and tell Elizabeth to take him some—no, wait. Elizabeth's gone to fetch your father. You help your sister finish her hairdo, and I'll go and greet Edward myself and see that he has a glass of cider. Don't be long now, Abby."

Mother swept from the room, and Deborah approached Abigail's chair.

"Would you like me to pin up the last few locks?"

"Oh, would you?"

Deborah reached for the silver-backed brush. Her gaze met that of her sister in the wall mirror. "Try to smile when you greet him, Abby. You look like a terrified rabbit."

"Oh, Debbie, I'm not sure I want to see Edward."

"That's silly. You'll have to see him sometime. He's home to stay."

Tears escaped the corners of Abigail's eyes and trailed down her cheeks. "But it's been so long. Debbie, I was seventeen when he left."

"I know." Deborah sank to her knees and pulled Abigail into her embrace.

Abby sobbed and squeezed her, then pulled away. "I'll ruin your dress."

"Here." Deborah reached for a muslin handkerchief on the dressing table and placed it in Abigail's hand.

"If only Mr. Hunter hadn't sent him away," Abigail moaned.

"You know he wanted his son to learn every aspect of the business before he began running it," Deborah said. "Edward was preparing to take over when his father retired. His commission as an officer on the *Egret* was intended to give him the experience he'd need to head a shipping company. The men wouldn't have respected him if he'd never been to sea."

"I know, but he'd been on one voyage with his father already. Why did Mr. Hunter have to send Edward on that horrid voyage to the Pacific?"

Deborah sighed. "Maturity, Abby. Experience. Look at Jacob. He was a lad, too, when the *Egret* left. But now he's a man, and he understands the business perfectly, so he's able—"

She stopped and looked into Abigail's stricken face.

"What will happen at Hunter Shipping now? They've given Jacob the place Edward would have had if he'd lived. I mean, if he'd—oh, Debbie, this is too awful, and I'm confused."

"There, now, you can't keep crying. Your eyes will be puffy and bloodshot. And you can't blame Mr. Hunter. The news devastated all of us, and it was his own son who went down with the *Egret* in that brutal storm. Or at least, we all thought he did. Jacob and the other men in his boat survived, and we all praised God for that. You can't hold it against Mr. Hunter for taking his nephew into the office afterward, when he thought his only son was lost."

"Edward's drowning broke his poor father's heart."

"Yes." Deborah picked up the hairbrush and began once more to pull it through Abigail's tresses, then pinned her hair up quickly. "If only Mr. Hunter had lived to see this day."

"He would be so happy," Abigail whispered.

"He certainly would be. There."

Abigail examined her image in the mirror, blotted the traces of tears from her cheeks, and stood.

"I guess it's time."

Chapter 2

Edward, what a joy to see you again!" Mrs. Bowman bustled into the parlor, and Edward jumped up.

"Thank you. I'm grateful to be here, ma'am."

She set down the tray she carried, took his hand, and smiled up at him. "Abigail will be right down. She was surprised at the news, of course. You understand."

"Of course." He sat when his hostess sat, perching on the edge of the upholstered chair, and accepted the cold glass of sweet cider she offered him.

"You must have been through a nightmare."

"Yes, ma'am. A very long nightmare." He wondered if he ought to launch into his story or wait until Abigail appeared.

From the hallway, he heard the front door open and close, and his hostess sprang up again. "That must be Dr. Bowman. Will you excuse me just a moment, Edward? I know he'd love to see you."

Edward stood up but said nothing as she hurried from the room. This was getting increasingly chaotic. All he'd wanted was a glimpse of Abigail's face and a moment alone with her, but he should have known he would have to wade through her family first.

The murmur of voices reached him, and then Dr. Bowman's deep voice rose in shock and pleasure. "What? You don't mean it!"

Abigail's father strode across the threshold and straight toward him, his hand outstretched in welcome.

"Edward! What a wonderful surprise!" The older man shook his hand with vigor, and Edward eyed him cautiously. He hadn't changed much. Perhaps his hair held a bit more gray. His square face bore the interested expression that inspired confidence in his patients. Edward had always liked the physician but was somewhat intimidated five years earlier, viewing him as his future father-in-law. His persistence and diligent labor in Hunter Shipping's office and warehouse had finally convinced Dr. Bowman that he was acceptable husband material for Abigail. Her father had relented and permitted the engagement just before Edward left on his voyage.

"It's good to see you, sir."

"Sit down." The doctor waved toward his chair, and Edward resumed his seat, more nervous than ever, as Dr. Bowman took a place on the sofa.

Mrs. Bowman, who had entered the room behind her husband, gave Edward a nod and a smile. "You'll excuse me, won't you? I must go and give some instructions about dinner to the hired girl."

"You've moved your practice out of the house, sir?" Edward asked.

"Yes, I've got a small surgery down on Union Street now. Convenient for the patients, and it saves the family the disturbance of all those people coming to the house. The short walk there and back gives me some exercise."

"You look well, sir."

"Thank you. I can't say as much for you." The doctor looked him over with a professional eye, and Edward tried not to fidget.

"So, tell me: What happened to you when the *Egret* foundered? And better yet, what miracle has restored you to us now?"

Edward decided that an abbreviated version of his adventure was in order. He would probably have to tell the story many times in the next few days, but short of Abigail herself, Dr. Bowman might be his most important audience.

"Well, sir, we'd done our trading and were ready to start home. Almost four years ago it was. We hit bad weather, which is not unusual, but it was a wild gale. The storm buffeted us about, and we lost a great deal of rigging; finally the mainmast went down. The captain could see the ship was lost, and he urged us all to get into the boats."

The doctor placed his elbow on the arm of the sofa and leaned his chin on his hand, watching Edward with his avid dark eyes.

Like Deborah's eyes, Edward thought. *Always searching. Wants to know everything.*

"Your cousin Jacob told us how you had to abandon ship," Dr. Bowman said.

"I heard he survived. I'm thankful for that," Edward said. "Jacob led the first boatload, and they got away from the *Egret* in the yawl. I held the longboat near the ship until the captain came down. He insisted on seeing all the men down first. It was difficult. . . ." He closed his eyes for a moment, remembering the howling wind and the boat lunging on the waves. In his mind he saw young Davy Wilkes leap over the side of the ship and land half in, half out of the longboat, with his thighbone broken.

"Did the captain survive, too, then?"

Edward opened his eyes, shaking off the memory. "At first he did. We had eight of us in the longboat. Jacob had a dozen or more in the yawl."

"Fourteen came home."

"That many? I'm glad. I knew a few drowned in the storm, trying to get into the boats. And we lost four men from the longboat before we reached land."

"Starvation?"

"Lack of water, mostly. One boy died of his injuries, and we lost one man over the side in rough water the first night."

"Jacob told us that after your boats became separated during the night he and his crew sailed on for several days, and then another ship picked them up."

"God be praised," Edward murmured. He had often prayed for his comrades and wondered whether they had escaped death.

A stir in the doorway drew his attention, and he realized that Deborah had returned. As he jumped up, she smiled at him, and again he felt the infectious warmth of her presence.

"Well, girls. About time," Dr. Bowman said.

Edward saw then that another young woman was entering behind Deborah, hanging back as though reluctant to break in on the scene. Her eyes were lowered, but when she glanced up as she came forward, he caught his breath.

"Abigail." His pulse hammered.

Deborah stepped aside, and Edward met Abigail in the middle of the room. She looked him in the eye then, her mouth a tight line and her eyelids swollen.

"Hello, Edward."

He reached for her hands, and she hesitated a moment, then let him take them. She hadn't changed, really, except for the shy, sorrowful air she bore. She was as lovely as he remembered. Thinner, perhaps, and more fragile. She had lost the gaiety he always associated with her. Indeed, Deborah exhibited far more pleasure at his appearance than Abigail did.

"I'm so glad. . . ." She turned away abruptly and pulled a handkerchief from her sleeve. "Forgive me," she sobbed.

Edward cleared his throat. "There's nothing to forgive. I realize this is a shock, my dear."

"There, now, sit down, girls," said their father. "Edward was just telling me how he and several others escaped the shipwreck."

"Do tell us," Deborah begged, guiding Abigail to sit with her on the sofa. Dr. Bowman took another chair, and Edward sat down again. "Your boat also was spared by the storm, then?"

"We drifted for two weeks." Edward glanced at Abigail, who was surreptitiously wiping away a tear.

Mrs. Bowman returned, and in the pause she asked, "Shall I bring tea?"

"Not for me, thank you," Edward said.

"Nor me," said the doctor. "It's too close to dinner."

The young women shook their heads, and she slipped into a chair near her husband.

"Please go on, Edward," his host urged.

"Well, sir, we had a small sail and a rudder, and we steered for the nearest land we knew of. We took on water constantly, and I was sure we would all perish. But finally we fetched up on an island."

"What island?" Dr. Bowman asked.

"A small one west of Chile, sir. Far west. It is called Spring Island after the water available there. It has been charted for many years, but not many go there, as it is off the usual shipping lanes."

"Four years!" Deborah stared at him, her lips parted and her eyes glistening. "You stayed on that remote place for four years?"

He nodded. "Nearly. I hoped we would be rescued soon, but after a few weeks we grew discouraged. We were just too far off course for most ships. The one that finally came had also suffered damage and put in for fresh water and a chance to make some repairs before resuming its voyage."

"The ship that rescued Jacob Price and the others searched for your party," Dr. Bowman said.

"Aye. I expect they did. But we'd gone a long ways before we struck land."

"How many of you were there?" Deborah asked.

"Four of us were left when we first landed. But. . ."

"Some of them died?" the doctor asked softly.

"Yes, sir. Alas, I was alone the last two winters." Edward's throat constricted, and he wished they would not ask him any more questions. Eventually he would have to tell all, but for now he wanted only to forget the island and gaze at Abigail.

She had said nothing since they were seated, and Edward wondered at her reserve. She had never been boisterous, but neither had she cringed from him as she seemed to be doing now. This was not going at all as he had imagined.

He drew a deep breath.

"By God's grace, I was found a few months past and carried home again." He turned toward her father. "I don't mean to be forward, but might I have a word with Abigail, sir?"

Mrs. Bowman looked at her husband, and the doctor stood, smiling.

"Of course. I must change my clothes for dinner. Will you stay and eat with us, Edward?"

Abigail's gaze flew to her father, and her features froze as though she dreaded Edward's response.

Edward hesitated. Abigail was definitely not throwing him any encouragement.

"Thank you, sir, but I must decline. I have yet to see my mother."

"Of course," said Dr. Bowman. "Please convey our respects to her."

"I must go to the kitchen," Mrs. Bowman said. "Do come see us again, Edward."

He watched them go, puzzling over what Mrs. Bowman's words might mean to a man who was engaged to marry her daughter. Deborah was also rising, but Abigail shot out her hand and grabbed her sister's wrist.

"Please stay, won't you, Debbie?"

"Well, I. . ." Deborah glanced at him and back to Abigail. "I need to change my clothes as well."

"Please," Abigail whispered, so low Edward barely heard.

Deborah swallowed hard, tossed him an apologetic glance, and settled once more on the sofa.

Is she afraid of me? Edward wondered. He knew his experience had changed him. He was thin and run-down physically, but his love for Abigail was unscathed. *I must be patient until she realizes I am the same man she loved five years ago.*

Deborah looked hard at her sister. When Abigail did not speak, she said, "Edward, I would like to hear more of your ordeal sometime, if it is not too distressing to speak of it."

He nodded. "Perhaps sometime after I've settled in and gotten used to being home again. It was a time of great testing and hardship. The isolation. . ."

"I'm so sorry you had to go through that." Deborah glanced at her sister again.

Abigail turned her attention on him, but her smile seemed to strain every muscle in her face to the point of pain.

"My dearest," he said quietly, leaning toward her. "I do hope you'll forgive me for speaking so frankly before your sister, but I must know—"

She pushed herself up from the sofa, clapping a hand to her temple.

"I'm sorry, Edward, but I don't feel well. Would you please excuse me?"

Edward leaped to his feet, but before he could reply, she had dashed for the door.

"Abby!" Deborah cried, but her sister was gone. Appalled at Abigail's behavior, Deborah turned back to face their guest. "Edward, I'm so sorry. That's not like her."

"She must be ill, indeed." He frowned, staring toward the empty doorway.

Deborah's heart went out to him. The forlorn dismay in his eyes wrenched every tender inclination she possessed.

"I'll go to her." She reached out and squeezed his hands. "Do, please, forgive her abruptness. I'm sure she wouldn't behave so if she were well. Perhaps you could come around again tomorrow."

"Yes, I shall. Please convey my apologies."

"You've nothing to apologize for."

Edward grimaced. "I'm afraid I must, or she wouldn't have reacted so. I seem to have lost my social graces. It would have been better to take a different approach rather than to shock you all." He took an uncertain step toward the door.

He looked so lost that Deborah gently took his arm and stayed beside him as far as the front door. He had no hat to retrieve, so she reached for the doorknob.

"Do come back tomorrow, Edward."

"Yes, I believe I will." Her heart ached as he turned his troubled eyes toward the stairs, then back to her. "But if Abigail is too ill to see me, you will tell me, won't you?"

"Yes, of course."

"Good. I don't want to be a bother."

His confusion and dejection made Deborah long to blurt out the truth. *Abby's promised to marry your cousin, but we still love you.* No, she couldn't say that. She glanced toward the stairway, wishing her father would appear to take over and tell Edward. Surely they shouldn't let him leave their house in ignorance. The whole town knew. Someone else would tell him. His mother, perhaps. He should not learn it that way.

But their father assumed Abby was doing her duty and explaining the situation to Edward herself. Perhaps Deborah should take him back into the parlor and beg him to wait while she fetched Father downstairs again. No, it was drawing close to dinnertime, and if Edward didn't leave the house soon, he'd still be here when Jacob arrived.

"Good day," Edward murmured. He was outside on the doorstep now.

What could she do? What could she say?

She caught her breath and stifled the words she wanted to shout. They nearly choked her. Instead, she managed to say, "I'm sure Abby will be all right once she gets over the jolt of your appearance. She ought to be able to receive you properly tomorrow."

He nodded and turned away, and she closed the door in misery, certain that she'd done the wrong thing.

Edward walked slowly down the path toward the street. What did this mean? Abigail seemed anything but glad to see him. Her blue eyes had remained downcast during most of their interview, and when she looked up, he saw something like panic harbored in them.

But she was still here at home with her parents. That in itself was an encouragement. His fear that she might have married was unfounded.

Lord, show me how to approach her tomorrow, he prayed silently as he stepped through the gate. *You know my wishes, dear Father, but. . .Your will be done.*

He pulled up suddenly as another man nearly collided with him.

"Sorry." He jerked away, but the man seized his arm and stopped him.

"Edward? Is it you?"

He turned to look at the man. Sudden joy leaped into his heart, and he flung his arms around his cousin.

"Jacob! I'm so glad to see you at last. The Bowmans told me you and your men made it."

Jacob gasped and pulled away from him, his eyes wide in disbelief and his mouth gaping. "I can't believe it! How can this be?"

Edward laughed, the first merriment he'd felt in a long time.

"It's wonderful to see you."

"But where. . .when. . . ?" Jacob shook his head and stood staring.

"I'm on my way home to see Mother. Come with me," Edward said.

Jacob looked longingly toward the house, then back at him. "I'm afraid I can't. I've a dinner engagement this evening. But perhaps I can get away early. You must tell me everything that's happened to you and the others."

"I'll be at home," Edward said. "We'll have a chance to discuss it soon." He wanted to get away, to have more time to think about his encounter with the Bowman family. And he must get to his mother right away. He'd sent a note to her as soon as the ship docked, but she would not forgive him if he lingered in the street, chatting with his cousin when he ought to be hurrying home to her embrace.

"All right," Jacob agreed. "Were you planning to go by the office tomorrow?"

"I might. Are you working there?"

"Well. . .yes. Listen, if you don't come in tomorrow, I'll come looking for you. I need to hear it all." He lifted the latch of the gate.

"You're going to the Bowmans' for dinner?" Edward asked.

"Well, yes." A flush washed Jacob's cheeks. "I say, Edward, have you been to see Abigail?"

"As a matter of fact, yes."

"Then she told you?"

Edward eyed him for a moment then cleared his throat.

"Told me what?"

Jacob looked toward the house, then back at him. "Edward, I. . ."

Edward's anxiety mounted to paralyzing torment as he took in Jacob's pale features. Why should his friend and cousin sound remorseful?

"I. . ." Jacob straightened his shoulders. "We all thought you were dead, Edward."

"So I've been told." This was it, then. This was why Abigail felt ill when she saw him.

"Yes, well, it's been a long time."

"Four years since the *Egret* sank."

"Yes. And for the past year—oh, Edward, I didn't mean any disrespect to you or. . .or any presumption, but. . .well, you see, I've been courting Abigail."

Chapter 3

Deborah knocked softly on the door to Abigail's room. Even through the six-panel pine door, she could hear her sister weeping. She opened it a crack and peeked in. Abigail lay facedown on her bed, crying into her pillow.

Deborah tiptoed in and sat on the edge of the bed.

"There, Abby. Don't take on so." She rubbed her sister's heaving shoulders, and the sobs grew quieter.

At last Abigail rolled over, her cheeks crimson and her eyes awash with tears.

"I suppose you think I'm horrible." Abigail sniffed and her mouth twisted into a grimace. "Oh, Debbie, I know I was unkind to him—and I'm sorry—but I just couldn't tell him. How am I supposed to deal with this situation? It's unthinkable."

"No, dear. I'm sure other women must have faced similar problems before."

"I just want to die." Abigail broke out in weeping once more, and Deborah gathered her into her arms.

After several minutes, Abigail leaned back and blew her nose on the clean handkerchief Deborah offered her.

"Look at me! I'm wretched, and Jacob will be here any minute for dinner. Maybe I should stay up here and not eat tonight."

"Don't you dare."

"But what do I say to him?"

"Well, that depends." Deborah sat back and studied her face. "Do you love Jacob?"

"Yes, of course, or else I wouldn't have agreed to marry him."

"And do you still love Edward?"

Her heart sank as Abigail hesitated.

"I'm not sure. I mean, I loved him when he went away, but he seems like a different person now."

"You were only in his presence a short time," Deborah chided. "What changes did you see in him?"

"Well. . ." Abigail smoothed her skirt and frowned. "Besides his looking a bit shaggy, you mean? And that jacket!"

Deborah smiled. "I expect someone cut his hair and found him a razor on the ship, and those were probably borrowed clothes."

"You're right, of course, but I found it disconcerting. Why didn't he go home first and—"

"I expect he didn't want to wait to see you."

Abigail drew a ragged breath. "There's more than that." She seized her sister's hand, her eyes pleading for understanding. "I think I'm a little afraid of him, Debbie. He's not nearly so docile as he was before."

"Docile? Honestly, Abby, I saw great longing and love in his face when you came into the room. He still dotes on you. I dare say he's been dreaming of this reunion for five years."

Abigail sobbed and put the handkerchief to her lips. "I want to do the right thing, but what is the right thing in this case? Though I didn't intend to, I find myself engaged to two men. What sort of hoyden would do that?"

"There, now, don't vex yourself. No one is going to think ill of you. You waited far longer than most women would to set your affections elsewhere. For three years after his disappearance, you mourned Edward. Even then, when Jacob began calling on you, you held him off for a long time. No one can fault you for your conduct on that score."

"Thank you. It means a lot to hear you say that." Abigail squeezed her hand. "But what should I do now? Should I break off my engagement to Jacob, or should I tell Edward things have changed and I am now committed to Jacob? What is the honorable thing to do?"

"I don't know. If it's not clear to you, you must pray and seek God's will about your dilemma. But I do know one thing."

"What is that?"

"You must tell Jacob tonight, and when Edward comes round tomorrow, you must be honest with him."

"What if he doesn't understand?"

"Did he understand you five years ago?"

"Well, yes, I thought so, but—we were so young, Debbie. Perhaps Father was right to urge Edward and me to put off an engagement until he returned from his voyage."

Deborah's heart twisted. How could Abby consider not marrying Edward now? He was the brightest, finest young man she'd ever known. They'd all mourned his loss with Abby. Yet they'd all felt relief this past year when she'd finally put aside her sorrow and risen from her anguished grief.

Deborah put her hand to her sister's cheek and wiped away a straggling tear. "Pray hard, then, and speak your heart to both men."

A soft rap sounded on the door, and Mother looked in. "Jacob has arrived, girls. Your father is entertaining him in the parlor. You'd best come down and greet him, as dinner will be served shortly."

Abigail stood and inhaled deeply. "I suppose I must go down and tell him that Edward has come back."

Her mother sighed. "You can stop worrying about that. He knows."

"But how—"

"He arrived a bit early, and he learned it when he saw his cousin leaving the house."

"He saw Edward?" Abigail grabbed the bedpost and clung to it.

Concerned that her sister would swoon, Deborah leaped to her side.

"Please, Mother," Abigail wailed. "Let me stay up here. I'm not hungry."

"None of that, now. It's bad enough you seem to have let Edward leave without explaining your situation to him. You mustn't neglect to speak to Jacob."

Deborah slipped her arm around Abigail's waist. "You'll feel better after you discuss it with him. Jacob is a reasonable man."

"Not to mention a very handsome one and devoted to you," her mother added. "Come, now."

During dinner, Deborah sensed that everyone was on edge. After a timid, "You've heard about Edward," from Abigail and Jacob's response that he was indeed aware of the marvelous news, the conversation grew a bit stilted. Deborah ate mechanically as she strove to find topics that would put them all at ease. Her father launched into a story about one of his patients, and the tension subsided.

As soon as the meal was over, Dr. Bowman said, "Jacob, will you join me in my study for coffee?"

"If you don't mind, sir," Jacob replied, "I'd like to speak to Abigail privately." He looked anxiously at his fiancée.

Deborah expected Abigail to find an excuse to decline, but instead, her sister said, "I will take a short stroll with you if Deborah accompanies us."

Her mother frowned. "Are you sure you are up to it, dear? You've had a shock today."

"I—" Abigail glanced at Jacob, then looked down at the linen napkin crumpled in her hand. "I think Mr. Price and I need a chance to discuss today's events."

"You're right," said Dr. Bowman. "With Debbie along, I have no objection. Just see them home early, young man."

"Thank you, sir." Jacob rose and pulled Abigail's chair out for her.

Deborah found the prospect of chaperoning while Abigail bared her heart to her suitor distasteful, but she knew that if she refused, her sister would probably put off clearing the air with Jacob. Resigned to the outing, she fetched her shawl and headed toward the harbor with the couple.

As they walked, Jacob kept to mundane remarks about the weather, not broaching the subject that concerned them all until he found a bench overlooking the water. They sat down, and he reached for Abigail's hand.

"Abigail, dearest," he began.

Deborah turned away and stared studiously at a sloop anchored beyond the cluster of fishing boats nearest the shore. It was not fully dark yet, and other people passed them, ambling peacefully along in the warm June evening.

"I must know how things stand with you and Edward," Jacob continued. "Surely you understand my turmoil. I know you pledged your love to me in good faith, but you also pledged yourself to my cousin. I shan't be able to sleep tonight if I don't know that you still love me and plan to become my wife."

A prolonged silence followed, and Deborah felt Jacob's distress. Even more, she felt Abigail's anguish. Her sister's shoulders began to shake, and the bench quivered. Deborah whirled and put her arms around Abigail.

"Really, Jacob, can't you be more considerate?"

Jacob coughed and stared at Deborah. "Forgive me, but my future is at stake here. Surely I have a right to know where I stand."

"And what about Abby? Hasn't she any rights?" By the shock in Jacob's eyes, Deborah knew she was coming at it a bit strong, but she couldn't help it, seeing her sister crushed by the weight of the decision that lay before her. Suddenly she wondered if her own secret preference for Edward was influencing her to fight so fiercely. Was she more committed to seeing Abigail have time to make a rational decision or for Edward to have time to make his case? She wouldn't think about that now. "Abby has had a severe shock, and a gentleman shouldn't clamor so urgently for answers."

Jacob sat back, his spine rigid against the bench.

Deborah stroked Abigail's hair and whispered, "There, now, dear. You need some time to think everything through and pray about it."

Jacob produced a clean handkerchief. Abigail took it with a murmured, "Thank you," and dabbed at her eyes.

Jacob sat forward, clasping his hands between his knees. He shot a sideways glance at Abigail, and when he caught Deborah's eye, she favored him with a meaningful glare.

He cleared his throat. "I suppose your sister is right, my dear. You are as startled and confused as I am. Would you say that a week is time enough for you to sort out your feelings on the matter?"

Abigail gulped and raised her lashes, meeting his gaze in the twilight. "A week?"

"Yes." Jacob reached for her hand, and Deborah turned away, feeling even more the unwanted companion.

"Abby, dearest, I love you more than life itself. When you grieved for Edward, I admired that. I saw your tender heart and your faithfulness to the man you loved. And I longed for that. I craved to have that devotion turned my way."

Abigail let out a soft sigh. "Oh, Jacob! I do care for you. You know that."

There was a soft smacking sound, and Deborah assumed he was kissing her hands. She turned even farther away, her cheeks flushing, and wished she were anywhere but on that bench.

"Oh, darling," Jacob said, "if your earlier attachment to Edward is stronger, then I suppose you should honor it. It's not in your character to deny it. But in my heart, I can't help hoping you will choose me. Edward is an honorable man, and I love him, too. I promise to hold no bitterness toward you whatever your decision."

"Thank you." Abigail's voice broke, and Deborah foresaw another deluge of tears. She jumped up and faced the startled Jacob.

"I believe it's time we returned to the house, Mr. Price."

"Oh, certainly."

Abigail stood and gathered her cloak about her, and they strolled away from the harbor, back toward the residential neighborhood. Deborah noticed that her sister kept her hand tucked through Jacob's arm as they walked.

They reached the Bowmans' door, and Jacob caressed Abigail's hand before releasing it. "Might I come to call again Sunday, Abby?"

"I. . .well, yes."

He nodded. "I'll see you then. Good night."

Deborah opened the door, and she and Abigail stepped into the hall. She hung up her shawl and turned to face her sister.

"Oh, Debbie, they are both fine men. Whatever shall I do?" Abigail burst into tears again.

"My dear, dear boy!"

Edward submitted to his mother's ferocious embrace. "I love you, Mother. I'm so sorry I wasn't here for you when Father was ill."

She stepped back and devoured him with her eyes. "It was a trial, but your sister was a great comfort to me. The Price family, too. Jacob and his parents helped me with everything, from the burial arrangements to finding new household help when the hired girl left to be married. And Jacob has kept the business running as smoothly as a sleigh on ice. Thanks to him, I have not wanted for money."

"I'm glad he's taken care of you." He noted how her hair had silvered, but her posture was still straight and her movements steady.

He let her lead him into the kitchen and sit him down at the table in the spot where his father always used to sit. All the while, thoughts about Jacob raced through his mind. It seemed his cousin had taken his place in many areas—his career, his duties as a son, and even his role as Abigail's future husband. He tried to squelch the jealousy that sprang up, forming a crushing weight on his chest. It was only the closeness of the room, he told himself, and the smoke from the fireplace and the cooking smells within the confined space that made him feel ill and claustrophobic.

His mother tied a calico apron over her gray skirt and pulled two kettles away from the fire.

"I hope you were not overset by the news of my return," he said.

She bustled about, filling a plate for him. "It was a shock of the best kind. I fell into my chair when I first opened your note, but Jenny Hapworth was here—she does the housework for me now. She brought me tea and let me dither on. I'm afraid I was overly exuberant for a woman my age."

He smiled and captured her hand as she set the plate before him.

"I should have come to you first."

"No, no, I understood perfectly. You had another errand that couldn't wait." She eyed him closely, her mouth drooping in an anxious frown. "How did you find Miss Bowman?"

"She. . .was a bit more distraught than you and perhaps not so exuberant."

His mother eyed him with compassion, then nodded. "I'm sorry. Well, I set about cooking and airing your room as soon as I got the news. I hope you haven't eaten."

"No, I had a glass of cider while at the Bowmans', but beyond that, I've had nothing since breakfast."

"My poor boy! I hope you still like roast mutton. We've no potatoes left, but there's plenty of biscuits and applesauce and a pudding for after."

He surveyed the plate. "I doubt I shall be able to eat all this. I'm not used to such bounty."

Tears sprang into his mother's eyes, and she ruffled his hair before hurrying to the fireplace to remove a steaming kettle of water.

"Tea or coffee?"

"Coffee, please, if you have it. I spent many evenings in my exile trying to recall the smell and taste of the brew."

He bowed his head and offered a silent prayer of thanks for his food and his homecoming.

The first bite of his mother's biscuit put him in euphoria. The outside was golden brown, the bottom firm, and the top soft and flaky. The inside was pure white and separated into tender layers. The wholesome, nutty flavor answered some craving he'd had for four years. Bread! So simple yet so exotic. During the last two months on shipboard, he'd had hard, crumbling biscuits with traces of mold. He'd gone ashore briefly in Boston a week ago, but the bread in the tavern he'd patronized was almost as dry as the sea biscuit.

He chewed slowly, looking at the hole he had bitten from the side of the biscuit. None of the shipboard food had come close to this. And a platter full of them awaited his pleasure, if he could hold them.

"Don't you want some butter?" Mother asked. She pushed the blue china butter dish closer to him, but he shook his head.

"It's perfect. Perhaps tomorrow or next week I'll put butter on one."

She smiled, and he was glad to see the old look of affection and satisfaction she'd habitually worn when watching her menfolk eat.

"If only your father had lived to see this day."

He searched her eyes and saw that her grief was well banked.

"On the last leg of my trip home, from Boston up to here, the ship's captain told me Father had died."

"I'm sorry you learned it that way."

"Oh, he was good about it. He'd known Father for years. In fact, I had met him before at the warehouse. They'd done business together for a long time. Captain Stebbins, out of Searsport."

"Of course." His mother took the seat beside him. "He's dined in this house."

Edward nodded. "He expressed his condolences to you as well. When did it happen, exactly?"

"Last July. Your father collapsed at the office. Jacob sent for Dr. Bowman right away, but it was too late. His heart, the doctor said."

"I'm so sorry. If I could have done anything to get word to you, I would have."

"Of course you would. Your father was crushed when we heard that you were dead. We both were, if the truth be told. Jacob came to visit us as soon as he returned home from the voyage and shared his memories of the time he had on shipboard with you before the storm."

Edward nodded. "We got along well. I was glad Jacob was on the ship. We spoke many times of how things would be when we came home. But we thought we'd sail back to Portland together on the *Egret* with a huge profit for Hunter Shipping."

"I. . .blamed your father for sending our only son off on a long voyage like that." She reached toward him quickly. "Please don't despise me."

"I never could, Mother."

"I admit that when we got news of your death, I was bitter toward him at first. But after a while, we worked through our sorrow, and I asked your father to forgive me. He was always a generous person, and so, of course, he did."

He patted her hand. "That's like Father. Your reaction was natural, I'm sure."

She rose and refilled his coffee, and he sipped it, savoring the rich flavor. "Mother, I've been told that Jacob is running the company now."

"Well, Mr. Daniels is still there. He heads the accounting department. Has three clerks under him. And your uncle Felix runs the warehouse. But yes, Jacob has been invaluable to Hunter Shipping."

Edward nodded. "I'm glad he was there."

"When your father died, he helped make a smooth transition in the management of the company." She sat down opposite him and held his gaze. "You see, we believed you were dead, son, so your father took Jacob into the office and mentored him in the trade. He'd decided to let Jacob take over the company when he was too old to run it anymore. Felix Price was agreeable, and it seemed the best your father could do since his only son was gone."

"I understand." Edward took another sip.

"But then, last year your father's heart gave out and he died. No one expected him to go so soon." She blinked at tears, and her voice trembled. "He was only fifty."

"So. . .what is the status of the company now?"

She sniffed and went on with a steadier voice. "Your father signed paperwork before his death, allowing me to own it. I'll be honest with you: I encouraged him to leave it to Jacob with the provision of a lifetime allowance for me. But your father wouldn't hear of it. He had the papers drawn up all legal about three years ago, after we'd given up hope you would ever be found. He told me that when he was gone I could do as I wished, but he wanted to keep the company in the Hunter name while he lived."

"And you didn't change that after he died?"

"No. I do respect Jacob, but somehow I just couldn't do it. I kept putting it off and thinking I'd take care of the transfer a little later."

"I'm surprised you were allowed to own the business."

"Well, your father made sure it was all legal. He left 10 percent to Jacob, and 5 percent to Mr. Daniels. He's been a good and faithful employee for more than forty years."

"And you hold the rest?"

"Yes, but I shall transfer it to you tomorrow. You must take me around to the office, and we'll see about the papers. There's a lawyer in town now. If you think it best, we can ask him to draw them up."

"There's no rush, Mother."

"Yes, there is. I want things as they should be. I know it has irked Mr. Daniels that technically I have the final say in business decisions. He and Jacob have to come here and tell me everything they plan to do before they can execute an idea. Jacob has been very courteous.

Well, they both have, but it's been awkward."

"I'm not sure I'm qualified—"

"Now, don't start that, Edward."

"But I didn't finish the training my father sent me to undertake."

"Nonsense. You've always had a good head for business. You spent years in the office with your father before you went away. You practically apprenticed in the warehouse. You'll take your proper place in this company. Period."

Edward managed a smile. "All right, Mother. I shall do my best and pray that you won't regret your decision."

"Now tell me about Abigail. You said you saw her this evening."

He sat back and drew a deep breath.

"Yes, I saw the whole family."

"And what did she tell you? Did you know that she was affianced to Jacob when you saw her?"

He bit his upper lip and picked up his spoon. "No. But I learned it soon after."

"I assume you want to claim your right as her betrothed. What did she say?"

"She didn't say much of anything. I believe she was in shock."

His mother clucked in disapproval.

"I shouldn't have gone there today." He sighed and put his hand to his forehead. "I ought to have come directly here and sent word there, instead of the other way around. Then she would have had time to compose herself."

"Was it very awful?"

"Frustrating. I had to give her father an account of my whereabouts for the last four years, since the *Egret* sank."

"That's a tale I want to hear soon but not tonight," his mother said.

"It's soon told. I was on a small, isolated isle in the Pacific. Dr. Bowman found it fascinating. And Deborah!" He looked up at her and smiled involuntarily. "I was overcome by the change in her. She was just a child when I left, but now she's—"

"A woman."

"Yes, indeed."

His mother nodded. "A stunning woman, though I don't believe she knows it yet. One of these sailor boys will steal her heart soon, I'll warrant."

"Oh, I doubt Dr. Bowman would allow a common sailor to call on her. He would have to be a boatswain, at least."

"Or a second mate?"

Edward chuckled. Second mate had been his rank on the *Egret*. "Ah, well, a captain wouldn't be too good for her. She's very outspoken. Not at all pretentious, but with a bearing that's almost regal. In the best sense of the word, of course."

His mother said nothing but got up to serve the dried plum pudding.

Chapter 4

The next morning, Edward walked to the graveyard near the church, accompanied by his mother. She had given away most of his old clothing, but she'd kept a few things that had belonged to his father. He wore a hat that he'd often seen his father wear and a suit that hung on him.

"You'll need to have some new shirts and drawers," his mother murmured. "Perhaps I can find some muslin and linen this afternoon."

Edward felt the blood rush to his cheeks. She was his mother, but still. One thing it would never be proper to discuss with her was his island wardrobe. Hearing her plan what he would wear for linens and woolens here in Maine would be embarrassing enough.

"Don't overdo, Mother. I'm not used to a large wardrobe."

"I'll have Jenny help me. You'll be going to the office and meeting lots of businessmen. You look as peaked as a crow's beak, and you can't impress clients if you're wearing clothes two sizes too large. Perhaps I can take in that suit, but that black wool is too hot for summer. It will do in the fall, but you must have something decent to wear now."

Edward didn't argue. It was just nine in the morning and only mid-June, but already the sun beat down on them, making him sweat beneath the layers of wool and linen. He'd supposed the northern climate would seem cool and refreshing to him after years in the tropical sun, but already he was finding the summer uncomfortably warm. Besides, his mother would undertake assembling a new wardrobe for him whether he liked it or not.

He opened the gate to the churchyard, and they walked between the monuments, mostly flat slabs of slate or granite standing in the turf. Each of the families associated with this church had an area where their dead were buried. Some had one large family marker with smaller stones delineating the individual graves.

The Hunter family plot was dominated by a big, rectangular granite stone. Several generations were buried near it, from the first Hunters who had settled in colonial times to the most recently departed. Deep purple violets grew at the foot of the stone in a hardy bunch, and the name HUNTER was deeply graven on it.

His mother led him beyond the older graves to a marker that read JEREMIAH HUNTER, 1769–1819, BELOVED HUSBAND AND FATHER.

His father's grave. Edward bowed his head for a moment in silent anguish, then stepped closer. His heart lurched as his gaze caught the line chiseled lower on the granite slab.

EDWARD HUNTER, 1796–1816, PRECIOUS SON.

He gulped for air and felt his mother's strong hand grasp his elbow.

"Are you all right, son?"

"Yes. It's. . .a bit unnerving to see my own name there with Father's."

"I'm sorry. I had that done after your father died, in memory of you. There's nothing buried there for you, of course. I can ask the stonecutter to chip it off."

"No, just leave it, and someday someone can change it to the proper date."

Edward took off his hat and fell to his knees. He placed his hand over the letters that formed his father's name. *Dear Lord, thank You for the parents You gave me. Help me to live up to their dreams.*

Edward took his mother home and left her in the care of Jenny, the hired girl. In the short time he had been home, he had learned that Jenny expected to be married at harvesttime, and his mother would once more have to find and break in new household help. Already she was putting the word out at church and throughout her social circle. Edward doubted it would take her long to find another maid. His mother was not demanding, and the chores of the small household wouldn't overtax a woman.

He was glad she had the sturdy house his grandfather had built. It was not as grand as some built by sea captains and shipping magnates, but it was comfortable. The two-story building was sided with pine clapboards, and two masonry chimneys flanked the small observation deck on top. Like many a seafaring man, Edward's grandfather had spent much time watching the harbor, and Grandmother was often found on the deck, gazing out toward Casco Bay when the captain was at sea.

Edward walked toward the shipping company's headquarters near the docks. When he was a block from the building, a chandler paused in unloading a pile of merchandise and stared at him.

"Edward Hunter. Is it you, lad, or am I seeing a ghost?"

Edward laughed. "It's me, Simeon. I've returned from the sea."

"But I attended your funeral several years past. You can't say nay to that."

"Yes, I've been told I was mourned and missed, but as you see, I was never buried."

A small crowd gathered as more men heard the news or came to see what the ruckus was about.

"Please excuse me," Edward said. "I'm glad to see you all again, but I've business to attend to at Hunter Shipping."

He pushed through the knot of onlookers, greeting the men he recognized, shaking a few hands, and murmuring, "Thank you so much. Good to be back."

The company's offices were on the far side of the warehouse, and he entered through the loading door, then stopped to sniff the air. Tea, lumber, tar, molasses, apples, and cinnamon. Now he was really home.

"Mr. Edward." One of the men recognized him and stepped toward him, grinning.

Edward smiled and clapped the older man on the shoulder. "Yes, Elijah, it's me."

"Mr. Price told us you was back." The laborer shook his head. " 'Tis a marvel, sir."

"Yes, indeed. Praise God, I'm alive and I'm home. Someday soon I'll come down to the dock and break bread with you all at nooning and tell you of my adventure."

"You do that, Mr. Edward."

Two other workers stacking bags marked RICE stopped to stare. Edward waved then turned toward the doorway that led to the offices.

A large man hopped down from a crate and blocked his path.

"Edward, my boy!"

"Uncle Felix!"

Edward submitted to a hug from Jacob's burly father, then pulled away, fighting for breath.

"My son told me last night you were alive and well." Uncle Felix slapped his shoulder and grinned. "A wondrous sight you are."

"Thank you, Uncle. I'm glad to see you're still here and carrying on."

"Oh yes, I'm fine. Fifty-three years old and still strong as an ox. Now, Jacob, he's a different sort than me. Started out down here with me, but you know, he's not made for hauling truck around the docks. He can do it, but he's made for higher things." Uncle Felix touched his temple and nodded. "Your father saw that, he did. Put my boy over in the office clerking, then sent him to sea. And now he's wearing fine clothes and keeping your inheritance safe for you. Don't forget that, boy."

"I won't." Edward eyed his uncle, wondering if he'd just received a warning to take care of his family. Uncle Felix had lived his life as a laborer, first as a fisherman. After he married Ruth Hunter, Edward's father had employed Felix at the warehouse for his sister's sake but had privately opined that Aunt Ruth had married beneath her. Still, love is love, and Father had always managed to get along with his brother-in-law. Ruth was happy to see her husband with a job safe on land.

Felix was a hearty, jovial man and a hard worker. He had risen to the overseer's post on merit, not just because of his marriage to the owner's sister. His wages had allowed him to buy a small clapboard house in the better part of town, and Aunt Ruth was content. Her three daughters had all made respectable marriages and provided the Prices with an assortment of grandchildren.

"Have you seen your sister's new babe?"

"Not yet," Edward said. "I sent Anne a message, and the family's coming to the house this evening."

"Ah, she must be pleased her brother's not drowned and dead."

"I'm sure she is. It's great to see you, Uncle Felix." Edward shook his hand and headed for the office.

"Bring your mother 'round for Sunday dinner!" his uncle called after him.

As Edward left the warehouse and stepped into the outer room where the clerks had their desks, he stopped. Several doors led off the main room, and one of them led to the private office that had long been his father's sanctum when he was owner and head of the company. But now the door stood open, and coming out of that office was his cousin, Jacob Price.

"Edward, I was hoping you'd come down today."

Jacob's greeting seemed a bit stilted, but Edward stepped toward him.

"Thank you. I hope I'm not intruding."

"How could you intrude in your own office?"

Edward said nothing but couldn't help looking beyond Jacob to the open door.

Jacob followed his gaze. "I was gathering up a few papers. You'll want this office, of course. Your father's desk and all." He stopped and pressed his lips together.

Edward glanced around and saw that the nearest clerk, while not looking at them, had paused with his pen hovering above the ledger on his desk, as though waiting to hear what would happen next.

"Could we have a word in private?"

"Of course." Jacob gestured for Edward to precede him into the inner office.

Edward stepped to the threshold and paused, taking a slow, deep breath. Memories of his father deluged him: the double window where his father had often stood looking out over the harbor to see which ships were docking, the shelves of ledgers that held the business records of Hunter Shipping for nearly a hundred years past, the large walnut desk his grandfather had brought from England—it was all just as it had been five years ago when his father had wished him well on the voyage.

He could almost see Father sitting behind the desk, sharpening a quill with his penknife. Displayed on the wall behind the desk were an old sextant and spyglass, mementos of the past captains Hunter, and a large chart of the New England coast.

It was all precisely the way he had remembered it. Except. . .

He turned to face Jacob. "I don't recall that painting over there."

Jacob looked where he nodded. "Oh yes. The winter landscape. It came on a ship from France, and I liked it. I thought it would look nice in here."

Edward took a few paces closer to examine it. He didn't recognize the artist's name, but the composition attracted him with its subdued purple and blue shadows in the snow. He kept silent, wondering if the painting belonged to Jacob or to Hunter Shipping, and at what cost. That led to the question of what Jacob was receiving as salary. Could the company afford to pay them both?

Jacob closed the door softly and stepped toward him.

"Edward, I want to assure you that if I'd known you had survived I never would have made myself at home in this room."

Edward turned and eyed him once more, searching his face for deceit or malice but finding none.

"You were within your rights. It's my understanding that my father asked you to take on a major role in the firm, as a replacement for me."

Jacob coughed and turned to the window. "It was something of the sort, yes." He shoved his hands into his pockets.

Edward stared at his back. Jacob's broadcloth coat hung perfectly from his shoulders, and his posture was straight. His blond hair curled against his collar, a fashionable length for the merchant class. He looked the part of a shipping magnate. But Jacob's head began to droop, and his shoulders slumped.

Edward walked over to stand beside him and placed his hand on Jacob's shoulder. "I've been told the business is running smoothly."

Jacob's gaze flitted to his face. "Yes, everything's fine. Of course, the company was hit hard when the *Egret* sank with her cargo four years ago, but your father was canny and made some good investments on the next few voyages with the other two ships. And I've been thinking for some time now of purchasing another vessel."

"Funds are available for that?"

"Well, yes. Daniels tells me they are. I've pretty much left the accounts to him, but we seem to be doing all right, Ed. Some of our enterprises are more profitable than others."

"Naturally."

Jacob's eyes picked up the glitter of the sunlight streaming through the window. "It was my thought to buy a ship before fall if profits continued this summer as they've been for the last year or so. Another schooner, perhaps. We purchased a small sloop before your father died that we use in coastal trade, but I think we're ready for another vessel with the tonnage of the *Egret* or larger."

Edward nodded. "I know nothing of the company's state at the moment. I'd appreciate it if you'd tutor me a little."

"Of course. Edward, I hope—" Jacob studied Edward's face with anxious blue eyes. "I hope you'll keep me on."

"I have no intention of turning you out, Jacob. I regret that my return is displacing you to some extent, but I see no reason why we can't work together."

"Are you certain?" Jacob's brow wrinkled, and his mouth held an anxious crook.

He's thinking of Abigail, Edward realized. Would the fact that they both loved the same woman come between them?

He walked to the bookshelves and gently touched the binding on his father's copy of Bowditch's *The American Practical Navigator*.

"We've always gotten on well, Jacob."

"So we have. And I'm delighted that you've returned."

Edward felt a tightness in his throat and gave a gentle cough. "I'm sure we'll work something out so that we can both earn our living here. As I said, you've proven your worth in the company. I have my mother's word on that, and I expect I'll have Mr. Daniels's confirmation soon."

"He'll show you the books, Edward. Anything you want to see. It took awhile for business to pick up after the peace was signed with England in '14, you know. Sometimes money was scarce, but we've pretty well recovered. Your father was pleased with the way our trade was going last year. If his heart had been stronger, he'd be here now to tell you this."

Edward raised one hand to curtail his cousin's words. "I'm sorry, but I'm feeling a bit emotional today, seeing my father's office and all for the first time since. . ." Edward swallowed hard then brushed his grief aside, determined to get down to business. "You know, I think I'd benefit by a short tour of the wharf."

"Of course." Jacob hurried toward the door. "We've expanded the store on the wharf, you know."

"Oh? I came in on Richardson's Wharf yesterday, and I didn't get a good look at ours."

"Well, our chandlery is twice as large as it was when you left, and I've leased space on the wharf for several other small shops. I hope you don't mind. Most are one-year leases, and it's good for business. Draws more people to our store."

"I'm sure it's fine, so long as we're doing well in the ships' supplies."

"Last year was our best year ever. And I've worked out a deal with Stephens's Ropewalk. They make us eight sizes of cordage, and we sell all we can get, both here in our store and in the West Indies trade."

"Rope." Edward nodded. "It's a good, sound product." His mind was racing. It seemed the company was doing better than ever under Jacob's supervision. He knew it was partly due to the general economic climate of the day, but it sowed a riot of thoughts and feelings. How could he take over when Jacob was doing so well? But this was still the shipping company his father and grandfather had built. Could he do as well as Jacob was doing? What would it mean to Jacob, financially and socially, if Edward demoted him? And would it make a difference to Abby? Should he base his business decisions on what she and, yes, even her father would think?

"Of course, lumber is still our mainstay," Jacob said. "But we've been shipping a larger variety of goods in the past two years. I'm telling you, Ed, having England off our backs has opened up a lot of new markets."

Edward smiled at his cousin's enthusiasm. "Well, if you have time this morning, why don't you walk over to the wharf with me and point out the improvements? Afterward, perhaps I can sit down with Mr. Daniels and get an overview of the financial end of things."

"I'd be pleased to do that." Jacob reached for the doorknob. "And, Edward, whatever you decide you want me to do for this firm, I'll accept your decision."

"You've worked hard, Jacob. I'm not sure what our course should be yet, but I won't forget that."

Jacob nodded, but his troubled frown told Edward his cousin was not so settled as his words implied. Edward followed him out into the bright June sunlight. The thought was unspoken, but he inferred that, while Jacob might feel obligated to relinquish the management of Hunter Shipping, he would not so willingly give up his claim to Abigail.

"I don't want to see him."

Abigail sat before her dressing table, her back turned to Deborah, stiff and unyielding, while Deborah sat on her sister's bed, attempting to count the stitches in her knitting.

"Let's not go through this again." Deborah turned her knitting at the end of the row. She couldn't knit anything required to fit someone—no stockings or gloves. Her stitches were much too tight, throwing the gauge off. But she could knit mufflers and rectangular coverlets for babies, and she was working on one for Frances Reading, whose husband had been killed in an accident at the distillery on Titcomb's Wharf a month ago. Deborah had bought the softest wool yarn she could find and dyed it a pale yellow with goldenrod. The blanket was turning out surprisingly well.

"You were less than courteous to Edward last night," she reminded Abigail. "Go down and be civil."

"Must I?"

"Oh, Abby, is this simply embarrassment over your behavior last night?" Deborah watched her sister's downcast eyes in the mirror. Getting no answer, she laid her yarn and needles aside and walked over to touch Abigail's shoulder. "It's not like you to be unkind."

Abigail's mouth clenched for an instant. "All right, I'll talk to him, but only if you promise to stay with me. Don't leave me alone with him."

"Why ever not?"

"I don't know. He seemed a bit. . .savage, I thought."

Deborah shook her head. "You're imagining things."

"But he was out there alone for years with nothing but seabirds and wolves."

"Wolves? Who said anything about wolves on his island?"

"Cannibals, then."

"Nonsense. I've always liked Edward and thought you were marrying the finest man on earth. I doubt he lost his good sense during his ordeal, though he was forced to give up many refinements."

Abigail wrinkled her nose at her reflection in the looking glass. "Oh, Debbie, I liked him, too."

"You told me then that you loved him."

"So I did." Abigail sighed. "I was thrilled that he'd noticed me and that he chose me from among all the other girls. But he's been gone so long, and he's changed."

"Give him a chance, dear. Have you made up your mind to marry Jacob? I don't want to see you discard Edward lightly. He's a wonderful man, and he's been through more than we know, though I'm quite sure we can discount wolves and cannibals."

"I know it, and I don't want to crush his spirit. I'm just not sure I can ever recapture the feelings I had for him five years ago."

"Well, he's been waiting fifteen minutes already. I do think you ought to go down without further delay."

"Come with me."

Deborah frowned. "I hate this chaperone business. It's not in my nature."

"Oh yes, I know. You're the free spirit of the family. But I don't wish to be alone with him."

"All right. But you must make a promise in return."

"What?"

"Treat him decently, as you would any nice gentleman caller."

"I'll pretend he's one of Father's friends."

It wasn't quite what Deborah had hoped for, and she laid a hand on her sister's sleeve.

"Well, keep in mind that whichever man you marry, Edward owns the business concern that will support your family."

Abigail's eyes widened. "I'm always civil, I hope."

Deborah scooped her knitting off the coverlet and shoved it into her workbag. She was longing to hear more of Edward's tale and decided to make the most of this encounter. The idea of his fighting for life against nature in a beautiful but terrible setting intrigued her. She hoped that this afternoon he would reveal more of his adventures.

They walked down the oak stairs together, their full skirts swishing. Abigail looked lovely in the pale blue gown that matched her bright eyes. Deborah was certain Edward would appreciate her beauty. Her cheeks were slightly flushed, and her golden hair shimmered. If only she wouldn't leave the room precipitately again.

At last Edward heard the sisters coming down the stairs. He jumped up and met them as they entered the parlor. Abigail smiled at him and let him take her hand for a moment. That was an improvement over their meeting last night.

In fact, she seemed much calmer, and she even murmured, "Edward, so kind of you to come this afternoon."

"It's a pleasure. I hope we can come to an understanding about. . .things."

He couldn't help staring at her. She was more beautiful than his most accurate mental images of her. While on the island, he had wondered if his mind exaggerated her charms and if he would be disappointed on his return to find that she was quite plain. But that was foolish. He'd known from the first time he set eyes on her that she was among the fairest of the city.

The blue of her gown enhanced her creamy complexion, and her hair, pulled back in honey-colored waves, enticed him to brush it with his fingertips to see if it were truly as soft as it appeared.

"Hello, Edward."

Deborah stepped forward and held her hand out to him, and he released Abigail's and focused on the younger sister. He noted anew that Deborah had become a well-favored woman, and he smiled at the gawky girl turned graceful beauty. No doubt most men would find it hard to choose between the two if asked which sister was lovelier.

"What are you grinning at, if I may be so bold?" she asked with a playful smile.

"I'm sorry. I just can't get over the change in you, Debbie—or Miss Deborah, I suppose I ought to call you now."

She waved that comment aside and sat down on the sofa next to Abigail.

"Nonsense. I grew up calling you Edward, and you always called me Debbie. We needn't commence using formalities now."

He laughed. "Thank you. That's a relief."

He settled into his chair greatly eased. Deborah, at least, was willing to see this interview run smoothly, and Abigail seemed to be in a better humor as well. The shock of his survival and return to Maine had dissipated. He hoped she was ready to discuss their future.

When he smiled at Abigail, she tendered a somewhat timid smile in return and clasped her hands in her lap. Her lips parted as though she would speak but then closed again, and she looked away.

"Well, ladies," Edward said, glancing at Deborah and back to Abigail, "I do apologize for any abruptness, but I think we all know it's important for me to understand your intentions, Abigail."

Abigail's eyes widened, and she turned toward her sister in dismay.

"Dear Edward," Deborah said, patting Abigail's hand, "you are rather forthcoming today. I was hoping, and I'm sure Abby was, too, that you'd tell us a bit more about your travels."

He swallowed hard. So, they were not going to make this simple.

"Deborah, Abigail, please forgive me for being so frank, but surely you can understand my anxiety. I spent some time with my cousin at the wharf this morning, and I must know. . . ." He left his chair and went to his knees at Abigail's side, reaching for her hands. "Dearest Abby, I simply have to know whether or not you still intend to marry me."

Chapter 5

Abigail pulled back and jerked her hands away, looking frantically to Deborah. Edward saw at once that he'd been too aggressive. He stood and walked to the empty fireplace, leaning on the mantelpiece and mentally flogging himself for being such a dolt.

"Edward," came Deborah's tentative voice, "perhaps we could come at this topic more subtly."

He blinked at her. Deborah was stroking her sister's hand and gazing at him with such an open, accepting smile that he suddenly wanted to do whatever he must to please her.

That wasn't quite right. He ought to strive to please Abigail, no matter what Deborah thought.

He brushed his hair off his brow. His mother had offered to cut it. Perhaps he should take her up on that this evening. It was shorter now than he'd worn it in solitude but was still long enough to annoy him when it fell into his eyes.

"Please sit down," Deborah continued. "I'm sure Abby is willing to discuss the agreement she made last evening with Mr. Price."

Abigail caught her breath and looked down at her hands once more, her face flushing a rich pink. Once again Edward found his gaze flickering from Abigail to Deborah and back. Abigail, the older sister, so self-assured and cordial to him in the past, seemed terrified of him. Deborah, the lively, teasing younger sister, had assumed the role of the placid peacemaker.

He hesitated, then went to his chair and sat facing them, his nerves at the breaking point. Sweat broke out on his forehead and his back. He wasn't used to being confined in layers of clothing, and the tense situation combined with the warm weather had him perspiring profusely.

"I'm sorry," he said. "If you please, Abigail, we shall proceed with the topic at the speed you wish."

"You said. . . ." Abigail's voice quivered, and she began again. "You said you spent the day with Jacob."

"Part of it. I had a tour of the company's wharf with him this morning, looking over the expansion of the store there and some repairs done to the mooring slips. Then Captain Moody hoisted a flag indicating that a ship was entering the harbor."

"We heard the commotion about noon," Deborah said. "Was it one of your ships?"

"No, it was a schooner from Liverpool, docking at Long Wharf. Jacob decided to go down there and see if she'd brought anything we'd want to purchase for our store. I went back to the office and had a session with Mr. Daniels, our chief accountant. Jacob had told him this morning that I was back, and he had the books all laid out for me to examine."

"And were things in order?" Abigail asked.

"Well, I've only had time to give the ledgers a cursory look at this point, but yes, I'd say Hunter Shipping has been under good management these last few years." He wondered suddenly if Abigail thought he might doubt Jacob's capability, and he knew that, whether she chose to marry him or not, he must put that question to rest. "Of course, my father ran things right up until his death last year, but since then, all indications are that Jacob and Mr. Daniels have done a fine job."

She nodded and lowered her eyes. He decided to leave it at that, though one small item he'd noticed during his quick glance at the books had prompted him to make a decision. He would go through all the financial records thoroughly, especially those of the last year, as soon as he had the opportunity.

"It must have been an emotional day for you," Deborah said.

Edward nodded. "Yes. Seeing all of the fellows I used to work beside, and of course noticing that some I used to work with are missing."

"Will you go to sea again?"

He paused, wondering just how to answer that question. Abigail also seemed to take an avid interest.

"I might. I'm not angry at the sea. God determines if a man will be safe or not, whether he's walking a cobbled street or an oaken deck. But if I were a married man, I doubt I would make another long voyage. Perhaps I would sail as far as the Caribbean if the business required it, but I wouldn't want to. . .be away from my family longer than that."

Abigail flushed once more, and he felt the blood rush to his own cheeks. Perhaps a change of subject was in order.

"I saw Henry Mitchell in the warehouse today. When I left, he was only a boy. Twelve years old then, he told me. Now he's a laborer for Hunter Shipping."

"His father was one of those who didn't return from the *Egret*'s voyage," Deborah said.

Edward nodded and bowed his head for a moment. "I know. Amos Mitchell was in the longboat with me and the others. But he. . .didn't survive our journey to the island."

"I'm sorry," Deborah said. "That must have been a terrible time."

"It was. We started out with eight, but only four of us made it ashore. Captain Trowbridge died soon after. He's buried there." Edward ran a hand through his hair. "I must go around to see his widow soon."

"Mrs. Trowbridge seemed despondent at first," Deborah said. "She knew one day her husband wouldn't return from a voyage, she said. But after the first year, she regained her vim. Her daughter Prudy and her family live with her in the big house now."

A sudden thought disturbed Edward. "I hope my returning hasn't given anyone false hope for their loved ones."

"No, I'm sure it hasn't."

"I must visit her tomorrow," he said, more to himself than to the ladies. How awful for the captain's wife to resign herself to her husband's death and then, four years later, to hear that one of the men she thought drowned with him had survived. For four years, Edward had lived with his failure to keep Captain Trowbridge alive. He'd respected the man and wished he could have done more to help him, but by the time they reached the island and fresh water, it was too late.

After a moment of heavy silence, Edward wondered if he ought to leave. It seemed every conversation led to depressing memories. He didn't want to throw the household into gloom, but neither did he want to make his exit without learning how Abigail felt toward him.

Deborah shifted and smoothed a ruffle on her skirt. "If you mind my asking, do say so, Edward, but I've been wondering. . . ."

"Yes?" He met her rich brown eyes and saw a twinkle there not unlike the expression she used to don when he teased her.

"Whatever did you eat on that island?"

He laughed. "At first, we thought we'd starve. But there were shellfish, and we caught some other fish. Gideon Bramwell became quite good at killing birds with a slingshot."

"Young Gideon was with you on the island?" Abigail stared at him in surprise.

"Yes, for the first two years. I. . .regret to say that he fell from a cliff while trying to raid a bird's nest for some eggs." He sighed and closed his eyes against the image of the plucky boy's mangled body lying in the surf below. Making a mental note to visit Gideon's mother as well, he strove for a more cheerful note. "We landed there in midsummer, and soon the fruit began to ripen. That was providential. And we found a few roots we could eat, and the leaves of one tree made a passable tea."

"So you weren't starving," Deborah said with a satisfied nod.

"No, although sometimes our rations were short. But as soon as we saw that we had fresh water and could find enough nourishment, we knew we could live there until a ship found us."

Abigail's brow furrowed. "Why did it take them so long?"

"From what I've heard, the first search was arduous but didn't extend to beyond where we'd actually drifted in the storm. They didn't think we could have gotten so far, but we had a sail. After we rode out the gale and had better weather, we made good headway. Even so, we were off the usual shipping routes by several hundred miles. No one would ever go to that island on purpose."

"But it had fresh water," Deborah mused.

"Yes, and that's exactly why the *Gladiator* came there and found me a few months ago. She had run into some corsairs and taken some heavy damage. Afterward, her captain didn't think he could make it to the next port, Santiago. So he consulted his charts for a place to drop anchor, do some repairs, and restock the water supply. I thank God he chose my island."

"But you were alone by then," Deborah said softly.

Edward nodded. "Yes. Captain Trowbridge was feverish when we landed, and he didn't last more than a few days. John Webber, Gideon Bramwell, and I kept each other company for more than a year. Then John cut himself badly while skinning a shark. His wound became infected. We tried everything we thought might help, but he died a few weeks later after much suffering."

"Such a pity," Abigail murmured.

"Yes. And then last year, I lost Gideon." Edward sighed. "That was my darkest hour. I thought I would die there as well, and no one would ever know what became of us. Our struggles in the storm and survival for so long were in vain. I fully expected to meet my end alone on that desolate shore."

"Did you remain in such low spirits for a year?" Deborah asked.

He recalled the turmoil and despair that had racked his heart, and the manner in which God had lifted it. "No. God is good, and He did not forsake me. He brought me another friend."

"A friend?" Abigail asked, and Deborah's eyes glittered with anticipation.

"Aye. His name was Kufu."

Both young women leaned forward, eager to hear his explanation.

"A native man?" Abigail asked.

"No."

"A monkey?" guessed Deborah.

"No, Kufu was a seagull. He arrived with a storm, and from how far he came over the sea, I've no way of knowing. His strength was spent, and he flew into my hut for sanctuary. He startled me, but when I saw that he was about done in, I let him rest and offered him some fish entrails and fruit. Before long, he was eating out of my hand."

"He stayed there with you?" Deborah's eyes lit up in delight.

"Yes. I gave him a name I'd heard a sailor call his parrot once, and Kufu was my constant companion from then until the *Gladiator* came."

"Why didn't you bring him home with you?" Deborah asked.

"Alas, he made the choice. He rode out to the ship with me in her longboat, riding on my shoulder. But once we were aboard and the crew raised anchor, he left me and flew back to the island."

They sat in silence for a moment; then Abigail asked, "Do you miss him?"

"I did at first, but now that I'm home again, I can't help feeling it is for the best. No doubt he will find others of his kind. He's strong again now. He has probably already left the island and flown back to wherever he came from. But I can't help believing God sent him to me when He did as a distraction and an encouragement. You see, Kufu needed me at first, so I fought to live. I had no idea how long I'd remain there."

"Four years," Deborah said.

"Yes. Well, close to that. More than three and a half years on that little piece of earth. And the last year alone, save for Kufu. But with God's help, I could have stayed there longer if necessary. So long as I remembered His goodness, I was willing to wait."

"That's a remarkable tale," Deborah said.

Abigail nodded. "Thank you for telling us. I. . .feel I understand things a bit better now."

Deborah stood. "Let me bring in some refreshment. I think we could all use a cup of tea."

"Not for me," Edward said quickly.

"Sweet cider, then?" Deborah asked.

"Yes, thank you." That sounded much better than anything hot. Edward leaned back in his chair and watched her bustle out the doorway.

It took him a second to realize that at last he was alone with Abigail.

As Deborah opened the kitchen door, her mother looked up from pouring hot water into her teapot.

"Time for a bit of refreshment in the parlor," Deborah explained.

"You've left them alone?"

Deborah chuckled at her grimace. "Yes, but both were calm when I made my retreat. I hope Abby is sensible enough to use this time to tell Edward what transpired between her and Jacob last night."

"Well, here, you can have this tea."

"No, Edward's feeling the heat, I think, though Abby might welcome a cup. I'll take some cool cider with Edward."

"There's a jug in the washroom."

Deborah opened the back door and stepped down into the cool, earthen-floored room at the rear of the house. Here was where the Bowman women and Elizabeth, the hired girl, did the family's laundry. Dug down into the ground two feet and well shaded, the washroom stayed a bit cooler than the kitchen on hot summer days, and Mrs. Bowman stored her milk and butter here, along with any other foods she wanted to keep cool.

Deborah found a jug of sweet cider nestled between the butter crock and the vinegar jug and carried it back into the kitchen.

"Take some of this gingerbread, too," her mother said. "I'll cut it for you."

Deborah brought dishes and forks to add to her tray. "Be sure to save some for Father."

"I will."

"Father's not home yet?" Deborah asked as she worked.

"No."

"He missed luncheon."

"Yes. He sent Peter round to tell me Mrs. Reading delivered a son, but the doctor was called almost immediately after the birth to the Collins farm, where one of the children met with an accident."

"Oh, dear. I hope it's not serious."

"That is my prayer," Mother said. "Do you suppose Abigail has made up her mind?"

"If so, she hasn't confided in me." Deborah carefully poured two glasses of cider and corked the jug. "I don't mind admitting that I hope she'll choose Edward. He has first claim, after all, and I always found him great fun."

"Hardly a reason to marry a man," her mother said. "Edward's a good lad. He's a hard worker, too. But then, so is Jacob. Your father's come to like Jacob a lot. He's steady."

"Edward's steady."

"Well, he was," she agreed, "but is he still? We don't know, do we?"

"Oh, come now, Mother. You know he was always a true friend and faithful in churchgoing. His father was training him in business, and he always obeyed and treated his parents with respect."

"That's true. They say a man will treat his wife the way he treats his mother, and I've no complaints about how Mrs. Hunter's son treated her before he. . . went away."

Deborah looked into her worried eyes and smiled. "Awkward, isn't it?"

"Yes, a bit. And if I'm having a hard time coming to terms with his being dead, then alive again, I guess we can't blame Abby for needing some time to settle her mind."

"Well, I have nothing against Jacob. He's a fine man, too. But Edward is different. I always thought he was special."

Her mother shot her an inquisitive glance, and for no reason, Deborah felt her cheeks redden. Her laden tray was ready, and she picked it up and escaped into the hallway. She paused at the open parlor door, hearing Abigail's soft tone.

"And so, I honestly don't know yet what I shall do," she said, a catch in her voice. "It's true I loved you dearly, but it's been a very long time; it's also true that I've developed feelings for your cousin. At first I thought it was wrong, but Mother and Father both assured me it was not sinful to. . .find love again after. . .losing the one I. . ."

She faltered, and Edward's low voice came. "I'm sorry I put you in such distress, Abby."

"I beg you to be patient, Edward, while I seek God's will in the matter."

"I shall," he replied. "And I'll pray for your peace where this is concerned."

"Thank you."

Abigail choked a bit on the words, and Deborah stepped forward. She hated to break in on them, but the weight of the tray was causing her wrists to ache.

When he spied her, Edward leaped up from the sofa where he'd been seated beside Abigail and took the tray from her, setting it on the side table. Deborah noted his grave expression as he looked to her for direction.

"Thank you. Abby, I brought you tea; I hope that's your preference."

She handed Edward his cider and gingerbread and settled back on the sofa with Abigail, placing her own cup and dish close at hand.

"Father's been called out to the Collins place," she announced. "The boy studying medicine with him brought Mother a message. I doubt he'll be home before evening."

Abigail's taut face smoothed into serenity. "Poor Father. He works too hard."

"He thrives on it," Deborah said.

"Your father is a remarkable man." Edward took the chair he'd occupied earlier and sipped his cider, then placed the cup on the table. "Won't you tell me about the folks in the neighborhood? Is Pastor Jordan still at the church?"

For the next half hour, they brought him up to date on the doings of their mutual acquaintances, and Deborah was pleased to see Abigail join in with a few anecdotes. She even laughed once, a musical chuckle, and Edward's eyes sparkled when he heard it.

Deborah longed to learn more about his exile on the distant island, but since she knew reverting to that subject would upset Abigail again, she tucked her questions away. Someday she would have a chance to talk to Edward privately. She had no doubt he would reveal the details of his sojourn to her. But for Abby, the topic was best put aside. Her quiet, well-ordered life had become chaos, and Deborah knew her sister needed time to sort it out.

Chapter 6

Four days later, Edward felt easier in his new role at Hunter Shipping. The men of the warehouse and docks, along with the sloop's crew, all seemed happy to have a Hunter once more giving the orders. The clerks in the office appeared to be a bit more unsettled by his reappearance, but he'd taken a few minutes to thank each man for his service and assure him that, so long as he continued to do his tasks well, his position was secure. Edward had no intention of making any sweeping changes in the office.

Mr. Daniels brought him the ledgers for the previous year on Monday morning, slipping quietly into the private office and laying them on a shelf near Edward's desk.

"The books you wished to look at, sir."

"Thank you." Edward glanced up from the correspondence he was reviewing. "Mr. Daniels, you saw this letter that came in from the shipwright in Bath?"

"Yes, sir."

"And you think we are in good shape to meet his needs?"

"Oh yes, sir. We've done quite a lot of business with him the last couple of years. Masts and spars for a small trading vessel he wants, and sails and cordage. Not a worry there, sir."

"Good. And the extra barrels of tar he asked about?"

"We have plenty."

"Excellent. Perhaps we should send the sloop up there this week, then."

Daniels ducked his head. "Very good, Mr. Hunter. Will you speak to Captain Jackson?"

Edward eyed the stack of ledgers on the shelf. That job would be less interesting and more exacting. Still, he needed to do it as soon as possible. He looked up at Daniels.

"Mr. Price can handle that, I think. I'll speak to him if he's in the office."

"I believe he stepped over to the wharf, sir."

Edward nodded. "Then I'll send a note over by one of the clerks. He can tell Captain Jackson to alert his crew and prepare to load the supplies for the shipwright." He reached for a quill and a scrap of paper.

An hour later, he was immersed in the ledgers, flipping back and forth between the accounts. Twice he went to the door and called for Daniels to come and explain an entry to him. The older man seemed a bit amused by his intense interest in the ledgers. Edward had studied accounting only in passing during his office training as a teenager and then only at his father's insistence. He'd been much more eager to get out on the wharf and sail up and down the coast on short trading voyages. But he knew his father had gone over the books closely at the end of each month and had spent several days at the close of each year reconciling all the accounts.

Once again he called Daniels to his side. "Did Mr. Price examine the books this year?"

"Oh no, sir," the older man replied, removing his pince-nez from the bridge of his nose. "Mr. Price is very good with the customers and the sailors, but he's not much for figures. He signs off on the payroll each month, but he's left most other matters in my hands."

Edward frowned. "My father always prepared a summary of the previous year's business in January."

Daniels cleared his throat. "Well, sir, I totaled things up and reported to Mr. Price on the year's income and expenses, and he seemed to think that was sufficient."

Edward wondered. He found nothing amiss as he scrutinized the columns of figures, but something still seemed the slightest bit out of order. He couldn't put his finger on it. Cargoes brought in on the sloop and the two schooners, the *Prosper* and the *Falcon*; wares bought from other ships that landed in Portland; goods sold in the chandlery and from the warehouse on market days; wages paid out to the men—the notations seemed endless.

At last he put the ledgers aside. He wondered if he could secure an interview with Abigail tonight. The week she'd told him Jacob had given her to make her decision was scarcely half over, yet he couldn't help feeling she was close to knowing her mind. He'd stopped by the Bowmans' modest brick house for a few minutes last evening, but he'd only had his fears confirmed. She was polite, not encouraging.

On the other hand, if he let her continue thinking it over, would his chances of coming out the victor be any better? His spirits were low, and he realized the shock of having to deal with all the changes at hand weighed heavily on him. He'd expected to come home and find his father here to guide him and Abigail ready to marry him. Instead he was bereft and lonely, and his future seemed bleak. He folded his hands on the top of the glossy walnut desk and bowed his head to pray.

He felt better when he had once again committed his future to God. Rising from the desk, he decided to amble across the street to the wharf and see if he could find Jacob.

Edward had spent the weekend visiting with his family. His sister, Anne, and her family had driven up from Saco in their farm wagon and spent a night at the Hunter house. Edward had made the acquaintance of his two-year-old nephew and Anne's new daughter, a babe of three months. On Sunday they had all taken dinner with Aunt Ruth and Uncle Felix Price. Jacob had excused himself shortly after the meal, and Edward had no doubt he headed to Dr. Bowman's residence. Perhaps it was time to speak openly about Abigail.

Edward didn't want to avoid his cousin. They worked at the same business, and he couldn't see any sense in not speaking to each other. So far they had kept any necessary communication brief. But Edward's hopes of being welcomed into the Bowman family circle decreased with each day, and there was no sense in not acknowledging that.

He found his cousin at the chandlery, helping the man who managed the store for them. The chandlery specialized in ships' supplies, and several of the warehouse laborers were carrying goods from the store out to the sloop.

"Jacob, could I speak to you?"

"Of course." Jacob handed the list to the chandler and followed Edward outside. The wind whipped their coats and the rigging of the sloop that lay secured at the side of the wharf. Edward took Jacob around the corner and into the lee of the building, letting it shelter them.

"What is it?" Jacob asked.

Edward sighed and leaned on a piling, looking off toward the next wharf. A brig was docked, and men scrambled over her decks, laying in supplies by the look of things. "We need to find room for an office for you."

"I'm getting along fine."

"No, you're not. I saw you bending over the apprentice clerk's desk to work on an order yesterday. You need your own desk and space to lay out your work. I've displaced you."

"Edward, there's no need—"

"I say there is." He turned to face Jacob. "You're a 10 percent partner in this company, and a valued member here. You're much better at some aspects of the business than I am. There's no reason we can't work together. We'll partition off some space at the end of the front room. It won't be as large as my office, but I daresay we can make you comfortable."

Jacob pursed his lips for a moment, studying Edward's face. "I won't say no to that proposal."

"Good. That's one thing we agree on."

"What do you mean by that?" Jacob leaned forward, frowning. "Ed, we've been friends since childhood, not to mention our blood ties. Can't we be frank with one another?"

"Yes, of course." Edward walked over to a stack of crates piled against the back wall of the store and sat down. Jacob hesitated a moment then joined him.

"You want honesty?" Edward asked. "All right, I'm getting tired of this game we're playing with Abigail, and I expect you are, too."

Jacob ran a finger around the inside of his collar, not meeting Edward's gaze. "Well, cousin, you know she's promised to give me her decision by Friday."

"Yes, well, we both know what she's going to say, don't we?"

"Do we?" Jacob stared at him, an open challenge charging the air between them.

Edward jumped up and strode to the edge of the pier. He shoved his hands into his pockets and stood still for a moment, then exhaled deeply. "This is difficult for me, but I've got to face facts. She loves you. She no longer. . ."

He clamped his lips together and stared out at the waves troubling the harbor. "She no longer feels about me the way she did five years ago. That much is obvious to me."

He heard Jacob's footsteps and knew he had come to stand just behind him.

"Edward, I never. . . Please, you've got to know I didn't intend to spoil anything for you."

"I know, I know." Edward swung around and forced a smile. The pain he had expected wasn't in his heart. Instead, he felt chagrin. Jacob's face bore a bulldoggish look that Edward had often seen Uncle Felix wear.

"I've seen it coming," Edward said. "I just didn't want to admit it. She loves you. And you'd better love her as much or more, because if I find out you don't. . ."

Jacob's lips drew back, and his brows lowered in a good-natured wince. He extended his hand, and Edward shook it.

"I love her," Jacob assured him. "I would do anything for her. You know I love sailing, but I shall never sail again unless it's a short hop up the coast on business. No more voyaging for me."

"That seems extreme."

"It's not. I'll never do to her what you did. Oh, I'm not blaming you for getting shipwrecked—it could as easily have been me on that island. But knowing Abigail as I do now, I can see that the mere prospect of me not returning from a voyage would kill her. I'm staying ashore for the rest of my life, Ed. For her sake."

"Does she know that?"

"Yes."

Edward drew in a deep breath. *Dear Lord, should I just give up altogether? If I promised to stay on land, would she change her mind? Should I even attempt to find out? God, give me wisdom.*

He walked once more to the edge of the wharf and leaned on the piling.

"I think Deborah is getting tired of it, too. Last night she made no secret she despises chaperoning her sister."

Jacob laughed. "Yes, she made her father supervise Abby and me on Sunday. But if Abby affirms that I'm her choice, I should get more private time with her soon."

Edward nodded and managed a feeble smile. His disappointment ached in his heart with a dull, constant throb. *So be it, Father in heaven. Give me Your peace, and bless their union.*

"I've made up my mind," Abigail announced at breakfast Thursday morning.

Deborah's stomach twisted, and she laid down her fork.

"About time," her father said, not looking up from his copy of the *Eastern Herald.*

Mother was more sympathetic. "And which young man can we anticipate becoming our son-in-law?"

"Jacob, of course," Deborah muttered.

"You needn't scowl at me." Abigail broke a small piece of crust off her toast and tossed the morsel across the table, hitting Deborah's shoulder.

"Abby!" their mother scolded.

Abigail turned back to her mother. "Deborah thinks she knows what is best for me, but this is something I must decide for myself."

Deborah felt the accusation was somewhat unjust. It was true she had hoped her sister would choose Edward, but she had never tried to persuade Abigail to do so.

"I haven't attempted to influence your decision."

"Haven't you? You're always telling me how fine and upstanding Edward is."

"I just think you need to consider all aspects of the two gentlemen's characters."

"I have," Abigail said. "And I have made up my mind. Both are admirable, but Jacob is more. . .civilized."

"That's ridiculous."

"Here, now," their father interrupted. "You sound like a gaggle of geese fighting over a handful of corn, not two genteel ladies."

Deborah sank lower in her chair. It wasn't easy to disturb her father's placid nature. Abigail's turmoil must have bothered him these past few days, no matter how calm he appeared.

"And when will you tell the favored gentleman?" their mother asked, smiling. Deborah imagined that in her mind she had already resumed the wedding plans interrupted so rudely a week ago.

"This evening. And I've asked Edward to come by this afternoon if he can get away from the office long enough." Abigail glanced at Deborah. "I thought I should give him a private audience before my renewed betrothal to Jacob becomes public."

It was less than Deborah had hoped for, but more than she'd feared.

"Do treat him gently. He's loved you for such a long time, Abby." Annoyed with her own tender emotions, Deborah blinked rapidly and succeeded in keeping back tears.

"I shall. Of course, you understand that when I say 'private,' I mean that you shall be present as a chaperone."

"Never."

"What?" Abigail's rosebud mouth hung open.

Before her sister could wail to their mother for support, Deborah said, "I've sat by and listened to both these poor men lay their hearts at your feet. I do not wish to be present when you dash Edward's hopes."

"But—"

"Surely you can do this one thing on your own."

Abigail frowned. "Perhaps Father will tell him for me. I could send him around to your surgery, Father."

The newspaper shivered, and a deep, foreboding voice came from behind it. "I shall do no such thing."

Abigail looked to the other end of the table.

"Nor I," said her mother.

Tears streamed down Abigail's cheeks. "You all think I'm horrid, don't you?"

"No." Her mother rose and began to stack the dishes. "Jacob is a splendid young man, and we shall be proud to have him in the family. But you must do your own work with Edward, Abby. Don't send him away thinking you are a coward."

Abigail inhaled and looked at Deborah.

Deborah tried not to return her gaze, but the sound of Abby's shaky breath pierced her armor.

"Please?" Abigail whispered.

Deborah threw down her napkin.

"All right, but this is the last time. I mean the *last*. Don't come looking for me tonight. I intend to be far away when Jacob reaps the reward of his persistence."

"Thank you, dear sister."

Deborah stamped her foot. "Abby, you aggravate me so. If I ever ask you to chaperone me, please remind me of this moment and say no."

"In order for that to happen, you must stop ignoring all the young men who hover around you after church every Sunday." Abigail's watery smile was as exasperating as her comment.

As Deborah stomped from the room, she glanced at her father, not trying to suppress the resentment she felt. Hiding behind that newspaper! He ought to have interfered. Sometimes she thought he used his medical practice as an excuse to avoid the feminine intrigues that seethed at home.

She was startled when his complacent voice came once more. "Perhaps she will do that when she finds one who matches the young man she's been defending so passionately."

Deborah stopped even with his chair and stared at him.

As he folded his newspaper precisely, his eyes turned her way, and he threw her a conspiratorial wink.

Chapter 7

For once, Abigail was waiting in the parlor before her guest arrived. She sat on the sofa, twisting her handkerchief.

Deborah stood at the window, watching for Edward. The sooner this was over with, the better.

"Do you hate me?"

Deborah sighed and let the sheer curtain fall back into place. "No. But I shall be disgusted with you if you're not frank and to the point with him."

"I'll try."

"Oh, Abby, pretend you are Father doing surgery. This is a necessary procedure. Make it clean and quick, will you?" She plopped down on one of the velvet-covered side chairs.

"Do you think he knows why I've invited him here?"

"Of course."

Abigail's eyes widened in surprise. "Really? Oh dear."

Deborah threw her hands up in resignation. "You love Jacob. That settles it. It would be wrong for you to accept Edward now. You can't marry a man you don't love."

"Well, yes." Abigail wiped an errant tear from her cheek. "So. . .you think it's all right?"

Deborah was glad her sister could not see the chaos in her heart at that moment. "I know you've thrashed this out with God."

"Yes, I have."

"Are you at peace with your decision?"

"I am."

Deborah moved to the sofa and slipped her arm around Abigail's shoulders. "Then this is right. Thank God, and carry it through."

Abigail squeezed her in a suffocating embrace. "I love you, Debbie."

"I know."

They leaped apart as the thud of the knocker echoed through the house.

"Oh, he's here." Abigail dabbed at her face with the wilted handkerchief.

"Calm down," Deborah advised. "Deep breaths. Elizabeth is getting the door."

A moment later, Edward stood in the doorway. He nodded to Deborah with a slight smile, then centered his attention on Abigail.

"Thank you for inviting me," he murmured as he advanced.

Abigail shoved her handkerchief up her sleeve and extended her hand to him.

"It was kind of you to come, Edward. Please, sit down."

She resumed her place on the sofa, and Deborah tiptoed to the window, where she sat down on the cushioned window seat.

She couldn't watch, and she wished she could plug her ears and not hear without being outrageously rude.

Abigail cleared her throat. One quick glance showed Deborah that Edward had sat down beside Abigail on the sofa but was keeping his distance.

He still has hope, Deborah thought. *This will crush him. And how will he feel toward Jacob now? They've been inseparable since boyhood. Will this drive them apart forever?*

She considered her closeness to Abigail. The events of the last week had tested their loyalty, but Deborah knew she would always love her sister. She hoped Edward and Jacob's bond was firm enough to take them through this and bring them out still friends on the other side.

"Edward, I. . ." Abigail cleared her throat.

Deborah stared out the window at the sunlit garden. How she wished she were the little phoebe perched on the syringa bush, chirping in blissful unawareness.

"Edward, I am ready to give you my decision."

Abigail's voice had an icy touch, and Deborah winced. She knew her sister found her task excruciating and had retreated into coldness to make it easier. Tears were no doubt lurking, and she wanted to complete the interview without breaking down.

"I'm ready." Edward's voice was as stony as hers, and Deborah's heart ached for him.

"I. . ."

The pause was too long, and Deborah gritted her teeth, eyes closed. *Tell him! Just tell him.*

After another long moment of silence, Edward's voice came, quiet and gentle now.

"Perhaps I can help you, my dear. You wish to say that you've decided to marry my cousin."

Abigail sighed and whispered, "Yes."

"And you. . .regret any pain you have caused me."

"Very much."

"But you feel this is the only true and honest thing you can do."

"Stop being so. . .so good!"

"How would you have me be?"

Something like a hiccup came from Abigail, and Deborah couldn't resist turning her head ever so slightly and peeking.

Edward was drawing her sister into his arms, but it was not an embrace of passion. Abigail laid her head on his strong shoulder and let her tears flow.

"It will be all right, you know," he said.

"I hope so."

"It will, dear. If God had wanted us together, He wouldn't have kept me away so long."

"Really?"

"Really. I think I saw that when I first came home. I simply didn't want to admit it. But there's no denying it. You love Jacob, and you were meant to be his wife."

He stroked Abigail's hair and leaned back against the sofa with a sigh.

More than ever, Deborah wished she were not in the room. Yet she was glad in a perverse way that she was allowed to see the true mettle Edward was made of. His heart was breaking, yet he was comforting the one who'd delivered the blow.

She turned back to the window view. The phoebe was gone, but a chipmunk was scurrying about the garden. She felt a tear slide down her cheek and brushed it away with her sleeve.

"So. . .you aren't angry with me?" Abigail asked.

"All is forgiven," he said.

"And Jacob?"

"There's no bitterness between us, nor will there be."

"Thank you, Edward."

The sofa creaked, and their clothing rustled. Deborah turned to see that both had risen.

"Would you please excuse me?" Abigail asked.

"Of course, my dear."

Edward bowed over her hand, then watched her leave the room.

Deborah wondered if he remembered she was there. Should she jump up and offer to fetch his hat? What was the etiquette for ushering out rejected suitors?

He turned slowly, and his thoughtful gaze rested on her in the window seat.

"It seems your duties are ended."

"Oh, yes." She hopped up, her face flushing. "I'm sorry, Edward. It was not my choice to witness that."

"I know." His smile was a bit thin, but even so, it set her pulse tripping. "I believe her declaration was final."

Deborah nodded. "I'm afraid so. She won't change her mind."

They stood for several seconds, looking at each other. At last, Deborah said softly, "My condolences."

"Thank you. Perhaps you'll be kind to me at the wedding, and we'll laugh together about this. That way, maybe folks won't gossip about my despair and desperation."

"Is that what you're feeling now?"

"One thing I learned in my long exile, Deborah, is that God alone controls my destiny."

"So. . .perhaps even this is a part of His providential plan for you?"

"I must say yes to that, decidedly yes, or deny the faith I've gained. It is disheartening now, but I'm sure God can use this disappointment to prepare me for a different future, just as He used the shipwreck to prepare me for this."

Deborah eyed him for a moment, gauging his mood. "Do you have to go back to the office right away?"

"No, I've nothing more exciting than a stack of ledgers to draw me."

"Would you care for lemonade? I'd love to hear more about your experience—if I haven't badgered you enough about it already."

He smiled and nodded. "Lemonade sounds refreshing."

The next hour flew as Deborah plied him with questions about the men who fled the shipwreck with him and about his life on the island. He brought her near weeping again, telling how they had drifted for days in the longboat. Three of the men in the longboat had died and one was lost overboard before they reached the island. He then changed his tone and recounted humorous incidents that he, Gideon, and John went through as they became accustomed to their island home.

"They wouldn't leave off calling me 'sir' at first," Edward said. "Finally I told them, 'Listen, fellows, if we're still here fifty years from now, with our gray beards down to our belts, are you still going to dodder around calling me "sir"?' And Gideon said, 'I'm not sure we'll have belts by then, sir. We may have to eat them if we don't find a way to catch more fish.'"

Deborah shook with laughter, then sobered. "When you were alone after Gideon fell off the cliff, how did you go on? You told me about Kufu, the bird that came to you, but still. . ."

Edward settled back in his chair and sighed. "It was very difficult at first. I thought I would go mad, being alone there. I kept repeating scripture portions to myself and composing imaginary letters to my parents and my sister. And of course, to Abigail."

"That helped you?"

"Yes. I pretended to write long letters, detailing my daily life. Gathering food, improving my shelter against the rainy season, climbing the hills to scout for sail." He shot her a sidelong glance. "I even wrote to you once."

"You did?"

"Yes. I thought it might amuse you. I drew a picture of my hut on a piece of bark, too, then tossed it in the surf, pretending it would float to you, along with my latest letter to. . ."

She smiled. "You must have floated a lot of letters to Abby."

"Hundreds. And later I'd find them washed up on shore down the beach." He sighed and pulled out the pocket watch that had been his father's. "It's getting on toward supper time. I must leave you."

"Won't you—"

He held up one hand to silence her invitation. "I don't think this is the night, but thank you."

She walked with him into the front hall and handed him his hat. It was new, she noted, not his father's old one. His fashion consciousness was probably linked to his hope to win Abigail's hand, but she didn't mind. She only knew that he would hold his own in looks and good manners if dropped in the middle of a group of businessmen and statesmen. And in a roomful of eligible women? Abigail was probably the only woman who wouldn't find him magnetic.

He stood before the door, looking down at her with a half smile on his lips, and she realized she had been staring at him again. Bad habit. She'd have to train herself out of it.

"I wonder, Deborah. . . ."

"Yes?"

His smile spread to his gleaming brown eyes. "I wonder if you and your mother and sister would care to tour Hunter Shipping tomorrow if the weather is fine."

She swallowed a lump that had suddenly cropped up in her throat. Had he not taken Abby seriously? She was sure he had.

"I. . .must discourage you, if you think my sister is not adamant in her choice."

"I'm sure she is. But I mentioned to your mother not long ago that we have some fine fabrics in the warehouse. I thought perhaps you ladies would enjoy coming to the office, and Jacob and I could show you about."

She stared up at him for a moment, amazed at his calmness. He bore his cousin no malice. Could she be as generous to Abby? Her heart fluttered, and she knew that her professed forgiveness of Abigail was genuine. She could give thanks to God for this turn of events. Surely this resolution was part of His greater plan.

Chapter 8

It was a bright, sunny day, and the breeze that fluttered in from Casco Bay kept the temperature comfortable. Edward rose early, unable to sleep well, and arrived at the office shortly after seven. He huddled over the ledgers, frowning and trying to find the elusive inconsistency he felt sure was there.

At five minutes to eight, he heard Daniels and the clerks enter the outer office, and a moment later he heard Jacob's brisk step. Edward opened his door, and Jacob came toward him, grinning.

"Still friends, Ed?"

"Of course." Edward grasped his hand. "Congratulations."

"Thank you. I can't tell you what it means to me that you're taking it this way."

Edward smiled. "I shall endeavor not to diminish your joy, cousin. What would you think of inviting all the Bowman ladies down here this afternoon?"

"I like it, but what for?"

He shrugged. "A tour of the place. Another chance to see your fiancée and to let her see you in your place of business. Let them look over the dress goods in the warehouse before we sell them all."

"Splendid idea! Will you make the arrangements?"

"Yes."

Jacob nodded. "Then I'll be in my office." He headed for the far corner of the large room, where two workmen were erecting a wall to enclose a cubicle for his new oak desk. He swung around, still smiling. "I don't suppose this will be finished by the time they get here? And decorated?"

Edward laughed. "Hardly. Would you rather wait until it's done?"

"No, no. Let's invite them today."

By way of an apprentice who swept the floors and sorted bins of hardware, Edward sent a note around to the Bowman house, asking the ladies if they would care to see the improvements at Hunter Shipping, in company with the owner and Mr. Price, and take tea afterward in the office.

The boy came back forty minutes later with a brief but courteous reply. Both the misses Bowman would await him at one o'clock. Their mother was otherwise engaged.

Edward hired a hack after lunch. He and Jacob arrived at the Bowman residence to find the ladies waiting. Abigail was dressed in a burgundy silk walking dress with a feathered hat and white gloves. Deborah's dress was a plain, dark blue cotton, topped with a crocheted shawl and a straw bonnet. Edward was not sure who was prettier—the elegant, refined lady Abigail or the wholesome, restless Deborah. Abigail seemed pleased that they would not have to walk all the way to the docks and back. Although it was a swift twenty-minute stroll for Edward, the commercial district near the harbor was not one that ladies frequented on foot.

"Riding will save you ladies from wearing out your slippers and making the strenuous uphill walk on the way home," Jacob said as he handed Abigail up into the enclosed carriage.

Deborah smiled at that, placing her sturdy leather shoe on the step and hopping up beside her sister, barely putting pressure on Edward's hand for assistance. He could almost read her thoughts: She was not one to glide about in delicate slippers and tire from a brisk walk.

As they rode slowly along the streets, Edward commented on how much the population and commerce of the town had increased during his five years' absence. He was glad he'd worn the new suit he'd had made at his mother's insistence. His hair was neatly trimmed now, too. Still, he could see that Jacob outdid him so far as Abigail was concerned. The greater part of her attention was devoted to his cousin.

When they reached their destination, Edward learned that Abigail had never been onto the wharf. Deborah, it seemed, had ventured there under escort. By whom, Edward did not ask. Abigail shrank from the edge, preferring to be safely flanked by Jacob and Deborah as they walked out past the tinker's shop and the dry goods, hardware, and candle shops to the company's large store. Edward followed a step behind. Sailors and stevedores passed them and stared. The ladies flushed, and Abigail clutched Jacob's arm.

Edward stared down the worst of the oglers and stepped forward to touch Deborah's sleeve.

"Miss Bowman?" He offered his arm. She hesitated only a moment, then laid her hand lightly in the crook of his elbow.

"Thank you," she whispered.

It felt odd having a lady other than his mother on his arm once more, but Edward decided it was pleasant. Deborah's eager anticipation spilled over in her face, and he knew few women he would rather squire about Portland.

As soon as they were inside the store, she pulled away from him, apparently feeling secure on her own now, and wandered about, examining everything. Abigail, however, clung to Jacob's arm and looked about timidly.

Deborah's fascination with the chandlery pleased Edward. She was a practical girl, and her face brightened as she surveyed the mounds of rope and canvas, piles of bolts and pins, and barrels of victuals suitable for ships' crews.

"Your father was a man of great foresight to build his store right on the wharf," she said.

"Actually, my grandfather started the chandlery here with a little shack that offered the most basic supplies. Father improved the establishment, and I have to give my cousin credit for the latest expansion. This entire section is new." He stretched out one arm, indicating the wing Jacob had added to house a wider selection of foods, containers, tools, and hardware.

"Do lots of people come here to buy?" Abigail's voice squeaked. She squeezed nearer to Jacob as a burly seaman pushed past them, nodding and eyeing the ladies.

"Yes," Jacob told her. "The store was begun to outfit Hunter ships and any others that docked at this wharf, but we're open to all customers."

Edward nodded. "That's right. We've built a reputation for offering a wide variety of goods. Of course, we're competing for the business of ships that aren't owned locally. When a vessel comes in from another port—say, Buenos Aires or New York or Amsterdam—we hope it will choose Hunter's Wharf for unloading and selling its cargo."

They left the store and ambled along the wharf toward the city. Abigail seemed more at ease and chatted quietly with Jacob. As they approached the street, Edward pointed up the hill toward the distant observatory tower, built a dozen years previously in Captain Moody's sheep pasture on Munjoy Hill.

"Look! See that flag? There's a ship coming in to dock."

"Is it one of your ships?" Deborah asked.

"I don't know yet. I hope it's the *Prosper*. We'll find out soon enough."

They crossed the busy street that ran along the waterfront, then entered the warehouse.

"This is where we stow outgoing cargo until it's loaded, and incoming until it's sold." Edward guided them out of the way of two men rolling casks down the aisle of crates and barrels. The containers were piled high, and he felt a little claustrophobic when walking between them. He glanced anxiously at Deborah, to see if she was feeling the closeness, but she took in the scene with glittering eyes.

"Well, now. If it isn't my beautiful future daughter-in-law."

They all turned and saw brawny Felix Price approaching with a grin splitting his tanned face. Beads of sweat stood on his brow, and he wiped his hands on his homespun trousers.

"Oh, Mr. Price." Abigail's breathless words were lost in the cavernous warehouse. She ducked her head in acknowledgment of Felix's boisterous greeting.

"I broke the news to my parents last night," Jacob said, his cheeks nearly as red as Abigail's.

"Afternoon, Uncle Felix," Edward said easily, but he kept a sharp watch on the man. Uncle Felix was rough enough that he wouldn't care whether he'd embarrassed his son and his employer or not. That didn't bother Edward, but he was concerned that his uncle had mortified Abigail by calling out such a teasing declaration before the workmen. Several of the laborers paused in their work and cast glances their way but turned back to their tasks when they saw Edward's stern gaze upon then.

"Hello." Abigail's face was by now crimson, but she took the meaty hand extended to her and dipped a curtsy.

Deborah greeted Felix with a charming smile. "Good day, Mr. Price."

"Well, Miss Debbie. What are you doing here? It's not Thursday."

Edward wondered what that meant, but Deborah merely told him, "We're touring Hunter Shipping."

"Well, now, ain't we grand?"

Deborah laughed, but Edward saw Jacob wince as Abigail squeezed his arm. He wondered if her fingernails were digging through Jacob's sleeve into his skin. Felix Price frightened her with his loud, breezy manner, it seemed. Edward wondered what that would bode when Abigail married Jacob.

It was true that his uncle was unpolished. Felix had been known as a ruffian in his youth. He'd fished for years, hauling a living from the ocean by brute force, and was known in those days for drinking quantities of ale when on land and occasionally using his fists in blustery tavern brawls. But Aunt Ruth had fallen in love with him. Though her social status and manner of living were lowered considerably on her wedding day, she still appeared to love him thirty years later and put up with him when his coarseness flared up. Somehow she'd maintained her gentility and was so well liked that Portland's most prestigious women still welcomed her into their parlors.

Felix was another story, and his friends were for the most part fishermen and dockworkers. His employment at Hunter Shipping for the past ten years gave him limited approval. Of course, he was always welcome in the Hunter home, but Felix did not presume on his in-laws' goodness and, for the most part, kept to his own circle. He was good at his job in the warehouse, the men respected him, and he kept the vast quantities of supplies in order.

"We're heading over to the office for tea, Uncle Felix," Edward said.

"Ah, tea for the ladies. I expect you gents have peppermint cakes and gingersnaps with your drinkables." Felix turned to the expanse of the warehouse and shouted, "Come, lads, clear the floor there! We've a ship docking in an hour's time! Look lively!"

They hustled Abigail and Deborah toward the steps leading up to the office, and Edward was thankful to shut the door and the noise behind them.

"You see that little room a-building over there?" Jacob asked Abigail, pointing to the far corner.

"Y–yes."

He smiled down at her. "That, my dear, is my new office. In a week or two when it's finished, I'll bring you down here again to see it."

"It's. . .awfully small, isn't it?"

Jacob laughed. "Well, yes, but it's more than Mr. Daniels, the accountant, has."

"What does he have?"

"A desk over there between the clerks and the record files."

Edward said nothing but caught Deborah's troubled glance. He wished he could reassure her, but he could only smile and lead them into his own office.

In the private room, one of the young clerks laid out tea for four on a small table opposite his desk.

"Abigail, would you mind pouring?" Edward asked.

"Not in the least, thank you."

There. This was going better. While outgoing Deborah might have felt at ease among the workers, Abigail could not hide her relief at escaping into the quiet, well-appointed office. He began to tell them about the nautical artifacts displayed on the walls, and soon she seemed to have regained her composure.

"That's a lovely painting," Abigail said, eyeing the winter landscape.

"Thank you." Edward glanced at his cousin. "I believe that belongs to Jacob and will find its home in his new office when it's finished."

"No need, Ed. Keep it in here if you like it. I only paid a few dollars for it, and it was company money."

Edward smiled. "We'll discuss it later." *After I look up the amount you paid for it,* he told himself. He did not doubt Jacob's word but felt he ought to go slowly in financial matters and verify what the staff told him. If all was as Jacob represented it, he would be glad to let his cousin have the pleasure of hanging the painting on the wall above his desk.

Deborah carried her cup and saucer to the window and peered out.

"You have a splendid view of the wharf and the harbor, Edward."

"Thank you. You've never been here before?"

"Not in the office."

"But you've seen the warehouse."

She smiled at him over her shoulder. "Yes, but Abby hasn't until today."

He smiled and turned to Abigail. "What did you think? We're a rough lot, I'm afraid."

She stirred a spoonful of sugar into her tea and glanced up at him from beneath long lashes. "It's. . .exciting, but I'm afraid I'm not used to such hubbub."

"No, I thought not. I hope our outing didn't unsettle you."

Jacob pulled his chair close to Abigail's. "Edward suggested you and Deborah might want to look over the fabrics we have on hand. I can ask my father to send some boys up here with the bolts if you wish."

"That might be nice," Abigail said, glancing at her sister.

"By all means," said Deborah. "I'm sure Abby will be needing some new dresses soon."

A few minutes later, two of the laborers came in with several bolts of material. They spread them on Edward's desk, and Abigail smiled at them.

"Mr. Price says that's the best of 'em, sir."

"Very good." Edward herded the men out the door.

"Thank you," said Abigail. "I didn't expect this privilege."

Edward shrugged. "You are welcome anytime, Abigail. Jacob can tell you if we get something in that he thinks you would like. When the *Falcon* returns from France, I expect there will be a great number of fancy goods on board."

"Debbie, look at this rose silk."

Deborah set her teacup down and went to join her sister at the desk.

"Edward. . ." Jacob was eyeing him uncertainly.

"Yes?" Edward matched his low tone.

"What do I do if she finds something to her liking?"

He shrugged. "Send it home with her, and send the bill to Dr. Bowman."

Jacob seemed a bit relieved, and Edward wondered, not for the first time, how his return was affecting Jacob's salary. He would have to go over the last few payrolls in detail.

A discreet knock sounded, and he went to the door.

"We've a ship docking, Mr. Hunter," said Daniels.

"We saw the flag before we came in. Is it the *Prosper*?"

Daniels frowned. "No, sir, it's the *Annabel*, out of Philadelphia. She's bringing textiles and wheat, and she hopes to take on lumber. The master's mate came ashore a few minutes ago in a boat. The ship will moor at our dock."

Edward rose. "Shall we take you home, ladies?"

"I'd love to see the ship dock." Deborah's eager brown eyes darted from him to the scene beyond the window.

"I told Mother we'd be home early," Abigail said with a note of reluctance. "Elizabeth was ill this morning, and we need to help with the dinner preparations."

Deborah sighed. "All right. I'd forgotten."

Edward went to the door and told one of the clerks to run out and secure a carriage for them. When he turned back, he saw that Jacob was gathering up the bolt of rose-colored material and smiling at Abigail. Her face bore the most serene expression Edward had seen her wear since his return. Instead of allowing pangs of jealousy or depression to assail him, he sent up a quick prayer of thanks.

"Jacob, perhaps you'd like to see the ladies home," he said. "I'll head for the wharf, and you can meet me there when you return."

"If you're sure you won't need me for half an hour."

"I'm sure."

Edward walked with them out the front door and around to where the hack was waiting. When Jacob and both ladies were aboard, he shut the door.

"I'll be back soon," Jacob said through the window.

"Fine. We'll go over the manifest together." Edward tipped his hat to the sisters and stood back. The driver flicked the reins and headed away from the harbor.

Edward stood still for another moment, trying to analyze his feelings. Why wasn't he upset today? The woman he'd loved for years had jilted him last night. He could only conclude that God had answered his prayers for peace.

As the coach turned out of the yard, Deborah leaned out the window and looked back, waving at him. Her hair had escaped the straw bonnet and flew about her rosy cheeks.

Edward couldn't help smiling. He lifted his hand and waved back.

Late that evening, Edward bent over the ledgers in his father's study at home. No matter how many times he went over the accounts, he could find no fault in Daniels's bookkeeping. Even the price of the painting Jacob had purchased was as he'd represented it. Still, something was amiss. Edward was sure of it. The *Prosper* had brought a good income to the company on every voyage until his father's death. Then she had made a run to the Caribbean that should have been profitable, but instead the goods sold barely covered the expenses for the voyage. Edward totaled the sales three times, then compared his figures to those of the schooner's previous voyages. Perhaps it was poor judgment in the goods purchased in the islands.

The next voyage had brought in a little more but was still far below the amount the *Prosper* usually earned. He then laid the figures side by side with the earnings of the *Falcon* and found that the European trade was far outearning the Caribbean voyages.

Edward ran a hand through his hair and looked at the clock. It was late, and he was tired. Perhaps things would make more sense in the morning.

But the next morning, he saw no more logic to the figures than he had the night before. The custom at Hunter Shipping was for the office staff to work a half day on Saturdays unless a ship was docking. Edward carried the ledgers back to the office and called Mr. Daniels into his private room.

"I see what you mean, Mr. Edward," Daniels admitted after Edward had carefully pointed out the troublesome amounts to him. "I did notice that the last couple of voyages were not so good for the *Prosper*, but I thought it was just one of those things that happens occasionally."

Edward shook his head. "I'm at a loss, Mr. Daniels. But I'm not sure the company ought to consider buying another ship if profits are falling."

"They've increased in other areas."

"Yes. The *Falcon* and the sloop have both done very well on their recent voyages." Edward leaned back in his chair. "I just don't understand it. The Caribbean trade has been our mainstay, and those cargoes were all good products."

"Not as much coffee as we like to get," Daniels mused. "Less of the high-profit items, more of low-profit goods like rice."

"Perhaps you can get me the copies of the *Prosper*'s manifests from these voyages," Edward said. "Now that you say that, I'd like to compare the percentages of different goods she brought back."

"Yes, sir. Perhaps it's just a matter of instructing Captain Stuart on what merchandise you want him to trade for."

Edward flipped the pages of the latest ledger once more. The arithmetic was flawless. Daniels supervised his clerks so closely that Edward was sure they wouldn't make a mistake or change the figures without the accountant noticing it. Daniels was past sixty years of age, and Jeremiah Hunter had treated him well. He earned a good salary and was now a part owner in Hunter Shipping. Edward decided that Daniels had little motive to cheat the company. But wouldn't a man of Captain Stuart's experience know what cargoes to buy? He'd made eight voyages for Hunter Shipping, and up until the last two, he'd seemed to know how to buy goods in high demand at a low price. Was it just a coincidence that the *Prosper* had barely made a profit on its last two voyages south?

Chapter 9

Deborah opened the Bowmans' front door a week later and found Edward and Jacob waiting on the doorstep. She had half expected Jacob to come around looking for Abby that evening, but it surprised her to see Edward with him. Of course, they had behaved cordially toward each other the day she and Abby toured the shipping company with them. Now Jacob was laughing at something his cousin had said, and they both turned to face her with smiles on their lips.

For the first time, Deborah saw a family resemblance. Edward was taller by two inches, and his hair and eyes much darker than Jacob's. But the nose was the same, she realized, and both had a somewhat obstinate set to their chins. Jacob's form was more compact, and his legs were shorter, like his father's. But both had broad, muscular shoulders and were clean shaven, though Edward had admitted to her and Abigail that he had worn a beard of necessity for nearly four years. She tried to picture him in a bushy, untrimmed beard, and that set her off in a chortle.

"What's so funny, miss?" Jacob asked, taking a stern posture and stiffening his back.

"Nothing you need to know. Won't you come in?" She forced her mouth into a more serious line as she took their hats. "Unfortunately, Abigail has gone with my mother to call on Mrs. Jordan. But they should be back soon, if you'd care to wait."

"Only if you'll join us," said Edward, and her heart lurched, though she knew he meant nothing special by it.

"What?" Jacob asked in mock horror. "Deborah sitting with us when she doesn't have to? Unheard of."

She showed them to the parlor, then hastened to the kitchen to fix tea. Hurrying back to her guests, Deborah paused in the front hall to glance in the looking glass. Edward had come back, even though Abby had turned him down. Her pulse surged. Did she dare think he enjoyed being here in spite of the blow he had recently received?

Although Edward was still reticent about some aspects of his voyage and sojourn on the island, Jacob was more than willing to talk. He was an excellent storyteller, and Deborah suspected that Abigail had not let him tell as many tales of the sea as he would have liked.

She listened avidly as Jacob recounted the damage sustained by the *Egret*. He coaxed Edward to tell his part of the story, claiming he'd been wondering about certain points.

"How did you find Spring Island? Was it by accident, or did you make for it?"

"It was the captain's choice," Edward said, settling back in his chair with a steaming cup of tea. "He'd brought a compass and a quadrant with him when he climbed down into the boat, as well as a chart and a copy of Bowditch's navigation tables."

"Ah!" Jacob eyes gleamed. "We had a compass, but that was the extent of our navigating tools."

"The winds weren't right for us to head for the Society Islands or the Marquesas," Edward said. "I suggested Hawaii, but Captain Trowbridge said it was more than a thousand miles away. We were much closer to this little island in the middle of nowhere. He wasn't sure we could fetch it, and it would have been disaster if we'd missed it. We all would have died of thirst in another day or two. But through God's grace and the captain's knowledge, we made it."

"It's too bad our boats were separated," Jacob said.

"Yes, but that was part of God's plan, too. I believe that now. He wanted me there with Gideon and John, and at the last of it, by myself for a good long while."

"It's hard for me to fathom why God would want that to happen," Jacob said. "Do you think He wanted the others to die like they did?"

Edward hesitated. "I don't know. He took them home, one by one, and each passing left a deep impression on the rest of us. The two fellows who were with me the longest didn't hold much with prayer and faith at first. John Webber was cocky and proud. He ran wild whenever we touched port. But the captain's testimony before he died influenced John to believe in Christ."

"Praise God," Deborah murmured.

"And when John cut his arm and began to get feverish, Gideon tended him like a baby. During that time, John urged Gideon to turn to the Lord. Afterward, Gideon came to me and told me he'd had a long talk with the Almighty, and he was a child of God from then on. We had precious fellowship together, Gideon and I."

"What a wonderful blessing." Deborah set her china cup down and folded her hands in her lap, ready to hear more.

"Yes. God used the storm and the wreck and all that happened afterward to draw those two men, at least, to Himself."

"I guess I can see that He brought good from it," Jacob said. "I'm glad they believed. It's still hard for me to thank God for letting the ship sink, though."

Deborah smiled at Edward, and he answered her, his eyes full of understanding. Their gazes locked for a long moment, and she felt warmth flooding through her chest and up to her face as the blood went to her cheeks.

Edward was such a dear brother in Christ. If only God would bring a man like him to love her the way Edward had loved Abby. She would not, could not, allow the thought to reach beyond that. On other occasions, she'd felt the flutter of longing in her heart when she and Edward conversed. They comprehended each other perfectly. Hadn't Abby felt that when she talked to him? How could she not yearn to be with him?

Even these thoughts made her feel uneasy, as she vaguely discerned an uncrossable line. Edward loved Abby. She could wish for a man like him, and she could wish for his future happiness, but she could not meld those two wishes into one. It would be scandalous.

She broke the stare with regret and caught Jacob's eye. He was settling against the back of his chair with a contented smile that she hoped wasn't a smirk.

Oh no! He's imagining things between Edward and me. Or was it her imagination? The sudden prospect that she had betrayed her sister by developing strong feelings for Edward slammed Deborah's heart. She was fooling herself if she refuted it.

What had Jacob seen, exactly? Worse yet, what did he think he had seen? She could not deny the undercurrent that had surged between her and Edward. But it wouldn't be proper to act upon it. Would it? Abby had definitely put an end to Edward's hopes and was planning her wedding to Jacob. It was wrong for Deborah to feel an attraction for her sister's rejected suitor. Of course, Edward didn't feel anything of the sort for her. Did he? And if he did, he was too much of a gentleman to do anything about it so soon. But Jacob's perception of what occurred was another matter entirely.

"Edward is considering sailing down to Portsmouth in our sloop soon to look at a ship for sale there," Jacob said.

Edward's features sobered. "Yes, we're thinking of adding one more vessel to our fleet. I'm looking over the accounts to be sure we're in good enough financial shape for that."

"I thought it was settled," Jacob said, turning toward him with his eyebrows arched. "You said you would go and size up the ship we spoke of."

Deborah saw Edward's troubled frown, but she decided this topic was a good distraction for Jacob. It was much better than the flutter of guilt she'd felt a moment ago. "When are you going?" she asked Edward.

"I'm not sure."

Jacob said, "We're waiting on our schooner the *Prosper*."

"We don't want to lay out any large sums of money until she brings in her cargo," Edward explained. "But Jacob expected her back several weeks ago. We've been watching for her since I returned."

"Where did she sail?" Deborah picked up the teapot, and Jacob held out his cup for her to refill.

"To the Caribbean," he said. "Captain Frost of the *Eden* brought me a packet of letters two months past. Said he'd met the *Prosper* a hundred miles north of Havana and exchanged mail with her. The report I received from our captain indicates the *Prosper* was doing fine at that time, but we've heard nothing since."

"Perhaps she's waiting on her return cargo," Deborah said.

Jacob winced and shook his head. "I wish I knew. If she's been pirated or sunk—"

"Let's not borrow trouble." Edward threw Deborah a reassuring smile.

"How many men aboard?" she asked.

"Twenty-four," said Edward.

Jacob sighed. "Both the Ramsey brothers are part of the crew, and Ivory Mason's son. Lots of local boys. The company can't afford to lose another ship, but beyond that, the loss of the crew would devastate this town."

"Then we must pray for the best," Deborah said.

"Yes." Edward gave his cousin a slight nod, as though he'd reached a decision. "As soon as she docks and the cargo is unloaded, I will run down to Portsmouth and look at the *Resolute*." He swiveled toward the hall, and Deborah heard the sound of the front door opening.

She jumped up. "That must be Mother and Abby."

Mrs. Bowman and Abigail joined them in the parlor, and Deborah hurried to the kitchen to get a fresh pot of tea and more cups. When she returned to the front room, all four were engaged in lively conversation about the choosing of Portland as the new state of Maine's capital and the preparations underway to celebrate statehood.

Deborah poured tea for Mother and Abigail and sat on a Windsor chair tucked near the hearth and watched them all. Edward and Jacob did not seem to compete for Abigail's favor. Both participated in the discussion equally, with courteous but opinionated contributions.

Edward turned to Deborah after a few minutes. "What do you think, Debbie? Should the people be taxed to build new government buildings?"

"Well, why not? We begged for statehood. We must bear the consequences."

She wondered if he was just being polite, including her in the conversation. But his smile made her feel that it was more than that. Edward cared what she thought. The idea that a man she esteemed found her thoughts worth considering brought on a surge of pleasure that was followed by a confusing blast of self-recrimination. She could not, must not consider Edward as anyone more than a friend at this time. It would shock society if he took up with the sister of the girl who had so recently rejected him. But the very idea made Deborah's chest tighten. If Edward *should* think of her in that way—it was too intoxicating to contemplate.

Edward turned his attention to her mother as she inquired about his family, and Deborah shrank into her corner and watched the others. Jacob was fully engrossed in Abigail. He even chatted with her for several minutes about the style of gown she was sewing for the new governor's upcoming ball.

Deborah searched Edward's profile for signs of jealousy but found none. He conversed with Deborah and her mother while Jacob and Abigail continued their chat in low tones, with eyes for no one else in the room. Deborah drew in a long, slow breath. Edward had not come here to pine for Abby or to torture himself by watching his cousin court the one he loved. And she doubted he found her mother's prattle about the neighbors overly absorbing.

She peeked at him. His attention to her mother's small talk was flawless, yet. . . He threw a quick smile her way, and Deborah's lungs suddenly felt too small to hold the same air he breathed.

Ten days later, Edward put on his hat and headed for the front door of his family home. He stopped with his hand on the marble knob.

"I hate to go off to the office and leave you alone, Mother. With Jenny away this morning—"

"What claptrap! Do you suppose I've never been alone before?"

"Well, no, but. . ." He looked her over and saw a capable, healthy woman with graying hair, a figure leaning toward stoutness, glinting brown eyes, and a determined scowl.

"Besides, I shan't be alone. You'll come home for dinner, and I expect Jenny to come soon after. And I shall have company for tea at half past three."

"Oh." Edward was taken aback by his gentle mother's spirited declaration. He supposed she had grown more independent of necessity since his father's death.

"Yes, and good company, too."

She seemed to be dangling that morsel in front of him, teasing him to jump at it, so he said rather cautiously, "Anyone I'm acquainted with?"

"Deborah Bowman comes to tea once a fortnight. She's more entertaining than a gossip, and more sympathetic than a parson. Today is Debbie's Tuesday, and there's no one I'd rather share a pot of tea with."

Edward smiled, wondering how this bit of information had managed to elude him. "You make me wish I were invited."

"Well, you're not."

He left the house, still savoring his mother's roguish behavior. She was back to her old self. Or perhaps not. This was a new self. She'd gained a verve that assured him she would be all right now, no matter what God placed in her path.

Her delight at the prospect of tea with Deborah was comforting, too. It told him she'd been enjoying the young woman's company for some time. Since his father's death, perhaps. Deborah was a good listener with an unfailingly cheerful outlook. Only once or twice had he seen her frown over Abigail's standoffish behavior toward him, tiny wrinkles in her smooth disposition. In fact, during the three weeks since Abigail had freed him of his need to look only at her, he'd been taking some rather long looks at Deborah and had decided that her character was altogether pleasing. She matched him in intellect and energy. The idea that Deborah had been bringing sunshine and friendship to his widowed mother brought a warm feeling to his heart.

It also reminded him of his duty to the families of the men of the *Egret.* He'd been to visit the captain's widow a couple of days after he arrived home. Several days later he called on Amos Mitchell's family, and yesterday morning he'd been to see Gideon Bramwell's parents. Those visits were difficult, but the appreciation showered on him told him those interviews had been essential. The parents and wives of the sailors wanted to know how their men had fared to the end.

Gideon Bramwell's mother wept openly when Edward told her about the young man's valiant struggles for survival and their camaraderie on the island. His father shed tears as well when Edward got to the recounting of Gideon's death. He didn't suffer, Edward assured them. His fall from the cliff was unexpected and swift. He died at once on the rocks, and his last act was one of trying to provide food for himself and Edward.

He would try to get to the Wilkes farm tomorrow. It was several miles out of town, but he could borrow a horse and ride out there. Davy's death must have been a severe blow to his parents and the other children. Edward had already discussed with Jacob and Mr. Daniels giving a sum of money to the families of the men who had died when the *Egret* foundered. He himself wanted to take to the Wilkeses the amount allotted to them and tell them how bravely the boy had met his end. It wouldn't be easy, and he wasn't sure how much to tell them about Davy's suffering after he shattered his leg while escaping the *Egret*. Best wait and see what their mood was, he decided. It had been four years, but they might still be angry or bitter toward the company. If the mother seemed resentful or distraught, he would keep to himself the details of the boy's infection and lingering death.

He sighed, knowing he must take a day from his arduous work at the office to accomplish that errand. For the past week he'd given all the time he could spare to his scrutiny of the company's records. It relieved him in some measure, as he'd concluded that Daniels was trustworthy beyond a doubt.

But his study had also given him cause for further dismay. Something was definitely odd about the *Prosper*'s recent record. The ship had been a gold mine for the past two or three years, but since his father's death, she had been marginally profitable. Since Jacob had taken the company's helm, something had gone amiss in the Caribbean trade. Edward didn't like to think his cousin was directly responsible, but he had to eliminate the possibility. He weighed the option of a frank confrontation with Jacob against waiting for the *Prosper* to come in and assessing her performance on the most recent voyage. The longer the ship was delayed, the darker his thoughts were running.

"Edward! Good morning!"

He looked up to see Pastor Jordan approaching him.

"May I walk with you?"

"Certainly. I'm only going to my office."

"I'm heading for a house down past the wharves," the pastor said. "An old salt who lives down there is ill, perhaps dying. Micah Carson."

"I know him," Edward said. "He worked for my father at one time."

"And how are things going with you?"

Edward gritted his teeth. "Well, you made the announcement in church on Sunday, so you know Miss Bowman has set her heart on another."

The pastor nodded, his features schooled to neutrality. "Yes. I wasn't surprised when Dr. Bowman came to see me and asked me to announce Abigail's upcoming marriage to Mr. Price, but I was concerned about you. How are you holding up?"

Edward sighed and looked at the kindly pastor. "The first time I saw her, several weeks ago, I thought I couldn't go on living if she wouldn't have me."

"And now?"

He shrugged, looking down the street toward the harbor. "Well, I'm still alive."

The pastor laid a hand on Edward's shoulder for a moment. "It's a difficult situation, son. I've been praying for you."

"Thank you. I believe the Lord has brought about what is best. I bear Jacob no malice."

"That's good. Look to God for guidance and keep a forgiving spirit."

"I believe I'm more than halfway there."

"Good. This is a time of transition, then, in your mind and in your heart."

"Yes. We are all sifting the meal, so to speak, trying to get the lumps out. Jacob and I had a long talk when I first got home. I've accepted this as God's will for all of us. Now I'm concentrating on the business."

"A big responsibility with your father gone."

"Yes. I'm going over all the records to make sure I know everything that's happened at Hunter Shipping since I went away. I'm afraid our accountant, Mr. Daniels, finds me a bit tedious with all the questions I've been asking him this last month."

"Ah, well, hard work can be a blessing in times of emotional turmoil."

"Would you keep praying for me, Pastor? There are a couple of matters giving me some anxiety."

"Oh? Anything I can help with?"

Edward thought for a moment about the discrepancy in the Caribbean trade. That was strictly a business affair. But the other—an image of Deborah listening avidly as he related his adventures—flitted through his mind. Her smile was so genuine, so yearning that he couldn't help being drawn to her. Just thinking of her these days caused his pulse to jump. Yes, the second one was a matter of the heart.

"Not specifically," he said, "but knowing you are praying for me will be an encouragement."

"Then rest easy," said the pastor. "I've been praying for your peace and a bright future for you ever since I learned you'd come home."

They had neared the harbor, and Edward looked out over the calm water of the estuary. The morning mist was disappearing off the sea. He drew a deep draft of the salty air. His problems with Abigail had dissipated much like the fog, and a new anticipation gripped him. What would God reveal for him, now that the future he'd expected was gone?

Chapter 10

Deborah climbed the attic stairs in the Hunter house, preceding her hostess to the door at the top. It opened onto the roof, where a small platform was enclosed by a decorative white railing. She looked out over the town, which in recent years had burgeoned into a city. The cupola on top of the new courthouse caught her eye. So many buildings that hadn't been there when Edward went away. And now the new statehouse was under construction next to the courthouse. Portland must seem huge to him.

When he'd left, the businesses were still reeling from the economic blow dealt by the recent war with England. But now Exchange Street bustled with new shops, the wharves were crowded with stores, and dozens of brigs and schooners filled the harbor. The fledgling legislature was putting the new state constitution in place. Manufacturing was booming—foundries, ropewalks, soap and candle works, and mills and builders. Everywhere one looked, an air of prosperity hung over Portland.

Mrs. Hunter came behind her, puffing up the last few stairs, and stepped up onto the widow's walk with Deborah.

"You have such a lovely view of the city and the harbor." Deborah turned to the west and leaned on the railing, letting the wind blow against her face, tugging and teasing at her hair and her straw bonnet. "You must be able to see almost as far as Captain Moody can."

"Oh no, the observatory is much higher than we are." Mrs. Hunter chuckled. "Have you ever been up there?"

"No."

"My husband took me up soon after it was built. We could see the White Mountains of New Hampshire. The captain said he can spot ships forty miles out to sea with his telescope."

Deborah turned and looked east toward the conical building that towered over Moody's homestead. Built on a rise that was one of the high points of the area, it rose majestically over the town, like a lighthouse that had given up the sea, wandered inland, and settled on a farm.

"It is a lot higher," she conceded, "but I like your house best. I can see all the church steeples, the courthouse, and the river and the back cove. Even the cemetery. But I'm right here in your peaceful house."

"Thank you, dear. It's been a snug home for many years. My husband's father saw that it was well built, and I've not had much trouble with it, though I expect Edward will need to have it reshingled before too many more years pass. You can see down there on the gable where the shingles look a bit ruffled."

Deborah squinted down at the edge of the roof. "Yes, I see the spot."

"If we get another bad storm with a high wind from the east, he may need to do it sooner," Mrs. Hunter said with a resigned smile. "But that's the way it is when you live near the sea. Wind, wind, wind."

Indeed, the gusts were pulling at Deborah's bonnet so sharply that she untied the wide strings that anchored it under her chin and took it off, holding it down against her skirt.

"Now you'll lose your hairpins." Mrs. Hunter raised her voice against the stiff breeze, but she was smiling.

"That's a lovely idea." Deborah reached up and probed her coiled hair, extracting several polished wooden pins and slipping them into her pocket. Her long brown locks tumbled about her shoulders and swirled around her face, tossed about by the restless air from the bay.

Mrs. Hunter laughed. "Ah, to be young again."

"Are you cold?" Deborah asked, noting that the older woman pulled her shawl tighter about her.

"Perhaps a bit."

"Then we must go down. I'm sure our tea is ready." Deborah took her hostess's arm and guided her back to the entrance.

Passing through the attic, Deborah noticed chests and disused furnishings crowding the room.

"The castoffs of many generations," Mrs. Hunter said with a smile. "I suppose I ought to go through it all and dispose of half of it, but it seems such a lot of trouble. I believe I'll let Edward do it one day."

Deborah smiled and ran her hand over a smooth old wooden frame. "Did you ever use this loom?"

"No, not me. That belonged to my late husband's grandmother. Lucy Hamblin Hunter, she was. They say she wove the finest linen in the province. Of course, there weren't too many weavers in Maine then to compete with her."

Deborah laughed. "I admire her patience. It's all I can do to crochet a doily."

"Sometime I will show you the table linen she wove. I have several pieces she made. Why, it must have been almost a hundred years ago now. They say she married her husband while he was in prison."

Deborah stared at her in the dim light, wondering if Mrs. Hunter was teasing her. "In prison? What for?"

"Murder. Nothing less. But he was acquitted, and he and Lucy lived a long and happy life together in a little cabin not many miles from here. It was their son who went to sea and became the first Captain Hunter."

"I like that story." Deborah took Mrs. Hunter's hand and walked slowly down the steps with her. When they had descended into the upstairs hall and the attic door was shut behind them, she said, "Thank you for taking me up. I do love it on the widow's walk."

Mrs. Hunter smiled and patted her arm. "It's a joy to me when I see your face light up. I don't go up so much myself. . . not since Jeremiah died, God rest his soul."

"You do miss him a lot, don't you?" Deborah walked slowly with her toward the main staircase.

"Every minute I miss him. I used to go up there and look over at the docks. I can see the warehouse from up there. Sometimes I would see him turning the corner of the street on his way home. I'd wave to him, then rush down the stairs to meet him." Her dreamy smile told Deborah she was off in another, more pleasant time. "But then, with him and Edward both dead, as we all supposed, I stopped going up to the roof. It seemed too morbid. I didn't want folks saying, 'There's the widow mourning her menfolk' and pitying me."

"People don't pity you," Deborah assured her. "You're far too alive. You don't mope about."

"Don't I?"

Mrs. Hunter's eyes twinkled, and Deborah laughed.

"No, you most decidedly don't."

"Well, in any event, climbing those stairs is getting to be quite an exertion for me."

"Come," Deborah said. "I smell something tasty."

A few minutes later, they were seated in Mrs. Hunter's cozy sitting room. Deborah much preferred it to the larger front parlor. This small, paneled room was full of bright cushions and enameled boxes of many colors and designs. She knew that Mr. Hunter had presented the boxes to his wife one at a time, either when he returned from a voyage or when a ship docked after a long trading excursion, laden with exotic wares. When Deborah visited, her hostess let her handle and admire them as much as she liked. She fingered the brightly painted ones from the Orient as the maid laid out their refreshment.

After Jenny had left the room, Deborah sat down and Mrs. Hunter poured out their tea.

"Quite an announcement after church on Sunday."

"Yes." Deborah busied herself with the sugar tongs, not sure she could meet the lady's gaze without bursting out in either laughter or tears. The public reading of the marriage intentions of Mr. Jacob Price and Miss Abigail Bowman had left her torn.

"You don't seem elated at the news. But then, neither do you seem dismayed."

Deborah couldn't help smiling then. "You must understand my mixed feelings. I'm happy for my sister, but only because she is happy."

"Tut! My nephew Jacob is a good lad. He's risen above his father's humble station. He has his mother's wits."

"It wasn't my intent to disparage Jacob," Deborah said. "I believe he will make Abby a good husband."

"But?"

"But I feel disappointed for Edward."

Mrs. Hunter snorted and set her teacup down. "Edward is not weeping. Neither should you be."

Deborah blinked. It was an alien concept that Edward might be pleased with Abby's rejection of him. Was he relieved to be freed from their engagement? She wondered what he had told his mother after Abby revealed her decision to him. Was it possible that in time he might think of courting another? Of course, that would be the natural course of things after his wounded heart had healed, but how feasible was it that he would be captivated by a woman he considered an adolescent tomboy? Deborah shoved the thoughts away. She didn't dare hope that he might turn his affections her way. He was a family friend now. That was all. It meant nothing, and she mustn't read too much into the recent visit he'd made with Jacob.

She reached for a raisin cake and smiled at her hostess. "All right. I shall cease mourning the rift between him and Abby."

"As is proper. This is a time to rejoice with your sister."

Deborah bit into the cake, considering that. For the past few days, she'd felt more like rejoicing than she had since the day she first saw Edward returned from the deeps. But she was afraid to let her heart run too far astray. Every time she thought much about Edward and her growing feelings for him, she felt guilty. And when she considered whether or not he might ever return them, she felt obliged to quickly stifle that train of thought. She would only lay herself open for disappointment if he did not reciprocate. Time to change the subject.

"Mm, this cake is delicious. Did you make it, or did Jenny?"

"She did," Mrs. Hunter said. "I'm lucky to have that girl. She has a proper touch with the bake oven. But neither she nor I can wait to try cooking on the new stove my son has ordered for me."

"You are getting a cookstove?"

"Yes, I am. It will be prodigious fun. Would you like to come round when it's here and practice with me?"

"I'd love to."

Mrs. Hunter nodded. "We can make a huge pot of chicken stew without stooping over a hearth or catching sparks on our skirts. We'll do it on a Thursday, and you and Abigail can take it around to the widows and orphans."

"That would be wonderful. Some of them are so poor they rarely have meat on their tables."

"Then we'll do it and bake a basket full of biscuits from white flour to go with it."

"That will be a scrumptious treat for them. Does this mean you will share with me your secret for making biscuits?"

Mrs. Hunter paused as if it were a novel thought, then smiled. "I believe I shall. But you must be careful whom you share it with."

"I shall indeed."

They shared a smile of conspiratorial friendship.

"Of course," Mrs. Hunter said primly, "if Edward had married your sister, I'd have told her."

The implications of this were not lost on Deborah, and she felt her face flush.

"Abby didn't mean to be unkind to him."

"Of course not. But my Edward was always adventurous, perhaps more than she realized. And I'll not deny his experience of the last five years has changed him. He's more passionate now, more eager to make his mark on the world. I suppose that's because he nearly lost the chance."

Deborah tilted her head to one side, mulling that over. Everyone had agreed that Jacob had done fine while he was in charge of the business, and Mrs. Hunter had no complaints about his management. But Edward would do better than fine. His plans for the company, which he'd discussed with her father after the service on Sunday, were ambitious and bold. He would put his heart into the business and run with it, making Hunter Shipping even greater if God would allow it.

"Perhaps you are right," she said to his mother. "His new passion is an extension of his fight for survival on the island."

"You see that, don't you? But your sister feels safer and more at home with Jacob's more placid nature." Mrs. Hunter nodded and raised her cup to her lips. "I expect they'll make a good match."

"I do hope so. I was a bit put out with her when she turned Edward down."

"No need of that. This is well and good."

"You believe that?"

"With all my heart." As the lady reached for a cookie, Jenny Hapworth hurried into the room, her eyes downcast.

"I'm sorry, ma'am, but one of the clerks just came up from the office with a note for you."

She held a slip of parchment out to Mrs. Hunter. Deborah used the interruption to pour more tea into her thin china cup.

"It's a ship." Mrs. Hunter's merry brown eyes filled with anticipation. "Edward sent this to tell me."

"One of their own ships?"

"He's not certain yet."

"Let's pray that it is the *Prosper*." Deborah set the teapot down with care.

"Yes, indeed."

Mrs. Hunter reached out to her, and they clasped hands.

"Father on high, smile upon us today and bring the wayward vessel the *Prosper* safely to port."

Deborah added her own quiet plea. "Dear Lord, please allow us to rejoice in the homecoming of the *Prosper* today. And if this is not that ship, then, Father, we beg You to keep all the men aboard her safe, wherever they be now, and draw her swiftly back to these shores."

They raised their heads and smiled hopefully at one another.

"Why don't you run up to the widow's walk?" Mrs. Hunter suggested. "I'm not up to making the climb again so soon, but you can go and watch."

"How will I know if it's the *Prosper*? She's probably still far down the bay."

"Here." Mrs. Hunter rose and took a small brass spyglass from the cherry sideboard. "You'll be able to see her when she rounds the point and enters the river, but before that, Captain Moody will know. He's already raised the flag for Hunter Shipping, letting the merchants know, so he's identified the vessel. Either he knows her by her lines, or she's hoisted a signal for him."

"That seems promising, doesn't it?"

"Yes, it does. Run along up, dear."

Deborah seized the spyglass and dashed up the two flights of stairs. The wind was worse than ever, and she hadn't bothered to put her hat or her shawl on. Her skirt billowed behind her as she faced east, and her hair whipped about, stinging her cheeks.

She turned to the sea first and tried to see what Moody had seen, but the headland opposite the town, across the Fore River, obstructed her view. So she trained the glass on Moody's observatory. Three banners were flying, but she picked out the one for Hunter's easily. Everyone in town knew the flags of the big shipping companies.

A sudden fear that it was not the long-awaited ship came over her, and she closed her eyes, sending up a frantic petition.

Father, please don't let them lose another ship. There's been enough grief and loss. Please!

Far in the distance, the prow of a ship rounded the cape and entered the river. She held the spyglass to her eye. The national flag flew from the mainmast—and below it the banner of Hunter Shipping!

She turned and ran down the stairs. Jenny and Mrs. Hunter stood in the front hall, where the stairs came down, and a thin boy was with them. Deborah's heart lurched with joy as she heard his pronouncement.

"She's the *Prosper*, all right! Mr. Edward's dancing a hornpipe on the wharf, ma'am."

Chapter 11

Edward carried a sack of sugar up the companionway to the deck of the *Prosper* and heaved it onto the stack near the gangplank. He went back to the hatch and watched two stevedores climb up and deposit their burdens on the pile.

That was it. The ship's cargo was unloaded. All of the previous day and most of this morning, his men had labored at stripping the hold. Under Uncle Felix's exacting command, they'd filled the warehouse and stacked hundreds of barrels and crates in the warehouse yard and along the wharf.

Now the merchants of Portland would swarm to the yard and the wharf to look over the goods and speak for those they wished to purchase.

Edward retrieved his jacket from where he'd hung it on a peg over one of the scuppers but didn't put it on. He was sweating and filthy from his effort. He knew Jacob was on the wharf checking off the manifest that listed the cargo. And Jacob was, without doubt, cool and neat, impeccably attired for a businessman.

That was all right, but Edward preferred to get in among the men and put his back into it. That gave him a better understanding of the men's work and boosted the laborers' opinion of him. It also made the ridiculously generous check Mr. Daniels had written him last week for his monthly salary more acceptable.

Had his father drawn that much from the company every month? His mother assured him that his father had when things were going well. In tight times, such as during the war with England or in the months following the loss of the *Egret* and her cargo, he took less. He always made sure the employees were paid first, from the dockhands to the ship captains. The clerks, the sailors, and the boy who swept the warehouse floor were paid before Mr. Hunter drew his check. That knowledge gave Edward a new appreciation for his responsibility as head of the firm. Scores of families depended on him and Hunter Shipping.

More than ever, he knew he must uncover the mystery of the *Prosper*'s lagging profits. He'd handled the cargo himself and watched every cask and bundle brought up from the hold. If all was not as it should be, now was the time to discover it.

He slung his jacket over one shoulder and headed down the gangplank. The men worked about him in an orderly swarm, toting the sacks, rolling the casks, piling crates on small carts, and pulling the carts along the wharf toward the warehouse.

Jacob called to him as he approached his post near the store.

"Well, Mr. Hunter, you've been exercising your muscles, I see!"

Edward flipped the dripping hair out of his eyes. "To the point of soreness. I've only been back in the office four weeks, and already I'm getting soft."

"Well, I can put you in the warehouse under my father if you wish. That used to be your position, did it not?"

"Yes, before I went to sea as a cabin boy at fourteen."

Jacob nodded with a wry smile. "I had much the same experience, as you know, and I can tell you I prefer the deck to the warehouse floor. Of course, the office is better than either."

Edward laughed. "It wouldn't hurt you to rub shoulders with your old cronies now and then."

"Probably not, but I have a dinner engagement later. I can't see a lady receiving a gentleman in your condition." Jacob's nose wrinkled as he eyed Edward's sweat-drenched shirt.

"That bad?" Edward pulled his chin in and looked down at his clothing. "You're right. Perhaps I'd better go home to wash up and change my clothes."

"Commendable idea," Jacob murmured. "I've put the word out that we'll be open to buyers at noon. Several well-placed merchants will wish to greet you this afternoon as they do their business, I'm sure."

Edward nodded and glanced about to make sure none of the workmen were near enough to overhear. "There's something we need to discuss later, Jacob."

His cousin's eyebrows shot upward. "Anything serious?"

"Perhaps."

Jacob nodded. "At the close of business, then."

Edward bypassed the office and went straight home. He'd have to start taking an extra shirt to work with him to have on hand for such occasions. One of the clerks could fetch him wash water; they heated tea water on a small stove. Yes, he would implement the plan at once. That way he could take all the exercise he wanted and not embarrass Jacob or Mr. Daniels when the upper-class customers came around.

Was this the day his mother had said Deborah would visit? No, that was Tuesday. Time blurred with the hectic unloading of the ship, but he was sure this wasn't the day. Still, he half hoped he would run into Deborah at the house. Looking down once more at his soiled clothing and realizing how filthy he was, he cringed. No, it would not be the best time to meet the woman he hoped most to impress.

The thought startled him, but at once the sharpness of it softened. Why hadn't he seen earlier what a wonderful person Deborah was? Not that she needed impressing. She would scoff at that idea. She didn't judge people by appearances. That first afternoon, when he'd gone to the Bowman house fresh off the ship, she'd welcomed him joyfully, bedraggled as he was.

The image of Deborah's subdued beauty leaped to his mind, her lovely brown eyes and gleaming mahogany hair. She didn't play up her attributes, and many people probably would say she was not as pretty as her sister. Edward had thought so, too, at one time. Now he was beginning to revise that opinion.

His mother thought she was beautiful, and she was a good judge of such things. "Deborah has looks that will last," she'd said just the other day. He hadn't told his mother about his newly kindled feelings for the younger Miss Bowman, but somehow she seemed to know. Deborah's name came into the dinner conversation almost every evening at the Hunter house.

Yes, she was lovely. On Sunday she had sat between Abigail and her mother in the family pew. Jacob sat with the family on Abigail's other side, but Edward didn't mind. He took his place beside his mother, but he had eyes only for Deborah, two rows ahead of them that morning. Her green gown was plainer than Abigail's flounced and frilled blue, but it enhanced her creamy skin and dark eyes. And he noticed that while Abby fidgeted during the sermon and cast veiled glances at Jacob throughout the hour, Deborah sat still and seemed to give her undivided attention to Pastor Jordan.

Traits he used to find amusing in Abigail—her flickering attention, her interest in fashion—he had attributed to her immaturity in the old days. But she was a grown woman now, and she had not changed. Deborah, on the other hand, seemed to have grown into a mixture of practicality and playfulness. She appeared to be unconcerned about her appearance beyond neatness and appropriate attire. He knew her to be loyal—look at the way she'd insisted Abby not slough him off. She was industrious, too; she often brought needlework with her to the parlor while entertaining guests when she could have sat idle, and on several occasions he'd seen her jump to aid her mother with some household task. If his mother's words were any indication, she was a reliable and sensible young woman.

As he approached his home, he tried to squelch all thoughts of Deborah. They still felt wrong somehow. For more than five years he'd dreamed of a future with Abigail. But the Abigail of his daydreams didn't match up with the Abigail he knew now. Was it possible that the Abigail he'd longed for during his years of exile was more like the actual Deborah?

In confusion, he bounded up the steps and into the house to greet his mother and explain why he had come home. He was grateful it was not Tuesday, after all. He wouldn't have the slightest idea what to say to Deborah.

An hour later, Edward was back at the warehouse, watching the commotion from the top of a loading platform as buyers thronged the premises, touching the fabrics, sampling the molasses, and sniffing the fruit. Market days at the warehouse were a jumble of colors and scents. When a ship docked, word spread in a flash through the town, and the buyers awaited word that the unloading was completed and the newly arrived wares were available for sale. The merchants hurried in to speak for quantities of goods for their stores, but individuals were just as ardently in search of a bargain at a low price.

His uncle came to stand beside Edward.

"There's your fortune, boy. Your ship came in at last, and all your financial obligations are met and then some."

"Yes," Edward agreed. "God be praised. She was delayed for loading and revictualing, and then she ran into muddy weather in the Caribbean and had to replace torn canvas."

Felix nodded. "Two days ago we feared she was lost—but she's here now, and all is well."

Edward nodded. He'd read Captain Stuart's report of the voyage, but even with the foul weather and other obstacles accounted for, the *Prosper* had made poor time. She'd brought back a full cargo, which seemed to make everyone else happy; however, the month lost on what should have been a quick run had cost the firm plenty, and Edward was not entirely satisfied with the list of products she'd delivered. He had already asked to have the ship's log on his desk by close of business today.

"Mr. Hunter!"

He turned toward Jacob's voice. His cousin always addressed him formally when employees or customers were listening. Jacob was below him on the floor of the warehouse, holding a long sheet of parchment and beckoning for him to join him and the two men with him.

Edward nodded to Uncle Felix and headed for the steep steps. Just as he was about to descend, he glanced out over the warehouse and halted.

A woman in a brown and blue plaid dress was making her way through the barrels of food and piles of bulging sacks near the door. It couldn't be—

She turned, and the sunlight streaming through the open door glinted on her rich, reddish brown hair. A young man was with her, a gangly, teenaged boy he didn't recognize, carrying a large basket. As he watched, Deborah began taking yams from a barrel and loading them into the basket.

"Edward? Are you coming down?"

Jacob had come to stand just beneath him, not quite masking his impatience. Edward hastened down the steps.

"I just saw Deborah."

Jacob swiveled around to look but seemed unconcerned.

"What's she doing here?"

"She often comes when we hold open market." Jacob turned and pushed people aside to reach the two men he'd been dealing with, and Edward followed, losing track of Deborah. Ladies didn't venture into a crush like this where bankers and dockhands mingled.

"You know Mr. Engle," Jacob said.

"Yes, hello." Edward shook hands with the gray-haired owner of a sawmill on the edge of the river.

"This is his supervisor, Mr. Park, who is in charge of the lumbering operation. They are interested in sending a load of lumber and barrel staves to St. Thomas."

Edward nodded. "The *Prosper* will put out for the Caribbean and Rio again in two weeks."

"Yes," Jacob said. "If you can have it on the wharf next week, we'll make room for it."

"What about your bigger ship?" Engle asked.

Jacob ducked his head in acknowledgment. "The *Falcon* will be in soon, but she plies the European trade for us. We've new cargo lined up for Amsterdam, LeHavre, Bordeaux, and Lisbon."

"Ah, then the *Prosper* it is. We've a large order. I hope you can take it all at once."

"Mr. Engle has shipped lumber with us before," Jacob said, and Edward nodded.

"Well, then, perhaps you could take these gentlemen into the office and arrange the transaction," he suggested, looking toward the front of the huge room, hoping to spot Deborah again.

"We hope to add a third schooner to our fleet soon," Jacob said to Engle and Park. "If that purchase works out, we'll add the *Resolute* to our West Indies trade."

"You boys are doing well," Park said. "When will you have the new ship?"

"If we decide to buy her, we should have her here inside a week," Jacob replied. "Mr. Hunter leaves tomorrow for Portsmouth to examine the vessel."

"Yes, but we're not certain yet we want to buy her," Edward said, scanning the crowd. "If we do, it will likely take us several weeks to refit her before she's ready to take on cargo."

His mind was only half on the conversation, and then only because he was afraid Jacob would promise cargo space where there was none as yet. He spotted the plaid material of Deborah's dress as the people close to her separated and surged around her.

"Could you gentlemen excuse me, please? There's someone I must have a word with."

He made his way as quickly as he could through the throng, but when he got to the crates of tea where he'd last seen her, she was gone. He gawked about, feeling foolish, but soon located her and the boy a few yards away.

"Deborah!" he called as he strode toward her, afraid he would lose her once more.

She turned toward him, and her face lit with pleasure.

"What a surprise to see you here."

"Hello, Edward. I'm often here of a Thursday."

"Indeed?"

"Yes. I would like you to meet Thomas Crowe. He assists me." She turned to the boy. "Thomas, this is Mr. Hunter."

The boy stared at him as Edward held out his hand and said, "Pleased to meet you." After a moment, Thomas shook his hand, then quickly withdrew it.

"Er. . .assists you with what, if I may ask?"

"With making my purchases."

Edward frowned and eyed the basket on her arm, then studied the larger one the boy was carrying. Surely the Bowmans had servants to do their shopping for them, and he doubted their household would need yams and tea in such quantities.

"This is a rowdy place for a lady, especially when a ship has newly docked. We get all sorts of people in here, Deborah."

She smiled. "I know it. That's part of what Thomas is for. Mother forbade me to come by myself."

"I still don't quite. . ." He looked pointedly at her heaped basket. "I mean, that's a lot of tea."

"Yes, it is."

He was at a loss for words, and she laughed at his expression.

"I see I shall have to educate you about my Thursday outings. But it's noisy in here. Perhaps you can visit the house another time, and we can discuss it."

Delight sprang up in his heart at her suggestion, but it was quickly followed by a thud of disappointment.

"I'm afraid I must decline that enticing offer."

"Oh?" She was clearly disappointed as well, and he was somewhat gratified.

"Now that the *Prosper* is in, Jacob wants me to leave immediately for Portsmouth to see about buying that other ship we mentioned."

"The *Resolute*," she said.

"Yes." It shouldn't surprise him that she remembered. "Please believe me, I would much rather spend the time in your parlor discussing your Thursday schedule or any other topic to your liking, but Jacob is right; if we don't act quickly, we'll lose this chance. In fact, we've already delayed action several weeks on this matter, and the *Resolute* may already be sold to someone else."

"Of course you must go," she said.

He nodded. "Thank you for understanding. I shall leave at high tide in the morning, and I expect to be gone several days, perhaps a week."

Her eyes seemed to lose a little of their glow, and he knew he had let her down. But she shook her head and smiled up at him. "Then we shall have to meet when you return. I'll pray you have a safe journey."

"Thank you." He hesitated, then looked at the boy again. "Er. . ."

"Oh, the provisions. You see, a couple of years ago, I began a service of sorts that occupies me on Thursdays."

"A service?"

"Yes. In the past, your father always allowed me to buy a few staples at wholesale each week or anytime a ship came in."

Edward was puzzled by this, but by now he knew that, Deborah being Deborah, she probably had a good reason.

She laughed. "I see that I shall have to tell you my secret in full. Just, please, don't spread it about, will you? It threatens their dignity."

"Whose?"

"The sailors' wives. Or widows, I should say."

"You are taking food to sailors' widows?"

"A little food and a great deal of conversation and company. That's what I do best."

"And my mother is one of your ladies?"

Her merry grin at that warmed him to his toes.

"No, your mother is in a special class by herself. She often helps me in my cause by donating clothing and foodstuffs. But you see, by obtaining food, clothing, and other goods at wholesale prices from the city's traders, I am able to help several families. . . . Well, to be plain, I help them survive."

Edward drew a deep breath. Deborah *would* undertake a cause like that. She saw a need in the seaside city, and instead of petitioning the community's leaders to meet it, she endeavored to help those she could.

"How many families?"

"I've given small aid to about a dozen so far."

"And the boy is part of this?" he asked.

Deborah flashed her smile toward Thomas. "He is the son of a brave man who died at sea."

"I'll soon be old enough to sail myself, sir," Thomas said. "But my mother wants me at home for now."

Edward could understand that. If the husband was lost, the wife would be slow to let her children take up the sailor's life.

"Each week he helps me carry the goods I buy to his mother's house, where I distribute them," Deborah said.

Edward nodded. He was seeing a new side of Deborah, and his impression of her sweet compassion combined with her energy and practical good sense only grew more defined.

"I'm glad my father promoted your efforts."

"Thank you. Your uncle let me continue to come here after Mr. Hunter died. I hope you don't mind. I probably should have asked you."

"No, that's fine. In fact. . ." He glanced toward where he had left Jacob, but his cousin was gone, no doubt into the office to set up the delivery and fees for transporting Engle's lumber. "In fact, I'd like to give you a load of provisions for these families. Just tell me what is needed, and I'll have a wagonload delivered."

Deborah opened her mouth, swallowed, then found her voice. "Thank you, that's very generous. But you can hardly do that every week, or you would lose money. What I usually do is go around and solicit private donations from my friends and some of the business owners in town. If you are willing to let me continue buying at wholesale, that is enough."

"But surely you have ladies who need more than tea and"—he peered into Thomas's basket—"and sugar. Let me this once give you a wagon full."

"Well. . ." She tilted her head toward her shoulder, considering.

Edward's heart leaped, and he longed to throw his arms around her. In that moment, he knew that life without Deborah would be boring and flat. In her world, there would never be a day without some joy, or at least the satisfaction of a worthy effort completed. That was a life he wanted to share.

"Perhaps a few things," she agreed. "Mrs. Lewis has a baby and could use some soft flannel. I hadn't looked at the yard goods yet."

"Yes! You shall have a bolt of flannel and one of calico. And some rice and coffee and all the salt fish and molasses you can use. And from now on, when you come to the warehouse to buy for your ladies, you will buy at cost."

"At cost?"

"My cost, not wholesale."

"Oh, Edward, you'll bankrupt yourself."

"Nonsense. You won't put a nick in all this." He waved his arm, encompassing the whole warehouse and almost hitting a merchant who was passing.

She hesitated, then nodded. "I shan't say no. Thank you."

He smiled. "That's fine. Pick out what you want today. And fill the wagon. I mean it. This day's goods are my gift to you and the families. I'll have one of the men drive the wagon around to the place where you distribute the lot."

"That would be the Crowe residence." She named a street in the poorest section of town.

He nodded, keeping his face straight so as not to embarrass the boy, but the thought of Deborah going there appalled him.

"I'll send a good man to drive the wagon and help unload when you get there. Will you ride on the wagon seat with him?"

"Oh no, Thomas and I shall walk."

"Do you. . .walk down there often?"

"Every week unless Abby goes with me. Then we take a hack."

He stood speechless for a moment. The thought of Abby joining this enterprise shocked him, but with persuasion from the earnest Deborah, he supposed even that was possible. His admiration for Deborah and his longing to be with her urged him to make a further overture. He drew a careful breath and reached for her arm, turning her slightly away from the boy.

"I was wondering," Edward said.

"Yes?"

"When I come back from Portsmouth, may I call on you?"

"You can visit my family anytime."

"No, I mean *you*, Deborah."

She caught her breath and looked away, staring off toward the open door of the warehouse, where clerks were totaling up a buyer's purchases and accepting payment.

"Deborah?"

"Mm?" Her face was crimson, but she turned toward him and raised her chin until her melting brown eyes looked into his face.

"If you'll permit it, I'd like to come next week to call on you. What do you say?"

She opened her mouth, but nothing came out. Was she wondering what Abigail would say? Or perhaps what her father's reaction would be?

She swallowed and tried again. "I would be delighted."

Edward smiled. "Then I shall look forward to it during my voyage to Portsmouth. Now, speak for your merchandise, and I'll arrange for the wagon."

She thanked him again and turned away. Edward watched her for a moment as she headed for the bolts of material in search of soft flannel for babies' diapers. He ought to insist that she stay out of that part of town.

He almost laughed at himself. She'd been doing this for two years while he had been off digging clams and carving sticks to kill time on Spring Island. And Abigail sometimes went with her! Unbelievable! He still couldn't picture Abby entering the humble huts of the sailors' widows. But Deborah. . . Yes, he could see her doing it.

Suddenly he wanted to hurry through the rest of this day. He wanted to put the voyage to Portsmouth behind him and come home quickly. Home to Deborah.

Chapter 12

It's got to be the tonnage," Edward said, frowning over the mass of papers he had spread across his desk. "Nothing else makes any sense."

"How so?" Jacob asked. He shuffled through the manifests, logs, and sales reports, looking a bit lost.

"On her last few voyages, the total cargo on the *Prosper* was a lower volume than capacity."

"Really? I didn't notice that." Jacob pushed aside one of the ledgers and picked up another sheet of paper.

"It wasn't much off, but on her first voyage last year, the cargo totaled up less tonnage than you'd expect. Then, on the second trip, when she docked last fall, there seems to have been a shortage again, unless I'm missing something. Take a look at the manifest. They could easily have loaded more coffee or molasses in the Indies."

Jacob sat down and puzzled over the papers Edward had indicated.

"But this doesn't prove that anything's amiss."

"Not in itself," Edward agreed. "But this latest cargo..."

"Oh, really, Ed." Jacob looked up at him with troubled eyes. "You helped unload her yourself. They had that ship filled to the gunwales."

He nodded, mulling it over in his mind. "Yes, but with what? You've told me several times you expected several tons of coffee to come in. Stuart brought us only a small supply. We could have sold ten times as much coffee today. But this cargo was heavy on rice and raw cotton, Jake. Products we don't make much on when we resell them."

Jacob pressed his lips together and inhaled, looking down at the papers once more. "Captain Stuart told me he got all he could. Should we have him in tomorrow and question him further about this?"

Edward frowned and sat on the corner of his desk. "I'm not sure. I've read his log, and though there's nothing obviously wrong there, it seems a bit vague in spots. He said they turned back for repairs at one point, but the time spent on what should have been a minor job doesn't fit." He stood up. "Let's talk to some of the other men."

Jacob smiled. "Jamie Sibley. He was on the *Egret* with us, remember?"

"Aye."

"He was always a good lad. I put him on the sloop last year, but for this current voyage, I made him the *Prosper*'s second mate."

"Perfect," said Edward. "He was with you in the *Egret*'s yawl."

"Yes. I wouldn't question his loyalty to me or Hunter Shipping."

Edward nodded, liking it more and more. "Let's go."

As they walked the quiet streets of the harbor, Edward's mind surged with questions. They came to the corner of the street where the Sibley family lived, and he paused.

"Jacob, I hope you'll forgive me, but I had to start at the top on this. I've been looking pretty hard at you and Mr. Daniels the past few weeks."

"At me and—oh, Ed."

"Yes, well, I had to be sure. At first I wasn't even certain anything was going on. But I'm sure now. You had nothing to do with it, though."

Jacob's hurt expression pierced him.

"Can you forgive me for doubting you?"

"Well, I suppose you had to. I mean, it's your company and your family. Abby, too. You had to be sure she wasn't marrying a rapscallion."

"Yes. But still. . . Well, I never really thought you could do something like that to Hunter Shipping. Why would you, after all, when it looked as though you'd end up with the whole business? But there were enough indicators to make me look over all the men in the office."

"Father, too, I suppose." Jacob bowed his head, and Edward wished he could deny it; however, the truth was he'd thought of Uncle Felix, too, and whether there was some way he could have shorted the company when cargoes came into the warehouse.

"I. . .decided he wouldn't do that, and anyway, the discrepancies originate with the bills of lading and manifests, I believe. This thievery has taken place before the ship docks; that's my belief."

Jacob nodded.

"I'd have taken you into my confidence sooner, but. . .well, as you say, I had to be certain." Edward extended his hand. "We're in this together now, and it feels good to have an ally at my back."

Jacob grasped his hand. "I'm here for you. Let's see what Jamie has to say."

The *Prosper*'s second mate left his family at dinner and joined them in the yard of the small house.

"Mr. Hunter. Mr. Price. How can I help you gents?" He eyed them uneasily.

"We're sorry to disturb you, Jamie," Jacob said with a smile. "My cousin and I just had a few questions we'd like to ask about your voyage. Nothing to worry about."

"It's my fault," Edward said. "As you know, I've been away for a while."

"Yes, sir," Jamie replied. "And glad I was to hear you was alive."

Edward nodded. "Thank you. Mr. Price has told me how you helped the men of the *Egret*'s yawl survive, and I believe he used good judgment in promoting you."

Jamie glanced at Jacob, then shuffled his feet, looking down as he pushed a pebble about with his toe. "Thank you, sir. I was glad for the opportunity."

"Well, I'm leaving tomorrow on a short trip in the company's sloop," Edward said. "Going to Portsmouth. You wouldn't like to go along, would you? I'll be looking at another schooner we're thinking of buying."

Jamie's face lit up. "Oh, yes, sir, I'd be privileged to make that run. And say, if you's buying another ship, will there be berths on her for a new voyage?"

"Tired of the *Prosper*?" Jacob asked.

Jamie looked down at his feet again. "She's a good ship, sir, but. . .I'd just as soon try something new."

Jacob reached out and touched the young man's shoulder. "Jamie, we've been through a lot together, and I know you'll be honest with me. Is something slippery going on with the *Prosper*?"

Jamie exhaled sharply and glanced Edward's way, then looked back to Jacob. "It started with the coffee."

"Coffee?"

Edward kept quiet and let Jacob continue the interview, since Jamie Sibley obviously felt more comfortable with him.

"Yes, sir, we took on a prodigious supply in Jamaica. Finest Brazilian coffee, they had. More than half our cargo."

Jacob cocked his head to one side. "But, Jamie, when we unloaded yesterday and today. . ."

Jamie nodded, his forehead furrowed with wrinkles. "I know, I know. But Captain Stuart. . ."

"What?" Jacob asked.

"Well, sir. . ."

They waited a long moment.

"We went to St. Augustine and off-loaded most of the coffee, sir."

"You sold the coffee in Florida?" Jacob shot Edward a glance, but Edward kept still.

"Y–yes, sir. I wasn't sure what was going on, but I supposed the captain had orders from you. After that, we headed south again, and that's when I heard him telling Mr. Rankin—"

"The first mate," Jacob said to Edward, and Jamie nodded.

"Yes, sir. I heard him tell Mr. Rankin we'd run back down there quick and fill up with coffee again, and. . .and none would be the wiser, sir."

"Meaning me, I suppose." Jacob shook his head. "It's true, then. Ed, I'm not as sharp as you are with figures, and the whole thing slipped past me. He's selling off part of the cargo and reloading afterward. That's why it took Stuart so long to get back here this voyage."

"Aye," said Jamie. "But when we got back to Jamaica, they had hardly any coffee left. The captain was in a black mood. We pushed on to Havana, but he couldn't get any there, either. We couldn't go all the way to Rio for it, so we took on cotton and rice and whatever else he could get."

Edward took a deep breath. "I suppose something similar happened on her two voyages last year?"

Jamie shrugged. "I wasn't on board then, sir, but yes, from what the other fellows have told me, I'd think so. They sold off a bit of the most expensive goods at some other port."

"And the captain thought they'd all keep quiet?" Jacob asked.

Jamie hesitated. "Well, sir, he gave out there'd be something extra in it for them, and he told me. . . . Well, he told me he'd give me something later, but I must keep mum about the extra dealings." He threw an uneasy glance at Edward. "I'm sorry. I been fretting on it these two days since we docked, thinking I ought to come and tell you gents. You coming here. . . Well, that tipped it for me. I should have come to you sooner."

Jacob clapped his shoulder. "All's forgiven, Jamie, so long as you understand you're siding with us now."

"We'll turn this over to the law," Edward added. "You might be needed to testify."

Jamie swallowed hard. "It won't sit well with the men."

"We'll get you out of here tomorrow on the sloop with Mr. Hunter," Jacob said. "I'll go to see the magistrate, and I won't mention your name unless it's necessary. When you come back from Portsmouth, you might need to write out a statement or some such."

"Somebody'd have to write it for me, sir."

Jacob nodded. "Yes, well, don't you worry, Jamie. When we're done, Captain Stuart won't be able to get another ship, and any man who's been in this with him will face the law as well."

"That amounts to the whole crew, sir." Jamie seemed appalled at what his confession had put in motion.

Edward said, "We'll bring the men in and question them, and any who own up and give evidence against the captain will be kept on."

Jamie sighed. "Thank you, sir. There's some as weren't even smart enough to catch on, and then there's some who was just scared of the captain and Mr. Rankin."

Edward nodded. "We'll take that into consideration. Now go back to your family and rest easy tonight, Jamie. Be on the wharf at dawn, and we'll sail for Portsmouth."

Edward and Jacob walked silently up the street and out of the harbor district.

"Can you handle things tomorrow?" Edward asked at last.

"I believe I can," Jacob said. "I'll take Mr. Daniels into my confidence and go around to the magistrate first thing."

Edward nodded. "Perhaps your father could help you question the sailors. They're all afraid of him, and he could put the fear of the law into most of those boys."

Jacob smiled. "That's a thought."

"If you want me to stay. . ."

"No. You take Jamie and go see about that ship. Now that we know what's been going on with the *Prosper*, there's no reason we can't add the *Resolute* to the fleet and press forward."

Deborah knocked on the door of the Hunter house and looked around as she waited. The garden was a riot of color. She knew Mrs. Hunter employed three servants to keep the house and grounds in order. It was the Tuesday between her usual visits for tea, and Deborah wondered if her hostess had invited her so she could show her the lovely gardens in bloom.

Jenny opened the door and smiled. "Hello, Miss Deborah. Mrs. Hunter has a lady with her in the sitting room."

"Oh, I beg your pardon," Deborah said. "I'll come back another day."

"No, no. She insisted I bring you right in." Jenny opened the door wide and motioned her inside, so Deborah entered and handed her a basket.

"A few late strawberries for Mrs. Hunter."

"Oh, she'll be pleased. Go right in, won't you?"

Deborah removed her gloves, wondering if she'd been invited on purpose to meet the other guest. Timidly she peered into the small room. Mrs. Hunter spied her at once and stood to greet her.

"Come in, come in." To the other woman in the room, she said, "This is Miss Bowman, the physician's daughter, an old acquaintance who has lately become a good friend of mine."

The other woman did not stand but accepted Deborah's hand. She was about fifty, Deborah supposed, and elegantly dressed in a tan silk day dress edged in deep, ruffled flounces. The lady looked her over sharply, giving her the feeling that she was under inspection. Her feathered hat drooped over one ear and set off her stylishly curled hair.

"How do you do," Deborah said.

"Bowman," the woman murmured. Louder, she said, "Are you the young woman who threw Edward Hunter over for his cousin?"

Deborah felt her face go scarlet. Mrs. Hunter also flushed. Her only aid to Deborah's discomfiture was an apologetic smile.

"Actually," Deborah said, releasing the lady's hand, "that would be my sister, Abigail. I am Deborah."

The lady nodded. "I see."

"Deborah, this is Mrs. King," Edward's mother said.

"Mrs. . . ." Deborah gulped and used her selection of a chair as an excuse not to meet the lady's eyes for a moment, while she grappled for her composure. *I've just been introduced to the governor's wife. Was I rude? Oh dear, I hope not! But she was rude first.* She swallowed again, gathered her skirts, sat down, and smiled.

"Let me give you your tea." Mrs. Hunter poured out a cup for her, and Deborah accepted it, suddenly conscious of the dark stains under her nails left by the many strawberries she'd hulled that morning for her mother's preserve making.

"Thank you."

"So your sister is the foolish chit who gave young Mr. Hunter the mitten?"

Mrs. Hunter smiled at her guests. "It's really for the best, you know, Ann. They were so young when Edward went to sea, and then he was away for five years. They both had time to mature while he was gone. And when he came back, they found they'd outgrown their childish infatuation."

Deborah tried to hold her smile but felt it slipping. This was too humiliating.

Mrs. King didn't seem to think so. "Well, I still say she missed a good opportunity. Of course, I haven't met her new intended groom. But I have met Edward, and any girl who would—"

"I'm surprised you heard about it all the way up in Bath," Mrs. Hunter said.

"We hear everything," Mrs. King stated. "Of course, my husband is in Portland much of the time now. We're taking a house here until his term is up. That's why I'm with him on this trip, you know. We're only staying at the Robisons' home until the place we're leasing is cleaned and our baggage arrives."

"How lovely," said Mrs. Hunter. "Your husband does need to be here in the thick of things just now."

"Yes. He's had many social invitations and no way to return them, so I'll be setting up housekeeping and scheduling some affairs."

"I'm so pleased that you had time to come and spend the afternoon with me," Mrs. Hunter said.

"Well, I enjoy getting out and about, and I always make time for old friends. I was hoping to see Edward, though. We've heard so much about his death-defying feat. Do you expect him home today?"

"I'm not sure." Mrs. Hunter glanced at Deborah with an inclusive smile. "Edward ran down the coast in the company's sloop a few days ago, but he should be back soon. I've asked the gentlemen at the office to send me a note the minute he returns."

"How do you dare let him go off again so soon?" Mrs. King shook her head and sipped her tea.

"It's only to Portsmouth, and I'm not worried about Edward. He's proven himself well able to survive even the most unfavorable circumstances. Isn't that right, Deborah?"

"Oh. . .yes, certainly. He's a very capable sailor."

"I suppose you have a point," Mrs. King said. "I'm so glad my husband doesn't sail on his ships, though. William sends them off full of apples and potatoes and lumber, and they come back filled with cotton and coal."

"How expedient," Mrs. Hunter said.

Deborah was startled when her hostess winked at her. Apparently Mrs. Hunter had the same thought she did—that the life Mrs. King led must be boring.

"Yes, well, the general has enough to do without floating around the globe. He was hoping to see your son, though. He tells me he's been meaning to call here since he heard of Edward's return but hasn't found time. So busy, with the new legislature meeting and all."

"Your husband is welcome anytime," Mrs. Hunter assured her. "Of course, Edward would be happy to see him and tell him of his misadventure. Perhaps we can have dinner here once we know what Edward's schedule will be."

"Good, good. That would be most pleasant. I hope to arrange some small dinner parties in the new house. It's a bit cramped, so large gatherings would be awkward. But there are a good many statesmen and merchants who've entertained General King over the past few months, and I simply must reciprocate to them and their wives. That will be my first order of business once we're settled."

"I'm sure the entire city looks forward to it," her hostess said. "Your affairs are always delightful. Now, Deborah, I do wish you'd tell me about your Thursday project. How are things going, dear?"

Deborah had relaxed, glad to be ignored, and she flinched when Mrs. Hunter drew attention to her again. "Very well, thank you."

She saw Mrs. King's inquisitive look and was about to explain her widows' aid endeavor when Jenny appeared in the doorway.

"Yes, Jenny, what is it?" Mrs. Hunter asked.

"The apprentice brought a note, ma'am, from the office."

"Oh, thank you."

Jenny handed her a folded sheet of paper, and Mrs. Hunter quickly opened it and scanned the contents. Deborah watched her face, unable to suppress an anxious stirring in her stomach. Had she been truthful when she agreed that she did not worry about Edward?

His mother smiled. "Captain Moody has raised a flag indicating he has spotted a vessel flying Hunter Shipping's colors approaching the harbor. This note is from Mr. Price, saying they are preparing a berth on the wharf."

"The *Resolute*?" Deborah breathed.

"I don't know, dear." Mrs. Hunter's eyes glittered with inspiration. "Say, why don't we go down to the wharf and see?"

"Go to the docks?" Mrs. King's arched eyebrows and shocked tone told Deborah the governor's wife did not approve of the enterprise.

"We'll take a carriage," Mrs. Hunter went on. "If Edward has come home again, this time he shall have folks to welcome him when he steps ashore."

"Marvelous!" Deborah clapped her hands together, glad that Mrs. Hunter was undaunted.

"But the docks," Mrs. King said. "Is it safe, my dear?"

"Of course." Mrs. Hunter reached for the bell pull. "The men on Hunter's Wharf all know me and respect my husband's memory."

As Jenny came to the door, Mrs. King stood and reached for her reticule. "I fear I must go back to the Robisons' house. We'll be dining out tonight, and I must catch a nap. Our journey here quite fatigued me."

"We'll drop you off on our way to the wharf." Mrs. Hunter's animated face fed Deborah's excitement. Edward was returning, and she would be on hand to greet him. Her parents would not object since she would be in the company of his mother.

"Jenny, send Mercer to bring a hack. We three ladies are going out."

Chapter 13

"Aunt Mary! So glad to see you today." Jacob opened the door of the hired carriage and gave Mrs. Hunter his hand. "And Deborah! Welcome."

"Thank you," Deborah said as she lifted her skirt and stepped carefully down.

"Come. I've brought my spyglass, and we can walk out past the store and have a good view down the river."

"Do you know yet what vessel it is?" Mrs. Hunter puffed as they walked the length of the long pier, but she would not allow Jacob to slacken the pace.

"Not for certain, but I think it's still too early for the *Falcon*."

They stood together waiting. Jacob turned his spyglass toward Captain Moody's tower.

"One of our ships. I haven't called many laborers in because we're not expecting to unload a cargo today. Although Edward might have picked up a few bundles in Portsmouth."

A sharp-eyed lad gave a whoop and waved toward the mouth of the Fore. Deborah squinted and saw a vessel pull out from behind the headland of Cape Elizabeth. It was too small for the schooner they'd hoped to see.

"That's our sloop." Jacob's voice drooped in disappointment. "Well, Edward's likely on board, so your trip is not wasted."

"I did hope we'd get a first glimpse of the company's new ship," Mrs. Hunter said. "Ah well, perhaps it wasn't all we'd hoped, and he passed on buying it."

"Or perhaps she was already sold." Jacob held the spyglass out to Deborah. "Would you like to take a look?"

"Thank you." She trained the lens on the distant sloop, searching its deck for a tall, broad-shouldered man whose dark hair whipped in the wind. None of the sailors she saw had Edward's stature or bearing.

She offered the glass to Mrs. Hunter. "Would you care to look?"

"Oh yes. Thanks, dear." Mrs. Hunter scanned the sloop. "I don't see Edward."

"Nor did I," said Deborah.

His mother turned and studied the observatory tower through the spyglass.

"Jacob."

"Yes, Aunt Mary?"

"Captain Moody's run up another signal."

"Oh?"

Mrs. Hunter handed him the spyglass, and Jacob turned to look toward the tower on Munjoy Hill.

"You're right!" Excitement fired his voice.

Deborah shaded her eyes with her hand and tried to make out the distant flag.

"It's our colors again. Either the *Falcon*'s come home in record time, or Edward's bought the *Resolute*."

They all waited as the sloop drew nearer, the wind carrying her against the current. As the vessel came in closer, Deborah could make out half a dozen men on the deck, bustling to make the mooring.

"Ahoy, Sibley!" Jacob cried to the man who seemed to be directing them. "Where's Mr. Hunter?"

"Yonder!" Sibley motioned behind him, down the river.

Deborah could hardly contain her excitement. Jacob handed her the spyglass and scurried to help tie up the sloop. She put the brass tube to her eye and focused on the point of land where the sloop had first appeared.

Empty water lay restless between the shores.

Suddenly a dark bulk poked into her circle of vision.

"There she is!" Mrs. Hunter cried.

Deborah lowered the spyglass. Far away but coming about toward them, a majestic ship under sail hove into sight. Deborah drew a sharp breath. "She's beautiful!"

"Magnificent. Larger than Mr. King's flagship, too."

Deborah chuckled at Mrs. Hunter's satisfied smile. She handed over the spyglass and watched the ship as the crew went aloft, ready to take in canvas.

"I see him!" Mrs. Hunter bounced on her toes. "He's standing amidships just under the mainsail. Look, Deborah! He's waving his hat."

The next half hour sped past as the *Resolute* settled into her new berth at the outer end of Hunter's Wharf. The gangplank was put in place, and Jacob led the ladies onto the deck.

Edward met them at the rail, grinning like a child who'd found a half dime, and assisted them in descending to the deck.

"Do you like her?" he shouted to Jacob, who hopped down on his own power.

"She's perfect! Everything Smith told me and more."

"And the best part is she's in wondrous shape. There's hardly anything to be done before we can put her to sea. She handles like a dream, Jake!"

Edward smiled down at Deborah, and she realized he was still holding her gloved hand. She pulled it away reluctantly.

"Oh, Ed, about that matter we discussed the evening before you left," Jacob said.

Deborah watched curiously as Edward sobered. "All went well?"

"Yes, things are in hand, and when the sloop docked, I told Jamie he has no cause to worry."

"And Stuart?" Edward asked.

"Justice is in motion. I'll tell you all about it later, but things are proceeding as we hoped."

Edward nodded. "That's good, then. Well, Mother, what do you think of the *Resolute*?"

"Makes me wish I were younger," Mrs. Hunter said, surveying the deck and the rigging. "I'd ask you to take me on her next voyage and relive the old days."

"You've been to sea?" Deborah asked.

"Oh yes. When my husband and I were first married, I took two voyages with him. It's something I remember fondly, though there were frightening moments. All in all, being with the captain and understanding his love of sailing was valuable to our marriage. And seeing other places and people so different from us New Englanders opened my eyes. I've never looked at folks the same since."

"I should like to make such a trip." Deborah sighed, then realized Edward was watching her.

"Perhaps you shall someday," he said.

She felt her face color and was alarmed when he took her arm and led her a few steps away from the others.

"I should like to come round this evening to call on you, if I may."

"Of course." A thought suddenly struck her. "Oh, Edward, I haven't told Father."

He sobered. "Do you think he'll object?"

"Why, no, I don't think so."

"Fine, then, I'll ask him. When will he be at home?"

She glanced around him and saw his mother carrying on a spirited conversation with Jacob as they walked toward the stairs leading up to the quarterdeck.

"By six, if his patients don't keep him. He's usually home for dinner."

"Good, I'll take dinner at home, then come around and see your father. If all is to his liking, we'll have some time together afterward."

Deborah felt her mouth go dry. She'd never been courted before, but she had no doubt that was Edward's intention.

"I. . .we. . ."

"Yes?" Edward's eyes twinkled as he gazed down at her.

"We may have to compete for space in the parlor with your cousin and Abby."

Edward laughed, and her heart lifted. "Have they set a date yet?"

"Yes. The eighteenth of August."

"Well, we'll turn the tables on them. You chaperoned your sister many an evening, and now it's her turn."

Deborah's heart skipped. Never in her life had she been in need of a chaperone, but a quick glance at Edward's gleaming dark eyes told her the time had come. Perhaps her mother would stop despairing of ever seeing her married. That thought was enough to send an anticipatory shiver through her.

Edward reached for her hands and squeezed them. "You blush most becomingly. Come. I'm supposed to be showing off my new schooner, and poor Jacob has had to haul Mother off so I could have a private word with you."

"Is that what he's doing?"

"Of course. But we'd better relieve him and let him get on with his official duties. He and Mr. Daniels will have some paperwork to do. We'll have to register the ship and decide what we want for crew and cargo for her first voyage under Hunter Shipping's colors." He pulled Deborah's hand through the crook of his arm and took her toward the companionway that led above, where Jacob and Mrs. Hunter were now inspecting the ship's wheel.

"Where will she sail?" Deborah asked.

"To the Indies, I think, unless Jacob has a full cargo waiting to be taken to some other place. Oh, they're coming down. I'll show you all the captain's cabin. It's quite spacious for the size of the ship."

"Would you captain her yourself?" Deborah asked.

"I might. Bringing her up from Portsmouth was a joy. I wouldn't mind going out again on her."

"What?" his mother barked, descending the last steps. "Did you say you're leaving again?"

"No, Mother. I merely said that with a deck like this one under his feet, a man feels like sailing."

"You're not going to hire a captain to handle this ship for you?"

"Of course we are," Jacob said, scowling at Edward. "I have several names. There are good men out there waiting for a ship."

Edward smiled. "Then I expect we'll get someone, Mother. We haven't had time to discuss any of that yet."

She looked at him, then down the length of the main deck. "She is a lovely vessel. I wouldn't blame you a bit if you wanted to sail her. But don't forget your family."

"I won't. Now come and see the captain's quarters. Whoever he may be, the master of this ship will be quite comfortable."

Deborah sighed as she viewed the neat cabin. Mrs. Hunter spun round on the carpeted floor, exclaiming over the polished wood of the built-in cupboards and drawers, the folding table, the curtained bunk, and the mullioned window in the stern of the ship.

"Oh, if we'd had a cabin like this on the *Hermia*, I'd have been the happiest bride on earth. As it was, we had a tiny room one-third this size, and your father insisted on keeping his trunk in the cabin. We could barely turn around and were always tripping over that chest."

Edward laughed. "I'll keep that in mind, Mother, if I ever ask a woman to share a cabin with me." He winked at Deborah, and she felt her blush shoot all the way to the tips of her ears.

"What shall I do if Father isn't home before Edward arrives?" Deborah threw an anxious glance at Abigail in the mirror as her sister brushed out her thick, dark hair.

"We'll just have a pleasant evening with two gentlemen callers, and Edward can speak to him tomorrow. Don't fret so."

Deborah smiled at Abby's reflection. "I'm not fretting."

"Yes, you are. You haven't been still for ten seconds since you sat down."

Deborah was surprised that her wayward tresses were obedient to Abby's gentle coaxing and lay in gentle waves about her forehead.

"Do you like it?" Abigail asked.

"I'm not sure. It doesn't look like me."

"Well, it's time you started paying more attention to your looks. You're very pretty, you know. If you'd dress up a little and guard your complexion from the sun, the young men would hang about our doorstep in droves."

"Not true."

"Well, at least half true. You'd have to stop treating them like chums as well."

"And how should I treat them?"

"Like fascinating men."

"Most of them are boring."

"You seem to find Edward interesting."

Deborah whirled around in dismay. "Does it upset you that he asked to come calling on me so soon after. . .after your decision?"

Abigail smiled and shook her head, patting at a stubborn strand of hair over Deborah's ear. "Why should that bother me? I have the man I want."

"Oh, Abby, it wasn't my intention to attract him."

"I know."

"Then why do I feel so awful?"

"No reason. You should feel pleased and honored. Edward is a fine man, as you've told me many times."

Deborah puzzled over her sister's serenity. "You seem so calm now, but a few weeks ago you were overwrought."

"Because I knew I loved Jacob and couldn't bear to hurt Edward. I couldn't help but wonder if it was my duty to marry him, even though it would rip my heart to shreds. But now, seeing that he's accepted the outcome, I feel much easier."

"You don't think it's horrid of him to want to pay attention to me so soon?"

Abigail's smile had a wise twist that Deborah had never seen before. "I expect that if I hadn't become attached to Jacob before Edward came home we still would have found eventually that we were not perfectly suited to each other."

"Really?"

"Yes. It might have taken us months to discover that, however. You see, God works things out."

Deborah nodded. "I'm sorry I was cross with you."

"You had a right to be. I didn't behave very well at first. But I also think that you and Edward have an admiration for one another that transcends the years of his absence."

"You do?"

Abby reached for a hairpin. "Mm-hmm. You know you've always adored him."

"Yes, I have. But he only saw me as your bother of a little sister."

"Perhaps, but he commented to me several times in the old days about how clever you were and what a beauty you would make some day."

The air Deborah gulped felt like a square lump.

"I never, ever thought he'd think of me as. . .a woman."

Abigail laughed and squeezed her shoulder. "You're so droll, Debbie. It's quite a relief to me that Edward's not crushed. It would have been miserable to see him at church and social functions for the rest of my life, with him slouching about and staring at me with those huge, dark eyes."

"Edward wouldn't do such a thing."

"Perhaps not, but he does have a melancholy tendency. You are just what he needs. I predict you'll keep him in high spirits. I never should have accomplished that."

Deborah started to protest, but Abigail picked up another hairpin. "Turn around and let me finish.

The image in the mirror stared back at Deborah with dark, anxious eyes. Her sister's skillful ministrations had brought her hair into a soft, becoming style. Would Edward think she was pretty?

"Thank you, Abby. I confess I'm a bit nervous."

"Well, you shouldn't be. You're much more suited to him in temperament than I ever was." Abigail tugged at her sleeve. "Stand up now. I think the red shawl will set off that white gown splendidly."

"Oh no, the red is too bright." Deborah already felt misgivings at wearing the new white dress. The neck, while not daring, was lower than she was accustomed to, and she feared her blush would become perpetual.

"It is not," Abigail insisted, holding up the shawl in question. "Red is all the fashion, and it goes very well with the delicate flower pattern of your gown."

"No, I think I'd better wear my gray shawl."

"Impossible. I'm wearing it." Abigail seized Deborah's usual dove gray wrap and threw it over her own shoulders. "It goes well with my green dress, don't you think?"

"Well. . ."

"Come on." Abigail took her hand and sidestepped toward the door. "I heard the knocker. Jacob's probably cooling his heels and waiting for his dinner."

Chapter 14

Edward arrived at the Bowman house amid a gray drizzle that brought an early dusk. The family was just leaving the dinner table. They had delayed the meal, hoping Dr. Bowman could join them, Deborah told him.

"Father was detained with a patient this evening," she explained.

Edward's disappointment at being unable to settle his business with the doctor was short-lived. The shy, hopeful smile she bestowed on him made all obstacles shrink.

"Ah. Then we shall pass a pleasant evening in spite of his absence, and perhaps I can have a word with him tomorrow."

Mrs. Bowman carried into the parlor a tray bearing coffee and a bowl of sugared walnuts. The young people settled down, with Abigail and Jacob on the sofa and Deborah and Edward in chairs opposite them, while Mrs. Bowman sat in the cushioned rocker near the hearth.

"It's chilly this evening," she said. "This rain."

"Would you like a fire, ma'am?" Edward asked. "I can kindle it for you."

"A fire in the parlor in July?" Mrs. Bowman shook her head.

"Must we be so frugal, Mother?" Abigail asked. "It's cold, and the fire's already laid for just such a night."

"All right, then." Mrs. Bowman edged her chair back to give Edward room to work. He pulled the painted fire screen aside, and soon a comforting blaze threw its warmth to them all.

They spent two hours in enjoyable conversation, mostly concerning the new government and the upcoming wedding. Mrs. Bowman seemed hesitant to discuss the latter topic when Abigail first brought it up, casting worried looks in Edward's direction.

He smiled, hoping to put her at ease. "My cousin has invited me to stand up with him for the ceremony. I'm looking forward to performing that duty."

After that, Mrs. Bowman relaxed and brought out her sewing. Deborah began to knit, glancing up only now and then.

"And Deborah shall have a new gown as well," Abigail said. "Lavender, I think. We're going to shop for material tomorrow."

"The one she's wearing now suits her admirably," Edward said.

Abigail smiled. "Isn't it lovely on her? But I want her to have something a little fancier. Mother, too."

Deborah stared at her knitting, her lips firmly closed. He supposed that hearing her appearance discussed was not at all to her liking, though he was pleased he'd had a chance to let her know he approved. Her hair was different tonight. Softer somehow, and it suited her sweet features.

"Really, dear. People don't make so much of a wedding," Mrs. Bowman said.

"No, but it's for the party afterward." Abigail laughed. "All the best people will come, and the women, at least, will be lavishly turned out. Why, Father said we may even invite Governor and Mrs. King."

"Oh dear," Deborah muttered.

"And, Edward," Abigail went on, turning a brilliant smile on him, "you must know your mother has offered her garden and parlors for the affair."

"Very gracious of her," said her mother. "We haven't much space here, but Mrs. Hunter insisted we hold a reception there for the young people."

"So she's told me," Edward said. "After all, Jacob is her favorite nephew."

Jacob chuckled. "Aunt Mary is quite excited about it. She and Mother are having a grand time planning the menu."

"She wanted to serve dinner for forty, but we told her that was too much for her," Abigail said.

"Oh, I don't know. She surprises me with her energy these days." Edward shook his head. "I think she does more entertaining now than she did when Father was alive."

"Her gardens are so beautiful that I could not refuse," Mrs. Bowman told him. "Most kind of her. Abigail and I are going over tomorrow afternoon after we finish our shopping to make plans with her and Mrs. Price."

Deborah's ball of yarn dropped to the floor and rolled a few feet. Edward stooped to retrieve it and held it loosely in his lap, letting slack out as she tugged the yarn. She looked at him, and he smiled, raising his eyebrows. Her dark eyes flashed gladness, then were hidden once more by her lowered lashes. She went on with her knitting, saying nothing but with the faint smile lingering on her lips, and he was content to hold the yarn and watch her.

At last, Mrs. Bowman rose, remarking on the lateness of the hour, and Edward looked to his cousin. Jacob seemed to be making preparations to leave, so Edward rose and offered to carry the tray to the kitchen. His hostess thanked him and went with him to show him where to place it.

When he came back into the front hall, Deborah stood by the stairway alone, and he guessed she had left the parlor to allow Jacob a moment alone with his betrothed. As he approached her, Deborah took a breath and smiled at him a bit shakily.

"Thank you for coming," she said, an unaccustomed crease marring her smooth brow.

"It was a pleasure, and I've thanked your mother for a stimulating evening."

"Discussing wedding plans?" Her doubt colored her tone. "My mother isn't used to entertaining on a large scale, and she's in a dither about this. I'm sure that wasn't the most fascinating conversation you've ever engaged in."

"I don't mind. I shall doubtless see some people there whom I haven't seen in five years or more. Now, if we can only keep Uncle Felix sober that day."

Her eyes widened in alarm, and he bent down to whisper, "Don't worry. Jacob and I have discussed it. We're hiring half a dozen of our strongest men to keep an eye on him the night before and make sure he stays clear of the taverns."

"What about the day of the wedding?"

"Mother won't allow a drop in the house, but even so, I'll detail several men to guard the punch and watch him."

"Thank you. It's not that I don't like him. . . ."

"I know," Edward said. "I like him, too, but I don't entirely trust him in matters of this nature." He reached for her hand, and Deborah turned her eyes upward and looked at him. "I will speak to your father tomorrow. Nothing shall prevent me."

Her lower lip quivered. Then she nodded. "Thank you."

A flood of longing came over him, and he considered for a fleeting moment pulling her into his arms.

No. Not yet.

He smiled and lifted her hand to his lips. "I spoke the truth when I said I enjoyed the evening."

Her luminous smile rewarded him, but at that moment, Abigail and Jacob emerged from the parlor. Abigail's face was flushed, and Edward was satisfied to note that her beauty no longer affected him. A spark of grateful gladness sprang up in his heart as he noted the happiness on his cousin's face.

"Ready to go, Edward?" Jacob asked. "I believe it's still raining, and I thought I'd hail a hack."

"Yes, I'll share with you."

The two young men said good-bye to the ladies, and Edward found himself whistling softly as he and Jacob strolled toward the corner in the drizzle.

"Feeling blithesome tonight, Ed?"

"A bit. And yourself?"

"Euphoric."

"Ah."

They spotted a horse and carriage a short distance down the cross street, and Jacob whistled and waved his hat. The driver pulled the horse around toward them.

"It does my heart good to see you and Abigail so happy," Edward confided when they were in the carriage.

"Thank you. Sometimes I still wonder if you truly don't mind."

"I don't."

Jacob smiled at him in the dim interior of the vehicle. "I'm beginning to believe that. You know, Ed, I never meant to be an interloper."

Edward smiled. "Of course not."

"But I wasn't about to give ground to you, not after. . . Well, my heart was hers already when you came back. Can't undo something like that."

"You can rest easy. I believe God has another future for me."

"Ah, yes. And not an unpleasant one, I think."

"You'll be married in a month," Edward said. "Where will you and Abigail be living afterward?"

"I've something in mind."

"Not with your parents, I hope."

"Oh no," Jacob said quickly. "I couldn't subject Abby to that, although Mother would love to have us there."

"I should say not. Your father scares her."

Jacob gritted his teeth and shrugged. "Not surprising. He scares me sometimes, too."

"Well, I only ask, because. . ." Edward swung round to meet his eyes. "Jacob, Mr. Daniels dropped your salary when I came home."

Jacob opened his mouth, then closed it and fidgeted with his watch fob. "Let's not get into that. I've found a modest house to lease for the next year, and Abigail is agreeable."

"But before I came back, she must have expected something much more lavish."

Jacob shook his head. "It doesn't matter."

"Yes, it does. When we left five years ago, you were first mate on a trading ship. You had the expectation of a nice salary with the firm when you came home and a profit from your private venture."

"So I did."

"But it was nowhere near what you were paid after my father named you his heir apparent."

"Edward!"

"Hear me out. I've looked at the books. I know you were paid considerably more last year than you were before. If Father had left the company to you outright instead of to my mother, you'd own Hunter Shipping now. You'd be taking home what I am now. Instead, I came back and usurped your place."

"I would hardly call it that."

"Fine, but at least admit that on your salary before I disappeared you never could have hoped to support a wife of Abigail's class."

Jacob's face colored. "It's true I'd have thought her beyond my reach in the old days. But—"

"I don't want you and Abby living in a hovel." Suddenly he realized that Jacob must have expected to inherit the Hunter home, too. When Jacob had first proposed to Abigail, he'd probably planned to live with her in the roomy and comfortable house where Edward and his mother lived.

"Really, Ed!" Jacob said. "My salary this past month was cut back to what I earned two years ago, it's true, but it's enough. I'll be able to maintain a respectable household."

"Respectable. Small, plain, not to say stark."

"Yes. And Abigail is not greedy. She understands that things will be a bit more spartan than we'd at first planned. She doesn't care, Edward."

"That's remarkable."

"Isn't it? But it's true. If she did care that much about money, she'd be marrying you instead of me."

Edward took a long, slow breath and sank back. He stared out the window at the dark, wet street and realized they were almost to his aunt and uncle's house.

He was glad Abigail had risen to the occasion and shown her willingness to accept a lower standard of living than she had anticipated. That fit in with the Abigail he remembered. He'd always found her amiable and supportive in the old days. Now she would fulfill that role at Jacob's side.

The driver stopped the hack before the Prices' small clapboard house.

"Look, Jacob, we'll speak more about this later," Edward said. "You've done admirable work for Hunter Shipping, and I expect you'll continue to do so. I doubt I could get along without you now, with the increase in trade we're seeing. With the *Resolute*, our profits will rise, and—well, when it comes right down to it, I'm willing to take less than Father was."

"No, Edward, stop being noble."

"I'm not. I had no idea how much Father drew for a salary. Mother tells me now that he invested much of it, and that kept them going during the war years, when shipping was at a standstill. But so long as Mother is comfortable now, I'd like to see the company pay you a salary that's commensurate with the work you do."

Jacob opened the door of the hack. "Thank you for saying that, but I won't hold you to it. We'll talk again, as you say."

"Fine," said Edward. "Now, quick, before you go, tell me what happened with Captain Stuart."

"They jailed him overnight, but he's engaged an attorney from Boston and is out on bail. I expect he'll be tried when the judge comes here next month."

"And the rest of the crew?"

"Most of the men admitted they knew about it but felt they had no choice. I'll go over the roster with you tomorrow. There are a few I think we'd be better off without, but most of the fellows are probably all right. However, Mr. Daniels agrees we should prosecute Stuart and Rankin to the fullest."

Edward nodded. "Good. We'll talk about it in the morning." He saw his stocky uncle Felix silhouetted in the doorway of the house, seeming too large for the little dwelling.

"Whattaya doin', wastin' money on a hack?" Felix roared.

"Tell him I'm paying!" Edward called to Jacob through the window.

Jacob turned back and grinned at his cousin. "Been at the ale, I'd say." He faced his father and shouted, "Hush, Father! It's Edward's money. Now, let's get inside."

Chapter 15

Edward walked from the harbor to Dr. Bowman's surgery the next morning. The small building on Union Street had been erected as a wheelwright's shop, but after the owner's untimely death, the doctor had bought it and refurbished it as a place to attend his patients. He'd kept the wide double door, but instead of wagons and buggies, it now admitted the injured and ill people who sought his services.

Edward entered, pulling off his hat, and looked around. Two women sat stone-faced on a bench near the door, one of them holding a fretful infant. A curtain of linen sheets stitched together stretched across the room, and from behind it, he heard the murmur of voices.

"Is the doctor in?" he asked the older woman, and she nodded toward the curtain.

Edward hesitated, then sat down on the far end of the bench.

A moan came from behind the sheets, followed by Dr. Bowman's hearty, "There, now, that's fine. Just keep the bandage on until you see me again. Come back Friday."

A man in tattered sailor's garb appeared from behind the curtain, holding his left forearm with his other hand. His dirty shirt was stained with blood, and he walked a bit unsteadily. The woman with the baby stood up and walked with him to the door.

A gangly young man who seemed hardly out of his teens poked his head from behind the curtain and looked at the other woman. "Dr. Bowman's ready to see you, mum."

The doctor appeared next, carrying a few instruments and some soiled linen. He dumped the linen into a large basket in the corner and set his tools on a small table, then poured water from a china pitcher into a washbowl and immersed his hands in it.

As he dried his hands, he looked around and saw Edward sitting on the bench.

"Well, lad, this is a surprise. Not ill, I hope."

"No," Edward said, rising. "I only wanted a word with you, sir."

The young man who assisted the doctor was taking fresh linen from a cupboard. Dr. Bowman glanced at the middle-aged woman who was waddling toward the curtained area. "I'll be right with you, Mrs. Atfield."

"I'm next in line, Doctor," she retorted.

"Yes, I'm well aware of that. I shan't be long." He smiled at Edward and whispered, "Here, let's step into my private office."

He opened a door in the side wall, and Edward chuckled, stepping out into a tiny backyard.

"Mrs. Atfield comes at least once a week for her dyspepsia," the doctor said. "It will still be there after we've had our say. How can I help you?"

Edward drew a breath; the tangy salt air seemed inadequate, and he felt a bit lightheaded. "Sir, I came to ask permission to court your daughter."

Dr. Bowman stared at him, and though Edward feared for a moment he was going to be censured, slowly the man's mouth curved and his eyes began to dance.

"I've heard that from you before."

"Yes, sir, you have. I was sincere then, and I am sincere now."

"Well, since you know I've promised my elder daughter to your cousin, I suppose there's only one conclusion for me to draw."

Edward's smile slipped out of his control. He was sure he looked the buffoon, but he couldn't help it. "Yes, sir. It's Deborah I'd like to court."

"Well, now. Sensible lad." Dr. Bowman slapped him on the shoulder. "I almost felt the family had taken a grievous loss last month when Abigail chose Jacob. But I see I was early in my conclusion. We get to keep both you boys." He nodded. "I'm pleased. So will Mrs. Bowman be."

"Thank you, sir."

"And I don't have to ask how Debbie feels."

"You don't, sir?"

"No, she's championed your cause from the start."

"That means a lot to me. We've been friends a long time, and I see a staunch loyalty in her, not to mention she's a lovely young woman now."

"Just don't ever let her feel she's your second choice, son."

Edward nodded. "I shall endeavor to let her know that she will be first in my heart from here on."

"Good. Very good." The doctor sighed. "And now I suppose I must get back to Mrs. Atfield. Why don't you join us for dinner this evening?"

"Thank you very much, sir." Edward shook the doctor's hand and watched him go back through the door. He walked around the corner of the building and headed for the harbor, smiling.

He had been thinking on and off for a week about Deborah's charity for sailors' widows, and his mind returned to it as he walked toward the wharves. He'd seen some of the poverty in the shabbier parts of town. Deborah didn't despair about it. She set about to alleviate the worst of it. Through careful inquiries, he'd learned that she not only gave food to those in need, but she also helped the women learn new skills and had even found jobs for a few.

She was like the biblical Ruth, he thought, who gleaned grain for the widowed Naomi. Willing to work hard to help others.

He'd intended to visit the widow of Abijah Crowe, one of the men who fled the *Egret* in the longboat with him and the only one whose family he had not yet contacted. To his surprise, he had heard Deborah mention the name Crowe the day he'd given her the wagonload of provisions, and now he wanted to learn whether Abijah Crowe's wife was one of the women to whom Deborah ministered. He decided the staff at Hunter Shipping would not miss him if he stayed away another hour.

He recalled the directions Deborah had given the day she collected her goods at the warehouse. By asking about in the neighborhood, he soon found the Crowe house. The humble cottage looked in need of repair; however, the front stoop was neat, and bright curtains hung at the window that faced the street. He knocked, wishing he had dressed differently—not in the tailed coat he wore to the office most days. But it was too late. The door creaked open, and he looked into the face of a thin woman with dull brown hair. Her cheeks were hollow and her hands bony.

"Hello," he said.

"What do you want?" Her eyes narrowed as she looked him over.

"Mrs. Crowe?"

"I be her."

"I'm Edward Hunter."

She stared at him blankly, and he thought she did not recognize the name.

He said, "I heard your name mentioned by Miss Bowman. Deborah Bowman."

The woman drew her shoulders back and scowled at him. "And?"

"Well, I wondered if you were possibly related to Abijah Crowe."

Her gaze pierced him, and he stared back.

"He were my late husband."

Edward sighed. "I was with Abijah on the *Egret*."

"I know it. I heared you came back after all this time."

He nodded. "After our ship sank, Abijah was with me and a few others in the ship's longboat."

She said nothing but continued to watch him, unblinking.

"I. . .meant to come and visit you earlier. I've tried to visit the families of all the men who were in my boat."

"Nancy Webber told me you came to see her."

"Yes. Her John and I were together on the island for quite some time, and we got along well. I was glad I could tell her what her husband meant to me in those days." Edward removed his hat and wiped the perspiration from his brow. It was nearing noon, and the sun's rays made him uncomfortably warm.

"Do you want to set a spell?" she asked.

"I should be glad to if you've no objection."

Mrs. Crowe turned and shuffled into the cottage, and he followed. Two children about five and seven years old scuttled out of the way and tumbled onto a bunk, where they crouched and stared at him.

Edward took the stool the woman indicated near the cold hearth, and she sat opposite him.

"Thought you weren't going to come here," she said.

"I'm sorry I put it off, ma'am. It took me awhile to get used to being home again, and I've been back at work the past few weeks. But I believe I've gotten round to all the other families. I'm sorry it took me so long to find you."

She nodded once and reached behind her for a ball of yarn and a carved wooden hook. As she began to crochet, Edward studied the yarn. It looked very familiar.

"My Abijah died in that boat," she said.

"Yes, ma'am, he did. I'm sorry. He was a good man and a good sailor."

She frowned but kept on hooking the yarn through the endless loops.

"He spoke of you and the children."

Her hands stilled, and she sniffed. "What did he say?"

"He asked the captain, at the end, to remember him to you. And he said he didn't want the children to grow up fatherless."

"The captain died, too," she said, not looking at him.

"Yes, ma'am, he did. Several days later. But I tried to remember all the messages the men had given him in case I ever made it home."

"How did he die?"

"Abijah?" Edward asked.

She nodded.

"I'm afraid it was lack of water, ma'am. We started out with very little, and we all suffered from it."

"It's a terrible death." Her ball of yarn dropped from her lap and skittered across the floor, and Edward jumped to catch it.

He took it back to Mrs. Crowe and handed it to her. "Deborah Bowman brought you this yarn."

Her eyebrows drew together. "You're the man who owned the ship. The man Miss Abigail was going to marry."

"You know her?"

"Surely. She comes here with her sister and helps with the sewing and tells stories to the kiddies."

He sat down again. "My father owned the *Egret*. And yes, I was betrothed to Abigail Bowman when I left here five years ago."

"But she found some other fellow she liked more." She shook her head. "I thought better of her than that."

Edward cleared his throat. "It wasn't quite like that, Mrs. Crowe. You see, my cousin was also on the ship with your husband and me, but when the *Egret* went down, he was in the other boat. His boat was picked up, and my cousin Mr. Price came home thinking I was dead. After several years of believing I had perished, Miss Bowman agreed to marry Mr. Price."

"She shouldn't, though. Not now that you're here."

"Well, I thought so myself at first, but God has shown me a better plan."

"A better plan?"

"Yes. I believe our heavenly Father brought them together in their grief and that He has another woman chosen to be my wife."

"Oh?" She looked doubtful, and he smiled.

"Yes, ma'am. This morning I've been making arrangements to call upon another young lady. Someone I think you'd approve of."

"I?"

He nodded.

"Not Miss Debbie?"

"Yes."

Mrs. Crowe began to smile at last. "She be a fine young lady."

"Indeed she is."

"She gets victuals for those as can't buy them, and she sews togs for the little ones. She even brought me fine cotton for curtains." The woman nodded toward her small window, and Edward turned to observe the red calico fabric that hung there.

He smiled at her. "She told me that she had friends down here."

Mrs. Crowe's chin came up several inches. "She does. And she ain't ashamed to claim them. Miss Debbie says anyone who believes in Jesus is her sister."

Edward nodded. He could almost hear her saying that. "I'm so glad she is your friend, and I wanted to bring you something." He reached into his coat pocket and brought out a small pouch of coins. "Mrs. Crowe, Hunter Shipping has made a gift to the family of each man who died when the *Egret* sank."

"Don't want no gifts."

"But, ma'am, your husband served the company well."

"Don't need no charity. Now Miss Debbie, she comes down here, she shares with us, and she sits and stitches with us. She shows us how to do things. She taught me to spin raw wool, she did. The food she brings is for them that's starving. This family's not starving."

"I'm glad to hear that. How do you live, ma'am?"

"My older son, John, goes out with Abe Fuller fishing every day, and Thomas, the next one down, he runs errands for the haberdasher and the butcher, and sometimes Captain Moody. We get by."

"That's commendable. I'm glad your sons are able to work. But this money that I've brought you isn't charity. It's coming to you for your husband's good service. He did his job on the *Egret* until the day she foundered, and if he'd made it home, he'd have been paid for every day of that work. Hunter Shipping owes your husband money, Mrs. Crowe. But since he's not here to receive it, I would like to give it to his heirs, meaning you and the children.

It's the pay he would have gotten for the days he worked, not a penny more."

She pursed her lips together. "My man was a good man."

"Yes, he was." Edward set the little pouch on the table near her, and she did not protest.

"You say he died in that boat before the captain died."

"Yes." Edward rubbed a hand across his forehead. The harsh memories deluged him once more, and he sent up a silent prayer for peace. "We were in the boat for a fortnight, ma'am. Your husband lasted ten days, I believe. Longer than a couple of the others."

"Was he in distress?" she whispered.

"We all were. I won't lie to you, ma'am. It was awful."

She nodded. "And he's buried at sea?"

"Yes, ma'am." He reached into his pocket again. "I believe this was his." He held out a small knife he had removed from Abijah Crowe's pocket before they lowered him over the side of the boat. "I used it during my time on the island and was thankful to have it. Very useful it was. In fact, I might not be alive now if it weren't for this. But now. . .well, I thought your older boy might like to have it."

She took the knife in her hand and stared down at it. It was a poorly forged blade with a handle of deer's antler. Tears welled in her eyes and spilled down her cheeks. " 'Twas Abijah's all right. Thank you."

Edward left after wishing her well. He walked along the shore, surveying the wharves and boats without seeing them. After ten minutes he stopped, realizing he had come to Hunter's Wharf. Instead of heading across the street to the office, he walked all the way to the end of the wharf, past several moored vessels and the shops and chandlery. At the end of the wharf, he halted and stood gazing down into the water that swirled around the massive pilings.

At last his duty to the families was concluded, though he knew he would have dealings with many of them again. Amos Mitchell's son was now his employee. He prayed he would never have to face Mrs. Mitchell again on such an errand.

He recalled Mrs. Crowe's face as she looked down at her dead husband's knife. He'd seen similar reactions when he had delivered mementos to other families. The captain's wife had accepted his compass and quadrant with dignity, but even so, her face had crumpled as she examined the items. Davy Wilkes hadn't had anything in his pockets, and Edward had sliced a button from his coat before they eased his body overboard. His mother had wept over that, saying she'd stitched it to his woolen coat a few days before he'd sailed.

For Gideon Bramwell's parents, he'd delivered the key the boy wore on a thong around his neck. Edward had thought it belonged to Gideon's sea chest, which was now at the bottom of the ocean, but his mother told him it belonged to the chest that the girl he loved had filled with household items and vowed never to open until he returned with the key.

For each one of the seven men in the boat with him, he'd managed to preserve some small item to convey back to their families. John Webber had carved a wooden chain from a piece of driftwood he found on the island. It was more than two feet long when he died. Edward had chopped off the excess wood and carried the chain home to Mrs. Webber. With Amos Mitchell, who was lost out of the small boat in high seas, Edward had only a misshapen hat left behind where he'd sat. For Isaac Towers, they'd found pinned inside his pocket a small emerald brooch he'd bought in Rio and was planning to take home to his wife.

What would they have brought home if it were me? Edward wondered. The trinkets he'd bought for Abigail and his mother were sunk and gone. His clothes had gone to rags, and the few tools he'd had on the island had belonged to others. In his excitement on being rescued, he'd brought only the grass pouch he'd woven to hold the mementos of the men. Just one other thing had made it home with him from the long adventure. He shoved his hand in his pocket and rubbed his thumb over the smooth, rounded shell he'd carried for several months now. He'd stooped to pick it up from the sand one morning, and when he straightened and glanced toward the sea, there, incredibly, was a ship under sail, making for his island. His ordeal was over. He had thrust the smooth shell into his pocket and run toward the surf, shouting and waving his arms. His isolation had ended.

He closed his eyes and inhaled the salty air, feeling the breeze on his face and the sun on his shoulders. It didn't matter that he'd lost all. What mattered was the way he handled what God had given back to him.

"Thank You, dear Father, for bringing me home. Use me in what is left of my life as You see fit."

Finally he opened his eyes and turned toward his office.

Chapter 16

Deborah's heart soared as she opened the front door to Edward.

I have the right to love him now. Thank You, Lord.

The answering light in Edward's eyes sent anticipation surging through her. Modesty said she should avert her gaze, but she couldn't look away. Instead, she smiled and reached for his hand, drawing him into the house.

"I'm so glad you're here. Abby is dining with the Price family tonight, but Father and Mother are eager to see you."

She led him to the dining room, where her parents greeted him.

"You see, I tore myself away from my patients this evening," Dr. Bowman said.

"I'm delighted, sir." Edward shook his hand and turned to his wife. "Thank you for your kind invitation, Mrs. Bowman."

"We're pleased you could come. Sit here, Edward, where Abigail usually sits. Jacob has carried her off to spend the evening with his family tonight."

A thin, sober-faced woman served them under gentle instruction from Mrs. Bowman. When the maid carried the platter of lamb in and set it before the doctor, her hands shook so that the china hit the table with a loud *clunk*, and the woman jumped, flushing to the roots of her hair.

"There, now," said Dr. Bowman. "A nice leg of lamb. Thank you, Mrs. . . What's the name again?" He looked around vaguely toward his wife.

"It's Mrs. Rafferty, Father," Deborah said.

"Ah, yes. And is there sauce?"

"Aye, sir." The woman curtsied and dashed for the kitchen.

"Mrs. Rafferty is a friend of mine," Deborah said to Edward, hoping he would understand that she meant one of her Thursday widows. "She told me that she hopes to earn a bit of money in service, so Mother agreed to train her."

"If she works out well, I may recommend her to your mother, Edward." Mrs. Bowman raised her eyebrows. "Has she found a replacement for Jenny Hapworth yet?"

"No, she hasn't. I'm sure she'd be happy to consider anyone you vouch for."

"She's green, but she's willing to learn."

Deborah smiled at him. "We have Elizabeth in during the day, but because Mother has no one to help serve dinner, we've been letting Mrs. Rafferty practice on us this week. Usually one of us helps her, but I think she's doing splendidly, don't you?"

At that moment, the maid cautiously pushed the door open and entered, bearing a steaming dish and a pewter ladle on a tray. She inched toward Dr. Bowman's end of the table and set the tray down with a sigh.

"Thank you," he said, reaching for the gravy.

Mrs. Rafferty dipped her head, then looked toward Mrs. Bowman.

"Perhaps Mr. Hunter would like more potatoes?" the mistress suggested.

"Oh no, ma'am, I'm fine," Edward assured her. "I don't eat as much as I used to."

"Short rations for a long spell will do that to you," the doctor said.

"But it's delicious," Edward said quickly, and Deborah smiled at him. "The biscuits are very light, too. Much like my mother's."

Deborah said nothing but knew her face was beaming. Mrs. Hunter had watched her bake twenty batches of biscuits one rainy day until Deborah's were identical to her own. The children of the fishermen's shacks had reaped the bounty of her cooking lesson, with their fill of biscuits delivered and distributed by Mrs. Hunter's gardener.

But her mother was not about to ignore a chance to brag about her talented daughter.

"Deborah made the biscuits, and aren't they flavorful? She baked the pie you'll be enjoying later as well."

Edward sent a look across the table that topped approval. Deborah could only interpret it as thorough admiration, and she whipped her napkin up to hide the silly grin that stretched across her face.

Her father began once more to ask Edward about his travels, and Edward obliged by recounting tales of the sea and the ports he had visited. Deborah listened, enthralled. What would it be like to travel to such strange places? She was sure her imagination was inadequate to show her the wonders Edward described.

"Are you happier on dry land?" Mrs. Bowman asked.

"In some ways." Edward reached for his water glass and shot Deborah a smile.

"Jacob says he'll stay ashore now," Dr. Bowman asserted. "I'm afraid Abby's making a landlubber out of him."

"There, now, that's all right," said his wife. "Jacob says one shipwreck was enough for him, and he doesn't mind not sailing anymore."

"We've plenty to keep him busy at the office," Edward said. "I doubt I would undertake any long Pacific voyages again, but I might take one of our company schooners to the West Indies."

"That's a profitable destination for you, is it not?" The doctor carved a second helping of lamb for himself.

"It's the backbone of our trade. The goods are perhaps not as exotic or expensive, but we can make more trips there and back."

"Volume," Dr. Bowman agreed.

When the meal was over, Mrs. Rafferty brought the coffee tray to the parlor, where Mrs. Bowman poured and the doctor continued the discussion with Edward about trading and the outlook of Hunter Shipping. Deborah felt sure he was pumping her caller about his financial prospects, and perhaps Jacob's as well, but Edward didn't seem to mind.

At last, Mrs. Bowman rose. "I must see Mrs. Rafferty before she leaves for the night. And, my dear, you said you would get a hack to drive her home."

Dr. Bowman took his cue and stood as well. "Yes, she can't walk all that way alone after dark. There, Edward, I've kept you rambling on about business all evening. I expect you young folks have other subjects to discuss."

Edward had jumped up when his hostess stood, and once more he shook hands with the doctor.

"Thank you for having me in, sir."

Her father laughed. "I expect I shall be seeing a lot more of you. Come around my little surgery anytime you wish to talk, Edward."

"Thank you. I will."

"And don't keep Deborah up too late."

"No, sir."

Edward watched the parents leave the room, then looked down at Deborah and took a deep breath.

"It seems I am to be trusted now without a chaperone."

She nodded. "You do seem to be well favored."

"Would it be too forward of me to sit beside you?"

She felt her throat tingle and swallowed hard, then managed to say, "Not at all."

He came around to the sofa and sat on the cushion next to her, suddenly very close, and Deborah's stomach fluttered.

"You haven't said much this evening."

She smiled at that. "Well, you know Father. When he gets onto a topic, he won't let go."

Edward nodded. "I saw him this morning."

She stared at the fire screen that covered the empty fireplace. "I thought you must have."

They sat in silence for a moment, and she wondered if she ought to ask the outcome of that encounter.

"He. . .seemed a little sad at the thought of an empty house," Edward said.

"A what?" She stared at him, at his rich brown eyes and the dear, disorderly lock of hair that fell over his forehead.

"Well, if both his daughters left home, I mean."

She turned away, but it was too late. The telltale blush had returned, though she'd determined not to let it.

He grasped her hand lightly, and joy shot through her.

"I don't expect they'll go so far away that they can't visit," she whispered.

"I seem to recall you saying you'd like to sail one day."

She nodded. "So I should."

"I know you'd love it. But I wouldn't entrust you to just any ship or any captain."

Feeling very daring, she said, "And to whom would you entrust me?"

"I believe the *Resolute* will make trade voyages to the Indies soon."

"How soon?"

"Well, Mr. Price, the second officer of Hunter Shipping, tells me she'll sail within the month under Captain Redding. But this winter, that is, after the hurricane season. . ."

Deborah found enough courage to look up into his face once more.

Edward smiled and lifted a hand to her cheek. His voice cracked as he continued. "Mr. Price tells me that she'll sail again then under a different master."

"Oh?"

"Yes."

"As you say, I shouldn't want to go with just anyone."

"By then the company thinks it can spare its owner for a few months, and the ship will sail under. . .Captain Hunter."

Deborah took two deep breaths, trying to calm her raging pulse before answering. "I hear he comes from one of the oldest Maine families and a long line of sea captains and ship owners."

"I've heard that, too. Farmers of the oldest stock turned sailors."

She felt his arm warm around her shoulders, and he eased toward her. A flash of panic struck her but then was gone. She had nothing to fear with Edward. She surrendered and leaned her head against his chest, where his broadcloth jacket parted to show his snowy linen shirt. With a deep sigh, he folded her in his embrace and laid his cheek on top of her head. She heard his heart beating as fast as hers.

"Deborah?"

"Yes?"

"I love you."

"And I've always loved you."

He tilted her chin up and searched her eyes for a moment, and her heart tripped as their gazes met. He bent to kiss her, and she luxuriated in the moment, resting in his arms.

"Can you forget the past?" he whispered.

"I doubt it. Not altogether. But we learn from the past."

"Yes."

He was silent, holding her close to his heart and stroking her hair. "I shall always love you," he said.

"And I you."

He pushed away and fumbled in his coat pocket. When he brought his hand out, a round, brown-speckled shell rested in his palm.

"What is it?" she asked. "I've never seen one like it."

"It's all I have from the island. The few other things we had I gave to the men's families for remembrances. But I'd like to give you this."

She took it and ran a finger over its hard, satiny curve. "Thank you."

"And I hope we'll sail together one day and find other mementos."

He went to one knee beside her and clasped her hands, with the shell hidden between her palm and his.

"I'd like to bring you another keepsake soon. A ring, dearest. Will you be my wife?"

Deborah caught her breath. Would her father object and say it was too soon?

A certainty overcame her misgivings. This was what she had waited for these many years. This was why she had reserved her heart from loving any others.

"Yes," she whispered. "I shall be honored."

He drew her toward him and kissed her once more, and Deborah knew her own solitude had ended, too.

Epilogue

A cool October breeze blew in off Casco Bay and ruffled the limbs of the trees around them. A tall maple waved its branches, and red and yellow leaves fluttered down into the Hunters' garden. Edward seized Deborah's hand, and she smiled at him, then looked down and waved at the people below.

They were mad to get married on the tiny rooftop platform, but this was Deborah's choice. Indian summer had hit the Maine coast, and she had reveled in the warm, clear autumn days the last two weeks had brought. Edward had agreed to her suggestion for the wedding venue as he agreed to nearly everything she asked, eager to please her in the tiniest detail. Still, it was a bit cooler today, and harsh weather was not far away.

The two of them, Pastor Jordan, their witnesses and parents were all the widow's walk could hold. The other guests filled the garden and spilled over onto the walk. A few of Deborah's Thursday ladies and their children even stood outside the neat white fence, gazing up at them with awe.

Jacob and Abigail joined them at the railing. Edward's mother and Dr. and Mrs. Bowman left the shelter of the stairway and came to stand beside them. Mrs. Hunter was swathed in a fur cape and a woolen hood, but still, Edward hoped the ceremony would be short.

"Perhaps this wasn't such a good idea," Abigail said to her sister.

"I'm sorry. Are you cold?" Deborah asked.

"A bit."

Jacob seemed to feel this was license to slip his arm around his wife of two months and hold her close to his side, and Edward winked at him.

"Let us begin," said the pastor. "Dearly beloved, we are gathered here in this unusual place. . . ."

They all chuckled, and the pastor went on with the timeless words.

Edward pulled Deborah's hand through the crook of his arm and held it firmly as they recited their vows.

As the ritual ended, they bowed their heads, and the pastor invoked God's blessing.

"You may kiss the bride."

Edward leaned down to kiss Deborah tenderly. He felt the change in wind as it rippled his hair and sent his necktie fluttering to the side. When they separated, he opened his eyes and automatically sought the observatory tower.

"A ship!"

"Hush, Edward," said Abigail. "This is your wedding day. Stop looking up there."

"You mustn't be thinking of business," Jacob agreed.

"But a ship is heading for our wharf, and it can't be one of ours."

Jacob squinted toward the fluttering signal.

"Spanish."

"You sure?" Edward frowned, wishing he had the spyglass.

"Don't worry," Jacob said. "My father's in the warehouse. He insisted on working today on the odds something like this would happen. He and the harbormaster will see to it."

Their parents stepped forward to embrace them.

"Come in out of the wind," Mrs. Hunter said, leading the way to the door. "I'll have

Hannah open the front door for our guests. We're serving in the double parlor, not the yard."

"I'm sorry it turned too chilly to eat outside," Deborah said, making her way cautiously down the steep attic stairs behind her mother-in-law.

"Don't fret," Mrs. Hunter replied. "I've planned on it all along. Can't trust the weather in these parts. But I'm glad you didn't plan dancing on the wharf, Deborah."

"Dancing on the wharf?" Abigail asked as they reached the hallway below. "What a novel idea."

Edward smiled and squeezed Deborah's hand. He'd have gone along with it if Deborah had wanted it, but she'd confided that her mother would find it too raucous, and it was just as well. It would have been chaos with a foreign ship landing during the reception for the newlyweds.

The parlor was already filled with distinguished guests. Governor and Mrs. King and the state's congressmen rubbed elbows with ship owners, merchants, and Dr. Bowman's patients. Edward's sister, Anne, greeted the couple with a radiant smile, and her husband brought their two little ones over to kiss their new aunt. Deborah's widowed friends hung back in the yard, too timid to enter at first, but Edward took his bride out to stand on the front porch and urge them inside, along with most of the men employed by Hunter Shipping, where he had declared a half holiday.

"We shall cut the cake in a moment." Deborah's eyes glowed as she hugged Mrs. Crowe. "Hannah Rafferty helped Mrs. Hunter bake it, and you must have a piece. All the children, too."

The ladies came inside at last, with downcast eyes, peeking up now and then at their opulent surroundings. Abigail went around with a basket of little bags of sweets, handing one to each child. The rooms were crowded, but Edward stationed himself at Deborah's side, knowing she was determined to speak to each guest. She greeted each poor widow as graciously as she did the congressmen's wives.

At last the guests began to slip away, and only the newlyweds' families were left.

Felix Price entered, filling the doorway with his bulk.

"Any cake left?" he roared.

"Yes, Father," Jacob told him. "We fed near a hundred people, but even so, I think we'll be eating cake for a week."

Aunt Ruth hurried to fix a plate for him, and Felix sought Edward out.

"Well, now, there ye be with your beautiful bride."

Deborah smiled up at him. "Thank you, Mr. Price. It was kind of you to tend to business while Edward and Jacob were otherwise occupied."

"You're welcome, lass. But you must call me Uncle." He glanced at Edward. "May I kiss the bride?"

Before he could respond, Deborah turned her cheek to Felix, and he planted a loud smack on it, then turned to Edward with a grin.

"It's a fine Spanish brigantine at your wharf this minute."

"What's in her hold?" Edward asked.

"Olives and their oil, sugar, grain, wheat, and oranges."

"Oranges?"

"Aye. They look to be all right. A few spoiled, but I think they picked them green."

Jacob shook his head. "We'll have to have market day tomorrow. I'll send word around to all the buyers."

"Half of them were here today," Edward said. "If we'd known half an hour ago, we could have told them all at once. But you're right; unload as soon as possible. Most of it will keep well, but the fruit has to be sold quickly."

"There's cork, too," Felix added. "Big bundles of it."

"Good, we can sell that for certain." Jacob extended his hand to Edward. "Sounds like I should get down to the wharf. Abby can go home with her parents. Don't worry, Edward, we'll turn a good profit on this cargo."

"Should I come down in the morning?" Edward asked, glancing at Deborah. She closed her lips tight but made no objection.

"Of course not!" Jacob glared at him as though he had uttered heresy. "You have two weeks' honeymoon before you and Deborah sail in the *Resolute*. And you are not to show your face at the office during that time."

Deborah laughed. "Oh, please, Jacob. If you think you can keep him away for two weeks, you're daft. Besides, we'll be going back and forth to the *Resolute* while you're loading her. I expect you might see both of us once or twice during the interval."

"Yes," Edward said, patting her hand. "I insisted Deborah decorate the cabin for her comfort and bring along plenty of clothing. We'll be making a few trips to bring our baggage to the ship and get things settled."

"Fine." Jacob stepped back, looking around the room and smiling when his gaze lit on Abby. "Just don't let me see you for a few days at least, Ed. You'll scandalize the clerks if you show your face within a week."

Felix roared with laughter as his wife approached with a plate of food and a glass of punch. Edward noted Deborah's scarlet cheeks and guided her into the hallway, then, seeing they hadn't been followed, up the stairs and into the room his mother had designated as Deborah's new sitting room. The chamber adjoined the large bedchamber they would share and was fitted out with delicate cherry furniture and bright hangings and cushions.

"Are you tired?" he asked. "I thought you might want to sit for a moment, here where it's quiet."

"No, I'm not tired, but I'm glad to have a minute in private with my husband."

He swept her into his arms, blocking from his mind the preparations, the ceremony, the chitchat with the guests. This was his reward for long patience. This exhilarating moment brought him such joy that he could not speak but held her tight, brushing his cheek against her silky hair and inhaling her scent.

"Hasn't it been a splendid day?" she whispered.

"Perfect."

He kissed her then as he had longed to kiss her for months now, prolonging the interlude and relishing the light pressure of her arms as they slid around him.

When he at last released her, she nestled in against his vest, and he cradled her there.

"You know," he murmured, "I never thought I'd want to go back to Spring Island, but now I'm thinking it wouldn't be so bad, if you were there with me."

She laughed and squeezed him. "If you want to be marooned again, Edward, and live a wild life as a castaway, that's fine with me. Just do take me with you."

"No fear." He stroked her soft, dark hair and kissed her brow. "I shan't let you out of my sight now that I've found you."

THE LIGHTKEEPER'S DAUGHTER

by Paige Winship Dooly

Dedication

Thanks Mom and Dad for your love and support through the years and for your encouragement when it came to my writing. I love you both!

Chapter 1

Little Cumberland Island, Georgia, 1867

I know Papa's coming back, Samson. Don't try to tell me otherwise."

Hollan climbed to the top of the largest sand dune with Samson following close at her side. As they neared the peak, he nudged past her and plopped onto the sand. She sank down beside him. Her stamina wasn't keeping up with the rapid improvements in her vision. They'd searched for her father as far as she dared. With her eyesight coming and going, she was afraid to go too far. "We just need to find him, that's all."

Samson released a small whine.

"With Mama it was different. I knew she was gone. My heart knew. But this time, with Papa—" She stopped a moment and gave her next words some thought, then shrugged. "I don't know. With him, it's different. He's out there somewhere. I'm sure of it. We just need to figure out where. It's only been a day."

Samson lifted his furry head and raised an eyebrow.

"You think I'm crazy, don't you, boy?" She reached over and ruffled his tawny fur before settling on her back beside him.

The cloudless blue sky overhead stretched in all directions. The gentle breeze blew in off the water, carrying with it the salty scent of the ocean. Hollan inhaled deeply.

Her vision had steadily improved during the past few months, going from nothing but blurred shapes, as it had been for most of the past three years, to dim but specific outlines of objects and people. She hadn't told her father about the improvements, not wanting to get his hopes up if the experience was fleeting, but every day brought her more clarity.

Until now.... This moment brought her colors and clarity and...

"Samson!" She shot to an upright position and looked around.

Samson raised his head and barked, alert for pending danger. When he didn't see any, he looked at her in confusion.

"I *saw* your eyebrow quirk! I can see you staring at me like I've finally lost my mind. I can see the sky and the water and—oh Samson! I can see it all!"

The ocean-side view spread before them. Hollan could see every detail clearly: the sea oats, the waterline, the birds, a faraway boat on the horizon.

"Samson, I can see the water." Hollan held her breath, afraid that if she moved wrong or breathed too deeply the vivid scene in front of her would melt away. "Not only can I hear the waves, I can see them."

The sun played across the water, causing it to sparkle. A fin cut through the surface, though from this distance Hollan couldn't tell if it belonged to a dolphin or a shark. The movement—straight up, then forward for a few feet, then straight down—more closely resembled that of a shark. Dolphins tended to move in arched patterns, rolling up over the surface and back down, and they usually appeared and disappeared over and over until they moved out of view. She longed to see a dolphin. It had been too long.

Samson didn't respond other than to stare. She leaned down and peered into his dark brown eyes. She hadn't looked into a set of eyes in more than three years, and Samson's doggy eyes were just beautiful. It was a perfect moment. Samson reacted to the direct contact by wagging his tail.

"I know, Sam. This is a gift. It's precious."

Her vision blurred, and she panicked, wiping quickly at her eyes. She stared down at her hands. Tears. She could see the crystal clear liquid on her fingers. Her vision wasn't receding. The tears caused the blur.

"If only I could see Papa, Sam." She looked into her dog's eyes again. "He'll come home soon, right?"

Samson laid his head on his paws and stared out over the water.

Dark storm clouds appeared on the horizon.

"The next storm is already on its way, boy. I guess we aren't going to get a break in the weather for as long as I'd hoped."

Hollan wanted to savor the view, but she knew with her vision coming and going she needed to do some chores while she was still able.

"Maybe he's not coming back." Hollan whispered aloud the words her heart had wondered about for the past three days. Words she hadn't wanted to voice because stating them might make them real. Each passing day caused her more concern. Her father had never left her, not even for a day, and there was no way he'd leave her now unless he had no choice. Had she lost him to the most recent violent storm? She'd lost her mother during a similar squall three years earlier. She pushed back her panic and forced herself to take a few deep breaths. Perhaps he'd only been hurt. But deep down she knew even if he'd been hurt, he would have found a way to get back to her. Just as he always had in the past.

She squeezed her eyes shut against the thought, warding off the image of her injured father needing her when she was unable to find him. The reality that she'd kept pressed against the back of her mind insisted on forcing its way forward. If her father had been injured enough not to make it back, surely he wouldn't be alive three days later. Their part of the island wasn't that big.

Hollan faced the ocean and listened to the harsh waves as they crashed against the sandy shore—the sound the last remnant of the most recent destructive storm. The beach would be scattered with debris—driftwood, seaweed, and other odds and ends that always washed ashore with the waves.

But she wouldn't know at the moment. Her vision had returned to its blurred state. She didn't worry about it too much. It had reappeared with vivid crispness several times during the past couple of days. The clarity stayed longer and came with more frequency each time. She prayed her vision would return in full at some point, but she'd adapted to not seeing, too.

She hadn't spent much time with God lately. The realization caused a catch in her heart. Her prayers at the moment were rote, but she told herself she'd do better in the future. She'd spent most of her time during the past three years just existing. Her uncle had to be very disappointed. He'd told her as much, but in her newly blind state, she hadn't really cared. And ever since, she'd drifted away from everyone except her father. And now he'd somehow drifted away from her. Maybe God was trying to get her attention.

The briny scent of the sea and the taste of salt on her lips reassured her that not everything had changed. But without her father, Hollan's small world would never be the same. Two facts prevailed and tried to drag her down into depression. Her vision had faded, and her father hadn't returned. She fought hard to keep her positive outlook, but it all felt so confusing.

While the familiar scents and sounds reassured, a tremor started at her leg and steadily worked its way through her stiff body. She wasn't cold. The warmth of the early autumn sun beat down on her shoulders. She wrapped her arms tightly around her torso, as if the action could stop the shaking. She was afraid that if she let go, she'd fall into a million pieces.

A bark in the distance announced Samson's arrival. Hollan whistled for him, and he barked a response. A few moments later, he brushed up against her. His panting gave away the exertion of his latest hunt.

"Still no sign of Papa, Sam?"

The dog only whined and leaned against her thigh. If Samson had found his master, he'd have let Hollan know.

"I didn't think so, boy, but we'll be fine. I still feel confident that Papa's out there somewhere." She reached down to rub his head. And they *would* be okay. Just as soon as she figured out a way to take over her father's job as lightkeeper, her life would steady and move forward again.

Hollan had no idea how long she stood there, staring sightlessly at the water, but when dark clouds covered the warmth of the sun, and dampness from the brisk ocean breeze permeated the light cotton of her long dress, the tremors turned to shivers of cold, and she urged Samson to move back toward their home.

My home, she corrected herself, her steps slow and careful. Now that she was alone—and until her father returned—she was in desperate need of a plan. She passed through the shadow of the lighthouse and raised a hand to caress the cool stone of its base. The lighthouse had remained dark through the majority of the war. They'd only recently resumed operations. She'd need to go up there soon and ready things for the night's work. Whenever her vision cleared, she hurried around and did everything necessary for the next few hours. She'd spent enough time in the lighthouse to do the basic chores even with her limited sight. When her vision dimmed, she was forced to let the lighthouse sit in darkness, too.

But first she needed to prepare a missive for her uncle. She continued toward the cottage, counting backward through the past few days. The supply boat—if it had fared well through the storm—would arrive later that afternoon. When the young captain, Fletcher, found her alone, he'd surely insist on bringing her back to the mainland. She'd argue with him, and he'd agree to search the island for her father, but after, even if she talked him out of forcing her away, she'd only have a day's worth of time to plan before her uncle descended.

The abrupt pain of her bare foot stubbing against the lowest stone step of the cottage pulled her from her musings. She reached forward to catch her balance against the wooden door, barely preventing a headfirst tumble into the garden to her left. The pain was intense, and she clenched her teeth, blowing a few panting breaths through tight lips to ward off the ache before tentatively putting weight on the aching appendage. She'd likely bruised some toes, but they'd soon be fine as long as she was careful. Though her vision was steadily improving, she needed to pay more attention to her surroundings.

A wry smile formed on her lips as she clung to the solidity of the door and hobbled up the final two steps. Hadn't her father said the same thing to her many times before? The thought brought him closer. Perhaps he wasn't so very far away. His words and teachings, especially the ones about Jesus and His unfailing presence lived on inside her. The thought brought her a moment of peace, but the reality of the reason for the thought again caused tears to threaten. She'd never before been alone. Though she was strong and resilient, she needed to have someone close by. Her father had taught her that with Jesus as her Savior, she'd never be truly alone. But while that was all good and well during his suppertime teachings, it didn't really seem to help right now when she lived alone in darkness and needed to find her way.

She shook away the panicked thoughts and chastised herself. More importantly, she needed to write her note before giving in to the cloying and ever-present grief and concern about her missing father.

The wind blew harder, and Hollan hurried to open the door, suddenly anxious to be safely tucked inside the dimly lit interior of the cottage. Samson nudged in front of her and trotted to his usual position near the dying embers of the fireplace. Hollan closed and secured the door then felt her way across the room until she bumped into the small dining table nestled against the far wall. She reached forward and located the lamp with one hand while the fingers of her other hand searched along the rough wood of the table for the nearby matches. The familiar routine soothed her.

Light flared, and she tested her eyes. Though she could see a dim outline of most items in the room, she couldn't see anything clearly.

She moved a few feet across the floor to the hearth and nudged Samson out of the way before leaning down—mindful of her dress hem—to carefully stoke the fire. Years of practice made the chore easy, and she took a few moments to bask in the warmth of the crackling wood. When the flames had dried her dress and heated her skin, she sighed and moved to sit at her small writing table, ready to carefully formulate the brief note for her uncle. The change from the light of the fire to the dimmer light of her writing table didn't help her mission. But in all reality, it didn't matter. Even without the contrast of moving from the bright fire to the blank paper, she could just barely see well enough to discern the letters as she formed them on the blank page. Though not an easy task, she did her best to make the note brief and her correspondence legible.

She considered walking down to the dock to meet Fletcher but decided it was best to wait for him to come to her while she rested her throbbing toes. If she were to stumble or get hurt on the path, it would only fuel Fletcher's potential determination to take her back with him. Instead, she'd sit tight and pray, with the hope that God would answer her prayer by providing her with a way to remain on the island.

Chapter 2

Jacob topped a slight rise and reined in his horse, scowling as he took in the view spread before him. He'd come home. He ignored the anxiety that invaded his thoughts as he contemplated the hostile reception he might receive and instead focused on the beauty of his surroundings. He'd missed the ocean. And if he had to admit it to himself, deep down he was glad to be back.

He had a lot of wrongs to right, and after one quick stop, he'd start the process with Hollan.

The dirt path he'd traveled led directly to the thin strip of water that separated the mainland from Little Cumberland Island. A larger dirt road bisected the path, leading to the tiny village where he'd grown up. Small fishing vessels bobbed on the dark blue water, each one filled with occupants in various stages of securing their catch. The fishermen pulled nets laden with their bounty from the salty water, while others prepared to toss their nets back in from a better vantage point. A few scattered figures walked along the shore, enjoying the brilliant day, some feeding the seagulls and others looking for seashells. Out on the island, the lighthouse stood tall on the distant horizon, keeping watch over the mouth of the Satilla River and the coast.

Jacob figured he should feel some sort of reluctance at the thought of returning home to the seaside town as a prodigal of sorts, but instead relief loosened the tightness from his shoulders now that he'd arrived at his destination. His burden felt much lighter.

Three years earlier, he'd left his hometown behind. By day he'd lived life as a traveling preacher. At night he'd scoured the surrounding towns, looking for his outlaw father and brothers. In both endeavors, he'd been full of expectations and enthusiasm. Yet life on the road had left him surprisingly empty and alone. He'd thought doing the Lord's work would bring him contentment no matter where he was and that by bringing his family to justice he would in some way undo the evils they'd committed. But instead the process had drained him.

He had one more brother to track, but for longer than he wanted to admit, the tug to return home had consumed him. When his brother's trail turned and led toward home, Jacob felt the first flicker of hope in a long time. He knew God had a plan for his return. And now that Jacob had returned, for the first time in a long time he felt reassuring peace flow through him. He felt confident that he'd soon locate David and that justice would prevail.

Jacob turned the horse and urged him toward the village. First order of business was to find his good friend and adviser, Edward Poe. He'd start at the tiny parsonage. Jacob held his head high as he rode, not missing the glances that followed his progress as he passed, nor did he miss the way the townspeople bent their heads close together to whisper as he moved by.

The double doors at the front of the small whitewashed church were propped wide open, and they welcomed Jacob inside. He swung down from his horse with a smile, secured him to one of the hitching posts that stood sentry under the shady magnolias flanking both sides of the front steps, and pulled his hat from his head. As he walked he slapped the dusty brim against his equally dusty pants in a vain effort to shake off the remnants of the trail. With a sense of anticipation, he moved forward and entered the cool interior of the worn clapboard building.

Edward sat at a small table in an alcove just inside the front of the church. He had one elbow propped against the surface, his hand resting against his forehead while his other hand clutched an open note. The parson's eyes were closed and his white-topped head bowed in apparent prayer over the missive.

Jacob remained silent until Edward lifted his head, finally aware of his presence.

"Jacob Swan!" Hurrying to his feet, Edward came forward and pulled Jacob into a warm embrace. "You've come home. After all this time and those few notes insinuating your intent, you finally followed through!"

"I did indeed." Jacob smiled at his mentor. "I couldn't find peace on the trail and decided I'd best come back before the good Lord found a more blunt way to send me home to my roots."

Jacob stood with arms crossed and feet squared and grinned at his favorite teacher.

Edward studied him. "You had some concerns about your return. Have those worries lessened?"

Jacob shook his head. He tried to fight off the urge to pace but finally gave in and moved a few steps away and back in the small space behind the pews. Edward followed his movements with knowing eyes.

"You're nervous about your reception."

Jacob glanced out the church doors, watching as a couple of people moved past the entrance. "I am. It's the only thing that's held me back from coming sooner. My family. . ."

"Your family made their choices, Jacob. Those choices weren't yours, and the people around here all know it."

"I'm not sure my neighbors will see it that way. The townspeople are already talking."

"Well, that's their problem to live with until they see the truth. And you know how they love to talk. In the meantime, all that matters is that you've come home. I know several people who will rejoice at that news, Ettie being one of them."

Jacob smiled at Edward's mention of his wife. "I look forward to seeing her. Before I do any visiting, though, I need to finish some details of my return. I'll need a place to live. I need to locate work—and even though you think my father's and brothers' actions won't be held against me, I suspect I'll have a hard time securing a job."

"Tell me something." Edward frowned as he mulled over Jacob's words. "With all your concerns, why did you come back?"

"The Lord called me here. I stayed away until I couldn't refuse, if that makes any sense. The past year has been hard. Each time I tried to ignore the quiet voice urging me to return, things became harder on the circuit. I'm tired, and I need a change. More than anything, I want to right my brothers' wrongs. I want to make up for my father's poor choices."

"I see." Edward nodded. "That's a pretty strong order. But to put things in perspective, it's not uncommon for a traveling preacher to wear out if he doesn't take time to stoke the fire—especially if he's chasing his own demons at the same time." He sent Jacob another knowing look. "And after so many years on the road, giving to everyone you come across, you need to be refreshed. You need a break, yet you need to find a way into the hearts and lives of the locals." He glanced at the note on the table, and his features transformed with excitement. "And I think I have just the solution."

Jacob's eyes narrowed. Edward's *solutions* always came with a price. Sometimes a very high price.

"Don't look so suspicious." Edward clapped him on the back and motioned to the rear pew. "I think your timely arrival might just be an answer to my prayer. Sit."

Jacob sat. How he'd gone from confident warrior to submissive schoolboy in a few short moments he didn't know.

Edward joined him. "You're not sure what the townspeople's feelings will be now that you've returned. Correct?"

"Yeeesss." Jacob drawled the word out, knowing his agreement came with a catch.

"If you were to marry one of the town's darlings, it would go a long way in clearing the path toward your redemption, would it not?"

"Marriage?" Jacob's voice rose in volume and pitch. He jumped to his feet, ready to flee. "You just said my family's actions were not my own. Now you're using the situation against me to force me into marriage?"

"You know I wouldn't force you to do anything."

"I didn't come home to marry."

"I'm sorry. Is there someone else, another woman who holds your heart?" Edward asked in surprise. "Is this the cause of your return?"

"Another woman? Of course not! You know there is only one woman for me. The only woman I'll ever love is Hollan. And my father's and brothers' actions ended any chance for that marriage. After what they did to Hollan and her family. . ." He shook his head. "I can't believe you asked if there was anyone else. I'm constantly on the move. When would I have time to build a relationship with a woman? There's no one out there waiting for me. My family's legacy chases away any desire I might have to marry." He ignored Edward's motion that he be seated and paced the room again. "Marriage is the furthest thing from my mind."

"You have no intention of settling down?"

"I do want to settle down. I just prefer to settle alone."

"And there's no one—besides Hollan—who holds your heart?"

Jacob hesitated before answering. He had a feeling his words were throwing him headfirst into Edward's plans. "No. You know my father was an evil man. I watched my father's actions pull the life from my mother. I watched him break my brothers with his cruelty and then watched my brothers hurt the women in their paths. I won't do that to anyone else."

"How many times do I have to remind you? You aren't your father or your brothers."

"I understand that, but I am my father's son. My brothers treated the women in their lives in the same exact manner as my father treated my mother. Or should I say, *mistreated*."

"You didn't agree with your family's lack of morals back then. Why do you think you'd be like them now?"

"I won't marry, Edward. I won't take on a carefree bride, just to make her into a miserable wife."

Edward's face fell. "I see."

Jacob stopped in his tracks, suspicious at his mentor's abrupt change of heart. It wasn't like him to give up so easily. Whatever Edward needed must be very important to him. And Jacob owed the man. . .owed him a lot. When all the other people in town turned their backs on him, Edward had given Jacob a home. More importantly, from the time he was a boy, Edward had taught Jacob about his faith. He'd shaped Jacob's whole future from that of an outlaw to one as God's chosen. He and Ettie had encouraged him during the years he fought in the war. There wasn't much Jacob could deny the older man. But marriage?

Jacob battled his inner thoughts and lost.

"What—or who—do you have in mind?" He folded his arms and spat the words out, hardly the picture of amiability, but marriage was a big request.

Edward walked over to the table and picked up the note. "I received this shortly before you arrived. I've been praying ever since."

Jacob pulled the paper from his mentor's hand and read the words carefully. His heart tightened with each word of the missive. "Hollan."

"Yes, Jacob. And she's all alone. Well, not exactly alone at the moment. I've sent Sylvia over to stay until I could find a better solution."

"Sylvia?"

"Hollan's mother's best friend. She's a widow. The night of your family's rampage, Hollan's mother passed away. Hollan was injured. Sylvia went over to care for Hollan and her father until Hollan could manage alone."

"I remember Sylvia." Jacob winced. "I'm glad she was there for Hollan. I never wanted her hurt."

Edward paused. "You still love Hollan."

"I will always love her, but that night when my family left town, things between us changed." He held out the note for Edward. Edward ignored it, letting the note burn a path through Jacob's fingers. *Hollan had touched this paper.* "Ettie would want to bring her home to the parsonage, wouldn't she?"

Edward nodded. "Of course. And Ettie would be ecstatic at the chance to fuss over Hollan. But do you really think Hollan would be happy with that arrangement? You know my niece. She loves her life on the island. Bringing her here would be the worst thing we could do."

Jacob felt the weight of responsibility press down on him.

"Surely there's another solution. If Sylvia is with her, I could go over and stay at the lighthouse. I could do the necessary work—I often helped Gunter with the lighthouse—while Hollan could remain in her home." His thoughts made so much sense that the burden lifted. Edward would have to see the perfection in his plan.

"Sylvia can't stay. She's only there for a few days. After that she'll return to the mainland. If I can't find another solution, Hollan will have to return with her. That'll break her heart. And she's already been through so much."

Guilt ricocheted through Jacob's heart. She'd been through so much because of him. If Jacob kept his gaze toward the door, he'd be able to walk away from the situation. His conscience and sense of obligation would likely send him right back in, but he'd have had a chance. Instead he looked into Edward's eyes, and the pleading there settled his fate. He couldn't tell him no. Not after everything Edward had done for him.

"I can't just go out there and man the lighthouse and watch over her from afar?"

"You know people would talk. It would add fuel to the fire regarding your relationship and would tarnish Hollan's reputation. Make things right, Jacob. Go out there and finish what you started."

"Marriage, huh?"

Edward nodded. "It would be the only way, for propriety's sake. And if you truly have no desire to marry for love, a marriage of convenience wouldn't be such a bad thing, would it?"

Jacob shrugged. "The only way I'd ever marry would be for love, but Hollan will never have me. You know how things ended. What my brother did—"

Edward cut him off. "Think about the good that will come of this. With or without this marriage, I'm sure in time you'll find your neighbors' acceptance. Without being married at that time, with your charm and handsome demeanor, the womenfolk will line the eligible ladies up at your door, trying to get you settled. If you marry Hollan, the process of acceptance will move more quickly, without all the matchmaking that will surely come your way."

Jacob shuddered.

Edward took the action as encouragement to continue. "You'll soon be able to relax on the island. You know Hollan is independent and undemanding. The situation will be perfect for both of you."

"Speaking of Hollan, how do you expect her to react when you arrive on the island with her new husband?"

Edward grinned. "She'll be so happy to be able to stay on her beloved island, she'll welcome the idea with open arms. She once loved you, Jacob. She'll soon learn to love you again. I'll explain things to her as soon as we arrive. She'll embrace the idea."

Jacob raised his hands in surrender. "I guess you'd best prepare to board my horse."

Chapter 3

We're doing *what*?" Hollan's words ended in a shriek. "I—you—what? No. No! I won't do this. You want me to marry a complete *stranger*?"

"Jacob's hardly a stranger, Hollan. You two were engaged. You've known him since you were young."

"Oh yes. I remember. Right before he ran off with his outlaw family after they pillaged the town. The night my mother. . ." Hollan let her voice drift away as she stomped away from her uncle and headed for her place of refuge—the sand dune overlooking the ocean—wanting to leave everyone behind. Her astute hearing told her that her uncle ignored the fact that she'd purposely left him in her dust and continued to follow along.

"He didn't run off with them. He went after them to bring them to justice."

Hollan spun to face him. "How can you want this for me? How will this *fix* my present situation? Our love disappeared along with him the night he left. An arrangement like this will only bring more problems." She figured her horrified words could be heard all the way to the mainland, but she didn't care. What was her uncle thinking? "There must be another way."

Her uncle raised his gentle voice so he could be heard above the wind that blew in off the water. "I'm open to suggestions, Hollan. You need to be reasonable. You know you can't stay out here alone. Do you have a better plan?"

Hollan would find one. She had to. Anything was better than an arranged marriage to someone she no longer knew. The man she'd known no longer existed, if he ever had. She hadn't seen Jacob in years. The night he left, Hollan had lost her mother, her vision, and Jacob's love. It was a night she never wanted to think about again.

The man had outlaw roots, plain and simple, and in the end, when it mattered the most, those outlaw tendencies seemed to come to the forefront. Why else would he run off with his outlaw family and leave her to pick up the pieces? It didn't matter how long or how well Uncle Edward had known the man. Hollan didn't want any part of this.

Soon after Jacob had left—after she'd recovered from her accident—she'd made the decision to never marry. With her visual difficulties, she'd feel like a burden in the eyes of whoever ended up with her. She'd lose her independence. Her mother had unraveled on that horrible night, and she could only imagine why. If her mother had been happy, why would she have jumped from the lighthouse?

For her uncle to be desperate enough to marry her off to an outlaw, she was in a worse situation than she'd ever imagined. Marriage in any situation wasn't a good idea, but this was oh-so-much worse.

"How can you not see that this isn't an option for me?" Her mother's desperate attempt to escape from their life closed the door on that idea for Hollan years ago.

"Your mother wasn't of sound mind, Hollan. The accident wasn't what you think. Your parents had a wonderful marriage."

"What changed that? If something could go so horribly wrong in their marriage, how am I to know the same thing won't happen to me?" A balmy wind blew around her. She breathed in the comforting scent. "And I already come along with enough of my own challenges—challenges that would cause undue burden even in the strongest of marriages.

Even in a marriage filled with love, which this one won't have."

"The two of you loved each other before. I know you can find your way back to each other and love again. As for your mother's accident, we do need to discuss it further, but now isn't the time. Just know her decision that night had nothing to do with her love for you or your father." Her uncle's speech ended, and he stood silently beside her.

Her father and Sylvia both wrote Hollan's mother's demise off to an unstable mind, but she couldn't understand that. Why hadn't her father been able to fix whatever was wrong? Why hadn't the need to be around for Hollan been enough to keep her mother's mind intact? What could be so awful that her mother thought the answer lay in plummeting from the deck that ran around the lighthouse? In any case, her family history didn't bode well for marriage, especially when marriage to her came with the additional challenge of dealing with a sightless wife.

Well, she amended, her heart jumping with a momentary lilt—*a* partially *sightless wife*. Her vision still improved daily, returning in bits and pieces. Even now she could see the outline of Sylvia's slightly curved figure to her left and her uncle's more barrel-shaped chest to her right. A bit of a distance away, the bright midmorning sun highlighted the tall figure of her husband-to-be.

Hollan turned toward her caretaker. "Sylvia, you'll stay on to help me, won't you? I'll make sure you're well paid for your time. And Fletcher can take over the lighthouse. You know you're both welcome here."

Fletcher was a good man and a hard worker. After dropping off her uncle and Jacob, he left with the supply boat to fulfill his normal workday, even after the long night of tending to the lighthouse.

Sylvia moved forward to place a reassuring hand against Hollan's cheek. "You know I can't stay, dear. We've had this talk. I'm needed in town, and Fletcher's work doesn't allow him to be out here on the island. He can't continue to work the lighthouse *and* run the boat. You'll be fine with your uncle's arrangement. You know he wouldn't do anything to hurt you."

"But Sylvia, I—"

Her caretaker dropped her voice to a whisper and leaned close as if Hollan hadn't spoken. "And we all know how much that man over there once loved you. You'll find your way back to him again." She planted a soft kiss on Hollan's cheek and moved back toward the house.

"But—Sylvia! Wait."

"I can't, darling. I need to pack up and be ready to go when Fletcher returns."

"Argh!" Hollan stomped her foot.

The action was rewarded with a deep chuckle from up the hill. *Jacob. The heartbreaking outlaw.* She ignored him and spun back around to her uncle.

"An outlaw, Uncle Edward? Is that really what my future has come to? Am I such a burden that only he will take me?"

"I don't consider you to be a burden at all. As a matter of fact, your aunt Ettie and I would like nothing more than to have you pack up and return to the mainland to stay with us. We can forget this conversation ever happened, and you can start anew in our home. You do have a choice."

Hollan turned away so he'd not see her face crumple at the dismal choices set before her. She loved her uncle and aunt, but she loved her island, too. "Marriage to an outlaw or I leave the only home I've ever known to start over again in town. And what a choice it is."

"Don't sound so despondent, dear one. You know I'd never do anything to hurt you. And Jacob isn't an outlaw."

"The history of the Swan family made it all the way out here, Uncle. I know what his family did."

"Their history isn't Jacob's. You knew him as a boy and as a young man. He's a good person. That hasn't changed. He wasn't with his brothers or father when they pillaged and set fire that night. Their actions have caused him enough pain, and I won't have you joining in with the townsfolk and judging him unfairly. Jacob is a wonderful man of God. He wants nothing more than to live in peace, free from the demons that pursue him. He only seeks quiet and relaxation. The marriage will be in name only, for propriety's sake. You both seem determined in your quest to avoid marriage. Perhaps this arrangement will protect you from the very institution you both abhor."

Hollan couldn't help but laugh. "Marriage will protect us from marriage? That makes no sense."

"Nothing much makes sense lately, Hollan." Her uncle sighed. "But if you're both sure you don't want to seek out love and settle down with someone else—someone else you care deeply for—then this arrangement is for the best. You'll have the protection you require and, in exchange, someone to run the lighthouse."

"And what will Jacob get?"

"The quiet life on the island will agree with Jacob and will salve the scars of his past. I have no doubt he'll like it here. The two of you loved each other before. I know you'll take care of each other, even if your love is gone. You'll see the good in him. And in time the townspeople will see it, too."

Hollan started to ask what scars he carried but figured with his family history it was obvious. When Jacob went to serve in the war, his brothers and father had evaded any type of service. They'd been suspected of pillaging and raiding local towns instead.

"If you don't want to agree to this arrangement, you'll need to head up to the house and pack your things. We'll leave late afternoon when Fletcher returns for his mother."

"I marry Jacob, or I leave the island." The whispered words blew away on the breeze. "I can't leave my island. It's all Samson and I have left. It's our home."

"Then you agree to the marriage?"

She thought hard, but no better solution came to her. "Yes, Uncle Edward. Prepare the way for my wedding. I guess I'll marry the outlaw."

"You'll marry a gentleman. I'll have you see it no other way."

"Perhaps you should reintroduce me to my groom." She folded her arms at her chest and refused to turn around to see if Jacob stood nearby. "Is he still standing on the hill listening?"

Her uncle chuckled. "No, he fled after your foot stomp. He's down the beach a bit with Samson."

"With Samson? The traitor."

They fell into step together and headed in that direction. The sound of the surf rose in volume as they neared the shore. Hollan's bare feet sank into the soft sand, and an impetuous thought made her smile. What would her new husband think of her perpetually shoeless state? Perhaps he'd never know. But with the loss of her sight, she needed to use each and every sense she could. She loved to feel the textures of the ground around her. And she found the sensation of sand beneath her toes to be her favorite sensation of all. She wouldn't have that pleasure in town. She'd made the right decision, even if it was scary and hard.

She stopped momentarily to breathe in the always-present, reassuring scent of her surroundings. Marriage couldn't be worse than losing the island. She'd come through this and be just fine on the other side. She was not her mother.

Her uncle's voice broke into her musings. "Samson seems content. He's retrieving sticks thrown into the water by Jacob. Maybe the animal sees the merit of the situation better than you do."

"Samson doesn't make up with anyone, Uncle Edward. You know that. All the changes of late must be muddling his little doggy brain."

"That dog has more brain than most men I know, your fiancé not included."

"My fiancé." She groaned.

"Your fiancé only for a short while." Her uncle's voice held a hint of laughter. "Before you have a chance to get used to the idea, your fiancé will be your spouse."

"Maybe I could have a bit more time to get used to the fiancé angle before we jump into marriage?" she asked hopefully.

"Take all the time you need. After reintroductions, you'll have the better part of the next hour to get used to the spouse part of the idea. You'll get through this just fine."

Hollan stopped, and Samson ran to her side. She ran a clammy hand self-consciously through her wind-tossed hair. The hot sun beat down on her back. What must her husband-to-be think of her? Did he, too, see the ceremony as "something to get through"? Would he someday mourn his loss of choice in handpicking a bride in the future? He'd already turned his back on her once. Would he spend the rest of his life regretting her?

She squared her shoulders and moved forward. She wouldn't be pathetic. Her fiancé would meet the independent woman who was his future wife.

Chapter 4

"Jacob, Hollan thought it best that you meet again before you marry."

The introduction felt odd, but as Edward led the beautiful but reluctant woman closer, Jacob realized she might as well be a stranger to him. Hollan had matured and grown even more beautiful, something he hadn't thought possible three short years earlier. She wore her auburn hair pulled up, but stray wisps blew around her face. She reached up to hold them tentatively away from her delicate features. He saw only a glimpse of her warm brown eyes before she looked away.

Jacob wondered if she felt as awkward in the situation as he did. Outwardly she seemed completely calm, but judging by her earlier response, she, too, felt the tension. And how could she not? Her life had taken on a myriad of changes in a very short time.

"Hollan." Jacob stepped forward. "The years have been good to you. I'm pleased to see you again." He winced. Perhaps those weren't the best choice of words to say to someone who'd lost almost everything they valued.

She reached a dainty hand his way, and he took it briefly in his own. She looked toward him, though her eyes didn't meet his. A slight smile tilted up the corners of her mouth as her chin dipped in a nod of acknowledgment. "I'm pleased to meet you again, too." The forced smile stayed in place as she bit out each word.

Jacob held back the laugh that threatened at her forced words. He wouldn't do anything to jeopardize their future together, but she was anything *but* pleased. Her choices had been reduced to a life in town away from everything she knew and loved or a life married to—as far as she was concerned—a complete and total stranger who had already wreaked havoc in her life once before. That their marriage came with her uncle's blessing didn't really matter at this point—he was a stranger to her all the same.

An unexpectedly protective urge slammed through him as he held her soft hand in his, even as he felt the strength in her own response. She squeezed his hand once and released him.

"I'll leave you two to get acquainted. I have several things to attend to before we do the ceremony."

Jacob didn't miss the momentary panic that moved across Hollan's face. She wasn't as calm as she tried to let on. He'd do his best to put her at ease, but in reality he was just as nervous and shaken up.

They stood quietly for a few moments as her uncle made his retreat. Jacob loved the man, owed him his life, and would do everything in his power to make things easier for his former fiancée.

"Shall we walk?"

"Walk?" Hollan stuttered over the word, glancing up the coast.

"You know, one foot in front of the other as we move along the shore?" He figured the distraction of movement would be better than awkwardly standing there. "We should at least try to get acquainted as your uncle suggested. It's been a long time. We have a lot to discuss."

"I suppose."

"If I may?" He reached for her hand and placed it against his bent arm. She stiffened, and he thought she might pull away, but then she relaxed and accepted his assistance. He felt the heat from her fingers through the rolled-up sleeves of his thin cotton shirt. The sensation was pleasantly familiar. He'd missed her touch. He suddenly realized this wouldn't be nearly as easy as he'd imagined. The heart of stone he'd envisioned at his core was suddenly turning to mush.

They began to walk, and he took care not to let the waves break against her long dark skirt. A few times he led her higher up the beach to avoid an especially aggressive wave.

"What did you want to talk about?"

"Guidelines." Which, based on his response to her touch, they now needed worse than ever.

Her brows drew together. Her hand tightened against his arm, and her steps faltered. "Guidelines? Such as?"

"I know you aren't exactly excited about this arrangement."

He hesitated when she laughed.

"That's an understatement." Remorse immediately replaced the smile. "I'm sorry. It can't be much easier for you. You're making a great sacrifice and doing me a huge favor by allowing me to remain here, for reasons I can't even imagine."

The way his emotions were tossing about—much like the faraway ship moved across the storm-tossed sea—it didn't make marriage to her feel like such a sacrifice. He cleared his throat. "I'll be fine. But I want you to have peace with the situation, at least as much peace as possible. I want to do what I can to make the adjustment easier for us both."

She stopped. "Why are you doing this? What's in it for you? I want to hear your reasons from you."

"I think that answer is obvious. I know your uncle went over it with you. But to reiterate, we each have something the other needs."

"And what would that be?"

He reached for her wrist as she pulled away. Her rapid pulse beat against his fingers. He prayed for the words that would help soothe her fears as he again tucked her hand firmly in place. They continued walking at a leisurely pace.

"You aren't the only one who's had a rough time of it. You know I owe your uncle a great deal. I owe you, too. The night I left town, after what my family did, I couldn't face you. I needed to get away." He didn't really want to hear the specific details of what his brothers had done, but he left her the opportunity to discuss that night if she needed to. Otherwise, the details would come out in time.

"And yet you've returned."

"Yes." He was surprised she didn't lash out or want to discuss the details. But perhaps she'd never want to discuss it. He glanced down at the sand as they walked, and a delicate shell caught his attention. He bent to pick it up. Most of the shells on the beach had been broken into jagged pieces by the strong tides before they ever finished their tumble to shore. He started to throw his find into the ocean, but instead he carried it as they walked along, turning the smooth object over and over with his fingers. This shell, which looked so delicate, had to be strong to have made it through the rough waters in one piece. It reminded him of the woman who walked beside him. "The trails didn't hold the answers I'd hoped for."

"And you expect to find the answers out here?"

"The answers will come in time. Here I'll find quiet and relaxation. At least that's what Edward tells me." He grinned her way, even though she wouldn't notice. The smile carried on his words. "I suppose that remains to be seen."

Judging by the effect the gently breaking waves about a dozen feet out were having on him, Uncle Edward was correct. He felt a peace here he hadn't felt on the mainland. Or maybe it was the gentle nature of the woman walking beside him that charmed his heart.

He hoped the feeling was mutual.

"I won't get in your way."

Not quite the response he'd envisioned and hoped for.

"I don't want you to avoid me. I don't want to force any changes on you."

"What *do* you want from me?"

"Pardon?"

"What are your expectations?"

"I have no expectations. I haven't had time to think of any."

"I guess that's true. Where do you plan to sleep?"

Again she had him grinning. "You don't tiptoe around your thoughts, do you?" He hadn't smiled this much in years.

"I try not to. You know my father. He taught me that if a question is good enough to think about, it's worthy of putting into words."

His father's teachings had been far different. "I always liked your father. But to answer your question"—he turned back and glanced at the lighthouse—"your uncle said there's a room at the base of the lighthouse that would serve well as my living quarters."

Her features relaxed as she released a soft sigh. He hadn't noticed she'd been holding her breath while waiting for his answer.

"Indeed. He's right. That will work out nicely. The room is already set up with a bed. My father would often stay out there during difficult weather. Except for the night he disappeared." Her voice tapered off. A scowl marred her features.

"Fletcher said he searched the island."

"He did. But I don't feel as if my father is gone." Her grip tightened against his arm. "When my mother—died, after I came to, I knew instantly that she was no longer with us."

"I'll continue to look for him. If he's here, we'll find him."

"Thank you." For the first time her smile appeared to be genuine. "Fletcher and Sylvia seem to think it's shock talking when I say that. My uncle surely thinks the same." She shrugged.

They turned and headed back toward the cottage, the silence around them broken only by the cries of the seagulls.

She abruptly appeared to shake off the melancholy mood along with whatever thoughts were on her mind by quickly changing the subject. "I'll make your meals of course."

"That would be nice."

A most charming blush colored her cheeks. "You can eat in your room or up in the lighthouse if you'd prefer, but I won't mind if you'd like to join me at mealtime, either. I'd appreciate the company." She dropped her hand from his arm and hugged her arms around her torso.

Though in all likelihood she was only trying to be charitable in order to please her uncle, and judging from her actions hoped he'd say no, he couldn't stop the words that instantly popped out in response to her invitation. "I'd like that."

"You would?" Surprised, she stumbled and would have fallen had he not grabbed her by the arm. "Well, then. . .ouch!"

He'd been so mesmerized by Hollan and her enticing personality that he hadn't paid enough attention to all the broken shells and the uneven shoreline on this part of the beach. He should have been more diligent. Edward was counting on him to keep Hollan safe.

"What happened?"

"I'm fine." She waved him away, a look of desperation on her face as she tilted her head and listened to the sounds.

Jacob could only hear the surf breaking at their feet along with the calls of seagulls from up ahead.

"We're almost back to the cottage. Sylvia has been feeding the gulls about this time every day, and I can hear them begging up near the lighthouse." She took a cautious step, gasped, and closed her eyes in pain.

"You're hurt. Let me have a look."

"No."

"You're soon to be my wife. I don't think it will hurt for me to take a look. One of the shells must have cut through your boot."

"I'm not wearing any boots." She sighed. Frustrated, she scrunched her fingers in her hair. More loosened tendrils of auburn hair blew around her face. "I like to feel the sand under my feet."

She started when he laughed out loud.

"You find the notion funny?"

"I find you to be quite funny." He scooped her up in his arms and carried her away from the shells.

"I beg your pardon! Jacob, put me down!"

He had no intention of putting her down. She felt too good in his arms. "I will as soon as we get past these broken shells." He settled her on a large piece of driftwood before dropping to his knees in the sand. "Let me see the damage."

With a sigh she allowed him to look at her foot.

"There's still a fragment embedded in your skin. You're bleeding. No wonder it hurt to walk." He gently tugged the shell loose, but Hollan still gasped and patted at his arm.

"Ah, that hurt!"

"Sorry. The fragment is out now, but you can't walk on your foot. You'll fill the cut with sand. Stay put for a moment." He pulled a handkerchief from his pocket and walked down to dip it in the water.

Hollan stood, apparently planning to follow him.

Some things never changed.

"Must you always be so stubborn?" he called. She'd been an opinionated handful since the first day he'd met her. "I said to stay put. The last thing you need is an infection, and these shells can give you a pretty nasty one if you aren't careful."

He hurried to where she'd settled back down on the log.

"And you're as boorish as ever." She crossed her arms as she huffed out the words.

He brushed at the wound, but the sand wouldn't come free. "I'm going to have to carry you back down to the water. You'll need to hold your skirt up while I dip your foot in the ocean."

"You'll do no such thing. If you'll lend me your handkerchief, I can make a bandage. When we get back to the cottage, I'll make a poultice out of herbs."

"I'm sure you will, and that'll be fine, just as soon as we get all the sand out." He didn't give her a chance to argue as he lifted her up in his arms.

"Put me down," she hissed.

He walked to the water's edge. "Ready?"

"No."

Ignoring her, he dipped her foot into the ocean, soaking her skirt hem with seawater in the process. "There. That ought to do it."

"My skirt is drenched."

"I said you'd need to hold it up."

She glared his way. "And I *said* I wasn't ready."

"Would you have ever been ready?"

"No."

"Exactly."

She balanced on one foot until an overzealous wave knocked her backward. Jacob steadied her.

Her breath came in small huffy bursts. She was angry.

"Now see?" She poked him in the chest with her index finger. "This is exactly the behavior I worried would come along with our marriage."

"If you're referring to the fact that I just cleaned your wound and saved you from a tumble in the water, your worries are for naught. Speaking of our marriage, you might have all the time in the world to stand here and argue, but I have a wedding to attend."

"Unfortunately, so do I, and I'm going to arrive looking like a drowned rat."

"I recall asking if you were ready."

"And I *recall* saying no." She started to hobble up the shore.

"Stubborn woman! You're going to get the wound full of sand again."

"I'll—"

He didn't give her a chance to finish. Instead he flung her over his shoulder like a sack of potatoes. She shrieked and pummeled him on the back as he stalked up the path with long strides.

He might as well face her uncle head-on. At the rate they were going, the wedding was likely off anyway. Jacob didn't like the thought. He still had feelings for the feisty woman in his arms. But less than an hour earlier, Edward had entrusted into Jacob's care a healthy, pristine niece. Jacob now returned her injured, wet, and angry. The whole ordeal was anything but peaceful and relaxing. In all honesty, dealing with the townspeople couldn't possibly be any more frustrating than this.

Jacob didn't relish the thought of facing her uncle with his obvious failure, but the sooner they got the ordeal over with, the sooner they could put this mistake behind them.

Chapter 5

Uncle Edward's booming laugh welcomed them back to the cottage. Hollan didn't need to see his face—a feat that would be impossible even if she could see, thanks to her present dangling-upside-down-over-Jacob's-shoulder position—to know that the laughter was at her expense.

"I'm thrilled that you find my situation so immensely amusing, but perhaps you could stop laughing long enough to make him put me down." Her indignation was wasted on the man. She couldn't be heard over the laughter with her face and voice muffled against the back of Jacob's shirt. She tried to ignore the strength of his muscles, but it was hard to do while feeling the solid resistance as she again pummeled her fists against his back.

Jacob apparently heard. Or maybe the hard pinch to his side alerted him to her fury. He dumped her unceremoniously on her feet, only mindful at the last moment of her injury. "Thought I was going to drop you on your sore foot, didn't you?"

His voice was low, for her ears only, and she shivered at the intimacy. His closeness unnerved her. She limped a few steps away.

"You're hurt!" Immediately contrite, her uncle appeared at her side.

"Of course I'm hurt. Do you think I'd let him carry me up the dunes in that humiliating manner for the fun of it?" She sent another ferocious glare in Jacob's general direction. She didn't miss his chuckle.

"She hardly *let* me do anything. I had to take matters into my own hands. And it's only a surface wound, Edward, nothing to be alarmed about. Hollan will be fine."

"*Only* a surface wound? At the beach you acted as if I'd bleed to death without your immediate intervention."

"No, I only said the wound would fill with sand and increase the risk of infection, which reminds me, you do need to let Sylvia apply that herbal poultice."

"Help her over to this chair, Jacob, and we'll get her taken care of." Edward summoned Sylvia, and after a quick peek at the wound, she hurried off for the supplies. "Fletcher arrived at the dock just before you two made your appearance. He should be here shortly. As soon as he is, we'll get this wedding started."

Hollan sputtered. "You mean you're still planning the wedding, even after all this?"

"Indeed. Why wouldn't I? Jacob just proved he could deal with you quite nicely."

"Deal with me? You consider slinging me over his shoulder against my wishes *dealing with me nicely*?"

"Compared to the alternative, yes. The gash isn't life threatening, but walking on it wouldn't have been wise at all. Jacob made the best decision for you, based on the options."

Hollan snorted and shifted in her chair, turning her back on both of them.

"Dear, have you changed your mind?" She heard concern buried beneath the humor as her uncle placed a hand on her shoulder. "If so, you can pack a small bag and leave on the boat with us. We can collect the rest of your things later. Jacob can stay and tend to the light."

Hollan considered his offer. The emotions she felt when Jacob stood nearby concerned her more than any of his actions. She knew he had only her best interests at heart. But she hadn't expected the old feelings to come rushing back in such a vivid way. A part of her she'd thought long dead had come back alive in his presence. The realization scared and unnerved her.

"No, I'll be fine." And she would be. She wasn't leaving her island. Samson plopped down beside her with a contented sigh, breaking the awkward moment. "Samson seems happy enough to hear he still has a home."

"He could have stayed out here with me." Jacob stood nearby, listening.

Hollan wished she could see Jacob's expression. Was he disappointed she hadn't taken her uncle up on his offer? Would he have preferred to stay at the lighthouse alone? She thought about it a moment and decided she didn't care. She hadn't made him come out to get hitched, and if he had his doubts, they were his problem to deal with.

"Aunt Ettie's going to be upset about missing the ceremony." She addressed the statement to her uncle.

"I asked if she wanted to come, but she was so sure you'd turn us down flat, I couldn't get her in the boat."

"She still hates it out here. She's never cared for the island."

"She loved your mother like a sister. And though she wanted to be here with you, she can't deal with coming to the island just yet. I think she fully expected you to return to the house with me."

"I understand. Tell her I'll be in to see her soon."

"She'll want to have you both over for dinner."

"We'd like that." Jacob spoke for them both. "Ettie is a wonderful cook."

Hollan wondered about the fact that it didn't bother her that he spoke of them as a couple. Instead, it felt natural. Comforting.

Sylvia arrived and busied herself with tending to the cut. Fletcher arrived at the cottage, and the men exited and walked over to the dunes. A short time later Sylvia had Hollan bandaged up and ready for the ceremony. She helped Hollan into her prettiest blue dress—a color Hollan belatedly remembered was Jacob's favorite. She blushed, wondering if he'd think she'd chosen it especially for him.

"You look beautiful, Hollan. Your mother would be proud."

Hollan hugged the older woman, not sure she agreed. Her mother would have wanted Hollan to marry for love. They'd talked about it many times before, back in the carefree days when she was happily engaged to Jacob. Though the man remained the same, the circumstances had changed.

When Hollan didn't answer, Sylvia cupped her cheeks. "Your mother would understand."

Hollan nodded her agreement. "I'd like to think so."

"Jacob is a good man. If you give him a chance, he'll make you very happy. I think God has something beautiful planned in all of this."

Though Hollan wasn't so sure about that, she hoped her friend was right.

They decided to say their vows on a dune overlooking the ocean. The whole situation felt surreal. The wedding, although very similar to the one in her dreams—the wedding she'd wanted the first time before Jacob left—seemed a farce. The man standing beside her was nothing more than a stranger, and only a handful of loved ones stood alongside to witness the event.

Other than those few *minor* details, she thought wryly, the afternoon couldn't have been more perfect for their ceremony. Hollan loved being serenaded by the seagulls that flew over their heads. The ever-present sound of the waves crashing onshore brought a familiar comforting reassurance. She knew the sounds inland would be similar—the small village was a coastal town after all—but she wouldn't hear the roar of the surf from the Atlantic Ocean. She wouldn't be able to tell weather conditions solely by the force of the waves hitting shore. She'd not be able to wade along the tide line, nor would she be able to wander freely as she did now.

She had Jacob to thank for that. His presence allowed her to remain where she wanted to be. She turned her attention to the man at her side. She wished she could see him more clearly. As it was, the sun silhouetted his broad shoulders, and she could tell he wasn't the skinny boy who'd left her behind. She wondered how the planes of his face had changed with the years. She felt sure her vision would clear again. She'd see him soon enough. And even if she didn't, she had the details of the past tucked away in her memory. His sea green eyes wouldn't have changed, but his hair apparently had. Judging by the way the strands blew around in the wind, he'd let it grow longer than before, but she imagined the strands were the same sun-kissed color they used to be. He never had been one to stay indoors any more than necessary.

Her uncle's voice intruded on her musings. "I think we're ready. We need to finish up and be on our way." The usually wordy man surprised her as he made quick work of the ceremony.

"Jacob, you may now kiss your bride."

Before Hollan could work up a full panic, Jacob leaned forward and gently touched his lips to hers in the most gentle of kisses. Against her will, her heart began to soar.

The first few days of their marriage were awkward to say the least. Jacob could see the strain as Hollan tried to work into a steady routine of normalcy. They started each day with breakfast. Hollan worked hard to have the meal on the table before he arrived at the cottage door.

"You aren't normally an early riser, are you?" Jacob asked during their meal on their fourth morning together.

"Why do you ask?" she questioned, hiding a yawn behind her hand.

He laughed. "You're about to fall asleep in your eggs. At first I figured you weren't sleeping well due to our new role as—neighbors."

"We aren't simple neighbors, and you know it." She swiped his half-eaten plate of food from in front of him and made her way to the counter. "We're in a completely unique situation, and I do find myself losing sleep trying to make sense of it all." She snatched up a rag and returned to the table, wiping hard at the crumbs.

"You trying to wipe clean through the wood?" He stayed her hand with his.

Her breathing hitched, and she quickly pulled away. "Don't you have a lighthouse to tend to?"

"Again the lack of subtlety." He enjoyed putting a blush on her cheeks. He stood and pushed in his chair. "But yes, I do need to wipe down the lens."

"Don't forget to trim the wicks. And refuel the lanterns."

"Did all that before coming in for breakfast. Some of us get up early."

"Or never go to bed at all," she muttered.

"I sleep. I just don't need a lot of it. I sneak in a few hours before dusk and in between work."

Hollan rolled her eyes.

"Let me know if you need me." He wondered if she'd ever truly need him. If she'd ever care about him the way she used to.

He closed the cottage door behind him and walked over to the lighthouse. He climbed the multitude of narrow stairs that led to the top level. The day was clear, and he could see a good ways out. As had become his habit, he went around the entire walkway, looking for any sign of Hollan's father. If the man hadn't washed out to sea, he didn't know what had happened to him. For Hollan's sake, he hoped they'd someday find out. Hollan told him the lighthouse inspector was due for a visit within the month, and if her father hadn't returned, they stood to lose the contract. In the meantime, he'd do everything he could to keep the light in good working order.

Jacob slipped into Hollan's father's cleaning coat. The lens had to be immaculate at all times in order to work properly. He first wiped away all loose particles of debris with a feather duster. He then used a fine cloth to carefully remove any smudges left by the oil. The prisms were delicate and easily scratched, so he always made sure to touch them with caution.

He spent longer than he'd intended on the job, and the sun tipped slightly toward the west before he headed to the cottage for the midday meal. Hollan waited in a chair out front, staring toward the horizon, her forehead creased with concern.

"Is something wrong?"

"It's getting ready to storm." She motioned toward a cloth-covered plate that sat on a small table tucked between the two chairs. Samson lifted his tawny head and wagged his tail in acknowledgment before lowering his chin back down to rest upon his front paws, his favorite napping position.

Jacob surveyed the horizon. He saw some dark clouds, but he knew Hollan and her father recognized the signs of a serious storm much better than he. "Will it be a bad one?"

"I'm not sure." She'd balled her handkerchief into a small mass. "I just know the weather's turned. The seagulls have taken refuge."

He hadn't noticed, but now that she mentioned it, the ever-present birds weren't anywhere around.

"Tell me what I need to do." He didn't bother with his plate.

She smiled, but the lines around her mouth betrayed her tension. "First of all, eat. If it's a big storm, you'll be busy later."

"Then talk to me while I eat." He lifted his plate onto his lap and took a bite of crab cake. It was delicately seasoned and cooked to perfection. She'd garnished the plate with a side of tomato that he'd picked fresh from her garden earlier in the day. "This crab cake is wonderful. The tomato looks good, too."

"Thank you," she said absently. Not one to be easily distracted when she had her mind set on something, she continued to stare toward the horizon. "Do you see any clouds?"

He glanced at the ocean as he took a sip of water. "There's a darkening of the sky way out, but otherwise it's blue."

"The storms move in quickly. We'll need to batten down everything we can. The chairs and table need to go in the storage building, along with anything loose. I'm sure the process is the same as the one you'd go through in town."

"You're thinking this will be a large storm?"

"According to the birds, yes. But we won't know how large till it hits."

For the first time, he saw a chink in her armor. She'd been great about their whole situation, but her nervousness over the storm's approach was palpable. He reached over and clasped her hand with his. "God is sufficient for all our needs, Hollan. Always remember that. We'll be fine."

She didn't look convinced. "I've lost both my mother and my father in storms. They'll never be my favorite thing."

"That's understandable."

The wind picked up. The cloth that had covered his plate blew off the table, and Jacob jumped up to chase it. He glanced back at the horizon and saw the churning clouds moving closer at a quick pace.

"It's coming," Hollan stated.

"Yes." He gathered the plate and his mug and carried them into the house. He returned for Hollan. "Come. You'll be more comfortable inside."

Hollan shook her head. "I'll help with the preparations. Do you need to do anything with the light? It'll be needed more than ever during the storm."

"I have everything ready."

They worked around the yard, stowing any loose gardening gear in the storage building. The sky darkened. Clouds passed over the cottage and covered the sun. Hollan shivered.

"I need to light the lanterns. Let me see you into the house."

"I'd like to wait out here if you don't mind. I'll move in before things get rough."

"As you wish. But I'd feel better if you waited inside."

"Will you wait out the storm in the lighthouse? Or would you"—she hesitated—"consider waiting it out with me?"

"I'll be back as soon as my duties are taken care of."

Relief flowed across her pretty features. "Thank you." She waved him away.

He hurried through the motions of lighting the wicks that he'd already trimmed to the perfect length. He'd need to return in about four hours to trim them again, but as he looked around everything else was in order. The rain had begun a few minutes earlier, but now it came down in earnest. His cozy room waiting below beckoned him—he'd be drenched before he ever reached Hollan—but he'd given her his word. He didn't want her sitting through the storm alone, frightened.

He'd just exited the door at the base of the lighthouse, when a gust of wind slammed it shut behind him. The wind pushed him along as he moved toward the cottage. Hollan waited in the doorway, anxiety written across her face.

"I'm here, Hollan. I'm coming. Stay put."

Samson heard Jacob and shoved his way through the narrow opening, knocking Hollan off balance.

"Samson, no!" Hollan lunged for the escaping dog. She struggled to retain her balance against the force of the storm, but the wind caught her skirts and twirled them in a tangle around her legs. Before Jacob could get to her, she fell, tumbling down the steps with a scream. Her head hit the stone walkway, and she lay unmoving in a crumpled heap.

Chapter 6

Samson turned at once, hurrying back to his mistress. Jacob pushed him aside and scooped Hollan up in his arms.

"C'mon, Samson, let's get her inside." Rain blew through the open doorway as Jacob entered. He hurried to deposit Hollan on the quilt-covered bed. He forced the door shut before turning to stoke the fire. Though the fire burned warm, the light wasn't bright enough for him to check Hollan for injuries.

He lit a lamp and placed it on a small table near the bed. Samson, panting, stood with his front paws on the edge of the bed. He whined and licked Hollan's hand.

"She'll be fine." Jacob hoped his words were the truth.

The dog looked unconvinced.

"Hollan, can you hear me?" Jacob caressed Hollan's cheek with the back of his hand.

She remained still, her skin pale against the bright pastels of the quilt. He'd give anything to see her brown eyes open to peer into his. A trickle of blood ran down the side of her cheek. With careful fingers, Jacob tenderly sifted through her hair until he found the wound. It didn't appear to be deep at first glance, but with the amount of blood loss, it needed his attention.

First, though, he had to get her out of her wet shoes and dress. "Samson, help me out here. Hollan will tan my hide if she thinks I took any liberties with her."

Samson turned tail and headed for the fire, though he did thump his tail three times in sympathy before curling up into a cozy ball. Or at least Jacob imagined the thumps were a show of sympathy.

"She's my wife, buddy. It's fine, really."

Then why, he asked himself, *am I talking to the dog like he can understand or even cares about my justification of what I'm about to do?*

"She'll get pneumonia if she continues to lie here in a wet dress."

Samson snorted, and Jacob figured it was the dog's way of laughing at his dilemma. Or maybe the sound was just a contented sigh because as a dog Samson didn't have to worry about such things. Or maybe it was just a random dog sound that had nothing at all to do with the crazy individual who was talking to him, trying to figure out the inner workings of a dog's brain when he really needed to be caring for the woman who lay helpless in front of him.

Jacob decided to ignore the irritating thoughts that were pummeling through his head, and with purpose he unhooked Hollan's boots and slipped them off her slender feet. Though he knew she hated it, she'd taken to wearing the boots ever since she cut her foot on the shell. He doubted the habit would continue after she healed.

Next his clumsy fingers unfastened enough tiny buttons down the front of her dress to rival the amount of stairs in the lighthouse before he was finally able to pull the wet material down and over Hollan's arms. He tugged it down over her waist and away from her motionless body. He was relieved to find her underclothes dry, so he was able to leave her covered. Her petticoat and camisole did a fine job of keeping her modesty intact. He did a cursory examination for further injuries before tucking the blankets around her. He slipped the wet quilt from the bed and with a sigh of relief that the deed was done, moved the quilt and the dress nearer to the fire to dry.

Jacob dipped some warm water from the pot that hung over the flame into a small bowl. A huge gust of wind blowing against the cottage made him jump. The storm was intensifying. It sounded like this one might turn into a full-fledged hurricane. At least in her present state, Hollan wouldn't worry about their safety.

The search for rags took a bit longer, but soon he was back at Hollan's side, ready to clean her wound. He said a quick prayer of thanks that he hadn't seen any other signs of injury while he settled her in. He could only pray the head wound wasn't as bad as it looked.

"It's already stopped bleeding, Samson. That's a good sign, don't you think?"

This time Samson didn't even bother to open an eye. Jacob found it reassuring that the dog didn't seem nervous about the storm.

"I'll take that as a sign that you trust she's in good hands," Jacob muttered as he cleaned the wound. Now that the bleeding had stopped, the cut didn't appear to be deep at all.

A lump was forming under the gash. Jacob was cautious as he smoothed Hollan's auburn hair away from her face. Even now she was so beautiful. "You're going to be all right, Hollan. I'm here with you."

He couldn't do anything more for her for the time being. He slipped into some of her father's dry clothes that he had found in a trunk across the room and hung his own clothes to dry. He finally settled in a chair beside Hollan's bed and began to pray.

Hollan opened her eyes and peered into the dusky gloom. The effort was rewarded by a shooting pain that forced her to close them again. She struggled to get her bearings. She remembered the storm and Samson slipping past her. She'd reached for him and had fallen. She had no memory beyond that, except for waking in the bed minutes earlier.

I hope the injury didn't affect my returning vision. Slowly, realization flowed over her. She'd opened her eyes and had *seen* into the gloom. She'd been able to see perfectly. The few images she'd been able to take in were engraved upon her mind. The fire burned low. Samson slept near the hearth, closer than was safe, as usual. Her dress and a quilt, along with a set of men's clothes, hung on the backs of chairs near the fire to dry.

Men's clothes hung by the fire? She noticed the sound of deep breathing from a chair pulled up close beside her. She opened her eyes again, slower this time to let her eyes acclimate, and for the first time in three years she stared fully into the handsome face of the man she'd once loved. Jacob was stronger, sturdier, but still as striking as ever.

"Jacob." She whispered the word softly, but his eyes flew open as soon as she uttered it.

"Hollan." He slipped from the chair and onto his knees beside her. "How do you feel?"

She couldn't stop looking at him. "Dizzy."

"You hit your head pretty good right about here." He touched his fingers near the wound then caressed lightly down her temple. "You gave Samson and me quite a scare."

"I'm sorry." She shivered at his touch. To cover her reaction, she reached up and felt the raised bump.

"I hardly think you meant to do it." He pulled her hand away from the wound and smiled. "I cleaned the injury, but you'll want to be careful. It will be tender for a few days."

"Thank you." She peered over his shoulder. He didn't release her hand. He was too close. She felt vulnerable. "Has the storm passed?"

"Not completely, but it has calmed down some."

Her head ached. She closed her eyes and listened to the rain pattering against the roof. The aroma of simmering stew set her mouth to watering. And Jacob hovered nearby. The thought made her tremble.

"You're shivering. Let me stoke the fire."

It wasn't the cold that caused her tremor. She felt plenty warm in the cocoon of blankets he'd apparently tucked around her. It was his gentle touch that made her shiver, that stoked a whole other fire and set forth a new longing within her, a longing for things to be as they had been before. Back when he wanted to marry her out of love, not obligation. Before he left town, before she'd lost her sight, and before she'd lost her parents.

She studied him as he moved about the hearth, stepping carefully over the sleeping dog. His hair was indeed longer. He'd pulled it away from his face, which accentuated his high cheekbones. He smiled as he worked, his features relaxed with relief. When he leaned in from the far side, the fire flared, and she could see the green of the eyes she'd missed looking into for so long.

A sudden panic ran through her. Her vision felt different this time. It felt permanent. She couldn't put her finger on the change, but she had peace that her vision would remain. What if, now that she could see again, Jacob decided she no longer needed him and he was free to move on? He could have their marriage annulled and return to his previous plans—whatever those plans might have been. Surely he had some. She wasn't ready for more changes. Not yet anyway.

"What are you thinking?"

Hollan jumped. She hadn't noticed him crossing the floor to her side.

"Tell me your thoughts. You looked scared there for a moment." He pulled his chair closer and settled beside her. "Whatever your concerns were, don't worry about a thing. I'm here, and I don't intend to leave."

So you say now. When you find out you don't have to watch out for me anymore, you might feel differently.

She so badly wanted to stare into his eyes. Instead she closed her own and feigned weariness. "If you don't mind, then, I'll rest for a little bit longer."

"Do you really want to sleep, or are you merely avoiding the truth?"

"The truth?" Did he still know her so well after all these years? Had he noticed the change in her as she savored the familiar sight of his face?

"I think I understand. You're uncomfortable with our arrangement, yet you fear being alone. I'm sure this isn't easy for you."

So he didn't know her vision had fully returned. If she kept it that way a bit longer—at least until she had her bearings about her and could come up with a new plan—it would give her more time to think things through. Her head hurt and everything felt too overwhelming. She'd be able to make better decisions in the next few days.

"I feared being alone through the storm far more than I fear your closeness." There. She'd said it. But she wasn't sure that was completely true. His presence brought about a sense of awareness and accentuated an emptiness she hadn't noticed before he'd arrived back on the island. Already his presence brought her a sense of peace that she didn't want to lose. The fear of losing him so soon rivaled the fear of the storm. "At least, for the moment I *think* that's true." She cringed. She should probably stop talking until she had more rest and could think through her words, *before* stating them, with a clear mind.

He leaned close, his lips near her ear, causing tiny bumps to rise up on her forearms. "My closeness makes you nervous?"

She ordered her eyes to remain closed, though she longed to open them and see his face. She could feel the warmth of his breath on her skin.

"Yes," she admitted through clenched teeth. The man was toying with her. She didn't feel as bad about keeping her returned vision a secret at this rate. Here she lay helpless in bed and he used the situation to his advantage. She held back her smile. Deep down she didn't really mind his teasing.

Now he raised a finger and caressed her cheek. His touch was so gentle, so considerate; the act caused tears to form in her eyes. Her emotions were all over the place.

She opened her eyes. "I have a confession to make. My vision comes and goes. For the moment my vision has returned."

His face lit up. "That's wonderful news!"

"It is, but I'm confused and overwhelmed." And that was the pure truth. Hollan hadn't felt so mixed up and inundated with changes since she'd lost her mother.

"Have you prayed about it?"

She released a small breath and stared at the beams that ran across the ceiling. "I haven't prayed about much of anything in a long, long time."

"You don't believe anymore? You've lost your faith?"

The disappointment and concern in his voice had her firing off the first answer that came to mind. "No!"

She hesitated before saying anything more and analyzed his question a bit more thoroughly. *Had* she lost her faith? At the very least, she'd buried it beneath the pile of rubble that had been her former life.

"I'm embarrassed to say I haven't given it much thought lately." Guilt pricked at her conscience. If her faith had been strong, would she have let it drift away so easily? Most people used their faith to get them through the tough times—they didn't forget about it completely. "What does that say about me?"

"It says you've been through a lot." He shifted his position. "Is God still in charge of your life?"

"I guess so. . . I mean, yes, I want Him to be. I haven't given it much thought before now."

"God understands anger. But you can't let the anger make you so bitter that you turn against Him."

"No, of course not. Yet that seems to be exactly what I've done. That night. . . I lost so much."

"I know what you lost." Jacob tightened his grip on her hand. "Do you want to tell me about it? I feel responsible."

"How could you be responsible when you weren't even here?" She hadn't meant the words to sound so venomous. It might help to talk about it, to share with Jacob what happened that night. "Mama and I were talking about the wedding when we heard a noise outside. Mama went to check. A storm lurked over the water, and the wind had started up. I stayed inside and continued to work on our dinner, and the next thing I knew, Papa came in through the door. He said he'd sent Mama inside."

She untwisted and smoothed the sheets she'd wrung tight with her hands. He reached over and massaged away the tension that had gathered in her clenched hands. His touch encouraged her to continue. He deserved to know. The experiences had shaped her into the person she was today.

"Mama hadn't returned, and we both knew something wasn't right. Papa was upset and ran to check the beach while I searched the grounds around the house. Neither one of us thought to check the lighthouse, because Papa had just come from there. After looking out over the dune, I turned to go back to the house and I saw a flash of color from the ledge that circles the light. Papa couldn't hear me, so I went up without him. Mama had been crying, and she stood at the rail, much too close to the edge with the storm brewing around us."

Her breath hitched.

Jacob wiped away a tear she hadn't realized she'd shed. "Maybe now isn't the best time. You need to rest, not get more upset."

His voice was husky, full of emotion, and she wondered at the remorse she heard in his tone.

"No, I need to do this." She took a deep breath. "I went out there, and the wind buffeted around me. It almost blew me over the edge. My mother didn't even acknowledge my presence. I called to her and tried to pull her back inside, but she shoved me away. I fell against the stone wall and hit my head. When I came to, I'd lost my sight and Mama all in one fell swoop. Papa saw us up there, but before he could get to the top, Mama had jumped."

"No one knows why?"

"No, we never found out. She took her secret to the grave." Her voice had dropped to a whisper, but now she laughed, the sound harsh in the silence. "What kind of mother does that to her child—even if the child is almost grown? What type of wife abandons her husband in such a painful way? How could she have done that to herself and to us?"

"Hollan, maybe she didn't jump. If the wind was that strong, maybe she fell over accidently."

"Why was she up there?"

"I don't have the answers to those questions, Hollan. I wish I did."

Hollan understood his confusion.

"I know. I don't really expect you to. But therein lies the reason for my silence and distance from God. It wasn't a conscious choice I made, but I stopped communicating with Him." She hesitated. "I haven't forgotten my father's and uncle's teachings. I've even talked to God a bit lately. But still I've drifted away."

"Now that you've realized this, are you ready to make things right with Him?"

She nodded. "I am. I want to find my way back."

"He'll calm your fears and will help you sort through all the changes you're experiencing." He chuckled. "Changes we're both going through. If we work as a team, perhaps we can make sense of it all and see what God has for us. Let me pray with you."

Jacob clasped her hand and leaned forward to rest his forehead against it. She clung to him like the lifeline he was. The strength and confidence in his warm voice as he prayed washed over her.

"Lord, we join together in prayer and thank You for keeping us safe through the storm. Help Hollan back into the fold, Lord, and use me to make the process easier. We ask that You bring Hollan clarity of mind and calm her fears in all situations. She wants You to take control of her life. Guide her in all things.... In Jesus' name, amen."

Hollan listened as he finished up his prayer and felt a sense of peace flow through her. She released to Him all the fears and concerns she'd carried. For the first time in a while, she felt the burdens she'd carried alone lift. She held only one small concern back for herself. She knew she was supposed to turn *everything* over to God, to let Him watch over all aspects of her life, but in this one small area she still felt she needed to keep control, at least for a little bit longer. For now, for just a little bit longer, she still felt the need to keep the permanent return of her vision a secret from Jacob.

Chapter 7

After two days in bed, Hollan couldn't wait any longer to get out and explore the island. She understood Jacob's overprotective nature after a blow to her head, but she wanted to get up. She had a lot to celebrate. Her *vision* had returned! It hadn't wavered once. She sent a covert glance at Jacob. And neither had the man she still loved. He'd returned and now stayed close to her side. But that all-important detail aside, at the moment she only wanted to see the places and things she loved through new eyes. And even better would be to see everything with Jacob by her side.

"We're going out to explore today." Hollan settled at the table, not leaving her comment up for debate. "I feel completely ready to go outside and breathe in some fresh air. If I have to stay inside another day, I'll surely go insane."

"You will, huh?" Jacob set an aromatic plate of eggs in front of her before taking his seat. "We certainly don't want that. A little fresh air won't hurt, but you'll need to take it slow."

"Yes, doc." She busied herself with eating, not wanting to waste a moment of the brilliant day that waited outside their doorstep. "Jacob, these eggs are wonderful. Where'd you learn to cook like this?"

"All over the place." He stabbed at an egg, and she took the moment to study him. His damp hair was slicked back from his forehead. "When you travel like I did, you meet up with a lot of different people. I had to work a lot of odd jobs in order to make ends meet."

"How did you end up choosing to do that? What made you decide to become a traveling preacher? I don't remember you ever talking about wanting to do such a thing."

What she really wanted to ask was why he'd left her behind. From the way he froze in place, fork halfway to his mouth while contemplating his answer, she knew she'd hit a sore spot.

"That night I left, a lot of bad things happened." He laid his fork down and reached over to toy with her hand. She had a hard time not staring into his eyes. She wanted to lose herself in them. But he couldn't know about the return of her vision. Not yet. She didn't want him to leave. She wasn't ready for that possibility. She needed more time. She needed to solidify their relationship.

"I remember."

"I know you do." He pulled his hand away and ran it through his hair, the gesture reassuringly familiar. "I couldn't face anyone after what my father and brothers did to the people of our town. So when they fled, I chased them up the trail. They scattered, and I tailed them one at a time. Each time I'd catch one, I turned him over to the law." He picked up his fork and used it to push the eggs back and forth, but he didn't eat any of them.

"That had to be hard." Hollan ached for him, for the pain he had to have felt each time he had to turn in a brother. "You found your father, too?"

"Someone else found him first. I found his body soon after."

"That's awful." What else could she say to that? Though she longed to know what had happened to her father, finding his body wasn't something she could imagine. She didn't want to contemplate it further. "And the others, what happened to them?"

"I found all but one. They'll spend a lot of time behind bars, if not worse. I didn't stick around to see what happened."

"Which one evaded you?"

"David."

He seemed to be studying her face for a reaction. She stared at his chin. His expression turned quizzical when she didn't have one.

"So you decided to let him go, and instead you returned home?"

"No, I trailed him back this way. I don't intend to stop looking until he joins our other brothers behind bars."

"So you're only here for a short while?"

"I married you, Hollan. I'm with you for life. I meant my vows when I said them."

Her heart leaped at his words. Maybe she wouldn't have to keep her secret as long as she thought. She tested him.

"But you were forced into the marriage. You might change your mind if. . ." She let her voice trail off, not sure what to say.

"If what?" His voice held a chuckle. "I made my commitment for life, Hollan."

He stood to gather their plates and moved out of her line of vision. Her *newly returned* vision. A hint of a smile broadened her lips. She savored the thought and forced herself not to track him with her eyes.

"Well, I don't know. What if you get bored? What if you catch your brother and want to travel again? I understand you wanted to return home and right the wrongs of your family, but once that's all behind you, maybe you'll want to wander again."

"Not likely." This time there was no humor after the statement. "A person can only wander for so long before life catches up with them. And in my case, it was time for me to return."

"So what about David?"

He helped her up from her chair and led the way to the door. "I'll know what to do when the time comes. God has led me to each of them in turn. I don't know why David came back. He already caused all the pain he possibly could. But for whatever reason, God has been urging me back this way for a while now, and I've ignored Him. Next thing I know, my quarry turned this way and led me home."

"Interesting." Hollan wished he'd come back because he missed her. But they were married and working on their new relationship. That had to be enough. She'd try to be patient and see what happened next.

"Enough of that. Let's go explore and see what the hurricane did to our home."

Our home. The words were so simple, yet they meant so much to her. She wasn't alone anymore.

Jacob tugged her toward the inland channel. "How about we start at the dock? I want to check the boat."

Hollan nodded her agreement.

Jacob led her down the path toward the water at a leisurely pace, walking slightly ahead. She held back just a bit, wanting to look around without him taking notice. She savored every single sight. The brilliant green of the trees stood out against the vivid blue of the sky. The seagulls circled overhead, scavenging for small crabs and fish. They neared the sandy beach, and the water lapped at the shore, tossing tiny shells and clams with the movement. The sea oats danced in the slight breeze. Hollan wanted to dance along with them. Pelicans and herons dove for their dinner in the distance. And decidedly the best view of all was that of Jacob walking just ahead of her. Her beloved Jacob. She studied his broad shoulders and the way his waist narrowed at the hips. The muscles in his arms flexed as he cleared debris from their path. The sun shone off his golden hair, which he'd again pulled back and tied at the nape of his neck. He was truly a striking man.

Jacob's grunt pulled her from her perusal. He'd stopped just ahead of her. She wanted to wrap her arms around him and press her cheek against his back, but instead she hurried to stand at his side. She glanced at the dock.

Only one thing seemed to be missing—one major thing. She put her hand to her forehead and scanned the open waters.

"The boat's gone." Jacob stated the obvious just before Hollan blurted it out. At the rate she was going, she'd surely clue him in about the return of her sight. Jacob didn't notice—he was too focused on the missing boat.

"Gone. . .where?"

Jacob reached over to clutch her hand. "I have no idea. I didn't think the storm would have done that much damage to this side of the island. It's more protected."

"Odd."

"Yes, it is." His voice held a funny tone.

"Are you thinking someone tampered with it?"

"I'm not sure. But it can't have floated off on its own."

"The supply boat won't be here for days. This means we're on our own until then."

"It looks that way." They'd reached the dock, and Jacob released her hand as he bent low to check out the dock and surrounding water. He stood back up, hands on hips, and glanced around again. "This is so strange. There's no sign of it at all."

"The storm likely blew it away. I doubt we'll ever find it."

"What now?"

"There's nothing we can do until Fletcher returns."

He clasped her hand again and led her down the shoreline path. His hand felt solid and reassuring. "Let's walk some more. Maybe it washed ashore. If so, we'll come across it. If not, I still want to see what other damage the storm did to our island."

They walked in silence, and more than once Hollan's eyes blurred with tears of happiness. A lizard skittered across the path and disappeared in the overgrown foliage to her left. A large turtle floated in the water just offshore. The water was so clear here that she could see the turtle's shadow on the sandy bottom as it moved along. A mockingbird sang from somewhere in the dense trees overhead. She'd missed these sights dearly. And because she never dared to walk very far, she'd missed a lot of the shoreline's sounds. Hollan took a deep breath, breathing in the salt-laden air. The vivid blue of the sky almost hurt her eyes, but she embraced the sensation. She'd never been happier to squint.

Jacob slowed. "Where does that path lead? I've never noticed it before."

"What path?"

Jacob tugged her inland, a small path barely visible through the dense jungle of palmettos and scrub that made most of the island impenetrable. "It leads through the undergrowth. It looks like at one time it would have been used quite often, but now it's almost completely overgrown."

"Sounds like the path to Amos's old place." Hollan was beginning to hate the farce she'd put into motion. If only she had complete surety that the return of her vision wouldn't cause a negative change in their budding friendship.

"Amos?" Jacob took the lead through the tunnel of vegetation. Hollan's skirts were snagged and tugged by the ends of the palmettos' sharp fronds. She didn't care. She'd happily sacrifice the old dress she wore for the experience and adventure of refamiliarizing herself with the interior of the island. Especially when it meant Jacob would hold her close against his side as he did now.

"He helped my grandfather when he first took over the lighthouse, before my father had the contract. He had a small shack somewhere around here."

"Let's find it."

"If it's even standing." She laughed. "It's been around for a long time, and you know how harsh the weather can be."

"It's still here."

Sure enough, it was. And it looked surprisingly solid. Of course she couldn't admit that to him.

The door screeched as he pulled it open. Hollan screamed as a bat flew out, barely skimming her head.

"Sorry about that." Jacob pulled her into a quick embrace. "It's gone now."

Hollan shuddered. She'd never liked the creatures of the night. Suddenly the area felt dark and oppressive. She couldn't imagine how much worse it would be if she couldn't see. Snakes loved to lurk on this section of the island, along with alligators and all sorts of other creatures.

"If you've seen enough, I'm ready to go back to the shore."

"No, actually, I want to look a little closer. Other than the bats—"

"Plural? I thought there was only one!" Hollan reached up and scrubbed at her hair with both hands. "They're gone, aren't they?" She spun in a circle.

"They all flew away. You're fine." She didn't comment on the chuckle she heard in his tone. He stood in the open doorway. "But it looks like someone has been here recently. The interior isn't as rough as I'd expect after all these years."

Hollan stepped closer and grabbed hold of Jacob's arm. "Someone or—something?"

"Someone. The floor is cleared, and there's a sign of fire. Let me duck inside."

"All the more reason to leave."

"I'll only be a moment."

"You do know there are snakes and gators around here? Don't leave me for long."

Hollan hugged her arms around her waist and scoured the area for signs of predators. A bubbling stream ran along the opposite side of the small clearing. Though she much preferred being outside in the open rather than being inside the tiny bat-infested cabin, her mind was quickly conjuring up quite a few alarming scenarios of possible creatures lurking at her feet.

"Um, Jacob? I'm hearing scurrying sounds in the brush. Not something I like to stand here and listen to. My imagination's racing out here."

"I'm ready." His sudden appearance at her side made her jump. "Let's get you out of here. But I'll be watching the place, and if someone is using this cabin, I'll find out."

"Sounds good to me. Meanwhile, I'll stick to waiting on one of the nice, clean, wide-open paths on the beach when you check."

Jacob laughed.

They cut across the island toward the ocean and reached the main path. Hollan breathed a sigh of relief. The sigh ended in a cough as she inhaled the sharp odor of rotting fish. Quite a few of them lay scattered at their feet. "Whoa. Lots of fish washed ashore in this area after the storm."

Jacob turned her way, eyes squinting, his forehead creased. Hollan covered quickly, waving her hand in front of her wrinkled nose.

He laughed. "It *is* a bit potent."

"It's the aroma of home. I like it."

"You are an island girl through and through, aren't you?"

"Always and forever." Hollan couldn't imagine living anywhere else. She didn't want to *think* about living anywhere else.

"Hollan, there's something we need to talk about."

Her heart plummeted. Here it came. She didn't want to hear what he had to say. "Oh listen! The waves are louder and the birds more vocal. We're nearing the ocean side, aren't we?"

"Yes." He squeezed her hand. "Hollan, don't change the subject."

Intent on savoring the newest view, she didn't answer. The Atlantic Ocean seemed to stretch out forever before her. Shells scattered at her feet, begging for her attention. She loved walking with Jacob, but she couldn't wait to make her escape in the near future and spend a morning enjoying her favorite pastime, looking for seashells and pirate treasure.

"Hollan?"

"I'm sorry." She kept her gaze down and moved forward.

"Anyway, as I was saying, we have to discuss what will happen if the lighthouse inspector arrives and decides that we can't stay."

She froze. "Decides we can't stay? Why would he decide that?" The panic made her voice rise. She hadn't even thought about that possibility.

"The contract for the lighthouse is with your father, not with us. I don't know how that all works, but he might have someone else in mind to take over for your father—now that he is missing."

"Well, he can just wait." She set her jaw, daring him to disagree. "We have no—*proof* that my father isn't coming back. Until we do, we need to protect his job."

"You have a point. We'll keep that as our plan for now." He gently guided her face to look up into his. "But you have to keep in mind that we might need an alternate plan."

Hollan carefully avoided his gaze after one quick glimpse of his beautiful green eyes. She had to end this farce—tomorrow. She wanted one more day to savor the sights and Jacob's presence before telling him how drastically things had changed. He seemed genuine in his commitment, but he didn't have all the facts. "There'll be no plan other than the one that allows us to stay on this island."

"As you wish." He smirked. "I suppose we can always move into Amos's place. Quarters might be tight, but I think we could make do. I certainly could."

Hollan stared straight ahead, but she felt the flush wash over her features. *Close quarters* would be an understatement. "There would be bugs and snakes and other equally horrible things. I couldn't even imagine."

"I'd batten it down. I'll make sure they don't get you."

"We'd have no beds. We'd have to—" The blush continued. "We'd have no room to move around."

"I'd hold you close and keep you safe."

Hollan didn't know what to say to that. She'd love to have him hold her close at night and keep her safe. But she wasn't sure she was ready for all the changes that would bring to their relationship. They were married after all, but she hadn't kept up with all the changes as it was. She needed them to take things slow. But he'd slept inside the cottage—albeit in a chair—for the past three nights. He'd watched over her since the hurricane. She didn't want to send him back to the lighthouse now.

"That might be—tolerable."

"Tolerable?" He choked on a laugh, his profile showing his dimples.

She shrugged. "I'd do my best to adapt."

"Tell me, which part might be merely tolerable? Living in the cabin?" He stepped close behind her and whispered in her ear. "Or being held in my arms at night?"

Hollan shivered. "If necessity mandated such a situation, I'd probably survive both conditions."

"You'd *probably* survive them?" Jacob laughed out loud. "That's nice to know."

He spun her around and pulled her close. She knew he was going to kiss her. She closed her eyes. He planted several soft kisses on her lips, and she felt herself respond and kiss him back.

"I've missed you, Hollan."

She asked the question that had bothered her for so long. "Then why'd you leave?"

"It's complicated. But my decision to leave that night had nothing to do with my feelings for you. My love for you has never changed."

Hollan's heart swelled. "I'm glad to know that."

"I'd like to tell you about it soon."

"Maybe tonight at dinner?"

"I don't know. You've had a busy morning, and I want you to rest. I think we need to get lunch, you need to lie down, and we'll see what the evening brings later."

"You're avoiding me."

"I wouldn't say I'm avoiding you exactly. . . . I'm just trying to give you the time to heal. Besides your head injury, you've lost your father. I want to take things slow. We have our whole life ahead of us, and there's no reason to hurry while we're muddling through all the changes."

"I have faith that my father is alive. My head injury is fine." Hollan's good spirits began to slip away. He was echoing her thoughts from a moment earlier that they needed to take things slow, yet now she found herself pushing forward. "When you use the word *muddling* as you just did, it feels as if you think you're stuck here in this awful. . .*quagmire*. . .or something with me."

"I'm not *stuck* in anything with you, Hollan, and I'm sorry if it came across that way." She leaned against his chest, and he rested his chin on her head. "I know I'm where God led me to be. I'm perfectly content to be where I am. I love being married to you, and I can only hope that in a very short time we'll be living as a married couple in every way."

"Then why—?"

"I won't take advantage of you in a vulnerable state. I want to make sure you're coming to me freely when we make this marriage real. I'll sleep in the lighthouse for tonight, and we'll see what tomorrow brings—tomorrow."

Disappointment rolled over Hollan, but she knew he was right. They'd work things out as they went. But she knew she'd miss his presence in the cottage tonight.

They circled around toward the dunes in front of their home, and Jacob led her directly toward a piece of driftwood. She panicked. If she stepped over it, he'd know. If she had to trip, she'd feel like an idiot. It served her right for her deceit.

She slowed just as she reached the limb and bent down to fumble with her boot.

"Is everything all right?"

"Everything is fine, thank you."

"So we can continue on?"

"Yes."

At that slower pace, she had no trouble kicking her foot toward the driftwood. Jacob stopped her.

"There's a piece of wood in front of us. Come this way, and we'll go around it."

"Thanks," she mumbled.

"We need to head up to the cottage."

"Let's keep going." Hollan wanted to see it all. Everything she'd missed seeing for the past three years.

"No. You need to get back and rest. And I need to check the lighthouse."

When she started to protest, he put a finger against her lips.

"You suffered a huge blow to the head. I don't want you to overtax yourself. We'll walk the other way in the morning." They continued in the direction of the dunes. "If you want us to save our post, we need to be ready and have things perfect at any given time."

"Good point." She sighed. "I'll come up with you." She couldn't wait to see the view from atop the lighthouse!

"You'll return to the cottage and sleep."

She made a disgruntled sound, and Jacob laughed. "You'll be up to par soon enough, wife. You need to have patience."

Wife. She grinned. "I'm up to par now. My tyrant of a husband just won't let me prove it."

Silence met her hasty retort, and she wondered if she had inadvertently offended him. Instead her eyes widened as Jacob leaned in for another gentle kiss. "I'm sure you have a lot to prove, wife, and I anticipate and look forward to each and every revelation."

He accentuated the word *revelation*. Was he insinuating something? Her guilt had her constantly returning to her deception. She stubbornly stood her ground. She liked things as they were. She didn't want to mess things up.

He captured her gaze with his own, and she swooned. She stepped backward. Jacob caught her by the arm. "Dizzy?"

"A—a bit maybe." She put a hand to her forehead and feigned exhaustion. No way would she admit that it was his kiss that threw her off balance. "I think you're right about my lying down."

"I'll get you settled then."

She ignored the laughter in his voice. She hadn't fooled him in the least.

Chapter 8

Hollan rose at dawn, determined to get an early start on her day. She figured the best way to effectively avoid Jacob would be to ease out the door well before their usual meeting time. He wouldn't be happy with her, but she needed some time alone. She wanted to be able to explore without hiding the fact that she could see. Today she'd tell him about the return of her vision—just as soon as she took this walk along the shore.

She had a feeling their relationship would take a turn for the better after she cleared the air. She looked forward to sharing her news. She hadn't liked sleeping alone in the cottage after having Jacob there the three nights before. She wanted their marriage to be real.

If Jacob felt she didn't need him anymore and he decided to move on, she'd work through the situation day by day, just as she'd dealt with every other challenge in her life. But she hoped and prayed he wouldn't decide that because she really did need him. She knew now that her love for him had never diminished; it had merely been buried somewhere deep inside.

Hollan stood before the mirror and smiled at her reflection. Today she could brush and style her auburn hair, and she would know what the end result actually looked like. She'd picked her favorite dress to wear and loved how the deep blue color she'd never seen before so perfectly matched the hue of the sea. Her brown eyes sparkled with excitement in the mirror's reflection. Soon she'd be walking along the beach, scouring the soft sand for shells. Seagulls called to her through the open cottage door. The waves pounded the shoreline in the distance, promising interesting treasure.

Mindful of the time, she hurried to prepare a batch of blueberry muffins. She arranged them on a plate and set a flowered bowl of butter and a matching one of jam beside them. Guilt had her scurrying to the garden for a pretty arrangement of flowers. Jacob likely wouldn't notice, but if he did, maybe he'd realize she'd taken the extra step to make her absence less harsh. Then again, he'd probably not even miss her and would be thrilled to have a morning meal without the awkwardness of their usual forced routine, though she had to admit their camaraderie felt more natural compared to before her accident. She now felt a certain comfort in the presence of her husband.

When she couldn't think of anything else to do, she hurried out the door. Samson tried to follow, but she knew his barking would draw Jacob's attention. She blocked him with her leg and forced the door shut behind her. The dog would get even by leading Jacob straight to her side but hopefully not before she'd had plenty of time to savor the beauty of her surroundings. And when they arrived, she'd happily share her news with Jacob, and she'd ask him to move into the cottage so they could properly live like the married couple they were.

Hollan wasted no time moving past the lighthouse and let out a sigh of relief after she'd cleared the stone walls. Once on the beach, she breathed even easier. No voice called out to stop her. No footsteps pounded down the hard-packed sand walkway in her wake.

Her bare feet sank deep into the coolness of the powdery soft sand at the water's edge, and she laughed out loud, wiggling her toes in order to bury them deeper. She wanted to do so many different things. She wanted to swim, to explore, and to merely sit and savor. But first she had to make haste and get far away from here. She followed the shore in the direction they'd been heading the previous day. A tide pool usually formed just around the curve of the farthest dune, and she hoped to find it alive with crawling creatures. While she didn't care for most of the land-type creatures, she loved each and every one of the aquatic types.

And suddenly there it was—the tide pool—spread out before her, sparkling in the morning sun. From a distance the tide pool looked placid, just a thin layer of water filling up the slight depression in the sand. But Hollan knew it would contain a whole underwater world full of sea creatures. Smiling, she dropped to her knees on the dry sand and studied the undersea world before her. She'd often wished in the past, as a little girl, that she could shrink down and be able to swim with the inhabitants. Now she was content just to be able to watch the miniature world. Everything she could see was a blessing and a privilege. She'd never take her vision for granted again.

Tiny coquina clams waved their siphons around, waiting for algae or plankton, not knowing they were a target themselves for the scavenging seagulls that flew overhead. Hermit crabs, their shells shiny and multicolored, glistened as they scurried across the bottom of the pool. A small blue crab lurked behind a rounded rock. A group of tiny fish swam together, twisting and turning with perfect precision. The scent of sea blew in on the breeze.

Hollan moved her fingers through the surface of the water, smiling as the clams pulled their siphons under the sand. The blue crab disappeared from sight when her hand's shadow moved too close. The hermit crabs pulled back into their shells. The fish darted away to the far side of the pool.

Something brushed against her foot, and she looked over to see a curious ghost crab hurrying away. It blended in with the color of the beach and disappeared down a tunnel dug into the sand nearby. She felt as if her favorite friends had all gathered to welcome her back. All these aquatic creatures she'd missed for so long. She sat and savored the sights.

Hollan settled onto her hip and curved her legs beneath her. She dug her fingers into the sand and let it sift through them as she breathed a heartfelt prayer of thanks for the return of her vision. She knew God had a purpose in returning her sight, but this moment defined why she personally valued the ability to see. Her entire world here at the beach revolved around the land and the creatures she loved so much.

She glanced up. Fluffy white clouds moved across the brilliant blue sky. The water wasn't quite as brown as it had been the day before. The sediment churned up by the storm was settling, allowing the water to return to its natural blue-green color.

Hollan wished she could throw caution to the wind and run out into the waves. But she wouldn't. Jacob would probably be along soon, looking for his errant wife.

Instead she stood slowly to her feet and began to move farther down the beach. She stayed close to the waterline, not wanting to miss a treasure. Though most shells lay in pieces, tossed and broken by the surf, a few choice shells made it through the treacherous waters. One particularly delicate-looking shell washed up at her feet. The wave flipped it upside down to show a perfect outer shell, the color bleached white by the sun.

Hollan picked it up, feeling a strange kinship with the item. She'd add it to her collection. She tucked the shell into her pocket. Several starfish and sea horses had washed in, too. She carefully lifted them and settled them back in the water. Most floated atop the water and drifted out to sea. But a few gave halfhearted efforts to swim before seeming to realize they were once again free to swim away to safety.

She was fully absorbed in her observations of the sea life at her feet. Hollan didn't notice the arrival of a large ship until the sound of men's voices carried to her from across the water. She stood watching the activity aboard ship, deciding it was likely a renegade privateer ship from the war. She knew from her father that a select few still sailed up and down the coast.

Fascinated, she raised her hand to her forehead, shading her eyes so she could study the magnificent vessel.

"What have we here, gentlemen?"

Hollan jumped and swung around as a voice spoke close behind her. The hair stood up on the back of her neck.

A rough-looking man stood just to her right, and a bit farther back three others stood and leered at her. None of them looked like gentlemen as far as she was concerned.

She slowly backed away. She hadn't heard the arrival of the small boat that was now pulled up behind her down the shore. A shiver passed through her. For the first time that day, she prayed for Jacob to hurry and find her.

"I think we have a damsel in distress," one of the men muttered. "We need to *rescue* her."

They erupted into a semblance of laughter, the sound rusty, as if they hadn't laughed in a very long time. The grating sounds sent another round of shivers down her spine.

"Thank you, but I'm not in need of rescue." She turned and hurried in the opposite direction, on a path that would lead her directly back to Jacob. She wanted to run headlong into his strong embrace and never leave the warmth of his protective arms again. She wanted to tell him about the return of her vision. She wanted to say that she loved him. She suddenly realized that if a person waited too long, things could happen that would prevent those moments from ever happening. She prayed this wasn't one of them. She'd just regained her vision. She didn't want to lose her life.

A rough hand grasped her shoulder and spun her around. "It's rude to walk away from someone when they're talking."

"It's rude to place your hand upon a woman you've never met. Please release me at once," Hollan gritted out through her teeth.

"Ah, we've caught ourselves a spunky one, men."

They all laughed.

"You haven't *caught* me at all. I'm not a fish." Hollan fought off a wave of fear and held her ground.

"Ah, that's good! She's not a fish." The closest man mocked her.

Hollan tried to jerk from his grasp. "My husband will be along at any moment, and he won't be any too pleased to find you taking liberties with me."

If only it was true. She had no idea when Jacob would come looking for her, or even if he'd look at all.

"Then we'd best get back to the ship at once."

Her momentary relief turned into full-fledged panic when the closest man grabbed her roughly by the arm and dragged her toward their small wooden craft. She fought with everything she had, but that wasn't much. She might as well have been a feather for all the good it did.

She managed one more glance over her shoulder before they forced her into the boat, but the beach behind her remained empty.

Jacob finished his morning chores and headed down for breakfast. He stopped by his tiny room, which was in dire need of cleaning, and hurried to freshen it up. He didn't think Hollan would mind if he took a few minutes to tidy things. And if he didn't take the time to clean it now, he knew she'd eventually make her way out and clean it for him. He made the small bed—the only item pushed against the north wall of the room—and gathered a few pieces of clothes into a pile. He went outside to dump the pitcher of water that had sat forgotten upon his small table on the opposite side of the room before returning to put everything else back in place. Hooks on the remaining wall—the one opposite the door—held the only other clothes he owned.

When he decided the room was clean enough, he bundled up the clothes to be washed and headed over to greet his wife. He needed to talk to her about several things. He laid his laundry down near the washtub. Hollan would insist on doing his laundry, but he'd insist just as hard on doing it himself. Until they lived in the same house as husband and wife, he wouldn't expect her to do his clothes. And that very topic was one he intended to bring up. He'd been lonely last night and wanted things to change.

His feelings for Hollan hadn't ever wavered. Though their marriage hadn't come about quite the way they'd planned, they were still married. It was silly to live apart as they were. He just hoped she returned his feelings.

If she didn't, he'd be patient and wait. In time she'd surely grow to love him the same way he loved her.

Samson barked from inside the cottage, and Jacob grinned. The dog had heard his arrival. Surprisingly, he didn't hear Hollan hush him as usual with her melodic lilting voice. He'd come to rely on the familiar sound at the start of his day.

The early morning sun beat down on his head. Though the autumn nights were cooling down, the days were staying warm. Judging by the way the sun heated his back, today would be a hot one. The cool interior of the cottage beckoned him.

Jacob knocked and pushed open the door. "Good morning."

Samson almost knocked him down in his hurry to get past and out into the yard, but Hollan didn't answer Jacob's greeting or bother to call Samson back.

With a whine, Samson wound himself around Jacob's legs.

"Hollan?" Jacob had a warning sensation that something wasn't right. He reached down and rubbed Samson on the head. "Where is she, boy?"

Samson glanced up at him with worried eyes.

Jacob moved into the empty room and let his eyes adjust to the dim interior. The table was set for one. The bed lay empty and neat. She'd taken time to pull the quilt up. She hadn't left in a hurry. The fire burned low, but she'd finished breakfast preparations before departing.

Maybe Fletcher had arrived early with the supply boat. Knowing Hollan, she'd have walked along with him to bring back supplies. Jacob glanced around. The few times he'd seen Fletcher, he hadn't wasted time. If he'd arrived at Hollan's door, he'd have carried something along. No sign of packages or supplies sat anywhere nearby.

He sighed. More than likely Hollan had left early in order to be alone. He tended to be a tad overbearing when it came to her. He knew she didn't like to be coddled, but he couldn't help himself. He hadn't protected her three years earlier when he'd needed to, and he didn't ever want to mess up again.

"Ah, I see." Jacob put his hands on his hips and looked at Samson. "She snuck out and left us both behind, is that it?" He walked to the table and surveyed the arrangement. "Well, we might as well show our appreciation as long as she went to the trouble of setting it all out."

The aroma of fresh-baked muffins permeated the room.

Samson wagged his tail. Jacob slipped into a chair and held a muffin high over his head. Samson stood on his hind legs, begged for a moment, then tired of the game and jumped to snatch the delicacy from Jacob's hand. He hurried away to eat his prize at his favorite place near the fire.

Jacob frowned and spread some butter on his own muffin. It was lonely here without Hollan. Without her presence, he'd have preferred to eat outside. But the flowers on the table showed the care she'd put into making the table pretty for him, and he wouldn't chance moving out front only to have her return and jump to the wrong conclusion.

As he ate, he mulled over his thoughts. He was sure Hollan was hiding something from him, and he was pretty sure he knew what her secret was. Ever since she'd recovered from her storm injuries, she'd been skittish. Something in her eyes had changed. She'd looked right into his eyes a few times before catching herself and turning away. He didn't want to jump to conclusions, either, but he was pretty sure she'd regained her vision, at least partially.

Why she wouldn't tell him, he didn't know. He'd tried to figure it out, but he'd stopped trying to understand her years ago. Whatever her reason, he'd find out soon enough.

He wanted to go after her but decided to give her a little more time. She'd been through some hard times. He wanted her to feel free and comfortable enough to confide in him whenever she decided the time was right. He wanted to move forward and have a life and a future with her. But a part of him worried that she might be having second thoughts. Maybe the return of her sight had her thinking she didn't need Jacob at all. If so, they needed to talk things out. She needed him, and he'd be the first to explain that fact to her.

Jacob wasn't one to tiptoe around a delicate circumstance—he preferred to plunge headfirst into every situation that crossed his path. He wouldn't do anything different with this one.

While he waited for her to return, he decided to tend the garden. A little hard work would clear his mind and help him think. The growing season was almost over, and only a few vegetables remained on the vines. He picked the tomatoes that were ready and put them in a nearby bucket. He pulled the last few weeds. Next year he'd like to expand the garden's size. If there would be a next year.

The thought led him back to wondering about Hollan.

He put down the hoe and walked over to the dunes. Hollan's small footprints led down toward the beach. The impressions of her bare feet showed that, once again, she'd left her boots behind.

Enough was enough. It was time for Jacob to go after his wife. He wanted to feel her in his arms.

He walked over to the cottage's open door. Samson lay sprawled just inside the cool interior.

"C'mon, boy. Want to go with me to find Hollan?"

Samson almost bowled him over in his hurry to get outside. Obviously he didn't intend to be left behind again. They headed up the path. Jacob stopped at the lighthouse door.

"I need to check on something first, boy. Stay."

Samson whined again but stayed where Jacob pointed. Jacob hurried up to the top of the lighthouse, no easy feat with the multiple stairs he had to climb. He stepped onto the platform that circled the top and looked out over the island. Samson lay where he left him down below.

He didn't see any sign of Hollan, but he did see a large ship offshore. An uneasy feeling settled over him. He walked a bit farther around the platform to a better vantage point. His breath caught as he located Hollan. A small boat had been pulled ashore.

His wife was so enraptured by whatever lay at her feet that she didn't appear to notice the men coming up from behind her. From the stealthy way they walked, he sensed they were up to no good.

"Hollan!" His voice blew away on the breeze. He spun on his heel and rushed back to the stairs. He forced himself not to take them two at a time, a recipe for disaster. He couldn't afford to take a tumble. Hollan would be gone forever if that happened. She might be even as it was.

Samson stood at the ready, the hair on the nape of his neck standing on end.

"Go, boy, go to Hollan."

The dog tore away over the dunes and disappeared from sight. Jacob followed along as quickly as he could. The sand pulled at his heavy boots, slowing him even as he pushed to go faster. He didn't have a weapon, and he had no idea what he'd do once he reached her. But he'd do whatever was necessary to keep his wife safe.

God, please protect Hollan. Help me reach her in time.

His feet slipped in the sand as he rounded the bend and approached the last place he'd seen his wife. He put his hand down to stop his tumble and landed on his knees. There was no sign of Hollan there now. The rowboat was halfway to the ship, too far away for him to have any hope of reaching it. From this distance, he couldn't tell if she was on board.

"Hollan!" No one aboard the small craft looked his way. The wind blew against him. They wouldn't hear him any more than Hollan had heard him from the lighthouse.

Samson stood chest deep at the water's edge and growled, confirming to Jacob what he already knew. Hollan was on the small boat.

Chapter 9

Hollan sat rigidly at the front of the small rowboat, glaring at her four captors. Two of them perched on the middle seat with their backs toward her while they rowed the small vessel closer to the large ship. The others sprawled on the remaining seat at the back of the boat, steadfastly glaring back at her. On closer observation she realized that one glared while the other tried his best to do the same through an obviously damaged eye. His left eye was swollen shut, and dark blue bruises spread outward from the edges.

She studied him, the smaller of the two, and winced. She vaguely remembered making the connection with her fist. "I'm truly sorry about your face."

An apology probably wouldn't make much difference at this time, but she figured she might as well try. She had no idea what awaited her aboard the ship, but surely arriving there after having assaulted one of the crew wouldn't work well in her favor.

The man didn't answer, but his good eye narrowed further.

"In my defense, you shouldn't sneak up behind a person like that. Surely you know the natural instinct is to swing around with a fist at the ready."

"I ne'er expected a lady to swing in such a way at all," the man muttered. He gingerly touched the area in question. "Or that a lady would connect with such accuracy."

"Because I'm a lady I'm supposed to just turn myself over to a bunch of scoundrels without a fight? Is that what you're saying?"

She folded her arms across her chest. Her bare foot tapped against the wooden floor with annoyance.

"It ain't polite to call people names, missy."

"It *isn't* polite to kidnap people, either." She raised one eyebrow and stared until he looked away.

The men in the middle rowed on without missing a beat. Each stroke brought them closer to their ship and farther away from Jacob. The methodical sound of their oars slapping against the water made Hollan want to scream. Every once in a while the wind would reverse and blow a whiff of their odor her way. She quickly figured out it was best to hold her breath under a direct assault and to breathe through her mouth the rest of the time.

Cloudless blue skies stretched high overhead. The sun shone down on the water, dappling on the tiny waves, just as it had when she was onshore. The gulls continued to scavenge for food. Nothing had changed, yet for her, nothing was the same.

While the injured man continued to look out over the water, the man beside him cleared his throat in an attempt to catch her attention. "Speakin' of faces, you're not sorry for mine?"

Hollan studied him for a moment and forced back the snide comment that first came to mind. She wasn't doing a very good job at keeping her thoughts kind. His perpetually bewildered expression wasn't likely any fault of his own. She noticed the bridge of his nose tilted at an odd angle, but she assumed it had been broken before. Then she noticed the trail of blood that led from his nose to his beard.

"Oh my." Her brows pulled close. "Did I do that to your nose, too?"

"You did."

"But when—?"

"You fought like a wildcat when we first grabbed you."

"Of course I did. Wouldn't you?"

"Then you snapped your head back into my nose."

"And I'm supposed to apologize to *you* for that? You grabbed me around the waist. Perhaps if you didn't snatch innocent women off beaches, you'd not end up injured."

"I told ya we should have left her there. She's gonna be nothin' but trouble." The man with the swollen eye returned his scowl to her.

"Couldn't leave her, Paxton. Cap'n gave us orders."

Hollan shook her head, trying to clear it. "He gave you orders to bring back a woman?"

"He gave us orders to bring back *you*." Swollen Eye—or Paxton—sneered.

"But how would he know about me?"

"Dunno. But he does, and you walked right into our arms."

"Hardly."

"Regardless, we didn't have any choice but to follow orders."

"You always have a choice," Hollan stated. "Are you nothing but slaves? This man—the captain—why would you allow him to order you around like that? Why would you want to do wrong on someone else's behalf?"

One of the men in the middle laughed. "It's his job to order us around." He glanced at the man beside him. "How dumb is this woman anyway?"

"I'm not dumb at all." Hollan tried to keep the hurt from her voice. "I'm only trying to understand why you'd choose to live this way."

Broken Nose gave her a sympathetic look. "There's no call to say mean things like that, Nate."

Hollan nodded. "Thank you. That was very kind."

He beamed at her. Nate sent her a glare.

"Look, if I had my way, you wouldn't be here at all. It's bad luck for a woman to go aboard ship. Just look at what's happened to Paxton and Jonathon." Nate nodded toward the men.

So the man with the broken nose is apparently named Jonathon. "If you believe that, then return me to shore."

Nate didn't answer. He just kept rowing toward the vessel. They were almost to the ship. If she wanted out of this situation, she needed to act fast.

"Paxton. Jonathon. Please. You seem like nice enough men."

They both looked away.

"Idiotic is more like it," Nate snarled. "Now sit tight and be quiet. You're going to see the captain, like it or not."

Panic threatened to overwhelm Hollan, but she forced it away. She had to keep her thoughts straight. She sat quietly, not moving until they bumped against the side of the larger vessel.

"Ladies first." Nate laughed. He stood and grabbed her by the arm, pulling her to her feet.

Hollan looked back at him, blank. "I'm sure I don't know what you mean."

He motioned at the rope ladder that dangled over the side of the ship. "See that ladder in front of you? Climb it."

"I will not." She sat back down and folded her arms.

"Oh, but you will." He grabbed her arm again.

"You're hurting me."

"I'll hurt you a lot worse if you don't do as I say and get up that ladder."

Tears of anger and frustration poured down Hollan's cheeks. She snatched at the ropes and began her ascent. The skirt of her dress, still drenched from her trek when they dragged her through the water, snagged at her feet. She'd made it halfway up when she lost her grip. With a scream of terror, she plunged to the boat below. The boat rocked wildly back and forth but didn't capsize.

"Miss, are you all right?" Jonathon helped her to her feet.

"I—I think so. Nate broke my fall." She turned to thank him, but he lay still on the bottom of the boat. "Nate?"

The other man, the only one she hadn't injured at this point, stared at her, speechless. "Nate was right. You *are* bad luck."

She rolled her eyes. "There's no such thing as bad luck."

The man leaned away from her, fear filling his face. "I don't know about you two"—he glanced over at Paxton and Jonathon—"but I'm not sticking around to see what she does next."

"Matt, what about Nate?"

"Leave 'im."

Matt turned and scaled the ladder and disappeared from sight in a way that left Hollan envious.

"I didn't mean to hurt him."

She took a step toward Jonathon. He looked from her to Paxton.

Paxton took advantage of her inattention and followed Matt up the ladder. "Don't let her get away, Jonathon."

"But—I—" Hollan had no idea where they thought she would go.

Paxton made it up the ladder with surprising grace and disappeared from sight.

"I guess it's just you and me, Jonathon." Hollan put on her most charming smile.

"You, me, and the dead man." Jonathon eased around Nate and headed for the ladder.

Hollan huffed out a breath. "He's not dead; I just knocked him unconscious—or something."

"No offense, ma'am. Deep down you seem like a nice lady and all. But I don't intend to stick around and see how you hurt the next man."

"I don't intend to hurt anyone!"

"All the same, you seem to have a knack."

Hollan knew if she let him go, she'd be free and she could escape. But the currents were rolling offshore as the tide went out, and she knew she'd never have the strength on her own to get back safely. She'd be washed out to sea, which at the moment actually sounded appealing compared to the thought of whatever unknown situation awaited her aboard ship.

Before she could think things through, she was suggesting an idea to Jonathon. "If you help me get back to shore, I'll help you start a new life. You don't have to do this."

He stopped. "I'd never make it off your island alive."

"Yes, you would. My husband and I would protect you."

Jonathon hesitated.

"Please."

His bewildered face glanced from her to the ship's rail and back.

"What's going on down there?" a voice called from above. The muzzle of a rifle edged into sight from over the rail.

Hollan glanced at Jonathon. "The captain?"

Jonathon nodded.

"Get the prisoner up here at once!" the voice bellowed.

"We have to go. I'm sorry." Jonathon took her arm, his touch gentle.

Hollan felt the panic welling. "We still have time. We can push off and go ashore. My husband will be waiting."

"He's a very good shot, ma'am. I'm truly sorry. We hafta do as he says."

Hollan let silent tears fall in resignation as she put decorum aside and climbed the ladder to the top.

A strong set of arms reached over the edge and pulled Hollan the last few feet up and over the top of the rail.

Hollan swung around and landed awkwardly on her hands and knees. "Thanks. I think."

"Welcome aboard the *Lucky Lady*."

"Funny choice of name for a boat since your entire crew begs to differ."

"Speaking of crew, it sounds like you might have an idea about what made them scatter."

The masculine voice sounded strangely familiar.

She ignored the offered hand and remained on her knees. She slowly raised her gaze. "David?"

"Indeed. Are you happy to see me?"

"I'm not sure." Would Jacob's brother show her favor? Had he changed his ways? Would he see to her safety, or would he continue his mutiny? She answered her own questions. He'd sent for her. And he certainly hadn't done so in order to congratulate her on her recent nuptials.

His laughter chilled her to the bone.

"Paxton!"

Paxton rounded a corner but kept his distance.

"Gather the rest of the men."

David didn't offer her further assistance. Hollan was content to remain on her knees—the more distance she could have between him and the rail, the better.

A few moments later her kidnappers reappeared.

David glanced at them and then looked again. "What happened to you?"

"*She* happened to us." Paxton pointed.

David stalked along the deck. "You're telling me this wisp of a woman gave one of you a black eye and the other a broken nose?"

"She did. And she kilt Nate." Jonathon sent her an apologetic look. "But I don't think she meant to do it."

"She killed—" David's eyes widened as he hurried to the side and peered down at the smaller craft where Nate still lay sprawled on the bottom of the boat. "But how?"

Hollan sighed. "I didn't kill him. He's merely unconscious." Her brows furrowed. "Or at least I think that's all it is."

"Well, don't just leave him down there. Someone bring him up."

"How we gonna do that, Cap'n?"

"Think of something."

Jonathon's studious expression made him look as if he was in pain. "We can wrap a rope around his neck and haul him up that way."

Hollan's eyes widened in horror.

Paxton rolled his own eyes. "That'd be called a noose, Jonathon. Wanna finish Nate off completely?"

"We'll tie it under his arms, then."

"That should work." Paxton glanced at Matt. "You climb down to the boat and tie the rope around him. Jonathon and I will pull him up."

David shook his head. "Or you *could* just raise the rowboat into place and then lift him over the side."

"Good idea, Cap'n. Makes more sense." Jonathon grimaced. "We can do that easy. We'll get right on it."

"See that you do." David stalked away toward the main deck, shaking his head. "And one of you take Hollan down below. Secure her in the hold."

"You go with her, Jonathon." Matt motioned her way. "Paxton and I will take care of Nate."

"Afraid to be alone with me, are you?" Hollan knew better than to goad Matt, but she couldn't resist. If the level of fear in his eyes when he looked at Hollan was any indication, the man still felt she had the ability to cause them all harm with nothing more than her presence.

"I'm not afraid of you, miss." Jonathon led the way. Hollan's moment of levity passed when she realized they were going below deck. The chances of escape were few, but if she remained below deck they'd be nonexistent.

"God is sufficient for all our needs, Hollan."

Hollan remembered Jacob's words from just before the hurricane. He'd been right then, and she felt sure God would bring her through this, too. A momentary sense of peace swept through her. Though this was a different kind of storm, the words couldn't be any truer.

Jonathon led the way, and Hollan stayed close at his heels. The ship's gloomy interior depressed her. It took a few minutes for her eyes to adjust. She could see the dim shapes of several other prisoners. Jonathon led her to a nearby pole and waited expectantly. Hollan stared back, not sure what it was he wanted her to do.

"You need to wrap your arms around the pole." Jonathon waved a piece of rope he'd snagged from a nearby hook. "I have to tie you up."

"Tie me—?" Hollan sputtered. Suddenly she realized the gravity of her situation. If she was tied up below deck and they set sail, Jacob would never find her. A sob forced its way through her terror. "But Jonathon—"

"I'm sorry, miss. I have to follow orders. I'll be back to check on you soon."

"Don't leave me in the dark. I've had nothing but darkness for so long. You don't understand."

"I really am sorry." He tied her hands around the pole and left to go above deck.

"Oh God, what am I to do?" Hollan whispered the words aloud. None of the emaciated men around her moved. She couldn't tell if they were dead or alive. Surely she hadn't been left alone in a room full of dead people. She shuddered. Based on the odors sifting around her, she wouldn't be surprised. Where was that sense of peace? It was as if she'd left it above deck before she descended. She felt as if she'd entered her own personal version of hell.

I will never forsake you. A gentle breeze caressed her hot skin. She looked around but saw nothing amiss. *God is here with me!* Hollan knew the fact as well as she knew her own name. She wasn't alone.

God had a plan for her. She didn't know what it was, but she rested in the knowledge that He'd led her here for a purpose.

"Hollan."

Had God spoken her name aloud?

She glanced around and saw movement to her right.

"Hollan." The raspy voice came again, stronger this time.

It couldn't be. Her mind must be playing tricks on her. But she hadn't imagined that voice.

"Papa?" Her voice broke. *Please, God, let it be so!*

"It's me, daughter."

Hollan pulled at her ties, but they only tightened.

"Papa!"

"Don't fight the ropes, Hollan. You'll only cause yourself pain."

"But, Papa, what are you doing here?"

"Same thing as you, apparently." His soft laugh flowed through her like a salve. "I've missed you so much. I know you had to worry."

"I knew you were alive." Hollan smiled into the darkness. God had indeed had a plan. He'd sent her to rescue her father.

Chapter 10

Jacob couldn't believe the mess his wife had gotten herself into this time. How could she not have seen the crew's arrival? He cringed as he thought through the words. Maybe her vision hadn't returned after all. And here he'd been thinking she was keeping something from him. He felt awful. He'd just found her again, and he wouldn't lose her now. He had to get her back.

The ship was too far out for him to swim to her, and though the tide was going out, he knew they'd never make it back to shore, even if he had their missing boat. The boat wouldn't have helped anyway. They kept it on the inland side of the island. He couldn't go after her. He'd never make it through the currents. He paced back and forth on the shore, trying to come up with a plan. Without his own boat, he had no choice but to watch as she floated away with the crew. He hadn't felt this helpless since the night his father and brothers had ransacked the town.

Samson remained at the water's edge, staring out over the ocean. Every once in a while he'd look at Jacob like, *Why aren't you* doing *something*?

Jacob returned to the dog's side and watched until the rowboat was too far away to see very well. Even if Hollan looked around, she wouldn't see him now.

He turned back and headed at a fast pace toward the lighthouse. Samson trotted alongside him. "We'll get her back, boy, don't worry."

Jacob sounded a lot more confident than he felt. He took the steps of the lighthouse two at a time. Maybe he couldn't go after her, but what he could do was keep watch, take notice of anything he could about the ship, and track their progress. When Fletcher came their way with the supply boat, Jacob would summon help.

The crew of the ship didn't appear to be in any hurry. They lingered offshore even as the sun set. The full moon tracked their progress as they curved around the end of the island and sailed toward the mouth of the river.

Jacob's heart skipped a beat. If the captain continued his present course, they'd soon be near the far side of the island. The channel narrowed on that side in a way that if Jacob left now, he might be able to get on board the ship.

The thud of heavy feet lumbering down the stairs pulled Hollan from a restless sleep. She found herself curled up on the filthy floor.

"Jacob." Her voice was hoarse as she whispered his name. Perhaps he'd found a way to come for her. She peered through the darkness but knew immediately that Jacob would never arrive in such a noisy fashion. Her heart sank. He'd come in quietly, not wanting to rouse suspicion, and would sneak her—and her father—away without anyone the wiser. Whoever descended the stairs now had no concerns about drawing attention. Quite the contrary, from the noise the person made on the stairs, he wanted to alert everyone to his presence.

Her legs were numb from hours spent in an awkward position. Earlier, during the night when she couldn't bear the thought of sitting or lying on the slimy wood floor, she'd placed her forehead against the pole and settled into a squat. She hadn't slept well at all. The tormented moans of the other prisoners had her on edge. Throughout the night the sound of tiny claws skittering across the floor made her shudder. She could well imagine what type of creature the scurrying feet belonged to. And the cloying heat and putrid odors permeated every breath she took.

Each time she'd doze off, she'd fall forward, and the motion would jerk her back awake. Exhaustion had her on edge. She didn't even want to imagine what David had planned for her. And she hoped she'd never find out. He wouldn't have anything in store for her if she could help it. She only had to figure out an escape plan before the madman sent for her.

"Cap'n wants to see you on deck."

The escape plan would have to wait.

Paxton stood beside her. When she couldn't rise on her own, he grabbed her arm and pulled her roughly to her feet. Her legs tingled.

"You seem to take great pleasure in yanking me around by my arm." His bad eye made him look demented in the dimness.

"A lot of things bring me great pleasure. Dealing with you does not."

"Leave her alone!"

Papa.

Her father's voice brought her a measure of peace, even though he couldn't do anything to help her at the moment. She had to focus on a plan that would get them both away from here. In the meantime, it wouldn't hurt to pray.

Lord, I'm not sure what is in store for me while You have me on this ship, but I pray that You'll protect us. Please help Jacob to know where we are, and keep my father safe.

She turned her attention to Paxton. "What does David want with me?"

Paxton shrugged as he untied the knots in the rope that held her hands prisoner. Once he released her, she almost fell on her face.

"You'll get your sea legs in due time."

"I don't intend to be around long enough for that to happen."

Paxton laughed. "I don't see that you have a choice."

"I'll find a way out of here."

"You will, huh? We'll see about that."

He half-dragged her to the stairs. They exited the stairwell onto the main deck, and the bright early morning light shot a dagger of pain through Hollan's head. She closed her eyes briefly, let them adjust, and then squinted through them. Her vision remained clear. She eased her eyes open after a moment and located David at the ship's helm.

She left Paxton's grasp and plowed forward. "David."

"Ah, good morning, Hollan. I trust you slept well?"

She ignored his ridiculous question and instead asked one of her own, echoing her earlier one to Paxton. "What do you want with me?"

"It seems I need to go up the inland channel. In order to do so, I'll happen to need a guide."

Hollan couldn't hold back her smirk. He needed a guide, and he'd chosen the least able person to comply. "You do realize I lost my eyesight three years ago?"

He glanced at her, his forehead wrinkled. "You can't see at all? If that were true, you wouldn't have found your way so easily to me just now."

"Whether I can or can't see right now doesn't matter. What does matter is that I haven't seen this pass or much of anything else since. You've chosen and kidnapped the wrong person to help you."

"You can stop looking so amused." David's scowl deepened. "I'm sure the pass hasn't changed all that much over the past three years."

"Do you seriously believe that?" Hollan's jaw dropped. "Do you not remember the storms we get around here? Nothing ever remains the same."

Not in the least. The storms damaged everything. Her experiences attested to that.

"Then you'd better pray the storms haven't changed the pass."

Hollan started to refuse. She wouldn't guide him anywhere.

"If you don't abide by my terms, your father will pay the price for your rebellion."

That quieted her. She wouldn't do anything to bring more pain to her father.

An idea began to formulate in her mind. When they rounded the end of the island to enter the pass, Jacob would be at the closest point to help them. At least he would be if he knew she was aboard the ship and he'd been tracking their progress.

She couldn't stand the thought of the alternative. If he hadn't figured out where she'd disappeared to, why would he care about one more ship offshore? She hadn't a clue where her father had gone when he'd disappeared. Why would Jacob have any idea about where she'd gone? Even if he went to look for her, she'd have disappeared just as completely as her father.

She decided that just in case Jacob hadn't figured out her whereabouts, her plan had to be something she could fulfill on her own. The pass was treacherous in the best of times. Maybe she could use that to her advantage.

"The currents are very strong at the mouth of the river."

"Thank you. We'll prepare for rougher waters. In the meantime, you'll remain below deck. I'll send for you when I'm ready."

Hollan thought hard. If she stayed above deck, she might have a chance to catch Jacob's attention. But if she went below, perhaps her father could help with suggestions to guide them through the channel. She didn't want to return to the stench of the dark, dank hold, but if she needed to, she'd make use of the option.

In the meantime, she'd try to stay above deck. "I'd prefer to remain up here if you don't mind."

"I don't recall giving you a choice."

"I'll stay out of the way." Hollan started for the rear of the ship. Maybe she'd spot Jacob and would at least be encouraged that he was looking for her. "I'll just settle in up there where I can observe the channel and the conditions."

A rough hand grabbed her arm. David leaned close. "You'll do as I say and go below."

His menacing blue eyes peered into hers. Hollan fought back a chill. The man's eyes were empty. He had no trace of heart or soul. The hold suddenly sounded inviting in light of this realization.

"Fine." She pulled her arm loose.

He pushed her forward toward Paxton. "Stow her below until we're ready."

The dirty hem of her dress tripped her as Paxton led the way downstairs.

Her father waited anxiously where she'd left him.

"Hollan. Are you well?"

"I'm fine, Papa."

He didn't speak again until Paxton had tied her wrists around the pole. As the man shuffled upstairs, her father leaned forward. "What did he want with you?"

"He wants me to guide him through the channel."

A soft chuckle carried over to her. "Did you explain?"

"I did. But, Papa—" She leaned nearer, wishing she could see him better in the darkness. "I can see clearly again. During the past couple of months, my vision would come and go, but now it stays."

"That's wonderful!"

"It is, but I'm not sure it'll help me guide the ship through the pass." She heard him change position. "Are *you* well, Father?"

"I'm fine." He shifted again. "Nothing the light of day won't fix, along with getting back to our island. I sorely miss your cooking."

Hollan laughed. "That says a lot, Papa. My cooking hasn't ever been all that great."

"I miss it all the same."

"Papa, what's going on? Why are you here?"

"David thought he could take me from my position as lightkeeper and use it to his advantage if he's captured. He wanted me to lead him through the inland waterway, but I refused." He let out a breath. "I refused to help the scoundrel. I had no idea he'd go after you next."

Her eyes had adjusted to the dim interior, but it was still pretty dark. "What are we going to do?"

"You're going to do exactly what they tell you. I don't want them angry with you. I don't want David to get violent. If he hurts you, you could lose your vision again—or worse. I won't have you risk that. Just do as he says, and let me figure something out."

Another figure stole quietly down the stairs. His furtive movements drew Hollan's attention. "Who is that, Papa?"

"I'm not sure. Keep quiet. Don't draw attention. I don't trust any of the crew around you."

Hollan settled low and huddled near the pole. The bulky figure carried a mop and moved through the men, stopping now and then to peer closely at each person as he passed. Hollan's heart beat quicker and sweat rolled down her face as the figure turned their way.

"Stay low, Hollan. Duck your head."

She did as her father instructed. The shadowy form loomed over her. He leaned close. Hollan kept her head down, praying she'd be left alone. The figure squatted down and leaned in close to her ear.

"Get away from her." Hollan's father's voice held a hint of panic.

Hollan knew it would kill him to watch if she was attacked and he couldn't do anything about it. She reacted instinctively, kicking the aggressor with her foot. A soft laugh rewarded her attempt.

"My darling wife. A bare foot does nothing to me. Though based on the stench of this hold, I might catch a nasty illness by connecting with your foot."

"Jacob?" A sob caught on Hollan's throat. "Is it really you?"

"It's me."

He wrapped his arms around her and held her close for a moment. She leaned nearer and drew in his scent. "You smell wonderful."

That comment drew a laugh out of him. "You seem to be in good humor. Are you all right?"

"I'm fine now that you're here." She savored the feel of his strong arms around her. She'd never take his presence or touch or encouragement for granted again.

"Want to tell me what you're doing here?"

"Rescuing him." She gestured toward her father in the dim light.

"Rescuing someone with your arms tied tightly around a pole. And whom would you be rescuing?"

"My father. He's alive, just as I said. What are *you* doing here?"

"Rescuing my wife and apparently helping her rescue her father."

Hollan laughed quietly. "I just about had my plan figured out."

Jacob trailed her arms to where they were tied around the post. "So I see. And your capture by the crew, that was all part of your plan?"

"Not exactly, but once it happened and I knew my father was here, I knew God brought me here for that purpose. I just needed to figure out what the plan was."

"Well I'm here now to help." Jacob put a finger against her lips. "Be quiet now; we don't want to draw any more attention our way. I'm going to be close, but I'll continue to pose as one of the crew until I get *my* plan figured out."

"Papa's right beside me, one pole over. He's a little worse for wear, but he says he's fine."

Jacob caressed Hollan's hair with a gentle hand before moving to her father's side. "Gunter? I'm so happy to see you're alive, sir."

Hollan grinned as she watched her two favorite men interact.

"I'm happy to see you, too. My daughter told me about your marriage and all that you've done for her. I appreciate that you took it upon yourself to watch out for her. It's not an easy task."

"Papa!"

"Well it's true. Now, Jacob, tell me what you've come up with to get us out of here."

"I haven't figured out the details on that myself. I saw the crew take Hollan, but I was too far away to do anything about it. I watched the ship from the lighthouse until I saw the present course. I was concentrating on getting aboard but didn't get far enough to figure out a rescue in the event I was successful. I've spent most of my time searching for your daughter aboard ship."

"Well son, you're aboard now and you've found my daughter, so you'd best get to figuring out our escape."

"Have you made friends with any of the other prisoners?"

"No. None of them have tried to communicate with me. I'm not even sure some of them are alive. From what I can tell, they're all worse off than I am. I think some of them are former crew members from whenever the present crew took over the ship."

"I see." Jacob moved back to Hollan's side and took her hand. "I'm going back up to have a look around. I'll return soon."

"Don't leave us."

Her father leaned forward. "They're coming for Hollan soon. They want her to lead them through the channel."

Jacob hesitated. "That might work."

"What might work?" Hollan didn't like his tone of voice.

"Hollan, if you're on deck, you'll be that much closer to escape."

"And if my eyesight falters?"

"We'll worry about that if and when it does."

"I won't leave without you and my father."

"We'll all go together. But I need you free and above deck." He turned to her father. "Do they check your ties often?"

"Never."

"Good. That'll work in our favor, too. I'm going to untie you. I don't want you to move until we're ready to go. Hollan, you'll have to get the ship stuck in a shallow, narrow part of the channel. Try to guide them close to the island. While they're unloading supplies in order to lighten the load, we'll make our move. I'll come down here to get your father. You get off ship and head for the cabin on the island."

"I won't leave without my father. I already told you that."

Papa motioned to her. "Hollan, you'll do as your husband says."

"But—"

"But nothing." Jacob's voice was calm but commanding. "If you're out of the way and safe, I can better help your father."

Hollan bit back her next words. They'd discuss this later. She watched as Jacob untied her father's hands.

"Try to stand. I want to see if you can walk."

Her father stood, but he wavered. Hollan wanted to cry. Her normally strong father was thin and very weak.

"I'll be fine. You go do what you need to do. I'll work on my stamina while you're gone."

"Hollan, I'll leave you tied up until the captain sends for you."

"Jacob." Hollan knew the next words wouldn't be easy for Jacob to hear.

Jacob paused.

"The captain—he's your brother. David."

"*David's* behind this?" Jacob spat. "Why am I not surprised?"

"Promise me you won't rush into anything."

"I won't worry about David until I have both you and your father safely ashore."

Hollan didn't like the innuendo behind his words. She had a feeling that as soon as Jacob had them safe, he'd risk his own life by going after his brother.

Chapter 11

Hollan didn't have to wait long before David summoned her. Paxton's heavy boots stomped down the stairs, echoing through the dim interior like a death sentence. She sent a frantic look at her father as the other man slopped through the muck and headed their way.

"It's going to be fine, Hollan. Jacob's watching out for you. God's on our side. Say your prayers and do what David says. Don't do anything dangerous. Let Jacob make the decisions that need to be made. Watch for him and be alert for any sign he sends you. He won't let anything happen to you."

"But if things don't go as we plan. . ."

"Our plans aren't what matter," her father interrupted her. "Do what you need to do, daughter. But above all else, keep your temper under control. Think before you act."

He lowered his voice as Paxton drew near. "Keep in mind what will happen to Jacob if you act in a rash manner. If he thinks you'll be hurt, he'll intervene before he's ready. The two of you are fully outnumbered by the crew. The timing for our escape needs to be perfect. If at all possible, do only what Jacob told you to do. Find a way to get the ship stuck on a sandbar and let him handle things from there. Remember what I've taught you about the currents. If you see your opportunity to get off the ship, take it and make your escape. Jacob and I will soon follow."

"But if you don't. . ."

"We will."

"*If* you don't. . . ?"

"Find a place to hide and watch for Fletcher to come."

"He's due back tomorrow."

"Then you'll go to him."

Paxton tripped over a body sprawled at his feet. He kicked at the immobile form.

Hollan glared at him as he continued his trek their way. The man was deplorable.

"Your emotions are written all over your face, Hollan, even in this dark place. Keep your thoughts hidden. If David thinks you're anything but compliant. . .it won't go well." Her father's quiet plea drifted her way. His gaunt face looked tortured for a moment. "Do this for your mother. David caused her to do what she did. I'll explain everything later. But we need to make things right. Do your part to get us safely off ship, and we'll talk when we meet back up."

Frustration edged through Hollan. She didn't know what the next few hours would bring, but she prayed they'd bring closure for all three of them.

"C'mon. Cap'n says it's time."

"Time for. . . ?" Hollan stalled.

"Let's go." Paxton ignored her comment and untied her. He reached for her arm.

Hollan scurried to her feet and backed away from him with her arms raised in defense. She knew her father would go after Paxton if he made any untoward moves. She couldn't let her father expose the fact that his hands were no longer tied.

"I'm ready. I don't need your assistance." The boat lurched, and Hollan pitched forward, plowing into him with her head.

Paxton let out his breath with a *whoosh.*

"Sorry. I didn't mean to." Hollan sent her father a quick glance and shrug. He remained in place, though his features were pained. "I lost my balance when the ship shifted."

"So I noticed," Paxton snapped. "See that you don't do it again."

"I'll do my best," Hollan snapped back.

She hadn't intended to get that close to the smelly man in the first place. As it was, she felt in dire need of a sweet-smelling bath. If she ever got out of here, she'd soak in an herb-filled bath for a full day. The hold's odors had permeated her nose and surely everything she wore. How her father had tolerated it for as long as he had she didn't know. It had to pain him to remain below deck, a free man, and not be able to do anything about it.

They exited the stairwell, and Hollan gasped for her first breath of fresh air topside. A gentle breeze blew her way, and even the fishy scent that rode along with it smelled pure after breathing in the stale air down below for the short time she'd been back down there. Now that the sun had risen higher in the sky, the day was clear and sunny. Inspiration bubbled up from deep inside. They had to make this work. Hollan wanted off the ship.

A movement to her left caught her attention. *Jacob.* He peeked up at her from beneath the rim of his hat. The bedraggled outfit he wore made him blend in perfectly with the crew. She twisted the corner of her mouth up in acknowledgment before diverting her gaze.

"What do you find so amusing?" Paxton glared around at the crew.

"There's nothing amusing about my situation. I'm simply rejoicing in the fact that I'm out of that pit for a time. Surely you can understand that."

Paxton scowled at her. "Don't try anything stupid. The captain doesn't tolerate anything close to what he considers mutiny."

Hollan didn't answer. She busied herself looking for Jonathon. Next to Jacob, he seemed her only ally. And though she wasn't sure his kindness would be enough to allow him to stand up against David and his crew, she had a feeling the man had a soft spot somewhere deep inside. If need be, she'd use that to both of their advantage.

"Are you ready?" David didn't waste time with pleasantries.

Hollan walked up beside him, shading her eyes with her hand as she scoured the water ahead of them. *How to best get the* Lucky Lady *stuck?* According to her father, it wouldn't be hard.

"We need to stay with the darker water. The path is narrow. Are you sure you don't want to turn around and go by sea?"

"What I want is for you to do as I ask. Don't question my decisions." He shifted his stance. "I have authorities looking for me on the open waters. I want to use this waterway to avoid a—shall we say—unpleasant outcome."

"You mean you want to avoid your imminent arrest." Hollan smiled up at him.

"I will not be arrested." His face turned purple. "I won't be captured alive."

She frowned. "Which means you'd prefer to be captured dead? But how will that benefit you or your crew? I'm not sure I understand."

"Must you always be talking?" He sighed with exasperation. "I don't intend to be captured at all. Now focus on the task before you."

Hollan laughed. "You sound like my father. That's his favorite thing to say."

David stared at her. "My crew doesn't dare to speak to me the way you do."

"Your crew? Is that what you call them? Better it be said that they are your slaves." She muttered the last part in a quieter voice, but he apparently heard her.

"Every man here has a right to leave anytime he chooses."

"Maybe—but only with a knife in his back or a bullet through his head."

David sputtered. "What gives you the right to speak to me like that? Your father has spoiled you. I'm not sure what my brother ever saw in a quick-tongued woman like you."

"Jacob saw my heart."

"And then, apparently, you drove him away."

"I didn't drive him away." His comment cut to her very soul. Jacob hadn't left her because of anything she'd done to him—had he? She shouldn't listen to this man. Her father told her to focus on the tasks set before her, and here she goaded the evil man instead of focusing on her responsibilities. She couldn't help spitting out one more remark. "That isn't true."

"Aw, have I hit a nerve?"

Hollan stared at the water ahead. "No, but you're about to hit that sandbar." She pointed a finger straight out in front of them.

David swore and spun the wheel hard to the left. Hollan hid her impertinent smile. A cough slightly behind and to her left drew her attention. Jacob worked nearby, and she was sure he'd overheard their discussion.

"You did that on purpose," David snapped.

"I did. I pointed out the obvious. But next time you'd rather I allow you to hit the object we're heading for?"

"No!" He reached up to adjust his hat then glared her way. "You're trying to distract me so we'll run aground."

"I'm hardly *trying* to distract you. Do you think I enjoy your attention?" Hollan huffed out a breath of exasperation. "And if my intent was to distract you so that you'd run the ship aground, *why* would I warn you when I saw the sandbar coming?"

"I guess you have a point."

She pushed her hair out of her face and gave a distracted wave toward their left. "You'll want to steer hard to the left for a bit. The current here runs strong and pushes to the right." Strong enough to embed them securely just off the island's shore if things worked out as she planned. Hollan set her mouth in a pout and crossed her arms in front of her.

"You don't have to sound so offended."

"And why shouldn't I after I save the ship from going aground only to have you berate me?"

The ship missed the sandbar and gently drifted to the left. David relaxed his hold, and the wheel spun out of his grip. They picked up speed as the current forced them into the smaller channel. "Wha—?"

He frantically fought the wheel. "I thought you said the current pushes to the right!" His voice rose in pitch and shook with anger. His eyes held a hint of panic.

They headed toward the island at a fast pace. Hollan sidled over to grab hold of the ship's rail. "Did I say the current pushes to the right? I meant you'd need to steer right because the current pushes to the left. Sorry." She raised her voice to be heard. "You can correct the ship's course, right?"

"You did this on purpose!" David screeched. "All hands on deck—*now!*"

Strong hands grabbed Hollan from behind and dragged her away from the captain. "Get down!"

Jacob's voice.

Hollan did as he said. She hadn't quite hunkered all the way down when the ship went hard aground. Barrels and crew went tumbling across deck. David flew to the right, cracked his head on the rail, and landed facedown, motionless.

"I need to go to him. I did this." Hollan's breath caught in her throat. Had her actions killed the man? She hadn't planned for anyone to get hurt. The ship listed heavily toward the mainland. "I didn't intend to hurt him."

"Well, he does intend to hurt you. Remember that. You're going nowhere but off this ship. As soon as you're clear, head for the cabin immediately." Jacob lifted her to her feet, and they took off across the deck at a run. He dodged both crew and debris as they went. No one looked their way with all the chaos. "David isn't worth your concern. Not right now."

"But my father."

"I'm sure your father is already on his way up here. I'll return to help him as soon as I get you safely on your way."

They reached the ladder. No one bothered with them as the crew frantically threw barrels and supplies off ship in an effort to stop her pitching.

Hollan peered cautiously over the side. "It's a long way down. Coming up was bad enough. My dress! The skirt will. . ."

Jacob snatched a knife from the sheath he wore around his waist and spun her around. He grabbed her skirt and hacked it off at the knees.

"Jacob!" Hollan sputtered.

"It's filthy and ruined. You'll move faster this way. Your skirt won't pull you under the water."

He resheathed the knife and eased her over the edge. "Hold the ladder tight. If you lose your grip, push off so you don't bump against the ship. Get away as quickly as possible in case she shifts. You don't want to be crushed beneath her."

"And there is a very pleasant thought with which to bid me good-bye."

"And a very likely scenario if you don't get out of the way." He hesitated and grasped her upper arms. "I love you, Hollan." He pulled her close for a quick peck on her lips. "Now go. Get out of sight. Move quickly."

She ducked below the ship's rail and headed carefully down the ladder. Her hands shook, and she prayed she'd not lose her grip. The ship's rounded sides made the endeavor awkward and hindered her descent. Her foot slipped, and she flailed for a moment before finding purchase again.

Just as she regained her footing, something large catapulted past her. She ducked with a scream. Another piece of her dress tore off as the large object shot past, but she was able to keep hold of the ladder.

Hollan lowered her foot again and felt for the next rope step. Something else fell from above, and again it barely missed her. A sob tore loose. Were they throwing things at her? Had they figured out the plan? Had someone noticed her missing?

She pushed herself to move faster but again lost her footing. This time her fingers slipped from their hold, too, and she plunged to the water below. The momentum sent her into a downward spiral under the water even as she fought to return to the surface. After a few panicked moments, her toes finally hit sand, and she pushed hard against the bottom. She broke through the surface of the water and gasped in a huge lungful of air.

A barrel splashed down beside her, barely missing her head. She swam in place and looked around for a safer location to wait out the barrage of debris. Only one area would offer her protection. She swam to the boat and hunkered down out of sight, slightly under the rounded side. If the ship shifted at all, she'd be crushed beneath it, just as Jacob had warned.

Jacob hurried across the tilting deck and prepared to go below just as Gunter surfaced. A small man with a crooked nose assisted him. Jacob raised an eyebrow in question.

"It's all right. Jonathon here offered me his assistance. He said he failed Hollan when she needed him, and he wanted to make things right with me." Gunter looked around. "Where is she?"

"I've already helped her over the edge. She should be well on her way to the shore." Another glance at Gunter's helper reassured Jacob that the man didn't have any ulterior motives. The man nervously watched the actions of the crew but didn't try to draw attention. David still lay where they'd left him. "We need to get out of here before he comes around. He isn't going to be in a very good mood."

"Does the man *have* a good mood?" Gunter muttered.

"Not that I've ever seen, but we don't want to be here to see what he does when his perpetually bad mood gets worse."

They helped Gunter to the side of the ship where Jacob had last seen Hollan. He peered over and saw no sign of her. Hopefully that meant she'd made it to safety. Two members of the crew appeared, carrying a large barrel between them. They staggered up beside Jacob.

"Can you give us a hand in gettin' this over? It's mighty heavy," one of the men gasped.

"Set it down." Panic coursed through Jacob. "Have you thrown other things over this side?"

"Yep. We needed to lighten the load."

Jacob leaned over and again searched the water for any sign of Hollan. If a barrel had hit her. . .

He saw a piece of fabric from her dress floating on the water, but he didn't see any other physical signs of her. Surely if she'd been hit she'd still be in sight. He breathed easier and looked at the men. "Not on this side, you don't."

The man surveyed him suspiciously. "Why not?"

Jonathon stepped up beside him. "Ya see how the ship lists? Ya might knock a hole in the side."

"Oh. I hadn't thought about that."

"Head on over there with the barrel"—Jacob pointed to the far side—"and I'll be right behind you to help."

The two men struggled to lift the large container.

Jacob rolled his eyes. "Can I offer a suggestion?"

One looked at the other. "I guess."

"Roll the barrel to the other side. Don't carry it."

"That might work." The deckhand looked skeptical. "We can try."

They laid it on its side and pushed.

"No, you'll want to—" Jacob shook his head as the barrel picked up pace on its journey across the deck. It took out two men before slamming into the wooden rail on the far side. "Never mind."

The men took off at a run, and Jacob quickly turned around. "Come on, we need to get out of here before someone else comes along."

Jonathon helped lift Gunter over the side. Jacob looked at Jonathon. "Are you coming with us?"

"No. I'm needed here. You go. I'll keep watch as I work, and I'll offer a diversion if need be."

"We appreciate it, Jonathon."

"Tell Hollan I'm sorry. I couldn't help her before, but I hope she's safe now."

"Thank you."

Jacob glanced around then slipped over the rail and followed Gunter down the ladder. He heard a soft *splash* below as Gunter entered the water. Jacob made quick work of dropping down beside him.

"Let's go. We need to get away from the ship."

"Jacob!"

Jacob glanced around and saw Hollan clinging to the large vessel's side.

"Woman! Don't you ever listen?"

"I *do* listen, but before I could get away, huge objects started raining down on me from above."

"I think we've stayed the falling objects. Let's get out of here."

They only had a short swim before their feet touched bottom. Jacob reached back and assisted Hollan until her feet reached solid ground.

"I'm fine, I'm fine. Go, go, go!" Hollan's panicked voice urged him on. She stepped up beside him and helped assist her father.

She started toward the shelter of the trees.

"Not that way. We need to stay in the water."

"They'll see us."

"Jonathon is helping from the ship. He won't let anyone approach this side. It's tilting away from us. The crew is busy on the other side, trying to lighten the load so the ship will rise off the sandbar."

"Why not go into the cover of the trees?"

"The foliage is too dense. We have to get to the path, but we need to stay in the water so they can't follow our tracks."

They reached a shallow creek and turned to follow it into the trees.

"We're safe for now, Hollan. Their guns won't reach this far. No one can see us."

Hollan's legs gave out. Jacob caught her and held her close.

"We're safe," he murmured again. "It's going to be okay."

"I need a quick rest." Gunter climbed out of the creek and sank to the ground nearby. He leaned against a tree. "What's the plan from here?"

"We'll go to Amos's cabin."

Hollan pulled her face away from Jacob's chest and looked up at him. Her eyes were smudged with exhaustion, but she stared directly at him. He watched her eyes soften as she surveyed his features. Her mouth broadened into a smile. "You're a sight for sore eyes."

"Your vision seemed to be intact the entire time we were on the ship. Is it fully restored?"

"At first it came back in bits and pieces, but yes, I can consistently see clearly now. And thank you."

"Why are you thanking me?"

"You came after me. You rescued us."

"You're my wife. I'll always come for you." He kissed the tip of her nose. "But about the return of your vision. . ."

She smirked and turned his words on him. "We'll discuss it later."

Gunter motioned for their attention. "If you two can try to concentrate, we do have some pretty angry men aboard that ship who would probably like to recapture us. I'd like to get some more space between them and us. I think I can walk some more now."

"Wait." Hollan looked up at Jacob. "You said the other day that the cabin looked like someone had been there."

"That would have been me," Gunter interrupted. "I cleaned it up and took shelter from a storm a short while back."

"I remember now." Hollan looked at her father. "You were gone all day, and I was so worried. If only I'd known then what the coming days would bring."

"Speaking of. . .we do need to move on," Jacob prompted.

Gunter stood to lead the way.

Jacob held Hollan back. "How long has it been since your vision returned? Since the day we walked around the island?"

"Before that." She frowned. "It was better when I woke up after hitting my head in the storm. I could see, but I wasn't sure my vision would stay."

"And you kept that from me? Why?" Jacob could hear the tremor in his voice. He wanted his wife to trust him, but apparently, after all he'd done in the past, she still didn't.

Hollan stared into his eyes. "I was afraid you'd think I didn't need you anymore. I was afraid you'd leave."

"So you trust me that little, even after I've told you repeatedly that I was here to stay."

"You did tell me that." Hollan nodded. "But that was when you thought I couldn't see. I wasn't sure things would stay the same if you knew. I needed more time."

"And when were you going to tell me?"

"The morning I was kidnapped."

"I see." Jacob stared back at her for a moment and then turned to stalk away up the path.

"That's it?" Hollan hurried to catch up with him. She grabbed his arm. "That's all you have to say?"

"I married you the moment I heard you were in need of a husband, Hollan. I stood by you through the hurricane, and I tended your injuries. I saved you from a ship full of rogues. If you don't trust me by now, after everything we've been through, I'm not sure I'll ever be able to regain your confidence."

Chapter 12

Jacob, wait!" Hollan's heart moved into her throat. She couldn't breathe. Her worst nightmare was coming true. Her deception had caused the exact scenario she'd wanted to avoid. She'd hurt Jacob, and now he didn't want to talk to her. "You kept saying you were here for me and that you wouldn't leave. But I wasn't sure if it was because you wanted to be here or because you had no choice."

"Not now, Hollan." Jacob continued to move ahead at a quick pace.

Hollan raised her voice. "I was afraid you'd leave if you knew I could see."

"I said not now." Jacob's words were clipped and cold.

Hollan dropped back and lagged behind. She could hardly see past her tears. She tried to tell herself it didn't matter, that with the return of her vision she'd be fine. She had her father back, and things could return to the way they'd been before this all happened. At least life would return to normal as soon as they figured out a way to rid themselves of David and his crew.

Hollan realized Jacob was right in that respect. This wasn't the time to worry about anything but their safety. They'd figure the rest out later. Even though she knew this all to be true, tears still forged their way down her cheeks.

The trio worked their way up the path, and Hollan wished for her boots. Chipped and broken shells lined the creek's bed, and the path wasn't any better. Hollan knew a cut from one of the shells could cause a serious infection. But she wasn't about to ask Jacob for his help. She hesitated and glanced around, trying to figure out a way to walk without causing injury or drawing Jacob's attention to her ineptness.

"Keep up, Hollan. We need to carry on."

Hollan snapped, "I have to find my way around the shells."

Jacob came back and abruptly swept her up into his arms. "You should have worn your boots."

"I'll try to remember that next time I walk the shore prior to getting unexpectedly kidnapped."

A vein throbbed in Jacob's throat, but he didn't comment further.

Still, her feet were scratched and sore by the time they reached the shack. Her tears of heartache had diminished, but the pain of Jacob's anger simmered under the surface.

Jacob set her down next to the small building in the clearing. Hollan wandered over to the edge of the stream and sat down, placing her sore feet in the cool water. She cupped some of the water into her hands to wash her face and scrubbed away all trace of her tears.

"I'm going inside to lie down." Her father's face was pale with exhaustion.

"I'll help you get settled." Hollan moved to stand, but her father waved her away.

"Let me be. I can manage to lie down without assistance. Rest your feet."

Jacob watched from a distance and waited until her father had entered the shack before coming up beside her. "You should have told me."

"About my feet or my vision?"

He squatted at her side. Hollan glanced up at him. The sun broke through the leaves, and one shaft highlighted the gold in his hair. His green eyes were lined with fatigue. "Both."

"I told you. I was going to tell you about my vision, but the crew got to me first."

"And your feet?"

"What good would it do to tell you? What could you have done? If I'd worn my boots, I wouldn't have had a problem. It was my problem alone to deal with, and my feet are fine." Her words sounded bitter, but he'd walked away from her. Why would she think to bother him with anything after that?

"To answer your second question, I would have done this"—his face took on a devious expression as he reached over and swept her up into his arms—"earlier than I did."

"Put me down!" she hissed while glancing at the shack.

"No."

"I'm a mess."

"You look fine to me."

"Then maybe we need to be concerned about *your* vision."

"My vision is fine."

"I just spent the night on a smelly ship."

"And you had a nice dunk in the water after. You look beautiful."

"*Beautiful?* My dress is torn and cut to pieces. My petticoats are in shreds. My feet are filthy, and my hair is a mess. How can you say such a thing?"

"I mean it. I went a lot of years without seeing you. I intend to enjoy every moment of seeing you now."

"You're finished being angry?"

"Do I look angry?" He raised his eyebrows up and down. "You aren't going to chase me away, Hollan."

Hollan rolled her eyes. "My father's going to come out and see us this way."

"Your father isn't coming out. He's exhausted." Jacob settled back against a tree with Hollan held securely in his arms. "And regardless, he's not going to take offense."

She laid her head on his shoulder and snuggled closer. Her heart felt full. "I didn't expect you to carry me through the woods. My feet hurt, but I'm fine. I would have dealt with sore feet."

"That's what I've been trying to tell you all along. Nothing—no problem—is yours to deal with alone. Not anymore. You have me to lean on now. I didn't marry you because you were blind. I didn't marry you because I felt sorry for you or because I felt there was no other choice. I married you because I love you. We'd planned to marry before I left. The pieces fell together when I returned, and I felt marriage to you was what God had brought me back here for. I'll carry you through any situation I need to."

Hollan stared at her reflection in the creek, afraid to meet his eyes. She knew she'd burst into tears. The stress of the past two weeks was taking its toll. She was exhausted from lack of sleep the night before and the anxiety caused by their escape. Her mind was a muddled mess.

"You need to rest. You barely recuperated from the blow to your head before you were taken. I'm sure you didn't sleep well on the ship."

The compassion in his voice was her undoing. A sob racked her body.

Jacob stroked her back. "I'm sorry," he crooned into her hair. "I didn't mean to make things worse."

"You didn't make things worse." She didn't want to talk. She just let him hold her while she stared into the water. The reflection there confirmed what she already knew. Her hair was a mess; her dress was dirty and torn. She looked awful. She likely smelled worse, even with her dip.

"You've made things so much better," she whispered.

"I haven't seen you cry before now."

"I haven't faced the reality of losing you before now."

He tilted her chin up. "I'm not leaving."

"You were so angry."

"Not angry, just frustrated."

His emerald eyes were so beautiful. He studied her.

"I don't want to make you frustrated."

He grinned. She'd forgotten about the way his dimples curved around his smile. "You've been making me frustrated since we were very young. I doubt anything's going to change in that respect."

"Oh."

He reached up to caress a strand of her hair.

She made a face and tried to swat him away.

His hand drifted down to her chin, and his thumb caressed her cheek. "Hollan, I'm going to disappoint you. You're going to frustrate me. But none of that will change the fact that we'll always love each other. Can you live with that?"

"I can," she whispered.

He slid his hand back to comb through her hair. He gently tugged her toward him as he leaned in for a kiss. "I can, too, very happily."

They sat forehead to forehead.

She breathed him in. "I'm so glad you're back."

"Me, too." He kissed her again and pulled away. "You need to rest."

"Don't leave."

He set her aside and tried to stand. She tugged him back down and leaned against him. He stroked her hair.

"I have to leave. Samson must be going nuts in the cottage. If the men come ashore—and I'm sure they will—the cottage will be their first target. I need to get Sam out of there and salvage some of our things."

"Poor Samson. I wondered how you got away without him."

"I had to lock him up." He seemed as hesitant about leaving as she was about watching him go. "Anyway, we need some supplies. I'll run up to the cottage and bring Samson back with me. We'll need food and clean clothes." He sent her a pointed look. "And I'll grab your boots and some more salve, too."

She laughed. She wanted to go with him, but no way would her feet allow that. Nor would Jacob. The brambles in the path would tear her to shreds. "Thank you. I appreciate your consideration. Just stay safe and hurry back quickly."

"I'll always hurry back to you."

Hollan could only nod.

"Do you want me to help you into the shack?"

"I'll stay out here, thank you. I'll have enough of the cabin when we have to go in there at dark."

"I'll hold you close and keep you safe."

Hollan blushed. "I'm sure you will. And my father will be right there on the other side, with me sandwiched in between. Sounds like a wonderful way to spend the night."

"Oh yeah, I suppose your father will be right there." Jacob's laugh told her he hadn't forgotten her father. He was teasing her again. "But we will make an excellent shield for you, protecting you from all that lurks in the dark."

Hollan shivered. "And there could be plenty of things lurking with David's crew wandering about."

"Last time we were here, you were worried about gators and snakes. Are you sure you don't want to go in with your father?"

"It was dark and creepy that day if I remember correctly, or at least it seemed so back then. Now I know scarier things lurk in the area. Today the clearing feels brighter and sun dappled. I'll stay here."

"Sun dappled?"

"Sun dappled."

Jacob walked over to where he'd placed his coat and folded it into a square. He placed it on the ground and motioned for her to lie down. "Go to sleep. When you wake up, I'll be here."

"Sounds nice," she murmured. She was already drifting off.

Jacob hurried back to the cottage and heard Samson barking frantically from inside. He released the dog, and Samson ran in circles around his legs.

"She's fine, boy. I have her safely stashed away. We need to get you to safety as well."

Jacob hurried inside to gather some clothes for Hollan and her father. He stuffed a day's worth of food into the bag, too. He quickly grabbed anything he found of value and took it all to his room in the base of the lighthouse. Larger, less expensive items he hid as best he could in the outbuilding. He kept Gunter's rifle and ammunition with him.

"C'mon, boy, I need to make one more stop by the lighthouse before I take you to Hollan."

Samson didn't need any encouragement.

Jacob hurried back into his room and added his clothes to the bag. He hefted it up and placed it outside.

"Stay." He pointed to the bag, and Samson sat beside it. "I'll only be a moment."

He'd come a long way since the day he'd watched the men take Hollan. He was back at the lighthouse. At least now he had Hollan safely tucked away and out of the grasp of David. Still, he needed to get back to her.

Jacob hurried up the stairs. The lighthouse gave him a full view of the stranded ship. The ship didn't list quite as badly and seemed to have stabilized, but it remained stuck on the sandbar. Perhaps his wife had done her job a bit too well.

He noticed the smaller boats from the ship were being lowered to the water. He searched the treetops for any sign of the shack, but it couldn't be found. They'd be safe as long as they could get to Fletcher before David and his crew got to them.

Jacob secured the lighthouse as well as he could and motioned for Samson to come. He didn't think the men would carry along the right tools to break into the tower, and he hid any of Gunter's tools he could find. He prayed the men would be too tired to try to gain entry to the lighthouse. The damage they could do in vengeance would be expensive to repair.

Jacob and Samson set off for the shack. They finally arrived, with Samson leading the way through the trees, into the small clearing. Hollan lay where Jacob had left her. He quietly opened the door to the shack and placed their supplies inside. Gunter's exhausted snores reverberated throughout the room.

Jacob closed the door and walked over to where Samson stood watch over Hollan. "I can take care of things from here, boy." He dropped down beside Hollan and pulled her close. He shut his eyes and listened to her breathe.

She shifted in his arms. "Jacob?"

"I told you I'd be back."

"I'm glad."

Samson nudged his way between them. Hollan laughed and petted him.

"I think I got everything we need."

"Good." She nestled against Jacob, still half asleep.

Jacob grinned.

"I think nothing short of the arrival of outlaws would wake you up right now."

Her auburn hair fell across her face, and he pushed it back. She squinted up at him, her brown eyes warm. "I'm awake."

"Ah, then you still must consider me an outlaw."

"Hardly." She tried to sit up. "More like a hero."

"Stay. We have nowhere to go." He captured her with his arm. "So I'm a hero now. I like that much better than being compared to my outlaw family."

"I apologize for that."

"You had reason to be upset."

"Perhaps just a bit of a reason." She changed the subject. "And what did my hero find out through his explorations?"

"The crew is just now leaving the ship." He felt her tense up. "They won't find us here. I knew where to look and couldn't see a thing. It'll be dusk before they reach the lighthouse. I'm pretty sure they'll head to the cottage for now. While I was up in the lighthouse, I tracked the path Fletcher's boat will travel if he shows up tomorrow. If they leave a man on watch, he'll see Fletcher coming this way."

"From the lighthouse?"

"Only if they can gain entry. I'm hoping they're too tired to try."

Jacob had left his hair down, and Hollan absentmindedly stroked it as she listened. Her touch made it hard to concentrate.

"We'll need to warn Fletcher."

"Yes. I figure if we can get an early start in the morning and stick close to the trees, we can intercept Fletcher before he makes it as far as the ship. We can hop aboard the supply boat and be out of here before David and his men get off the dune."

"That sounds fine."

He leaned on his lower arm, put his other hand against his heart, and feigned surprise. " 'That sounds fine'?" he mimicked. "You don't want to add to the plan or take something away?"

"Very funny." She pushed him back down and laid her head on his chest. Samson wiggled closer. "I trust you."

"You do?" Jacob sat halfway up again. "You trust me completely this time?"

"I do. We've been through a lot during the past week, and you've stuck by me through it all. You didn't have to risk your life to rescue me, but you did. I do trust you."

"Thank you, Hollan. Your trust means everything to me. I'll never break that trust again."

She settled back against him just as Samson let out a low growl.

Jacob glanced at him and saw the hair raised on the back of the dog's neck. The dog growled again.

A gravelly voice sounded from behind them. "What do we have here?"

Chapter 13

Samson barked.

"Samson, it's just Papa." Hollan laughed. "Your sudden appearance and hoarse voice must have startled him, Papa."

Samson jumped to his feet and wagged his tail as he sheepishly hurried over to his master.

Hollan surveyed her father. "Are you feeling better?"

He definitely looked better now that he'd had some sleep.

"I feel much better."

"Good." Hollan turned to Jacob. "You said you brought more of our clothes back with you?"

"They're in the shack." Jacob's voice was groggy. He hadn't moved from his place on the ground.

"I think I'll go a ways up the stream to bathe and change."

"Don't go far," Jacob warned. He yawned. "I'll rest while you're gone."

"Stay within calling range, Hollan." Her father's face creased with worry. "The men might come ashore."

"I'll be close by, Papa."

"Actually, I think I'll tag along and freshen up myself. That way I'll be nearby if you need me."

Hollan rolled her eyes. She might be a married woman now, but her father apparently didn't see her as such. "As you wish, Papa."

She knew he'd worry the whole time she was gone if he didn't accompany her. And truth be told, she didn't want her father far away after being apart from him in such a way.

They gathered their supplies and walked up the overgrown path. Hollan stopped and pointed out a small pool in the creek. "This looks like a perfect place. I'll stay here."

"Good. You'll be protected and safe. No one can get through this foliage. Jacob is just down the path behind us. And I'll go a bit ahead and stand guard from that angle."

"Thank you, Papa." She stopped and handed him a bar of lye soap. "I'm sure you can use some freshening up, too. You were on that ship longer than I."

"I can't wait to get in the water and then put on some fresh clothes. If we could light a fire, I'd burn these."

"Burying them will do just as well," Hollan teased.

Her father walked off, and Hollan savored the time alone. She slipped into the cool water and lathered up her hair. She scrubbed her body twice, just to make sure the filth of the ship was gone from her skin. Her skin tingled when she exited the water and dressed in fresh clothes.

She leaned back against a sun-warmed rock and contemplated the past few days while she waited for her father. She had her father back. The thought made her smile. More surprisingly, she had Jacob back. And for the first time, she felt confident that he meant it when he said he'd stay. He'd changed a lot during the past three years. They still needed to talk about why he'd left her in the first place. And she needed her father's explanation about what had happened to her mother.

The warmth of the late afternoon sun lulled her into a drowsy state. She listened to the sound of the birds in the trees. The wind rustled through the bushes. At least, Hollan hoped it was the wind. She knew the gators came out at dusk and willed her father to hurry.

She heard footsteps along the path and shrank down behind the rock.

"Hollan?"

"Papa? Oh, I'm glad you came back."

"Did something happen?" He glanced around.

"No." She smiled. "I'm just hearing things in the scrub. I'm ready to head back to Jacob. I don't want to meet up with an alligator any more than I want to meet up with David and his men."

Jacob woke up as they neared the small clearing and rubbed his eyes. "Is everything okay?"

"Just fine." Hollan smoothed her clean pink skirt and settled down beside him. He studied her fresh-scrubbed appearance. She couldn't help teasing him. "Everything meet your approval?"

"Indeed." He grinned. "I'm trying to figure out if you're the same woman who walked away from here a short while back."

"One and the same."

"I think I'd better follow suit." He hopped up to his feet. "Stay close to your father."

"You stay close to shore and make sure to be careful."

"What's the matter? You don't want me to end up as gator bait?"

She shuddered. "That's not exactly something to joke about."

"We have a bit of daylight left. I'll be fine."

"See that you are. I have some questions to ask when you return."

"Sounds serious."

"Maybe. But it's a conversation that's been a long time in coming."

"You're right." He nodded. "It has. We'll talk when I get back." He gathered his clothes and walked up the path from where they'd just come.

Hollan bent down and busied herself with cleaning and wrapping her sore feet.

"We need to talk, too, Hollan. Now's as good a time as any."

Hollan glanced back at her father. "About Mama?"

"Yes." He eased himself down beside her. "The night she—fell—from the lighthouse, something happened. Something bad."

"You don't have to tell me, Papa."

"I want to tell you. You need to know. You need to understand that she didn't do what she did to hurt you. She was hurting so badly, I don't think she gave anything else much thought."

"She'd just left the cottage. What could have happened?"

"David waited just outside, and he grabbed her. . . ." Her father stopped, his face both pained and angry.

"Papa, you don't have to do this."

"Yes, I do." He waved her words away. "David grabbed her, and he abused her. He—hurt—your mother. He violated her body. I was so close by, but I had no idea."

"Oh, Papa. I had no idea either."

"She didn't want you to know." He shook his head. "I was supposed to watch out for her, but I wasn't there for her in her time of greatest need."

"You didn't know."

"That doesn't change things in my mind."

"What happened next?"

"I went into a rage. I told her to go back inside, and I went after the vile man."

"But you didn't find him?"

"No. And I heard you calling, and I was afraid for you."

"Why would David want to hurt Mama?"

"I don't know. I'll never know. He and his brothers and their father hurt a lot of people that night, for no reason anyone has ever been able to figure out."

"I know what happened." Jacob stood at the edge of the path, his voice tortured. "I think I'm starting to understand."

They both spun around to look at him. He dropped his things beside the door of the shack and walked closer.

He sank down beside Hollan and took her hand. "He'd come to hurt you."

"But why? I didn't even really know him. Why would he want to hurt me?"

"Because hurting you would be the best way to hurt me." Jacob shook his head. "David hated that I was different from him and our father. He constantly goaded me and tried to get me to go along with them as they destroyed everyone in their path. I wouldn't have any part of it, and I spent most of my time with your uncle and aunt."

"I knew your family was rough, but I had no idea they were that bad."

"I didn't want you to know."

"Oh."

"You were my refuge. You were the bright spot in my life. I didn't want to dirty that up with my family's reputation."

"It wouldn't have changed anything between us."

"I know. I just didn't want to sully what we had when we were together. Regardless, things weren't good at home. That last night, they'd decided to skip town. The law was coming down on them, and they knew it was time to move on. I heard them talking and planning. David asked me to go along, and I refused. I tried to talk them out of it, and I tried to tell them about my beliefs. I told them it wasn't too late to start fresh. David laughed in my face. They didn't want anything to do with any of it. I said I didn't want anything to do with their deeds. I had you, and I had my life there in town. I had no reason to run."

Hollan saw the muscle working in Jacob's jaw. "What happened next?"

He struggled for control. "David said he was going after you, that maybe he'd just take you with him instead. He hated that he couldn't control me. He hated that I was so different. He wanted to be in control of everything."

"Oh, Jacob." Hollan tried to grasp everything he was telling her. The raw emotion on his face clearly showed his pain. "What did you do?"

"I went into a rage, just like your father did later. I'm not proud of the fact. David has a tendency to bring out the worst in a man."

"But I don't blame you. You were totally justified."

"David laughed and said he didn't really want to take you with them. . .he'd just take what he wanted from you and would leave it at that."

He looked at her. Hollan continued to hold his arm.

"I went after David. All three of them, my dad and my other two brothers, jumped me while David hit me from behind."

Hollan closed her eyes against the horrific image of Jacob being held by his own father and brothers while another brother attacked him. "That's atrocious."

"They knocked me unconscious." He blew out a breath. "When I woke up, your uncle was bent over me and they were gone. It was daylight. My head was pretty messed up. I croaked out your name and your uncle said you'd been traumatized and it would be best if I left you alone for a bit."

He threw a small stone into the creek and watched the water ripple out from where it landed. Hollan remained quiet, figuring he needed time to gather his thoughts before continuing.

"I figured—based on his comment—that David had succeeded in getting what he was after. I figured your uncle's phrasing was his way of telling me to leave you alone."

"So you just left?"

"No, I couldn't travel. I was in and out of consciousness for a few more days, and your aunt and uncle cared for me. When I was finally well, I asked about you again."

He shrugged. "Your uncle again repeated that you needed some time. You'd been injured. The whole town had been wronged. I had to go after my brothers. I couldn't let them get away with what they'd done."

"I had been injured. Just not as you thought. The weather was awful, and my mother was standing at the edge of the platform on top of the lighthouse. I was afraid she'd fall. I tried to take hold of her arm, to pull her back, but she just shook me away like I didn't matter. I fell and hit my head. When I woke up, I couldn't see. We hoped it would only be for a short time, that maybe it was caused from the trauma of everything that happened, but after several days passed. . .we had to accept that the loss of vision might be permanent."

"I'm so sorry."

Hollan nodded. "What happened after my uncle told you I still needed time?"

"I decided I'd go after my father and brothers. I wanted to find my own justice."

"But you didn't. You went to the law."

"You're right, I did. As I rode after them, God shook some sense into me. He placed some good people in my path. I decided I would bring them to justice, but I'd do it the right way. I didn't want to become like them."

Hollan's voice was soft. "So, you didn't leave me because you didn't want me. You left because you thought you'd lost me."

"Exactly." He took her hand in his. "I never stopped loving you, Hollan. I just thought I'd lost you because of what my brother did. I thought when your uncle said to give you time, you didn't want to see me again."

"But David never came to me. . . ."

Her father spoke up. "Yes, he did."

Hollan was bewildered. "No, he didn't—"

"But he did. . . ."

She glanced back and forth between them. Realization dawned. Her breath hitched. "He got Mama instead."

Her father nodded.

"Mama wasn't his intended victim. He thought she was me. Then it was my fault David hurt her."

Jacob pulled her close. "No, it wasn't your fault at all."

She pushed him away. "It was! He'd come for me. Mama went out there. . . ."

"And in the storm, she looked so much like you that David mistook her for you." Her father nodded again. "Hollan, your mother wouldn't have had it any other way. She told me as much. She said he kept saying your name, even as she fought him. She said she was glad it was her he'd found, not you. She didn't blame you, and you can't blame yourself."

Horrified tears poured down Hollan's cheeks. "Then why did she do what she did?"

"I don't know. She was hurt, angry, devastated. She begged me not to go after him. Not with the rage I was in. If I'd only stayed with her. . ."

"You can't blame yourself either, Papa." Hollan reached up to wipe her tears, but Jacob got to them first.

"Hollan, I don't think she jumped of her own free will. Now that we've all shared our views of that night, I think your mother must have gone up to the top of the lighthouse to get away from everything, to feel safe. You were in the cottage. She wouldn't want you to see how distraught she was. Your mother didn't leave you intentionally."

"I think you may be right." Hollan nodded slowly. She turned to her father. "Papa, if you won't let me blame myself, you can't take that blame either."

"None of us are to blame. It took me three years to realize that." Jacob caressed her fingers with his thumb. His golden hair glistened. He surveyed her, looking deep into her eyes. She couldn't pull her gaze away from his. "Only God can judge them for their sins. The law can try them for their crimes. Our responsibility is to forgive."

"It's hard."

"It is, but if you don't forgive. . .if you hold the anger and bitterness in. . . you'll become just like them. Don't let them win."

She turned to her father. "Papa?"

"Your husband is right, Hollan. As hard as it is to hear, Jacob speaks the truth. David needs to be brought to justice, but as soon as that's accomplished, we need to go on with our lives. We need to move forward. God has blessed us through all this."

"I guess He has, hasn't He? I'll still have to work through the anger toward David, but God restored my vision. He brought Jacob back to me." She smiled up at him.

"He led me back to you," Jacob agreed.

"And He allowed you both to find me," her father added.

"So we're all in agreement." Hollan stared back and forth between both men. "But what now? How do we bring David to justice?"

Her father considered her question. "We leave first thing in the morning and intercept Fletcher."

"What if he can't make it? What if he can't get away? The hurricane might have caused a lot of damage."

Jacob surveyed her expression. "You have something on your mind."

"Yes." She raised an eyebrow. "I do."

"I'm afraid to ask. . .but. . ." Her father's blue eyes twinkled. "Are you gonna fill us in?"

"David and his crew rowed ashore to get over here, right?"

"Right."

"They'd have to leave their boats onshore, wouldn't they?"

"I believe they would."

Jacob exchanged a look with her father. "Are you thinking what I'm thinking?"

Her father nodded. "I'm pretty sure I am."

They both looked back at her.

Jacob spoke first. "If they did leave the boats onshore, they'd surely have a guard."

"Guards can be bribed." Hollan shrugged. "Or overthrown."

Jacob laughed. "You say that like it's such a simple thing. And you're volunteering us for the job?"

"I'll do my part." Hollan tipped up her chin and dared him to cut her out of the plans.

"What did you have in mind?"

"I could sashay over and distract whoever it is while you two strike from behind."

"My wife is villainous!"

Hollan snorted. "I'm not. I'm just willing to do whatever needs to be done."

Gunter sat in contemplative silence.

"Papa?"

"I don't want to use you as bait. These men are very dangerous. Now they're both dangerous and angry."

"Do you have a better plan?"

"Well, I don't as of now, but I bet we can come up with one before dawn."

Jacob leaned forward and rested his arm on his knee. "They'll be watching for us. If we leave before daybreak, we'll have a better chance of getting away."

Hollan grabbed his sleeve. "And if we catch them off guard, maybe we can just slip away with one of the boats. David didn't seem to hire the brightest of men for his crew."

"That's because anyone with a lick of sense would have stayed far away from him."

"Jonathon actually has a heart," Hollan disagreed. "I don't know why he's with them."

They sat in silence for a few minutes.

"Jacob. . .Papa. . ."

Both men answered in unison. "What?"

"What if Jonathon volunteered for the watch?"

Jacob thought for a moment. "The odds are against that, Hollan."

"I know. But just think. God has protected us so far. What if He's put the next step into place by giving us Jonathon as a guard?"

"It could happen. And if not, I'm sure He has a plan for us to get out of here to safety."

"We won't know until we get there."

"You want to go now?"

"Why not? What better time? We've all slept. We'll sleep better if we get to the mainland. They won't expect us to act until morning. And they have to be exhausted, too. They worked hard all day trying to unload the ship. David told me he wanted to go up the inland canal because officials were looking for him. He won't want to stay around very long."

Gunter exchanged a look with Jacob. "I think the lady is on to something."

She smiled with relief. "So we act tonight? Now? I think I'll go crazy if we have to sit here any longer."

"You'll be okay walking through the area in the dark? I know you aren't real fond of it here, even in the daylight."

"I'm fonder of the thought of walking away than I am of spending the night here in that shack. And I have my boots on this time."

Jacob stood and pulled her to her feet. She dusted off her skirt. Gunter joined them.

"Let's get something to eat then see what the shoreline holds."

Chapter 14

The moon barely provided enough light through all the foliage for them to see as they walked down the overgrown path. Hollan stayed close to Jacob and clutched the hem of his shirt. Gunter followed close behind.

They neared the shore and walked quietly along the trees. Even Samson seemed to understand the gravity of the situation as he kept pace beside Hollan. She appreciated the solid warmth of his body as he pressed against her leg. She kept a firm hand on the nape of his neck. If anything lurked in the bushes, Samson would warn them in plenty of time.

They'd debated leaving him behind, but with no way to secure the shack's door, he'd break free and end up tagging along anyway. At least this way they had a semblance of control over the situation.

The large outline of David's ship loomed high against the horizon, its features eerie in the moonlight. The smaller boats were pulled up on shore, just as they'd hoped, and Hollan didn't see any sign of a watchman.

"No one seems to be around," Hollan whispered. "Maybe they're so cocky they don't expect us to steal—I mean, borrow—one."

"If so, it's more likely they were too tired or too drunk and they didn't give it a thought," Jacob interjected.

"Perhaps it's a mixture of both," her father agreed.

Jacob glanced back at Hollan, the moonlight highlighting the smirk on his face. "And surely my dear brother wouldn't have an issue with us borrowing one of his boats."

"Yes, he's so accommodating and thoughtful." The sarcasm rolled off Hollan's tongue.

They huddled at the edge of the trees.

"I've been wondering. How *did* David get a boat so quickly?" Hollan asked. "If you followed him here. . . ?"

"I told you I had to argue with God a bit before I headed back. David had time to secure the vessel. As to how, I'm sure it wasn't by legal means. The crew might belong to the ship—and it's a skeleton crew at that—but I doubt the ship belongs to my brother."

"Well said." Hollan was ready to leave the island. "Let's keep going."

They slowly crept along the edge of the curved beach that contained the rowboats. "If no one is here, we'll just hop in and go, is that the plan?" Hollan asked. "The area appears to be deserted." She couldn't wait to get out of there.

Samson let out a low growl.

"Then again, we could be wrong," Hollan hissed as the dark form of a man rose up from where he'd apparently been sleeping on the bottom of one of the boats.

They all ducked in unison.

"Who's out there?"

"It's Jonathon!" Hollan whispered, then stood and started to answer.

Jacob yanked her back down and shook his head then put a finger to his lips. Hollan nodded.

"We need to make sure he's alone."

"Of course. I'm sorry."

They waited in silence. No one else moved or answered. Jonathon stood and stepped out of the beached boat and headed for the trees. Samson growled again, and Hollan returned her hand to the nape of his neck.

"He's coming this way!" she hissed.

Jacob held up a hand. Hollan quieted. Her heart beat quickly in her chest as she watched her husband's actions. He crouched in the shadows and followed Jonathon's movements with scrutinizing eyes.

When Jonathon stood within reach of them, Jacob lunged forward and grabbed the man around the neck. He pulled him close against his chest.

"Jonathon. Don't make a sound. Is there anyone else here with you?" Jacob asked in a quiet voice.

"No, I'm in charge of the boats." Jonathon sounded rattled.

Hollan's heart went out to the man. "It's okay, Jonathon. It's just us."

Jacob loosened his grip, but Jonathon didn't move.

"You shouldn't oughta sneak up on a man like that," he groused. "A man could drop dead from fright. I didn't want to stay out here in the first place. It's spooky."

"Says the man who kidnapped me from a beach," Hollan pointed out.

"Fair enough." Jonathon shifted on his feet. He didn't exude any of the cockiness that David liked to portray. "I do apologize for that. But I couldn't go against the other men. They'd have killed me on the spot."

"I'm glad they didn't." Hollan's voice softened. She didn't blame Jonathon for not helping. But she did hope he'd help them now. "You can make it up to me, though."

"How's that?" His voice held a hint of distrust.

"You can let us have a boat, let us get away."

"Oh, I don't know. David would be so angry."

"Then go with us. We'll take you to safety."

"I don't think there's a place safe enough to get away from David."

"If we can get to the authorities, David will be captured by the law. You'll be safe. Think about it, Jonathon! Won't you feel good knowing you're on the right side of the law for a change?"

"I ain't never been on that side that I can remember. . . ." Jonathon sounded dubious.

"Jonathon. God put you here to help us. I'm sure of it. If you help us, we can help you."

"No offense, ma'am, but David's the one who put me here, not God."

"That's how it might look to you"—Hollan reached for his arm—"but I feel sure God put you here to help us. We can help each other. Come with us, help us paddle through the channel, and we'll hide you in a safe place when we get to town."

"I didn't know there was a town nearby."

"It isn't exactly a town, per se, but there's a small church and a building that's used as a general store. There's an acting sheriff. The townsfolk look out for each other. You'd be welcome there."

He hesitated.

"You don't want to let God down, do you? We need you to help us."

"You're sure I'll be safe?"

"Yes. But we need to leave right now."

"On the open water, at night? With a woman on board?"

"You can't possibly still blame *me* for all the problems after you kidnapped me. There's no such thing as bad luck. Everything that happened to you, Paxton, and Nate was caused by your own actions. And as for nighttime travel, there's enough moonlight to see pretty well. We know the waters, and this stretch won't be difficult at all. It's just a little ways away."

Jonathon didn't answer. Hollan didn't know what they'd do if he refused. She didn't want to see the man hurt and didn't know that Jacob and her father even had it in them to hurt a man. She had a feeling, though, that if pushed into a corner, when it came to her safety against Jonathon's, Jacob's protective instinct would kick in.

"Please? This would more than make up for the kidnapping." Hollan prayed for the right words. "If you help us escape now, the law will see that you assisted us. Otherwise, you might be charged with kidnapping along with the others when they're caught. And they will be caught, if not right now, then soon. David said the officials were after him."

"You're sure we'll get away?"

"Do you expect David or any of his men to come check on you tonight?"

"No, they won't be coming around till morning."

"Then we need to go now."

Jonathon nodded and led the way to the farthest boat. "If they catch us, I'll tell them you threatened me with that shotgun Jacob's carrying."

"Nice to know you have our backs," Hollan muttered.

Jacob bent down to help push the boat into the water. "I don't intend to let them catch us."

Hollan settled into the seat at the bow, the same place she'd sat when David's men first took her from shore. She patted the seat and with a whine Samson climbed in with her. He settled at Hollan's feet on the floor.

Jacob and Gunter took the middle seat, and Jonathon took the rear.

"Wait," Hollan hissed. "What about the men in the hold?"

"None of them made it," Jonathon said. "If it makes you feel better, they weren't much better than David and his crew. They were privateers during and after the war."

Hollan shuddered. "I'm not sure that makes me feel better, but thank you."

"Hollan, you'll have to watch for debris and sandbars," Jacob instructed. "We'll stay close to shore, but you'll have to guide us if you see anything coming our way."

Hollan shifted in her seat so she could see where they were going.

They traveled slowly. The gentle current worked with them. Hollan was glad Jonathon had come along. Though he wasn't a large man, he was burly, and his added strength as they rowed didn't hurt as they made progress.

"I have a confession to make." Jonathon's hesitant voice sounded loud in the silence. He laid his oar across his lap.

Jacob and her father stopped rowing, but they continued to drift along. They all stared at the man as they waited.

"We ran into a man on our way over this afternoon."

A chill passed through Hollan. "A man?"

"Yes. He came across on a flatboat just as we neared your island in our rowboats."

"A flatboat. . .like a supply boat?"

"Yes'm." Jonathon shifted nervously in his seat and set the boat to rocking.

"Sit still!" Jacob commanded. "What happened to this man?"

"David. . .um. . .well, he and some of the men sort of took advantage of him."

"Took advantage?" Hollan asked, confused.

"They beat him and stole his load from the boat."

Hollan's heart pounded. "Where is he?"

"I don't know. After stealing the supplies, they left him aboard his boat and sent it downstream. Last I saw him, the supply boat was floating this way."

"If the current caught Fletcher, he could be well on his way out to sea." The anger in Jacob's voice was palpable.

"I didn't do it," Jonathon defended.

"You might as well have if you just stood by and let it happen," Jacob accused.

Jonathon looked down and didn't say anything more.

Jacob ran a hand through his golden hair. "I'm sorry. You didn't have a choice. They would have just beaten you and added you to the boat with Fletcher or worse."

"We need to find him." Her father's voice was full of resolve. His comment was a command.

"We need to get closer to the other side. We've been fighting the same current his boat would have. It keeps pushing us to the east. The shapes of the vessels are different, so his boat would have flowed more smoothly across the water. There's a chance we'll pass him on the far side."

"If he didn't capsize or fall off."

"He was pretty well centered when they sent his boat off," Jonathon said quietly.

They crossed the channel and headed toward land. Hollan felt vulnerable out in the open, even though she knew no one could possibly be nearby. The moon glistened off the top of the water. She prayed Fletcher would be all right and that they would find him.

Though Hollan longed to dangle her fingers in the water, she knew better than to do it at night. She rested her elbow on her knee and put her chin on her fist as she watched the water for obstacles. She searched the shore for any sign of the supply boat. The lateness of the hour caught up with her, and she struggled to stay awake.

Lord, help me to focus and do my part. I'm so tired. I don't want to let the men down or fall asleep in my seat.

Just as she finished the prayer, a large shape rose up from the water and then rolled back down in front of her. Hollan smiled. A dolphin! She hadn't seen one in three years, and here this one was swimming in front of them as if directing their boat across the waters. Any thoughts of sleep drifted away as she watched the magnificent creature. Each time he ducked below, she hoped he'd surface again. As long as she could see him, she'd know there wasn't anything in front of them.

Finally the dolphin did a half turn and swam away from the boat. Hollan wanted to beg him to return. But as she looked up, she noticed a structure ahead of them.

"I see the dock! And Fletcher's boat is there." Hollan all but bounced on her seat as they neared their destination.

"Sit still, girl, before you swamp us," her father's good-natured voice called from the middle seat. "Looks like Fletcher made it back."

"What a relief."

"Strange," Jonathon said. "It looked like they did him in."

"Fletcher is a very strong man. He must have recovered from the blows and made his way back home," Jacob stated.

"I sure hope so. I'd feel a lot better."

"We'll know soon. We'll check on him as soon as we get in." Jacob dragged his oar in the water, spinning them around. The current pushed them closer to shore.

"Now to see how the town has fared."

They pulled the boat up against the dock. Jacob jumped out to secure it. He helped Hollan from the boat, and the other two men joined them. Samson ran happily from one end of the dock to the other.

Fletcher's boat was tied securely to the pier. There was no sign of the man on the dock or in the water nearby.

"Where do we go from here?" Jonathon asked nervously.

"We don't have far to go," Hollan assured him. "We'll go to my uncle's house. It's just up the road from here."

"It's the middle of the night. Will he be upset to find all of us at his door?"

Hollan grimaced. "He's the reverend of the church. He's used to late-night calls."

They trudged along the sandy path, the moonlight leading the way. Samson ran ahead. Every so often he'd return to check on them, and then off he'd go again. An alligator bellowed from the marsh to their right, and Hollan shivered. Jacob wrapped a reassuring arm around her shoulders.

Hollan let out a sigh of relief when they reached civilization, though the houses they passed were all dark. As they neared the row of buildings that composed the town, Jacob stopped. "I want to alert the sheriff. I doubt David would be so brass as to come here in the morning, but it's best not to take a chance."

"I'll head up the road. I'll wait for you there." Jonathon backed away.

"Nonsense." Hollan grabbed his arm. "You'll stay here with us."

She could feel his muscles tense when the sheriff opened the door.

"What's going on?" The gruff voice made her want to run, too, but she stood firm.

Jacob nodded toward Hollan. "Pastor Edward's niece here was kidnapped from the beach yesterday by my brother and his crew of men. They met with some misfortune and ran their boat ashore and have now moved into the cottage at the lighthouse."

"I see." The sheriff looked at each of them in turn. "Fletcher apparently met up with the same group on his way to your place. He made it back, but he's in pretty bad shape."

"Where is he?" Hollan asked.

"They took him to Doc when they first found him, but he's at his mother's now. We were going to put together a posse at first light and go over to check on you. At least now we can concentrate on the hurricane repairs. Where are you all headed?"

"We're headed for Edward's place, and we'll stay there for the night."

"I'll make sure to keep an eye out for anything suspicious."

"Thank you." Jacob reached out his hand, and the sheriff shook it. "When do you think you'll be able to secure the island? David said they were wanted. That's the reason he attempted the channel as it was."

"You said no one's in harm's way?"

"No, and David and his men aren't going anywhere fast. They're stuck there. Unless they decide to come over here."

"I'll set up watch, but I doubt David will come here. He's still a wanted man. We're still repairing damage from the storm. We need to secure the homes that are open to the elements. I'd guess we have about two to three more days, and then we'll gather up a posse."

"Three days?" Hollan asked in disbelief. "The cottage and lighthouse could be in shambles if you wait that long!"

"Hollan, it'll be fine." Her father laid a reassuring hand on her shoulder. "We're safe, and that's what matters most."

"What about the ships, Papa? Who will keep them safe? The lighthouse needs to guide them."

"Gunter? Is that you?" The sheriff leaned forward with his lantern.

"Yes, Sheriff Roberts, it's me."

"I'm glad to see you safe. Parson Edward said you were missing."

"David and his crew took me just before the storm hit. Hollan and Jacob came to my rescue."

"Only after they kidnapped me!" Hollan filled in. "But Jacob came for us both."

"I'm sorry this happened to you." The sheriff lifted his lantern and stared at Jonathon. "And who do we have here?"

"Jonathon, sir." Jonathon's voice quaked under the sheriff's perusal.

"That don't tell me much."

Hollan hurried to intervene. "He helped us escape. He's from the ship."

"Did you now? I'm glad to hear that. We'll need to talk in the morning. I'll have some questions for you."

"Yes, sir." Relief tinged Jonathon's words. "I'll be here."

Sheriff Roberts looked at Jacob. "Swan. It's good to have you home. Edward told me about the marriage. Congratulations to you both."

They thanked him.

"Go on with you now. We'll all get some sleep, and I'll see you in the morning."

They walked up the road toward Edward's place.

"Your uncle has room enough for all of us?" Jonathon asked.

"He does. He'll probably put you men up in the church, and I'll stay in their home."

"Will you be safe there?" Jonathon continued with his questions. "David is a dangerous man."

"Yes, she'll be safe," Jacob interrupted. "I intend to make sure of it."

"Jacob, you need to get some sleep. I'll be fine. David won't know where we are. He surely won't dare to come after us."

"I agree. Most likely he won't. But I'm not taking any chances. If I have to sit on Edward's front porch, I'll do so in order to know that you're safe."

"Then perhaps we'll all stay in their home. They have several extra rooms."

"We'll see what Edward says. But I can guarantee if you're staying in that house, I'll be right there with you."

Edward answered his door and welcomed them in. Ettie pulled Hollan into her arms and cried when she saw Gunter.

"My brother!" Edward's eyes moistened as he took in the sight of Gunter. "You're alive."

"I'm fine. Or I will be after a bit of rest."

"You look well, Hollan." Edward beamed. "Married life must agree with you."

Hollan smiled up at Jacob. "Much to my surprise, it does."

"And Jacob. Is island life everything you hoped it would be? Did you find it to be a balm to your weary soul?"

Hollan laughed out loud.

"You find the question amusing?" Her uncle looked confused.

Jacob looked at Hollan, and they shared another smile. "Life on the island has been interesting to say the least. Two things stand out at the moment, though. Hollan has her sight back, and Gunter is safe."

"Hollan!" Ettie's tears continued. "I'm so happy, sweetheart. Let me look at you."

"More importantly, Auntie, let *me* look at *you*."

"We have a lot to catch up on."

"Indeed we do."

Aunt Ettie turned to Hollan's father.

"Gunter"—she gave him a little poke—"you gave us all quite a scare."

Uncle Edward raised his hands. "I'm glad we've all had a moment to catch up, but I'm sure you didn't make your way out here in the middle of the night to share your good news."

Chapter 15

Gunter and Hollan were kidnapped by my brother David." The words rolled off Jacob's tongue.

A vein in Edward's neck began to throb. "Hasn't that boy caused y'all enough grief?"

"He's hardly a boy anymore, Ed," Ettie corrected. "But he does need to be stopped."

"Where is he now?"

Hollan answered, "He's on the island."

"Then we need to go after him. I'll get the sheriff."

"We've already talked to the sheriff, Uncle Edward. We're meeting him again first thing in the morning."

"Hmmph."

"There's more." Hollan knew her uncle and aunt were very close to Fletcher and Sylvia. "Fletcher apparently brought our supplies over about the same time David and his men came ashore. They stole everything he had, beat him, and left him for dead."

"Oh dear me." Ettie's hand was at her throat, and she fanned herself.

"Now, dear, sit down before you get yourself too worked up." Uncle Edward helped her over to the settee. "Where's Fletcher now?"

Jacob shifted on his feet. He looked tired enough to fall over. "According to the sheriff, he's home with Sylvia. We intend to go out there in the morning, too."

"I'll be going with you." Edward sighed. "Ettie and I were at the Black place all day. We had no idea."

"Poor Sylvia, dealing with this all alone." Ettie kept shaking her head.

"She's a strong woman, Ettie. I'm sure she's fine."

Hollan listened to them talk. "Well, I'm glad Sylvia was here to care for Fletcher." A plan began to formulate in Hollan's mind. If the menfolk were too busy to go over and capture an outlaw, she'd talk to Sylvia about flushing them out somehow. Surely the woman would be just as incensed as Hollan after what happened to her son. "She has to be furious at David."

"As well she should be," Ettie huffed.

Ah, yes. Hollan would surely have an ally in Sylvia. Ettie was upset, and it wasn't even her son hurt, though Hollan was like a daughter to her.

The simple facts were her father wasn't well, the lighthouse was unattended, and local seafarers were unsafe as long as they had no light to guide them. Hollan glanced at her father. He'd paled and now looked exhausted. She hurried to his side. "Papa?"

"I'm just tired. I suppose all the excitement of the past few weeks is catching up with me."

"Well, let's get you tucked into bed, then." Ettie was on her feet and acting as hostess, leading the weary Gunter to a room at the back of the house. "And you two take the room upstairs across from ours—Hollan's room when she stays here," she called as she retreated down the hallway.

Hollan darted her eyes to Jacob.

"If you don't mind, I'd rather stay down here where I can watch the door. Let Hollan sleep in the bed. She needs a good night's sleep."

"As do you," Hollan quipped. "You've lost several nights' sleep."

"I'll be fine. Like I told you before, between the war and the traveling, I've learned to sleep in snatches."

"Jonathon." Ettie's no-nonsense voice as she came up the hall made the man jump. "You'll settle into the room across from Gunter. Follow me to the back of the house, and I'll show you the way."

Jonathon blushed. "Oh no, ma'am. I'll be fine on the porch or in a shed if you have one out back. I haven't slept on the likes of a bed in longer than I can remember."

"Then it's high time you had a good night's sleep. Tonight you'll be blessed with a bed."

"I've already been blessed in many ways tonight." Jonathon glanced at Hollan.

She smiled back at him. "You deserve it, Jonathon. You helped save us. Tomorrow I'll make a celebration breakfast in your honor."

"I'm not sure I earned such an honor."

"You've more than earned it, Jonathon," Hollan encouraged.

"You brought our niece home safe and sound. We will celebrate."

Jonathon beamed.

Edward walked with Ettie and Jonathon as they headed for the back of the house, leaving Hollan and Jacob temporarily alone.

"Thank you for volunteering to stand watch. That saved us an awkward situation."

"I volunteered to stand watch because I want to know you're safe. Otherwise I would have grabbed Ettie's suggestion before you could have said anything about it."

"Oh," Hollan croaked.

He stepped closer, and his green eyes stared into hers with such intensity she figured he could read her deepest thoughts. "And when we get this all taken care of, I expect to start all over with this marriage. This time we'll do it right."

"I see."

Jacob laughed. "My wife appears to be tongue-tied for the first time ever."

Hollan mashed the toe of her boot into a knothole on the floor. "And what am I to say to such talk? I wonder. . . ."

"What?"

"Would it be possible to have our wedding ceremony over?" She felt silly asking. "I'd love to have Aunt Ettie there this time around. And our friends. . ."

"If that's what it takes to set this marriage straight."

"Your intensity embarrasses me." Hollan stepped away but laughed. She might as well get used to it.

He moved closer still. "It isn't my intent to embarrass you. But you should know my thoughts. We'll start our marriage again, and we'll do it right this time."

"I'd like that."

"Good." He grinned. "Now get up to bed. We have a busy day tomorrow."

Hollan woke later than she'd planned the next morning, after the long and tiring night. She couldn't wait to talk to Sylvia. She wanted to check on Fletcher. But she also wanted to ask for Sylvia's assistance in ridding their lives of David. If Jacob wouldn't go along with her, and the townsmen still wouldn't go after David after all that he'd done, she'd find a way to capture him herself. Surely after a night's sleep, Jacob, the sheriff, and the townspeople would agree this couldn't wait.

A few minutes later she listened as Jacob dashed her dreams of going home soon.

"We can't do this yet. The town needs to be secured, then we'll worry about the island.

People will lose their life's belongings if we don't fix their roofs before the next storm rolls through."

"Jacob, why are you standing against me in this? Our life has been in turmoil far too long and all because of David."

"I'm not standing against you, Hollan. But we need to have a plan. David's not going anywhere. The ship is stuck for now."

"But I want to go home. I want our life to get back to normal. I want to enjoy the return of my vision in the place I love."

"Oh. . .and here I thought you were in a hurry to get back so you could officially start your life with me."

Hollan blushed. "You know I want that, too. But first we need to rid the island of David."

Jacob refused to budge.

She tried her ace in the hole. "The lighthouse is unattended. At least, it's unattended if they haven't broken into it yet. They've probably destroyed everything I hold of value. I could lose everything I own, too."

"I admit that bothers me." Jacob paced as he always did when stressed. "But the lighthouse is well secured, and I'm pretty sure they won't be able to get in. I'll replace anything we lose."

"You're 'pretty sure' they won't get in?" Hollan raised an eyebrow. "Do you realize how long it will take to replace the lens if they find a way to damage it?"

The scent of fried ham and eggs wafted into the room from the kitchen. Hollan's mouth watered, momentarily distracting her.

"Hollan. We can't go back until we put a plan in place. Gunter, Jonathon, and I will talk to the sheriff as soon as we've eaten breakfast. I want you to stay here and wait with Ettie. Understand?"

"I need to go see Sylvia."

Jacob's face lit up. "That's a wonderful plan. You spend your time with Sylvia and Fletcher while we menfolk come up with our plan."

Hollan scowled.

Jonathon walked into the room. He looked uncomfortable. "Good morning."

"Is everything all right?" Hollan hurried over to his side.

"I'm not used to waking up in a—home. It's unnerving."

Hollan smiled at Jacob. "I'm sure it is. Aunt Ettie has breakfast ready, and we were just heading that way. Do you want to clean up and meet us in the kitchen?"

Jonathon nodded and shuffled toward the back of the house while Hollan and Jacob headed for the kitchen.

Hollan hesitated in the doorway. "Aunt Ettie? If you don't mind, I'd like to go on over and see how Sylvia and Fletcher fared last night."

"Before you eat?" Jacob frowned.

Her aunt looked up from the biscuits she was pulling from the oven. "Can't you wait, dear? I'd planned to walk over with you."

"Father needs someone here. I'll stay if you'd like. . . ." She made her voice wistful.

"But you'd really rather go yourself." She sighed. "I know how important Sylvia is to you. I'll stay here with Gunter. You go on ahead."

"If you're sure. . ."

"Go on. Here"—Aunt Ettie grabbed a biscuit and smeared it with jam—"at least eat this on the way."

Hollan took the biscuit and gave her aunt a grateful look. She glanced at Jacob and tried to hide the guilt she was sure he could read in her eyes. "I'll be going then. I'll see you. . .after?"

"After? Oh, right. We'll talk to the sheriff and meet up with you later." He shrugged, though he still looked perplexed. Or did he look suspicious?

Most likely Hollan was merely feeling guilty.

She headed out the door and up the sandy path. The late morning sun beat down upon her back, and the day promised to be clear. The marshes on either side of the road were bustling with activity. Butterflies flitted from plant to plant. A lizard darted across the path right in front of her. A bit farther Hollan saw a snake slither through the tall reeds at her side.

The lizards and butterflies didn't bother her, but after the snake sighting, Hollan picked up her pace. It took the better part of an hour before Sylvia's small cabin was just around the bend.

"Hollan! What a pleasant surprise." Sylvia had been sitting on her front porch, sipping from a steaming mug, but now she hurried to her feet. She tilted her head and studied Hollan for a moment.

Hollan stared back and grinned.

The wind blew Sylvia's hair. Suddenly her hand flew to her chest. "You can see again."

"Yes, I can see again." She smiled at her friend for a moment then sobered. "I heard about Fletcher. How's he doing?"

A cloud passed over Sylvia's face. "He'll be fine, no thanks to whoever harmed him. We were so worried about you."

"I'm fine. . .and I know who did this to him."

Sylvia slapped her mug down with a *thump*. "You tell me, and I'll go after them on my own!"

"You don't have to go alone. I'd love to go with you." Hollan walked up the steps and placed a hand on Sylvia's arm. "The man responsible for hurting Fletcher kidnapped my father and me. He's also responsible for what happened to my mother."

"What a horrid person. How do you know?"

Hollan told her friend what had happened.

"We must put a stop to this."

"I agree, but Jacob says the town isn't in any shape to help us out. And he's right. People need a roof over their heads before the next storm hits."

"But a very dangerous man is lurking out there, waiting to hurt his next victim. We won't be safe until the authorities get him under control."

"I agree, but that isn't my only concern. The ships aren't safe without the lighthouse."

They exchanged a mischievous glance.

"Do you have a plan?" Sylvia took another sip from the mug. "You aren't thinking of going alone. . . ?"

"No–o–o," Hollan drawled. "But I *am* thinking of going over with help." She sent Sylvia a meaningful look.

"We don't want to put ourselves in danger."

"I know that island like the back of my hand."

"The menfolk will be so upset."

"I'm willing to take that chance. I'm pretty upset myself that we have to sit here and do nothing while those outlaws ruin what little I have left from my previous life."

"This isn't a decision to make lightly, dear."

"I'm not making it lightly." Hollan put her hands on her hips. "David has hurt too many people. If we don't act, someone else will be hurt. I saw the look in Jacob's eyes, Sylvia. He's telling me he has to wait to act, but I'm afraid he'll go alone and he'll confront David. I don't want him hurt on my behalf."

"Yet you're willing to be hurt on his behalf?"

"I don't intend to get hurt. But yes, I'd do anything for him. He's been here for me through everything we've endured of late. I owe him."

"But you don't think it'll upset him if something happens to you?"

"I don't intend for anything to happen to you or to me. I plan to use a little subterfuge. I'm not going to confront David."

Doubt crept across Sylvia's features. "Subterfuge?" She raised an eyebrow.

"I just want to set a bonfire as a warning to sailors entering the mouth of the river. We might not be able to use the lighthouse to show them the island's location, but we can light a huge fire on the beach that will serve the same purpose. They'll see the fire and know land is nearby."

"I don't know. Maybe we should just wait for the men to figure this out."

"And let Jacob sneak over on his own?" Hollan shook her head. "I won't chance that. We have to watch out for the sailors. At least help me set a warning fire on the shore. David said he and his crew are wanted. If men on ships are searching for them, I'd like to do my best to protect those men and lead them our way."

They stared at each other for a few more moments. Hollan prayed Sylvia would come along. "Please, Sylvia."

"Perhaps you just solved your own dilemma." Sylvia waved her hands and sighed. "I can't exactly sit by and let you do this alone."

"You're coming with me?"

"I suppose I am."

"And Fletcher will be all right if you leave him?"

"He'll be fine. He's sleeping. Let me run inside and make sure he has everything he needs. Then we'll make our plans. We don't want to get over there too early either. We need to do this under the protection of dusk."

"Sylvia—"

"Yes?" Hollan's friend stopped and turned around.

"Thank you."

"Sweetheart, I don't want you to take responsibility for what we're about to do. I'm doing this for you, yes, but also for your mother, Fletcher, and myself. I'm doing this for all of us. I want the man responsible for hurting my son behind bars."

Hollan smiled. "I understand. And I intend to do my best to see that happen, too."

Chapter 16

"We need to put in here," Hollan whispered. "We don't want David's crew to see us if anyone's on watch."

"I hardly think you need to whisper, Hollan. We're in the middle of a marsh."

"Must you remind me?" Hollan shuddered. If the reeds, taller than their boat, didn't clue her in, the stench of the stagnant water surely did. "Maybe I'm whispering so the creatures don't know we're here. Maybe it has nothing to do with David and his men hearing us."

Sylvia laughed. Hollan's nerves were shot, and she said crazy things when she was stressed and tired.

They'd commandeered Fletcher's supply boat for the trip. Sylvia was accustomed to piloting the flat-bottomed boat. She felt it would allow them to skirt the shallower water and hug the shore more closely. It would also hold the most supplies. Sylvia had been right on every count. Hollan knew she'd made the right decision when she invited the woman along.

They worked together to guide the front of the boat alongside the shore around the bend from where David's men had placed their boats. The watery ground was marshy. Hollan pushed back her fears of snakes and alligators and maneuvered the flatboat deep into the swaying reeds and grasses. They were able to secure the boat mostly out of sight. Hollan jumped into the water, saturating her boots, and tied the vessel to a low-lying tree.

"Tie both ends of the boat securely, dear. Otherwise it will swing back and forth and might work its way loose. We don't want it to be damaged."

Hollan shuddered. "You're right. I want to be sure we have a way off this island."

After doing what Sylvia told her, Hollan helped the older woman off the boat. They gathered their supplies. Sylvia had prepared well for the expedition. They were stocked with weapons, food, and various types of gear, the use of which Hollan didn't even understand.

The sun sat low on the horizon.

"Tell me what you have planned before we leave here," Sylvia requested. "We might not be able to talk as freely later."

"Well, I'd hoped to be here much earlier than this. But since you and I wasted time chatting—"

"Planning and preparing, dear. That wasn't a waste of time."

"Whatever you want to call it, it set us way off track," Hollan replied.

"Not necessarily. The dusk will keep us covered. They're drinking men. They should be well into their indulgences by now."

Which will put us into even greater danger if we get caught. Hollan felt responsible for Sylvia's well-being. It was one thing to deal with evil men. It was another thing entirely to deal with drunken evil men.

Hollan nodded. "I suppose we'd best be on our way."

"Let's pray first."

Sylvia said a quick prayer for their safety and for justice to be served. As soon as she finished, she motioned to Hollan with her hand. "Lead the way. I'd like to get out of here before nightfall."

"Me, too." Hollan didn't need to be asked twice. She was in her least favorite place on the island. The swampy, marshy grounds were home to all sorts of creatures she didn't want to think about, let alone meet. She avoided the area like the plague in broad daylight, so being here after dark was a nightmare.

They didn't talk; they just made haste while walking through the scrub. Hollan pushed through far more spiderwebs than she wanted to think about. Her skin crawled as she wondered about the spiders that lived in the webs. The cooler weather might have chased them off, but she couldn't be sure.

She did a little jig as she walked.

Sylvia's soft laugh flowed through the evening air. "You're fine, Hollan. I see no spiders on your dress or hair." She knew about Hollan's fear of spiders, and she also knew how much Hollan hated this area.

The older woman clucked her tongue. "Love certainly is a mysterious thing."

"Pardon?" Hollan called over her shoulder, not slowing her pace.

"I know how you feel about this area. Yet you're willing to brave it for Jacob."

"I'm braving it in order to right the wrongs David has brought upon our families."

"How far do you plan to go?" Sylvia was out of breath. Hollan needed to slow her pace for the older woman.

"Not much farther. We're nearly at the end of the island now."

"And what are we doing here?"

Hollan stopped a few feet away. "We'll set up a bonfire." She moved her arms in an arc, gesturing toward the beach. The moon was climbing upward, reflecting off the water. Stars studded the sky. The only sound was that of the water lapping gently against the shore.

"Why here?" Sylvia frowned.

"We're at the bay end of the island. If any ships come through here tonight, they'll be able to see where we are. Even better, the outlaws shouldn't be able to see us. We might not have use of the lighthouse, but we can warn the ships' captains of the island's danger from here."

"Good idea."

They busied themselves with gathering all the driftwood they could find.

"I want the fire to be big so it can be seen and so the outlaws can't easily put it out if they do see it."

"Another good idea."

They placed Spanish moss throughout the wood, and Hollan set it on fire. The fire flared, dimmed, and as she held her breath, flared again. Suddenly it caught and made its way through the pile of wood.

"It's magnificent!" Hollan trilled. "And the warmth feels wonderful against the night's chill."

"Indeed it does." Sylvia stared out over the darkened beach. "Only one problem comes to mind."

"What's that?" Hollan asked, turning to look at Sylvia with a smile. No problem could possibly dim her satisfaction now. She'd reached her goal to warn the sailors. Anyone drifting along the shore would see the bonfire and veer away from the land. Their main task had been accomplished.

"A large and very angry group of men seems to be headed our way."

Hollan looked up, and her heart leaped into her throat. Sylvia spoke the truth, and they didn't have time to hide. The men carried torches, and according to their well-defined silhouettes, they also carried very big guns.

Jacob couldn't wait to get his hands on Hollan. He glanced at her father, wondering how the man had ever survived her. "I specifically told her to stay with Sylvia."

"Yes, you said to stay with Sylvia, which is exactly what she did." Gunter's forehead was creased with worry, but admiration for his daughter's spunk put a spark in his eyes. "In time, son, you'll learn to be more careful when choosing your words."

"I chose my words carefully this morning. Hollan deliberately chose to ignore them and twist them to her own benefit."

"Yes."

"Yes? That's all you have to say about it?" Jacob stomped along the path. The group of men walking with them tailed behind. They couldn't hear the conversation between Gunter and Jacob.

"You should know Hollan well enough by now to know she doesn't take well to direct commands."

"I'm her husband."

"And I'm her father. Apparently those two facts don't mean a lot to her when the time comes to make her decisions. Hollan has always acted first and thought later."

"We'll be changing that as soon as I have her safe."

Gunter's only response was an annoying chuckle. "We'll see about that, Jacob. The girl has a mind of her own."

Jacob sighed and pushed his hair back from his face. "I know. And I love her for it. I just don't like it when she puts herself in danger."

"God has His hand on you both. He won't fail Hollan—or us—now."

"You're right." Jacob sighed. "It's just that she makes me crazy with worry when she pulls a stunt like this. I want her home safe, knitting or sewing like a normal woman, but here she is ready to take on a band of roving privateers!"

"I would imagine that when Hollan continues to see her faith is safe with you, Jacob, she'll learn to settle down and let you lead."

"I certainly hope so, sir. I can't take much more of this."

"Meaning?" Gunter raised an eyebrow.

"Meaning, I want my wife safe at home."

"I understand. And I think we'll get her there tonight."

The sheriff walked up to join them. "Any idea what Hollan and Sylvia would have planned?"

"I know she was worried about the lighthouse not being lit. She wanted the seafarers to remain safe. She hated that the light was off during most of the war. She was also worried the men would destroy the cottage and everything in it."

They continued to work their way along the beach. The boats were pulled ashore just as they'd been the night before. It didn't seem as if Jonathon had been replaced by another guard.

Jacob glanced at Hollan's father. The man was pale but hanging in there. "Gunter, what do you think the chances are that David hasn't even missed Jonathon?"

"Pretty fair, I'd say, based on the fact that no one's been sent in his place."

They wove around the boats and continued along the shore, heading for the far end of the island.

The sheriff looked at Jacob again. "Which concern of your wife's would be the priority?"

"I think she'd worry first about the safety of others. My guess is she'll take care of the lighthouse situation first."

"Would she try to get into the lighthouse? Surely she'd know she'd be trapped inside as soon as the light was lit."

Jacob's heart dropped to his toes. What if his brother recreated the situation he'd been in with Hollan's mother? Jacob would throttle Hollan if she survived this! He'd never felt so much concern for another person. He couldn't lose her. Not now. Not after everything they'd been through. Not ever.

"You look ready to take on the outlaws single-handedly," Gunter observed.

"I feel like I could do just that. If they hurt Hollan. . ."

"She'll be fine, son. We're here now, and we'll find them. And although Hollan is contrary and impetuous, she's also very smart. She won't allow herself to be boxed into a corner."

"So how do you think she'll protect the lighthouse without endangering herself?" Jacob hoped with everything in him that Gunter was right.

"I believe—if I know my daughter—she'll set a bonfire on the beach."

"A bonfire, huh?" Sheriff Roberts rubbed his chin. "The fire would warn any captain of the island's dangers."

Jacob pointed ahead. "And it would lead my brother directly to Hollan's side."

"What do we do now?" Hollan panicked. "My plan was that we'd set the fire and then move away the other direction. We'd go into hiding and make the next plan."

"I think we better figure out another plan and fast." Sylvia's voice was shaky.

They'd left their weapons in the trees. They couldn't get them now. In unison, they began to back away.

"We could always turn around and run for it."

Sylvia's laugh held no humor. "Yes, we'd run with a throng of angry men chasing after us with guns. We'd not likely get very far."

"Then we stand tall and go out fighting."

"I don't much like that plan either. Don't you have anything else?"

"No. I have nothing."

The men were getting closer. Hollan reached over and took Sylvia's hand. Not the most heroic gesture, but she drew comfort from her friend's presence.

"We need to pray!" The urgency in Sylvia's voice sent a chill down Hollan's spine.

Hollan heard Sylvia whisper a prayer for their safety. The words had no meaning in Hollan's terrified brain. She didn't want to be in David's custody again, especially now. He'd surely be angry about the ship going aground and about their escape.

The men continued to move closer.

"I'm starting to think we made a really bad decision in coming here."

The sneers on the men's faces scared Hollan to her toes.

"You're just starting to think that? I came to that conclusion when we first saw the throng of men coming our way."

The men neared the far side of the bonfire. Suddenly, as quickly as they'd appeared, they stopped and started to back away.

"Pray again, Sylvia, I think your prayers are working."

"I've already said my prayer, Hollan. I don't need to repeat myself to God."

The men looked wary and then alarmed. They turned heel and began to run.

"I don't understand."

"Me, either." Sylvia laughed. "But I like it!"

"I do, too." Hollan grinned with relief. "If and when we get out of this situation, let's not ever get ourselves into another."

A deep male voice whispered into Hollan's ear, "Is that a promise?"

Hollan screamed.

Jacob leaned around her. "Don't be afraid, Hollan. It's only me."

"You?" Hollan spun around. Her father, the sheriff, Uncle Edward—and almost every man from town—formed a line that stretched across the beach.

"Papa." Her father grinned at her. He didn't seem too angry. Jacob, on the other hand—he seemed angry enough for the both of them. He was possibly angry enough for the entire group.

"Well, I guess now we know why they turned and ran."

"Hollan. We'll discuss this later."

"That's all right," Hollan hedged. "We don't really have to discuss it at all. Let's just let bygones be bygones and start fresh like you said."

"We *will* discuss this." The fire reflected in his eyes and intensified the emerald-green color. His golden hair hung loose in wild curls that danced across his shoulders. He towered over her, looking every bit the outlaw rogue she'd imagined him to be on their wedding day.

A commotion up ahead interrupted their conversation.

"What is it?" Hollan stood on her tiptoes but still couldn't see. Some of the men who had gone ahead returned.

"It seems the bonfire offered a much-needed diversion for the naval patrol. They were able to make landfall and sneak in behind David and his men. They're rounding them up as we speak."

A cheer rose up from Hollan's friends.

"But how—?"

The sheriff walked up with a huge grin on his face. "They knew where David was all along. They only needed the perfect break to come in and overwhelm them. Hollan, your bonfire created that diversion."

Hollan smirked at Jacob.

He quirked up the corner of his mouth and shrugged his shoulder.

Most of the men were drifting back the other direction. They were ready to head home.

Her father, Sylvia, and the sheriff walked ahead. Jacob and Hollan followed at a more leisurely pace.

"You know what this means." Jacob took Hollan's hand in his own.

"We can go home." Tears filled Hollan's eyes as she said the words. "Finally, after everything that's happened, we can go home."

"I like the sound of that, wife."

"That is, if we have a home left to go back to."

"Our cottage is tougher than a few crusty outlaws." Jacob smiled. "Our home will withstand more than that." He stopped and pulled her into his arms. "More importantly. . .home for me is wherever you are."

"Oh Jacob, that's so sweet." Hollan considered his words. "But it's also very true. I feel the same exact way."

Epilogue

Once again Hollan faced Jacob on a dune overlooking the ocean. This time nothing about the situation felt surreal. The wedding *was* the wedding of her dreams. And the man who stood beside her was as familiar to her as her own face. All of her loved ones stood alongside them to witness the event.

Their house—now put back in order after their adventure—and the untouched lighthouse stood sentry behind them. Samson ran between all the people, savoring their attention and happy to be back home.

The afternoon couldn't have been more perfect for their ceremony. The seagulls serenaded as they flew overhead. The ever-present sound of the waves crashing onshore brought a familiar comforting reassurance. Hollan would never tire of the roar of the surf from the Atlantic Ocean. She couldn't wait to wade along the tide line with her husband.

She turned her attention to the man at her side. She saw him clearly. She drank in his dimpled smile, his sparkling green eyes, and the way his golden hair blew in the wind. The sun silhouetted his broad shoulders and proved he wasn't the skinny boy who'd left three years before. The planes of Jacob's face had indeed changed with the years, but the changes were all for the better. And Hollan knew from recent experience that Jacob still didn't like to stay indoors any more than necessary, which accounted for his sun-kissed skin.

Her uncle's voice intruded on her musings. "Hollan. Jacob. I think we're all about ready. Let's do this ceremony right."

"We're ready, too," Jacob said with a grin. He gently squeezed Hollan's hand.

She nodded.

Uncle Edward smiled at her. "No regrets?"

"Never. Not a one."

"Jacob, has life on the island been everything you thought it would be?" Uncle Edward asked.

For a moment, Jacob could only laugh. Hollan watched him with a frown.

"Edward, we've been through a hurricane, I saved Hollan's life—more than once. I watched her captured at the hands of outlaws. I helped her escape. We slept outside with all the bugs on the Georgia coast and the various creepy-crawlies and reptiles. We found out about Fletcher's attack and were chased again by the outlaws. . . ."

"When you put it that way"—Hollan's heart plummeted—"I'm not even sure why you'd want to stay. Why *did* you keep coming for me, even when I put us in danger?"

"My unending love and protection of you is similar to God's unending love and sacrifice for us. Hollan, as long as God allows me the privilege, I'll be right here to pull you away from any danger that comes our way."

Hollan smiled.

"And Edward, to answer your question—" Jacob looked at them both, but his eyes settled on Hollan. The look of love he sent her filled her heart to bursting. "This experience has been everything I imagined and more."

"I'm glad to hear it, son." Uncle Edward slapped Jacob on the back and turned to welcome their guests.

Again he made quick work of the ceremony.

"Jacob, you may now kiss your bride."

Hollan grinned up at him. This was the perfect moment.

Jacob leaned forward and touched his lips to hers in the most gentle of kisses. Hollan's heart soared.

RESTORATION

by Cathy Marie Hake

Dedication

For those who gave an unseen part of themselves away in service to our country and the women who love them through it all. May the day come when wounds heal by the grace of God.

Chapter 1

Virginia, 1918

Tonight, when they're asleep, I'll burn it. Russell Diamond stared at his uniform in the drawer. He hadn't intended to find it, but now that he'd stumbled across it, Russell was certain of the action he had to take. No one would have to know—at least, not for a long while. By then, maybe he'd have the words to smooth over the whole situation.

The olive drabs looked so innocuous, all pressed and clean—just as they had the day he'd first put them on. By the time he got home, the uniform still held blood, mud, and sweat, as well as sea salt from the quick "laundering" it was given aboard the passenger liner the army used to transport the wounded back from Le Havre. Russell loved his country, but he hated war. He wanted no reminder of what he'd seen and done. For now, he took care to glide the bottom drawer of the walnut wardrobe shut and headed for the backyard.

Not many folks had an orchard for a backyard. Big, old, beautiful peach and apricot trees near the house gave way to younger apple trees farther away. Dad had planted a dozen of the apples the year he and Mom married—mostly because he didn't care for the taste of peaches.

Mom and Dad sat on the porch swing, sipping lemonade and enjoying the sunset. Russell didn't feel like talking, so he bobbed a curt nod and plowed on past them. His leg ached as he limped at his best speed. He knew he should have been warmer to his parents, but it wasn't in him. Instead of ruining their pleasant evening, he'd go off on his own. Snagging a pair of buckets and slipping out of sight, he hoped they'd assume he was off to weed a bit.

Among the trees, with peach, apricot, and nectarine blossoms drifting down on him in a gentle Virginia breeze, Russell sat on the ground and jerked weeds until the first pail overflowed. He set it aside and collected more to fill the second. The pain in his leg intensified, but he kept working. Coming across a withered apple core, Russell pitched it into the bucket with the bitter knowledge that he'd missed harvest this past year.

It's too late—or far too early, he thought wryly, *for even gathering any windfall.* Mom always took the bird-pecked or bruised fruit and turned it into sweet cider, cinnamon applesauce, peach jam. . .something. She could find the good in even the worst of situations. *But she was never in war.*

Russell continued to scan for weeds. Anything—anything to keep him busy so he wouldn't have to think.

He finally sat and leaned against a tree his father had planted the Sunday after Russell's birth. At twenty, it was vibrant and straight—a contrast to the dried up, gnarled way Russell felt inside. Home was just the same as always—Dad working at Diamond Emporium, Mom busy with charitable tasks and cooking far too much food. Sis had married one of Buttonhole's fine young men, and they'd be blessed with a baby in a few months. Folks visited over picket fences with their neighbors, bachelors still had a special pew at the back of the sanctuary, and old Mrs. Blanchard still missed about every fifth or sixth note as she played the piano in her parlor.

But I've changed. I'm different. I'll never be the same.

Pain rolled over him again. Russell closed his eyes and let his head fall back against the rough bark. Minutes passed; memories swelled. Everything suddenly shifted when a soft footstep sounded. Russell jolted and grabbed for a rifle that wasn't there.

"Son."

"Dad." He rasped that single word and tried to act casual as he pulled his arm back into his lap, but his heart still thundered.

Dad's step faltered; then he sauntered the last fifteen yards or so, weaving past trees. *He can't stride through his own orchard because of me—I've taken away the pleasure he always took in his evening strolls.*

In days gone by, Dad would have reached out to give a fatherly squeeze to Russell's shoulder, but he'd learned sudden moves and sounds set Russell on edge, so he didn't venture any form of touch. Russell ached for the missing contact.

"Your mother and I would like to talk with you."

"Yes, sir." *The time's come.* Russell got to his feet and walked in silence beside Dad until they reached the back porch. *Dad's slowing his pace to compensate for my limp.* Russell resented the need for it.

Mom, her hair in its usual mussed bun and her apron slightly askew, patted the seat of the porch swing next to her. He sat there, and she handed him a glass of lemonade.

"Thanks, Mom."

Russell could feel her studying him in the waning light. Dad set to lighting a lamp. Unable to look them in the eyes, Russell watched his father's hands as he performed the simple task. Once done, Dad sat on an old wooden chair.

"You're hurting, Son—and I'm not talking about your leg."

Russell shifted his gaze and stared at a droplet of water meandering down the side of his glass. His father's quiet words were so typical of him—direct, open, and unadorned. The very stark quality of them made the truth all that much more painful. The distraction of watching such a mundane thing allowed Russell to consider a response. Finally he opted for honesty. "Yes."

"We knew going away would. . .be hard on you." Mom practiced no artifice, and her candor and sincerity had been qualities he'd come to admire very early on. It tore at him that she felt the need to measure her words so carefully.

Until this evening, he hadn't known she'd also been watching her actions just as cautiously. Mom hadn't washed and hung his uniform back in his wardrobe; she'd laundered it and quietly slipped it away in the bottom of the wardrobe in Sis's old room. If he hadn't been looking for the battered old valise they kept in the drawer, he wouldn't have seen the painstakingly folded olive drab pants and shirt just awhile ago.

Russell chugged down the lemonade, mostly because it bought him a few more moments. He set aside the glass then looked from one parent to the other. "I mean no disrespect. This is hard." He drew in a deep breath. "I can't stay here anymore."

Mom wrapped both of her arms around his right arm and leaned her head on his shoulder. She was holding on tight, just as she had the evening before he took the train to leave as a soldier. "You haven't finished healing yet. The cast just came off. Wait. Stay just a little while until you're more stable."

He'd known she'd resist his plan, but Russell still knew what he had to do. Dad searched his eyes, and Russell couldn't take the scrutiny. He looked away and subtly shook his head. Waiting was out of the question.

"Have you prayed about it?" His father's face looked drawn.

Russell couldn't lie, even though he knew the truth would burden them. He'd not taken the matter to God—in fact, he and the Almighty were on very shaky terms. "No."

Mom gasped, and Russell knew he'd let her down. Her voice showed it when she finally said in a strained tone, "Aw, honey."

Mom's faith was deep and dear to her; he'd strayed from the path of righteousness. It was one of the biggest reasons he couldn't live here.

"You should still stay, Russell." She rubbed her cheek on his shoulder. "It takes time when a man's been hurt for his body and soul to settle with all he's gone through. We understand. It doesn't change how we feel about you."

Russell gently separated from her and stood. He and his father exchanged a momentary look—one that silently agreed to shield Mom from as much of the pain as they could. Russell dipped his head and pressed a kiss on her hair. "I love you, too." The scent of peaches and cloves that always clung to her gave him a scrap of comfort.

Dad took a deep breath and let it out slowly. "We have something else to discuss."

Though he wanted to escape to the solitude of his bedroom, Russell forced himself to sit back down on the swing. One last night, he'd sit here. He'd discipline himself to pretend things weren't so bad. It was the least he could do.

"A letter came today," Dad said. "My great-uncle Timothy passed on. The family house belonged to him. He boarded up the place, and no one's lived in it for several years. The day we learned you were coming home, he wrote his will and left the house and all of his wealth to you, Russell."

"Money won't cure what ails me."

"No, it won't." Dad sighed. "And I'm glad you have the wisdom to see that, but you said you need to leave. You'll always have a place to come back to here, but in the meantime, you have a home and funds to take care of yourself."

Russell nodded. Words seemed futile, and Mom seemed far too fragile.

Mom tilted her head and looked up at him. She tried her best to give him a brave smile even though tears glossed her eyes. "Think on this more. Sleep on it. Your dad and I will pray." Pain radiated from her as she added, "If you still feel you have to go, we'll be supportive."

They all sat together as night engulfed the yard. Crickets chirped and cicadas whirred. The wind soughed through the branches. He'd left as a boy and come back a man—but for this one evening, Russell relished the one thing that he'd not been stripped of: the unvarnished, uncomplicated, unconditional love of his family.

If he stayed here, the ache in his soul would ruin that. He knew he had to go.

Crack! Lorelei Goetz looked down at the two pieces of glass in her hand and grimaced. They hadn't broken along the line she'd scored. Setting down the smaller segment, she focused her attention on the larger. If she tapped it a bit more with the ball end of her scoring tool, she might still get the cut.

Minuscule glass slivers caught the sunlight pouring in through her workroom window, turning the edge of her table into a kaleidoscope of red, gold, and blue. She paused for a second to appreciate the prisms the clear shards added to the mix. Papa had called them the beams of joy. He'd taught her the art of stained glass, and at times like this, it was bittersweet to see the beauty but not have him here to share it.

"You start early today, *Ja*?"

Lorelei looked over her shoulder and smiled. "Ja, Mama. I'd like to finish this window a few days early if I can. Mr. Grun said he'd be going to Portsmouth next week, and he'd be willing to deliver it for me."

He mother smiled and nodded. "*Wunderbar!* He will be very careful. Herr Grun is a kind man."

Lorelei turned back to the glass. "Yes, Mama, he is." She paused a moment then added in a firm tone, "It doesn't mean I'm going to pack up and go marry his cousin in South Dakota.

This is our home—yours and mine. We're staying here."

Mama clucked her tongue. "You are a pretty girl, my Lori. There is no reason for you to spend your days breaking glass and putting it back together when you could be married and having babies. Your papa would want you to."

"Yes," Lorelei agreed pensively. "Papa would have been a wonderful grandpa."

Taking advantage of the opening, her mother rushed to add, "I was married and had you by the time I was your age."

"Twenty isn't old, Mama, and Papa also wanted me to find a man who would love me the way he loved you. He told me not to settle on anything less than a perfect fit—not in a window, not in my marriage."

"If only he were here. He would talk sense into you. There is a difference between wishes and wisdom, Lori."

She turned around. "Mama, what's wrong?"

Her mother came into the workroom and perched on a wooden stool. She looked like a chickadee—a plump, compact woman with brown and gray hair; she wore a faded gray apron over a brown and black dress. Instead of folding her arms as she'd normally do, she shoved them into the apron pocket—a sure sign she was worried. Instead of speaking, she shrugged.

Lorelei set down the glass, blew on her hands to remove any glass slivers, then went to her mother. "Mama, we have each other."

"But we have little else!" Her mother blurted out the words then bit her lip.

"You're worried about money?"

"Yes, but more—I'm worried about you. So many still look at us as the enemy."

The injustice of that hurt. Papa had gone to fight for America, yet because they had German ancestors, still spoke German at home, and had a German last name, folks reviled them. It wasn't until after Papa died and the government sent a soldier in a fancy uniform to give them shiny medals in Papa's honor that many of the townspeople finally shifted from hostility to wariness.

"There are hard feelings—ones that won't fade for a long time. Too many of the young men refuse to be seen with a German girl even just for a date. They won't want you for a wife." Mama pasted on a smile. "If you go to South Dakota, you will have a husband and children."

"Arranged marriages ended in the Dark Ages. I'm happy here with you. We'll pray that if God has a husband in mind for me, He'll bring him to our doorstep."

Mama shook her head. "What am I to do with you? Men are not like bottles of milk that get delivered to your porch."

Lorelei laughed and gave her mother a peck on the cheek. "Last Sunday, the pastor told us to seek God's will and to pray specifically, in faith."

Mama finally pulled her hands out of her apron pocket and rubbed her legs. "Child, I'm going to end up with flat knees from all of the hours I spend kneeling in prayer for you."

Chapter 2

"Son." His father's voice carried grim determination. "I want a promise from you."

Russell stood near the backyard porch steps, by the barrel Mom grew strawberries in. He plucked a dried leaf from one of the plants. Mom was inside, putting together some food for him to take. From how red and puffy her eyes had looked at breakfast, he knew she'd been up half the night weeping. He'd come out here because. . .well, because.

"You write your mom. Let her know how you're doing."

Swallowing hard, Russell lifted his chin and stared at Dad. He gave a curt nod. "You have my word."

"And you have my word that if you need me, I'll be there. If it would help, I'm ready to come along right now—just me. I have a sense that you're fighting mightily to shield Mom from things."

Knocking the heel of his hand against the barrel, Russell cleared his throat. Dad had built the emporium from a failing, little, backwater shop into a thriving concern. For him to be willing to leave it all at the drop of a hat underscored the love he felt. "Dad, I appreciate the offer, but you were right last night. I have to be alone."

"Son, you're not alone; God is with you."

"I told you last night—I'm not talking to God anymore."

"I heard you." His dad came down the steps and plucked a strawberry. He dusted it off gently and popped it into his mouth.

He chose the fresh, sweet berry; I'm standing here clutching the dead leaf. Russell let out a bitter laugh.

Dad shoved his hands in his pockets and didn't take offense at Russell's mirthless reaction. "It's not your leg that's troubling you; it's the ugliness you endured. It's a soldier's burden, one I hoped you'd be spared. My great-uncle Tim was battle scarred and struggled mightily with his feelings and his faith."

"I don't remember much of him—just that he didn't get married until he was real old."

"He took what little was left of the family shipping business after the war and threw himself into rebuilding it. Business and the sea were his lifeblood, but his escape—his refuge—was the old family house."

"He left it."

"Originally, he went back home after the war. With time, he finally found peace there. When his wife developed consumption, the doctor recommended they move. It wasn't until then he left. You'll find peace there, Son. I have faith."

"I heard old Mr. Sibony has a matched pair of geldings he wants to sell." Russell hoped his father would go along with the change of subject. "I figure I'll just ride to the coast."

Shortly thereafter, with a blanket tied to the rear of his saddle and packs tied to the second gelding, Russell left Buttonhole. Following the directions he'd been given, he rode for two days until he passed through a seaside town and arrived at the outskirts where the road branched off. To the right, he spotted a charming little cottage with two chimneys, a budding garden, and sheets on the clothesline, snapping in the stiff breeze. That breeze also carried a woman's voice.

He didn't want to deal with others, so instead of following the curving dirt road, he cut across a spread that once must have been a well-kept lawn. He could see stables in the distance off another fork in the road, but ahead loomed the old Newcomb house.

Russell halted the horses near a clump of overgrown shrubs and studied the house. He listened intently for any sounds of inhabitants and heard none. Not a single track or footprint marred the earth. Satisfied the place hadn't been approached from this direction, he tethered the geldings and reconnoitered on foot.

He continued to scan the ground for signs of footprints and the windows for faces or moving curtains. Several of the windows were cracked. A few panes were missing entirely. What glass remained intact looked murky with age-old, undisturbed dust. *Good. No one's been here.*

Water would be his most basic need, so he strode down a weed-encrusted cobblestone path to a well. Someone had wisely fitted a cover over the well for safety's sake. Russell nodded approvingly. He dragged it to the side, looked about for a rope and bucket, and realized neither was present. Inhaling deeply, he could smell the sweet, damp aroma of fresh water. He flipped a small stone in and heard a satisfying splash.

Russell made his way to the front of the house and allowed himself to look up and assess the architecture. It must have once been a graceful place—a large antebellum mansion meant for rearing a big family. It would accommodate sizable crowds, and from family stories he'd heard, the Newcombs had done considerable entertaining.

The roof lacked a plethora of shingles, warning Russell the inside undoubtedly suffered water damage. Some of the upper story's windows were cracked; a few were even missing. The ground-floor windows had been boarded up, and sections of clapboard on the seaward side of the house looked thoroughly rotten. The veranda sagged here and there.

It looks like I feel.

Dad had told him his great-uncle had found refuge here after the ravages of the War Between the States. *It can be my hideaway now, too. There's plenty of work to be done, and it doesn't matter how long it takes.*

Russell trod carefully—not just because of his leg, but because the steps and veranda sported broken or missing planks. He curled his hands around a gray, weathered board and yanked. Nails squealed, and the piece pulled free. After that, he pried two more slashes of wood free and revealed a leaded-glass window. Russell rubbed dirt from the panes and peered inside.

Cloth lay over a lump he presumed to be a piece of furniture, looking like a gray-shrouded ghost. This had to be the foyer. *How did I imagine I'd find refuge in this desolate old place?*

Russell plotted a course across the veranda and yanked several boards down from across the front door. Whoever had driven the nails in had meant them to stay. It took considerable effort to clear the door. When revealed, the entrance boasted a matching pair of panels that bore elegant carvings of dogwood blossoms. The doors showed no evidence of a lock, but Russell still expected significant resistance when he simultaneously twisted and pushed both door handles. To his great surprise, though, the doors groaned loudly then swung open with ease.

Russell forced himself not to press against the doorway, to pan across the foyer with his rifle. The fact that he didn't have his rifle had a lot to do with why he refrained from the action. The habits he'd developed to survive had become ingrained. Russell wondered if he'd ever get over feeling the need to exercise such extreme vigilance. He entered the house, then closed the doors behind himself.

And promptly sneezed.

The sound echoed up the great wooden staircase, into all of the rooms, then died out. Dust, inches thick, covered every surface in sight. Not a footprint marred the floors; no handprints disturbed the stair rails or doorsills. Enveloped in nothing but dust and silence, Russell closed his eyes and let his shoulders slump. At least he'd found the solitude he craved.

"It's beautiful," Mama said in a hushed voice as she looked at the nearly finished window on Lorelei's worktable.

Lorelei painstakingly rubbed one of the hand-painted segments with a soft cotton rag. She'd spent hours on that one piece because the angel's wings needed to convey the shelter of God's provision of protection. "I'm happy with the way it turned out."

"Your papa would be so proud."

Lorelei ached as she heard the tears in her mother's voice. The pain of losing him was still fresh. "It makes me feel close to him, working on these windows. I sent him a sketch of this one in my last letter."

Mama hugged her. They huddled close in the workshop, surrounded by a pair of sturdy tables, frames, lead cames, pieces of glass, and assorted tools of the trade. Papa had loved working on church windows, and they both felt surrounded by echoes of his love whenever they were in the workshop.

When Papa had gone to war, they couldn't afford to stay in town. Rent was too high. Then, too, having a German last name and accent didn't exactly make them welcome. A friend of Lorelei's had told them about this cottage. Lorelei had walked out to it that very day, looked over the little cottage, and decided it would suit their needs admirably. As far as she was concerned, the workshop cinched the deal.

She'd found the attorney who handled the property, and he'd gotten special permission from the old man who owned the place to rent it. The rent was ridiculously low, and Lorelei suspected it was a move of compassionate pity; but since the budget looked grim and orders for windows were slow, she'd thanked God and signed the papers for a long-term lease.

She'd worried she'd lose that special feeling of being close to Papa when they moved, but her fears were unfounded. Even Mama, after they'd settled the last soldering rod into place, remarked that it all felt "right."

"Did you know," Mama whispered in a tight voice, "after we lost Johann Junior, your papa painted his face for an angel in the church window?"

Lorelei gave her mother a playful squeeze. "Not until he and I went to Richmond to install another window at that church. I saw it and asked Papa why he'd painted my pesky brother as an angel."

Mama pushed away and clucked her tongue in her special way that she used to try to induce shame.

"You're not fooling me, Mama. You only make that sound when you know you'll end up laughing if you talk!"

"Oh, my Lori." Mama reached up and patted Lorelei's cheek. "You are God's gift to me. When the shadows of life fall across my heart, you cast them away with your sunny laugh."

"Let's hope my laugh lasts long enough for us to run out and get the sheets off the line. It looks like we're about to get a spring shower!"

They scampered outside. Lorelei ran ahead while her mother grabbed the wicker laundry basket. By the time Mama met her by the clothesline, she'd gathered the slips and underwear they'd made from carefully bleached flour sacks and pillowcases. Lorelei dumped them into the basket, then started whipping the clothespins off one end of the sheet while Mama dislodged them from the other. Ocean winds were unreliable and often grew brisk enough to sweep any unsecured items right off the line, so they'd learned to secure everything—just in case.

She and Mama had the simple chore down to a quick routine. She matched the two bottom corners while Mama matched the two top ones. They'd snap the sheet, fold it in half lengthwise again, then meet in the middle. Today, as the first sprinkles hit, they dumped that sheet into the basket instead of finishing the folds.

Lorelei laughed as she skidded around the clothesline and yanked the next sheet. Her action sent clothespins pinging into the air like crickets.

"Your Sunday dress! Get it first," Mama called as she pulled her own Sunday-best black skirt free from the pins.

The skies opened up with a flash shower. They threw the last few items into the basket, each grabbed a handle, and they ran to the house. Mama stared at the basket, then scowled at Lori. "In South Dakota, they would not have storms from the ocean."

"In South Dakota, they don't have sunrises over the ocean, either."

"Hmpf."

Lorelei pretended Mama's reaction was to the top layer of laundry that had gotten soggy. "I'll help you hang up whatever is still damp. I have some twine in the workshop."

"You will do more on that window. I will hang the clothes." Mama wrinkled her nose. "I'll let you do the ironing later while I read the Bible."

"I ought to have time to do that later this afternoon since God is watering the garden for us." Lorelei took a few steps closer to the window and tilted her head as if doing so would help her see around a clump of trees. "I thought I saw a man walking a horse."

"Sweetheart, no one would be out in this rain, walking a horse—riding one, maybe." Mama raised her hands, palms upward in a who-knows gesture. "But not walking it. If the horse were lame, the man would have stopped back at the Rimmons' instead of coming up this old road."

Lorelei didn't see anything more. German Americans suffered all sorts of persecution, and the newspaper habitually carried articles denouncing the "Huns." Since they'd moved out here, no one had bothered them, but Lorelei still felt wary.

"Usually, I am the one who worries," Mama teased. "I tell you, no one is out there."

"I suppose you're right." Still, Lorelei folded her arms and tried to rub away the shivery feeling that wasn't from the rain.

Chapter 3

Pure, sweet, clean rain. Russell had just finished walking through the entire house, including the attic, when the spring storm hit. He'd moved from room to room, shutting doors in hopes that the stiff breeze wouldn't find too many cracks and blow the dust around that had him sneezing repeatedly. He'd have to tackle the chambers one at a time, collecting the worst of the grime before he tried to air out the house. He'd grown up doing a lot of dusting and cleaning for Dad at the emporium; he knew the routine well.

Russell headed for the kitchen, having decided that he could open the large windows and push open the door. The draft ought to race through and blast out a fair bit of the mess. An ancient straw broom in a small closet by the pantry came in handy. He used it to dislodge a pair of massive cobwebs that swagged like fishing nets from the ceiling to the stove and worktable. He'd need somewhere to set his gear, so he whisked off the tabletop and cast aside the broom.

Unsteady due to his healing leg, he loped outside toward the shrubs to fetch the geldings. "Hey, boys." The large workhorses lifted their heads and snuffled. "You've kept busy, haven't you?" Russell stroked the closest one's damp withers.

The horses didn't mind the rain in the least. From the looks of the uneven grasses, they'd satisfied themselves by foraging. "Come on. I have a place in mind for you." He'd not checked out the stable yet, and Russell refused to keep his mounts there until it was cleared out and held fresh water. The horses obediently walked along as Russell led them to an ivy-covered overhang off the small wing near the kitchen. Half a dozen old, large urns lay there, tipped on their sides. Russell dumped out what little dirt remained in them then set them upright to collect the downpour from the roof. He swiftly unburdened the first horse of the saddle and the second one of the bundles, then went back inside.

The pump in the kitchen needed to be primed, but he rather doubted it would work even then. The gaskets and cups inside must have rotted out long ago. Determined to work through the fiery pain in his leg, Russell dragged a tottering wooden chair toward the cabinets. He dropped heavily onto it then jerked open each drawer and cupboard within reach.

A single plate. A chipped mug. A coffee can filled with mismatched knives and forks. . . battered pieces. *Like me.* He gathered them into a pile and left them when he happened along a set of large mixing bowls. Russell swiped the bowls under the water cascading from the roof, then started collecting drinking water in them.

That task accomplished, he recalled other receptacles he'd spotted during his tour. Soon his odd collection of pans, wash pitchers, two slop jars, a metal milk pail, and a battered steel washtub sat in strategic spots throughout the house, catching leaks. It made for an odd symphony of pings, drips, and drumming sounds, but something about it took the edge off his restlessness.

Aware he couldn't clean the whole place in a single day, Russell decided to focus on the largest bedchamber upstairs. The dust nearly choked him, so he tied a kerchief over his nose and mouth, then yanked the fancy draperies from the rods. He dragged them across the floor to help get rid of a goodly portion of the grit, then dropped them over the banister into a heap on the floor of the foyer. Just that small amount of handling had the fabric disintegrating.

"What am I doing?" His words echoed in the house as he looked down at the billowing dust he'd sent into the air. "I'm not going to find peace here."

Thunder boomed over the roof.

I have nowhere else to go. May as well make this place habitable. Russell figured he'd do better to shake out a blanket or sheet and hang it over the window. He thought of the sheets he'd seen on the neighbor's clothesline and felt a pang of envy for how fresh and clean they'd be. He'd be sleeping wrapped in a blanket tonight—much as he had in the trenches.

Russell shook off that awful analogy, surveyed the room, and quickly settled on priorities. He retrieved the broom and used it to sweep down the walls. Cobwebs and dirt banished, the walls looked the same shade as the sky when it went from blue to that first tint of twilight lavender. The floor was, to his relief, sound as could be. It creaked here and there, but that didn't much matter. He could fill the spots with talcum to solve that paltry irritation.

Russell limped about, using the water collected from the leaks to sluice off the bedroom floor. He quickly swept out the tiled upstairs washroom and bathtub, then used the next round of water to do a cursory wash down of that room, too.

Clothes damp from rainwater and sweat, Russell sat on the old tub's edge. *At least no one is here to witness how weak I am.* The notion of being out of shape stuck in his craw. Tall, broad-shouldered, and well-muscled, he'd never been limited. *I refuse to give in now.* He shoved away from the tub and left the room, his uneven gait ringing like a never-ending taunt on the tiled floor.

He braced himself in the door to the hallway. *This is my haven? This? Supposedly Uncle Timothy found contentment here, but I can't see how. Maybe he was just better at fooling folks into thinking he was at peace. He left it behind as empty and forgotten as a snake leaves its old skin.*

Russell's leg ached abominably, but he refused to acknowledge it. He headed for the kitchen, opened the door, and saw the horses contentedly drinking out of the urn. He stuck his hands out into the rain, scrubbed his face, and turned back toward the house. Mom had slipped in some of those little tablets she considered to be cure-alls. He shook two of the Bayer aspirin into his palm, shuddered at the bitter taste, and washed them down with rainwater.

Hungry, Russell unwrapped the last two slices of bread Mom had sent along. He had canned provisions, as well, but for now, he didn't much care what he ate. No matter what he put in his mouth, it all tasted like sawdust. Even Mom's famous peach jam failed to give him any pleasure.

Russell looked about the kitchen and let out a deep sigh. This old place was a filthy hulk. His survey of the structure showed the roof and veranda needed immediate and extensive attention, but the rest of the house was fairly sound.

He didn't dare try to start a fire in one of the fireplaces or the stove. Even if there weren't nests in the flues or stovepipe, he didn't have much in the way of usable fuel. Then, too, the wooden structure was dry as could be. One spark, and the whole place would become a torch. He'd need to varnish, paint, and polish the place from top to bottom to protect it.

Time. It would take time—not just days or weeks, but months. That was okay with him. He had the time. He needed the time. *Even after I restore every last inch of this old house, I'm not sure I'll find this place to be a refuge.*

The drumming and pinging in the pots called him back to action. Using the broom as a cane of sorts, he grabbed his baggage and limped back upstairs. The water went into the tub; then he set the pans back in place to catch more.

Russell ventured back into one of the smaller bedrooms. Gritting his teeth against a wave of pain, he leaned against the doorframe and rested a moment. He bent forward, kneaded his thigh to break a cramp, and grunted as he straightened up.

After knocking his way through gargantuan cobwebs, Russell pulled out a dismantled metal bed frame and dragged the parts to his bedchamber where he put the pieces back together. A bedroom door lay across the springs. He sat on it. "Rock hard," he groused. "You'd think they'd have left at least one decent mattress behind."

He'd worn himself out. Russell unrolled both thick wool blankets, used them to form a mattress, then pulled a jacket over himself for a cover. He stared out the window at the rain and realized it was only midafternoon.

Unaccustomed to being unwell, he'd pushed himself all morning in an effort to tamp down any memories or thoughts. Now he'd pay for it. The rest of the day and night stretched ahead, and he had nothing to occupy his hands. Against his will, his mind started heading down the tormenting paths he'd worked so hard to avoid.

"Mama, I'm sure someone is up at the big house."

"You said that yesterday, and then the Rimmons' boy came by, looking for their cow."

Lorelei shrugged. "I know."

"So why are you so jumpy? Do you feel we are not safe out here, away from the town?"

"I wouldn't have rented the cottage if I thought we weren't going to be safe, Mama."

Mama bobbed her head in agreement. She sliced cabbage into thin ribbons—some to be coleslaw, the rest to become sauerkraut. She snorted. "Besides, no one would come here to make trouble. That old house is a wreck, and we're too poor to rob."

"The way you're wielding that knife, no one would dare bother us."

"I'd offer them some of my coleslaw and make the enemy my friend, just as the Bible tells me to."

Lorelei shredded carrots. "Where does the Bible talk about coleslaw?"

Mama tried not to smile, but her eyes twinkled. She set down the knife and drummed her fingers on the cutting board. "You shouldn't concern yourself with that. Concentrate on where the Bible talks about children respecting their parents and girls getting married."

Dumping the carrots into the bowl with the cabbage, Lorelei teased, "Mama, don't tell me the Bible mentions South Dakota along with your coleslaw."

Mama pursed her lips and pretended to think on it for a minute. "Remember in Proverbs where it says a meal of herbs in harmony is better than a fatted calf with a contentious wife?"

"I thought we were praying for God to deliver a man to our porch."

"Oh, so that is why you keep thinking you see a man."

Mama's sly look made Lorelei shiver. "Mama, you'd better not be doing anything more than praying. If I find out you've been trying to help God by playing matchmaker, I'm going to be perturbed."

"When have I had a chance to be a matchmaker?" Mama tossed mayonnaise and only a skimpy bit of sugar into the bowl, then started to stir. "Once a week, we go to church. The iceman and the milkman come to make deliveries, but they are both married. I'm going to go to my grave without ever becoming a grandmother."

Lorelei dipped a fork into the bowl, swiped a sample of the coleslaw, and ate it. "Since you're hinting that we have only a matter of hours or days left before God calls us home, I'd go to my grave happy, having tasted your cooking. It's heavenly."

"Heaven should be filled with the sound of children laughing, not the taste of a humble salad."

Though they carried on the conversation as if it were a lark, Lorelei knew her mother was serious. She'd been talking about the future and marriage nonstop ever since Monday's storm. Once Mama got a notion in her mind, it was there to stay. Unwilling to continue the conversation, Lorelei took off her apron and hung it on the hook behind the kitchen door. "It'll be another thirty minutes before the casserole is done cooking. I'll go work on that window a bit more."

"You do that. Be sure to keep your eyes open for that strange man."

"So you do think someone's here!"

Mama shook her head. "No, Lori, I don't." She turned away and added in a pained voice, "It would be nice to have a man at our table again."

In the months since Papa had left, then after they learned he'd died, Lorelei discovered that Mama would turn to her if she wanted consolation. When Mama spun around the other way, she wanted to be left alone. Respecting her mother's desire for privacy, Lorelei slipped outside.

Lord, this hurts so badly. I miss Papa terribly, and Mama pretends she is okay when I know her heart is broken. Please help us.

Chapter 4

"Mabel, get on out here." While the storekeeper shouted those words, he kept staring at Russell.

A rawboned woman muttered something under her breath as she came out of the back room. A two-inch brooch secured a red, white, and blue ribbon to her bodice. Russell didn't have to see the picture on the brooch to know it was their son. He braced himself for what he knew would come next.

"We got us a soldier!" The storekeeper came around the counter, headed for Russell, and rubbed his hands in delight. "I can tell by the set of your shoulders—that military bearing is unmistakable."

Russell's stomach started to churn. He hadn't thought to eat before he came, and the emptiness in his belly underscored how little he cared about even the most basic things now. *I just want to buy some stuff and leave.*

The woman shocked Russell when she threw herself at him and hugged him like a long-lost son. "You dear boy! Where were you? Did you meet my Herbert?"

"Herbert Molstead. He's with the First Division." The storekeeper's voice rang with pride. "Eighteenth Infantry Regiment."

Russell awkwardly patted the woman even though he wanted nothing more than to get out of there. "Sorry. I was with the Twenty-eighth."

"Oh." Disappointment creased her face, but she still clung to him.

"Twenty-eighth? That's under Bullard! We got us a whiz-bang hero, Mabel. They beat the socks off the Krauts at Cantigny." The man stood a bit straighter and stuck out his hand. "A pleasure to be in your company, young man."

Still patting the woman with his left hand, Russell reached out and shook hands. "Sir."

"Mabel, turn loose of him and let him tell us all about it."

The last thing Russell wanted to do was talk about the war. These people wanted to hear stories about glory and victory; his memories were gory and vicious. He gently pulled free and indicated the brooch. "What do you hear from Herbert?"

"That boy." Mabel Molstead tsked. "He said he's up to his ankles in mud all of the time."

"Trenches," her husband added knowingly. "Mama's sure he'll catch a cold. She sent him socks."

"I'm sure he'll appreciate them." Russell wanted out of there. He quickly revised his plans. Not wanting to let anyone know he'd taken up residence, he'd ridden to a town just north in order to buy supplies.

On the way there, he'd decided to buy a buckboard so he could haul a mattress back to the estate. Knowing the buckboard would enable him to transport supplies made it a good investment, and the thought of having a comfortable, soft mattress lightened his mood.

Now those things didn't matter. What he needed most was to get away.

"Oh! Oh, mercy me. You would still be over there unless..." Mrs. Molstead's voice died out.

Mr. Molstead cleared his throat. "Yes, well, then. We've been nattering on, and I didn't even ask what you came in to buy."

"Just a few basics." Russell spied a folding cot and reached for it. "Do you have bread, or is there a local bakery?"

Ten minutes—an eternity—later, he secured packs to one horse and mounted up on the other.

"Here, son. The missus wanted you to have this." Mr. Molstead held up a pair of home-knit socks.

"Much obliged." Russell forced a smile, nodded, and rode off. He'd barely accomplished a thing coming here. No mattress, scant repair materials, and the groceries would last only a few days—especially since he didn't have an icebox. At least he'd gotten parts to repair his pump.

Since his last name was Diamond, the Molsteads wouldn't connect him with the Newcomb family or house. He'd still have his refuge. That and the thought of sleeping on the cot gave Russell grim satisfaction.

"I can see what you mean, Miss Goetz." The sheriff frowned at the big old house. "Someone's definitely torn down most of the boards. Footprints are fresh, too. I'll go in and take a look-see."

Lorelei nodded. As soon as the sheriff crossed the veranda and stepped foot into the mansion, she scampered up behind him.

"Miss, you'd best not come in here. No telling what I'll find."

"You've taken the county championship for pistol marksmanship for the past three years, Mr. Clem."

His chest puffed out a bit. "Could be whoever's squatting here is outside. Stay close so I know where you are."

"All right." Chills chased down her spine. Lorelei glanced about the entryway.

"Only one fella," the sheriff whispered. "See? One set of boot prints. Dust in here is thick. He's got a bum leg—see how the stride's uneven?"

"Looks like he's gone upstairs a few times." Dust still coated the stairs, but in a very thin layer that bore fresh scuffle marks.

"We'll check downstairs first." Sheriff took his pistol from the holster. "You stay right behind me. Even if he's not here right now, no telling if the floorboards are rotten."

Lorelei felt a spurt of relief that he'd thought of that potential problem. She'd been gawking around from the moment she'd entered and now paid more attention to the floor. She tapped her toe, sending puffs of dust swirling about her worn shoes. "This is marble."

Sheriff started toward the left. "Typical enough of these old houses. Rest of the place ought to be fancy wood floors. No linoleum in the olden days, you know."

"I'd not thought of such a thing." She carefully followed his footsteps through a parlor, then into what must have been a ballroom. The long room at the back of the house where the windows overlooked the ocean held an enormous buffet and a few chairs. "They must have had splendid suppers here."

"Kitchen's likely through these doors." Sheriff Clem cast her a warning look. "The evidence from the outside and the footprints show he's been in there a fair bit. You stay back." A minute later, he called, "It's okay in here."

So far, the rest of the downstairs hadn't been disturbed in ages. Gray tan dust clung to every surface, giving a dismal air to what once must have been exceptional beauty. She couldn't tell what furniture formed the lumpy shapes under canvas sheets. The sheriff didn't bother to search beneath them because none of the footsteps that stood out in shocking relief on the floors ever approached the abandoned pieces.

Lorelei couldn't believe the difference as she sidled into the kitchen. Clean. The walls, counter, and floor gleamed from a fresh scrubbing. The iron cookstove off to the side was big enough to prepare food for an army. A small hodgepodge of dishes peeked through the glass-fronted doors on one cabinet, and stacks of canned food, neat as a row of soldiers, sat in another.

"Whoever this is, is planning to stay a good long while." The sheriff nosed into the pantry and tilted his head toward another door. "Best be getting on with the search."

An entrance to the other wing hadn't been traversed, so they bypassed it and peeked through the rest of the downstairs, including what had to be one of the most dismal sights Lorelei had ever seen: book-filled shelves in a library, a treasure trove left ignored in the passage of time.

Once upstairs, they discovered the squatter had trundled up and down the hall a few times, but the most noteworthy thing was that he'd scoured the master bedchamber and made it into his own place. A bureau, a table-sized Turkish rug, and a cot showed the mysterious occupant had made an effort to create a tidy, functional place for himself.

"See that cot? Made up right and tight—the military way. We got us a soldier boy here, Miss Goetz. Gotta be careful. Some men go to war and come back teched in the head. Could be a dangerous situation. I'll see if I can't catch this fella, but until I do, you and your mama might be wise to stay in town."

Lorelei stood in the room and closed her eyes. Sadness swamped her. She opened them and blinked away the tears that threatened. "Whoever this is, he has been here awhile and never bothered us."

"Never know." Sheriff Clem shook his head ponderously and escorted her out of the room. "I reckon you and your mother can ask around to see who'll take you in for a few days until I can come back and lie in wait for this soldier boy. I've got me some important things to do for the rest of the week. 'Bout middle of next week, I could see my way clear to coming to set a trap for this trespasser."

Her step faltered at the top of the stairs. She stopped and pled, "Must we do anything? Maybe he just needs to rest awhile before he's on his way."

"Trespassing is a crime—and before you let that tender heart of yours come up with excuses, no one had to post signs. The boards on the doors and windows gave the message loud and clear."

They descended the gritty stairs and went back outside. Sheriff kicked one of the boards that must've once blocked the front door. "Suppose I'd be ten kinds a fool to bother tacking that back up. If he's just resting up, he'd best be gone by next week." His brows beetled, and he gave her a meaningful look.

"I'll talk to Mama and see what she thinks."

He nodded. "You do that, Miss Goetz. It shouldn't take you long to pack a few necessities and walk to town."

The sheriff mounted up and tipped his hat. He rode off down the lawn and across past the shrubs and took the shortcut to town through the wooded area. For all of his warnings and concerns, he'd not offered to give Lorelei a ride back to her cottage.

She hadn't expected him to. He had two sons in the American Expeditionary Force "over there." Like so many townsfolk, he couldn't quite ignore her last name, accent, or Nordic coloring. He'd done his duty by coming out here to investigate, but the delay in any attempt to apprehend the trespasser because he had "important" things to do made it clear he'd rather wash his hands of the affair.

Russell winced as he exited the narrow passageway. Once he closed the secret door, he limped to the window and braced himself as he watched the man ride off and leave the girl behind.

He'd heard them coming and slipped into the hideaway. Dad had told the story of how the black sheep of the family had experienced spiritual revival and used that passage to get into the house and borrow some keepsakes so he could reproduce them. The missing items had caused Great-Uncle Duncan to suspect one of the maids was a thief. Once matters had been ironed out, Duncan had ended up marrying the maid. Aunt Brigit had been one of Dad's favorites. As soon as he'd prepared a decent place to sleep, Russell had remembered that family lore and located the secret passageway.

Prying busybodies. They had no call to bother him. He'd kept entirely to himself.

Russell watched as the girl walked the weed-encrusted gravel road that arched around toward the main thoroughfare. She moved gracefully, with a fluid step that made her hem sway. Cutting across the grass would have saved her time and distance. Why would she stay on the path, and why hadn't the sheriff given her a ride back to the cottage? For all of his brave talk about safety, the sheriff had done nothing. He'd left the girl behind, alone.

Pretty thing, too. Tall and willowy. Had sunbeam yellow hair. She halted for a moment, stooped, and rose. Even from her profile, he could see her smile. She held up something and pursed her lips. *Wishing on a dandelion?* "Honey, don't you know wishes and prayers are for children?"

He startled himself by speaking those words aloud. He'd heard everything the sheriff had said while they'd been in the house, but her voice had been too soft for Russell to hear most of what she'd said. The lawman had called her Miss Gets.

Before enlisting, Russell had worked at his father's emporium. He recognized the material of Miss Gets's dress—one of the economy prints that sold for a paltry three cents per yard three years ago. Money must be tight.

But the sheriff was right—she and her mother shouldn't be living out here alone. Russell knew the caretaker's cottage they inhabited was part of his property. He'd write a letter to his attorney and tell him the place wasn't for rent any longer.

Chapter 5

"There's definitely someone living up at the big house, Mama." Lorelei tugged the baby blue table oilcloth straight, then put a small vase of pansies in the center.

"It is not our concern. We have no responsibility for that old place."

"I didn't want to worry you, so I went to town and asked the sheriff to meet me there. We went inside."

Mama whirled around so quickly from rinsing radishes, she showered water in an arc around the kitchen. "Lori!"

"It was perfectly safe. You know Sheriff Clem. He even wore his pistol. He walked ahead of me every step of the way."

Mama turned away, banged her hands on the sink to supposedly shake off the water, then came toward the table. The effort she put into wiping her hands off on the dish towel told Lorelei she was trying to control her temper. "What did you think you were doing, to walk into danger like that? Do not tell me Mr. Clem would protect you. He is one who believed your father went to fight with the Germans. Even after the army delivered those medals saying Johann was a brave American soldier who died for this country, Mr. Clem did not apologize for his ugly lies."

"His wife always talks to us at church."

Mama sighed. "What am I to do with you, child? You want to believe good of everyone. The world is not like that. It is why Jesus came—because man is sinful. You cannot give away your trust so easily."

"I need to talk with you about that very thing." The chair scraped the battered linoleum floor as Lorelei pulled it out. She sat down and patted the table in an invitation for Mama to join her.

Mama sat down and folded her hands on the table. Just as quickly as she folded them, she unfolded them and reached out to hold Lorelei's hand. "What is it?"

"Until Sheriff Clem can meet the man who's living at the big house, he thinks we should move back to town. He said it's not safe here for us."

Mama didn't say anything, but her hold tightened.

"I promised him I'd speak with you about it." Lorelei leaned forward. "Mama, I don't want to go back to town. I wouldn't have the workshop, and it's important for me to honor my promises to complete the windows on time."

"Your safety is more important than a thousand windows."

"I feel that way about you, too, Mama." She shrugged. "I don't feel scared at all out here. Even when I was in the mansion, I didn't worry."

"Tell me then why the sheriff thinks we are unsafe here."

"From what we saw, only one man is there. Mama, he's probably a soldier. Sheriff Clem judged the footprints to be made by a lame man. More than that..." She paused and tapped her temple. "The sheriff thinks he could be dangerous because war can change men."

"This is true. It can." Mama ran her forefinger down Lorelei's arm. "You have been thinking. I can see it in your eyes."

"I have." Lorelei leaned forward. "Mama, if Papa had come home from war with an injury, we wouldn't love him any less."

"Of course not."

"I was thinking, if the injury wasn't a physical one—if his mind or spirit was hurt—we would still love him."

"So you are thinking this soldier man hiding in that old house might bear an unseen wound. Though the sheriff's warning seems prudent, your heart tells you otherwise."

Lorelei smiled. "Oh, Mama, I was hoping you'd understand."

"This isn't something you decide without prayer. While you make sandwiches, I'll read the Bible. We can pray and talk about it during lunch."

Papa had always read the Bible and said family prayers at the close of supper. When he'd shipped overseas, Mama had reasoned that France was six hours ahead of Virginia, so if they had their devotions at lunch, it would be at the same time Papa was. That way, they'd all read the same chapters and worship together as a family.

Mama started reading from the second chapter of Nehemiah:

Wherefore the king said unto me, Why is thy countenance sad, seeing thou art not sick? this is nothing else but sorrow of heart. Then I was very sore afraid, and said unto the king, Let the king live for ever: why should not my countenance be sad, when the city, the place of my fathers' sepulchres, lieth waste, and the gates thereof are consumed with fire? Then the king said unto me, For what dost thou make request? So I prayed to the God of heaven. And I said unto the king, If it please the king, and if thy servant have found favour in thy sight, that thou wouldest send me unto Judah, unto the city of my fathers' sepulchres, that I may build it.

Lorelei drew in a deep breath and let it out slowly. "Mama, those verses—they never really meant anything to me before. This time, they jump out. If this man has a sorrow of the heart, I want to help."

Resting her hand on the thin pages of the open Bible, Mama fell silent.

Lorelei wanted to plead her case. The verses spoke so clearly to her of a man who had suffered and needed to find a safe home again. Still, the decision wasn't hers to make—at least, not alone. Whatever they did, Mama needed to feel at peace, too. Mind racing, Lorelei thought of things she could say that might convince her mother to agree to befriend the stranger. Failing that, she thought of people in town Mama might stay with if she felt scared.

The knife cut through the bread at a slant, creating uneven slices that told of her impatience. Mayonnaise. Lettuce and tomatoes fresh from the garden. Some salami. It took only seconds to make lunch, but in that time, Lorelei prepared an argument worthy of being heard by the Supreme Court. She turned back to her mother.

"Don't," Mama said softly. "I know what you want, Lori, but this is not about what we want; it is about what God would have us do."

Lorelei let out a guilty laugh. "You're right. Still, Mama, there can't be anything wrong with leaving a little food for him."

"How do you know he's hungry?"

"There hasn't been any smoke from the chimney or stovepipe."

"So you are imagining this soldier is going without his daily bread?" Mama shook her head. "Lorelei, if you feed him, you encourage him to stay."

"He's not a stray cat!" Lorelei set the plates on the table and let out a short laugh. "It's too bad he's not. Have you seen how many field mice we've had around here?"

"Deer, rabbits, gophers. . ." Mama gazed out the window. "They're going to eat up half of my garden."

"He's living up there and hasn't stolen a single thing from the garden, Mama. Did you notice? It would have been so easy for him to help himself—especially at night."

"If you weren't so talented at making such beautiful windows, I would say your time is wasted here and you should stay in town and sell things. You could make a poor man buy a wallet!"

Lorelei laughed guiltily. "Okay. So let's pray and eat."

They stretched their hands across the table to meet in the middle. Mama's hands felt cool, slightly rough, and reassuring. Even so, Lorelei missed Papa's big strong hands turning their grasp into a triangle.

"Heiliger Vater in Himmel," Mama began. She always prayed in German.

Holy Father in heaven. The rest of the prayer poured forth, but Lorelei clung to the very first words. War had robbed her of her beloved earthly father, but he'd taught her to rely on her heavenly Father—and that brought solace in times like this.

Russell froze as he heard footsteps on the veranda. They were tentative. *Because someone is sneaking up on me? No. The weight is too slight, the shoes heeled. If the woman is scared, why would she bother to come here?*

He heard her next few steps, and realization dawned. She tested each step she took before putting her full weight on it—wisely checking to see if the rotting boards were safe. The footsteps finally stopped, only to be replaced with three uncertain knocks on the door.

He'd hoped the sheriff's warning would be sufficient. Clearly, someone had ignored it and decided to get snoopy. Folks were like that, but Russell didn't want to be around anyone. He refused to go answer the door. He stood stock-still and waited until he heard the woman leave the veranda. A wry smile twisted his mouth. She made faster time on her retreat. More likely, she was scared of him rather than it simply being a matter of her retracing her steps so she'd use the boards she knew to be safe.

He quietly crossed the parlor and drew back the very edge of the heavy draperies. From that vantage point, he could see the lissome blond sauntering back down the road. Her flour sack dress swayed with each step, swishing gently from side to side in a uniquely feminine way. Odd, how many little things he'd forgotten while living in the muddy trenches with men.

About twenty feet from the house, she turned around and gave a fleeting look at the porch. A smile chased across her face; then she looked up at the upstairs windows. Her smile faltered, but Russell felt a stab of relief that she didn't sense where he stood. He didn't want any connection to anyone.

"Go home, Buttercup," he whispered. "You don't belong here."

As if she heard him, she whirled around and walked out of sight.

He'd been going from room to room, trying to decide which projects needed immediate attention and what could wait. He'd been up on the roof. The whole thing needed to be stripped down to the base and completely reboarded and reshingled. Russell couldn't haul the wood up and do the work alone, and he didn't want to have to deal with others, which led him to the dismaying conclusion that he'd need to hire others to come do the task.

While in town, he'd go ahead and purchase supplies for several other repairs. In fact, he'd buy a buckboard. By loading it high, Russell reckoned he'd be able to stock up on enough that he'd be able to avoid making several trips.

Last night, as he fell asleep, he'd already made a mental list of half a dozen items he needed. Upon awakening and walking around, he'd added to that list until he needed to actually write down everything. Tomorrow or the next day, he'd grit his teeth and ride in.

For now, he'd leave the parlor and library as they stood. Due to the way the wind blew off the ocean and their intact windows, those two rooms had the least amount of grime in them. Russell took a quick peek under the heavy sailcloth at an ornate set of nesting tables. Once the rest of the room was restored, these would make a nice addition to the furniture.

Then again, so little furniture remained that he'd have to be satisfied with what was on hand unless he went to town to shop for more or made it himself.

Russell chewed on the tip of the pencil, then scrawled on the paper, "boards for porch." He couldn't risk someone falling through the disintegrating planks. Maybe he hadn't wanted to do that as a first project, but given the curiosity factor of his neighbor and the sheriff, he didn't have much choice.

In the meantime, he'd go ahead and shore up the existing porch for safety's sake. A fistful of nails, his hammer, and the boards he'd ripped from the windows would do the trick. Russell opened the front door and stopped cold.

A small basket sat there, a rust-colored gingham cloth covering its contents.

Russell wanted to ignore it. If he accepted a neighbor's gift, he'd end up having to interact and be sociable. The thought curdled his stomach. He stepped over the basket and avoided looking at it again as he assessed the planks. As he scanned the boards and visually measured their lengths and condition, the basket kept coming back in view.

Seeing it was bad enough; smelling it was worse. The aroma of fresh-baked bread sneaked past the cloth covering and tempted him to eat his fill. Russell swallowed and turned away. One nail. Two. Three. He banged each in place and lied to himself with each of them. *I don't want bread. I don't. Not a bite.*

He sat back on his heels and studied the porch a bit more. *The first week I was in Buttonhole, your mama stopped by with a big old basket of corn bread, chicken stew, jam, and applesauce.* His father told that story often enough. Mama was famous for her baskets. Russell had grown up watching her cook far too much, then slip extra loaves of bread, jars of soup and jam, vegetables, and cookies into her baskets and set out to deliver them to whomever she fancied might need them.

"I'm not a charity case." He punctuated his rough words with a few bangs of the hammer. The basket jumped.

Try as he might, he couldn't ignore the aroma. Russell argued with himself, hated his weakness, but still leaned back, snatched the wicker handle, and yanked the basket onto his thighs. He swept off the checkered napkin and inhaled. Several slices of bread, a pint jar of jam, an earthenware crock of baked beans, another of coleslaw, and a savory, two-inch-round length of bratwurst filled the basket to overflowing.

His lap was full, but his heart and stomach ached with emptiness. Russell stared at the offering. When he saw the neatly printed label on the jar of jam, he lost the battle. Peach jam. How many hundreds of jars of peach jam had Mama cooked and delivered? She'd done so in her special way—with that gentleness of wanting to be kind to another. The young woman—Buttercup—had done the selfsame thing. That fact slipped past his defenses.

Russell scooted backward until his spine rested against the house, unscrewed the lid, and dipped his finger into the jam.

Russell waited until night fell. He'd kept busy all day, then washed up. Round about midnight, he slipped out of the mansion and approached the small cottage on the edge of the property. At least two hours had passed since the lamps in the cottage had gone out, so he felt certain the women were fast asleep.

He knew two women lived there. The laundry on the line broadcast that fact. He'd also been spying from his attic window. Buttercup lived there—probably with her mother, from the looks of things. A pathetically small woodpile slumped along the back fence, one of the two chimneys lacked a few bricks at the top, and the place needed basic repairs.

Carefully, quietly, Russell walked from his home to the cottage with his arms full. He stacked several logs onto their woodpile and carried a few more to their back porch. He wouldn't need all that much for himself, and he'd have all summer and autumn to chop more. It was the least he could do as repayment for the food they'd given.

By returning the basket and dishes and leaving wood, he turned their charity into a barter. Satisfied with that arrangement, he turned to go home.

A small whimper stopped him in his tracks.

Chapter 6

"Poor girl," he said as he approached the small form. Fifteen minutes later, Russell carefully peeled his shirt from around the mutt and gently petted her between the ears. Glad he'd cleaned out the stovepipes the day before, Russell started a fire in the stove to provide some radiant heat for the dog and to boil water to cleanse her wounds.

The poor beast looked like she'd been struck by a motorcar. One hind leg and her tail were injured—just how seriously, Russell couldn't tell. The dog seemed to sense Russell meant to help her. She weakly licked his hand as he finished bathing away the dirt and blood. After dipping a white cotton dishcloth into the boiling water several times, Russell tore it into strips and used them as bandages. It wasn't until he finished that he let out a rueful laugh.

"You're going to have a limp just like me. Same leg, even. We're a sad pair."

The dog yawned and rested her muzzle on his thigh. Russell stroked her ears. "I guess I'm stuck with you."

Sunday morning, Lorelei left a basket on the porch of the big house and scurried back down the road. She and Mama needed to hurry so they wouldn't be late for church. This was the third basket she'd left for the strange soldier.

Both times she'd left baskets, he'd returned them along with doing a chore as payment. They now had plenty of firewood and the well sported a new rope and bucket. Lorelei didn't want him to think he had to barter for the food they gave, but it was nice to have someone see to the details that slipped her notice or strained her abilities.

Mama came out of the cottage and tucked a hanky into her purse. "Hurry. We don't want to be late for church."

"We'll be on time."

Mama wrinkled her nose. "I want to be there a little bit early. It's past time for Sheriff Clem to tell us what he's found out about the man up at the house."

"He hasn't bothered to do anything more, Mama."

"Unless he benefits, the sheriff lets matters slide." Mama fell into step with her. "He claims to be busy, but most afternoons, he either sits at the counter at Phoebe's drinking free coffee, or he goes off to play poker at David McGee's."

Lorelei laughed. "I suppose we ought to be glad he's coming to church. Perhaps his heart will be touched."

"Maybe we can ask Mr. Rawlin about the house." Mama walked around one side of a mud puddle while Lorelei went around the other. "He's in charge of the property. When we wanted to rent the cottage, we had to work with him."

Lorelei nodded. Mr. Rawlin had taken care of the matter—even though she'd suspected he didn't want to lease to them. "Maybe he could rent the place to the soldier. It would be a fair trade if he could stay there for all of the cleaning and repairs he's doing."

Mama stopped. A stricken look chased across her face. "We ought to have invited him to come to worship with us."

"I did, Mama. I slipped a note in with the basket on Friday."

"I'll be back soon." Russell petted the dog as he spoke. She'd lapped up half of the can of beef broth. "They've gone off to church, so I'll slip down to the cottage. I'll be back before you know it."

The unbandaged tip of her tail wagged weakly on the kitchen floor. Russell didn't know exactly what to do for her, but he'd applied the first aid he'd been taught and hoped it would be enough to let the dog heal.

Russell had wanted the women to leave for church, and he'd hoped it would be late enough in the morning that the ground would have dried from any dew. Ever since he'd returned home, Russell couldn't stomach the smell of morning-damp earth. Rain didn't bother him: It carried a sweetness to it that helped. But he'd spent too many frigid predawn hours in the trenches with the loamy smell of dirt overpowering him.

He stepped outside and breathed through his mouth to minimize his sense of smell. *Okay. It's okay.* He let out a sigh of relief, then hefted a few scrap lengths of planking over his shoulder and grabbed a small crate containing nails, a hammer, folding measuring stick, pencil, and saw. On the way to the cottage, he managed to stumble twice due to his weak leg. Anger welled up. Though no one had witnessed his awkwardness, Russell still hated it and all it brought back. He went to the front of the cottage and dumped the boards with a satisfying clatter.

Then he saw it: the flag in the front window. The background was white, just like the draperies, which is why he hadn't seen it from far off. In the center was a star—but not the blue one that proclaimed the family had a son, brother, or father at war. This one featured a gold star carefully stitched over that blue one—a heartbreaking testament that their man wouldn't be coming home.

Russell stood and stared at the flag. Fury welled up. He took another look at the small porch and went into a frenzy, completely shattering the warped boards and dismantling the entire structure. As soon as he pried the last board free, he stared at the mess he'd created. What was supposed to have been the simple replacement of a few boards had resulted in this galling destruction. He'd been enraged at the loss these women had suffered, but his actions had only caused more problems. He let out a long, deep sigh.

He couldn't very well go into town on Sunday and buy boards, but tomorrow he'd be able to get the lumber to do the job. Then again, he didn't dare leave the porch as it was. He searched about for wood.

A stack of storm windows lay on the leeward side of a fair-sized workshop. Russell selected those with the sturdiest wood and carried them to the front door. By setting them in place, he created a temporary walkway. Anxious to leave before they returned from church, he left a note under the front door.

"Miss Goetz, I need to speak with you for a moment." Mr. Rawlin looked at her steadily as his wife bustled away to claim their youngsters from Sunday school.

"Oh, good." She slipped out of the pew, into the aisle. Mr. Rawlin invariably discussed matters out of earshot. She figured as an attorney, he had to guard his tongue and weigh his words more carefully. That being the case, she waited to mention anything about the stranger staying at the house until they got outside.

"The sheriff mentioned someone's living up at the big house," Mr. Rawlin said.

"Yes. He's fixing things up and cleaning."

The attorney nodded sagely. "Makes perfect sense. He's undoubtedly the new owner. The old one died, and I contacted his heir—a great-great-nephew." He smoothed his tie. "He's a good man—a war hero. I'm sure you and your mother will be safe."

"Thank you. He hasn't troubled us at all."

He hasn't troubled us at all. Lorelei's words echoed back in her shocked mind as she stared in horror at the porch when she and Mama got home. *I spoke too soon.*

"Mercy, mercy!" Mama blotted her forehead with her hanky. "Will you look at that!"

"I am." The two words caught in her throat and came out in a strangled croak.

"That just proves it."

Lorelei bowed her head in defeat. She and Mama would have to find somewhere else to live—but where?

"God provides our every need." Mama smiled. "That old porch—you are slender, and it doesn't mind you, but it's started to creak and groan under my feet. I was nervous to use the front door anymore." Nimble as a mountain goat, she climbed the three makeshift steps, crossed the storm window "porch," and opened the front door.

"Mama, be careful."

Mama turned around. Her eyes twinkled—a rare event these days. "You're too late to say that, Lori. Come now. Oh, look! We have a message here."

Lorelei joined her mother in a flash. On the back of a long list of tools and supplies, in a bold scrawl done in pencil, he'd written, "Wood was rotting and dangerous. Be careful. Will finish soon."

"Isn't that nice of him?"

"Yes, it is, Mama."

"What a pity that he didn't come to church, though."

It was too late by the time he spotted her. Busy thinking about what more he could do for Mutt, Russell hadn't paid attention. Monday morning, he went out the front door and nearly knocked over the girl. "Whoa!" He instinctively grabbed her arms to keep her from tumbling backward.

She let out a gasp, then got her footing. Color flooded her cheeks even though he released her. "Excuse me. I brought you this." She nudged the basket into his arms and stepped back. "Your list. . .tools and wood and things. . ." She nervously moistened her lips. "I thought you might want it back."

He nodded curtly.

"I–I heard a woofing sound when I came the other day. There is a bone for your dog."

His chin came up. *She's been spying on me.*

"Thank you for the firewood and the porch." She'd inched back toward the steps, and the morning sun glinted on her pale hair and necklace—a very plain, rather small, silver cross. "It is very kind of you to help us, sir." He gave no reply, so she whispered, "Good-bye."

As she walked off, Russell stared at her back and felt a bolt of hatred nearly consume him. *She's German.*

Chapter 7

As he rode down the path toward town, Russell cast a quick look at the cottage. He'd given his word that he'd repair the porch, and he'd honor it. Then again, he owned the property. He didn't want anyone living there—especially not the enemy. He sought out the lawyer's shingle as he rode down Main Street.

"Mr. Diamond." The attorney reached out to shake hands.

Russell automatically scanned to be sure Mr. Rawlin didn't have a knife or pistol in his other hand. The notion was ludicrous, but life in the trenches taught a man to be cautious. Satisfied no danger existed, Russell shook hands and refused the proffered seat.

"What can I help you with?"

"I don't want anyone on my property. Get rid of the renters."

Mr. Rawlin slowly eased back to lean against his big mahogany desk. "I'm afraid that's not possible. Your great-great-uncle signed a ten-year lease with the Goetz women."

"Ten years!"

Drumming his fingers on the desktop on either side of his hips, the attorney nodded. "It was old Timothy Newcomb's idea. I confess, I tried to talk him out of it. Stubborn old man wouldn't be swayed. He wanted to be sure the women would have a safe haven. I suppose by now you've determined they are of German heritage."

Russell folded his arms across his chest.

Mr. Rawlin heaved a sigh. "I confess, at the start, I wasn't any happier about it than you are."

"Then find a way to break the deal."

The attorney shook his head. "Johann Goetz gave his life for this country. Last year, when the War Board started gearing up for us to enter the Great War, they knew they'd need reliable men who spoke German. Being close to D.C. as we are, they had a few scouts come out and nose around. Johann was a shade older than they wanted—thirty-nine—but they needed him, and he went."

Russell didn't move an inch or say a word.

"Gossips whispered plenty. Your great-uncle always had the *Gazette* mailed to him. It's featured several articles about the vandalism against Germans in this area. Just north of here, a German was lynched, and the jury found the men who did it innocent. In that same edition, a letter to the editor hinted that Mr. Goetz went off to fight with the Jerries." He paused. When Russell said nothing, the lawyer continued, "Just about that time, Lorelei came to me and asked to rent the cottage. I didn't want to, but as a professional I had to set aside my own feelings and serve my client. I contacted him, and he gave me instructions."

"A decade was extreme." Russell scowled at him.

"I thought so, too, but that's what your uncle specified. He was worried someone might take a mind to smash up her place like they have others."

"From the looks of things, no one bothers them at all."

"Perhaps because they moved out of town. Problems happen—especially here along the coast where folks have lost their sons at sea even before we got sucked into the war."

Russell had heard of such events. He thought of the star flag in the cottage window. *But anyone could put that up. It doesn't actually prove their man was fighting with the Americans.*

"Most of the gossip stopped when posthumous awards arrived for Mr. Goetz," Rawlin continued. "Your uncle figured it's been hard on those women and that they deserved better."

The star stitched on the flag in the window was gold. Russell couldn't argue with what he'd been told. If anything, he owed that widow and her daughter some help—it was a soldier's duty to see to a fallen comrade's family.

"The bank is expecting you to come by and put your signature on file." Clearly, the attorney chose not to press the issue of his renters any further. "The inheritance is in your name, and you can draw on it as you see fit." He glanced down at the papers in front of himself and read the latest bank balance.

Russell stared at the papers in shock. *Dad told me I'd have enough to live on. He didn't tell me I'd be rich. Ten men couldn't squander that much money in their lifetimes.*

"I took the liberty of opening an account for you at Sanders' Mercantile so you can get supplies. Did you require anything else?"

"No." Russell started to walk out. He stopped at the door and turned. "The house needs to be reroofed immediately. Do you recommend anyone?"

"Want it done cheap, or want it done right?"

"Right." Even if he hadn't inherited a fortune, he would have given that answer, but the fact that the lawyer even bothered to ask the question seemed bizarre.

Rawlin jerked his thumb toward the north. "Pinkus Bayley. Gray house with the red shutters. Don't let his age fool you. He used to be a shipwright. He can gather the best men in short order. Let him buy the supplies—he'll get a better deal."

"Thanks."

The livery had hitches for his team and a sound-looking buckboard. The man in charge sat on a stool, showing a couple of strapping teens how to splice rope. "Don't suppose you got any work out there at your place, do you?" one of the youngsters asked.

"My boys are hard workers," the livery owner added.

Russell didn't want people all over his place. Then again, he'd have the crew doing the roofing. *I might as well get it all over at once and be done with it.* "My stable's a wreck. Needs a thorough cleaning."

The younger lad's voice cracked and went up several notes. "We're used to mucking out stables. You came to the right place to hire yourself some workers."

"Show up tomorrow—two hours after daybreak. I'll pay you two bucks a day apiece." Russell watched how their eyes lit up. "For that kind of money, I expect you to be men—not boys who need directions."

"We can do it!"

"Fine. I've got things to see to here in town. My horses could stand for some decent feed—corn and oats. I'll be about two hours, so take care of them now, then have them hitched and ready to go."

At the feed store, Russell arranged for corn, oats, and hay to be delivered at the end of the week. By then, the stable would be ready to hold the supplies.

Next, Russell stopped by the post office and mailed a letter to his mother. He'd taken pains to write more than the fact that he'd arrived at the mansion. After two paragraphs, he'd included as much as he could concoct, then signed, "Love, Russell." It wouldn't win a prize, but it fulfilled his promise. He hoped it would settle Mama's fears.

By the time he reached the diner, Russell's leg ached abominably. He slid into a seat and ignored the assessing looks of others by staring sightlessly at the menu. It would be like every other menu nowadays—featuring so-called patriotic dishes like victory burgers and liberty cabbage, and a reminder about meatless Mondays and wheatless Wednesdays.

"Have you decided what you want?"

"I'll have the blue plate special," he ordered without glancing up. In an attempt to keep from having to strike up a conversation, he pulled the list from his pocket and reviewed it. When the waitress slid a plate of liver and onions in front of him, he winced.

A brawny, middle-aged man swaggered up, grabbed the plate, and shoved it back at the waitress. "That's not fit for eatin'. Give him meat and 'taters. Bring me a steak while you're at it." He slid into the seat opposite Russell and leaned back with more show than a rodeo pony. "Chester Gimley. Figured you'd be lookin' to have someone do the work out at that old place. I can do anything you want. Cheap."

"And I reckon," the waitress said as she thumped the plate back down in front of Russell, "Mr. Diamond can eat anything he orders. In case you didn't notice, he's concentrating on his work."

"Mind your own business, Myrtle."

"Gimley?" Russell looked at him, and the stranger's eyes brightened with greed. "I don't hold with a man treating a woman with disrespect."

Gimley went ruddy and blustered, but he didn't apologize.

Russell deliberately picked up his knife and fork and cut into the revolting slab of liver. He took a big bite, promptly washed it down with his coffee, and realized it didn't taste any better or worse than anything else he'd had in weeks. He ate because he needed to, but everything got stuck halfway down and had to be washed past the ever-present ball in his throat.

Gimley snorted derisively, shoved away from the table, and stomped off.

Half an hour later, Russell left the diner with his stomach churning. He stopped at the gray house with the red shutters, struck a deal with old Pinkus Bayley to replace the roof, and gladly accepted a glass of bicarbonate before he left.

The mercantile made him suffer a momentary pang of homesickness. Dad's emporium carried the same wondrous mixture of aromas—briny pickles, sweet, fresh fruit, the tang of new leather goods, and the honest scent of soap. Drawing the list from his pocket, Russell started searching for the items. In a matter of minutes, Mr. Sanders and his daughter, Olivia, were both helping him. It didn't take long before his order filled the entire counter and formed an appreciable heap on the floor.

Staples, eggs, produce, three one-pound cans of coffee, and a crate overflowing with cans and jars of food sat next to a frying pan, cast iron pots, and a kettle.

"Looks like you're feeding an army," Mr. Sanders teased.

Russell ignored the comment and added molasses to the supplies. The beans Buttercup had brought in the first basket had been sweetened a tad with molasses, and he'd had a hankering for more. *I can make them for myself. I don't want her cooking for me.*

"I have just the thing for you: Kirby's Ezee 'Grasshopper' vacuum cleaner." Olivia demonstrated it and added, "It requires no electricity."

Russell hastily propped it against the icebox. Doing so knocked the Johnson's Prepared Wax for the floor from atop the stack and created quite a ruckus.

Russell startled at the sound and broke out in a cold sweat. For a few horrible moments, he was in the trenches again, hearing the clatter of equipment. His heart raced, and he kept clutching his fists as he reminded himself that he didn't need to grab his rifle or knife. Everything within him screamed to retreat, yet Miss Olivia stood there giggling behind her hand while her father unrolled a mattress for his inspection.

The mattress. I need the mattress. I have to get this stuff so I can stay home and not come back for a long time. Russell snatched the dipper from the water bucket and gulped several mouthfuls, then croaked, "The mattress is fine. I'll take it."

Folks in the store chattered just like they did back in Dad's place. Russell knew it was all just neighborly talk—snoopy, helpful, good-natured. Nonetheless, he was on edge. He'd turned down at least half a dozen housekeeping offers and didn't care what they thought his total bill would come to.

". . .sheets, a pillow, and blankets?"

Russell realized Mr. Sanders had asked him a question. He nodded and rasped, "Add it all up and put it on my account. I'll go fetch my buckboard." He got out of there as fast as he could limp.

Lorelei hoed the garden and watched the road. He'd taken both horses and headed toward town. She wanted to ask her neighbor a favor, and it had taken her hours to build up her courage after he'd scared her this morning. She heard the trundling sound of a wagon and the jingle of harnesses before he came into view.

As she wiped her hands on a rag, Lorelei went to stand in the middle of the road. Mr. Diamond looked about as cheerful as a thundercloud when he pulled the team to a stop.

"Mr. Diamond, I have a favor I'd like to ask of you." When he made no reply, Lorelei wrapped her arms about her waist and forged on. *Nothing ventured, nothing gained.* "Mama and I garden. We've planted a Victory Garden—like they have in England—and many folks in town buy our produce. I wanted to ask you to let me sharecrop a tiny section of your land."

"I'll think about it."

His reply surprised her. She'd braced herself for a flat refusal and dared to hope for agreement. Never once had she thought he might delay making a decision. Lorelei blinked at him for a moment, then tucked a wind-whipped strand of hair behind her ear. "Thank you."

He stared off to the side. His eyes carried a haunted look, and the set of his jaw didn't invite further conversation. In fact, the raspy quality to his voice made it sound as if he rarely spoke.

Lorelei sidled off the path and watched as he nickered and the handsome pair of geldings set the buckboard in motion. She'd wanted to intercept him without Mama overhearing the request. Worried as she was about money, Mama would get her hopes up or be in a dither that the neighbor would deduce their finances were strained. This way, Mama wouldn't know a thing if he refused them.

Lorelei went back to the garden and picked up the hoe. She carried it to a small shed, then washed up at the pump and went back to the workshop.

Mama was sweeping the workroom floor. Lorelei stooped, held the dustpan, and smiled at the tinkling sound as all of the tiny bits hit the thin steel. "In my fanciful moments, I imagine that's what the angels' laughter sounds like."

Mama smoothed her hair. "Ah, my Lori. It takes so little to make you happy."

"You're the one who taught me to count my blessings." She rose and dumped the sweepings into the wastebasket as she began to sing:

Count your blessings, name them one by one;
Count your blessings, see what God hath done;
Count your blessings, name them one by one;
Count your many blessings, see what God hath done.

Mama had joined in on the last two lines. Afterward, she brushed away a tear. *"Du bist mein Segen, Lorelei."*

"You're my blessing, too, Mama."

"It would be nice to have the blessing of more orders." Mama fiddled with the last remaining order slip on the board.

"Papa always said, 'God will provide.' He'd want us to have faith."

"Yes, he would." Mama tugged a hanky out of her sleeve and wiped her cheeks. "I will take some lettuce and cabbage into town tomorrow. It will buy more flour for us."

"See? God provides."

Sleep didn't come easily or well for Russell. Even on his new mattress, he'd jerk awake and reach for his rifle. He'd rolled out of bed before dawn and made a pot of coffee. As he finished the last sip, wagons rolled up.

I told them not to come until two hours after daybreak. Irritated, Russell thumped down his empty mug and went outside.

"She's a beauty," Pinkus Bayley said as he admired the old house. "We'll have her looking grand as can be in no time at all."

"Warn your men that the veranda is rotting in places and they'll need to test their footing. I don't want anyone breaking a leg."

"Hear that, men?" Pinkus clapped his hands and rubbed them together. Russell estimated it was more out of eagerness to begin than from a need to warm them. "Even from here, I can see you're right. We'll take it clear down to the joists and put up all new slats, felt, tar paper, and shingles."

"I'll set a water bucket and dipper here for the men."

"Jim-dandy idea." Pinkus turned back to his men. "Daniel, go check out the chimneys to be sure they're sound. Jake and Ed, I want you to scythe the grass over yonder. We'll dump the old shingles and rotten wood there. We'll have us a bonfire when the job's finished."

The liveryman's sons rode up together on a swaybacked mare. *Can't anyone in this town follow directions or tell time?* Russell took them over to the stable and pulled open one of the creaky, weathered doors.

"We'll oil the hinges, Mr. Diamond," the elder boy said as he put his weight behind the companion door and got it to budge. "Pa said we need to be sure to wash down everything after we clean it out. No putting your team in here until then, else they're like to take sick."

Russell frowned at the boys' worn shoes. "Might be snakes in here. I'm sure every last spider in Virginia is. Go on back to town and tell Mr. Sanders to put you in boots."

The boys exchanged a worried look.

"A man pays for the tools and equipment for jobs on his place. Boots—sturdy boots—are a necessity. He's to put them on my account."

"Pa don't cotton to folks takin' charity."

Russell gave the boys a steely-eyed look. "I don't cotton to someone else giving orders to my hired help. While you're here, you'll do as I say."

"Yessir."

Russell headed back toward the house. The work there literally started with a crash bang. Shingles and boards slid off the roof and smashed onto the earth. Pinkus jerked his chin toward Russell.

"Yeah?"

"Most of the chimneys are in fair condition. The mortar needs some patching, but that's not much. The one to the parlor needs to be torn down at least to the bottom floor and rebuilt. It's about to topple. I'll need to be getting sand and gravel to make cement and a load of bricks. Daniel's best as they come on chimneys. After we're done, he'll clean 'em all. Until then, don't set any fires."

"Okay." Russell squinted toward the cottage. *It's my property, and I'm responsible for it.* "Have Daniel repair and clean the chimney over at the caretaker's cottage while he's out here."

"Aye. Fine notion. My men brought lunch buckets today, but most often, folks feed them when they work. Mrs. Goetz is a dandy cook. Think you can talk her into setting up our dinners?"

"We'll see." Russell looked back at the top of his house. The smallest effort made shingles come loose and skid. Much to his relief, all of the men were wearing safety ropes.

Pinkus cupped his gnarled hands and shouted, "Ed! Wind and rain pattern would hit the southeast corner hardest. I expect the boards there are weak. Don't go over there. You've eaten too many of your wife's noodles!"

The men chuckled, and Russell knew he'd gotten the right man for the job.

Pinkus slanted him a sly look. "I know what you're thinking. I'm older than dirt. Seventy-one. Fought in the War Between the States."

Russell didn't reply to that revelation, though it surprised him.

"When I got home, I didn't want to talk to a soul." Pinkus squinted at the roof and rubbed his chin. "I reckon folks are makin' pests of themselves. I told my men they're to concentrate on this job, not on whatever's happening 'over there.'"

Russell froze. The old man's insight stunned him.

"I'm glad you're takin' care of the Goetz women. Things are tight for them 'specially since they lost Johann. Admirable Christians, staunch Americans. You gonna have little Lorelei replace your broken windows?"

"Windows?"

"She took on her father's trade. Good at it, too. A dab hand at glazing windows and puts together some mighty fine stained-glass church windows. From the looks of it, you have plenty of cracked and broken panes."

"One thing at a time." Russell didn't want to have anyone here at all—let alone a woman. A pretty woman.

One who was German.

They parted, and Pinkus went to holler orders to his men as Russell trudged toward the caretaker's cottage. He started toward the front door, then recalled he'd torn the porch to shreds. As he knocked on the back door, he secretly hoped no one would be home.

Chapter 8

Pale blue, striped curtains with cherries dotting them parted. Buttercup—*Lorelei,* he corrected himself since he'd learned her name from Pinkus—peeked out. She smiled and opened the door.

"Why, hello."

"Is your mother here?"

"No, she went to town today. Can I help you?"

Russell shifted his weight from both feet onto just the left. His right leg ached. "I need to speak with her."

"She should be home later." She bit her lip for a second. "Is something wrong?"

"No." He hated to have to ask for help. Waiting only meant he'd have to come back. "I'm going to need dinner for the workmen each day. 'Round about noon—something good and filling. Counting the boys cleaning out the stable, there are ten of us. Do you think your mother could cook?"

"Yes. Yes! Mama loves to cook. We have a wagon. I can help her pull the food up to the house."

"You can't very well walk into town and drag back the rest of what you'll need in a kids' wagon. Can you drive a buckboard?"

Her eyes sparkled as she nodded.

"Do you have an icebox?"

"Yes. Ice is delivered every Thursday."

"We won't need food today. Starting tomorrow at noon, I want solid meals. No skimping. I'll give your mother a note for the butcher and the mercantile so she can get whatever she needs." At that moment, Russell realized the mercantile wouldn't be a problem, but the butcher might well be ugly about selling meat to a German. He added, "I'll make it clear she's my cook and feeding my workmen, so there shouldn't be a problem with her buying the necessary bulk."

Lorelei smiled. "It will be a lot of food. How many days will they be working?"

"Two weeks." Her question took him by surprise. He'd expected her to ask how much he'd pay. "New York housemaids earn eighteen dollars a week." He'd decided twenty would be fair, but Pinkus's words echoed in his mind. *Things are tight. Lost Johann. . .* A closer look showed Lorelei's dress and shoes were both nearly worn out.

"Eighteen dollars!" Her eyes grew huge. "But that is New York."

"I'm sure cooks make far more, and I'm asking your mother to feed several hungry men, even if it's only one meal a day. Tell her I'll pay thirty a week on top of whatever the food costs."

He spun around and made it down the steps before she stammered, "Do you have dishes and tableware enough for ten men at your house?"

Dishes and tableware enough, he repeated to himself. *It's not just her voice that sounds German. She puts the words together wrong.*

"We have dishes if you don't." She spoke the words softly, tentatively.

Russell thought of the mismatched left-behinds he'd gathered. He didn't own enough to have one guest at his table, let alone nearly a dozen. The notion of doing any formal entertaining left him cold, but he refused to depend on someone else for anything as basic as table service. "Get dishes. None of those painted steel things—real ones."

"Fancy china?"

Having worked at Diamond Emporium and ordered stock through catalogs, he knew far more than most men ever would concerning domestic goods. He could handle this. Relieved to be dealing with something straightforward and unemotional, Russell turned.

"Haviland. They have an everyday pattern called Ranson that will do. If that's not available, get Spode's Tower."

"Ranson," she repeated in a tone that matched her astonished expression. She leaned into the doorsill. "What about glasses and such?"

"A case of whatever pressed glass they have on hand. I'll probably use most of the glasses to mix paint or clean brushes. When the house was locked up, they left a mishmash of cutlery that ought to work, so don't bother getting any silverware."

"Very well."

That settled, he turned to leave. The women would feed the workers, and he could make himself scarce by continuing to work on the interior of the house. He said over his shoulder, "I'll also have the boys plow a garden for you once they're done cleaning the stable."

"Thank you!"

"I'll have the buckboard here in ten minutes."

"Make it twenty minutes, Mr. Diamond. I have cinnamon rolls in the oven."

Lorelei laughed at how the pots rattled and the toy wagon wheel squeaked as she pulled it up the road. The combination made for a comical symphony, and she delighted in the music because it reminded her of how God had provided this opportunity for them to make money. This wasn't a tiny sum, either—it was enough to provide for a little while.

Mama would be coming in ten minutes, after the tarts came out of the oven. The men could start in on the main part of the meal first.

Mr. Diamond left his buckboard parked in the yard to serve as a buffet table of sorts. She reached it, spread a cheery scarlet tablecloth over the bed, and started arranging the dishes.

"Chow time!" one of the men hollered to the others.

It wasn't necessary for him to shout. Two of the men had seen her coming and whistled. Part of her wanted to smile at how silly it was for them to do that, but the other part felt embarrassed. It didn't feel any better to have them all crowding around as she put a big roasting pan on the buckboard table.

"What did you fix us?"

"Today," she said as she picked up a kettle and a big saucepan by their handles and plunked them on either side of the roaster, "is pot roast, braised potatoes and baked carrots, peas, salad, and rolls."

"Got any gravy?"

"In the speckled pot that's still in my wagon." She didn't bother to get it. No less than three men dove to grab the gravy. They were all hardworking men, but when it came to food, they acted like starving little boys.

Old Mr. Bayley cast a woebegone look at the now-empty wagon. "No dessert?"

Lorelei smiled. He was such a nice man. "Mama knows you like berry tarts. She's taking them out of the oven in a few minutes."

The men heaped food on their plates and sat in the dirt to eat. Mr. Diamond wasn't anywhere to be seen, and Lorelei feared the men would dive in for seconds before he had a chance to get anything. She took a plate, placed generous portions of everything on it, and went around the back of the house toward what she'd learned was the kitchen.

A chair propped the back door open. "Mr. Diamond! I'm leaving food here for you." She stayed on the doorstep and peeked inside. The kitchen was homey, and the scarred cutting board made Lorelei think many happy hours had been spent in this room. The sensibly arranged room held a huge, ancient stove. Beside it lay a bedraggled-looking, heavily bandaged dog.

"Oh, you poor baby!" She remained outside, set the plate on the chair, and tugged a little piece of the roast free. "Here, puppy. Are you hungry?"

The dog barely paused to sniff, then gobbled it. The very tip of her tail, free of a bandage, swished to and fro in a sign of pleasure.

"What are you doing in here?"

Lorelei jumped at the harsh sound of Mr. Diamond's voice and whirled to face him. "You were not there. I saved food for you."

"You don't belong here."

He cast a disparaging look at the food and made an impatient sound. "Not just here in the house. You don't belong up here at all. You had to hear the men whistling at you."

Embarrassment washed from her bosom to her scalp in a scorching wave.

"It's foolhardy for you to deliver dinner alone. I hired your mother, not you. From now on, she's to bring the food. You can come only if she's with you."

"You are here, as is Mr. Bayley. I am safe enough."

"No one is ever safe." His voice rang with pain and bitterness.

"God is with me."

His face hardened, and his eyes narrowed as he shot back, "Where was God when your father died?"

Russell helped Mrs. Goetz put the empty dishes from yet another fine meal into the wagon. Today's corned beef and cabbage, soda bread, and carrot cake tasted wonderful. Truth be told, she'd managed to bring something different every day so far, each meal far surpassing what he'd expected when they struck their bargain.

Rationing and food "rules" restricted what women cooked. Mrs. Goetz studiously adhered to the government's recommendations, but it never seemed as if her meals lacked anything at all. Fish and fowl dominated the menu instead of beef—just as the pamphlets advised. On "Meatless Mondays," she made hearty soup from Lorelei's vegetable garden or filling casseroles. On "Wheatless Wednesdays," she'd serve chicken with potatoes or rice and make puddings or baked apples for dessert. With sugar and butter being limited so more could be sent overseas, she still managed to use honey, molasses, currants and raisins, and cooking oil so creatively that the men actually asked for the recipes for their wives to use.

She deserved praise for her hard work, but Russell wasn't in much of a mood to talk.

"I'm leaving this here for your dog." Mrs. Goetz set a small earthenware bowl on the buckboard. "Lorelei scraped from yesterday's chicken bones the marrow and made a special gruel. It helps the puppy grow healthy again."

"Thanks."

"Lori and I—we are grateful to you for plowing the garden for us."

"She was planting stuff yesterday."

"No. She was mixing in ash and horse droppings to enrich the soil." Mrs. Goetz curled her fingers through the handle of the toy wagon and crammed her other fist into her apron pocket. "She will have to come with me here tomorrow to get the buckboard. I must go to town for more food, and I do not drive."

It was the first time anything had been said about Lorelei not coming up to the house anymore. For a whole week, she'd stayed down at the cottage. Clearly, Lorelei helped cook the enormous meals, but never once had she ventured anywhere near the mansion.

Russell fought with himself over whether to go talk to her. He'd spoken in anger, and in doing so, he'd caused her grief to deepen. The memories of how she'd flinched at his words and the tears that filled her eyes haunted him. Her hand had trembled as she lifted it to touch the small silver cross hanging on a fragile chain about her neck. *Almost as if she were trying to shield her faith from my cruel onslaught.*

"How many more days do you need me to make the lunches? It looks good—this roof of yours. The men are working hard and fast. They will be done soon."

"Another week." He cleared his throat. "They'll also be repairing your roof and chimney, but I'll do the porch myself."

Mrs. Goetz shook her head. "No."

"I understand you're worried about whether it's safe to have the men there. Perhaps you could make a few meals ahead and go into town with your daughter so she's not around them."

"This is not the problem." Aching pride showed in her careworn face and squared shoulders. "We do not want anything from you."

"What's that supposed to mean? It's my property. I'll do whatever I deem fit."

Tears silvered her eyes, making him remember how Lorelei's had glistened. "Patching a porch does not fix hurt feelings."

He inwardly winced at that observation and didn't pretend to misunderstand what she was saying. "I made your daughter cry. It won't happen again."

"My Lori has a big heart. She cares easily for others."

He shook his head. "Not after how I spoke to her. She's been glad to keep her distance."

"That is where you are wrong, Russell. Lorelei wants to bear your burden as a Christian should, but you have made it clear you want nothing to do with her or with God."

"She's not responsible for me or my soul."

"You are responsible for your soul," the older woman said in a matter-of-fact tone. "But as Christ's followers, we believe we are our brothers' keepers. You were trying to be mindful of her safety when you told her not to come alone." She hitched her shoulder. "That time, you were being your sister's keeper."

Her comment didn't amuse him. "I upset her. You can tell her I'm sorry. Warn her I'm going to work on the porch so she can avoid me."

"Lorelei needs no warning. Perfect love—the kind God gives us in His name that we are to show one another—this special caring knows no fear."

Mrs. Goetz left, pulling the wagon behind her. Russell watched her leave. What would it be like to live without fear?

"Here, girl. Come to me. Yes. Good girl." Lorelei crooned softly to the dog and knelt to capture her. No longer bandaged, the brown and white mutt still looked. . . well, like a mutt. One ear cocked up while the other flopped to the side. One haunch bore partially healed scrapes and was missing most of the fur. "What are you doing out alone?"

Lorelei gathered her in the basket of her arms, rose, and realized she'd never be able to carry the dog back to Mr. Diamond's house. He cared for this dog, and once he discovered she was missing, he'd be worried. Lorelei's gaze fell on the wagon. She managed to lay the dog in it, then worried she might hop out once the wheel started squeaking. Once she finished tying down the dog, she grabbed the handle, steeled herself with a deep breath, and headed toward the forbidden mansion.

Soon she started to sing:

Are you ever burdened with a load of care?
Does the cross seem heavy you are called to bear?
Count your many blessings, every doubt will fly,
And you will be singing as the days go by.

"What are you. . ." Mr. Diamond's voice died out as he strode down the drive. His gait seemed steadier, his limp far less noticeable. His forehead creased, then he let out a disbelieving bark of a laugh. "My dog is wearing your apron?"

Chapter 9

It was the only way I could be sure she wouldn't bound out. She is healing well, but I didn't think her strong enough to walk back here." Lorelei started to untie the apron strings she'd wound around the wagon to keep the dog inside.

Mr. Diamond knelt on the other side of the wagon and loosened a stubborn knot. "How did you get out, girl?"

The dog woofed and licked his hand.

"She probably smelled your cooking. I can't blame her for following her nose. Old Pinkus Bayley told me the men are taking their time to do a good job, but they might be working a tad slower than usual because of the food you're making."

"Mr. Bayley is a kindhearted man."

"And I'm not."

His words jolted Lorelei. She didn't know what to say. *Jesus, please give me the right words. I need Your wisdom and kindness.*

Mr. Diamond looked at her and said gruffly, "I'm not proud of how things went last week. I had no call to say what I did. Whatever gentility I once had is long gone. Stay away from me. I had the good sense to leave home so I wouldn't hurt those I love; this is my refuge. Once I have this place fixed, I won't have to bother with anyone else."

"It is no sin to hurt inside or to question God, Mr. Diamond." Her apron wadded in her hands as she quietly confessed, "God has heard more than a few of my questions and knows my grief. I would be wrong to judge you, let alone find you guilty of what I have done myself."

"I saw your tears." Each word grated out of him. "You walked out of my kitchen weeping—because of me."

She closed her eyes for a moment, then opened them. "It was because of you. In this, you are right; but you are also wrong. I didn't cry for myself. I cried because I cannot imagine the pain you try to bear alone. In Psalms, it says the Good Shepherd is with us when we walk through the valley of the shadow of death. Many days and nights—even in the midst of my sorrow and questions—that has been my only comfort. I have been angry, and I have asked, 'Why?' but I have always leaned on the assurance that God is beside me. My heart aches to think you are without that comfort."

"You can't expect me to find peace when I've lived though war."

"Peace is not a place; it is a serenity that comes when we trust God that He will make all things right in His time."

He shook his head sadly. "Buttercup, I meant it. Keep your distance."

Buttercup—I like that he called me such a beautiful name. Deep inside, this man longs for good things. She reached out to pet his dog. "When you doctored her and bandaged her, did she try to bite you?"

Lightning fast, he reacted. "I'm not a stray dog for you to heal."

"No, you are not, but just as you understood she didn't mean to hurt you, I also accept that you reacted out of pain. Now that I see what is in your heart, I'm not afraid."

Pinkus sauntered up. "Good, good. The two of you are talking. Lorelei, knock some sense into this stubborn man's head. Tell him to hire me to paint the place after you put in the new windows."

Lorelei felt her face grow warm. "I cannot do this, Mr. Bayley." She'd secretly hoped Mr. Diamond would give her the commission to replace his broken windows. The job would bring in enough money for her to slip some into the savings sock. Now, though, since Mr. Diamond had made it clear he wanted nothing to do with her, she couldn't very well make a bid for the work.

"Why not?" The old man's face crinkled into a hundred wrinkles as he turned to Russell. "You unhappy with the job my men have been doing?"

"I'm pleased. The roof and chimneys look good."

"Then what's the holdup? While we do the roof and chimney over at the cottage, Lorelei can get to work on your windows up here."

"I didn't order the paint yet," Mr. Diamond said.

Something about the set of his jaw made Lorelei take a second look. He put down the dog, and as the dog gingerly tested standing again, realization dawned. *He's offended because his leg is weak. Climbing the ladder will be too hard, but he doesn't want anyone to treat him like a cripple.*

Lorelei sat in the wagon and folded her hands in her lap. "What colors did you decide on, Mr. Diamond? When you paint the inside of your house, will you do different colors for the rooms?"

"He can paint them whatever color he fancies. Don't make no nevermind to me," Mr. Bayley snorted. "And the outside—well, to my way of thinking, it would be a crying shame to paint this grand old woman anything other than white." He directed his attention back toward Mr. Diamond. "Russ, reason it through. By the time you buy ladders and scaffolding, you pert near hired my crew to do the outside of this place. They could really use the work, and you have plenty that needs doing on the inside to keep you busy."

Clearly, the old man's reasoning went a long way toward salvaging Mr. Diamond's pride. Mr. Diamond hooked his thumbs through belt loops and drawled, "Slate. I want slate for some of the detail work."

"Slate blue or slate gray?" Lorelei ruffled the fur between the dog's ears.

"Isn't it the same?" both men asked in unison.

She shook her head. "What colors do you want inside?"

"Back to that, eh?" Bayley chuckled.

"Well, if he wants to use silver, pink, and black inside, then he should use slate gray." She tilted her head toward Mr. Diamond. "If you want to use blues, lavender, and gold, you should use blue slate."

"Sounds to me like the lass knows what she's talking about. She going to do the windows before we set to painting?"

"I need to go back home." Lorelei wondered why she'd bothered to try to look so casual. She stood and reached for the wagon handle, the whole time feeling embarrassed that her neighbor didn't want her around and hadn't offered her the job. "Good-bye."

"What's awrong with her?" Mr. Bayley muttered as she dragged the wagon down the gravel.

Mr. Diamond mumbled something, but Lorelei couldn't tell precisely what he said. Then again, maybe that was best. *Perhaps he has been too polite to say it, but the real reason he doesn't want me around is the same reason others have shunned us. Yes, he asked Mama to cook, but he was desperate. The truth is, he doesn't think I'm American; he thinks I am the enemy.*

"Miss Goetz?" Russell stood in the doorway of what looked to be her workshop. Lorelei was welding something on a table, and he'd waited until she put the soldering iron down so she wouldn't burn herself. In those moments, he'd promised himself that he would mind his words so he didn't hurt her again.

"Yes?" She glanced over her shoulder at him.

"I'd like to speak with you."

"Come around toward the window." She swept her hand in a fluid gesture. "I have not swept and do not want you to get glass in your shoes."

He walked around the perimeter of the room and hated how his uneven gait sounded on the cement floor. If Lorelei noticed it, she managed to hide her reaction. She sat on a tall stool, had a pencil shoved haphazardly into her hair, and wore a supple leather apron that nearly covered her everyday dress.

As far as he knew, she owned three dresses—a "Sunday-best" gray and black one and two "everyday" dresses. He strongly suspected the sunshine yellow dress had been her Sunday best until she'd needed to make the gray-and-black-striped one for mourning.

"What are you making?"

She fussed with the edge of the window. "A piece for the Mariners' Chapel."

"Can we hold it up so I can see the design?"

"I need to weld a few more places before it can be moved."

"Okay. I'll wait." He watched as she exchanged the soldering iron for another that she had waiting on a potbelly-type affair. Even with all the windows and both doors open, the heat made the workroom feel sticky and hot. *But that thing isn't enough to keep this big drafty room warm in the winter. I'll have to put in a larger one. Maybe she'd rather have a second one in the opposite corner.*

"There's another stool. You are welcome to have a seat." She bent over her task and concentrated on each action with precision that made her features take on an intensity that caused her eyes to glow. The heat from soldering and her passion for what she did made her cheeks rosy.

"You love what you do."

"It was a gift from my papa. He taught me."

He didn't want to talk about her father. He'd seen too much death in his short time in the trenches to want to think of it now. Instead, Russell tried to keep the conversation focused on her work. "What is this one called?"

"Fishers of Men."

"Do you design them yourself, or do you have a book of samples?"

"Each window is a new opportunity. I talk to the person who commissions it and see what they have in mind; then I make sketches and have them select what pleases them." She handled the flux, soldering wire, and iron with a deftness that bespoke many hours of practice.

"The racks there for storing your glass are clever."

She laughed. "You are teasing me."

"I'm serious." He looked at the wooden fixtures that held a veritable rainbow of glass panes in an orderly vertical array. *The attorney said my uncle feared her place might be vandalized. No wonder he worried. All this glass. . .*

"Every business has to organize the material," she said in a practical tone.

Her words pulled him away from imagining what danger she and her mother might have been in, in town. He didn't want to think of that, and conversing about how she had things set up seemed easy enough. "You can see everything, and it doesn't take much storage space."

She glanced up from her work. Her eyes danced with unrestrained humor. "Some were broken when we moved here, so I use noodle-drying racks on the end to hold the smaller pieces."

"Noodle-drying racks?" He took a closer look. "No wonder you thought I was teasing you."

Setting aside the soldering iron, she offered, "We can lift this now so you can see it if you are still interested."

"Let me help."

"Just a minute, please." She rotated a crank, and a length of sturdy rope snaked down from a pulley hanging from a ceiling beam. The rope forked into two equal lengths. Each held substantial hooks. "This will make it easy." She stood on one of the rungs of her stool and stretched forward as far as she could.

"I'm closer." He took the hooks and threaded them through rings she'd affixed to the top of the window. "There."

Slowly, carefully, she operated the crank until the window hung suspended in space. "Come to this side so you can see the sun coming through the panes."

Russell didn't need to be asked twice. He'd already gotten the general flavor of the piece and wanted to see its full splendor. He reached her side and looked at the work in awe. Boats floated on rippled glass that looked just like water. The fishes' scales were iridescent, and the faces on Christ and the men He'd called to become His disciples had been painted with undeniable artistry. "Incredible."

"You like it?" She watched him eagerly, clearly wanting to see his reaction.

"That belongs in a museum."

"There is a second one." The implicit offer came out in a shy admission.

"Show me!"

She left his side, went to another crank, and raised another piece off a nearby sturdy table. In the foreground, a young sailor gripped a ship's wheel. Jesus stood behind him, one hand on the sailor's shoulder, the other extended, pointing the way. The thin black paint stroked on the glass gave grain to the "wood," folds to the "cloth," and strands to "hair."

"You're such a wonderful artist. What will you do for my house?"

Lorelei gave him a wary look.

"You don't just do religious windows, do you? What about something old-fashioned?"

"You would have to show me which window." She still looked less than eager.

"Lorelei—I'd like to call you by your given name, if you don't mind." She nodded her permission. "I couldn't put you in a dangerous situation. I worried you might get hurt, climbing a ladder and trying to glaze the windows."

"That is not the only reason." She turned away. Her shoulders were hiked clear up to her ears with the tension that sang through her. "I would not have a lie between us. It is better to be honest, even when it hurts."

He sighed. "All right. I'm sure you guessed it anyway. Your mom and I had a discussion. You've got a tender heart, Lorelei. I decided to keep my distance because I don't want my bitterness to poison you."

"Then why are you here now?"

"Because Pinkus showed me how I can remove the window frames and bring them to you. You'll be working from home, and I won't show up if I'm in a bad mood."

She looked doubtful, so he pressed, "Next week, while the men are working on your roof and chimney, you and your mom can come to my place. You can number all of the windows and measure them. We can decide on some of the places to hang some of these masterpieces, then we'll all go to town and buy whatever glass and supplies you'll need."

"Tell me, Mr. Diamond—"

"Russell. Call me Russell."

"Tell me, Russell." She paused as if to bolster her nerve, then blurted out, "Do you really want us at your home? Many do not, because they think we are German."

"I'm English and Irish; you're German. We're both American."

His answer came too quickly—as if he'd rehearsed it. Lorelei paused. *Do I want to pursue this or let it go?*

He shifted his weight and looked uncomfortable. Her silence must have prodded him because he began to speak again. "I admit, the first time you spoke and I heard your accent, it surprised me."

"It was not a happy surprise."

He exhaled slowly. "No, it wasn't. I won't bother lying. Heines. Huns. Krauts. I've heard it all, and I've even said it myself. Living like a rat in trenches, soldiers are crude and desperate. They have to build up hatred so they can kill the enemy. It isn't easy to come home and hear echoes of your enemy in your neighbor's voice."

I am not your enemy."

"Of course you aren't. I've come to know that full well." Russell's features tautened. "I've seen the gold star in your window. I know you've paid the ultimate price for our country."

Lorelei bowed her head. Her eyes and nose stung with tears. "Papa wanted to go. He loved America and wanted to help."

Russell cleared his throat. "Then there's no problem with me hiring you to replace my windows or commission stained glass—unless you're already backlogged."

"Fishers of Men was the last piece I had on order." She pasted a brave smile on her face and hoped he wouldn't ask why she didn't have stacks of orders waiting. Before the war, they'd always been backlogged with commissions; now, no one wanted to do business with German Americans.

Russell nodded. "It's selfish, but I'm glad. I need you to work for me."

"I am able to start on your house right away."

"I have to go get paint in a few days. We can pick up some windowpanes while we're at it. How do you keep the glass from breaking when you transport it?"

"It's not easy. Sometimes one of the neighbors who has a motorcar drives for me. When we moved here, I layered straw in the bed of a wagon, then laid the glass between our blankets." She cast a glance at the noodle-drying racks. "The pieces that broke, I kept. I can use them still."

"Are you able to match glass?"

"Sometimes. Why do you ask?"

"There's a leaded-glass window in the parlor that has a few bars of color here and there. I like the effect, but about half of the window is broken. Temporarily, I'll have you replace the whole thing with plain glass, but eventually I'd like to have you restore it."

"If you show me, I can see what kind of glass it is. Even if there is none in town, we could put in a special order. I should warn you, red glass is most expensive. Gold is used to make the red glass, thought it would not seem so to look at it."

He gave her a look she couldn't interpret, and Lorelei felt gauche for having to broach the subject. "You have much work to do, and the cost must be a great burden. I wanted to let you know so I can keep my windows for you affordable."

"I see."

"I could replace the regular windows for you first, because those will be cheapest. When the new garden plot begins to yield a harvest, Mama and I can sell your share or can it for you, and you will end up with a little bit more money."

He scanned her workshop and pointed at a dowel. "What are those metal, snakelike things?"

"Lead cames. They are the channels the glass fits into and come in different widths and shapes. The U shape is for the edges, and the H shape is for the middle." She smiled. "Like when you put together a puzzle—the inside pieces must have nooks and crannies to hold on to one another, but the border must be smooth."

"When I got here, you were using solder and flux."

"Yes." *Such an intelligent man, gathering information so he can calculate the costs of materials.* "When I do more delicate work, I sometimes use copper foil. If you have any lamps which are in need of repair, that would probably be the technique I would employ."

"Where do you buy all of this stuff?"

"The store is starting to order it for me again." As soon as the words were out of her mouth, Lorelei regretted them.

Russell's eyes narrowed. "Starting to? What does that mean?"

"It is of no consequence now."

He tilted her face up to his. "They persecuted you for being German, didn't they?"

"No longer. And during the time I needed things, Mr. Bayley was most helpful. He very kindly used his connections with stores in other towns to obtain whatever I lacked."

"So the old codger is really a guardian angel in disguise, huh?"

Russell's tone was warm and rich with approval, so the words didn't seem disrespectful in the least. Lorelei smiled and nodded.

"We'll go to town day after tomorrow." She detected a slight edge to his voice as he added, "Make a list. Don't worry about which stores we'll go to."

"I need to ask Mama. She might need my help with the cooking or something."

"Lorelei, it would have been dishonorable for me to come speak with you if I hadn't already gotten her approval."

"Oh." She looked into his unfathomable eyes. "I did not mean to insult your integrity."

"No offense taken."

"Well?" Mama stood in the doorway. "What do you—oh, Lori! The window ist wunderbar!"

"You like it?" Lorelei vacillated between being delighted that her mother loved the work and being worried that Russell would get upset at hearing a few German words.

"Ja!" Mama waggled her finger at Russell. "I told you my girl, she makes beautiful windows."

"She does. I'll be here day after tomorrow to take her to get supplies. Perhaps you could come with us to the house now so she can get a feel for what she's going to need."

"I cannot go. I have food almost ready for the stove—potato soup, green beans fresh from the garden, and bread, of course. It is just humble food, but perhaps you should eat supper here."

Lorelei watched indecision flit across his handsome features. "Put it in the wagon. You can use my stove. I need to fire up the oven, anyway. Mutt is sleeping next to it at night."

"This is good, yes. We can come together this way." Mama bobbed her head approvingly. She spun about and headed back to their cottage.

Russell sat on a stool out of the way as Lorelei took care of the small oven so the fire would go out, then let down the stained-glass windows and put things away. "Where's your broom, Lorelei?"

She shook her head. "I am odd. I prefer to sweep in the morning, before I start to work. The little slivers of glass welcome me, and I like the way the morning sun turns them all into sparkles. It makes me happy to start to work again each day."

"Are we ready?" Mama stood in the doorway again.

"Not yet." Russell slid off the stool. "I'm virtually living in the dark. I have one lamp. It would probably be wise for us to take one of your lamps or a candle along so I can get you back here safely."

Lorelei slanted him a funny look. "This, coming from a man who leaves logs in our woodpile at night?"

Russell woke, rolled out of bed, and grimaced as his leg cramped. He'd overdone it yesterday, and he'd pay for it dearly today; but since he'd spoken with Lorelei and they'd cleared the air, he felt better.

He'd wondered yesterday if she'd just been in a good mood after finishing that incredible window, so he'd gone down to the garden and tried to act casual as he watched her garden. "Russell! Hello!" Lorelei's warm smile had drawn him closer.

"I'll hold that." He'd taken the bucket off her arm and watched as she deftly started filling it with beans. To his surprise, the smell of soil hadn't bothered him. He'd absently picked some of the string beans and added them to the harvest. After that, they'd each filled a whole basket with tomatoes. He'd spoken very little; she had chattered sunnily and hummed under her breath. Contentment had radiated from her, and he'd basked in it.

Unwilling to lose the ease he found in her company, he'd urged her to come measure more windows last evening before they'd make the trip to buy supplies. Mrs. Goetz had invited herself along and again made supper for all of them, then puttered around the downstairs as if she belonged there. Only after she'd left had he discovered Mrs. Goetz had worked wonders in the parlor.

Rubbing the morning stubble on his face and staring down at the fresh scars on his leg, he willed away the pain—but the pain didn't obey. The doctors had removed whatever shrapnel they could, and they'd set his leg—but his leg had healed an inch shorter, and some of the shrapnel remained in place.

I have my leg. I'll take the pain. Russell shuddered at the memory of them discussing amputation. He'd shouted himself raw, telling them not to do it. In the end, they'd been worried about infection and damaging nerves, so they'd left shrapnel behind—a permanent reminder of war. *As if my memories and limp aren't enough.*

In a sour mood, he glared at daybreak's first ribbons of light streaming through the window. The blanket that normally hung there was missing, and he jolted. *The windows!* Today he and Lorelei would go into the village and get the supplies to do more work on his house.

Dressed but with his shirt hanging open, Russell hobbled into his kitchen. The aroma of coffee sped his uneven gait. Mutt's head lifted, and her ears perked up. Slowly, she struggled to her feet and headed for the door. Russell let her out and grinned at the stove.

Just before she'd left last night, Lorelei had put a pot of coffee on the back of the stove. "It has far too much water. During the night, the banked embers in the stove will cause the extra water to steam away. You will start your day with a good cup of coffee."

Mmm. He reached for a cup and could hardly wait to get a mouthful. It was a fine trick—one he'd remember, just as he'd keep a big kettle of water on the stove each night so he'd have warm water with which to wash and shave in the mornings.

By the time he hitched the horses and drove the buckboard to the cottage, Russell came to a stunning realization: For the first time since he'd come home, he didn't mind being with other people.

Well, not exactly. He didn't want to cope with everyone in town, but he found an odd comfort in Lorelei's company and an undemanding nurturing in her mother's presence. Odd, but he felt a kinship with them: They didn't want to have to interact with some of the people in town any more than he did. *If Lorelei can face those people, I can, too.*

Lorelei laughed the minute Russell drove up. "So you brought your friend?"

He twisted and urged the dog to sit in the back of the buckboard. "Silly dog is starting to follow me everywhere. She jumped aboard as I was leaving."

"You have doctored her well, that she can jump." She hefted a bushel of vegetables and swung it into the buckboard. "Mama said you told her we could take the produce to town to sell."

Russell got down and wrested the next bushel from her. "Give me that."

Mama came out of the cottage, crossed the brand-new, brick-edged cement veranda he'd made, and started for the buckboard. Russell made an irritated sound, went to her, and grabbed the box of quart-sized canning jars from her. "What do you think you're doing?"

"Taking the produce to town, as you told me I could." She toddled along beside him. "You brought the dog. Do you think whoever the owner is will claim her?"

He stiffened for an instant, then shrugged. "We'll see."

Once they reached town, it didn't take long to unload the produce at the mercantile. The money went toward their store account, so Lorelei turned toward the paint. Russell stopped her. "Did you need anything?"

"Not today, thank you."

He stared at her, then asked in an undertone, "I should have asked before we got here. What do you need?"

"Just two days ago, Mama and I came with your buckboard to buy the food to feed your workers. Our kitchen is quite full. If you have the paint, we can go on to get the glass."

"Okay."

Russell barely finished loading the paint into the buckboard when an energetic group of boys raced up and encircled him. "Is it true? Were you in the war? Did you kill a bunch of Krauts?"

Lorelei saw sweat bead on his forehead and upper lip as the boys continued to pepper him with questions. The haunted look about his eyes intensified, yet he remained completely silent.

"We want to hear all about it!"

"Not from me." Russell pushed past them and helped Mama into the buckboard.

"Heroes do not boast, boys," Lorelei said softly as she slipped past the boys. As they drove off, she leaned forward and whispered to Russell, "We can get the glass another day."

"No." His voice was low and harsh. "Whatever needs doing is getting done on this trip."

Chapter 11

Lorelei rolled the putty into a long, smooth, snakelike cord, then carefully positioned it along the edge of the glass. Once she laid it there, she used her putty knife to press the doughy substance into place and smoothed it so the seal would be sound and the glass secure.

Windowpane after windowpane, she'd done this. A simple skill, glazing a window didn't take a lot of thought, but each one gave her a sense of satisfaction. This particular window sash held four panes; two were originals, and she'd replaced the other pair. The original ones had a faint undertone of lavender to them, and she'd searched among all the panes of available glass to match it. Old glass often had ripples, bubbles, or a tint to it, and on the day they'd gone to buy glass, Russell had said he wanted to restore the house to be comfortably livable but have it maintain its old flair. He'd been genuinely pleased at the notion of trying to approximate color matches instead of doing wholesale replacement of all the windows.

Russell. Ever since that day when the boys wanted him to talk about the war, he's become more reserved.

"Ready for lunch?" Mama asked from behind her.

"In just a minute."

Mama's footsteps died out, and Lorelei carefully replaced the lid on the putty can before going to the cottage. Once there, she washed up.

"You stopped singing today," Mama said as she fished corn on the cob from the kettle with a pair of tongs. "Usually you sing as you work. What worries you?"

"Russell."

"Ahh." Mama's voice held a wealth of understanding.

"For a while, I thought maybe he just needed to meet people. He started being more sociable for a little while, but then he got grumpy again. He's all by himself up at that house, day in and day out. It's not good, Mama."

"He's hurting. Not his leg—his heart. Men who go to fight can do this. Some call it 'shell shocked,' but he is not crazy in the head or dangerous. He has curled away from the world because his soul is wounded."

"His soul won't heal if he doesn't read his Bible or go to church, but I can't push him. I feel like God is asking me to be patient and gentle with him."

"God reveals Himself in many ways. It is for us to be right with the Lord so we can be light in the darkness."

"He won't talk at all about the war."

"I can imagine why not. A man who has witnessed the brutality of combat can bear wounds that only the Lord sees. Deep wounds don't heal rapidly."

"He came here to get away from those he loves. He told me he did it so he wouldn't hurt them. Perhaps this is a relapse of the pain that initially brought him to this place."

"We will pray. God is faithful. He will not let this warrior's wounds fester forever. There will come a time of healing."

"That is what is needed," Lorelei agreed. "A prayer for restoration."

The smell of sawdust filled the air. Russell moved down one more step and started to sand the next baluster. Mutt scooted down beside him. The dog shadowed his every move. Russell surveyed his work. He'd gotten almost all of this side of the stairs done; the other side had taken four days. Inch by inch, he'd been stripping varnish, sanding, pulling the wood in the house down to bare grain.

The wind off the ocean felt far stiffer today. He welcomed the refreshing change. Most of the month, record-breaking temperatures had scorched the coast. The marble floor of the entryway helped keep the center portion of the house cooler, so he'd purposefully planned to work in this area during the peak of the heat.

The sound of glasses clinking together made him pause.

"Russell!" Lorelei stood in the open front door with a huge smile on her face. "Look at how much work you have done!"

Mutt gave a happy yip of recognition and scuttled down the stairs to her side.

Russell stood and dusted off the front of his shirt and sleeves. "No, look at how much work you've done." He walked toward her and shook his head. "I told you, I don't need this."

"We agreed to sharecrop." She pressed the crate into his arms. "You will not take your portion of the money; the least we can do is see to it you have food put up in your pantry. Mama said you are to come to supper tonight."

"Your mother would have me eat supper with you every night. She must think I'm starving."

Lorelei laughed as she passed the crate full of jars to him. "Can you blame her? We saw the charcoal you tried to feed this dog. If that is your idea of a roast, it is a wonder both of you survive!"

The sound of horses made them both turn around. Pinkus Bayley rode right up to the veranda. "Folks," he greeted them curtly, " 'member how I insisted on the men making new storm shutters? Well, I brought the liveryman's boys to help you get 'em up and batten down the hatches. We've got us a big storm brewin', and the drop on my barometer makes me think it'll be a hurricane."

"Oh, my." The color drained from Lorelei's face. "I have heard they are fearsome things."

"Never been in one?" Pinkus shook his head. "Lock the covers on your wells to keep debris out, and board up the windows. You got a basement, just in case it gets bad?"

Russell set aside the jars. "I do. Lorelei, run down to get your mother. Grab kerosene, lamps, candles, and some blankets. Haul it back here in the wagon." He shook the old man's hand. "Thanks for rounding up help."

"Glad to do it." Pinkus nodded. "Those of us on the windward side of town are seeing boats make for storm anchor, but I reckoned those of you out here didn't know. Ships are reporting North Carolina's getting hit hard, and they've measured higher than thirty-four knot winds. Hurricane flags went up an hour ago. I'm going on to warn the Rimmons."

Four hours later, the boys had fastened the storm shutters built onto the upper windows and affixed the ones made for the lower ones. Russell helped them board up the windows down at the Goetzes' cottage. The boys had refused his offer to stay, delightedly accepted five-dollar bills apiece as payment, and ridden back home.

"I just filled the bathtub," Lorelei called from upstairs as he came inside. "It's cold in the basement. If you don't mind, I'll take the blankets from your beds and drop them down to you."

"There's only one bed. It's in the last room on the right." He turned as Mrs. Goetz emerged from the basement. "Is the fire in the stove out?"

"Ja. But first, I made a good stew and plenty of hot coffee. We will have a good meal as we endure this storm, but I have closed the flue so we will not have smoke come in."

RESTORATION

The winds had been picking up steadily. Soon they shrieked, and rain pelted the house. As it sat atop a hill overlooking the ocean, the house groaned in the fury. He'd put it off for as long as he could, but Russell knew the time had come. He led the women to the basement door, sent them down along with the dog, then stared into the dank, dusty darkness. He broke out in a cold sweat. *It's like the trenches.*

Chapter 12

Wind howled louder. Lorelei pulled her sweater closed, more for comfort than for warmth, as Russell shut the door and descended the steps. She saw his steps falter. *His leg! The steps are steep, and it's dark.*

Lorelei grabbed a lamp and hastened to the base of the stairs to light his way. She forced a laugh. "Promise you won't be mad when you get down here and see where Mutt is."

Russell paused and scanned the dim basement.

"Look at the cot."

"We need more light in here." His harsh words echoed in the enclosed space.

"Ja, this I am seeing to." Mama laughed. "Seeing to—that was funny." She turned with two more lighted lamps, came toward the stairs, and handed one to Russell.

He breathes too fast. His face is sweaty. Lorelei shuffled back a bit. "You've worked hard for our safety, and we're trapping you on those stairs. Come. Sit and rest now."

He descended the last step and made a sharp turn to the left. Wordlessly, he prowled the basement, inspecting every last inch. The stairs marked the center of a narrow, fifteen-foot room. One end opened into a small, square room.

"This room, since it already has shelves, we thought was perfect for storing everything." Lorelei scanned what had probably served as an additional pantry in years gone by. "Do you think we have enough?"

Russell barely paid attention to the crate of canned food, the odd assortment of buckets and pitchers filled with water, and the folded stack of blankets. He grabbed a tin of kerosene and shook it. "Almost full."

"Yes. We also brought a box of candles." *Why is he so concerned about light?*

He exited the storage room and looked about as if he hadn't seen the main room before. He walked the full length and stopped by the clunky vacuum cleaner.

"Mama, she coughs when she gets around too much dust," Lorelei said. "I didn't have time enough to clean well, but the worst of the dust is gathered and gone."

He nodded. "There's not much of anything down here."

Mama sat down in one of the three chairs they'd brought down and patted the seat of another. "Come. Sit. Lorelei is right. You have worked hard. There is nothing to do now but wait."

Russell shook his head. "Things down here look fine for a fall-back position if the need is present. For now, we'll stay in the entryway."

"But is that safe?" Mama fretted.

He'd already started toward the stairs. "It's in the center of the house, away from the wind pattern."

Lorelei and her mother exchanged baffled glances.

"Hand me the coffeepot and the stew," Russell called from the top of the stairs. "I don't want you to spill and scorch yourselves."

They settled in the curved area of the entryway in the shelter of the staircase. Instead of sitting with them, Russell kept prowling around. He came back with something each time—an overstuffed chair from the parlor for Mama, a small table from the library for their food. After his fifth or sixth trip, Mama grabbed his arm.

"Come. Have coffee with us."

"Yes," Lorelei agreed. "You've done more than enough to make us safe and comfortable."

Russell sat on a wooden chair he'd brought from upstairs. He accepted a mug of coffee, curled his big capable hands around it, and took a big gulp. Mutt settled on the floor beside him. "Raining pretty good out there now."

"Does that mean it's started?" Lorelei listened as the wind whistled through the shutters.

"Perhaps." He shrugged. "Hurricanes can also have bands of rain clouds that come before the brunt of the storm. We'll sit tight."

"This is a good place to be." Mama craned her neck and studied the area. "It is like being in the cleft of the rock. I don't remember where that is in the Bible."

"Exodus thirty-three." Russell jerked his cup up to his mouth and took another drink.

"Let's read it." Lorelei strove to hide her surprise at how quickly he'd rapped out the citation. She took a small Bible from the pocket of her apron. "I tucked this in before we left the house. Exodus thirty-three. . ." She ran her finger down the page until she reached the passage.

"Starting at verse twenty-one. 'And the Lord said, Behold, there is a place by me, and thou shalt stand upon a rock: And it shall come to pass, while my glory passeth by, that I will put thee in a clift of the rock, and will cover thee with my hand while I pass by: And I will take away mine hand, and thou shalt see my back parts: but my face shall not be seen.' "

Russell didn't seem to be in the least bit interested in the scripture, but the fact that he'd known precisely where to find the verse hinted that he'd spent considerable time in the Word at some point.

Mama began to hum. She paused and smiled at Russell. "This is your house. You do not mind if we sing, do you?"

He shrugged.

Mama began to sing, and Lorelei joined in:

A wonderful Savior is Jesus my Lord,
A wonderful Savior to me;
He hideth my soul in the cleft of the rock,
Where rivers of pleasure I see.

He hideth my soul in the cleft of the rock
That shadows a dry, thirsty land;
He hideth my life with the depths of His love,
And covers me there with His hand,
And covers me there with His hand.

As they finished the last line, Russell leaned forward and reached for the coffeepot. Lorelei grabbed it and poured more for him. He'd tolerated the hymn, but clearly, he hadn't enjoyed the lyrics.

Instead of letting things fall into awkward silence, she said, "You've done much to the house. What will you do next?"

"I'm stripping the wood." He reached up and curled his fingers around one of the balusters. "Think I'll strip wallpaper out of the parlor, then do a lot of staining and painting."

"The wallpaper is ready to come down in there," Mama agreed. "If you mix vinegar and water, then put it on the paper with a sponge, it will make the glue let go."

"Vinegar?"

Mama nodded. "The day you do this, you will smell like the pickles or sauerkraut."

When he chuckled, relief poured through Lorelei. She settled back. "What color will you paint the parlor, and what will you do about curtains?"

Gusts of wind and rain pelted the house. They discussed his plans, gave suggestions, and finally ate stew. When Mama yawned, Russell took a second lamp, lit it, and ordered Mutt to stay before he walked off.

"I think he's getting the cot, Mama. I'll go get the blankets from that little room in the basement."

"Do you need the lamp?"

"No, Russell has one. It'll only take a minute."

Lorelei descended the stairs, took a few steps, and let out a gasp as something knocked her to the floor and hands closed around her throat.

Chapter 13

"Rus-sell." His name came out in a breathless whisper. It took another second for him to realize his assailant wasn't fighting back. Long strands of hair filled his hands, too. *Lorelei!*

Russell let go and rolled to his knees. "Are you all right?"

Lorelei lay there, her eyes huge with fright, yet she nodded.

"Can you breathe?" He anxiously brushed her hair back as remorse clawed at him.

"Yes."

"Did I hurt you? Can you move?"

She rolled to the side and started to push herself into a sitting position. "You surprised me is all."

Gently as he could, Russell pushed her back down. He dragged the kerosene lantern he'd left on the floor closer. Even as he gently turned her head so he could examine her neck, she protested.

"Truly, Russell, I am fine."

Fear turned to anger. "Why did you sneak up on me?"

"The blankets—they're down here."

"If I'd had another second or my trench knife, you'd be dead."

She shook her head and rested her hand on his arm. "No, Russell. You would never hurt me."

"Buttercup, you have more faith than brains." He stood and loomed over her. "Go back upstairs."

She took his hand and got to her feet. He braced her, afraid she might suddenly collapse, sick at the thought she'd cower from him. Lorelei rested her hand in the center of his chest—more, it seemed to still the thundering beneath her palm than to steady herself. Standing there, she looked so fragile, so feminine. He'd scared the wits out of her, yet she smiled up at him and acted as if her heartbeat didn't match his. Being down here scared him; being around her scared him even more.

"I'll get the blankets, and you can get the cot," she decided.

He clamped his hands around her waist, lifted, and set her halfway up the stairs. "Get going."

She took hold of the stair rail, so he let go and turned his back on her.

"I'll wait here. If you go get the blankets, you can hand them to me."

"Stubborn woman."

Her laughter warmed the basement. "Yes, I am."

She's not leaving me down here alone. Russell didn't know whether to be relieved or mad. He strode to the small room, grabbed the blankets, and stomped back. "Here. Scat."

"Yessir!" Humor tinted her voice.

He grabbed the cot he'd been folding, snatched the lamp, and sped up the stairs. Though desperate to be out of there, he still wasn't ready to let matters alone. Russell set up the cot with a few practiced moves, then tugged Lorelei's hand. She lost balance and tumbled into his arms with a surprised cry. He laid her on the cot.

"What is this?" Mrs. Goetz hopped to her feet.

"Loosen your daughter's collar and check her out. I practically broke her neck." Russell paced away and kept his back turned.

As soon as the storm's gone, they'll be gone—and I'll make sure they don't come back. I could have killed her.

"A week," Lorelei grumbled under her breath. "A whole week, and he still barely speaks to me." She scored the glass, tapped along the underside with her cutting tool, then snapped it neatly into two pieces. Ever since he'd set upon her in the basement, Russell had kept his distance.

"Now, Lori," her mother chided as she cleaned one of the windows, "don't be so impatient. Russell Diamond is a good man. He's been very busy clearing away all of those branches which fell—and didn't he cut them into logs for our very own fireplace and stove?"

"Yes, Mama. You don't have to convince me that he has many fine qualities."

"Well, you have been very busy, too. You were in town most every day, fixing windows that storm broke." Mama smiled. "I still thank God that it did not worsen and become all we feared."

"If that was a storm, I don't want to live through a hurricane!" Lorelei walked to the glass rack and selected a small scrap of green to use for a leaf. As she decided how to cut it to use the swirl pattern in the glass to its best advantage, she added, "God heard us when we were singing that He covered us with His hand."

"Ja, so this is true." Mama finished the window and set aside her rag. "And what about the gardens? I thought for sure the plants would all blow away."

"Having the gardens by the hedges helped. They served as a windbreak. If you take produce into town tomorrow, could you please tell Mr. Rawlin that this window is done? Maybe he can drive out to get it."

A shadow fell on the workroom. She glanced up. "Russell!"

"How big is the window?"

"Come see." She gestured to him.

He ordered Mutt to stay in the doorway, walked around the edge of the workroom as he had before, then came to her side to look at it. "Pretty, but not big at all."

"No, it's not." She nudged a piece into alignment. "Teddy broke one just like it when he was playing ball. It belongs to Miss Florina."

Russell winced. "I broke a neighbor's window once. Worked long and hard to pay for it." He stuffed his hands in his pockets and looked decidedly uncomfortable. "I. . .um. . .came to ask a favor."

"That is what neighbors are for."

"I don't know about that. I got a letter from home."

"Is everything okay?" Mama blurted out.

"Yes." He shot her a kind smile, and Lorelei liked him all the more for how nice he always was to Mama. "To put it in a nutshell, my mom and sister have decided they need to come see the house. It's nowhere near ready to have visitors, and I'm not even sure what I need to get."

"Curtains, towels, beds, and bedding for two rooms," Lorelei said at once.

"I like to sew." Mama smiled. "You get many yards of nice fabric, and I can make curtains and pillows and a cushion for a chair in each room."

Russell held his hand up in surrender. "Wait! I figured I'd have you come shopping with me tomorrow. We'll deliver the window while we're at it."

"Stay for supper. You need to eat better." Mama shook her finger at him and headed toward the door. "And come for breakfast. It will be a long day tomorrow."

His head pounded unmercifully, his leg ached, and Russell knew they'd barely begun. He shot Lorelei a get-me-out-of-here glare.

"No, thank you, Mrs. Whorter. I am positive he won't want Chinese urns." She picked up a crystal vase and turned it toward the sun. It cast myriad rainbows about them. Unlike everything else in the store, it was American-made instead of imported. "This Heisey vase is the last thing. You will pack it with the rest so we can pick it up in an hour?"

"Yes. Of course." Mrs. Whorter set the vase on the counter next to an appreciable pile of towels and toiletries, then gave her a shrewd look.

"Good. We've got to get moving." Russell got out of Whorter's Imports and collapsed on a bench on the boardwalk.

"This is moving?" Lorelei plopped down beside him and giggled.

"I have to recover. I kept wanting to sneeze." He scrubbed his hand across his nose to try to stop the tingling from all the perfumed soaps, powders, and whatnots. "What's wrong with getting all of that stuff at the mercantile?"

"Nothing." Lorelei tugged on the edge of her glove. "But Mrs. Whorter is a widow, and it is nice to give her business. We can go to the mercantile after we go to the china shop—unless you want to use those everyday plates we already bought for when we were feeding the workmen."

"I'm only doing this once. Since I have your help, we'll get the fancy china today."

Ten minutes later, Lorelei somehow managed to get Mrs. Sweeny to seat Russell in a dining chair at a table. "Now, then," Lorelei said, "it is easier to picture the place setting."

She coordinated so well things that made it all go together—the Garland pattern of the Fostoria crystal carried the same graceful motion as the swags between the historical cameos on the Virginia pattern of the Lenox china. The Mount Vernon pattern of Lunt silverware featured the same style of curve.

Even a year ago, this would have irritated him to no end. Now, having a young lady set pretty things on the table before him, worry about whether it harmonized with the other pieces, the soft rise and fall of her sweet voice, the graceful little gestures—it all rolled over him like a balm. War did that to a man, made him aware of the gentling effect women exerted in an otherwise savage world.

Lorelei shifted, bit her lip, and replaced the goblet with another. "There. What do you think?"

I think I'd like to stretch this moment for a long while. Russell lifted the plate to assure himself he'd not been woolgathering and misheard the pattern name. "Virginia." Russell raised a teasing brow. "The silver is Mount Vernon. Are you going for a theme here?"

"Of course." Lorelei set a pair of candlesticks nearby and crooked her head to examine the match. "You told me you were restoring the house. The patterns are old-fashioned looking and honor your heritage. Isn't that what you want?"

"I have the Hanover pattern," Mrs. Sweeny held out a plate with a touch of red amidst heavy gold embellishment around the edge. She cast a sideways glance at Lorelei, and her voice took on a decided bite. "It might suit your heritage, too."

Russell didn't like the undercurrent. He pushed to his feet and tucked Lorelei behind himself as if to protect her from any cruelty. One ugly comment, and the peace he'd craved died instantly. Once again, he was a warrior, and he'd defend Buttercup from anyone who dared pose any threat or unkindness toward her.

"The lady already showed her preference. We'll just go elsewhere—"

"No! Oh no, there's no need for that." Mrs. Sweeny blanched. "I misspoke."

"Yes, you did. Years ago, Americans didn't want my Irish ancestors to immigrate here. I went to war because our country believes all men are created equal." As he spoke, Lorelei shifted to stand beside him. His arm went about her waist, and he tucked her close to shelter her. "It would be unspeakable if the freedoms we fight for were denied the citizens at home."

"Yes. Of course you're right."

Russell dared to look at Lorelei. Her eyes glistened with tears, but instead of looking pained, she glowed.

"Russell, your words are so wise. Papa would have been so glad to know such a good man as you. For those things, he went to fight, too."

"We don't have to do business here."

Lorelei traced the tip of her forefinger on one of the cameo pictures on the salad plate. "Mrs. Sweeny is sorry. Even before America entered the war, her son's ship was hit by a German U-boat."

Lorelei obviously didn't want to make a scene, and Russell knew it would be best to follow her lead. He bought the china and led her out of the china shop, silently vowing he'd never spend another cent there.

As they waited at the corner for a buggy to pass before they crossed the street, Lorelei turned her face toward the sunshine. The joy on her face sent pangs of envy through him.

"Is there some specific charitable cause I should know about at the next store?"

Lorelei spluttered, then laughed. "Russell, even when you are wry, your wit tickles me."

He smiled back at her. She made being grumpy seem so ridiculously selfish. Few were the people he knew who could laugh at themselves; Lorelei did so regularly. She also coaxed him out of being in a bad mood simply with her sunny disposition.

They'd dropped her mother off at the mercantile in the first place. While they were taking care of the other matters, Mrs. Goetz was supposed to arrange for several other items. Now Lorelei and her mother chattered like birds on a clothesline, and Lorelei kept insisting that Russell make a decision between two things. Finally he leaned back against the counter and folded his arms across his chest.

"This must be done today so the house is ready for your guests," Lorelei scolded playfully.

Russell turned to Mr. Sanders. "I've got dozens of rooms to furnish, and she's fussing like I wouldn't have someplace to stick another bedstead. Just take all of the stuff and dump it in my buckboard. If it won't fit, deliver it."

"But you didn't decide on the material!" Lorelei's mother glowered at him.

He gave Mr. Sanders a yet-another-tempest-in-a-teacup look. The storekeeper grinned as Russell said, "Just throw the whole bolt of whatever fabrics she liked on there, too. Now give me a bottle of Bayer aspirin. Domestic matters are a headache."

Lorelei waited until they reached the mansion and started to unload the wagon. Mama had taken an armful of goods into the house before she tapped Russell on the shoulder. He turned around, holding a gleaming teakettle.

"What?"

"Your headache—is it all you have? Is anything else bothering you? In Boston, the navy is having many cases of the grippe."

"I heard about that. They're calling it the Spanish Influenza. You don't need to fret. I'm fine. Besides, there haven't been any cases down here or out west, so you can stop worrying."

A heavily laden wagon trundled up, and a young man jumped down. "Mr. Sanders ordered me to help carry all of this in. Where do you want it all?"

For the next two days, Lorelei and her mother went up to Russell's house. Russell was more than generous each time they worked for him, and the sock with their savings finally bulged.

Lace curtains hung in the parlor, and Mama had sewn new cushions for the window seat. She'd salvaged the material on the underside of the cushions and made pillows that still matched the old settee they'd uncovered. Russell had already stripped the wallpaper and freshly stained the floor, so he painted the walls a creamy color and nodded appreciatively as Lorelei filled the Heisey crystal vase with a fistful of black-eyed Susans.

She'd concentrated on the bedrooms. He'd painted each of them a pale shade of green. An ornate, white, wrought iron bedstead in one room was covered with a deep green counterpane. It had taken very little time for Lorelei to stitch hems in the dark green material, and after she'd hung the draperies, she'd pulled them open with white, tasseled cords. The room had no bedside table, so she'd tossed a tablecloth over a barrel and set a flowery, globed lantern on it.

The other room boasted cabbage rose bedding and curtains, and fresh, fluffy towels graced the washroom bars.

"What do you think of this?" Russell knocked on the top of a small chest of drawers. "I'm finding stuff in the attic that looks salvageable. When I first got here, I didn't bother looking there, but since I'm going to need some furnishings, that place is full of stuff."

"That will be nice. Can you sand and stain it, or would it be easier to paint it white?"

"The grain's nice. I'll stain it. There are a few washstands and eight or nine chairs up there I'll bring down and either stain or paint."

"Your mother and sister—do they come from far away?"

He straightened suddenly. "Buttonhole. They live in Buttonhole."

"I am sure they will be very glad to see you." She gestured in a wide arc. "When they see all you have done—"

"That's the idea," he said curtly.

Lorelei quietly studied him, then asked, "Do you believe they will be so busy looking at your house that they will not see the trouble in your eyes and heart?"

Chapter 14

Russell's face hardened, and he gave no reply other than to turn and carry the piece down the stairs and into the empty ballroom he used as his workshop.

Lorelei sat down at the top of the stairs. *Heavenly Father, Your voice holds together the universe. Please speak in a way that will soothe Russell's hurting soul. I dared to hope he'd been improving, but I was wrong. The changes were only on the outside, while inside he's so very broken. You, God—only You can heal the hurt he carries.*

"You're Diamond?" A purser from the railroad scuttled up to Russell.

"Yes." Russell kept searching the trickle of folks disembarking.

"I was asked to give you this message. The phone and telegraph line to Buttonhole blew over in the gale, and the new one's not working."

Russell accepted the envelope and ripped it open. Just seeing his father's strong script brought back memories:

Dear Russell,

Your mother and sister have both come down with a fever and are staying home. Mom says not to worry, that she'll come next week. She's missed you sorely, as have I. She complains your letters are too short. I would complain, too, but I'm no better, as you can see from this. We pray for you daily and trust the Lord to give you strength and peace.

Love,
Dad

P.S. We've sent some furniture to you. It once belonged in your house, and we wanted you to have these pieces.

Russell had dreaded seeing his mother, knowing full well Lorelei was right. Mom was far too perceptive to be deceived by a pretty bedroom and fragrant soap. She'd admire them, enjoy them, but she'd fuss over his leg and fret over how he'd changed.

What was a man to do? He'd gone to war with high ideals and heroic plans. He'd believed in God and country—well, country was still here, but where was God? Where was He when men all around were dying? The first day out, Jonesy—Russell's childhood friend—had stood up and crumpled back into the trench, dead from a sniper's bullet. Men he considered brothers had died all around him.

The very first man Russell had killed had a rosary spill from his pocket. He'd undoubtedly thought God was with him, too. From that day on, Russell hadn't opened the Bible Dad had given him right before he'd left.

That had been the first of many lives Russell had taken. Kill or be killed—it was the most basic rule of warfare. The Bible said God created man in His image, and man was nothing but a bloodthirsty, cruel animal.

Mom and Dad lived such innocent lives. Their world was simple, their faith unshaken. Russell couldn't bear to look them in the eye and let them see what he'd become. Body, mind, and soul, he'd come home battered in ways no one would ever comprehend.

One more week of respite. . .but at what cost? *Is Mom really all right? And Sis? Is it the Spanish Flu?*

"Sir? Mr. Diamond." The purser scowled at him. "You need to claim your crates and sign for them."

"Sure. Fine."

He'd cleaned up an old buggy from the stable to come claim Sis and Mom. Clearly, he'd never manage the furniture. Russell arranged with the livery to deliver the large crates.

The house felt eerily empty when he got home. Once the oak secretary, rocking chair, and hall tree were in place, the feeling of loneliness intensified. Dad had often sat at the secretary, going over order forms. Mom had loved the rocking chair. The hall tree had no umbrellas, hats, or jackets on it to give it a homey air. As far as companionship, Mutt usually was all Russell wanted or needed, but tonight he felt alone.

Russell couldn't sleep. He worried about his mom and sister. Had Dad taken sick, too? Russell purposefully didn't read magazines or newspapers because the major features were all about the war. Even so, he'd overheard stories about the influenza up in Boston. It killed strapping, healthy soldiers.

Did I tell Mom I loved her before I left?

"Hop in. I'm going to town to make a telephone call."

Lorelei took hold of Russell's hand and nimbly climbed into the buggy. "Telephones are amazing, aren't they? Hearing a voice over wires—it doesn't seem possible."

"My dad had one put in his emporium. I always thought it was a nuisance, because whenever anyone called, it fell to me to answer it and take messages."

Lorelei chuckled. "So now who will have to take the message?"

"I'm calling my dad. Mom didn't come yesterday. She and my sister are both sick."

Lorelei twisted on the seat to face him. "Oh, Russell, I am so sorry to hear this. I will have to pray for them."

"You do that, Buttercup." His voice sounded grim, and he said nothing more the rest of the way to town. As soon as they entered the mercantile, Russell beelined to the telephone on the rear wall.

Lorelei decided to buy ten-pound bags of flour and sugar instead of five pounds since she'd have a ride home and she and Mama hadn't bought any for themselves in a while. Then, too, she asked for a dozen brown eggs. Folks chatted and jabbered as usual. One of Mrs. Sweeny's sons had received a battlefield promotion.

After he finished his phone call, Russell prowled around the farthest aisles of the store. Noting his dark expression, Lorelei ventured over to him.

"How is your mother?"

"Dad said it's a nasty cold—nothing more." He didn't meet her eyes. "While I'm in town, I want to stock up. It'll take time. Is that a problem?"

"Not at all." She laughed. "With the unexpected ride, I'll still get home sooner."

By the time they left, Lorelei knew for certain they couldn't have wedged one more thing in the buggy. As it was, she held a crate on her lap that contained the oddest assortment of canned food she'd ever beheld. "Your larder will be full for at least a year with all of this."

"Don't blame me." He fished a can of chipped beef from the crate and held it up. "Mutt's the hungry one."

"She is by your side all of the time. How did you make her stay home?"

"It wasn't easy. Listen, Mom sent apples from our orchard back home. I'll eat a few, but they'll mostly spoil. Can you and your mom use them?"

"But of course. Oh. . .I should have bought more canning jars."

"I'll get you some if you promise to make cinnamon applesauce."

Lorelei laughed. "This applesauce—"

"Cinnamon applesauce."

"This cinnamon applesauce—I suppose it is also for your very hungry dog?"

Chapter 15

Russell carried Lorelei's measly ten-pound bags of sugar and flour into the cottage, barged into the kitchen, and started opening cabinets. "Where do these go?"

"In the canisters, silly." Lorelei put down the eggs and gave her mother a hug.

"You will stay for lunch." Mrs. Goetz made it more of an order than an invitation, but he'd been counting on that.

"I can't stay long, what with that stuff in the buggy. Let me help." He opened the pantry and scanned the shelves. *They hardly have anything on them.* He cleared his throat. "What do you want?"

"I want you to sit down," Mrs. Goetz said as she pulled out a chair.

"Yes." Lorelei's eyes sparkled with humor. "Having seen your roast, Mama is sure your cooking would give us stomachaches."

"I'm never going to hear the end of that roast, am I?"

Lorelei and her mother said in unison, "No."

At dusk, they stood side by side and said the same thing. "No, Russell."

He rotated his shoulders, but the action didn't relieve the stress. As soon as he'd finished lunch, he'd driven the buggy to his back door, unloaded the contents, then changed his socks to the ones Mrs. Molstead had knitted. He'd unhitched the horses from the buggy and changed them over to the buckboard.

It had taken considerable fortitude to drive north to the Molsteads' store. He'd done it for Lorelei, though.

Only, Lorelei acted anything but pleased.

Russell folded his arms across his chest and glowered at the woman. "I didn't want to tell you this, but you're backing me into a corner. I have information that the flu is spreading."

"You don't read the newspaper, Russell." Lorelei made a dismissive gesture. "So far, they think it will stay up North. No one expects it to come down here, and experts say it will never go to San Francisco, either."

He'd hoped they'd simply accept what he told them. Clearly, Lorelei needed to be set straight. "You know I spoke with my dad on the telephone. He's got contacts all over because of the orders he places for his store. He said it's spreading—faster than folks realize. Dad's not one to panic, but he's not letting Mom or my sis come visit. That says plenty to me. After I spoke with him, I placed a few calls myself."

"You truly are worried." Lorelei gave him a compassionate smile.

"I am." He didn't mince words. "You're going to have to cooperate with me, because the less often we go to town, the lower the chances are that we'll contract it."

"But influenza strikes the feeble, the old, and the very young," Mrs. Goetz reasoned.

"Not this one. People fifteen through forty are getting hit the worst." He hated scaring them, but he had no choice. "It's killing them in a matter of a day or two."

Russell didn't give the women a chance to demur. He hefted twenty-five-pound bags of sugar and flour onto his shoulder and headed toward their kitchen door. Prices—especially of sugar—were high, so folks had been cutting back and buying smaller bags. He, on the other hand, was willing to pay top dollar, and the Molsteads gladly sold him as much as he wanted. Fatigue and the extra weight of the sacks made his limp worse. A sardonic smile twisted his mouth. His bum leg had provided a good excuse to buy several bottles of aspirin.

Glass clinked behind him. Funny, how he'd come to associate Lorelei with that sound. "Russell," she said in her singsongy voice, "I hope you bought some cinnamon for the applesauce I'll put in these."

He shouldered the door open and dumped his burden near their pantry, and more than just the weight on his back lifted. He smiled at her. "Are four big tins enough?"

"Four!"

The shock in her voice still rang in Russell's mind as he crawled into bed that night. Exhausted as could be, he lay there and experienced the oddest sensation—security. He'd not felt this way since he'd gone off to war. For the first time in ages, he'd been able to control matters and take action to make a difference.

The sickening knot in his stomach and the tension in his muscles eased as he closed his eyes and recalled his last glimpse of the Goetzes' kitchen. By the time he'd left, every last cabinet and shelf there had bulged with provender. Astonishment and gratitude had shone in Lorelei's eyes as she bid him sweet dreams when he walked past her toward the door. He rubbed his aching leg and let out a sigh. *She'll be safe now.*

"All set." The iceman shut the door to the icebox and pulled a newspaper from his pocket. "Here's the paper. News is bad all over. The missus said to thank you for the pumpkins."

Mama handed him a burlap sack containing more bounty from their garden. "She is welcome. They grew well this year."

Lorelei sat on the new porch and opened the newspaper. Mama came out and settled on the chair. She started to shuck corn. "Read to me."

"Things look bad in the North," Lorelei said as she scanned the headlines. She didn't tell Mama about the article of another German store being vandalized.

"So Russell was right about the influenza?"

"Yes. Boston canceled its Liberty Bond parades and sporting events. In New York, they closed the theaters and symphony halls. The stock market is only open half day. The influenza is awful in Europe, too. They've canceled schools!"

"So terrible this is!"

Lorelei read aloud, and as she turned the page, Mama called out, "Good day, Russell!"

"How can you say it's good with what you're reading?" He waved his arm toward the newspaper.

Lorelei watched his gait as he approached. *He barely limps at all anymore. . .or is it just that I've grown accustomed to his walk? No. It is better, because on the days it pains him, I can tell by his bearing.*

"The day is beautiful, crisp, with the lovely autumn air and weak sunshine. The news is bad. Perhaps the church is doing something. We will see on Sunday."

"You can't be thinking of going to church!" Russell halted by the porch steps, leaned forward, and snatched the newspaper from Lorelei. "Public gatherings help spread the disease." He turned and appealed to Mrs. Goetz. "You've lost your husband; you can't possibly endanger your daughter!"

Lorelei folded her arms in her lap. *Dear Lord, let this be an opening.* "Will you make a deal with us, Russell? If we do not go to town for church, will you come to our house and worship with us?"

"Is that what it'll take?"

Lorelei glanced back at Mama, saw her nod, and turned back to him. "We would be pleased."

"Fine. Sunday." He stomped off.

"You know, it will be hard for him," Mama said softly. "He knows the Bible, but his faith is faltering."

"I know. He got angry when I was singing, 'Great Is Thy Faithfulness' out in the garden last week. He's still a soldier, but the battlefield is his soul."

"The Holy Ghost is wooing him. Maybe God will make something good happen out of all of this bad."

"With God, all things are possible." Lorelei scooted backward and reached up. Her fingers closed around her mother's corn-silk-tassel-covered hand. "Let's pray, Mama."

"What was I thinking?" Russell angrily opened a can of chipped beef and dumped it in a bowl for Mutt. Russell plopped the bowl on the floor for the dog and didn't worry about the gravy that slopped over the edge. Mutt would make short work of it. He twisted and threw the empty can into the wastepaper basket with total disgust. "What under the sun was I thinking to agree to that ridiculous proposition?"

I care about them. The truth nearly knocked him off his feet. It was dangerous to care. How many friends had he made on the battlefield, only to lose them? How often had he shared a cold, miserable trench with someone, only to see him die? *This flu—it's killing people. It could claim any of us.*

The safest thing is not to grow attached. Even though she's freshly widowed, Mrs. Goetz has a pleasant outlook on life and a gentle warmth. As for Lorelei. . .

Russell didn't want to admit it to himself, but the truth glared at him. He yanked out a chair and dropped into it. *She has a way about her—a compassion and joy for living that lights the dark corners of my heart. It's too late for me to keep from caring. I'll be sure to keep as much distance as possible.*

Really, it wouldn't be all that hard. He'd been essentially solitary since he'd arrived. Other than interacting with the workmen as necessary, Russell made a point of not socializing. All he'd do was walk down to the cottage for an hour or so on Sunday mornings, then ignore his neighbors the rest of the week.

Satisfied with that decision, he stood and tugged open a cupboard door. Scanning the cans of food, Russell felt a twist of disgust. Overseas, he'd eaten out of tins for months and promised himself he'd never eat out of them once he got home. Now that he was home, it didn't matter. Nothing tasted good. For the most part, he ate only because hunger forced him to. The meals Lorelei and her mother made were the exception. Russell couldn't figure out why he suddenly developed a decent appetite and appreciated the flavor of their food. He grabbed a can of tuna and wrinkled his nose as he opened it. It occurred to him that anything he didn't have to fix or something fresh ought to rightfully be more appealing. *But when I've eaten at the diner, that might as well have been sawdust.*

He peeled off the lid and didn't bother to drain the can or mix it with anything. Hunched over the counter, he scooped out bites and shoveled them into his mouth.

Why did I agree to worship with them? I left the battlefield in France, but I'm still at war—only this is a personal war. I'm fighting with my soul, with God. Tradition and convention aren't good enough, and I'm not going to pretend.

Russell spent a sleepless night and a hectic day. He tried to find something to take his mind off the fact that he'd gotten roped into Sunday worship. Mucking out the stable and grooming both horses, raking and burning leaves—the heavy physical labor didn't distract him in the least.

The library beckoned—the one room he'd left entirely alone. Heavy draperies blocked out the sunlight, and sailcloth drooped in forlorn, dusty shrouds over the bookcases. Methodically, he removed and folded each piece of sailcloth from the outside to the middle, effectively capturing the worst of the dust. Whoever had closed up the house had taken great pains to try to preserve the books. Russell finally stretched his back and wiped his hands on the thighs of his jeans. He'd gotten a lot done—even if he'd been thinking of Lorelei all the while.

The next morning, he grudgingly put on a tie and walked to the cottage. Mutt trotted alongside him, and he figured it would be all right. *She'll probably behave better than I will.*

Lorelei opened the door, and a combination of aromas from the kitchen and her light, floral perfume greeted him. Her eyes sparkled. "We waited breakfast on you. There's even some applesauce—cinnamon applesauce."

He cracked a grim smile. They'd tried to do their part to make this comfortable. After breakfast, they moved from the kitchen table to the small parlor.

Lorelei smoothed her Sunday-best dress. "I thought to have us sing a bit, read a passage of scripture, and pray."

Russell shuffled his feet and cleared his throat. "Ladies, I'll not be a hypocrite. I won't sing the words to those hymns. I don't feel them, and a man ought not misrepresent himself to the Lord or to others."

Mrs. Goetz smoothly invited, "Then listen and hum. You can appreciate the music even if the lyrics don't quite match your thoughts."

Satisfied with that compromise, Russell sat down and hummed old, familiar hymns. Lorelei lovingly opened her Bible and paused a moment as she fingered the ribbon marking the passages she'd selected. She didn't start reading from the left page where the Psalms began. Instead, she shifted the Bible slightly and began reading. "Psalm four: 'Hear me when I call, O God of my righteousness: thou hast enlarged me when I was in distress; have mercy upon me, and hear my prayer. . . .' "

Three psalms she read, her expressive voice rising and falling, carrying a range of emotions that made the psalmist come alive. Before now, the Psalms had never been much more than pretty words to Russell. The depth and complexity in the verses struck several nerves.

After Lorelei finished reading, Mrs. Goetz prayed. Lorelei had once told him that her mother usually prayed in German, but at the meals they'd shared, she prayed in English. Even so, then, as today, she occasionally slipped and called God *Vater* instead of Father. Her prayer, so honest and intimate, made the ache in his heart double.

Seconds after saying, "Amen," Mrs. Goetz smiled at him. "Russell, you will stay for dinner?"

"I can't. I have to go." He stood and saw the surprise, shock, and chagrin on Lorelei's face. He couldn't help it. He had to get out of there, shift his thinking, and shut down the unexpected flood of emotions he felt from hearing David's words, the hymns, and prayer.

At home, the haunting passages played through his mind. He'd never appreciated how David was a warrior. He'd been besieged, seen comrades fall. *I will both lay me down in peace, and sleep: for thou, Lord, only makest me dwell in safety. . . .* The words from the psalm nagged him, taunted, and wouldn't let go. Even after enduring combat, killing and seeing his own men perish, David could lie down in peace—and he slept. *Oh, to have my head hit the pillow and not relive the horror of what I saw and did!*

David the soldier was also David the musician, the one who sang unto the Lord. *I can't sing. Nothing flows from me but anger and sadness. How did David manage?*

As the week went by, Russell found himself humming as the words of hymns Lorelei and her mother had sung seeped into his memory. "Abide with me! Fast falls the eventide. The darkness deepens. . ." Russell knew all about darkness—not just the pitch black of night, but the ugliness of the soul. In the silent moments when Russell paused from his work to rub his leg or catch his breath, he'd recall the lyrics again and again. "Lord, with me abide. . . ."

The next Sunday, he took a harmonica to worship, hoping to drown out the lyrics. He didn't want to remember how he'd once treasured those hymns and believed them, had held faith in a loving God. Russell hoped if he concentrated on playing, the lyrics wouldn't continually intrude upon his conscience, but nothing could drown out the sweet blend of Lorelei and her mother's voices as they worshiped the God they loved so dearly—the same one who turned His face away and allowed Russell to wallow in the aftermath of man's ultimate evil.

No matter how hard he worked, regardless of the physical difficulty or the mental acuity required for a task, Russell couldn't free himself from the persistent reminders and memories of what Lorelei and her mother sang, read, or said. Between the songs of reverence and praise and the scriptures, he left the Goetz cottage and lived with the echoes of worship all week long.

Daytime was hard enough; nights grew nearly impossible. Russell would lie in bed and fight to find a comfortable position. His leg troubled him after the exertions of the day, and that pain only compounded his inability to sleep well. He'd toss and turn, besieged by flashes of battlefield memories. Jolting awake, he'd struggle to reorient himself. In the moments after he established that he was safe in his bed, he'd try to substitute a different vision in his mind. Time and again, his thoughts would go to Lorelei as she held up a stained-glass window of Christ or as she read her Bible. Lorelei laughing. Sun shimmering on her golden hair as she bowed her head in prayer. She had the peace he craved. It didn't take a genius to figure out her peace ran soul deep—but the problem was, his trouble plumbed the depths of his soul.

Each Sunday, he kept his promise and went to their cottage. At first it was just to keep them safe, but in the following weeks it became a habit. Sunday morning became the only way he marked time. He'd left home and family behind in search of a refuge, to get away from others; yet he paid a weekly visit to his neighbors, sat in their parlor, and examined how others in the Bible had endured the separation from God he was experiencing.

Most of all, Russell identified with David. He'd lost his friend Jonathan. He'd gone to battle, been brave, then shook with fear. Psalm after psalm revealed the ups and downs he'd experienced—the joys, the sorrows, the fears, the depression. David was just as likely to cry in grief and sorrow as he was to sing in victory.

David—David had known the ugliness that lurked not only in other men's souls, but in his own, too. War had forced Russell to do things he'd never imagined himself doing. He'd slain—even rejoiced and taken pride in causing his enemies' deaths. That fact plagued him. . . but King David—the warrior, the psalmist—had done the same thing. And Lorelei had said David was a man after God's heart.

Right and wrong—they once were so clear. Now Russell struggled to reconcile a loving God with all He allowed to happen. As time passed, Russell's anger started to give way to unspeakable sorrow.

David had times of darkness when he couldn't see God's face. Why had he still called out to God? *And why can't I?* Russell shook his head. *I can't.*

Chapter 16

"It's cold in here."

Lorelei nodded absently and tapped a nail into the surface to keep the next piece of glass in place.

"Why didn't you light the fire?" Russell tromped across the workroom toward the potbelly stove.

"Please, don't light it." She looked over her shoulder at him. "The newspaper says it is best to leave the house cold. They think it kills the microorganisms for the influenza."

"The cold will kill you before it kills the germs. You don't dare catch a chill. It'll weaken your lungs and make you a prime target." He opened the grated front of the small stove, then slammed it shut.

"Come look at this window. I've been working on it for your parlor. Remember the pieces I couldn't match? I've removed the original edge, cut and used those pieces, and reformed the border with this opalescent gold. See how the amber makes the vertical lines shimmer?"

"What about that spot in the middle?"

"I couldn't quite make the glass stretch far enough, so I decided we'd put jewels here, here, and there." She touched the empty spots.

"Jewels?"

"Yes." She pulled a box from a shelf off to her right and opened the lid.

"Oh. Bauble things."

She laughed. "There are plain, smooth, round ones, or we can use faceted ones. What do you prefer?"

He reached over her shoulder and used his forefinger to push the jewels around in the box until he found one that appealed to him. "This kind." He picked it up and set it on her work board. "Yeah. I like that a lot."

"I agree. We need two more." Before he could respond, Lorelei hurriedly added, "In fact, there are many supplies I need to buy—more lead cames, more solder, and emery so I can smooth out the chips on some of your pieces in order to repair them best."

"Make a list. I'll go to town."

"I knew you'd offer, but it won't work. I need to look at the things and decide for myself." She could see the fire in his eyes, so she hastily added, "If I'm to stay out of town, at least I should have the things necessary to keep myself busy."

"Don't you understand?" Russell glowered at her. "My mother and sister just had a simple cold and fever. Even after they recovered, they stayed in Buttonhole, because by then, Dad wouldn't let them get on the train. It's utter foolishness to mix with people."

"I'm getting essentials, not going to a party."

"Lo-ri!" The frantic pitch of Mama's voice sounded from the house.

"Coming, Mama!" She started toward the house, and Russell rushed alongside her. "What is it?"

"We need to go check on Russell. Mutt is here. Perhaps something is wrong."

"Nothing's wrong, Mrs. Goetz." Russell brushed past Lorelei.

Her mother threw her arms around him and burst into tears. "I was so worried for you!"

"Shh," he murmured. Lorelei watched as he awkwardly embraced Mama. Seeing Mama's stark fear and how his tender nature surfaced touched her deeply. After a few minutes, Mama calmed down, and he announced, "Enough of this. I'm worried about the two of you, and you're worried about me. My cooking is so bad, I'm likely to kill myself with something I fix. I'm moving you into my house."

"You can't mean it." Lorelei stared at him in shock.

Crafty as a fox, he ignored her and spoke to Mama. "Lorelei can share my workroom downstairs to do the windows. It will make it easier than creating them here and moving them."

"This would be good."

Lorelei slipped an errant hairpin back into place. "I can't finish this window or start on more until I have my supplies."

I lost the battle but won the war. Russell shot Lorelei a surreptitious look as he drove the buckboard toward town. Her mother stayed home to pack up their necessary belongings. "This is a short trip."

"You've said that twice since we left home."

"I mean it." As they reached the edge of town, Russell felt her stiffen. "What is it?"

"The cemetery."

He leaned forward to look past her. Perfectly manicured grass normally graced the lot, but now it was pockmarked with multiple new graves.

"Mrs. Sweeny has black crepe on her door, but the stars on her flag are still white." Lorelei grabbed his arm. "Everyone is wearing masks."

Russell grimly hitched the horses outside the mercantile. "Stay put, and don't visit with anyone." He tied a bandana over the lower portion of his face and went inside. Moments later, he emerged with an entire bolt of cotton gauze. Hastily, he hacked at it with his pocketknife and folded the freed portion into a mask that he secured over her nose and mouth.

"Russell, look around us. There are posters in the windows, warning of contagion and how to battle it."

"It's bad, Buttercup." He squeezed her hand. "Give me the list. I'll leave it with Mr. Sanders. He'll fill the order while we take care of everything else. I want to get out of here as quickly as possible."

At the hardware store, they found everything they needed for her windows and the repairs Russell was making. The china shop was closed, and a black wreath hung from the door. Lorelei's eyes filled with tears. "I used to walk down the street and see the star flags in the window. Now there is black crepe everywhere."

Just then, a wagon started down the street. Two plain pine caskets rattled on it, and Mr. Sweeny sat in the back with them as the preacher drove the team.

"What time does the funeral start?" Lorelei asked in a subdued voice.

The pastor shook his head. "New orders are out. Family only. No church services—only fifteen-minute graveside commitments."

Russell reached around and tugged Lorelei into the lee of his body. He could feel her shaking. "We'll go home now."

"No, Russell. We must help."

He knew that look in her eye and the streak of stubbornness that ran straight through her. Instead of arguing, Russell let out a sigh. He searched for something that would satisfy her without putting her in danger.

"Tell you what, Buttercup. We'll go to the butcher and the mercantile. I'll load up and buy the biggest kettle they have and every last canning jar. You and your mother can bake bread and make soup. I'll bring it to town."

"Here you go." Mrs. Goetz set one last paper-wrapped bundle in the bed of the buckboard. Flour streaked her apron, and she tried to brush it off. "You're starting out late today. The sun is setting earlier, too. If it gets too late, unhitch the wagon and ride home. The horses know the way."

"You go on in and rest. You're working too hard."

"Broth and bread are easy to make."

"You've made plenty of both for the past two weeks."

She pressed her hand to the bib of her apron. "In my heart, I make many more prayers than any loaves of bread. I pray God keeps you safe, Russell."

He reached town and took the list of homes from the light post. The pastor had arranged to hang a roster from a string he'd knotted around the post, telling Russell which families needed bread and soup. He'd drop off the food on their porches and pick up the jars from the previous day.

Each day the list grew longer. Russell worked his way across town from one street to the next. Folks didn't stop to visit—they scurried away, eyes big with fear above the ever-present gauze masks. At the last stop, Russell walked up to the door. To his surprise, little Arnie was sitting on the stoop. The five-year-old had been the first in his family to come down sick. He'd only gotten out of bed two days ago.

"Arnie, it's late for you to be up."

Arnie looked up, and Russell's heart skipped several beats. The little boy's face was ashen, and his eyes huge. Dried tear runnels etched his cheeks. "Mommy won't wake up."

Russell knocked, then invited himself inside. A quick check revealed the worst: Both of Arnie's parents and his baby sister were dead. It would be foolish to take anything out of the diseased home, so Russell took off his shirt, wrapped the little boy in it, and headed toward the parsonage.

The pastor took one look at Arnie and bowed his head in grief. He paused a moment, then motioned Russell inside.

"No one's left at his house." Russell chose his words carefully as he lowered the child onto the couch. Arnie wouldn't let go of him, though, so he sat on the horsehair-stuffed cushion and kept the boy in his lap. "What about the rest of his family?"

The pastor wearily rubbed his forehead and sat in a nearby chair. "They've already passed on. He doesn't have anyone. All the families who were able to help out are overburdened. I can't see any choice. Arnie will need to go to Tepfield."

"Tepfield?" Russell gave the parson an appalled look. An orphanage was never a good arrangement, but in the midst of the epidemic, it would amount to cruel neglect at the best and death at the worst. Over in France, Russell had hated seeing the ragged orphans wandering about hungry, frightened, and alone. He refused to resign an American child to that fate. He took a deep breath. "I'll take him."

"Do you know the way?"

Russell shook his head. "No, I meant I'll take him home with me."

"Praise be to God!"

Russell rose. "It's not temporary. I won't have him relocated later. He's been through enough."

"I agree." As the pastor led them back outside, he offered, "I'll handle the arrangements so you'll be assigned as his guardian."

Russell nodded. The commitment he'd just made ought to be staggering, but even amid the sorrow surrounding the situation, the decision felt right. He set off for home. Along the way, Arnie snuggled in his lap. "That house has a star. Daddy says they have a boy in the war."

"Yes, they do."

Arnie pointed out house after house, mentioning the star flags. "There's a lellow star at that house. That means they gave a son."

Russell wondered if Arnie understood what that meant. *So much death. So much heartache. Why, God? Why?*

The horses walked slowly since it had grown dark. They went past an open field. Arnie pointed up at the sky. "Look. Lots of stars. God has lots of boys like me."

"Yes, He does."

Arnie nudged Russell's chin. "Lookie. A big lellow star. God gave a Son, too."

It was all Russell could do to keep from roaring in his agony. Instead, he tightened his hold on Arnie. "What if I take you home and let you be my boy now?"

Chapter 17

Please, Lord, bring him home. It's grown so late. Keep Russell healthy and safe. He's been through so much, Father. Show him Your mercy and grace. The sound of the buckboard and horses jolted her. *Thank You, Almighty Father!*

Lorelei raced out onto the veranda. "Russell!"

"I brought home a nice little fellow." Something about his tone and the sorrow in Russell's eyes made Lorelei's breath catch. "Arnie's going to be my boy now."

She reached up and accepted Arnie. Russell had sacrificed his shirt to bundle the small boy. "You look tired, Arnie. Let me carry you into the kitchen. I'll make you a nice, warm snack; then we can put you to bed."

Arnie clung to Russell while Lorelei spooned chicken noodle soup into him. Mama didn't bother filling the bathtub; the kitchen was warm, so she pumped water into the sink, added hot water from the stove's reservoir until it was just the right temperature, then sang quietly as she bathed the boy.

Lorelei went upstairs to set up the cot, and Russell called to her, "Put it in the little parlor off my bedroom so I can hear him during the night."

After she did as Russell requested, Lorelei came downstairs to catch Russell burning his shirt and Arnie's clothing. Neither of them said a word.

Mama came in with Arnie bundled in a towel. "Russell, our little boy needs to borrow one of your undershirts. Tomorrow I will sew some handsome clothes for him."

"I seem to recall trunks up in the attic with old clothes in them." Russell stood and gently took Arnie from Mrs. Goetz. "I'll tuck him in tonight and search for stuff for him first thing in the morning."

A short while later, Lorelei and her mother went up to bed. They peeked in on Arnie. Russell sat on the settee by the sleeping child's cot, looking as if the weight of the world had fallen on his shoulders. Mutt lay curled at his feet.

"You look so domestic," Lorelei whispered.

He raked his fingers through his hair in agitation. "He doesn't have anyone. Pastor said there isn't anyone left in his whole family. I promised I'd watch over him, but I can't do it alone. I can keep him warm and fed, but I don't have the love and solace he'll need."

Lorelei opened her mouth to refute his words, but Mama silenced her with a touch and said, "We will help you. Arnie needs a whole family, and together, with God's loving help, we will become what he needs."

"I'll fix up this little room for him. He was afraid to be by himself."

"We can do that tomorrow. For now, let's all get some rest." Lorelei gently ruffled Arnie's hair and smoothed his blankets. "No fair going to the attic alone, Russell. I want to see what's stored up there."

He leaned his head back on the settee and said, "There's something else."

Lorelei dreaded what else might have gone wrong. *Lord, please don't let him have lost someone dear to him. He can't take it.*

"Buttonhole is almost decimated by the epidemic. I got a telegram from my dad. So far, you and I have done well by staying isolated, and I'm thinking about having my mom load up some of my cousins who are the most vulnerable and having them come to stay here."

"This is something to pray about," Mama said sagely.

"We'll go back to our cottage. You'll have plenty of room." Lorelei smiled at him.

He bolted upright. "No! I thought you just promised to help me with Arnie. I just wanted to know if you'd mind having more people underfoot."

"God blessed you with a mansion, Russell. I think it would be a sin to leave rooms empty when they could harbor children who need a safe place."

"I'll think on it more tonight."

"And we'll pray," Mama said. She shook her finger at Russell. "I get to look in that attic tomorrow, too. If we are going to fix up more bedrooms, I might find things up there we can use."

"Look at these!" Lorelei dusted off a pair of pineapple-topped bedsteads. "They'd be wonderful together in one of the larger bedrooms. It is odd, though, these pineapples."

"They're an old American symbol of welcome," Russell said absently as he lifted an old ceramic chamber pot.

Arnie, who clung to Russell's leg, announced, "I don't got one of those under my new bed."

"Then it must be yours." Russell chuckled.

Lorelei knelt and smoothed her hand over another piece of wood. "What is an altar doing up here?"

"Family lore is, the church burned down the night one of my ancestors proposed. He ran into the church and saved the altar for his bride's sake. He knew she'd want it for their wedding."

"Yes. Yes, I believe this. Part of it is burned."

Mama bent over a trunk that was pressed way beneath the eaves. "The top of this has had much rain, but inside it looks good. There are clothes here—old ones that belonged to a woman." She dug deeper. "Oh, bless the Lord! There are clothes here for a little boy!"

"Count your many blessings," Lorelei started to sing.

"Mommy sings that song to me. When is Mommy going to come get me?"

Russell sat on the floor of the attic and tugged Arnie around so the boy stood eye to eye with him. "Mommy was very sick. Daddy, too."

"And Baby 'Liz'beth."

"They died, Arnie. Do you know what that means?"

Lorelei knelt on the floor and said, "It means they sleep in heaven now with Jesus."

Arnie's eyes filled up with tears. "But what 'bout me?"

"You're going to sleep in your new room here," Russell said. "You're going to be my boy now."

The little boy's face puckered. "Am I 'posed to put lellow stars in the window?"

Mama came over and opened her hand. Three golden buttons in the shape of stars lay nestled in her palm. "Better than that, sweetheart. You'll wear the yellow stars."

"I'm going." Lorelei set down her soldering iron so hard, the pieces of glass jumped. The room that had once been an enormous parlor and ballroom rang with her words.

"Don't be so stubborn. It's for your own good."

"You are my friend, not my father," she said hotly. "You cannot make me go to my room like a naughty child." *Even if you want to. . .*

"See reason."

"I am seeing reason. It will be necessary to get essentials."

"For crying in a bucket, Lorelei, I'm losing my patience. I have enough china and silver to feed an army."

"But you do not have towels enough, nor sheets. You don't even have mattresses for the beds! I know what to get; you do not. Of course I should go to town."

He stared at her. "I'll tell you what: My dad and mom own a mercantile. You make a list, and I'll have them fill a freight wagon. I'd rather have them ride here than come by train, anyway."

Jaw clenched to the point that the tiny muscles on the side of his cheek twitched, he bent over a little chest of drawers and resumed sanding it with long, heavy strokes. The grating *swish* against the sudden hush in the room sounded unnaturally loud.

The patter of little feet echoed on the marble entryway, giving warning that Arnie had awakened from his nap and would be with them in an instant. The little boy burst into the workroom and zoomed toward Russell. "There you are. I thought you were gone."

Russell let go of the sandpaper, knelt, and opened his arms wide. Arnie ran straight to him and hung on tight. His eyes and voice were filled with tears. "Don't leave me."

"Leave you?" Russell pulled away and gave the little boy a playful shake as he repeated in a voice full of patently mock outrage, "Leave you? Do you know what I've been doing this morning while you slept in?"

Arnie shook his head.

Russell thumped his palm on the top of the chest of drawers. "I was fixing this for your bedroom. You'll need it to hold the clothes Mrs. Goetz found for you."

Arnie stood on tiptoe and stared at the compact wooden piece. "What're you doing to it?"

"I didn't want you to get any splinters, so I'm sanding it."

"Can I help?"

Lorelei watched as Russell opened his arms and heart to Arnie. It came as such a surprise. He was normally so standoffish—but there he was, a tall, broad-shouldered, gruff man with a tattered-looking mutt on one side and an orphaned little boy on the other.

He'll make a good father.

The thought sent streaks of warmth through her. *Deep inside Russell, there is tenderness and goodness.* Surely, there must be hope for him. She pensively brushed flux on the joints she needed to solder. *Jesus, You are the lover of our souls. Please shower Your love on this man. Wash away the pain and doubts, and allow his spirit to flourish again.*

"Are you thinking about what to put on the list?" Russell's words made her look up. "I'll need to go place the telephone call this afternoon. While I'm there, I'll deliver the soup and bread and can pick up a few of the smaller things at the mercantile."

"You'll wear a mask the whole time?"

He nodded.

"Me, too." Arnie bobbed his head, a miniature replica of Russell.

Lorelei gave Russell a startled look. He wouldn't let her go to town; he couldn't possibly allow Arnie to. In those tense seconds, Arnie's eyes widened, and he grabbed a fistful of Russell's pant leg.

"Hey, now, buddy." Russell shifted and gave Lorelei a bail-me-out-of-this look.

"Russell doesn't want me to go to town, either." She came around the worktable and sighed. "I suppose we'll have to keep each other company and watch Mutt for him until he gets home tonight. In just a few days, some big, big boys and girls are coming to visit. We can surprise Russell with how much we get done on the bedrooms for them."

"It's about lunchtime." Russell ruffled Arnie's hair. "You can help us think of things our guests will need to bring."

"I didn't bring nothing."

"You most certainly did!" Lorelei laughed at Arnie. "You brought Russell back home in the dark!"

"Everybody's settled in for the night."

Russell didn't turn toward his mother's voice. Instead, he continued to stare out the bank of windows at the back of the house, out into the darkness where the sky and ocean met. *Moon flecks on the water and stars in the sky make it almost impossible to tell them apart.*

Lots of stars. God has lots of boys like me. Arnie's words kept echoing in his memory. *Lookie. A big lellow star. God gave a Son, too.*

"You have a beautiful view of the stars," Mom said as she stood beside him. She snuggled into his side. The top of her bun tickled his jaw, and she smelled like the peach soap he'd bought especially for her. "Thanks for inviting us to come, honey. I've missed you so much. Your father sends his love."

He pressed a kiss on her temple. "You're tired, Mom. Go to bed."

"My room is lovely. Did Lorelei help you with it?"

Lorelei had moved out of that very room and in with her mother. Still, Russell didn't want his mom playing matchmaker. "Lorelei and her mother did it together, just as they worked on the other bedrooms."

He'd managed to turn her around and walk her toward the entryway. She stopped and smiled. "The hall tree looks wonderful here."

"It does. Thanks for sending it. I want this mansion to look as much to period as I can make it."

"While we're here, the kids can help. Alan and Philip could help you paint and work outside—especially cut back some of the shrubs and pull out the dried weeds."

"I'll keep 'em busy."

"I brought bolts of fabric. I'll have the girls sew each day, and they can help in the kitchen."

"Mrs. Goetz will appreciate it. The town just started using the local dance hall as a makeshift hospital. Late each afternoon, I deliver soup and bread to it instead of going to individual homes as I used to."

"But is that safe?"

"It limits any exposure, and everyone has to help out." He took her arm and forced a chuckle as he escorted her up the stairs. "I can't believe you'd fret. I've spent my entire life watching you make baskets and deliver them to everyone in Buttonhole who had so much as a bruise, bump, or boil."

"Those aren't catching, Russell."

"Nothing's killed me yet." Once he said the bitter words, he regretted them—they were truthful, but he'd promised himself he'd shield his mother and cousins from the ugliness inside. They'd just arrived early this evening, and he'd already stepped far over the line.

Chapter 18

Lorelei smiled as she watched Mrs. Diamond organize her nieces. She'd sent the dark-haired one to the kitchen to help Mama make bread. "Beatrice, Beatrice," Lorelei chanted under her breath to remember who was who.

Three girls, two boys, and Russell's mama made for quite an addition to the house. They ranged from thirteen to seventeen, and all had the look of children setting out on a holiday adventure instead of ones hiding from a terrible epidemic.

"Lacey, I know you girls brought your sewing boxes. Go fetch them and bring them to the parlor. Adele, wipe down the dining table so there's nothing sticky left from breakfast. We'll use that as a cutting table."

Lacey is blond, and Adele is the youngest.

While the girls all scattered to do as they were bid, Mrs. Diamond walked over to Lorelei's worktable. "Oh, this window is lovely, just lovely. Where is it going?"

"In the smaller parlor, just on the other side of that wall."

"I'm surprised at how few windows needed to be replaced. After the house sat vacant for so long, I expected it to be a hideous mess."

"Russell has done considerable work. He's put on a new roof, painted the outside, replaced more than fifty panes of glass, rebuilt the veranda. . ." She made a spiraling gesture. "So many more things, too. It used to look like a magnificent bridal gown that somehow ended up with torn lace, smudges of dirt and mud, and a sagging hem. Now when I look at the house, I see what the mansions in heaven must be like."

"Will you be doing any more stained glass for the house?"

Lorelei nodded. "Russell found an old photograph when he took the drawers out of one of the washstands. It showed that there used to be large, floral windows on either side of the front door. I'm to reproduce them, but first he must decide on the colors. Perhaps you could help him."

"Evidently my son hasn't told you my embarrassing secret."

"Russell is discreet. He would not speak badly of anyone."

Mrs. Diamond picked up a little scrap of glass and held it up to the light. Her voice lilted with merriment. "I love pretty things, but when it comes to putting them together, I'm hopeless. Why, when my husband courted me, he actually had to point out that my clothing was ragged and faded as a beggar's."

"You cannot mean this!"

Mrs. Diamond laughed and nodded. "It's the absolute truth. In fact, I was hoping you'd help me look at the bolts of cloth we brought along so I can start the girls sewing some quilts and pillows or cushions for the rooms. That bedroom I'm in is utterly charming, so I know you have an eye for these things."

"The bedroom where Adele and Lacey sleep needs curtains. Perhaps that would be a good project to do first. I have the measurements of the windows, so that will make it easy."

Mrs. Diamond set down the piece of glass and nodded. "Wonderful idea. I'm sure they'll enjoy decorating their room. I want to keep the children busy so they'll not get into trouble or be too homesick."

"Russell once mentioned he has a list of things he wishes to do. Perhaps you could read it to see what might make good projects."

"Aunt Rose, do you know where Russell is?"

They turned toward the door. A younger version of Russell stood there, still at the gangly stage where he was all knees and elbows. His voice cracked midsentence as he added, "I found a bunch of paint in one of the stalls, and I was thinking we could spruce up the stable. Russell has a pair of geldings out there."

"Out exploring, Philip?"

"Yes." He shrugged. "This is a nifty old place. Russell must be having a great time fixing it up."

Lorelei had seen Russell work. He wasn't having a great time at all—the work was demanding and pressed him to his limits. Nonetheless, he determinedly forged ahead. Sometimes she watched him as he toiled, and she'd arrived at the conclusion that he pressed himself until exhaustion would allow him to sleep. Still, he slept poorly. Every single night, he groaned or shouted out in his dreams. Refusing to reveal any of those facts, Lorelei looked about the room and said, "He's put much care into this place."

Philip wandered across the floor and gawked around. "It was too dark to see much yesterday. My dad said he'd been by a couple years ago, and the place was nothing but a dirty wreck. He ordered me to test the floors to be sure they hadn't rotted, but I can see that's not necessary."

"Russell replaced the veranda here and the porch down at the cottage." Lorelei noted the envious gleam in Philip's eyes and added, "Russell mentioned some of the rooms in the attic sustained rain damage. If you are as skilled as Russell, you might wish to ask him if he could use your help in repairing them."

"Wow. Yeah. I'd like that. I brought some tools along—in case he needed that kind of help."

"You said my son has a list of projects?" Mrs. Diamond shot Lorelei a conspiratorial glance.

"Perhaps we could ask him to show it to us at lunch. Mama always told me a man is easier to deal with when his stomach is full."

Philip sniffed and grinned. "Smells like the bread is out of the oven. The kitchen is like a big city bakery—loaves and loaves all laid out and more dough ready to bake."

Lorelei laughed. "Mama loves to cook. You should ask her about her cinnamon rolls. She would be happy to make you some."

"Really?"

Lacey, having entered the room with the sewing baskets, chimed in, "Cinnamon rolls?"

"Now I don't know. . . ." Russell's mother shook her head.

Lorelei laughed. "I'm sure. They're Mama's favorite, so it would give her a good excuse."

Russell called from the window, "What's going on in there, and why does someone need an excuse?"

Lorelei rolled over and blinked at the shaft of sunlight creeping though the chink between the halves of her curtains. *Lord, it's Your day today. Russell isn't going to let anyone go to town. Will You please grant him some comfort as we worship here with the children?*

She yawned and burrowed beneath the quilt for a few more minutes, mentally going through a list of hymns they might sing. "Stand up, stand up for Jesus, ye soldiers. . ." No, that wouldn't do. "Onward, Christian soldiers. . ." Lorelei grimaced. She'd never noticed how many songs used words like "soldier" or "battle."

Heavenly Father, help us to keep this day of worship holy and special. Let it unfold according to Your will, and make me sensitive to what You would have us say, do, sing, and read. Russell is hurting, and he needs Your healing touch. The children all miss their parents. Arnie clings to Russell, to Mama, and to me because he is so afraid of losing any of us. Tender Shepherd, we need Your touch and mercy. Guide and direct us, I pray. Amen.

"You're awake, Lori?" Mama whispered.

"Yes, Mama."

"I dreamed of your papa reading the Bible to us. Remember how he smoothed the ribbon back into the pages when he was done?"

"Every time." The memory made sorrow wash over her.

"I was thinking about how I wished the ribbon on that Silver Star medal the government brought us for your Papa was smooth, deep blue satin instead of striped grosgrain." Mama rolled over. Tears glossed her eyes. "I decided to put blue satin in the box the medal came in."

Tears spilled down Mama's cheeks as Lorelei reached over and pulled her into a tight hug. When she found her voice again, she whispered, "That's a nice idea, Mama."

A little while later, when they'd regained their composure, Mama sat on the bedside and combed her hair as she said, "Russell's mother tells me he got a medal, too—the same as your papa's."

"I'm not surprised. He's a man of honor and courage." Lorelei bent to tie her shoes and added quietly, "But I don't think we'd better ask him about his medal. He doesn't want to talk about the war."

"His eyes hold much hurt, Lori."

"So does his soul." She straightened. "Which makes me wonder, what shall we do for worship today?"

"I know just the right verses." Mama gave her a watery smile. "And Rose Diamond has a lovely voice. She can help us decide on some hymns."

They slipped downstairs, and Mama stirred up the fire she'd banked in the stove last night. Lorelei opened the kitchen door and pulled in the milk Mr. Rimmon had delivered. Before the epidemic, he'd delivered a single half-gallon bottle to each house twice a week. Now he left a half-full, ten-gallon tin milk can each dawn. He'd already strained it and left half a gallon of cream, too, so they could churn their own butter.

"Hi!" Arnie skipped through the kitchen, accompanied by Mutt. Only a step behind, Russell nodded and turned the knob to let them out. The three of them were nearly inseparable, and Mama and Mrs. Diamond both thought it slightly scandalous that Russell allowed the dog to sleep at the foot of Arnie's bed, but no one dared interfere since the three of them seemed to need each other.

Soon the kitchen smelled of yeast from the bread dough and cinnamon from the rolls. Beatrice sat in a chair over by the window, using the Daisy paddle-wheel churn. Mrs. Diamond had Adele setting the table as Lacey rearranged the parlor for "church." Alan and Philip went to muck out the stable. The routine in the household hadn't taken long to establish, and it carried with it a comfortable air. It didn't take much longer before everyone sat down to breakfast.

After the meal, Russell ordered the boys to carry their chairs to the parlor for worship. Everyone found a seat, and Mrs. Diamond led the singing. True to form, Russell didn't sing, but he played his harmonica.

Russell lifted Arnie onto his lap to stop him from squirming as Mrs. Goetz started reading from the second chapter of Nehemiah.

Wherefore the king said unto me, Why is thy countenance sad, seeing thou art not sick? this is nothing else but sorrow of heart. Then I was very sore afraid, and said unto the king, Let the king live for ever: why should not my countenance be sad, when the city, the place of my fathers' sepulchres, lieth waste, and the gates thereof are consumed with fire? Then the king said unto me, For what dost thou make request? So I prayed to the God of heaven. And I said unto the king, If it please the king, and if thy servant have found favour in thy sight, that thou wouldest send me unto Judah, unto the city of my fathers' sepulchres, that I may build it.

Russell stared at the worn Bible in her lap. He couldn't recall hearing that passage before now. *Sorrow of the heart. Yes, that said it well. And I'm also rebuilding what belonged to my ancestors. Nehemiah felt this way, too?*

"Russell is rebuilding." Adele smiled at him.

Arnie waved across the room at her, which seemed to serve better than the stingy smile Russell himself barely managed. *What am I doing with all of these tenderhearted children here?*

Alan cleared his throat. "I'm thinking of that verse about building a house. I don't recall where it is."

"The one about whether you build a house on rock or sand?"

"That's a nice one, but not the one that I had in mind. It's about laboring in vain if God isn't building the house."

Russell cleared his throat. "That's Psalm 127:1: 'Except the Lord build the house, they labour in vain that build it: except the Lord keep the city, the watchman waketh but in vain.' "

Mom patted Alan on the arm. "Russell's mind is like a camera. He need see something only once, and he remembers it forever."

And there are things I wish I'd never seen and wouldn't remember. . . . He stared at the floor. The autumn sun streamed through the stained-glass window Lorelei had restored, and the golden segments she'd cleverly borrowed from the border and stretched to fit by using the amber jewels he chose ended up casting a golden cross on the far wall.

Lorelei suggested, "Let's finish with sentence prayers. Anyone who would like can join in."

The prayers and the glass-cast golden cross don't bother me, he realized with shock. When he'd first come back from France, those things would have set him on edge. Now, after weeks of quiet worship and hearing Lorelei read the Word of God aloud, he'd let go of most of his anger. At times it still surged, but for the most part, a profound emptiness replaced the rage.

Their faith is touching, innocent. I was like that once. A sense of loss swamped him. He held Arnie and rested his chin on the little boy's soft hair. Wrapping his arms tighter, he realized how much he wanted Arnie to grow up believing that Jesus loved him. Lorelei's sweet, husky voice chimed in with a word of prayer.

Russell's leg ached, but his heart ached more. *Even if I can't patch together my own faith, I want this little guy to have the assurance and security Lorelei has.*

"Russell, I brought you your jacket." Lorelei knew she needed to speak before she approached him. He'd been lost in thought, and sudden sounds and movement always resulted in startling or angering him. The past week had been particularly bad. He'd been going to town and digging graves, coming home only to get the bread and soup, then returning again late in the evening. The bleakness in his eyes and the groans in his sleep bore testimony to the great cost of the work he'd done.

"The air, it is chilly much of the day now. It is good that we have so much wood piled up for the winter." Slowly, she walked across the veranda and out into the yard.

Russell pushed away from the tree and shrugged into his jacket. "Thanks."

"You are troubled."

"I'm not decent company, Lorelei. Go back inside."

An undertone of anguish in his voice made her stay. "I didn't ask if you were good company. If I wanted pleasant companions, there are plenty in the house."

"Are they getting under your skin?"

She laughed. "I just said they were pleasant companions, Russell. Your mother is a wonderful woman, and your cousins are delightful. My place is not with them right now; my place is to be with a friend who is hurting."

"Who's hurt?" He stiffened as he barked the question.

Lorelei paused a moment, then quietly answered, "You."

Chapter 19

Lord, I felt led to come out to Russell, but I feel so unsure of why You have me here. I have no understanding of the pain he feels or what to say to him.

"My leg's never going to get better." He snorted. "I'm going to limp for the rest of my life. The shrapnel left in there is too close to the nerves and arteries to mess with, so the ache's permanent. I'm a cripple. There. Did that clear the air?"

"The ache, this I am sorry for. The limp—it has gotten better over the months you have lived here. It does not keep you from doing the things you wish. Your body serves you well, Russell, and you use your strength and talents for others. I hold no pity for you, only gratitude. You have a battle raging inside you, yet you had the kindness and courage to think of others."

"Don't fool yourself. I came out here because I was thinking only of myself."

"You need time alone. What is wrong about that? There have been days when I sought solitude in my sorrow and confusion."

"Buttercup." His voice sounded ragged. She liked how he occasionally called her such a pretty name, even if he said it in a jaded tone. Somewhere deep inside, it meant that he still longed for good things, even if he denied himself.

"Yes?"

"I'm as splintered and jagged as the broken glass you sweep up. You don't know what you're dealing with."

"What I know is that even when glass is shattered, the pieces can be fit together in a new way to make something beautiful."

Russell shook his head. "Not me."

"You must be patient. Papa used to patiently fit the pieces of a window together. He refused to hurry. These things take time. He taught me that if something is to last, it must be tended with diligence now—whether it is a window or a soul."

"You still believe in fairy tales, Lorelei."

"I'm a grown woman, Russell. I didn't fight in a war, but I have lost my father, and I've worked hard to make a living and provide for my mother. I believe in God's love. I believe in family. I believe in friends. The pattern I envisioned for my life was shattered, but I chose to put the pieces back together. The picture is different, but the Source of my light never changed."

He smashed his fist into the trunk of the tree. "My friends died! Don't you get it? All around me, my friends bled and died. I used my rifle, my trench knife, even my bare hands, and killed Germans—men who had families and friends back in their hometowns. I've seen slaughter, I've slain, and I'm sick of death."

Lorelei quietly reached over and curled her hand around his wrist. He yanked free, but she persisted and took his wrist again. Gently, she brushed bark off his skinned knuckles. "You are hurting enough on the inside, Russell. Don't hurt yourself on the outside, too."

"There's blood on my hands and in my soul." He pulled free.

"Only the Living Water can wash that away." She folded her arms around her ribs. "Once, I told you the red glass was the most expensive. Right now, the only color you see in the window of your soul is red. Christ already paid the price to purify it. Regardless of the color, though, know that I care for you as a friend. Your pain doesn't frighten me away."

Russell sat at the head of the supper table long after the meal was over and everyone had left the dining room. Arnie didn't want to leave his side, but Adele promised to teach him how to play checkers. Laughter and chatter drifted across the marble entryway and into the dining room. The swinging door to the kitchen sat ajar, allowing a wedge of light and the musical conversation between Lorelei and their mothers.

At the first lunch they all shared, Mom, Mrs. Goetz, and Lorelei had created a schedule of chores. They'd all insisted on taking a turn at dishes, too. Mom and Mrs. Goetz spent a couple hours each day in the library, clearing off bookshelves and oiling the wood. In another day or so, that room would be an inviting haven of peace.

The girls rotated into the kitchen for a day, then sewed for two. They hadn't decided on any particular room—they'd stitched in the parlor, in a bedroom, on the veranda—so no matter where he turned, Russell seemed to run into someone. Simple, gathered cotton curtains hung from the windows in the kitchen, bedrooms, and washroom, and the duvets in the girls' rooms bore new, matching covers. A lacy, tatted doily lay in the center of the dining table beneath the mum-filled Heisey crystal vase.

The boys eagerly traipsed through the house and over the estate, then voiced which projects appealed to them the most. After the first day, Russell had decided he'd make assignments so he'd know where they were and what they were doing; finding Philip "fixing" the stairs to the attic reinforced the need for that decision.

So far, the washroom and four bedrooms sported fresh coats of paint, a wobbly chair's legs now measured even, and two doors that used to sag and stick had been planed and rehung. The stable sported a fresh coat of barn red paint, and most of the shrubs had been cut back to manageable level. Once set to work, the boys did fairly well. Their exuberance sometimes eclipsed their judgment, but overall, they hadn't been too much trouble.

How did I ever end up with this troop in my barracks? He stared at the hodgepodge of chairs about the table. Counting Lorelei, Mrs. Goetz, Arnie, his mother, and five cousins, he'd taken on responsibility for nine other people. *And to think I came here to get away from everyone.*

He let out a burdened sigh. His father hadn't asked him to take on these guests; he'd simply revealed how bad things were in Buttonhole and asked how Russell was doing since he lived so far on the outskirts of a town. Survival: the first rule of war—and they were fighting a deadly enemy in the form of an epidemic. Russell knew he'd made the right decision. It didn't make it any easier, though, when he craved solitude.

Suddenly rifle fire split the night air.

"Sniper!" He dove out of his chair and crawled to the doorway. "Down! Down! Everybody down!"

His pulse thundered in his ears as feet pounded on the floor.

"Russell? What's wrong?"

Someone burst through the front door. Russell grabbed Lorelei and yanked her to the floor. She tumbled over him, and he shoved her into the corner where she'd be safest.

"Alan bagged a buck! Come see!"

Sweat poured down Russell's temples, and tension made him jump as Lorelei gently rubbed his back. "A deer, Russell. Alan hunted a deer. In your yard in Virginia, Russell. You're home, not in the war."

A shudder rippled through him. It took another second or two to fully understand her. He bolted to his feet, yanked her upright, and strode as fast as his limp allowed him out to the front yard.

Alan stood over a buck on the far side of the hedges, chest thrust out and shoulders squared with pride. "How do you like this?"

Russell grabbed the rifle from him. "I don't."

"We'll have venison roast, and Mrs. Goetz can make stews for the folks in town."

"That's no excuse. None at all," Russell bit out. Memories of what a rifle shell could do to a human being burst through his memory, making his voice harsh. "In this light, you couldn't be sure what you were shooting. Do you understand me?"

"Hey, I was just trying—"

"No excuse," Russell repeated himself through gritted teeth. He stared at Philip. "If you have a weapon, you're to give it to me now. No one hunts without my permission."

Arnie started to sniffle. Lorelei stooped, pulled him into her arms, and rose. She patted his back and cooed, "It's okay, honey. It's okay. He's not mad at you. Russell worried that someone got hurt because he cares about us."

"You children go back inside." His mother gave the order firmly. Spreading her arms wide, she herded them toward the house and didn't leave any chance for objections.

Alan stood belligerently over his kill. Russell's hand curled tighter around the stock of the rifle he'd carefully kept aimed at the ground. He stared at Alan until the teen looked away, then commanded, "This is your kill—you dress it."

"I. . .um. . .don't know how."

"Then it's time you learn."

"I could help." Lorelei's soft, husky voice startled Russell. He shot her a strained look. She set Arnie on the ground and gave his little backside a pat to send him on his way.

The last thing I need is for her to weaken my stance with the kids—if that's possible.

Russell shook his head. "This is Alan's mess. He's not a child; he's a young man. A responsible young man handles his own affairs."

The next evening, Mama and Mrs. Diamond declared it was a celebration night. All the rooms on the second floor and the three maids' bedrooms in the attic were painted. The occupied rooms all had curtains; refurbished furniture; spreads, duvets, or quilts; and pictures. Beatrice had shown remarkable artistic flair, and her works hung here and there.

Mrs. Diamond fixed a big venison roast while Mama used bread crumbs to make dressing. Lorelei passed the okra over Arnie's head to Russell and teased, "Now aren't you glad you gave us that garden?"

"He's more likely to be thankful there are a bunch of us at the table to eat the okra." Mrs. Diamond laughed. "Russell doesn't care for it."

Lorelei gaped at him.

He cleared his throat. "I'd like some of your beans, though. Between the corn and beans you canned, I'm still glad you garden."

Mrs. Diamond took the bowl of green beans from Philip and passed them to her son. "Like father, like son. Did Russell ever tell you I have a fruit orchard?"

Lorelei nodded. "He shared the apples you sent."

"Mom makes peach everything—jam, tarts, pies," Russell began.

"Don't forget her cobbler!" Philip tacked on.

"Yes, well, Russell's father had me fooled about liking peaches for the longest time. It wasn't until he asked me to marry him that he confessed he can't stand the taste of peaches!"

While others laughed, Lorelei felt a twang of worry. "Did you give me the apples because you don't like them? Is that why you want cinnamon in your applesauce—to hide the flavor?"

"Love them." Russell tipped his head to the side and gave her an assessing look. "That apple I'm smelling—it's not the cider you're drinking?"

Arnie piped up, "Nope! Lorelei made apple doodle. It's a s'prise."

"Strudel," Lorelei corrected softly as she saw the deliciously greedy spark in Russell's eyes.

"You told!" Arnie glared up at her. "Now it's not a s'prise."

After dessert, everyone played musical chairs in the entryway with Russell controlling the tunes on the gramophone; then everyone bundled up and went outside.

A big pile of leaves and logs lay ready. Russell supervised Alan as he lit it. Sugar prices made candy cost an arm and a leg; marshmallows were a rarity. The bag of marshmallows Russell's mother brought out to toast counted as the highlight of the whole evening.

"Uh-oh. I burned mine!" Arnie's face puckered.

"Yum! Just the way I like it!" Russell swiped the charred, gooey mess and popped it into his mouth. "I suppose you like them all golden perfect like Lorelei's, don't you, Arnie?"

"Uhn-huh." The boy nodded.

"Shh. We have to be sneaky," Russell said in a stage whisper. He grabbed Lorelei's stick, and she obligingly let out a shriek.

"Lorelei, Russell has a marshmallow on his stick," Adele tattled. "He hasn't roasted it yet."

"What's sauce for the goose," Lorelei said as she tried to grab Russell's marshmallow.

Quickly, they were "fencing" with marshmallow-tipped sticks. Russell and Lorelei became the judges as they set up matches between the cousins. Arnie fought the boys, who gladly got on their knees to make for a fair fight.

After the final cry of "Touché!" they toasted the last few marshmallows and sat around the fire as it died down to mere embers. They sang "Shenandoah" and "Shoo Fly" and ended the evening with Arnie's request, "Twinkle, Twinkle, Little Star."

Russell poured water on the embers, and Alan raked the ground to guarantee they'd extinguished the fire entirely. Alan started coughing from the smoke.

Lacey giggled. "Don't pretend the smoke is bothering you. Lorelei is practically in a cloud of it, and she's not coughing."

"She's used to it." Russell stood with his arms akimbo and stared at her. The look in his eyes sent sparks through her. "Everyone knows smoke follows beauty."

Russell lay in his bed and closed his eyes. Instead of the hideous scenes of war that usually flashed across his mind, he pictured Lorelei with a speck of apple strudel on her lower lip. For the first time since he'd come home, he felt the knot in his chest loosen. He'd been able to horse around and laugh tonight—and it was because of Lorelei.

Arnie's cot squeaked as he tossed about in the little parlor. Accustomed to the little boy's restlessness, Mutt snuffled and settled back in. Lorelei had marked Arnie's height on the pantry door frame this morning—just another one of her little ways of making sure Arnie felt secure about this being his new home. She'd made this old house a home with her warmth, laughter, and hard work.

The house creaked as it always did—the settling sounds of old timbers easing after the burden of a day. *Like I do.* He smiled wryly.

Somewhere in the house, someone coughed. Russell rolled over, yawned, and drifted off to sleep.

"Russell. Russell! Wake up." Lorelei stood over him, her beautiful hair streaming like ribbons down past her waist. She shook his shoulder again. Desperation tainted her sweet voice. "I need your help. It's Alan."

Chapter 20

"There. That's better." Lorelei eased Beatrice back onto the pillows she'd piled beneath her shoulders to ease the coughing. Unsure if it made any difference, Lorelei still kept pillows piled beneath the shoulders and heads of four of the kids and Mrs. Diamond. They'd all come down with the flu in the past day and a half.

At first, Russell moved Alan into the nursery in an attempt to isolate him. By daybreak, all the teens except Adele were also sick. They'd been brought here, too. Russell argued hotly with Lorelei that she shouldn't help, that she'd get sick, too. She'd turned around, made a gauze mask, and returned. Since then, he'd not been able to send her away. With the girls sick, Russell needed a woman to help with their care.

They'd transformed the big nursery into a sick ward. Mama kept Adele and Arnie away from the doorway and delivered broth, tea, and fresh linen and towels.

"S–sorry." Mrs. Diamond rasped after being violently ill.

"Shh. It is nothing." Lorelei supported her head and held a glass to her lips. "Sip. Rinse your mouth. You will feel better for it."

"I want my mama," Lacey whimpered in her fever-cracked voice.

Lorelei watched as Russell tenderly sponged her blue-tinged face and made soothing sounds. They'd been going from bed to bed, doing their best to control the fever, ease the cough, and keep their patients hydrated. When Russell had first put up supplies, fearing the epidemic, he'd bought quinine and aspirin. The posters in town advised using both, so they'd diligently dosed each patient.

By afternoon, everyone except Alan seemed stable. Lorelei knew from the newspapers that many who died of the ravaging disease did so within the first day. As long as she and Russell kept them medicated and hydrated, they ought to pull through—all except for Alan.

Russell sat by Alan's bedside, hollow-eyed with grief. From Alan's rattled, irregular breathing, Lorelei knew he had little time left unless God intervened. She went over and sat on the opposite side of the bed. Taking up a damp cloth, she fought tears as she sponged his parched, hot skin.

"Eternal Father, we've done our best. You know how we love Alan. Please, Lord, if it be Your will, heal this young man."

Alan opened his eyes. They were glazed, yet he feebly reached for Lorelei's hand. "God is love."

"Yes. Yes, God is love."

Russell made an agonized sound. He stood, paced away, and came back. Standing over the bed, he muttered, "This is my fault."

"No, Russell. You did your best. You tried to protect these children."

"I made him take half of that buck to the Rimmons. Rimmon's son brought milk today—because his father is down with the flu. If I hadn't been so stubborn and—"

"Stop! You were right to want a young man to be responsible for his actions, and you were right to share the meat with a family who needed it. Life isn't lived on our power. We aren't in control, and we don't bear responsibility for tragedies like this."

"Then God is to blame." Russell buried his head in his hands. "God allows the war; God allows illness." He lifted his face. "How can you serve Him when He refuses to protect His own children? Look at Alan. Just look at him!"

"I see a young man in God's hands." Her mask didn't successfully muffle her sob. "I want him to recover and sit at your table again, but if he does not, I know his heart is right with the Lord and I will someday feast with him in heaven. This I cling to. It is the hope Jesus bought for us on the cross."

"That's where we're different—you still hope. Me? I've learned otherwise."

"Leave him alone, Lori," Mama said softly.

"I can't." Lorelei slipped past her mother and headed toward the large oak tree. It was barren of leaves, and a fresh mound of dirt beneath it carried a lovingly made wooden cross that lay beside a small collection of old family headstones. The pastor had come out and performed the funeral. Russell refused to come inside after the burial. He'd been out there ever since, and sunset had given way to dusk; then the moon rose. Still, he stood alone beneath the barren branches, staring at the grave.

Lorelei said nothing at all. Leaves crunched beneath her shoes as she walked to his side and silently slipped her hand into his.

"It's too cold out here for you." Even as his words rejected her, his fingers curled about hers.

"My hand is warmer than yours."

"So is your heart. Go back inside, Lorelei. The chill inside me will freeze you. I've already caused enough heartache and damage."

"You've done no such thing."

He let out a gusty sigh and said nothing more.

"Come inside. Your mother needs to see you before she goes back to bed."

He cast a quick look at the second story of the house. "Her light's on. Your mom will take care of her. She'll sleep better in her own room tonight."

"I'll peek in on her during the night."

He looked down at her. "Just like you slip in to tug Arnie's covers up higher?"

"You knew I do that?"

"Buttercup, you're like a guardian angel around here. I don't think anyone does anything without you hovering over their shoulder." The gentle look on his face hardened. "But you can stop hovering over me. I'm a lost cause. God and I—we weren't on speaking terms before this happened." He gestured toward the fresh grave. "Now—well, now it's plain as can be that He's cursed me for what I've done."

"God isn't that way, Russell. God is faithful. His character is unchanging. Bad things happen in life—things we cannot understand. They hurt, but God is with us during the hurt to give us consolation. If there is distance between you and Him, He is not the one who pulled away."

"That's some snappy theology you've worked out."

His words cut her to the core. Lorelei gulped, then closed her eyes. *Please, God, give me wisdom so I speak only the words You would have me say.*

"Lost, Buttercup? It's not easy to try to make sense of it all when things go wrong. I've given up. There's no use pursuing God when all He does is turn His back on me."

"God does not turn His back!" She staggered back from his bitter words. "You once told me you gave your heart to Jesus when you were a boy. So now you think to snatch it back because life is hard? Is that all a vow means to you?"

He glared at her stonily.

"Think of what a vow is. It does not say you will be true to your words only if all pleases you. I think of my parents. When they wed, they promised for better and worse, for richer and poorer, in sickness and in health. When things were hard for them, they did not blame each other, pull apart, and curl in opposite corners. They clung together and gave their all."

"That's what marriage is."

"Yes. Two people make a promise to one another, and you expect them to keep their word. How can you think a vow made to God is less binding? You, Russell, made a vow to God. It was an eternal one—that no matter what life brought, you would follow Him. Instead of thinking of yourself, it is time for you to start serving Him."

"What more does He want?" Russell slashed the air with his hand in sheer frustration. "I've done everything I can. I deliver food. I dig graves. I've adopted an orphan."

"Your deeds are not what He wants. He wants your heart."

The air hissed out of his lungs. He flinched as if she'd struck him.

Lorelei watched the pain in his eyes. Even in the moonlight, the deep anguish he felt shone in them. She'd spoken the truth. The message wasn't a gentle one, and part of her wanted to soften the impact, but she couldn't water down the foundational truth. Until Russell chose to yield control to God, he'd fight a painful and losing battle.

After a prolonged silence, she murmured, "I left supper for you in the warming box." With a heavy heart, she walked back inside.

In the next two weeks, Russell worked from first light to well after dark. Arnie, shaken by another death, trailed after him like a second shadow. His cousins all leaned on him to be strong. "You're like the Rock of Gibraltar," Philip said as Russell helped him back upstairs after his first meal at the family table.

A rock? I can't let them see that I'm like a million grains of shifting, sinking sand. They depend on me.

Even with all his hard work, Lorelei's words rang in his ears. *Your deeds are not what He wants. He wants your heart.*

One evening, he came back from delivering food in town to find Philip in the large parlor, working on refinishing a piece of furniture. At first, Russell couldn't see what it was. By the time he reached a decent vantage point, Philip turned. "I saw this in the attic and decided it needed to be repaired."

Russell stared at the burned altar.

The teen reverently ran his palm across the surface. "When I saw it, I felt closer to Alan." His voice cracked, "I remember his last words."

" 'God is love,' " Russell remembered aloud.

Nodding his head, Philip started to sand the singed wood. Drawn to his side, Russell studied the damage. "We can fix it, can't we?" Philip asked.

"It won't be the same as new." Russell thumbed an edge. "I can plane it, and you could rout the edge. Then we can sand it to even out this other surface. A little putty and darker stain will cover any of the imperfections."

Late into the night, they worked on the altar. Every spare moment in the next three days went toward restoring it. Finally, late at night, all alone, Russell ran a polishing cloth over the surface. Though he'd put Arnie to bed upstairs, the little guy had crept back downstairs and fallen asleep beneath Russell's jacket on a small sofa. Arnie stirred and sat up. He rubbed his eyes.

"Russell?"

"Yeah, buddy?"

Arnie padded over and snuggled close. He wrapped his little arm around Russell's neck and curled his other hand around the edge of the altar. "Can we pray at this one, just like we do at the one in church?"

Chapter 21

Russell's breath caught. *I'm not equipped to do this. God, why are You putting me in this position?* One look at Arnie's innocent eyes forced Russell to tamp down his own doubts. "Would you like to?"

Arnie nodded. He slithered onto his knees, folded his hands, and frowned. "I'm too short."

"Here." Russell knelt on one knee and crooked the other up. He lifted Arnie to sit on it, and the little boy then folded his hands and rested them on the altar.

"That's right," Arnie said happily. He closed his eyes tightly and dove right in. "God, it's me, Arnie. You got my daddy and mommy and Baby 'Liz'beth with you. Please take good care of them. Russell takes good care of me. Night-night. Amen."

"Amen." Russell hugged him tightly. "Now go on up to bed."

"Yessir."

Russell sat on the floor by the altar as despair washed over him. *If only my soul could be restored like this house and altar. If only my faith were that simple and pure.*

"The paper in town says the flu is still bad, but it's not claiming as many folks as it did in October," Russell said when he got home one evening.

"How much longer will it last?" His mother took a sip of tea.

Russell shrugged. "No one can say."

"I want to go home," Beatrice said quietly. "It's been good of you to have us stay, but in the end, it didn't make any difference. I'm homesick." She laughed. "I'd even be glad to have Mama scold me for slacking on my chores."

Lorelei cut Arnie's meat and didn't participate in the conversation. The Diamonds needed to make this decision on their own.

"Going home by wagon is going to be too taxing," Russell said.

His mother nodded. "We'll go by train."

"Tomorrow is Sunday," Mama said.

"We'll leave Monday," Mrs. Diamond decided.

After everyone left the table, Russell remained, as had become his custom. Lorelei started to clear the dishes. "Mama and I will return to the cottage, too."

His head shot up. "Why?"

"Because it is time."

"Arnie needs you!"

Silently, Lorelei left him and went to the kitchen. Alone and up to her elbows in suds, she scrubbed a plate and fought back her disappointment. *Why couldn't you need me, Russell?* Tears stung her eyes and nose.

Mama came in, picked up a dish towel, and started to dry dishes. "There was a time, I thought Russell was the answer to my prayers. You reminded me the pastor said we should pray specifically, and I did—just as you said—that God would put a husband for you on our cottage porch. Russell fixed that porch. I hoped with time, his heart would mend, too, Lori. It hasn't.

"You cannot be with a man who has hardened his heart against God. It is too hard for you to be under his roof and not set your affections on him. With his strength and kindness, he will woo you, but it is not what God would bless. On Monday, we will move back home, too."

Heartbroken, Lorelei whispered, "I know. I've already told him."

"It's over!" Russell didn't bother to knock. He plowed straight into the cottage and repeated, "It's over!"

"What?"

He swept Lorelei up and swung her around. "The war! They declared armistice! It's over!"

"Praise God!" Mama said from the kitchen doorway.

As Russell set Lorelei down, he still couldn't contain his relief. He held her shoulders and planted an exuberant kiss on her cheek. She gave him a shocked look, but he laughed and grabbed her mother in an enveloping hug. "It's done."

Arnie tugged on his slacks. "Do we get to cel'brate with marshmallows?"

"Better than that. We'll go to town. If you all promise to wear masks and stay away from others, we'll go in tomorrow. They're planning music in the park and a parade."

Arnie scratched his knee. "Daddy had mag'zines. They showed soldiers marching, marching, marching in parades. You gonna wear your soldier clothes, Russell?"

The question jolted him. Russell hadn't thought about his uniform since the night he'd happened across it before he left home. The very thought of ever putting it on again made him sick inside.

"The war is over, Arnie." Lorelei poked the little boy in the belly and made him laugh. "No more uniforms. What if we decorate the buggy? How would that be?"

"Terrific!"

Indeed, the buggy did look terrific. Russell chuckled as he hitched the geldings to it the next afternoon. "You folks outdid yourselves. This is the fanciest buggy in all of Virginia!"

Even the black crepe on doors and fresh graves in the cemetery didn't dampen spirits. Folks from all around came to town to revel in the good news. The gauze masks couldn't muffle the shouts of victory. The War to End All Wars was over. Never again would man engage in such brutality.

For the first time in months, Russell felt a glimmer of hope for the future.

Lorelei carefully cleaned each piece of glass, then wrapped the edges with copper foil. Once the foil cupped the edges, she used her crimper to burnish it in place. She'd decided to do this window as a gift for Russell—a thanks for his generosity. The copper foil allowed her to make this far more intricate, and she'd constructed it so he could place it in the library window since he often slipped into that room when he needed to ponder matters.

"What are you up to now?"

His voice startled her. She jumped and let out a gasp.

"Sorry. I didn't mean to scare you. Hey—you cut yourself!"

"It's nothing." She set down the small piece of ruby glass and grabbed a rag. "I'm used to cutting myself. It's just part of the job."

He encircled her wrist with his hand and turned the finger toward the light. "Poor finger. If this happened to Arnie, he'd want me to kiss it better."

"I'm not Arnie." She pulled away. A shiver ran through her, so she reached over and grabbed her sweater.

"No, you're not." Russell held the sweater for her. "I came over to talk with you about that."

"That I am not Arnie?" She glanced at her finger, decided it wasn't going to bother her and didn't need any bandaging, and set back to work on the window.

Russell chuckled. "No. Arnie's in with your mother. They get along famously."

"They do," Lorelei agreed. She tucked a finished piece in place and started to foil the edges of a deep green leaf.

"Will you please stop messing with that and look at me?"

Surprised at his request, she laid down the leaf and foil, then turned toward him.

"Arnie misses you up at the house. I miss you more."

His admission stunned her. Lorelei blinked at him in utter surprise.

Russell leaned forward. He traced her hairline with his forefinger and quietly said, "Buttercup, we've been through a lot together."

"We have." The tenderness in his touch and voice made her want to lean closer.

"I'm not very good with fancy words." He cupped her cheek. "But, Lorelei, I can be myself around you. There isn't anyone else I can say that about. You listen and are honest about what you think. I don't know another gal in the world with a heart as big as yours."

"Russell, those are fancy words. Kind ones. Your praise means much to me."

His eyes darkened as he rubbed his thumb across her lips. "And my love? Does that mean much to you? I want to marry you, Lorelei."

She sucked in a shocked breath. His words thundered in her ears, made her world tilt crazily.

"Don't you love me, too?" His voice dropped an octave as he asked those words in a velvety voice.

The chill she'd felt earlier doubled. Lorelei stepped back and wrapped her arms around herself. "Yes. No." She shook her head. "Russell, it does not matter how I feel. My love for you is strong, but my love for God makes such a marriage impossible."

His brow furrowed. "What is that supposed to mean?"

Hot tears scorched down her cheeks. Everything inside trembled as she searched for the right words. "Russell, the man I marry must love God. In marriage, two become one. My heart and body tell me such a union would be wonderful, but my soul tells me no. We would not be a good match because there is this difference between us. Faith matters. It matters much."

"It doesn't have to. I'll go to church if that's what bothers you. You can continue to say grace at meals and bring up our children with Bible reading." He got off the stool and came closer. Cupping her shoulders, he drew her close. "I wouldn't expect you to give up anything that is dear to you."

"But—"

"Your mother—she'd move in with us. She'll make a wonderful grandma for Arnie, don't you think?"

His words broke her heart. Lorelei pressed a hand to her mouth to hold back a sob.

He brushed away her tears. "Buttercup, this was supposed to be a happy moment. Things are looking up."

"My heart says yes, but my soul says no. Russell, you honor me with this proposal, but I cannot accept it. A woman should not marry a man in hopes of changing him. It is unwise. Though I love you, marriage would be wrong because the Lord is my Shepherd, but He is your enemy."

She could barely see him through her tears. Her legs felt rubbery, and she blindly reached behind herself for the table to keep herself from falling.

"If that's how you feel." Russell's voice sounded grim, muffled.

Instead of bracing her, the table slid. The sound of glass shattering filled her ears as the world tilted and everything went dark.

Chapter 22

"Mom!" Russell burst into the cottage with Lorelei draped limply across his arms. Ever since he'd come to the realization that he loved Lorelei, he'd begun to think of her mother as his, too. The horror on her face cut him to the core. "She fainted. She's running a fever."

"Put her in bed. Go get the quinine and aspirin." Mrs. Goetz hurried into the bedroom and yanked back the covers.

By the time Russell returned, Lorelei was dressed in a lawn nightgown and covered by a sheet. Her mother worriedly sponged her wrists and face. "She is so hot. Too hot. Please, Russell, hold her up so I can make her take your medicine."

Of the people he'd seen with the flu, no one had been as sick as Lorelei—no one except Alan. Russell sat at the bedside, nearly crazed with grief. He couldn't bear to lose Lorelei. He trickled broth into her, held her head when she was sick, sponged her to control the fever. Nothing helped.

She grew weaker by the hour. Her coloring changed to the telltale bluish white that indicated she didn't have long.

Russell stared at her and remembered when Alan was at this point. He'd whispered, "God is love."

Lorelei believes that, too. My beautiful Lorelei, whose world is so full of light and color. Her soul sparkles with the joy of the Lord.

What do I believe? He'd tried to make bargains with God in the trenches. *If You spare me and my buddy, I'll... Get me out of here and... Make this war end...* Now he sat at the bedside of the woman he'd grown to love. His hands and heart were empty.

I can't bargain. I never could. I have nothing to offer God. I have no power. You are God, and I am a man—one who cannot bear to lose this woman.

Lorelei had spoken of vows and promises and commitment. *When things got rough, I failed to rely on the Lord. I tried to live on my own terms, and I turned on God. What kind of fool have I been?*

He took the Bible Lorelei kept at her bedside and started to read where a blue ribbon that was purpled with age lay between the pages in the eighth chapter of Mark:

> *And when he had called the people unto him with his disciples also, he said unto them, Whosoever will come after me, let him deny himself, and take up his cross, and follow me. For whosoever will save his life shall lose it; but whosoever shall lose his life for my sake and the gospel's, the same shall save it. For what shall it profit a man, if he shall gain the whole world, and lose his own soul? Or what shall a man give in exchange for his soul? Whosoever therefore shall be ashamed of me and of my words in this adulterous and sinful generation; of him also shall the Son of man be ashamed, when he cometh in the glory of his Father with the holy angels.*

The words cut to the depths of his soul. He had nothing to exchange with God...nothing to give but a heart that was jaded and aching. The man in him wanted to bargain still—to beg God for this sweet woman's life—but that wasn't right. He couldn't make a deal with God.

Sovereign, Almighty God owed him nothing. If in His grace He spared Lorelei, it would be a blessing beyond all hope, but if He didn't spare her. . .

Even then, I will serve You, Lord.

Russell slipped onto his knees. He closed both hands around Lorelei's and prayed. "Father, take my wayward heart and make it Yours. I beg Your forgiveness for letting anger and pride separate me from You. Lord, I love this woman. I promise to follow You no matter what her fate. She said there is always the hope of eternity—of being seated together at the banqueting table in heaven. Our only hope now is in Your promise of eternity and salvation. Merciful God, be with us, I pray."

Wrapped in her nightgown and two blankets and propped in the corner of the couch, Lorelei swallowed the apple cider and hummed appreciatively.

"Thirsty, Buttercup?"

"Yes." She sipped more as Russell held the glass to her lips.

He sat next to her and played with the tip of her frazzled braid. "You're looking miles better."

She managed a weak laugh. "That is a terrible thing to say. As you carried me out here, I saw my reflection in the mirror. I'm a fright!"

"You're beautiful." He scanned her face slowly. "I need to tell you something."

Please, no. Please, Russell, don't ask me to marry you again. It nearly tore my heart out, telling you no last time. I'm too weak right now for this.

"While you were sick, I did a lot of soul searching. I didn't like what I saw. Things have changed. I've recommitted myself to God."

"Oh, Russell!"

"It's not supposed to make you cry." A lopsided grin tilted his mouth.

"They are happy tears."

His woodsy, masculine scent enveloped her as he leaned closer and used the corner of the sheet to dab her cheeks. His voice deepened. "Before you got sick, I told you I love you. Do you remember?"

She nodded slowly.

He looked into her eyes. "You were right to refuse my proposal. We wouldn't have had the bond in our marriage that God gives to His children."

"I didn't want to hurt you, Russell. I never wanted to hurt you."

"Shh. I know. Because you stood firm in your faith, you challenged me. It wasn't in a spirit of cruelty—you held up a mirror to my soul and forced me to look at myself."

"Since I met you, I've held a burden for you. God gave me a special passage to lean upon."

"Tell me."

She felt weak as water. Without her saying a word, Russell tucked her into his side and pressed her head to his shoulder. She closed her eyes at the security and serenity she felt in that moment, then recited softly, "It's in the first chapter of Second Corinthians. 'Blessed be God, even the Father of our Lord Jesus Christ, the Father of mercies, and the God of all comfort; who comforteth us in all our tribulation, that we may be able to comfort them which are in any trouble, by the comfort wherewith we ourselves are comforted of God. For as the sufferings of Christ abound in us, so our consolation also aboundeth by Christ.' "

"We've had plenty of tribulation. I'm ready for that comfort and consolation." He pressed a kiss to her temple. "Lorelei, my heart overflows with love for you. Will you marry me?"

"I love you, too, Russell. Being your wife would be an honor."

Epilogue

July 3, 1919

"The altar is our something old," Lorelei told Russell's mother as she showed her the grand parlor where the wedding was to be held the next day. Once, it had been the workroom she and Russell shared. Now it would serve as a wedding chapel.

Though outbreaks of the flu had lessened, quarantine laws made it impossible to use the church. Family members and a few close friends would come to the mansion for the nuptials, and Lorelei loved the fact that she and Russell would still have an altar for their wedding.

"And you have a beautiful new gown." Mrs. Diamond smiled.

"The something borrowed is Mama's lace hanky, and something blue is from Papa's Bible. I'm using the ribbon marker from it for my g—" She stopped abruptly as Russell entered the room. Heat suffused her cheeks at the thought that he'd almost overheard her speaking of such a thing.

"Everything set to your satisfaction?" He looked about.

"Not exactly." Mrs. Diamond's words shocked Lorelei. Walking toward her son, she said, "Lorelei thinks that beautiful altar is her something old. To my way of thinking, the bride is supposed to wear something old."

Russell wore a smug smile. "I've got that covered." He gave his mother a peck on the cheek; then she left the room. Russell took Lorelei's hand and tugged her to the window. A veritable rainbow of color shimmered around them from the stained glass. He pulled a frayed scarlet cord out of his pocket.

Three tiny hearts dangled from it.

"This has been in the family for seventy-seven years. I'd like you to tie it in your bridal bouquet. Maybe it's not exactly wearing it, but I think carrying it qualifies for the tradition."

"Three hearts. . .for God, you, and me?"

He smiled. "I knew you'd understand." He kissed her, then cupped her face in his hands and shook his head. "In the myth of Lorelei, she was a siren who called men to their destruction. You, my sweet siren, were the voice God used to call me to restoration."

The next afternoon, sun showered through the window onto the altar where they sealed their marriage with a heartfelt kiss.

"Now?" Arnie asked as he wiggled off to the side.

Lorelei laughed as Russell motioned for him to come. "Yes, now."

Arnie pulled two roses from Lorelei's bouquet and turned to the small crowd. "I got a s'prise. I'm 'dopted, so Rus—I mean, Dad—said I get to give these to my new grandmas."

They had a lovely wedding supper, and as a special celebration that night, Russell arranged for fireworks to be shot off the main lawn for the guests' enjoyment. He and Lorelei stood by the window of their bedroom and held each other in the sparkling showers of light.

She walked her fingers up the buttons of his shirt. "It's Independence Day. I've heard men think marriage takes away their freedom."

"Not this man." He captured her hand and kissed the backs of her fingers. "I've found liberty from doubt and anger. It's not just the world that's at peace, Lorelei. I'm at peace."

"And I'm in love."

With a full heart and in a finished home that love had restored, he swept her into his arms and kissed her.

About the Authors

Lynn A. Coleman is an award-winning author who makes her home in Florida, with her husband of thirty-six years.

Mary Davis is a full-time fiction writer who enjoys going into schools and talking to kids about writing. Mary lives near Colorado's Rocky Mountains with her husband, three children, and six pets.

Susan Page Davis is the author of more than forty novels, in the romance, mystery, suspense, and historical romance genres. A Maine native, she now lives in western Kentucky with her husband, Jim, a retired news editor. They are the parents of six, and the grandparents of nine fantastic kids. She is a past winner of the Carol Award, the Will Rogers Medallion for Western Fiction, and the Inspirational Readers' Choice Award. Susan was named Favorite Author of the Year in the 18th Annual Heartsong Awards. Visit her website at: www.susanpagedavis.com.

Paige Winship Dooly is the author of over a dozen books and novellas. She enjoys living in the coastal Deep South with her family, after having grown up in the sometimes extremely cold Midwest. She is happily married to her high school sweetheart and loves their life of adventure in a full house with six homeschooled children and two dogs.

Cathy Marie Hake is a Southern California native. She met her two loves at church: Jesus and her husband, Christopher. An RN, she loved working in oncology as well as teaching Lamaze. Health issues forced her to retire, but God opened new possibilities with writing. Since their children have moved out and are married, Cathy and Chris dote on dogs they rescue from a local shelter. A sentimental pack rat, Cathy enjoys scrapbooking and collecting antiques. "I'm easily distracted during prayer, so I devote certain tasks and chores to specific requests or persons so I can keep faithful in my prayer life." Since her first book in 2000, she's been on multiple bestseller and readers' favorite lists.